PRAISE FOR ROBERT NEWCOMB

A March into Darkness

"Wonderfully captures the imagination."
—*Publishers Weekly*

Savage Messiah

"Meticulously planned action . . . another mega-fantasy along the lines of Robert Jordan's *Wheel of Time.*"
—*Booklist*

"Magic, intrigue, and plenty of action."
—*Library Journal*

The Scrolls of the Ancients

"Plenty of adventure and magic . . . continues Robert Newcomb's tradition of mixing adventure with an interesting and well-realized magical world."
—SF Site

By Robert Newcomb

THE CHRONICLES OF BLOOD AND STONE
The Fifth Sorceress
The Gates of Dawn
The Scrolls of the Ancients

THE DESTINIES OF BLOOD AND STONE
Savage Messiah
A March into Darkness
The Rise of the Blood Royal

A MARCH INTO DARKNESS

VOLUME II OF THE DESTINIES OF BLOOD AND STONE

ROBERT NEWCOMB

BALLANTINE BOOKS • NEW YORK

A March into Darkness is a work of fiction. Names, places, and incidents either are products of the author's imagination or are used fictitiously.

2008 Del Rey Books Mass Market Edition

Published in the United States by Del Rey Books, an imprint of The Random House Publishing Group, a division of Random House, Inc., New York.

This book contains an excerpt from the forthcoming hardcover edition of *The Rise of the Blood Royal* by Robert Newcomb. This excerpt has been set for this edition only and may not reflect the final content of the forthcoming edition.

Originally published in hardcover in the United States by Del Rey Books, an imprint of The Random House Publishing Group, a division of Random House, Inc., in 2007.

Map illustration by Russ Charpentier

ISBN 978-0-345-47710-1

Printed in the United States of America

www.delreybooks.com

OPM 9 8 7 6 5 4 3 2 1

This one is for Robert Strom
You will be missed. . . .

Contents

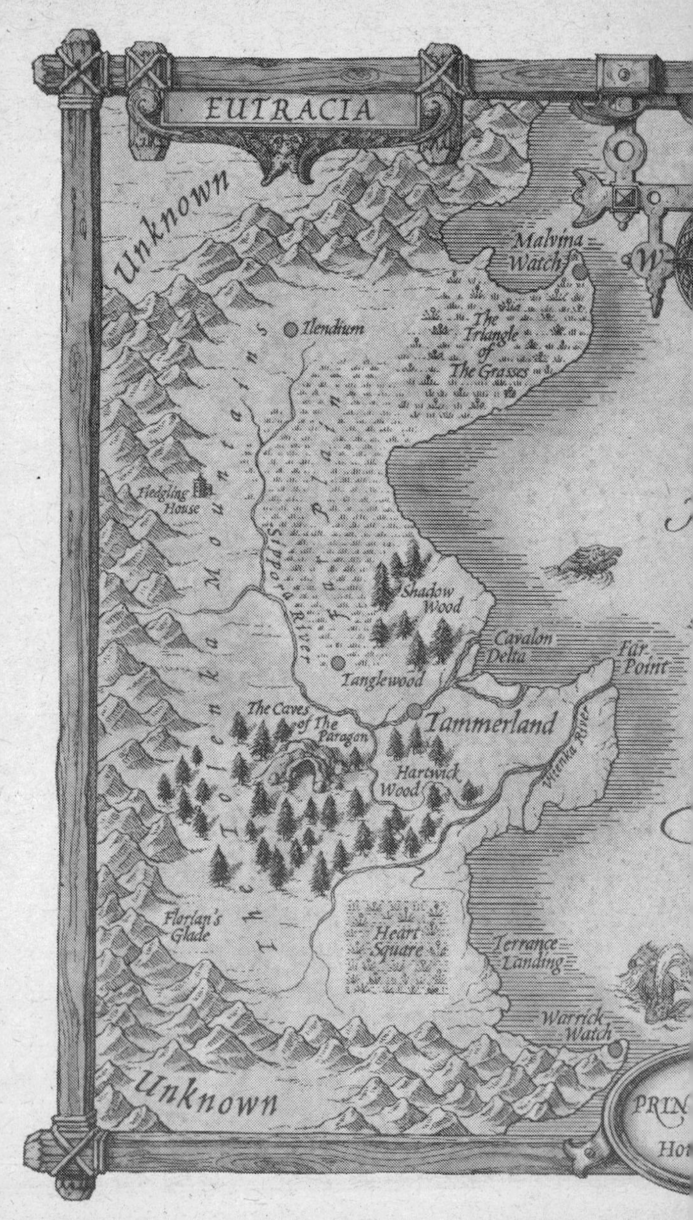
EUTRACIA
Unknown
Malvina Watch
Ilendium
The Triangle of The Grasses
Fledgling House
Silent Mountains
Sippora River
Shadow Wood
Cavalon Delta
Far Point
Tanglewood
The Caves of The Paragon
Tammerland
Hartwick Wood
Florian's Glade
Heart Square
Terrance Landing
Warrick Watch
Unknown
PRIN
Ho

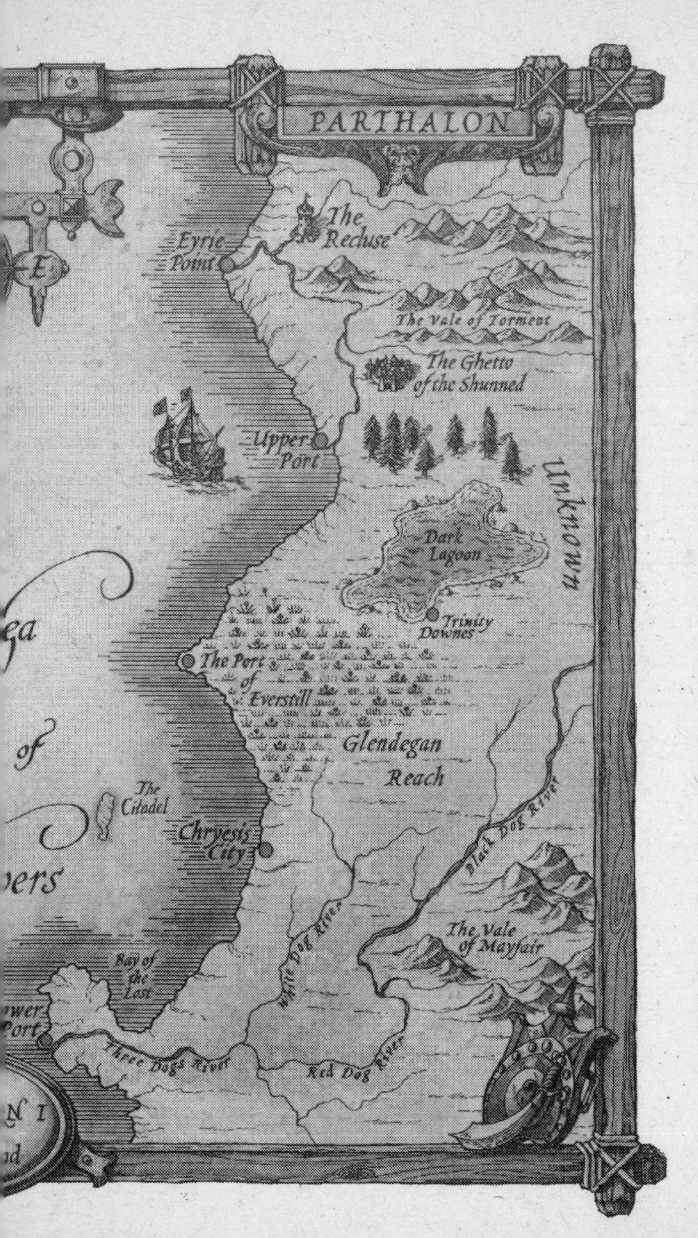
PARTHALON
The Recluse
Eyrie Point
The Vale of Torment
The Ghetto of the Shunned
Upper Port
Unknown
Dark Lagoon
Trinity Downes
The Port of Everstill
Glendegan Reach
The Citadel
Chryesis City
Black Dog River
The Vale of Mayfair
White Dog River
Bay of the Last
Three Dogs River
Red Dog River

A MARCH INTO DARKNESS

Volume II of The Destinies of Blood and Stone

I

THE DARKLING

Chapter I

Should the Jin'Sai *somehow prevail against the* Enseterat, *even then his trials will have only begun. For a Vagaries servant shall come to taunt him, and he will seduce the* Jin'Sai *into following him on a march into darkness.*

—PAGE 242, CHAPTER VI OF THE VIGORS

GAIUS WAS UNUSUALLY FAIR FOR A MINION WARRIOR. HE WAS clean-shaven, with light brown hair and green eyes. Recently promoted to the rank of captain, he commanded the eleven warriors stationed near the magnificent azure pass that had been carved into the rugged Tolenka Mountains. Eager to impress his superiors, he took his first command seriously.

Seated by the campfire with five fellow warriors, he looked up at the mountainside. He could easily see the pass shimmering in the night. Six more warriors were camped up there, watching it. Even from its great distance up the mountainside, the pass's magnificent rays flooded the plains below.

Gaius and his troops had been stationed here for nearly two months, but the pass had yet to relinquish any secrets. As he looked back down at the fire, he wondered whether it ever would. Those were riddles for wizards to unravel, and far beyond a warrior's knowledge.

Tristan, Wigg, Faegan, and the sorceress Jessamay had arrived in Minion litters to view the pass just after the *Jin'Sai* and his forces turned back Wulfgar's invasion for the second and final time. Ox and Traax had accompanied them. Although his written reports to the *Jin'Sai* had said little since his posting here, Gaius still sent them along at regular intervals.

By now it was widely known that the *Jin'Sai* was a widower. During his visit, each of the warriors had expressed his or her heartfelt condolences. His face grim, Tristan had thanked them, then ordered that his group be taken to view the pass. Gaius had climbed aboard and directed the litter bearers up the mountainside.

On reaching the site they all disembarked. They walked to face the glowing pass while the wizard Faegan levitated his chair on wheels, following along behind. The entire mountainside had been scorched black and barren. Even now, warm cinders crunched beneath their boots. There were no trees, no brush, and no grass—just the strange pass, shimmering brightly against the face of the granite mountainside. Because their habitats had been decimated, all the forest creatures had fled.

They'll never return, Gaius thought as the group approached the strange phenomenon. *The craft is at work here, and somehow they know it.*

When they saw the group coming, the six warriors guarding the pass came to attention. At first no one spoke. As everyone stood before the pass's wondrous presence, it was almost like there could be nothing left to say.

The deep gap was barred by a brilliant azure wall, its aura so bright that it hurt everyone's eyes. It stretched silently from one mountain sidewall to the other—a distance of about twenty meters. Looking up, they could see no limit to its height, for it disappeared into the dense fog that always crouched atop the mountain peaks.

The pass's flat surface was smooth as glass. As the visitors gazed into its depths they could see white shards of light shooting to and fro, as if begging to be released to the outside world. It was a wondrous, awful thing. No matter how many times Gaius came here, he was stunned by its majesty.

Knowing that his place was with his troops, the captain stayed behind as he watched the inspection party approach the glowing wall. He saw the wizards point at it and speak anxiously to one another. Tristan said something to the wizard in the chair, and the mystic nodded.

Gaius watched the *Jin'Sai* unsheathe his dreggan. As the blade cleared its scabbard, for several moments its unmistakable ring filled the air. With another nod from Faegan, the prince walked closer.

Gaius held his breath as the prince drove his sword directly into the glowing wall. The blade disappeared effortlessly, like it had entered the still surface of some countryside pond.

As the prince steadily held his weapon, the light shards on the pass's other side started gathering around it. They danced to the dreggan like it was a lightning rod, but they did it no harm. With a final nod from the wizard, Tristan withdrew the blade and sheathed it. Again the wizards and the sorceress huddled together, talking in urgent tones. Finally turning away from the pass, the *Jin'Sai* ordered a return to the base camp.

The royal party stayed the night, and everyone feasted. As the smell of roasted venison filled the air, much akulee—the dark, bitter brew of the Minions—was consumed. Although they spoke little about what they had seen, Wigg, Faegan, and Jessamay had been sociable enough.

But the *Jin'Sai* was another matter. He had eaten little, then gone off to be alone at the camp's far edge. He sat there for hours before finally falling asleep, holding the gold medallion around his neck and drinking akulee while he stared into the darkness. The two wizards and sorceress had looked at him often.

At dawn the inspection party had thanked Gaius, then flown back to Tammerland. Before leaving, the *Jin'Sai* had instructed Gaius to keep the reports coming, no matter how sparse they might be. The captain had answered with a smart click of his heels.

His thoughts returning to the present, Gaius again looked up the mountainside. The pass's azure rays still flooded the ground around him. He had no idea how long he and his warriors would be stationed here, but they would gladly do their duty until ordered otherwise.

Gaius took a last pull on the akulee jug, then wiped his mouth with his forearm. Lying down by the fire with the others, he finally fell asleep.

AS THE PASS THROUGH THE TOLENKAS CONTINUED TO SHIMMER, three of the six warriors stationed nearby lay asleep by the fire. The other three sat on camp stools playing at cards. It would be dawn soon. Then they would sleep while the others stood guard.

Being posted to this desolate place had quickly become tiresome, even for diligent Minion warriors. The wall of azure light never wavered, never threatened. Silent and beautiful, for them it had become nothing more than what it appeared—a seemingly harmless construct of the craft. Even the usually wary Minions had begun taking its harmlessness for granted.

Without the warriors noticing, a thin white line started silently climbing up the middle of the azure wall. Starting at the ground, it soon stretched as high as the eye could see and disappeared into the fog. Still the three warriors did not turn around. The line quickly parted the wall into halves, revealing a space that was dark and endless.

As an intruder came through the gap, still the warriors did not notice. A mounted black stallion stepped silently forward to a place about five meters from the fire. The vapor from the stallion's nostrils streamed in the cool night air.

The warrior named Eranan was the first to jump to his feet and draw his sword. Startled, the other two quickly followed.

Without hesitation the rider raised one arm. With a muffled explosion, Eranan's insides burst through his chest and abdomen. His fellow warriors watched in horror as his vitals slipped wetly from beneath his body armor and fell to the ground. Without saying a word, Eranan dropped his sword to fall facedown, dead where he lay.

Drawing their dreggans, the other warriors ran to attack the intruder. Before they could near him, they died in the same hideous fashion as had Eranan. Rising sleepily from their places by the fire, two more warriors perished before they grasped what was happening.

The lone surviving Minion charged, swinging his dreggan for all he was worth. Surprisingly, the murderer did nothing to stop him. Sure that he was about to take the intruder down, the Minion smiled menacingly.

The dreggan blade came whistling around, slashing into the rider's right shoulder. But as it did, the warrior felt no resistance against it.

Doing no harm, the dreggan flowed through the intruder's body, then down through his mount as though they were ghosts, burying itself into the trunk of a nearby tree. The warrior frantically struggled to free the blade, but could not. His eyes wide, he looked up at the miraculous opponent who had just bested him. The being's face was hideous, terrifying.

"Who are you?" the warrior demanded.

Staring down at his bewildered enemy, the being atop the horse smiled. He raised one arm.

"I am a Darkling," he said quietly. "But you won't live to tell anyone."

The warrior's organs exploded like those of his fellows, and he fell dead to the ground. His dreggan—still caught in the tree trunk—glinted softly in the light of the three red moons.

Saying nothing more, the rider guided his horse down to where Gaius and the five other Minions were camped. The dark gap in the pass sealed itself, leaving no trace of the exit that had just formed.

In the end, the sleeping warriors at the bottom of the mountainside would fare no better than their brothers.

CHAPTER II

DESPITE THE COOLNESS OF THE NIGHT, TRISTAN WAS SWEATING. ITS blade shining in the moonlight, his dreggan felt cool to the touch as he held it vertically before his body. A stout Eutracian maple tree was at his back. He had been hiding at the edge of the forest for some time. Taking a deep breath, he peered around the tree trunk.

Wigg and Jessamay were quickly making their way down the hill. The crippled wizard Faegan was close behind, levitating his wooden wheelchair as he went. The trio would soon near the nondescript cottage in the clearing. Then they would know.

Gritting his teeth, Tristan chafed at being left behind. For the last two months each of these deadly encounters had been the same. He and the others were always ordered to stay back, while the mystics went in first. More often than not their fanatical prey chose to die, rather than surrender. The few who had been taken alive were interned in the depths of the Redoubt.

As the three mystics hurried, Faegan cloaked their endowed blood. Even so, the adepts neared the cottage with extreme care. Light could be seen coming from its windows, and smoke gently curled its way free from the stone chimney. It was an idyllic picture, belying the deadly nature of those hiding inside.

Desperately wanting to act, Tristan looked over at Traax and Shailiha. Their expressions told him that they were equally eager to go charging down. They all had their individual scores to settle—Tristan most of all.

Looking deeper into the woods, Tristan saw more eager Minions, crouched in hiding and awaiting his orders. He doubted that the extra warriors would be needed, for the scouts he had sent here yesterday had reported that only two souls inhabited the cottage. But if the fugitives were of the craft they could prove deadly. His hands tightening around his sword hilt, he looked back down at the scene.

Their backs flattened against the cottage's front wall, Wigg and Jessamay waited anxiously for Faegan. Finally landing his chair directly before the cottage door, the crippled wizard raised his hands. Twin azure bolts shot from his fingers, brilliantly illuminating the night.

Faegan used the twin bolts to free the door hinges from their frame. Lifting his hands into the air, he cast the door to the grass. Tristan held his breath as he watched the wizards and sorceress charge inside.

At first nothing happened. Then Wigg's warning came roaring out into the night. Tristan raced down the hill. As he approached the cottage, bolts of azure energy screamed from the windows. Then the roof exploded into the air, and three of the cottage's four walls tumbled into ruin. The blast took Tristan off his feet, throwing him hard to the ground. What remained of the cottage crumbled into flaming debris. Burning wood and charred stone landed all around him.

Tristan slowly came to all fours. He looked up to see Traax, Shailiha, and Ox come running. As his vision cleared, they helped him to his feet. Traax handed him his sword.

"Are you all right?" Shailiha asked anxiously.

Tristan ran one hand through his dark hair. "I . . . believe so," he answered. But as his mind cleared, a terrible foreboding took him.

"Wigg . . . ," he breathed. As fast as his legs could carry him, he again started running toward the inferno.

Soon the heat was too much, forcing him to a skidding stop.

Trying to enter the crumbling cottage was unthinkable. The last timber suddenly fell in, leveling the dwelling for good.

Shailiha came to stand with Tristan, and she took him by the hand. His body was shaking with hate, and tears filled his eyes.

"What happened?" she asked quietly as she sheathed her sword.

Tristan angrily slid his dreggan into the scabbard lying across his back. He looked down at the ground.

"Whoever was inside that cottage chose to die, rather than be captured," he answered grimly. "Did you see those azure streaks come tearing out of the windows? That explosion was generated by the craft. Despite their amazing gifts, our friends never stood a chance." His hands balling up into fists, the *Jin'Sai* closed his eyes.

"Oh ye of little faith!" a gravelly voice suddenly called out from the darkness. A familiar cackle followed.

Everyone spun around to see Faegan approaching. He was again levitating his wooden chair. In the light of the burning cottage they saw that he was dirty from head to toe, but smiling broadly. Wigg and Jessamay—each equally filthy—were following along behind.

Tristan let go a sigh of relief. Shailiha ran to greet them. Faegan and Jessamay beamed back with the sheer joy of being alive. Embarrassed by Shailiha's enthusiastic embrace, Wigg cleared his throat, then busily smoothed out the hem of his singed robe.

While the cottage remains crackled and burned, Tristan, Ox, and Traax walked over. By now the warriors hiding in the woods had joined them. Faegan gave Tristan a conspiratorial wink, but it was clear that the *Jin'Sai* was not amused. The prince crossed his arms over his chest.

"I'd say you three have some explaining to do," he said. "How did you manage to survive that explosion?"

"We managed to take cover behind the rear wall, which we strengthened with the craft." Obviously pleased with himself, Faegan smiled again.

Shailiha scowled. "I don't understand," she protested. "How did you know that there would be an explosion? And what made you believe that you would be able to get out in time? It must have been close!"

"Indeed," Wigg answered.

As the First Wizard and Jessamay walked closer, the others

could see that their hair and clothing had been singed. The Paragon—the bloodred jewel that helped to empower both sides of the craft—hung securely from a gold chain lying around Wigg's neck. Seeing that the gemstone was safe, Tristan finally relaxed.

"When we stormed the cottage, we saw two men sitting at a table," Wigg added. "I recognized them as onetime consuls of the Redoubt. When a ball of energy started to form between them, I wasted no time in causing the windows to blow out so we could run for cover. We were lucky, but the two consuls died immediately. I think that was their intent from the beginning. I am sorry to see them perish. They might have told us much."

Reaching down into one knee boot, Tristan retrieved a ragged piece of parchment. He held it to the moonlight as he glanced down the page.

"This was the last consular safe house on Satine's list," he said. "But that does not mean that it was the last of the consuls." His face grim, he closed his hand around the parchment and crushed it to pieces.

"This simply isn't good enough," he said menacingly. "I want them all."

Wigg cleared his throat. "We may as well return to camp," he said cheerfully. "Our work here is done. I for one am so hungry that my ribs must be showing through!"

"I agree!" Faegan added. "I could do with a bit of Minion cooking myself—crude as it might be!"

But as the group turned to go, the *Jin'Sai* stayed put. He turned to look at the remains of the burning cottage. Sensing his frustration, Shailiha walked over and snaked one arm through his.

"Come, Brother," she said gently. "There is nothing more to be done here."

When Tristan turned she saw his eyes start to well up. Holding him a bit closer, she accompanied him back to the Minion campsite.

"HE WORRIES ME," SHAILIHA SAID SOFTLY.

As she sat by the campfire with the First Wizard, the princess pulled her knees up under her chin. It was a perfect evening. The nighttime sky was full of stars; the tree frogs sang pleasantly. Her soft brown jerkin and matching trousers were helping to keep her warm, while the campfire added to her sense of security.

Several Minion tents dotted the ground nearby, and the occasional flying patrol could be seen highlighted against the three red moons. Reaching up, the princess tossed a handful of her long blond hair over one shoulder.

The roasted pheasants the Minions prepared had been wonderful, and the princess had consumed a bit more than her share of red wine. Ox and Traax were off seeing to the sentries; Faegan and Jessamay had retired. They would all be home late tomorrow. The princess would be glad to hold her daughter Morganna in her arms again.

She looked over at Tristan. He had again eaten little, then gone off to be alone, sitting with his back up against a tree. He was monotonously sharpening his dreggan blade with a whetstone. As the stone slid down the sword's edge time after time, the crown prince of Eutracia simply stared into space, like he was the only person left in the world. Since the death of his beloved Celeste, they all knew that when he was like this, it was best to leave him alone.

Sighing, Shailiha looked over at the First Wizard.

"You have been with him when he endured so many of his losses," she said softly. "Each time he has returned to us. Will he do so this time as well?"

Taking a deep breath, Wigg leaned over to rearrange his robe. As he did, the Paragon dangled forward to twinkle in the firelight.

"Yes, but I cannot be sure when," Wigg answered.

"How can you know?" Shailiha asked.

"Because he must," Wigg answered simply. "He understands that. His nation needs him. His blood has finally returned to its natural state, and his training in the craft must start. More important, he is the reigning *Jin'Sai*. Despite his recent behavior he understands his destiny far better than ever before." Pausing for a moment, Wigg picked up a nearby stick to casually poke at the fire.

"He worries us all," the wizard went on. "His personal losses have been huge. He so loved his parents, and the late Directorate of Wizards. He loved Lionel and Geldon, too. But he loved Celeste in that special way that only lovers' hearts can become entangled. She was the single greatest loss of his life. His blood has such strength that I believe he loves more deeply, hates more deeply, and struggles against his enemies with more intensity than the rest of us could ever know. We must be patient with him. But besides the fact he so loved Celeste and that she was his wife, there is another, even more meaningful reason why he grieves so deeply for her."

"Why?" the princess asked.

"Because he feels responsible for her death," Wigg answered. "It was, after all, their physical act of love that began her slow demise. Had he never lain with her, she might be alive today."

Shailiha looked back at her brother. For the first time in a long while, it finally seemed that their nation had found peace. Despite everyone's losses they should all be happy and looking forward to their futures. And they were—except for Tristan. As she again looked into the fire, her mind was taken back to the unimaginable series of events that had brought them all to this remote campsite in the woods.

Wulfgar's second invasion of Eutracia had been defeated, but at a huge cost. The *Enseterat* had attacked Tammerland with two full armies and a fleet of the magical Black Ships that could do wondrous things. The resulting war had cost many Minion troops. It would take an entire generation to replace them.

Much of Tammerland had been ravaged by fire and by the destructive creatures Wulfgar had loosed on the city. Lionel and Geldon had been killed by the assassin Satine, whom Wulfgar had hired to kill the members of the Conclave of the Vigors shortly before the invasion. Serena—Wulfgar's widow—still lived in the island fortress on the other side of the Sea of Whispers. She alone possessed the fabled Scroll of the Vagaries.

But perhaps the most ominous development was the appearance of the azure pass that had been cut through the Tolenka Mountains by the wounded Orb of the Vigors, as the orb rained its destructive energy down on the land. Tristan had later used the craft to heal the orb and destroy Wulfgar. But the secrets of the pass—and what lay beyond it—remained mysteries. Wulfgar had nearly succeeded in his insane plans. Despite the losses, however, good things had also been born of that struggle.

After Tristan killed Satine, Wigg's search of her body produced a crumpled parchment. There were thirteen names and matching locations listed on it. Even more interesting was the series of secret code phrases associated with each of them.

Wigg recognized the names immediately. To everyone's surprise, each one identified a onetime consul of the Redoubt. The list also revealed a series of safe houses in which Satine could hide as she went about her grisly work. The network of endowed spies lying in wait throughout Eutracia had finally been brought to light. But the bottom of the list was ragged, indicating that Satine had ripped away one or more of the names. This concerned them all, but there was nothing to be done about it.

Tristan had been right. Even though tonight's cottage had been the final safe house on the list, that didn't mean that the last of the traitorous consuls had been dealt with. The few who had been taken alive awaited questioning in the Redoubt.

She thought back to the night when Tristan defeated Wulfgar, and healed the Orb of the Vigors. Despite the carnage and destruction, things had ended on a glorious turn of events. His blood having been turned from azure back to red, Tristan used the last of the spells in his blood signature to miraculously heal the warriors who had been wounded in battle, and also heal those unfortunate citizens stricken by the orb.

As a result the jubilant populace—long wary of the prince and the Minion warriors at his command—again regarded Tristan as their rightful leader. They had even come to accept the flying warriors as their protectors.

The people of Eutracia again appreciated magic for the good things that it could do, rather than fearing it for the evil. Watching the citizens and the Minion warriors working side by side to rebuild the palace and the city had been a heartwarming thing. A grand masquerade ball had been scheduled to celebrate the royal residence's completion. It would be the first real palace social event since the ill-fated night of Tristan's aborted coronation ceremony.

An added result of this new peaceful period had been a rebirth of culture and prosperity in Eutracia. Shops again buzzed with activity. Crime in Tammerland had been drastically reduced because of the Minion patrols that Tristan ordered to wander about the city. Long overdue taxes and vital goods again flowed into the capital. Vital trade had resumed not only between Eutracia's far-flung provinces, but up and down her coastline as well.

"A kisa for your thoughts," Wigg said, bringing the princess back to the present. Looking over at his craggy profile, she smiled.

"I was just thinking about how much things have changed," she answered. "And about how much we've all lost, yet also gained." She looked over at Tristan again, to see that he was still painstakingly sharpening his sword. His silhouette dark against the moonlight, he did not look back.

"Do you think that the peace will hold?" she asked.

"For a time," Wigg answered. "But periods like this have always been fragile. Several things still threaten our security."

Wigg took a deep breath. "We must secure the Scroll of the Vagaries," he added, "and Serena must be dealt with. I am sure that she is of highly endowed blood, and that makes her immensely dangerous. Wulfgar would have never chosen her as his queen otherwise. There is simply no telling how much craft training she might have already had. From that mission you and Tyranny carried out at the Citadel not long ago, we also know that she is pregnant. That means that there will soon be another child in the world of your family's bloodline. As long as Serena controls the other scroll and has gifted consuls working in her service, we will always be in danger.

"Our recent examination of the azure pass also concerns us greatly," Wigg added. "The terrible hordes Wulfgar used to attack Tammerland came through there, but we have yet to learn any of its secrets. Who knows what other horrors may lie in wait behind that glowing wall? Faegan, Jessamay, and I think that the calculations needed to breach the pass might be found in the Scroll of the Vagaries. But would having them do more harm than good? Only time will tell."

Summoning a mental image of Shawna the Short rocking Morganna in her arms, Shailiha smiled. For no good reason, Wigg again poked at the fire.

"There are other things to consider," he said, "things that easily eclipse our storming of the Citadel, or whether the calculations we seek to breach the pass can be found in the other scroll." He looked over at Tristan again, then back into the fire.

"And they all have to do with the amazing revelations about you, your brother, and your destinies," he added.

Shailiha nodded. "The things that the Scroll Master told him," she offered.

"That's right. When Tristan explained them to me just before he finally destroyed the *Enseterat,* at first I couldn't believe my ears. We are still trying to come to grips with what they might mean. His training should start soon, but Faegan, Jessamay, and I would much prefer to see his heart lighten before we start. His full attention and willingness to learn will be crucial. But there is no telling when that might be."

Turning from the fire, Wigg looked at Shailiha. "You know how stubborn he can be," he added.

Shailiha understood Wigg's worries. During his time with the Scroll Master, Tristan had learned not only where Forestallments came to reside after a blood signature's human host dies, but also that there had been many other *Jin'Sais* and *Jin'Saious* who had arrived long before he and she. Every one, the Scroll Master said, had failed in their attempts to unite the two sides of the craft.

The Scroll Master also told Tristan that Celeste—despite how much Tristan loved her—was not his destiny. Had she lived, he would have been forced to leave her for the good of the craft. Another love would come to him, and it would be a love like no other. When Tristan saw her he would know. It would be she who would become his true love, and bear his children. And when she arrived to take part in his life, she would not be what he expected.

Shailiha knew that Tristan did not want to believe that. Nor did the First Wizard, she guessed. But the word of the young Scroll Master was not to be doubted. Despite how much he had loved Celeste, Tristan found himself having to accept these painful facts.

When Tristan finally finds this new woman, will he be able to love her in the way that the Scroll Master foretold? Shailiha wondered. *Or will Celeste's memory continue to so crowd his heart that there will be no room for anyone else?*

Perhaps most important, in a painful application of the craft the young Scroll Master had used the spells given him by the Ones Who Came Before to change Tristan's blood back to red. He would now be able to wear the Paragon and start translating the Prophecies—the third and final volume of the Tome that only he or Shailiha were destined to read.

But before that process started, the wizards and Jessamay had agreed that the consular safe houses needed to be wiped out. Each time they approached one it had been all they could do to convince the prince not to go charging in, trying to kill every consul he could find. Since Celeste's death he seemed to possess an even deeper, more blinding hatred of all things connected to the Vagaries, and he mercilessly acted on it with every opportunity.

Shailiha often wondered what her late parents would think of her and Tristan helping to round up and sometimes kill former Redoubt consuls. Sometimes she felt like their parents' spirits were looking down on her and her brother, watching them struggle to fulfill their destinies.

She looked back at Tristan. His silhouette dark in the moonlight, he continued to hone the already razor-sharp blade. Sensing his pain, Shailiha closed her eyes.

CHAPTER III

SECRETS AND GIFTS, SHE THOUGHT AS SHE QUIETLY WALKED THE corridors. *That is all I have left of what my lord so graciously bestowed upon me. But the secrets and gifts that remain in my heart and in my blood signature shall be enough to pluck my revenge from the ashes.*

As she walked, she clutched a withered rose to her breast, and a tear came to one eye. The droplet slowly traced its way down one cheek.

Soon, my love, she thought. *Soon I will avenge your death.*

Serena walked slowly down the Citadel hallways, her black silk gown rustling pleasantly as she went. Dark ringlets lay on her shoulders. Although her blue eyes were tinged with grief, they also carried a commitment to see the Heretics' goals attained. She would struggle until her efforts ended either in the death of the *Jin'Sai,* or in her own. Wiping the tear from her face, she walked on.

Two months had passed since Wulfgar's unsuccessful invasion of Eutracia. The rose that he had bound to his life force before departing the Citadel had told Serena his fate. If the rose withered, she would know he had died, and she would be the new ruler of the Citadel.

When the impossible had happened, and the rose had died before her very eyes, she had been in her private chambers, taking tea. Her grip had faltered, and her teacup had smashed upon the floor as she cried her grief to the heavens. Without a doubt, she knew: The *Enseterat* was dead.

At that very moment, a searing pain had racked her belly, its strength so great that she was sure she would die as well. The first of the horrible contractions came quickly as her endowed blood surged hotly through her veins. Then she felt something inside her slip.

Collapsing to the floor, she began to bleed and give birth. Just moments before she fell unconscious, she managed to place an azure field around the little corpse that lay there beside her like a bloodied doll.

Summoned by her screams, her servants soon found her. Teetering on the cusp of death, Serena lingered under the care of her worried consuls for two more days.

On the third day her consciousness sensed the Heretics of the Guild for the first time, as their voices roused her from her nether-sleep. Opening her eyes, she commandingly raised one arm to order her shocked servants from the room. After they had gone, she closed her eyes again.

"Serena," she heard.

"I am here," she thought, innately understanding that she would not need to speak to make her thoughts known. Then her losses stabbed her heart again, hurting so badly that she could hardly bear it.

"My husband and child are dead," she told them.

"We know," the choir of voices answered. *"In his twisted eagerness to rule the craft, the* Jin'Sai *killed them both."*

Serena took a quick breath. *"How?"* she asked.

"He used the Orb of the Vigors to destroy Wulfgar," they answered. *"The unexpected might of their clash had been underestimated—even by us. It had been aeons since your world witnessed such a titanic struggle of the craft. But the Ones cannot commune with the* Jin'Sai *again, for the Forestallment required to do so is lost to his blood."*

"What of my child?" Serena asked. *"I still do not understand."*

"When the Enseterat *died, your blood could withstand it; the vulnerable blood of your unborn child could not. But take heart. Wulfgar granted you many Forestallments before he died. You are a fully empowered sorceress, and your blood is strong. Any additional Forestallments required for your purposes can be gleaned from the Vagaries scroll. If you act soon enough, victory can still be ours."*

She smiled for the first time since the death of her family. *"What do you wish of me?"* she asked. *"My life is yours."*

"We know, Daughter," they responded. *"Your mission will be a complicated one, and must be accomplished in steps. Listen as we tell you what to do first."*

As she lay near death, Serena was astounded by what she heard. Nonetheless it all made perfect sense. The task before her would be enormous. But the rewards would be, as well.

When the Heretics had finished speaking to her, she bid them good-bye. From that moment on, her strength and vitality had returned quickly. That had been seven weeks ago. She had accomplished much since then.

Reaching her destination, the queen of the Vagaries stopped before a pair of tall twin doors. A wreath of flowering red cat's paw hung on each one. She pointed an index finger. At her bidding the heavy locks turned over and the doors parted. Serena walked into the room. The doors shut heavily behind her.

She paused for a moment to look around. Everything was just as she had left it. The room was to be perfectly maintained at all times. If she found the slightest thing disturbed, the handmaidens responsible for maintaining this place would die.

The chamber was large and well lit. Sunlight streamed in through numerous skylights; songbirds could be heard warbling in the outer yard. The brick floor was covered with fresh red rose petals. On the dawn of each new day the old petals were removed, then carefully replaced. Their familiar aroma permeated the air. Two specially chosen handmaidens stood in the far corners. As Serena looked at them, they bowed.

Finally satisfied, she again lifted her gown to stride through the lush foliage and toward the center of the room. When she reached the altar she stopped to look down. Her eyes immediately filled with tears.

The pink marble altar was just large enough to support a small body. An azure glow surrounded it. Reaching through the aura, the bereaved sorceress stroked her daughter's cold cheek.

The tiny body was covered by a black silk sheet. More rose petals littered the shroud and surrounding altar top. Small and frail-looking, the dead baby girl lay peacefully atop the stone. The child's eyes were closed in death. A small wisp of downy brown hair adorned the crown of her head. Had she lived, she would have been named Clarice.

In memory of the child's father, Serena had ordered the floor covered with rose petals of the same variety Wulfgar had chosen to signal his demise. The glow she had conjured over the little corpse would ensure that the body remained perpetually preserved. The spell's calculations had been purposely convoluted to avoid tampering, and Serena was sure that only she could unravel it. She turned and looked at her handmaidens.

"These petals upon which I stand," she said. "They were fresh this morning?"

One of the handmaidens bowed. "Yes, Your Grace," she answered.

Serena returned her gaze to her daughter's lifeless form. "Good," she replied. Silence filled the room again.

She suddenly heard someone knocking on the double doors of the crypt. Earlier this morning she had summoned the only two other people she would allow into this room without killing them outright.

"Enter," she called out.

The doors parted to show two men. She bid them enter.

Two servants walked into the room. They bowed to their queen, then to the little corpse. *"When you are in this sacred place you are to bow to my child as well,"* Serena had warned them. Given their queen's mental state, they knew better than to disobey.

Serena looked commandingly at them. Einar, her senior consul, was dressed in his familiar dark blue robe. Tall and whippet lean, his dark brown eyes stared back at her with confidence. She watched him lower the hood of his robe to expose his sharp features and cruel-looking mouth. Serena trusted and respected Einar. His loyalty to her late husband had been unshakable.

Reznik was another matter. Serena found his kind to be greasy, unpleasant creatures, but she tolerated the partial adepts here on her small island because she found their gifts useful. At fifty Seasons of New Life, Reznik had a wrinkled face, a thick middle, and a balding head. A circular fringe of graying hair fell to his shoulders. Yellow teeth, a hooked nose, and limpid brown eyes finished the unappealing picture. As if suddenly needing something to do, he nervously ran his wet palms down the front of his bloody smock.

Also known as the Corporeals, his group had been granted sanctuary by Wulfgar. There were nearly two hundred of Reznik's kind here on the island. Corporeals possessed partial, left-leaning blood signatures. They specialized in producing dark wares of the craft that they sold for profit. With no market left in Eutracia for their deadly wares, they gladly served the new queen of the Vagaries at the Citadel. Despite how much Serena looked down on them, even she had become impressed by their unique abilities.

As the leader of the Corporeals, Reznik was an expert herbmaster, potion blender, and cutter-healer. But he had little experience with royalty, and now he made the mistake of speaking first.

"Has the new Vagaries servant entered Eutracia?" he asked.

Serena glared angrily at him, then turned to look at the handmaidens. They each quickly looked at the floor. She turned back to glare at the Corporeal.

"Not here, you fool!" she admonished him. "Follow me."

She strode past the two men, then caused the doors to open. As she walked out into the daylight, her servants followed. The twin doors shut heavily behind them. Saying nothing, Serena led them through the Citadel's inner ward.

The island fortress was a majestic place. The Citadel walls rose straight up from the island's rock. The many interior buildings and turrets were interconnected by an ornate series of catwalks suspended high in the air. Manicured gardens and majestic fountains dotted the grounds. There had been many nights when she and Wulfgar had walked these grounds, talking and dreaming of the day when they would rule the craft, and watch their daughter grow to womanhood. But those days were no more.

Her mind often drifted back to her early captivity in this remote place—days that later led to her enlightened worship of the Vagaries. She loved following their dark teachings. Before departing for Eutracia, Wulfgar had granted her the Forestallment that allowed her communion with the Heretics. She knew her gifts were easily a match for those of the Redoubt wizards. And as the Heretics had told her, not one of her Conclave enemies could commune with the Ones—an advantage she would use wisely in the days ahead.

Still, disadvantages loomed. The demonslavers—the macabre army Wulfgar had employed to invade Eutracia—were all dead, leaving the Citadel largely unguarded. The majestic Black Ships in which Wulfgar had transported his army had also been lost to her. But she still had nearly one hundred consuls at her command, plus the Corporeals. Most important, she possessed the Scroll of the Vagaries—the ancient document containing every Vagaries Forestallment calculation known to man.

She knew that the Conclave would try to take the scroll from her. But by then she would be ready for them. Soon the Redoubt wizards would be dealing with an entirely new host of problems, the likes of which they had never seen.

Choosing a stone bench beneath a willowberry tree, she sat down. As the breeze ruffled her mourning gown she reached down to smooth out the dress. Einar and Reznik came to stand before her. When she was satisfied, she looked up at Reznik.

"Never discuss our plans before my handmaidens," she said. "You and your people are merely guests here. I will kill you without remorse if you violate my confidence again."

The blood rushed from Reznik's face. "Yes—yes of course, Your Grace," he stammered. "You have my deepest apologies."

Serena nodded. "Now to answer your question," she said. "Yes, the Darkling has arrived in Eutracia. By now he should be about his mission."

Einar smiled. "That is indeed good news," he said.

"Yes," Serena answered. "The *Jin'Sai* and his Conclave are about to get the shock of their lives. I wish I could be there to see it." She suddenly remembered the little corpse lying in state in the crypt, and her face darkened. "Though it will never make up for Clarice's death," she added softly. Einar and Reznik waited while she composed herself.

"Is there news regarding the project I entrusted to you?" she asked her consul at last.

Einar sighed. "The issues are complex," he answered. "We have done almost all that can be accomplished here at the Citadel. Once we have traveled to Parthalon, the real research can start. But as you know, before we leave we must be sure that the Citadel is protected. The Redoubt wizards and the *Jin'Sai* and *Jin'Saiou* will soon come for the scroll—and for you."

Serena nodded. "Keep me informed. Your work is vital to the Heretics' plan." She again looked at Reznik.

"And you?" she asked. "Have you and your group been helpful to my consuls?"

"We have been as much aid as our limited gifts allow, Your Grace," Reznik answered. "The going is slow, but Einar and I believe that we are on the right track. Every Valrenkian is doing what he or she can to aid the cause."

Serena nodded. "Good," she said. "Leave me. I have much to consider and I wish to be alone." With deep bows, the two men left for their respective research areas.

Finally alone, Serena looked around. The birds were singing again, and the early-afternoon sun felt good on her face. Standing, she looked up to the barbican surrounding the fortress. She gently levitated herself.

Higher and higher she soared as the sea breeze billowed her black gown. She landed gently atop one of the wall guard paths, then turned west to look out over the Sea of Whispers.

The dark blue ocean tide was high. From where she stood she could smell the salt air and hear the waves crashing in their endless assault against the shore. The white gulls called noisily to one another as they sought out their next meal.

Enjoy what peaceful time you have left, Jin'Sai, she thought. *You will soon pay for your crimes.*

CHAPTER IV

"NO, NO, *NO!*" WIGG CRIED OUT, RAISING HIS HANDS IN FRUSTRATION. "You're losing her again!"

Seeing that it was already too late, the First Wizard braced himself.

The great ship fell a good ten meters through the air, then slammed mightily back down onto the ocean. The impact shot seawater plumes high into the sky, and the vessel heeled hard to starboard. Faegan's chair on wheels nearly tipped over. Wigg slipped to one knee. Seawater fell down, drenching everyone again.

It was plain to see that the two wizards were becoming furious. For her part, it was all Jessamay could do to keep from howling outright. Twice this morning she had already laughed uproariously, adding to the wizards' growing aggravation and embarrassment.

Sister Adrian stood nearby with a sheepish look on her face. Her red acolyte robe lay soaked against her skin, making her plump figure look thinner. Her sandy hair lying wet on her shoulders, she pursed her lips, then looked toward the deck.

She would have to try harder next time. If she didn't succeed soon, she feared that the First Wizard's head might explode with frustration.

It was a sunny day in Eutracia, and the sea winds were light. It was a perfect time to start the acolyte's training, the two wizards had decided. But as they stood on the drenched deck, they were starting to have their doubts about this project.

With the consuls' safe houses finally dealt with, the group had returned to Tammerland two days ago. They were all glad to be home, but many important actions still awaited the Conclave's attention. By mutual agreement, the most vital of these was to devise the plan of attack against the Citadel.

There was more than one reason why capturing the Vagaries scroll had become so important. Without it, Serena and her traitorous consuls would be far less powerful. Wigg and Faegan were acutely aware that the longer she held the document, the greater the likelihood that she would imbue herself with yet more Forestallments. And with the scroll safely in the hands of the Conclave, other Vagaries practitioners would find themselves at a distinct disadvantage. But no matter the Conclave's battle plan, the siege of the Citadel would be problematic. With the bulk of the Minion armada destroyed, the Black Ships would have to take them there.

Providing I ever get these monstrous vessels to obey my com-

mands, Adrian thought. She had to admit that as the morning wore on, she was becoming less and less optimistic.

Fuming and stamping about like a wet hen, Wigg angrily shook the water from his robe. Then he reached over one shoulder to grasp the braided queue of gray hair falling down his back. After squeezing out the seawater, he tossed the braid back again.

Adrian heard a strange noise. She turned to see several fish flopping around on the deck. Pointing a finger at them, she called the craft and tossed them overboard.

Faegan tilted his head. Inserting a finger into one ear, he tried to free some trapped seawater from his ear canal. His gray hair lay all about his shoulders. Finally overcome, Jessamay just had to laugh again. Wigg scowled.

"What's so funny?" he demanded. "This is serious work!"

"That might be," she answered, "but I just can't help it!"

The blond-haired sorceress was as wet and frustrated as the others, but it didn't seem to bother her. Smiling, she placed her arms akimbo.

"You should see yourselves!" she exclaimed. "Wigg, I haven't seen you this perplexed since you were a boy! You had just accidentally blown up your father's laboratory. As I remember, Faegan was in on it with you. You two were inseparable, even then! Let me remember—what was it that you miscreants were trying to do? Ah, yes—something about perfecting a spell that would allow you the power to turn lead into gold. I thought your father was going to kill you both!"

"I remember," Wigg grumbled. He looked down at Faegan to see the crippled wizard still trying to drain his ear.

"They were *your* calculations, you know!" Wigg hollered at him.

Faegan looked up crookedly. "Oh?" he shot back. "Just who can remember back that far, eh?"

Wigg quickly pointed a bony index finger. "You can!" he thundered back. "Or have you forgotten about your power of Consummate Recollection?"

"Uh, excuse me," Adrian said as she walked nearer. "With all due respect, this isn't getting us anyplace. Our goal was to teach me how to empower the Black Ships—not to fight among ourselves, remember?"

Sighing, Wigg rubbed his brow. “Yes, yes, I know,” he said. “But you aren’t grasping the concept.”

All morning, Wigg, Faegan, and Jessamay had been trying to teach Adrian how to fly one of the Black Ships. Six of the huge vessels had survived Wulfgar’s attack on Tammerland. The five others lay quietly at anchor nearby. If the Conclave’s plans were to succeed, the ships would be needed soon.

Each ship was easily four or five times the size of the largest that had once served the Eutracian fleet. Every part, including the sails, was solid black. Each of the ships’ five black masts rose dozens of meters into the air. Eight full decks lay below their topsides. Despite their huge size, these potent vessels could not only rise from the sea, but fly through the air with great speed. Due to other enchantments, they were nearly impervious to traditional forms of attack. One Black Ship is easily the equivalent of many normal vessels, Wigg was fond of saying.

Several weeks earlier, Tristan had ordered that a bright red image of the Paragon be painted onto each ship’s huge foresail. It had taken an entire Minion host more than a week to finish the job. When freed to the wind, they were an amazing sight.

The ships were all more than three hundred years old. Once the mainstays of the Directorate of Wizards’ battle fleet, they had been sunk by the Coven during the Sorceresses’ War. Using a Forestallment found in the Scroll of the Vagaries, Wulfgar had raised them and pressed them into his service. Now spoils of war, they were again firmly in the control of the Conclave. But the specialized gifts of those trained in the craft were required to unleash their amazing abilities.

Walking back over to her three teachers, Adrian looked at them humbly. Seawater still dripping from his robe, Wigg shot her a questioning glance.

“Are you ready to try again?” he asked.

Adrian nodded. “Yes, but I believe it would help if you explained the theory once more.”

“Very well,” he answered. Taking a deep breath, he looked into her eyes.

“As I have told you, this is a binary spell,” he started, “and they can be tricky. ‘Binary’ means two parts. As you can imagine, tri-spells and quadra-spells are even more difficult. In this case you are not trying to levitate the ship, then push it forward over the waves. Instead, you must change the atmospheric conditions surrounding her. Using the calculations we provided, first you must create a strong vacuum, just above the ship. If the spell is strong enough, the vacuum will attract the ship, causing her to rise.

"Performing the second part of the spell—while also maintaining the first—is the truly delicate part," he went on to say. "You must simultaneously enlarge the vacuum and cause it to flow down toward the bow. Only then will she hover while being pulled forward. Instead of the wind pushing her from behind, this vessel is *pulled* into the emptiness of the morphing vacuums. And as we have already seen, if both parts of the calculations are not properly maintained, then the spell fractures, and the ship falls back into the sea. Now then, shall we try again?"

Nodding, Adrian recalled the complicated series of calculations. She raised her arms.

At once the ship started to rise. She wobbled a bit as her massive hull laboriously left the ocean surface. Dripping seawater from bow to stern, she slowly climbed about twenty meters into the air.

Wigg, Faegan, and Jessamay could see the strain on Adrian's face. Walking closer, the First Wizard knew that the most difficult moment had again come.

"Good!" he said gently. Her concentration firmly locked on her work, Adrian did not look at him.

"Now," Wigg said, "while maintaining the current vacuum, enlarge it and draw it down toward the ship's bow."

Straining to keep her focus, Adrian did as the wizard asked. This time the spell seemed to hold.

"Don't be alarmed when she starts to move forward," Wigg whispered.

No sooner had the wizard spoken than the great vessel started to glide over the waves. A joyous look overcame Adrian's face.

"Good!" Wigg shouted. "But continue to concentrate! We can celebrate later!"

As the vessel gained speed, Jessamay and Faegan came nearer. The air rushing by them began teasing their hair and clothes. Smiling broadly, the crippled wizard slapped one hand down on the arm of his chair.

"I believe she's got it!" he exclaimed. He gave Wigg a knowing wink. Wigg nodded, then looked back at Adrian.

"Since things are going so well, let's try some basic maneuvers," he said. He knew that Adrian was tiring, but pushing her would help strengthen her newfound talent.

During the next hour, Wigg showed Adrian how to change the ship's speed, direction, and hull pitch by altering the vacuum's intensity and shape. Now that she had the knack of it, Adrian was performing brilliantly. So much so that Wigg decided it was time for another test.

"While continuing to sustain the spells, walk to the bow and guide us home," he ordered. "If you feel yourself tiring, shout out at once. We will quickly augment your power."

Adrian slowly lowered her arms. She was beaming with pride. *So far so good,* she thought.

She walked to the bow, and steadied herself by grabbing part of the rigging. The other three mystics felt the huge ship start to carve a gentle turn in the air. Soon she was pointing straight toward the Eutracian coast.

Satisfied, Wigg walked over to the port gunwale. Jessamay came to join him. For several moments they didn't speak, choosing instead to simply enjoy the wondrous sensation.

Jessamay smiled. "It's been a long time since we stood on these decks, eh, First Wizard?" she asked. "Then again, in some ways it seems like only yesterday."

Wigg turned to look at her. She expected to see a smile on his face, but only sadness showed.

"A long time indeed," he answered. "It's good to have you back."

"You miss Celeste terribly, don't you?" Jessamay asked.

Wigg looked back out to sea. "Yes," he answered. "She was my only child. Perhaps the hardest part is that I knew her so briefly. She suddenly came into my life as a fully grown adult, only to age quickly, then die in my arms."

Taking a deep breath, he paused for a moment as the sea wind continued to harass his robe. "A father isn't supposed to outlive his child," he added quietly.

Jessamay placed a hand over his. "I know," she answered.

Wigg returned his gaze to Jessamay and took in her long, curly blond hair, blue eyes, and slim figure. She was pretty, in a wholesome, country-girl sort of way. Her simple green shirt, dark trousers, and black boots enhanced that impression. Three centuries earlier, Wigg had granted her the time enchantments. At the time she had been thirty-five Seasons of New Life. Even though she was nearly as old as he, she didn't look it—a fact everyone had trouble remembering. But her power was formidable, and the wizards knew that her gifts and knowledge would soon prove invaluable.

Suddenly they heard Adrian cry out. With a frightened look on her face, she turned toward them. The Black Ship was slowly but inexorably gliding down toward the ocean.

"I can't hold her!" Adrian shouted. "I'm too tired!"

Smiling, Wigg looked over at Jessamay. "Would you like to do the honors, or shall I?"

"I'll take her," Jessamay answered. "It has been three hundred years since I tried, but I used to be pretty good at this! Let's see how much speed I can get out of this old bucket!"

Jessamay hurried to stand beside the acolyte. She said something to Adrian, and the tired First Sister gratefully started unraveling her spell. After summoning the spell's lengthy calculations, Jessamay took over for her.

At once the great ship regained altitude, and her speed rose markedly. Gathering his robe against the strengthening wind, Wigg was suddenly reminded of how fast these amazing vessels could fly, given the proper mystic to captain them. With Jessamay at the helm they would be home in minutes.

Then other, more dangerous thoughts revisited him. Turning west, he looked out over the ocean again. His mind started unknowingly echoing some of the same concerns that had teased Serena, only two days before.

The enemy lies out there, he thought. *Only the Afterlife knows what new horrors await us.* Turning back to the east, the ancient wizard watched the Eutracian coast grow closer.

CHAPTER V

BRENT WAS DOING HIS BEST TO IMPALE A WORM ONTO HIS FISHING hook, just as his father had shown him. But the slimy little creature kept wiggling about, adding to the difficulty. Every time Brent tried, the worm somehow seemed to outsmart him. Slipping from his grip, it plopped into the Sippora River. Brent guessed that his father would not be pleased.

Instead, the lean, middle-aged man only smiled. Reaching into his bait box, he produced another worm and handed it to his son. He considered doing the job for him, but he wanted the boy to learn on his own.

Brent took the worm and started the frustrating process again. At seven Seasons of New Life, he found preparing the hook far less fun than dangling the line in the water and waiting for a fish to come along.

Finally succeeding, he beamed a smile up at his father, then lowered his line into the swift-moving Sippora. The river was fairly shallow here, making this a perfect place to find Eutracian trout.

Alfred watched Brent's line go out and take the bait downstream. When it had traveled far enough, Alfred told his son to stop letting it go. The red-and-white cork attached to the line bobbed happily as it fought the current.

The late-afternoon sun slanted across the water; it would be time soon to return to their small village of Charningham. Many such farming hamlets bordered the Sippora. Lying well to the north, Charningham had been spared the wrath of the orb's recent rampage. Rumor had it that Prince Tristan had somehow used the craft to heal the orb and restore the river's vitality. Everyone had been grateful for the good news.

Alfred looked up from his line. He and Brent were sitting on wooden chairs, atop a stone bridge stretching over a curved neck in the river. A farmer by trade, Alfred owned much of the surrounding land. To the east, Charningham stretched out before them. Colorful wildflowers dotted the intervening fields for nearly as far as the eye could see.

Evening was fast approaching. Cicadas and tree frogs sang happily. The Sippora burbled noisily, adding its unique contribution to nature's chorus. The river pulled on Alfred's fishing line, gently reminding him to pay attention.

Looking down, he affectionately tousled Brent's blond hair. They already had two trout in the quiver, and the last one was still flapping about. One more and they would go home.

Annabelle could do miraculous things with trout. Tonight's dinner might be late, but definitely worth the trouble.

That was when things suddenly changed.

The Sippora River impossibly stopped flowing. Alfred had often seen the river meander or rush, depending on the season. But this was different. A curious expression on his face, Brent looked up at his father.

Then the breeze abruptly quieted. So did the singing of the cicadas and tree frogs.

Everything suddenly carried a deathly stillness about it, like nature herself had somehow lost her never-ending vitality. Rising from his chair, Alfred looked downstream. His hands tightened around his fishing rod.

Dark and unmoving, a rider could be seen on the western bank. Dressed all in black, he simply waited there, staring at Alfred and Brent. The black stallion's coat shone in the growing moonlight; vapor streamed whitely from his nostrils. Alfred couldn't see the rider's face. Grasping Brent's shoulders, Alfred spun him around.

"We're leaving!" he said quickly. "Grab up your pole!"

A questioning look crossed Brent's face, but he did as he was told. Alfred snatched up the bait box and quiver, then literally started pulling his son off the bridge. At the same time the intruder spurred his horse into the still river and started coming upstream. Reaching the end of the bridge, the father and son stepped to the ground.

As Alfred turned to look, his face fell. It would be useless to try to outrun the stranger. Charningham was a quarter of a league away, and there was no one about to help. All he could do was wait, and pray that the rider meant them no harm.

As if reading his mind, the lone rider slowed his mount to a walk. The intruder quietly exited the river. As he watched him approach, Alfred's mouth fell open.

With every step the being's horse took, the surrounding grass and wildflowers withered and died.

The rider prodded his horse closer. A battle axe hung at his left hip, and a war shield was tied to his saddle. Even now the river refused to flow, the night creatures remained silent, and the breeze had not returned.

Alfred looked into the rider's face. A shock went through his system; he took a step back and put an arm around his son.

Alfred tried to find his voice. "Who are you?" he asked.

"Call me Xanthus," the leader answered. "I come from another world—a world you couldn't possibly imagine. The answers to your questions will do you no good, for I can tell that your blood is unendowed. So inquire no more."

"What do you want?" Alfred whispered.

Xanthus smiled. "I want you," he answered. The voice possessed a strangely macabre, hollow timbre. If a dead man could speak, it seemed that this was what he would sound like.

"Why?" Alfred asked.

"For no other reason than you are the first Eutracians I have encountered," Xanthus answered. "My orders are specific." He turned in his saddle and looked east.

"Charningham?" he asked.

Nervously, Alfred nodded.

Xanthus leaned forward in his saddle. "How many souls live there?" he asked.

Alfred's dread grew. "About one thousand."

"A sizable enough audience with which to start," Xanthus replied cryptically.

"What do you mean?" Alfred asked.

"You will learn that soon enough. You are coming with me."

At once Alfred felt his body rise into the air. Struggle as he might he couldn't overcome the invisible grip that tossed him onto the stallion's back behind Xanthus. Speaking and moving had become impossible. He could only watch as Brent, screaming, was hauled into the air and deposited on the horse's back just behind him. And then the scream was cut off as Brent, too, was frozen in place.

Xanthus turned his horse toward Charningham. The grass and flowers in their path died quickly, turning brown. The sun, its golden rays reddening, slowly slipped behind the Tolenka Mountains.

Hoping he and his son might somehow survive the night, Alfred closed his eyes. There was no one around to observe as the horse and its riders vanished.

With the Darkling gone, the Sippora River slowly started flowing again. The breeze returned. The tree frogs and cicadas sang. Inside the abandoned fishing quiver, the most recently caught trout finally gave in to the inevitable, and died.

* * *

"ARE YOU RESTING COMFORTABLY?" THE VOICE ASKED.

It was an absurd inquiry. The false concern, born only of malice, was taunting; its tone was completely devoid of compassion.

Night had fallen in Charningham. The only light came from the flickering torches Xanthus had lit—no doubt for dramatic effect. The town square was a mass of people; it seemed to Brent that every person he knew was there with him. All those who had resisted the Darkling's demand to attend him in the town square were dead, killed outright, their bodies left lying in pools of blood. Brent was mute with horror. Tears filling his eyes, he clung unashamedly to his mother's skirts. He could feel her legs trembling.

Shuddering, Brent looked down at his father.

Alfred lay in the square's center with his back against one of the large stones forming the plaza floor. Two men and two women lay at even intervals beside him. The Darkling sat on horseback, glowering over them. No one spoke; no one moved.

Iron shoes clip-clopped on the stones as Xanthus spurred his horse to stand before Alfred. A hush descended over the crowd.

"I asked you a question," Xanthus said. "Are you resting comfortably?"

Despite his partial paralysis, Alfred did his best to look up at his captor. "What do you want?" he asked. "We have little money to give you! We know nothing about the craft! Please—leave us in peace!"

"By the time I leave here, you will have found everlasting peace, I assure you," Xanthus answered.

Xanthus' ominous words made Alfred's skin crawl. He tried again to move, but it was no use.

"At least let the two women go!" he begged.

"No," Xanthus answered simply.

"But we have done you no wrong!" one of the other men screamed. "What in the name of the Afterlife do you want?"

"Ah, yes," Xanthus said. "The Afterlife—a concept you humans refer to often, but know so little about." Raising his dark head, he looked around the crowd.

"Despite your frequent references to it, who among you mindless sheep can explain it, eh?" he added. The silent crowd simply stared at him in dread.

"Just as I thought." He looked back down at Alfred. "Don't

worry. You will become fully acquainted with the Afterlife's workings soon enough. In some ways, I envy you."

"What do you want?" Alfred demanded again. Fearing the worst, he strained to find Annabelle and Brent in the crowd.

"The answer is simple," Xanthus said. "I want you five to die. It is going to take a long time, and your fellow citizens shall provide the audience. It is no more complicated than that."

Saying nothing more, the Darkling raised one arm.

Alfred started to hear a grinding sound. When he finally realized what was happening, his eyes bulged and his breath caught.

One of the massive stones of the plaza floor was lifting into the air. Dropping loose soil from its dark underside, it came to float directly above him. Even in the uncertain light of the torches, he could make out the worms, maggots, and other crawling creatures still attached to it, milling about on the stone's slick underside. Expecting the stone to come crashing down on him, Alfred closed his eyes.

But the stone did not fall. Instead it lowered slowly, its crushing weight starving his lungs bit by bit. His face was spared. But as the excruciating pain rose, he felt his sternum and several ribs snap. The pressure sent the wriggling creatures crawling free from the stone and onto his face.

Shaking his head wildly from side to side, Alfred screamed. Gasping for breath, he looked up at Xanthus.

"What—what do you want from us?" he whispered. He was barely able to get the words out.

Under the stone's overpowering weight, his veins began hemorrhaging; blood rivulets trickled from his nose, eyes, and ears. Unable to watch, Brent turned away, retreating farther into his mother's skirt folds. His entire body was shaking. Like his father, he could barely breathe.

"I have already told you," Xanthus said. "Be still, for my ears hear no begging. My eyes see no pain. My heart feels no remorse."

Another large stone came floating into the air. The other captives started begging. But they soon learned that the stone was not meant for one of them. Some in the crowd spoke up, pleading that the torture be stopped. But Xanthus ignored them.

As the second stone's weight was added to the first, the remaining air was pushed from Alfred's lungs. Several more ribs snapped, and both his shoulders dislocated. His heart, crushed, beat its last. A final death rattle escaped his lungs. His eyes were open wide, but unseeing.

Annabelle fainted; a nearby man caught her in his arms. For several long moments, Brent's wailing was the only sound in the square.

Suddenly a man rushed from the crowd. He was brandishing a sword, which he pointed directly at the Darkling.

"You're insane!" he growled. "If you don't stop this madness, I'll kill you!"

Xanthus didn't say a word. Raising one arm, he used the craft to levitate the fellow into the air. The man's fingers opened, and his sword clattered to the ground. His body stiffened; his eyes rolled back in his head. As if he were controlled by some unseen puppeteer—and in a way, he was—his body started dancing about wildly. Then his limbs began to break.

First the arms then the legs snapped, their glistening bones rupturing the skin in grisly, compound fractures. Blood flew, spattering the crowd nearby.

Suddenly the man's eyes went wide. His body arched, and then, with a sudden, swift motion, his back broke.

The body fell to the ground. Xanthus wheeled his horse around and glared at the crowd. Some sobbed; others hung their heads in shame. An elderly matron pulled Brent close to her.

"Is there anyone else who dares to be heroic?" Xanthus shouted. Silence filled the square.

"Good," he said simply, and walked his mount back toward the remaining captives.

It took three more hours to kill the four others. When it was done, Xanthus climbed down from his horse and removed the clothing covering the upper half of his body.

He was no longer the ghostly apparition the unfortunate Minion warriors had fought at the azure pass. He now appeared human, his body flesh and blood. Kneeling on the ground, facing west toward the Tolenkas, he removed a black, knotted line from his discarded clothing and began to flagellate himself.

Those in the crowd who had not already fainted watched, frozen by the Darkling's spell, though shock and horror would probably have kept them silent and unmoving even without the use of the craft.

As the cords ripped into his back, he showed no pain, no slacking in his self-discipline. On and on it went, his strokes perfectly spaced, until he had finished one hundred lashes. As the moonlight beamed down, his blood ran into the thirsty dirt lying between the square's remaining stones.

The Darkling stood and placed the bloody cords into a pocket, then donned his clothing again. The azure glow revisited him, returning his body to its original form. Xanthus released the crowd from his spell. The dazed citizens cowered as he walked back toward them.

"My work here is done," he said, "but yours is not. My mandate to you is this: Assemble a group of your most trusted citizens, then ride hard for Tammerland. You are to request an emergency audience before the Conclave of Vigors. Tell them what happened here by the power I, a Darkling, hold. Tell the *Jin'Sai* that it will do no good to try and find me, because I can vanish like dust on the wind. I will visit him soon enough. If you disobey me, I will return to this place and more of you will die."

He pointed to a nearby tree, and one of its branches tore loose to float in the air. As the flying branch approached, Xanthus drew his axe and cut it in half with a single motion. The two pieces fell to the ground. From a pocket he withdrew a white scroll bound with a bloodred ribbon. He tossed the scroll to the ground.

"See that the *Jin'Sai* is given the scroll and one of the cut branches," he ordered. "He will understand."

With a final glare at the crowd, Xanthus mounted his horse and headed out of town. As if bowing in shame, the foliage lining the street withered as he passed.

Just as the monster slipped into the darkness, he vanished.

CHAPTER VI

THREE DAYS LATER, TRISTAN SAT ALONE ON HIS PRIVATE BALCONY, looking out on the newly landscaped grounds of the rebuilt palace. It was morning in Eutracia, and he wore only a blue silk robe. He was tired; sleeping had been difficult again last night. A lavish breakfast brought by Shawna the Short sat untouched before him. Shawna would be beside herself when she learned that he hadn't eaten, but he just wasn't hungry. He took a sip of lukewarm tea, then returned his gaze to the palace grounds. He sat there for some time, remembering.

Finally he stood and walked into the rooms that he had briefly shared with Celeste. The familiar scent of myrrh still clung to the bedsheets and pillowcases. It often caused haunting memories of her to enter his dreams. He sometimes awakened in the night, expecting to find her lying there beside him. When he remembered that she was no more, the tears always came, making him feel even more alone in the darkness.

He shrugged off his robe and dropped it onto an empty chair, then dressed. As he took up his dreggan a thought struck him. He slowly slid the sword from its scabbard.

The Conclave was convening this morning to discuss the impending attack on the Citadel and other important matters. *How much longer would he need physical weapons like this?* he wondered as he stared at the shiny, razor-sharp blade.

Faegan, Wigg, and the late Redoubt Wizards had abandoned the use of physical weapons once their gifts had become fully realized. When he was trained, would he do the same? He always felt naked without his sword and knives, and couldn't imagine being without them. Sheathing the blade, he tossed the sword onto the four-poster bed.

He walked to the fireplace. On the mantel rested the urn containing Celeste's ashes. Beside it lay her farewell letter. There was no reason to read it again—he knew it line by line. He closed his eyes for a moment, then turned away and walked back to the balcony to lean against the railing.

His recent behavior was hurting people he loved. He knew that, but sometimes the pain welled up so much that he couldn't help it. Had his sorrow been only for Celeste, it would have been devastating enough. But when he also remembered the many others who had sacrificed their lives to the Vagaries, his sorrow morphed into sullenness, his sullenness sometimes deteriorating into outright rage.

Worse, until the Acolytes of the Redoubt learned to empower the Black Ships, there seemed little for him to do. Since the return of the Coven, Tristan had been a man of action, intent on destroying Vagaries practitioners wherever he found them. Whenever there was no enemy to fight, his restless spirit died a little. Eutracia was enjoying a peaceful time, and for that he was grateful. But without an enemy to face, this newfound peace was frustrating him.

The question that had haunted him since his experiences in the Well of Forestallments again came to mind. Who would she be, this woman the Scroll Master said would finally capture his heart? Where would she come from; what would she be like? Could he ever love someone more than he had loved Celeste? The mere thought was almost unbearable.

A knock came on the door, firm, insistent.

"Enter!" he called.

The doors parted to show Shailiha and Tyranny. Shailiha was wearing a simple green gown, with matching slippers and a Eutracian freshwater pearl strand. Her long blond hair caressed her shoulders. Tyranny was dressed as she had been since Tristan first met her, in black knee boots; striped, formfitting trousers; and a short leather jacket, its collar reaching nearly to her jaw. A sword hung at her left hip; a sheathed dagger lay tied down to her right thigh. Her short, dark, urchinlike hair looked as unruly as ever.

Tristan nodded to them. Shailiha gave her twin brother a cheerful smile.

"We've come to collect you!" she announced. "The meeting starts soon."

"I'm aware," he answered. He walked to the bed to take up his weapons.

A sudden idea came to the princess. Crooking a finger at Tyranny, Shailiha smiled and beckoned her to stand by Tristan's wardrobe. Quietly she opened the double doors and looked inside.

Since the Coven's return, it seemed that Tristan lived in nothing but his simple scuffed knee boots, black trousers, and matching leather vest. The wardrobe was full of beautiful finery that had hung unused for far too long. After examining the abandoned garments, she turned to her brother. There was an impish look on her face.

"I have an idea!" It was abundantly clear that she was trying to cheer him up.

"The masquerade ball is tonight! The palace will be full of

people. It's going to be grand, just like the old days! Why not let me help you choose something to wear?"

Having finally adjusted the dreggan baldric and knife quiver to his satisfaction, Tristan turned. He scowled when he saw the open wardrobe full of useless puffery.

He had forgotten all about the ball. In fact, he wished he could cancel it entirely. It had been the wizards' idea. The nation had finally healed, they said. It was time to celebrate the peace by opening the palace to the populace, even if it was only for one night.

In the end, Tristan had reluctantly agreed. He knew his presence would be mandatory. But that didn't mean he liked it.

The prince glowered at his sister. She countered his glare by folding her arms across her chest and impatiently tapping one foot on the floor. Tyranny smiled.

Tristan shook his head. "I hadn't thought about it," he answered.

Shailiha walked over. Pointing to his worn clothes, she shook her head and made a disapproving, clucking sound.

"Please don't tell me you're going to wear *those*!" she exclaimed. "There will be more than a smattering of young ladies there, eager for your attention! You have to look your best!"

The moment the words left her mouth, she realized how insensitive she had just been. Tristan's face darkened. Trying to warn Shailiha, Tyranny cleared her throat.

The princess immediately went to her brother. She took his hands into hers.

"I'm so sorry," she said quietly. "I should have known better." She pulled him to her.

He closed his eyes again. "I should know better, too," he answered gently. "You also understand what it means to lose the love of your life."

"I know how much you hurt," she whispered. "But each day gets a little easier. You'll just have to trust me on that."

Silent moments passed as he tried to believe her. Finally she let him go.

Gathering himself up, Tristan took a deep breath. "Now then," he said, "I must oversee the meeting."

He held out an arm to each of the women.

"By all means," Shailiha answered.

The princess gave Tyranny a wink; then, with a look of mock ferociousness, she pointed her index finger into the air.

"We must not be late!" she said, imitating Wigg. "Such meetings are of the utmost importance!" Tyranny and Tristan laughed.

It is good to hear him laugh, Shailiha thought as they walked to the door. *Especially now that it happens so rarely.*

Entering the hallway, the trio headed for the Redoubt.

TRISTAN LOOKED ACROSS THE HIGHLY POLISHED TABLE, FIRST AT Wigg, then at Faegan. "Give me a progress report on the acolytes," he said. "How soon can the Black Ships sail?"

Wigg placed his gnarled hands flat on the table. The Paragon, hanging on a cord around his neck, twinkled in the candlelight.

"Two more weeks," he said firmly. Then he added, "I know how badly you want to attack, but any sooner and we cannot guarantee that all the acolytes will be ready."

He looked over at the First Sister. "Adrian has learned quickly, despite a few mishaps. If the others do as well, the ships' seaworthiness will soon be ensured."

Taking a moment to think, the prince looked past the table at the flames dancing in the blue marble fireplace. He purposely kept his eyes away from the empty chair to his right—Celeste's chair. Her name was still inscribed on the back as a painful reminder of her absence. Pulling his thoughts together, he addressed Traax.

"How many fighting warriors do we still command?" he asked.

The Minion commander shook his head. "Not the number I would like," he answered glumly. "Wulfgar's second invasion force slaughtered too many."

Tristan wasn't in the mood for half answers. *"How many?"* he asked once more.

Traax sat up a little straighter. "I'm sorry, my lord," he said. "At best—including the female warrior-healers led by Duvessa—we might summon fifty thousand. As you are aware, we do not know whether that will be enough to take the Citadel. Even worse, there are hardly enough fletchers, armorers, healers, cooks, and so on to support them."

Tristan was about to respond when an insistent knocking came at the doors. Ox entered at Tristan's command, and it was plain to see that the gigantic warrior was worried about something.

"What is it?" Tristan asked.

Ox bowed. "I be sorry to intrude," he said in his broken Eutracian. "Visitors come to palace gates to request audience before Conclave. At first me not want to let them in. But they seem in bad way. They ride hard to get here. Lose three horses to the pace, they claim. I put them in Chamber of Supplication, then give them food and water. They wait for you there."

"What do they want?" Abbey asked.

"Me not sure," Ox answered. "But they say they must see entire Conclave—especially *Jin'Sai.*"

Tristan looked around the table. "Does anyone know what this is about?" he asked. They all shook their heads.

Tristan looked back at Ox. "They wish to see us *all,* you say?"

The warrior nodded. "Me believe that you should go. There be ten of them."

Tristan nodded. "Very well," he announced, and led the way out.

It took some time for the Conclave members to navigate the serpentine hallways that led to the Chamber of Supplication. On the way they passed dozens of servants—cooks, housekeepers, musicians—all hurrying to finish the preparations for that night's masquerade ball.

Tristan sighed. *We should be attacking the Citadel,* he fretted. *Instead, we will be foolishly feasting and dancing until dawn.* Quickening his pace, he rounded the final corner to stop before the pair of massive doors that barred the way into the Chamber of Supplication. Each door was adorned with a golden roaring lion superimposed by a golden Eutracian broadsword: Together, they comprised the House of Galland's heraldry. At Tristan's signal, the two Minion guards on duty swung the doors open. He quickly led his group into the room.

The recently renovated chamber sparkled with cleanliness. The morning breeze flowed through opened stained-glass windows, gently moving the patterned draperies. The smell of fresh-cut flowers permeated the air. Pillars of sunlight streamed in, highlighting the violet walls and ceiling, and the black-and-white checkerboard floor. Hundreds of upholstered chairs sat in neat rows on the floor before the dais. This was the hall where the late king and the onetime Directorate of Wizards had heard specific requests from the populace. Such meetings had always occurred on the first of each month. Supplicants by the hundreds had always arrived, each seemingly bearing a request more urgent than the last. If the need had been found to be in the nation's best interests, it was often granted. The wizards had yet to suggest that Tristan reinstate this old custom, but he knew it would be only a matter of time before they did.

Tristan made his way to the dais, where a row of high-backed chairs waited. From that vantage point, he looked down at the people who had come to see him. Although not one seemed injured, they all looked to be in a bad way, and all of them—five men, four women, and one young boy—were so intent upon a table that had been laid with food and drink that they hadn't even noticed the arrival of the Conclave members. Watching them eat, Tristan realized that Ox had done the right thing by bringing them here.

Tristan decided he wanted Shailiha at his right side and Wigg at his left. As he directed them to their seats, the beleaguered citizens below finally realized that the Conclave had entered the room. Plates and goblets were set back on the table with a clatter.

A middle-aged woman with dark hair clambered up the carpeted steps to stand directly before the prince. A blond-haired boy of about seven Seasons of New Life followed her. They looked filthy and exhausted.

The woman started crying. To Tristan's surprise, she threw herself at his feet, wrapping her arms around his knee boots. Bending down, he gently lifted her chin so she could look up at him.

"You're safe here," he said quietly. "What troubles you so?"

There was more than terror in her eyes. This woman was also grieving some awful loss. The little boy came to stand by her side. A worn haversack lay slung over one of his shoulders. Awestruck by royalty, he respectfully removed his weathered cap, then looked to the floor.

"Something terrible has happened, my liege," the woman said in a quavering voice. "Charningham—our village—so many dead . . ." Her voice trailed off into more weeping.

Tristan turned to look at Wigg.

"I am Wigg, the First Wizard," Wigg said gently. "What is your name?"

Trying to compose herself, the woman scrubbed her face with

her palms. "I am Annabelle," she answered weakly. "This is my son, Brent. My husband and four others were tortured and killed four days ago by a strange being of the craft. He told us to come here, to give the Conclave a warning. I have never seen anything like him. He wasn't human . . ."

Tristan helped the woman to her feet; she buried her face in his shoulder. He ordered Ox to fetch chairs from the chamber floor. Soon all ten visitors sat on the dais, facing the Conclave members.

"Please tell us what happened," the prince said. "Leave nothing unsaid."

For the next hour, the refugees related the tale. Brent told about seeing the Darkling—Xanthus—cross the Sippora River, and then how he and his father had been taken back to Charningham. The adults described the savage torture, the senseless killings, and the Darkling's bizarre self-mutilation. Finally Annabelle recounted the warnings Xanthus had given them, and how they were to be conveyed to the Conclave. When the group finally finished, the only sound came from the swishing window curtains as they obeyed the afternoon breeze.

Tristan looked over at Wigg, Faegan, and Jessamay. If anyone knew what these beleaguered people were talking about, it would be they. "What is a Darkling?" he asked.

"I do not know," Wigg answered. The First Wizard looked at Faegan, then Jessamay. They both shook their heads. Wigg looked back at Annabelle.

"Did Xanthus say where he was going next?" he asked.

The widow shook her head. "Only that if the prince did not obey, there would be more sacrifices," she answered. "But he did say that there was no use trying to find him, for he could become 'dust on the wind.' As he rode out of town, all the foliage in his path died. Then he simply disappeared."

His eyes alight with curiosity, Faegan wheeled his chair closer. "What did you just say?" he asked anxiously. "About the foliage, I mean."

"All the plants around him die," Brent answered for his mother. "Even big trees wither. It was the same with the Sippora when his horse came wading toward father and me. It simply stopped flowing." His eyes filled with tears, and he bravely brushed them away.

Just then Brent remembered something. After fishing about in his haversack, he produced a section of tree branch and a rolled-up scroll. The branch, hardy Eutracian maple, was about twice as thick as a grown man's thumb. One end was ragged, showing where it had been ripped away from its host. The other end was cut diagonally, its severed edge smooth as glass. The scroll was bound by a bloodred ribbon.

Brent handed the branch and the scroll to the prince. "Xanthus told me to give these to you. He said that you would know what they meant."

Tristan took them. He placed the scroll in his lap, then closely examined the branch. A grim expression came over his face. He realized that he wouldn't need to unroll the scroll. Lowering his head, he said nothing.

Shailiha gave her brother a puzzled look. "It's only some freshly cut maple," she said. "How important could it possibly be?"

Tristan looked over at his sister. "Frederick never told you?" he asked.

The princess shook her head. Frederick had been her husband, and Morganna's father. He had also been Tristan's best friend and the commander of the Royal Guard. He had fallen at the hands of the Coven on the night of Tristan's aborted coronation.

Shailiha looked curiously at the tree branch. She had no idea what Tristan was talking about. "What does it signify?" she asked again.

"Indeed," Wigg added. "Enlighten us all."

Tristan had heard stories, but that was all: Even though he knew what the items symbolized, he couldn't believe they had been presented to him. Looking back at Brent, Tristan held up the branch.

"Did you see Xanthus cut this?" he asked.

The boy nodded. "It was amazing."

Tristan nodded. "I can only imagine," he whispered. He turned to face the Conclave.

"This is a warning," he said simply. "Xanthus is coming for me. He is telling me that he can best me in combat. He therefore expects me to surrender to him without a fight."

Faegan wheeled his chair closer. "Tell us," he said.

"These two symbols involve a tale of the Royal Guard," Tristan explained. "Anyone who has taken Guard training is familiar with the fable. Wigg likely knows of it, too. It goes something like this:

"Long ago, an arrogant young Royal Guard captain challenged his elderly sword instructor to a duel. He apparently felt embarrassed for having his technique harshly criticized before his fellow officers. He sent a servant with a message for the instructor to meet him at dawn, with his second and his broadsword."

Tristan looked over at the wizards. "Duels were once commonplace, weren't they?" he asked.

"Yes," Wigg answered. "A barbaric custom, more often about revenge than honor. The Directorate eventually outlawed the practice."

Tristan nodded. "Anyway, when the young servant found the master and repeated his captain's demands, the sword master said nothing. Instead, he chose to reply physically, rather than verbally."

Interested as she was in all combat-related knowledge, Tyranny edged her chair closer. "What did he do?" she asked.

"The master tore a branch from a Eutracian maple tree, then tossed it into the air. With one swift movement, he pulled his sword from its scabbard and cleaved the branch before it touched the ground. The branch was sliced diagonally, just as this one has been. The cut was perfect in every respect. Since then, it is said that every Royal Guard member has tried to successfully duplicate that feat. To this day, no one has ever done so."

"And then?" Shailiha asked.

"Saying nothing, the master picked up the cut branch and handed it to the captain's servant. He also gave him a scroll, bound by a red ribbon. Then he simply turned and walked away. When the captain heard the story and saw the perfect cut, he wisely rescinded his challenge."

"I understand the branch's meaning," Abbey said, "but what purpose does the scroll serve?"

Tristan handed it to her. "The red ribbon signifies the recipient's spilled blood, should the scroll's message not be heeded," he said. "Read it for yourself."

As Abbey untied the ribbon and unrolled the document, several eager Conclave members left their seats to come peer over her shoulder. After looking at the unrolled scroll, Abbey scowled. The scroll was blank.

"Why send someone a blank scroll?" she asked. "It communicates nothing."

Tristan shook his head. "You're wrong," he said softly. "To those of us who understand, it says everything."

He took the scroll back from her. "Just as in the story I told you, this blank scroll presented to me represents the other half of Xanthus' message," he said.

"And that is . . . ?" Traax asked.

"That he has mastered the final stage of his weapons training," Tristan answered. "Its teachings have supposedly never been put into writing. To keep this highest instruction secret, it was only handed down orally, from master to student. It is also said that such teachings are long lost. The Old Eutracian word for this final stage is *K'Shari*. Roughly translated, it means 'The Eye of the Storm.'

"The blank scroll tells me that he has attained *K'Shari,* with the axe being his apparent weapon of choice. In other words, his technique has become effortless. Like this parchment's serene emptiness, during battle his mind remains as placid as a hurricane's eye while violence swirls all about him. The cut tree branch represents his prowess's physical side. The empty parchment signifies the mental discipline he has gained. Xanthus might well be the foremost weapons master in the world." He paused to let that sink in.

"There was supposedly a saying among those few who had reached the state of *K'Shari,*" he went on. " 'My ears hear no begging. My eyes see no pain. My heart feels no remorse.' This was their credo."

Annabelle's eyes suddenly went wide. "Those were his exact words," she whispered, "when he was torturing Alfred. Despite the horrific acts he was performing, he seemed completely at peace."

For several long moments everyone was silent. Then Brent looked from the cut branch to Tristan, and to the golden sword hilt rising up from behind the prince's right shoulder.

"Everyone says that you are a marvelous swordsman," the boy said respectfully. "Perhaps the finest in Eutracia. Can you cut a branch that way?"

Tristan shook his head. "Not even with a dreggan. I know. I've tried."

"And making matters worse, Xanthus also commands the craft," Adrian added. "But what is a Darkling? Where did he come from? And most important, why is he here?"

With a deep sigh, Faegan pulled thoughtfully on his beard. "That is impossible to say," he answered. "But I fear we will be meeting him soon enough, whether we wish to or not."

"If his powers are as strong as they seem, it is only logical to assume that he can also cloak his blood," Tristan mused. "Not to mention that he can become invisible. Like he warned us, trying to search him out would be pointless."

He looked at Annabelle. "Xanthus carried an axe and shield, you say?" he asked.

Annabelle nodded. "The axe was the weapon he used to cut the tree branch in midair. The blade moved so fast that it was only a blur."

Tristan looked down at the weary refugees. He knew that Wigg, Faegan, and Jessamay would be itching to discuss all of this in private. Suddenly the attack on the Citadel didn't seem so important.

He gestured to Ox. The giant Minion clicked his boot heels together.

"Find adequate quarters and fresh clothing for these people," Tristan ordered. "Until we better understand this new danger, they will be guests at the palace."

"I live to serve," Ox said.

Tristan looked back at his visitors. "Forgive me for making decisions on your behalf," he said gently. "But unless you strongly disagree, I believe it best that you stay here—at least for now. I realize that some of you have lost loved ones," he added. "We respect the fact that you are in mourning. But if you would like to attend tonight's ball, you are welcome."

As Ox led them from the room, Tristan turned to face the Conclave.

"We should return to the meeting room," he said. "It seems there is far more for us to discuss."

As the Conclave members moved to depart, Tristan picked up the perfectly cut tree branch and the blank scroll. He regarded them closely.

So the legend is true, he thought. K'Shari *exists, after all. And one of its practitioners is coming.* Lifting his face, he stared out over the vacant hall.

Just how good is this being? he wondered.

Still clutching the branch and the scroll, he started the long walk back to the Redoubt.

CHAPTER VII

AS HE WALKED ACROSS BARGAINERS' SQUARE, LOTHAR OF THE House of Fletcher felt his stomach growl. His dark eyes started searching out various food stalls. Soon he smelled freshly fried turkey, and his decision was made. But the stall where it was being cooked had already drawn a crowd. He knew that turkey legs always sold fast at a public execution. Today would be no exception.

When people saw who was coming, some made way. Rudely elbowing the others aside, Lothar glared at the elderly vendor.

"How much?" he demanded.

The vendor recognized Lothar. He immediately smiled—not because he wanted to, but because he realized that it would be in his best interests. The vendor stank of grease and oil. The turkey smell would permeate his clothes, his house, and perhaps even his soul, Lothar guessed.

Using wooden tongs, the vendor fished around in the boiling oil to retrieve a large, dripping leg. With a smile, he held it enticingly before Lothar. As if on command, Lothar's stomach growled again, louder this time.

"Three kisa," the vendor announced.

The stall's proprietor had clearly seen better days. He was missing two front teeth, one ear, and a good deal of his hair. Lothar found himself hoping that none of the vendor's disappearing facial features had recently found their way into the turkey pot. Trying to stay in Lothar's good graces, the vendor widened his crooked grin.

"But for the master of Tammerland's debtors' prison, I'll charge only two," he added wryly.

"Wrong," Lothar growled back. "For the master of Tammerland's debtors' prison, you'll charge nothing."

Reaching out, he swiped the turkey leg from the vendor's grip, tongs and all. He blew on it to cool it, then took a large bite. He found it to his liking. Seasoned drippings ran down his chin, which he daintily wiped with an embroidered handkerchief.

Everyone in the crowd knew better than to protest Lothar's thievery, so they remained still. Lothar was a powerful man. People on his wrong side could disappear for long periods of time—perhaps forever. He arrogantly pointed the half-eaten leg at the old vendor as though it were some kind of weapon.

"You'd best not protest the price I just paid," he warned. "If you do, I might have to dust off several outstanding debtors' warrants in your name. I'm sure you wouldn't want that, eh?"

Despite the heat rising from his pot, the vendor's face blanched. He gave Lothar a short, respectful bow.

"No, m'lord," he answered quietly. "I'm always happy to accommodate one of Tammerland's most respected officials."

Answering only with a grunt, Lothar took another bite of turkey, then turned away to find the executioner.

It was midafternoon in Eutracia, and the sun was high. Bargainers' Square was busy, and the impending execution added to the congestion. Once a hotbed of thieves, whores, drunkenness, and gambling, since the newfound peace, Tammerland's largest square had become somewhat more respectable.

The prince's roving Minions had helped to a great degree. Their eyes attentive and their swords always at the ready, a dark-winged patrol narrowly crossed Lothar's path. Smiling unctuously, he gave them a short but secretly insincere bow. In truth he hated the wandering warriors, for their presence only made his thievery more difficult.

But if one knew where to look, all the vices that had once been sold so openly here could still be had. That pleased Lothar immensely, for vice always brought debt—and it was debt that brought him wealth. Contentedly munching his turkey leg, he crossed the street to stand before a shop window.

The reflection staring back at him was tall, with a hugely fat stomach. Knowing it would only make him appear more obese, he resisted the urge to turn sideways. Taking a deep breath, Lothar pulled his gut in for a moment. But such pretenses had no lasting effect, so he gave up, letting his belly sag over his belt again. In truth, he didn't care how fat he became. He always bought his women, anyway. Even in the newly upright Bargainers' Square, rich men never lacked for affection.

No one had ever accused Lothar of handsomeness. The face staring back at him was jowly, and pale from spending so much time indoors. What remained of his dark hair lay slicked down across his shiny skull. His eyes were brown and his hooked nose long. His breeches, shirt, and waistcoat were of the finest material. Looking down, he could barely see the tips of his shoes for his protruding abdomen. But he knew that they were so brightly shined that his face would have been reflected in their tops. Tossing the ravaged turkey bone into the street, he got his great bulk moving again.

As he neared the executioner's station, the crowd thickened. He smiled. Despite the new sense of goodwill, there still seemed to be no shortage of those wishing to see their fellow man suffer. *Good,* he thought. *That always makes for more business.* Wending his way through the crowd, his mind turned to how he had risen to his position in life, and how he had cleverly used that position to enhance his ever-growing wealth.

Crime adjudication had long been an illicit income source for those who arrested, tried, and punished Eutracia's criminal element. The late Directorate had tried more than once to wipe out the corruption, but to no avail. Unless the wizards were willing to look into every crime personally—something they hadn't the time to do—oftentimes only a well-placed bribe determined a person's guilt or innocence. More often than not, the wealthy went free. With all but one Directorate wizard dead, the situation had worsened.

In most Eutracian towns, whoever administered justice also kept the bulk of the fines and forfeitures. It was a highly flawed system, literally begging thievery and corruption. Trials and punishments were public matters. But the identification, arrest, and imprisonment of the accused were details usually kept secret until then. As a result, town officials quarreled violently over who controlled the various jurisdictions. But Lothar's situation was unique, in that he alone held sway over every debtor's warrant in Tammerland. He also decided who did or did not go to debtors' jail. He profited by every opportunity—sometimes more than once.

Young and seeking work, Lothar had become a debtors' prison guard. The reigning provost had been old, sodden with liquor, and seemingly unaware of the unexploited chances for profit that his position offered.

But Lothar quickly saw what the old man did not. He saved every kisa he could—enough to eventually bribe the town burgher. Just before the old provost finally died, the crooked burgher awarded Lothar the post. That had been eight years ago, and Lothar's wealth and stature had grown with each passing Season of New Life.

Other than his meager salary, there were illicit ways he profited from his position. The simplest was outright intimidation, such as he had just applied to the turkey vendor. He knew every shop owner who had outstanding debtors' warrants filed against him or her. There were so many of them that he had paid for little from his own pocket for nearly five years. The understanding was simple. If they continued to supply him with what he needed, they remained free.

His many prisoners provided the other methods of profit taking. He alone had total control over who went in and who came out. Staying out cost a steep price; getting out commanded an even higher one. Oftentimes a person paid to remain free, only to be imprisoned anyway—especially if he or she had acquaintances that were well off.

Once inside, the prisoners' relatives and friends would then be asked to contribute funds to secure his or her release, and the warrants would be quashed. Even a prisoner's general treatment usually depended on yet more bribes, paid in the meantime. As one might imagine, these techniques yielded even greater profits if the internees' relatives and friends had outstanding debtors' warrants as well.

And so the vicious cycle went round and round, making Lothar not only wealthy, but feared. Having no wife or children to support helped his ill-gotten gains grow all the faster.

Pushing through the crowd, he wended his way to a small table that had been placed in the street. The town executioner, dressed all in black, sat there looking over some papers.

The fellow's "civic responsibilities" included such talents as performing hangings, beheadings, slowly drowning victims in the dunking pool, and burning criminals at the stake. The crime determined the punishment. Today's victim was a convicted horse thief, his crime punishable by a protracted, fatal dunking.

Lothar grinned down at the executioner. Even though the man wore a black hood, Lothar knew him well. Unknown to the spectators, the fellow was also an accomplished torturer.

Branding bare skin, flogging, precisely lopping off limbs and digits, and slowly extracting teeth and fingernails were but a few of the fellow's favorite techniques. Lothar could attest to the man's expertise, because on more than one occasion he had employed him for his own reasons. Kisa always flowed far more easily from debtor prisoners' friends and relatives after watching him work on a loved one for an hour or so.

"Good morning," Lothar said, being careful not to mention the fellow by name. The executioner looked up grudgingly from his paperwork.

"What's so good about it, sir?" the hooded man asked. "It's bleedin' hot out here today. Dunkings take more time and effort than a quick hanging or beheading. A bleedin'pain in the arse, they are."

Lothar turned to look at the dunking pool, lying off to one side of the square. The blindfolded horse thief was already tied to the chair. He was being roundly shouted at and pelted with rotten eggs, fruit, and vegetables—yet another custom performed at Eutracian executions. Lothar looked back to the executioner.

"Why complain?" he asked. "At least you'll earn a fee today. And some extra as well, if you're smart." Hoping to put the other man in a more receptive mood, he reached into his pocket and jangled some coins together.

He knew that the executioner would possess the list naming the persons due for execution, and when they were to be killed. Always accompanying that list was another one—the next-of-kin list. Criminals facing execution usually carried unresolved debts; it was simply their nature. Such undisclosed debts might justify swearing out a new warrant or two. By Eutracian law, a recently deceased person's debts became his relatives' responsibility.

If Lothar could get the most recent lists, they would provide yet another income source. Not only would they reveal relatives belonging to the same family house, but also those who did not share the same last name—information he might not otherwise have. With the deceased's debts later transferred to his relatives, after some added research Lothar could then swear out additional warrants. From there the process would go on. He and the executioner had done business this way many times, but usually not on an open street and certainly never just before an execution. He wanted those lists badly, and before it became too late for him to act on them.

"What do you want?" the hooded man asked. "I'm about to start the dunking."

"You know what I want," Lothar whispered.

The man in the hood looked around furtively, then back up at the grotesquely fat jailor. His eyes widened behind the hood's peepholes.

"Now?" the man whispered back. "Are you bleedin' crazy?"

Lothar looked around again. The crowd anticipating the dunking had grown larger. Some of the vendors had taken their wares afoot, wandering among the eager spectators while shouting out their prices. Curious children had been lifted atop their parents' shoulders, so that they could better see what was going on. The atmosphere was becoming more carnival-like by the moment. The dunking would start soon. In fact, Lothar was counting on it. Given the rising sense of urgency, the executioner would have to decide quickly.

"I realize the timing isn't perfect," Lothar said. "But business is business."

Removing a leather cinch bag from his trousers' pocket, he dropped it on the tabletop. It fell heavily, the clinking coins inside providing an enticing tune.

"I understand your concern," Lothar whispered, "so I have chosen to be generous. That bag holds twice the standard fee. Take it or leave it."

The executioner thought for a moment. He glanced around again. "Twice as much, you say?" he asked.

"Yes," Lothar answered. "I suggest you take it. For all I know, the fellow in the dunking chair might be a relative of yours and have outstanding warrants. It wouldn't be the first time, would it?"

After shuffling through his papers for a moment, the executioner selected two parchments and quickly folded them. He slipped them to Lothar. The leather cinch bag disappeared in a flash.

"Now go away!" he insisted angrily. "I have work to do!"

"By all means," Lothar said smoothly as he secured the parchments in a waistcoat pocket. After giving the hooded man a slight bow, he again started wending his way through the crowd.

Inordinately pleased with himself, he started walking back toward the debtors' prison. There was an especially appealing group of new inmates that he wanted to revisit. He had been looking forward to the occasion all day. They were about to provide him with his greatest coup of all time. For among his many other ventures, Lothar was also a slave trader.

As Lothar rounded a corner leading away from Bargainers' Square, he heard the condemned man scream, followed by the first splash of the dunking chair. If the executioner did his job properly, it would take several hours before the criminal's lungs completely filled with water. *One must never disappoint the masses,* he thought.

As Lothar took his fourth step down the side street, the crowd roared.

THROWING HER BLOND HAIR OVER ONE SHOULDER, MALLORY turned to look between the prison door bars. She and the others had been taken two days ago. Escape seemed a distant dream. When they had awakened here, their memories of capture had been a hazy blur. The only reason they knew they were being held in Tammerland's debtors' prison was because of the occasional bits of conversation gleaned from passing guards.

The girls were terrified by the leering men. Some guards had gone so far as stopping before the bars to make obscene gestures; others described outright the kinds of things they wanted to do to the girls. Shuddering as much from fear as from the dampness, Mallory retreated deeper into the room to join her friends.

There were eight girls here. Their journey to this place and the reasons for it had been a living nightmare. It had begun months ago, at a place called Fledgling House. The endowed girls were all that remained of a larger group of gifted students. At one time they had been endowed female trainees of the craft. Taught in secret, they had been destined to join a sisterhood of women older than they—the fabled Acolytes of the Redoubt.

These eight remaining girls were the daughters of Redoubt consuls, and their true identities were known only to a few special people. Handpicked at five years of age, each one had been selected for her above-average intelligence and deep wish to learn the craft. Then they were sent to the secret castle called Fledgling House. It lay to the north, near the slopes of the Tolenka Mountains. But with their caretakers dead, the girls had suddenly been forced to fend for themselves. They soon realized that becoming full-fledged acolytes would be almost impossible.

Their nightmare had begun one day during the previous Season of Harvest. The girls had been playing on the Fledgling House lawns when the sky suddenly darkened with strange creatures. An evil-looking man was riding one, his face leering, predatory.

As the awful beasts descended, Duncan—the consul who oversaw their training in the craft—was killed before their eyes. Martha, their loving matron, was sent flying away to Tammerland atop one of the horrible birds. At that time, the girls ranged in age from six to eighteen. Now nineteen, Mallory was the oldest and best trained. Since that fateful day, the others looked to her for leadership.

But she didn't feel like a leader as she wended her way deeper into the dingy cell. She had gotten the girls this far, only to wind up in a filthy debtors' prison with no way out.

Mallory was worldly enough to understand that because the jailor did not know their real identities, no one would be coming to pay off their "debts." She bristled at that lie. They owed nothing to anyone—a fact she would gladly shout to the heavens if only they could escape this place. They were a mere half day's walk from the royal palace. But because they were locked inside this gruesome prison, the Redoubt might as well be a thousand leagues away.

At first she had briefly considered telling the leering jailor who they were. But then she thought better of it, fearing that it would only worsen their plight. Even Lothar would fear trying to bargain with the Redoubt wizards for their release. His solution might well be to kill them outright, simply to get them off his hands. And so Mallory remained silent about their true identities. But if only she could somehow inform the acolytes or the wizards, she knew that the mystics would tear this place apart to save them.

Because the jailor did not understand the girls' importance, Mallory had also wondered why he had taken them prisoner in the first place, for they had no debts. But after overhearing the guards she learned the answer. They were to be sold into sexual slavery as soon as Lothar could arrange it. Several of the lecherous guards had as much as said so.

The girls' memories of their capture at Fledgling House existed only as short, dreamlike snips in time. Some recalled a beautiful-looking man in a glistening white robe. As her own fragmented remembrances resurfaced, Mallory winced, then locked them away again. It was probably best that they could not remember everything, she realized. The entire tale might be too much for the younger girls to bear.

Even so, they all remembered waking up one day in one of the elaborate Fledgling House chambers. No one was about, and the place was stripped of food. Worse, the Season of Crystal was due to arrive. The thirty confused girls realized that if they stayed there, they would starve. So they started walking toward the only other refuge of magic that they knew—the Tammerland Redoubt. If they could reach the Redoubt they would be cared for.

Leaving Fledgling House, they wisely decided to travel alongside the Sippora River's meandering banks. The journey would take longer that way, but they hoped that they could catch fish as they went, and use the river water for drinking and washing. People in the villages lining the riverbanks would surely help them on their way, Mallory had reasoned.

But as they neared the river they learned that strange aberrances of the craft were afoot. A great gouge had been carved into the earth, wending its way west toward the Tolenka Mountains. The river was boiling, and of no use to them. Living on their wits, they employed their weakening gifts to trap animals for food, and to divine water.

Given the land's recent decimation, such devices proved inadequate. By the time they joined the last refugee column trudging its way toward Tammerland, twenty-two of the girls had died. Despite the fact that they had been weakened by starvation, Mallory and a few older girls had done their best to bury their friends where they fell.

The fleeing villagers graciously shared what little food they had. As they all traveled south, the girls slowly regained some strength. By the time they entered the capital, much of Tammerland had been mysteriously burned to the ground and newly rebuilt. For the provincial young girls, it was like walking into a dream world. After learning the way to the royal palace, they immediately set off, hoping that their travails were finally over.

Then they had encountered the kindly old tavern keeper who offered to help them. Seeing the disheveled girls walking across Bargainers' Square, he had beckoned them into his small establishment. *"Come in,"* he had said. *"The place isn't much. But please sit for a while away from the sun, and have some free rootberryade. It will do you all good before you resume your journeys."*

The tavern was a dark, dirty place, but to the wayward girls it seemed a palace. The old man could tell that they were refugees, as were so many others in the streets these days. Giving them something to drink was the least he could do, he said. The man's wife was a pleasant woman, with a dark gray bun and a broad white apron. Smiling, she presented the girls with glasses of cold rootberryade. They drank it greedily, then asked for more. That was the last thing they remembered.

Mallory had been the first to awaken on the prison floor. As her mind cleared, she realized that they had all been drugged. She later met Lothar during his first disturbing meeting with them. Soon after that she heard the guards talking. Putting things together, she quickly understood that the old tavern owner, his wife, and Lothar were in league with one another.

As Mallory sadly shook her head she wondered how many other people had suffered this fate. If only she could escape, then find her way to the palace. She could return with the wizards, and that vile jailor would truly suffer.

As she reached the cell's rear wall, several large rats ran across the floor. The younger girls shrieked, but Mallory didn't care. A girl named Magdalene raised an arm to employ the craft against the rats, but Mallory quickly reached out to stop her. The look in her eyes meant business.

"No!" she whispered sternly. "You know our agreement! There is to be no craft use until we are ready! We simply cannot afford to tip our hand! Our powers are weak enough already, and we can't risk draining them further! Whether you like it or not, that includes you!"

Magdalene glared angrily at Mallory before finally lowering her arm. At sixteen Seasons of New Life, she was third oldest among them. Mallory didn't like Magdalene. For no good reason, Magdalene always thought herself to be special. Worse yet, she was quick to use the craft first and ask questions later. She had been that way in all her classes at Fledgling House. Sometimes Master Duncan had become so frustrated with her that he threatened to expel her and send her back to her father. Rather surprisingly, the threats never seemed to faze Magdalene.

Mallory gave her another harsh look. "Remember—no use of the craft until we are ready," she repeated.

Offering their support, the other girls gathered closer. Several of them looked at Magdalene with disdain. As usual, Magdalene didn't seem to care.

"If she tries anything like that again, stop her," Mallory told the others. Leaving Magdalene to stew in her own juices, Mallory walked over to see how her best friend was doing.

Ariana was seventeen. Ever since their grueling journey started, she had been Mallory's right arm. Mallory was the most powerful among them. But Ariana was the most learned—especially concerning spell formation.

Master Duncan had often said that in all of Fledgling House, Ariana had no equal in that discipline. Mallory had even overheard Duncan whisper to Martha that when it came to spell writing, Ariana had already surpassed many consuls he had known. It was this same talent that Mallory was counting on.

Ariana was on her knees, facing the cellar's far wall. She was tall for her age, with long dark hair. She disliked Magdalene even more than Mallory did. Several times during their journey the two girls had nearly come to blows. Looking up from her work, she smiled.

"I heard that browbeating you gave her," she said. "Good for you."

Mallory shrugged her shoulders. "I didn't enjoy it, but someone has to keep her in line." A faint smile crossed her face. "If I left her to you, only the Afterlife knows what you'd do," she added, then looked down at Ariana's work. "How is it going?" she asked.

Ariana dropped the charcoal piece she had found, then stood. She gazed over at Magdalene for a moment. Still seething from the lecture Mallory had given her, Magdalene sneered back. Sighing, Ariana rubbed her face.

"The work is slow," she answered. She looked around the cramped cell, then back into Mallory's blue eyes.

"These aren't the best working conditions, you know," she added. "Even if I were back at Fledgling House, this spell would be difficult to formulate on my own. And having had nothing substantial to eat since we left the school has not helped our mental or physical abilities," she added. She shook her head.

"Why am I telling you this?" she asked. "You know these things as well as anyone. But even if I can produce the spell, there's no telling whether you will be strong enough to work it successfully."

"I know," Mallory said. "But it's all we have."

Ariana kneeled again and took up her charcoal. The wall before her held esoteric numbers and symbols by the dozens. To Mallory's surprise, Ariana shook her head, then used one hand to scrub away all her recent formulations. She looked back up at Mallory with tired eyes.

"This latest series is just another dead end," she said quietly. "I'm sorry, but this is one that Duncan had yet to teach us. So I must figure it out on my own."

"I understand," Mallory answered. "But you must hurry! I don't know how much time we have left."

Ariana was about to answer when they heard a guard call out. "You!" he shouted.

Standing, Ariana narrowed her eyes. "Me?" she asked.

"No, no!" the guard shouted back. "The pretty blond bitch, standing next to you! Come 'ere!"

Mallory cringed. She didn't know what he wanted, but she didn't dare disobey. Summoning up her courage, she walked to the cell door. All the other girls could do was to watch in dread. Ariana gave her a supportive glance.

As Mallory approached the door she became slightly relieved. The guard had brought them something to eat. It wasn't much—mere bowls of gruel and flasks of water. Neither would provide enough nutrients to significantly augment their gifts. But it would keep them alive another day, and staying alive in this awful place was the first order of business.

As Mallory approached, the smell coming from even such

simple food started her stomach growling. The nearer she came, the more the guard leered.

The guard placed the food tray on the floor, then used one hobnailed boot to shove it through the small gap between the barred door and the floor. He hadn't shaved for days, and smelled of stale liquor. A jagged scar ran down one cheek. His eyes were menacing, predatory.

Mallory bent down to pick up the tray. As she stood with it in her arms, the guard's left hand shot between the bars. Grabbing Mallory by the neck, he squeezed. The pain was excruciating. She could barely breathe. The guard brought his face nearer.

"Come closer," he breathed, "or things will only go worse for you."

Trying to think through the pain, Mallory realized that if she tried to fight him she might drop the tray. Regardless of the food's quality, they needed it to keep what strength the girls still had remaining. Using the craft against the guard was not an option, because they needed to keep their identities secret until the last moment. She knew that the other girls would desperately want to help her, but she also hoped that they would have the good sense not to try.

Not knowing what else to do, she obeyed. As her face neared the bars she could better smell his stink. His hand tightened around her throat a bit more.

"Hold still, bitch," he whispered. "Don't fight me. If you do, I'll see to it that not one of you eats for a week." Smiling evilly, he licked his lips.

Mallory felt his other hand slip beneath what remained of her tattered school dress. Trying to control her emotions, she closed her eyes. Some of the other girls in the cell started to cry. As he probed her, she did her best to remember Duncan, Martha, and the good times she had known.

On and on it went, the guard's dirty fingers violating her in every way he could without being on her side of the door. Finally it was finished.

Mallory opened her eyes, but she held fast, unflinching in her gaze. For the first time in her young life, she truly knew what it was to hate—to hate so much she could kill.

The guard raised his rapacious hand before his face to luxuriate in her scent. Smiling, he finally let her go. Struggling for breath, Mallory took two paces back, nearly dropping the precious tray.

"Such a treasure you are," the guard said. He looked her up and down lasciviously. "I'll remember you," he whispered. "And I'll be back."

As she glared at him, Mallory memorized his face. He finally turned and walked down the hall, his heel strikes fading away amid the flickering shadows.

For the others' sake, Mallory forced back her tears. As she carried the tray into the cell, Ariana touched her on the arm.

"Are you all right?" she whispered.

"No," Mallory answered softly. "But I will be." Turning her head, she looked back to the cell door. "Once he's dead," she added menacingly. She looked back at Ariana.

"Hurry," she whispered simply.

Squaring her shoulders, she walked the food to the other girls.

CHAPTER VIII

AS TRISTAN WALKED DOWN THE PALACE HALLS, IT SEEMED THAT the entire castle had come alive. It felt good to him to see the place bustling again, even if he did have to attend tonight's masquerade ball.

When his mother, father, and the wizards of the Directorate had lived, the palace always seemed to be in a state of activity. With the arrival of peace, it was starting to become that way again, and tonight's impending ball was adding much to the general excitement. Servants, cooks, musicians, acrobats, jugglers, and others responsible for preparing the evening's festivities filled the halls. As expected, many felt obliged to stop and speak with him.

Wending his way through the hubbub, Tristan tried to acknowledge as many people as he could, but he was already late.

He smirked as he imagined the scowl he would get from Wigg—not to mention the mischievous looks Tyranny, Shailiha, and Faegan would contribute when he finally reached the Great Hall.

Tristan flagged down a waiter carrying a tray laden with wine. With a bow the waiter held it out to him. Tristan took a glass and quickly downed the contents, then grabbed another. If he had to attend this event, his unfair share from the palace wine cellars would help ease the boredom. After giving the waiter a smile, he continued on.

The newly rebuilt palace was a revelation. During the Coven of Sorceresses' unexpected return and the subsequent struggles with Nicholas and Wulfgar, much of the structure had been destroyed. But the combined efforts of countless Minion and citizen laborers had brought the castle to an even greater magnificence.

All seven hundred rooms had been repaired and redecorated as needed. It seemed that everywhere Tristan looked he saw new furniture, artwork, rugs, and tapestries. He sighed as he wished that his parents could be here to see it all. Then he again noticed the servants' black-and-white formal attire, and he smirked.

Despite Shailiha's earlier coaxing, he had adamantly refused to change clothes. Even his weapons still hung over his right shoulder. If he must be put on display tonight, then he would do it on his own terms, no matter what anybody said about it. Just then, Wigg crossed his mind. The First Wizard always placed great importance on such public affairs. He was bound to be incensed when he saw that Tristan hadn't trussed himself up in some ridiculous costume to match the occasion.

But Tristan decided he couldn't be angry with him. Wigg was more than three hundred years old. He had been the royal advisor and leader of the Directorate during the reigns of nearly a dozen Eutracian kings and queens, including Tristan's mother and father. Such traditions were an established way of life for the wizard. But Tristan still rejected them as boring and tedious.

As he neared the Great Hall he started to see guests. Each of their costumes seemed more sumptuous than the last. Even the Minions were in disguise—a rather incongruous notion, because it was impossible to hide their dark wings. It gladdened his heart to see Eutracians and Minions mixing so well. Less than two years ago, this gathering would have been impossible.

At first he was surprised to find the Minion women so stunning. Their body armor gone, they were dressed in human, female attire. Despite the obvious alterations for their wings, they wore the garments well. He smiled to himself as he wondered how Ox, Traax, and Duvessa would be dressed.

As he made his way through the crowd, he realized that wearing no mask put him at a disadvantage. As expected, guests began recognizing him. Disguised as they were, it was difficult to know how to respond to their greetings. After an older man lowered his mask to show Tristan that he was in fact Tammerland's mayor, the rather embarrassed prince decided it was time to even the odds.

Ducking into a room off the hallway, he closed the door. He put down his wineglass, then reached beneath his vest to produce his only concession to the masquerade—a simple black mask that covered the upper half of his face. He quickly tied its string around the back of his head. Picking up his glass, he walked to a mirror hanging on the opposite wall.

The image staring back at him looked far more like some menacing highwayman than it did a member of the royal house. Then his memories crept in again, and he looked to the floor. Closing his eyes, he rolled the half-empty wineglass back and forth between his palms, thinking.

If only Celeste was here. How ravishing she would look! If she was on my arm, I wouldn't care how long the ball lasted. Doing his best to shelve his sadness, he squared his shoulders, then reentered the busy hallway.

The crushing flow of people and warriors had become even stronger, but at least this time nearly everyone was going in the same direction. The ball would start soon, and the Great Hall would be packed with revelers. With his mask on, fewer people recognized him. But he would still be late. As he wended his way through the crowd, his thoughts turned to earlier that day.

When today's second Conclave meeting had adjourned, he had stayed behind for a time, thinking. Although the members had been able to talk freely, no one had been able to offer an explanation about Xanthus. Even Wigg, Faegan, and Jessamay were at a loss. Glad to finally be alone, Tristan had gazed into the fireplace and come to some conclusions of his own.

The deaths in Charningham had been horrific and unprovoked. Clearly, Xanthus needed to be stopped and his motives brought to light. But how did one do that when the quarry was a ghost, able to vanish at will? Then there was the disturbing matter of the freshly cut branch and the blank scroll. Their meanings clear, the two symbols sat quietly atop the meeting room table.

He soon found his mind returning to that awful day in Parthalon, when he had killed Kluge and become the lord of the Minions. Kluge had been the strongest opponent he had ever met. Tristan had barely escaped with his life.

But where Kluge's technique had been that of a raging beast, Xanthus' would not be. When his axe was in his hands, Xanthus would become the consummate warrior—a veritable magician of the combative arts. Kluge had reveled in his kills. But Xanthus' attainment of *K'Shari* would keep his heart and mind placid, unfeeling, and perfect in his deadliness. In the end, Xanthus would be far more dangerous.

Tristan had turned to see his dreggan and throwing knives hanging over his chair back. The weapons gleamed beautifully in the firelight. Then he looked into the fire again.

I cannot beat this creature, this Darkling, he realized. *If he comes for me and I resist him, I will die.*

Even so, one thing had become abundantly clear. Xanthus was of the Vagaries. The dark side of the craft was again on the march in Eutracia, and it had to be stopped.

The sound of music returned Tristan's mind to the present as he finally neared the Great Hall. Knowing better than to try to go through the giant doors and fight his way across the room, he opened a nearby alcove door and quickly closed it behind him.

He was soon standing in a well-lit antechamber just off the hall's dais. With luck, he might be able to slip into his chair without too many guests noticing that he was late. Walking across the chamber, he opened the door and stepped onto the dais.

Other than on the day of his ill-fated coronation, Tristan had never seen the Great Hall decorated so beautifully. The room was covered by a domed ceiling of stained glass through which light cascaded in a dizzying array of colors. The floor was a vast sea of black-and-white checkerboard marble squares. Giant variegated columns, so thick around that it would take ten men holding hands to surround just one, flanked the entire length of two opposing walls from ceiling to floor. Thick garlands of purple ginger lily were wound around each one, and strung from one to the next. Scores of golden chandeliers and standing candelabras provided light from their glowing flames. Several large indoor fountains playfully shot water streams into the air. The water tumbled back into surrounding pools holding fish of every color and description. A musicians' pit near one end of the dais held twenty men and women. The musicians were busily playing melodies for the whirling dancers.

While hundreds of costumed revelers wheeled to the music, liveried waiters and waitresses mingled politely on the sidelines, offering up silver trays laden with food and drink. Against the room's walls sat many buffet tables that were loaded with yet more delicacies.

Shaking his head, Tristan snorted. Each table had to be twenty meters long. The moment a platter became empty, palace cooks or gnome wives quickly bustled in, carrying ever-more-sumptuous treats.

Meant only for the Conclave members, ten high-backed chairs sat atop the dais. A line of citizens and warriors eager to greet the Conclave stretched from the room's far reaches, all the way forward along one wall, then up and across the dais. As the people and the warriors approached, another liveried servant accepted their engraved invitations, then loudly announced their names. As he took in the line's length, Tristan groaned. Then he smiled behind his mask as he heard the servant struggle, trying to correctly pronounce one of the Minion warriors' more exotic names.

Four Conclave members' chairs were conspicuously empty—those that had once belonged to Geldon and Celeste, plus Tyranny's and his own. Tyranny must also be late, he assumed. Although Geldon and Celeste could not be present, Tristan had insisted that their chairs be included as a sign of their sacrifices to the Vigors. He walked across the dais, to sit down between Wigg and Shailiha.

Like Tristan, it seemed that Wigg had granted no concession to the masquerade besides his highly ornate mask. How much teasing had the First Wizard been forced to endure from Abbey before finally donning it? Tristan wondered. For a moment he considered whether it was real or conjured, then decided that it didn't matter. It was beautifully made of crinkled gold foil, with black, sweeping eyebrows that gave it a rather disparaging expression. *How appropriate,* Tristan thought with a smile.

Wigg looked at him and said nothing. He didn't have to—

Tristan knew full well that the expression on the wizard's face and mask would match perfectly.

Shailiha was stunning. She was dressed in a dark blue gown, and her long blond hair graced either shoulder. Her matching blue shoes were decorated with indigo sapphires. Her gold medallion exactly matching his hung brightly around her neck. One edge of her mask was attached to a handle. The full mask was bloodred, adorned with white feathers where the eyebrows would normally be. The eye holes slanted up at the far corners, giving it a seductive quality. Tristan smiled at her from behind his mask; she smiled back.

"You're late!" she whispered. "In the name of the Afterlife, can't you ever be on time? Wigg must be furious!"

"Naturally," Tristan answered back. "That's his job."

He gladly drank in his twin sister's beauty once more. She would have no lack of suitors tonight, and for that he was glad. She had been lonely since Frederick's death, and enough time had gone by. Tristan knew that no one would deny her the right to be happy again.

Holding the mask before her face, Shailiha smiled as a man approached from the receiving line. As the man lowered his mask, the princess immediately remembered the handsome fellow as Count Tomasso, from the province of Ephyra.

When the count bowed, his blue eyes flashed in the candlelight. As Shailiha extended her hand, he lightly brushed his lips across the back of her satin elbow glove.

"Good evening, Your Highness," he said smoothly. Then he turned to Tristan. "My liege," he said.

"Count Tomasso," Tristan acknowledged simply. The count again focused his eyes on Shailiha.

"I trust your dance card is not yet filled?" he asked. "It would be such a shame to come so far, only to be denied."

Shailiha knew she could afford a revealing smile, as long as it was safely hidden behind her mask. Reaching to the floor, she retrieved her dance card and a quill. She handed them to the count.

"I believe there might be one or two left," she answered, trying her best to sound nonchalant. "You'll have to see for yourself."

The count glanced at the card. "One only," he answered happily. "The last one, as it happens. I will be looking forward to it."

After writing his name on the card, he handed it back to the princess.

"Until then," he said.

Working his way down the receiving line, he stopped to politely recognize the other Conclave members. Snorting out another soft laugh, Tristan looked over at his sister.

"You'll have to see for yourself?" he chided her. "With such a wonderful come-hither attitude as that, I'm surprised there's a man in the entire place who wants to dance with you!"

Shailiha smiled from behind her mask, then promptly shoved one elbow into the prince's ribs. He winced.

"I must be doing something right," she teased right back. "My dance card is full, but yours is empty. Doesn't that tell you anything?"

"It tells me that things are just as I want them," he answered. There had come a welcome lull in the receiving line. Taking another sip of wine, he cast his dark eyes back toward the spectacular scene.

"By the way," he asked, "where's Tyranny? It's not like her to be late."

Shailiha pointed toward the twirling dancers. "She's down there, somewhere," she answered, "and whirling madly, no doubt. It seems she has been popular tonight. I didn't even know she could dance."

Tristan raised an eyebrow. "Is that so?" he asked softly. "I didn't know she could, either."

Curious, Tristan searched for her. But amid the disguised revelers, finding her was impossible, so he stopped trying. Then he noticed several fliers of the fields—the giant, endowed Eutracian butterflies—soaring high above the crowd. He was delighted to see them.

"Wigg let you bring the fliers here?" he asked Shailiha. "That surprises me."

Lowering her mask, she gave her brother a conspiratorial wink. "I believed they would make a nice addition to the ball," she said. "So I brokered a deal with him."

Tristan scowled. "Just how did you manage that?" he asked. "Wigg isn't one to make deals."

"Abbey was hounding him mercilessly about wearing a full costume," she answered. "I suggested that in return for allowing the fliers to attend, he could wear only his usual gray robe, plus a mask. It worked."

Smiling, Tristan looked back up at the bevy of huge colorful butterflies. Each one's body as long as a man's forearm, they swooped and darted effortlessly. Knowing that Shailiha could silently communicate with them, he looked over at her.

"Call Caprice down," he said. "It has been some time since I've seen her."

Closing her eyes, Shailiha used her only active Forestallment to call down her personal flier. At once a violet-and-yellow one left the others to soar toward the Conclave. When Tristan realized that she was coming toward him, he raised a forearm. Caprice landed on his arm, then gently folded her diaphanous wings.

Shailiha closed her eyes again, then smiled. "She says that she is happy to see you," his sister told him.

Still amazed by his sister's gift, Tristan smiled. "As am I to see her," he said.

Gently shaking his arm, he cast Caprice back into the air. She soared to rejoin her kind. Just then Wigg leaned toward him.

"You're late!" he whispered. "And you're out of costume, to boot!"

Sighing, Tristan took another sip of wine. Stretching his long legs, he casually crossed one boot over the other.

"So I've already been told," he answered. "Anyway, I'm here now. And by the way, I don't think much of your costume, either." He gave Wigg a short, knowing smile. "Abbey can't be very happy with you," he added.

"That doesn't matter!" the wizard pressed. "You could learn a great deal about royal decorum from your sister!"

Tristan could tell that Wigg was about to launch into a full-blown lecture when the music suddenly stopped. Wondering why, everyone looked to the orchestra pit.

The leader had come to the center of the dance floor. Wondering what was going on, the slowing dancers formed a circle around him. Once he had everyone's attention, the orchestra leader cleared his voice.

"As everyone knows, it is an old Eutracian custom that one dance shall be in the form of an auction, the proceeds going to the Tammerland orphanage," he announced. "But tonight we are going to do something a bit different. Rather than the gentlemen bidding on the ladies as partners, things will be reversed. Tonight the ladies will be bidding for the men!"

Spontaneous laughter and applause erupted. It was clear that the crowd was delighted. But Tristan's reaction was another matter. He glared at his sister.

"This is your doing, isn't it?" he asked sternly.

Trying to stifle her glee, Shailiha bit her lower lip. "I'll never tell," she whispered from behind her mask. Everyone's eyes soon returned to the orchestra leader.

"So who among you lovely ladies would like to get things started?" he shouted. "Now then, don't be shy! It's all for a good cause, you know!"

"Ten kisa for the First Wizard!" one woman hollered. "I've always wanted to dance with a wizard! I hear they can be very light on their feet!"

As the crowd erupted into laughter, Tristan heard Wigg groan. The prince smiled evilly.

"Fifteen for Faegan!" another woman shouted. "With or without his chair!"

The crowd laughed good-naturedly. Curious, Tristan leaned forward to glance down the line of Conclave members. Unlike Wigg, the mischievous Faegan had lowered his mask and was grinning from ear to ear.

"Seventeen for Traax!" another called out. More congratulatory applause followed.

Urgently elbowing her husband out of the way, an especially rotund woman stepped forward. She lowered her mask to show a hooked nose and far too much rouge adorning her cheeks. With a coy look on her face, she stared straight at the prince. Fearing the worst, Tristan swallowed hard.

"Twenty for the prince!" the woman shouted. The crowd cheered.

Lowering her mask a bit, Shailiha leaned toward her brother. The catty expression on her face was plain to see.

"I'd be careful if I were you," she whispered. "She must mean business—she just paid twenty kisa for you. Watch your feet. One wrong step and they might be crushed beyond recognition."

Tristan scowled. "Twenty kisa, eh?" he mused. "I'd gladly pay one hundred not to have to go down there!"

Then another woman came forward. She was tall, and her red dress was stunning. Her handheld mask was white, with pink overtones. Wondering who she might be, Tristan leaned forward a bit. The unidentified woman looked over at the orchestra leader.

"One thousand kisa for the prince!" she shouted. "And don't worry—I'm good for it!"

A hush came over the crowd as they all wondered who the rich mystery woman might be. Then they started applauding. Taking another step forward, the winning bidder lowered her mask. When Tristan saw her face, his eyes went wide. He sat back in his chair.

It was Tyranny.

Tristan looked over at his sister. "This is your doing again, isn't it?" he asked.

To his surprise, Shailiha seemed as shocked as he. She shook her head.

"I knew she wanted to dance with you tonight," she said, "but not this badly." She smiled again. "Your duty is clear. One thousand kisa will go far for the orphanage. Besides, she's right about one thing," she added softly.

Tristan raised an eyebrow. "What is that?" he asked.

"She can afford it," the princess answered with a smile.

As the bidding for other men continued, Tyranny walked to the dais. Smiling, she curtsied, then reached one gloved hand out toward Tristan.

"Shall we?" she asked.

For several moments Tristan simply stared at her. He had never seen Tyranny so lovely. Even though he suspected that her dress belonged to Shailiha, the privateer seemed to be a totally different woman. The only reminders of her piratical nature were her familiar gold hoop earrings. Relieved to have been rescued from the unappealing matron, he smiled.

"By all means," he said. He took her hand and placed his other one behind his back as he escorted her to the center of the floor.

Bowing respectfully, the crowd quickly gave way for the stunning couple. As Tristan took Tyranny in his arms she beamed back at him. Leaning in, he placed his mouth near her ear.

"I certainly hope this will be worth one thousand kisa," he whispered.

A gentler look suddenly overcame Tyranny's face. "Of that I have no doubt, my liege," she answered softly.

With the auction concluded, the conductor was again standing before the musicians. Tristan looked his way.

"A waltz, if you please," the prince suggested. With a nod from the conductor, the musicians started playing.

Even though he cared little for dancing, Tristan had always been good at it. As he led Tyranny around the floor, he was surprised to find her his equal, if not better. She followed every command effortlessly, gracefully. According to custom, the other dancers let the dashing couple command the entire floor. After two graceful turns, Tristan gave the signal for the others to join in. Soon the floor was alive with elegant dancers, and the lovely waltz was carrying them all away.

Her mask in one hand behind Tristan's shoulder, Tyranny looked the prince in the eyes. Tristan smiled.

"I had no idea you were such a wonderful dancer," he said. Turning with the music, he led them toward a spot that would yield a bit more room. Tyranny followed his every motion like they were one.

"Where did you learn?" he asked.

"From my parents," she answered. "They were marvelous dancers. I wish you could have seen them together!" Showing her lovely neck, she threw her head back and laughed. "I might be mostly seagoing wildcat, but that doesn't mean I'm completely ignorant of social graces," she said coyly.

Sending her whirling, Tristan brought her to her toes, then wheeled her around again. As he did, he realized that for the first time in a long while he was starting to enjoy himself.

"By the way, is Scars here?" he asked. Tristan suspected that even tonight her giant first mate would be near his captain.

"Yes," she answered, "he's here somewhere." Then her infectious laugh came again. "But you know, although I've known him forever, I can't tell you whether he can dance. I love him like a brother—you know that. Even so, I don't imagine that Scars' dancing would be a pretty picture, do you? I pity the poor girl he might hold too tightly! And may the Afterlife forbid him stepping on her feet!"

For the first time in months, Tristan laughed out loud. It felt good—as if the dense fog surrounding his heart was finally starting to lift.

"Yes!" he said, amid his own laughter. "I suppose you're right!"

Tristan took a moment to look around. Then he smiled and laughed a bit more. Wheeling Tyranny leftward so that she could take a better look, he motioned with his chin. She also grinned at what she saw.

The two wizards had levitated themselves and their partners high into the air. At first the two women accompanying them seemed terrified. Realizing they had nothing to fear, they soon settled down. Then Wigg's partner suddenly blushed, and she urgently whispered something into the wizard's ear. After whispering back to her, Wigg smiled and he called a spell that effectively prevented the guests on the ballroom floor from sneaking looks under the ladies' dresses.

Tristan realized that it was much like watching all four dancers slide and twirl atop an invisible glass floor that was suspended high in the air. Having left his chair behind, Faegan dutifully held his delighted partner in his arms as his useless legs dangled below him.

Waving one arm, Tristan caught Faegan's eye, then winked. Understanding, the old wizard nodded. Tristan and Tyranny were promptly lifted into the air to join them. Soon all six were the center of attention.

Amazing, the prince thought as he looked into Tyranny's delighted face. He had been right about the invisible floor. It provided just enough support to twirl Tyranny about, but also gave a feeling of being lighter than air.

Smiling, Tyranny leaned closer. "This is definitely worth one thousand kisa!" she exclaimed.

Smiling broadly, Tristan looked back down at the swirling dancers to notice the heavyset woman whom Tyranny had so easily outbid. With her arms crossed atop her plentiful breasts and her face beet red, she was fuming. Looking farther across the room, he saw young Brent. Despite his recent trauma, the boy seemed mesmerized by the spectacle. That gave the prince an idea.

He decided to ask the wizards to test Brent's blood. Odds were that it would not be endowed. But if it was, and his mother consented, perhaps Wigg would consider allowing him to join the consuls' sons being taught the craft in the Redoubt Nursery. It seemed the least they could do. After all, the boy had just lost his father.

Just then Tristan heard Brent scream, the young boy's shrieks so loud that they easily rose above the music. As he stopped dancing, Tristan quickly looked around, but he could find nothing amiss.

Looking back at Tyranny, Tristan saw the blood drain from her face. She clearly understood—but he still hadn't grasped it. He looked down again to see that the dancing had stopped. The orchestra slowly stilled, its final strains waning away into nothingness.

Tristan was about to demand an answer from Tyranny when Brent screamed again, then pointed to the variegated columns lining the room's walls. As Tristan looked, the breath caught in his lungs. All the decorative ginger lily wound around the columns was dying before his eyes.

Tristan snapped his head around to look at a buffet table lying against the nearest wall. All the brightly colored flowers and decorative plants atop it were dying as well. Turning brown, their stems slowly slumped over in awkward death postures.

Then Tristan remembered what Brent had told the Conclave about his capture. Suddenly things became clear. Tristan frantically turned to look at Wigg.

From their vantage point high above the floor, the wizards urgently searched the room. But even they could detect no alien presence. The still-unknowing guests were happily murmuring among themselves as they wondered what was going on. "Another clever parlor trick by our wondrous wizards," Tristan heard one man say. But Tristan knew that this was no illusion. The stakes had just become deadly serious.

Just then all six dancers were lowered to the floor, and Faegan returned to his chair. Faegan urgently shook his head, telling the prince that it had not been his or Wigg's doing. Hearing Wigg cry out, Tristan looked back over to him.

To everyone's horror, the Paragon was being lifted from around the First Wizard's neck. Wigg quickly raised one hand to employ the craft. But try as he might, stopping the stone's ascent was impossible—even for him. Faegan and Jessamay tried to help augment Wigg's powers with their own, but to no avail.

Everyone could only watch as the Paragon glided to an empty spot above the checkerboard floor. Many gasped as the golden chain disappeared link by link, and was followed by the stone. The wizards looked aghast at the prince, who then cast his eyes back toward the dais. Those Conclave members still seated seemed as stunned as everyone else.

Drawing their swords, Traax, Ox, and several more male and female warriors started cautiously making for the floor's center. Tristan raised one arm, ordering them to stop where they were.

An irregular, shimmering shape started to form in the air. It slowly grew until its outer edges were about two meters wide. Then the shimmering vanished to slowly show an intruder. As he materialized, Brent screamed again and ran to his mother.

A mounted figure had brazenly invaded the room. The intruder's black stallion stood stock-still as white vapor streamed from its nostrils. The rider wore a soft black robe with its hood pulled up over his head. A black leather duster covered the robe and reached down past his saddle stirrups. He seemed to have no face, and the depths of his hood seemed limitless. Even the previously unsuspecting partyers had quieted as they realized that this dark being was not a welcome guest.

Tristan detected a slow movement by his side. Looking over, he saw Tyranny surreptitiously slip one hand beneath the folds of her gown. Understanding that she was reaching for a weapon, he locked his eyes on hers and shook his head.

Tristan started to approach the rider. In response, the intruder gently spurred his horse forward several steps. Tristan didn't reach for the weapons lying across his back. His wary eyes went to the axe and shield that were tied to the being's saddle. Despite the ominous circumstances, he found them magnificent. When Tristan looked into the rider's face, he was shocked by what he saw.

The deep space inside the hood was dark as night—with two eerie exceptions. The being's eyes glowed azure, as they stared back calmly. No skull held the orbs—they simply floated there in the hood's dark recesses. Tristan had never seen anything like them. Then the being smiled, exposing his equally grotesque, glowing teeth. The effect was chilling.

Xanthus, Tristan thought.

Suddenly he heard Wigg's familiar heel strikes, followed by the squeaky wheels of Faegan's chair. Turning around, Tristan looked them both in the eye and shook his head. They reluctantly stopped approaching.

When Tristan turned back to look at Xanthus, his blood ran cold. Xanthus was wearing the stolen vial around his neck.

Tristan could only hope that the stone was safely inside the pewter vial, and that the vial was filled with red water from the Caves of the Paragon. When the stone was removed from its human host, only the red, thick water could sustain its life—but not indefinitely. He forced himself to look back into the macabre eyes.

"Xanthus," he said, trying to control his anger. He looked over at Brent, then back at the Darkling. "We got your message," he added nastily.

"And also the branch and the scroll, I hope?" Xanthus asked. His voice was hollow, dead-sounding. Tristan nodded.

"Then you understand about *K'Shari*?"

"Yes."

Xanthus nodded his approval. "Good—that simplifies my task."

Tristan stood his ground, waiting.

"Then you also know why I have come," Xanthus said.

"You have come for me," the prince answered, "and you have stolen the Paragon. What I don't know is why. And why did those innocent people in Charningham have to die? Surely they meant you no harm."

Xanthus didn't respond. His jaw set, Tristan arrogantly looked into Xanthus' eerie eyes.

"Who sent you?" he asked softly.

The Darkling's bizarre smile surfaced again. He spurred his horse another two steps closer, then leaned one arm down on his saddle pommel.

"My masters are the Heretics of the Guild," he answered softly. "Unless I'm mistaken, you have heard of them. They request the pleasure of your company, *Jin'Sai.*"

Tristan took a quick breath. He didn't know why the Heretics had sent this abominable creature to him. But his heart told him that if he went with this being he would never return.

He turned to look at Shailiha. Her face was a mixture of fear and rage. She slowly shook her head, telling him not to go. Tristan looked back at Xanthus.

"Why do they want me?" he asked.

"All in good time," Xanthus answered.

Wigg and Faegan approached to stand on either side of the prince. "Why have you taken the Paragon?" Wigg asked. His voice was shaking with rage. "Do you truly understand the significance of what lies around your neck?"

"Yes, wizard," Xanthus answered. "I too can employ the craft."

"And if the *Jin'Sai* does not follow you?" Faegan asked.

"Then I will commit even greater atrocities," he said, "making those in Charningham seem like mere child's play. The *Jin'Sai will* accompany me. I could take him by force, but the Heretics have willed it otherwise. Unless he accompanies me this night, the horrors will grow. As a start, killing the revelers in this room will do nicely. Make no mistake, wizards—my gifts are of the Heretics. No one on the Tolenkas' eastern side has the power to stop me. Trying to do so would only result in your deaths, and the deaths of many others. Is that what you want?" Xanthus paused for a moment.

"There is something else you have failed to consider," he added softly.

"And that is?" Faegan asked.

"I possess the stone. I can vanish, cloaking my blood so well that your modest gifts will never find me. If I leave here without the *Jin'Sai,* not only will the atrocities recommence, but whatever hope you might have of recovering the Paragon will vanish with me. You see, I am to take the *Jin'Sai* to a place that your simple minds would find unimaginable. Allow the *Jin'Sai* to accompany me, and you might see your prince and your precious Paragon again. Do not, and the Heretics won't be so generous with their mercy."

Faegan wheeled his chair a bit closer. "What guarantee do we have that you'll keep your word?" he demanded.

Like he was lecturing some dullard schoolboy, Xanthus shook his head. "Fools," he said. "I have given no word to keep."

"Is it true that you have attained *K'Shari*?" Tristan asked. "Before I believe you I want a demonstration of your presumed gift. But I demand that you leave the guests alone. They have done you no harm."

"If you insist," the Darkling said.

Xanthus pointed to the battle axe tied to his saddle. The leather straps securing it untied themselves. He opened his palm, and the axe flew into his hand. He looked back at the prince.

"My ears hear no begging," he said. "My eyes see no pain. My heart feels no remorse." Then his glowing eyes bored straight into Tristan's. "The bluish green one, I think," he said.

Without taking his gaze from Tristan, Xanthus launched his axe into the air. Suddenly realizing his mistake, Tristan could do nothing but watch.

The axe caught a blue-and-green flier in midflight, slicing its body in two as though it had been tissue paper. The axe flew on, its blade crashing into a marble column lining one wall, its impact so great that it nearly cracked the gigantic support in half. For a moment Tristan wondered whether the massive column might give way. Stunned by what they had just seen, guests scurried away from it.

Its wings still beating pitifully, what remained of the flier tumbled to the floor. Faegan cried out; Shailiha screamed. As the broken butterfly convulsed, violet blood ran from her severed innards. Then her two halves stopped moving and died. The Great Hall became quiet as a tomb.

Again without looking up, Xanthus raised one hand. The axe hauntingly levered free from the cracked column and flew back to him. Xanthus calmly caught it in his palm. Violet flier blood ran down the axe's handle, onto his hand.

"You bastard!" Faegan screamed. His eyes were bulging, and his face was red. He wheeled his chair closer. "How dare you! Why did it have to be a flier? Are you insane?"

His mind raging past rational thought, Faegan pushed his chair closer yet. The old wizard loved the fliers with all his heart. Now one had died unnecessarily at the hands of some endowed madman. For that Xanthus would pay.

"A moving target is the only true test of my skill," Xanthus answered casually. "Cutting something in half as it travels through the air commands a certain degree of respect." He looked back at the prince. "*You* understand, don't you, *Jin'Sai*?"

Faegan had reached the breaking point, and he impulsively raised his arms. Twin azure bolts left his hands to go screaming across the room toward Xanthus. Tristan felt the bolts' searing heat as they narrowly missed him and continued on toward their target.

The twin strikes passed harmlessly through Xanthus' body. Tristan watched in horror as they continued, unfettered.

Before the unsuspecting guests at the hall's rear could react, Faegan's bolts tore into them and they were blown off their feet, their bodies literally torn to shreds. Five died instantly. Many nearby cried out in agony from scalding burns. Other guests started to scream; some fainted away. Blood trails crawled their way across the black-and-white checkerboard floor.

Some guests instinctively tried to flee the room, but they found that the doors wouldn't open. Tristan could only imagine that the Darkling had used the craft to lock them. Alarmed by the strange noises coming from the Great Hall, Minion sentries on the doors' opposite sides called out in concern and started pounding on them. But Tristan understood that it didn't matter how many warriors might barge into the room. If they threatened Xanthus, he would kill them all.

Without warning, the Darkling raised a skeletal hand. An azure bolt streaked from his palm to go flying straight toward Faegan.

The crippled wizard raised his arms in a try to ward it off, but he was too late. Xanthus' bolt blew Faegan's chair apart, throwing the wizard three meters into the air. Thrown rearward, Faegan crashed hard against Tristan's empty chair, then finally landed atop the dais floor and didn't move.

Wigg ran across the floor to his friend. Wasting no time, Jessamay, Abbey, Adrian, and Duvessa all hurried to the room's other end, to see what might be done for the wounded guests.

His rage nearly overtaking him, Tristan glared angrily at the monster seated atop the black horse. He desperately wanted to go for his throwing knives, but he knew better than to try. Many surviving guests were cowering in the room's corners. The air was smoky from Xanthus' and Faegan's bolts, and its charred scent harassed his senses. Pieces of Faegan's chair lay scattered across the floor, some of them lying in pools of blood.

Looking up, Tristan saw that the remaining fliers had attached themselves to the ceiling corners in an attempt to keep from harm. His jaw hardened as he saw the blood from the dead guests' mangled bodies approaching his boots.

Tristan removed his mask and dropped it to the floor. He looked back at Xanthus. The Darkling slowly lowered his arm. His glowing eyes confident, he smiled again.

"It is time for us to leave, *Jin'Sai,*" he said. "Unless you want to see more of these puny humans die."

"Is the crippled wizard dead?" Tristan demanded.

"I don't know," Xanthus answered. "Nor do I care. *Your* welfare is my only concern."

Tristan looked back at Wigg. The First Wizard paused in his examination of Faegan to look at the prince and gravely shook his head.

"Give me a moment to consult with my Conclave," he demanded.

"Very well," Xanthus answered. "I grant you five of your world's minutes."

Taking Tyranny by the hand, Tristan walked her to the dais. Wigg was kneeling over Faegan's body. The First Wizard's eyes were closed. His ten fingertips lay on either side of Faegan's head. The lower half of Faegan's robe was burned away, showing his hideously mangled legs.

Everyone knew better than to speak during Wigg's examination, so they stayed silent. Finally Wigg removed his fingers from Faegan's skull and opened his eyes. Desperately anxious for an answer, the others huddled nearer.

Tristan looked frantically into the First Wizard's eyes. "Is he—"

"No," Wigg whispered, hoping that Xanthus wouldn't hear him. "Faegan lives, but barely. Xanthus' bolt struck Faegan's chair, but part of the bolt's energy was transferred to Faegan's body. His brain and nervous system are severely shocked, and his heartbeat is wildly irregular. If I can get him to the Redoubt, Jessamay and I might be able to save him. If not, he will die."

Tristan turned to glare at Xanthus, then looked back at Wigg. "Something doesn't make sense," he said.

"What is that?" Shailiha asked.

"It's obvious that Xanthus has attained *K'Shari,*" Tristan answered. "It is said that those possessing that discipline never miss. And yet, his bolt struck Faegan's chair, so—"

"Xanthus never intended to kill him," Tyranny interrupted. "But if he really was sent here by the Heretics, why didn't they order him to destroy us all, right here and now?"

Tristan shook his head. "I don't know," he whispered back. "There is far more to this than meets the eye. If Xanthus or the Heretics wanted me dead, I would be." He looked into Shailiha's face.

"It seems that there is only one way to find out," he added gravely.

Shailiha vehemently shook her head. "No!" she exclaimed. "You mustn't! I won't let you! No one knows what that monstrosity has planned for you!"

"The princess is right, my lord!" Traax insisted. "There are at least one hundred male and female warriors in this room, most still carrying their dreggans! With one word from you, they will all attack Xanthus at once!"

Tristan shook his head. "Don't you see?" he asked. "If Faegan's bolts couldn't harm him, then how could a dreggan do so? Besides, if he is attacked he might vanish, and we could lose the Paragon forever. No, my friend—he would only kill more of us in the process. There has already been too much death."

Tristan looked back at Wigg. "I'm right, aren't I?" he asked.

Wigg sadly closed his eyes, then opened them again. When he did they were shiny with tears.

"Yes," he answered. "No matter how many of us attack, I fear we cannot defeat this creature. If his gifts truly are of the Heretics, we would be foolish to try. Even combining my gifts with Jessamay's and Adrian's would likely do little good. Despite how much I fear for you, I can see no other course but to let you go."

"Then I shall," Tristan said. "I know that I might never return. Either way, these are my orders: First, Shailiha is now the Conclave leader and reigning sovereign. She is also lord of the Minions. Her word is law. Respect her orders as you would my own. Second, speed your plans to attack the Citadel. If it is at all possible, take Serena alive, and capture the Scroll of the Vagaries. It is my belief that Wulfgar's widow has much to do with this."

"Your time is up, *Jin'Sai*!" Xanthus suddenly cried out. "Must more people die because of your indecisiveness?"

Tristan turned to gaze into the monster's glowing eyes. "Harm no one else!" he shouted. "I will go with you!"

Xanthus grinned, his teeth showing grotesquely in the hood's recesses.

Reaching out, Shailiha took her twin brother into her arms. She held him close, like she was never going to let go. She placed her mouth to his ear.

"I will find you," she whispered, her voice cracking, "just as you once had to find me. I swear it."

"No!" he whispered back. "Promise me that you will attack the Citadel!" Nodding sadly, she finally released him.

Knowing there was little left to say, Tristan nodded at Wigg. Wigg swallowed hard, then nodded back.

Just as Tristan turned to go, Tyranny stepped nearer. She pulled him to her, then kissed him hard on the mouth. She slowly let him go. For the first time since meeting her, he could see that she was shaking.

Rather than seeming surprised, Tristan smiled gently. "I know," he said quietly. "I always have."

Stepping off the dais, he walked to where Xanthus sat astride his mount. He looked again into the dark hood.

"I demand to keep my weapons," he said.

"Granted," Xanthus answered. "As you have no doubt surmised, you cannot harm me with them."

Tristan watched in dread as Xanthus raised a bony, glowing hand. Wondering whether the being was about to cause yet more mayhem and death, he held his breath. The answer surprised him. Another shimmering shape started to appear. It slowly coalesced to take a familiar form.

Shadow, Tristan's black stallion, soon stood where the shimmering had once been. A recent gift from the Minion warriors of Parthalon, the horse danced about a bit as he took in his new surroundings. Shadow was wearing the shiny black tack the warriors had also given the prince. Tristan walked over, grasped the bridle, and rubbed the stallion's face. Shadow slowly calmed.

After gazing around the disheveled room, Tristan threw himself up into the saddle. As he wheeled Shadow around, the stallion's iron shoes clip-clopped on the marble floor. Tristan took a last look at the Conclave members, then walked Shadow up alongside Xanthus' horse.

"It is time, *Jin'Sai,*" Xanthus said. In a voice that was almost kind, he added, "We travel to a place beyond description. Obey my every word, and many of your long-held questions will be answered."

Side by side, Tristan and Xanthus walked their horses toward the rear of the Great Hall. With every step they took, what living foliage still adorned the room withered, then died.

As they neared the far wall, both riders disappeared.

II

THE FLEDGLINGS

Chapter IX

It is for my lost Fledglings that I fear the most. With Duncan's death and the abandonment of Fledgling House, my precious girls might be anywhere. I am not the young girl I once was, and my remaining days grow short. My greatest hope is that I can somehow see my Fledglings again, before I go to the Afterlife.

—FROM THE PRIVATE DIARIES OF MARTHA, ONETIME MATRON OF FLEDGLING HOUSE

STANDING ATOP ONE OF THE CITADEL'S BARBICANS, SERENA LOOKED toward the heavens. It was almost midnight, and the sky was angry. Dark clouds gathered ominously, blotting out Eutracia's three magenta moons. The wind harassed her hair and gown, and the Sea of Whispers crashed mightily in its endless assault against the rocky shore. His hands clasped before him, Einar waited quietly by her side.

I will soon need to summon the craft to remain standing against this wind, Serena thought. *The storm is gathering, just as the Heretics said it would.*

The Heretics had again communed with her yesterday. As she remembered their words, the heavenly voices seemed as clear tonight as they had then.

"Although the Jin'Sai *travels with the Darkling, the Conclave plans to move against you,"* the Heretics had told her. *"You must summon your allies, so that the Citadel is unassailable while Einar and the Valrenkian visit Parthalon. Work the craft tomorrow at midnight, for there will be a great storm. If you fail, all that we wish to do might be rent asunder by the Conclave. We will grant you the proper Forestallment calculations needed to ensure your success."*

She had gone to her knees and lowered her head. There had

been much more to their message; she had listened intently. When the Heretics had finished relaying their instructions, she'd told them she would obey.

At first, the combination of azure letters, numbers, and symbols had seemed incomprehensible. But as they had continued to enter her mind she'd started to recognize the elegant thread of genius winding through them. She'd quickly realized that she would need Einar's help to impart them into her blood signature. It would have to happen soon.

After sending a handmaiden to summon Einar to the Scriptorium, Serena had walked there alone. The Scriptorium was a place of research, where many documents left behind by the Heretics lay in safekeeping. It was there too that she kept the consummately precious Scroll of the Vagaries. As she entered, several consuls in their blue robes nodded reverently, then returned to their work.

Ensconced high in one of the fortress's corner turrets, the Scriptorium was built of tan stone. Bookcases lining the walls held hundreds of texts and scrolls, some still laden with centuries' worth of dust. Several dozen desks sat in neat rows, their tops laden with more scrolls, texts, and tools of the craft. Golden candelabras, their candles enchanted to burn forever and without producing smoke, graced the desks' working surfaces.

Because the hour was late, consuls occupied only a few of the desks. She knew that they would be compiling the results of today's experiments. Other consuls were busy clearing away the physical remains of Einar and Reznik's research. Blood could still be seen here and there on the floor. She clearly understood that Reznik had been right about his warning to her. What they needed could no longer be found on the island. The Heretics had been right in telling her to send Einar and Reznik to Parthalon.

She walked to a consul's desk and looked down. The man quickly abandoned his work to stand before her. He bowed.

"Fetch me a fresh parchment," she ordered.

The consul scurried to do his queen's bidding. He opened one of the many desk drawers, selected a clean sheet, then hurried back. Lowering his head, he offered it up.

Serna took the parchment and walked across the room. By now every consul was watching her. Calling the craft, she caused the parchment to rise into the air.

She stepped closer, then shut her eyes as she recalled the magnificent formula. As the azure calculations started swirling in her mind, she concentrated harder, bringing them to the fore. When she was satisfied that she had summoned the entire formula, she pointed to the parchment. A thin azure bolt leaped from her fingertip to the paper. She opened her eyes.

The blank paper started to smoke as she burned the formula into it. Line after line seared its way into the sheet. When she finished, her small azure bolt disappeared. Smoke drifted lazily toward the open windows. Knowing that the consuls would be eager to view her creation, she looked over at them.

"You may approach," she said. "Come witness some of the Heretics' wisdom."

The consuls quickly left their desks to crowd around her. Some gasped at what they saw. They had never imagined such a complex solution. It was like looking into the minds of the Heretics themselves.

"It is a beautiful thing indeed, Your Grace," Einar said.

Looking up, Serena saw her lead consul approaching. He smiled at her. She smiled back.

"It is, isn't it?" she replied. She looked at the lesser consuls. "Leave us," she said. "Our discussion is not for your ears."

After bowing, the consuls left the room. Einar read the hovering parchment, his dark eyes eagerly absorbing every nuance.

"Amazing," he breathed. As he scanned the formula, Serena informed him of her recent communion with the Heretics.

He turned to look into Serena's eyes. Despite his admiration for the calculations and the reasons for their use, concern showed on his face. Taking a deep breath, he clasped his hands before him.

"Your Grace understands the risks involved when placing this formula into your blood?" he asked. "The Forestallment it will produce will be especially powerful. This could easily bring about your death, to say nothing of the exquisite pain."

Serena did not answer. Instead, she turned away, and returned to the window, then looked out over the restless sea. She stood there for some time, watching and remembering. When she turned back, her expression had softened. She looked around the Scriptorium, then back at Einar.

"It was not so long ago—in this same room, in fact—that you infused a similar spell into someone's blood. It was a spell that had also been gifted to us by the Heretics—one that also promised huge gains in our struggle against the Vigors. I'm sure I needn't remind you further."

A contrite look came over Einar's face. "I remember, Your Grace," he answered. "My only concern was for your welfare." Yielding to her authority, he bowed.

Einar would never forget the night she had mentioned. At long last, the formula for the index of the Scroll of the Vagaries had been acquired. Once imbued into Wulfgar's blood, it would grant him the ability to immediately search out and identify any of the thousands of formulas written on the scroll. It had been a huge leap forward in their understanding of the Vagaries.

The Forestallments Wulfgar's blood carried were a direct result of the *Enseterat* allowing Einar to imbue the index formula into his blood. He could then choose whatever spells he wished, granting them to his queen. He had done so with great care.

Einar had seen Serena's blood signature only once—the day that she had miscarried her child. Literally hundreds of Forestallment branches were evident. Coupled with her inordinately high blood quality, she was truly a living force of the craft. He believed that her gifts even surpassed those of Failee, the late First Mistress of the Coven of Sorceresses. Looking into her eyes, he saw the same unsatisfied hunger burning there that had once consumed Wulfgar.

Even so, Einar was hesitant. His similar use of the craft on Wulfgar had taken nearly all night; the intense pain had nearly killed Wulfgar. Worrying Einar even more was the fact that Serena's blood quality—although inordinately high—was not her late husband's equal.

Wulfgar's death had been a horrible shock to them all. Serena's majestic gifts, and her dead baby girl still lying among those rose petals in the crypt, were all that remained of him. In the end, perhaps the only way to honor Wulfgar's memory would be to honor his grieving widow's desires.

Serena had searched Einar's face with her piercing eyes. "The *Enseterat* was your lord and my husband," she had said quietly. "He was willing to risk all to honor the Heretics' wishes. Shall I do less?"

"I understand," Einar had answered. "When would you like to start?"

"Immediately," she had answered. "Our enemies across the sea do not tarry. Neither shall we." Her mood suddenly darkening, she looked sternly into his eyes. "But before we begin, I want you to take a solemn vow," she said.

"Anything, Your Grace. You know that."

"Should I die this night, promise me that you will continue with our work. To the death, if need be. The *Jin'Śai* must pay for his crimes."

Einar had bowed slightly. "I promise," he had answered, "even unto death."

The cold sea wind brought her back to the present, and Serena looked around. From her place atop the wall she saw that the sea was even higher now and the clouds thicker, the wind stronger. Even the saucy gulls had scattered, their keen senses telling them that something ominous was brewing. It was time.

She had never felt more alive. Although she had nearly died the night before, the suffering she had endured to accept the formula into her blood had been worth the price. Aside from the mysteries of the craft, she was about to partly rule over the world's most potent force. She would command nature herself. Even more, she would twist it to suit her needs, creating something never before seen in the world.

The queen of the Vagaries raised her arms. Calling on her new Forestallment, she began employing the craft.

The wind rose mightily, surpassing its earlier ferocity by far. Seawater violently splashed its way up from the shoreline to touch her mourning dress and her skin. Einar also found himself forced to call the craft, simply to avoid being blown off the wall's guard path. White tentacles of lightning snaked wildly across the sky, their accompanying thunder booming in his ears.

Looking skyward, Serena raised and joined her hands. The dark clouds frantically converged. Raising her hands higher, she caused a single cloud to become even darker. As the wind howled and the lightning flashed, the giant cloud started to spin, whirling itself into a vortex that encompassed the entire nighttime sky.

Einar's jaw dropped. The huge, spinning cloud was unlike anything he had ever seen. It was so dark and thick that it seemed to have real substance. Serena spread her fingers. A lightning bolt suddenly shot its way directly through the cloud's center. The massive cloud started spewing rain with tremendous force. It fell heavily, like dripping candle wax might. When the droplets neared the earth they started changing shape, growing in size until they blotted out the night sky. As the first of the things formed, he looked on in wonder.

Each of the drops widened to become a slim, flat oblong. They reminded Einar of another of nature's creatures, but he couldn't place them. Then they widened farther at their sides. Slender, graceful tails grew from their rears.

When the first of them came to hover before its new mistress, Einar suddenly remembered. It looked like a deadly ocean ray he had once seen. Its life finally expired, it had washed up on the Citadel's shoreline. This new being was similar in every respect, save for its larger size.

More of its fully realized brothers came to join it. One of them rose in the dark sky to reveal its underbelly. Although its topside was light gray like the fortress, its underside was of the darkest black, with small, scattered pinpricks of white.

Near its body's top edge, a pair of glowing, dark eyes stared back confidently. There were no nostrils or mouth. It hovered before them gracefully, kept aloft by the outer edges of its smooth, undulating body. It was a beautiful, yet terrifying thing. As the rain continued to fall, more of them formed. Einar estimated that there must be tens of thousands of them.

Serena slowly lowered her hands. The dark cloud stopped spinning and vanished. The lightning and thunder slowly faded away to show a clear night sky, and the Sea of Whispers calmed. Their dark eyes glistening, the vast horde of beings Serena had created hovered quietly. Einar stepped closer to Serena. He placed his mouth near her ear.

"Permission to speak?" he whispered.

Serena nodded. "These beings are our servants. They will not harm us."

Reaching out, she beckoned one closer. The edges of its body rippling gracefully, the amazing creature complied. Serena stretched forth one hand to stroke its velvety skin. The creature let go a sort of soft, cooing sound. *Almost like a mother and child,* Einar thought.

"What are they called?" he asked.

"The Heretics call them envelopers."

"Envelopers," Einar mused. "Why is that?"

Serna turned to him. "Did you bring the two Valrenkians I asked for?"

Einar nodded. "They wait in the corner guardhouse."

"They are each expendable?"

"Yes. One is an old woman near death, and the other is a boy of feeble mind. Reznik has confirmed their uselessness."

"Good," she replied. "Bring them."

Einar walked down the path toward the stone guard post. One such post sat wherever two or more fortress walls intersected. Employing the craft, he unlocked the squeaky door.

Inside, an old woman dressed in brown rags sat hunched over a table. A young boy with vacant eyes and uncontrolled drool running down his chin wandered aimlessly about the stark confines. His clothing was mostly red. Two consuls stood nearby, watching them. Einar gestured to the consuls.

"Bring them," he ordered.

The consuls grabbed the woman and the boy, and started manhandling them toward the door. The old woman screamed, alarming the boy. As they struggled, Einar scowled at the consuls.

"Use the craft if you must!" he shouted. "Just get them outside!"

Soon the two captives became more compliant and started shuffling along. As the group neared, Serena held up one hand.

"That's far enough," she said. "You will soon understand why. Leave them there and return to me."

Einar and the consuls did as they were told. Unsure of their fates, the woman and boy huddled together. As the boy started to cry, the woman smoothed his hair and spoke softly to him. Einar found the similarity striking.

Again, just like a mother and child, he thought.

Serena turned toward the nearest of her envelopers. "Go," she said simply.

Widening its undulating wings, the enveloper streaked toward its victims. Its speed was amazing. It quickly wrapped its body around them. Then the screaming started.

Einar could see nothing of the woman or the boy, save for occasional glimpses of their boots. He guessed from their muffled screams that they must be struggling, but it was impossible to tell.

As the enveloper's deadly embrace held them fast, Einar looked down at the victims' feet again. Despite his years of experience with the craft, he felt himself becoming sick. Realizing that he should never show such weaknesses to Serena, he again called on the craft to help steady his legs.

Blood and other body fluids started running to the pathway. The two pairs of boots seemed to somehow lose their shape, and their tops slowly turned earthward. The enveloper finally released its grip. Einar watched as the woman's and the boy's stripped bones rattled to the walkway amid their wet clothing and flopped-over boots. Nothing else remained.

"Now you understand," Serena said.

"What we just witnessed," Einar breathed. "That is how they take their sustenance?"

"Yes," Serena answered. Raising one hand, she bid her creation to join the others. The enveloper immediately obeyed.

"But surely we cannot feed so many," Einar protested. "Despite your dislike for the Valrenkians, we still need them."

"Yes," Serena answered. "For the time being the envelopers will hunt the surrounding sea. But soon they will leave us. Then they will have all the food they could possibly need." Serena turned back to look up at her creations. "Protect," she said simply.

The thousands of dark beings flew upward to start patrolling the skies over the island and the sea. As they went, their undersides perfectly matched the night—so much so that in mere moments, they had disappeared from view. Einar suddenly recognized that the small specks of white on their underbellies had been simulated stars. Mightily impressed, he shook his head.

"Will they be so well hidden during the day?" he asked.

Serena nodded. "Their topsides will take on the appearance of the sea, the ground, or the fortress," she answered, "depending on the terrain over which they fly. Their underbellies will take on the sky's ever-changing look, be it day or night."

Einar looked up again. Although he knew that they were up there, the envelopers were nowhere to be seen. He had to admit that he felt safer, knowing that they were overhead. A quick smile graced his lips. Should the *Jin'Sai*'s forces approach, they would never see the monsters until it was too late.

"All of the envelopers will accompany you on your journey," Serena said. "When added to the creatures already awaiting you, your work will be well protected."

Her words stunned Einar. "But mistress!" he protested. "Who

will protect you from the Conclave's forces, should they attack the Citadel?"

"Your loyalty to me is admirable, but do not fret," she answered. "The Heretics have plans to grant me another form of protection. You will also take the Vagaries scroll with you. Your destination is the last place on earth that the Conclave will think of searching for it. To them, it will be hiding in plain sight, as it were." She turned away from her lead consul and looked out over the sea.

"I am tired," Serena said. "I will retire."

Einar bowed. "Your Grace," he said reverently.

After nodding to him, Serena levitated from the guard path, her gown billowing as she went. Einar watched her land on the inner ward, then walk away.

Looking up again, Einar used the craft to augment his eyesight, trying to find the envelopers. He stood there for another full hour, dutifully searching the skies.

He never found one.

CHAPTER X

"ARE YOU READY TO SEE THEM?" LOTHAR ASKED. "BECAUSE THEY are so choice, at first I considered keeping one or two for myself. Especially the one called Mallory. They're all a bit dirty and thin, but that can be easily rectified. I'd bet that they're all virgins—yet another selling point. Before we talk price, you can check if you want. I'm sure the guards would be happy to help."

Lothar confidently put his feet up on his desk. His highly polished shoes shone in the candlelight. Then he took the cigar from his mouth and blew softly on its lighted end. Tobacco bits clung to his fat lips, adding to the gluttonous impression.

The woman sitting across from him was trying to remain nonchalant. But she knew that Lothar was in the catbird seat. She hated the fat jailor, but her brothel in Bargainers' Square needed fresh replacements. Unless she got them, she would soon be out of business altogether. Her remaining girls would have no place to go, and for that she would be sorry.

Worse, Lothar understood her plight. He was a regular visitor to her house of ill repute. He knew how few girls remained because of attrition from the orb, and that she had lost many customers. In turn, she knew his price would be even higher than usual. Even so, she refused to be bullied.

"I might not want all eight," she countered. "It will depend on their ages, general appearance, and how outrageous your price is."

Smiling, Lothar reached out to pour two glasses of wine. Just then they heard a distant scream filter down the hall and through the office doorway.

Soon begging and sobbing started, their sounds so faint that neither she nor Lothar could tell what the victim was pleading for. Then they heard a harsh slap. Things went quiet again. The woman across the desk looked hard into Lothar's face.

"That had best not be coming from one of my prospective purchases," she said skeptically. "Are you sure that your guards aren't taking liberties?"

"Quite sure," Lothar answered. "But they are interrogating a lady debtor who refuses to give up the last name of her family's opposite side. She's rather attractive, as it happens. Anyway, once we have the name, only then may the guards use her as a pastime. My rules about such things are specific. Any guard who breaks them is subject to death. But they also need to feed the inner man occasionally. You of all people should know that a slice off a cut loaf is never missed, eh?" Taking a sip of wine, he smiled at her like he commanded the entire world.

Ignoring her wine, Mary of the House of Broderick glared back at Lothar with hatred. She was a madam—that much was true. But she was no killer, torturer, or extortionist. Unfortunate conditions dictated that she must do business with him, so she would.

If there was such a thing as a madam with a conscience, it was Mary. Sold by uncaring parents into the trade at the tender age of twelve, over the years she had learned firsthand how to run a prosperous bordello. But even when times were good, it was a closely run thing. Her personal turning point had come six years ago, after being cruelly abused by a customer.

As she lay in bed fighting for her young life, the doctor summoned to her side had told her that although she would live, she would never bear children. Her madam had taken pity on her. She allowed her to stop servicing clients and took her under her wing, teaching her the trade firsthand.

Mary had sworn a solemn vow right there and then. When *her* girls had earned enough to pay off the price of their purchase, they could leave freely. Years later in her own establishment, some of her girls chose to leave, and some did not. But no matter their preference, she was always fair with them. In her own strange way she loved them like they were the children she'd never had.

She could have gotten her girls directly from the street, as did her competitors. But she knew how badly Lothar's prisoners were treated. She wanted to help as many as she could, before they met even crueler fates at his hands. So she did business with the greasy jailor, despite how much she loathed him. His high prices cut deeply into her profits, but it was worth it.

At forty Seasons of New Life Mary was still a handsome woman, even though her previous years in the trade had stolen the bloom from her cheeks. Dark red ringlets fell to her shoulders. A stylish hat sat cocked to one side atop her head, its diaphanous veil hanging down before her face. Wishing to keep as much of her anonymity as possible, she wore it every time she visited here. Her conservatively tailored dress and equally fashionable shoes made her look more like the wife of some respected burgher or barrister than a bordello proprietor. She liked it that way.

Lothar took another sip of wine. Bluish cigar smoke left his wide nostrils to drift toward the ceiling.

"Now then, do you want to see them or not?" he asked.

Always wary where Lothar was concerned, Mary thought for a moment. "Eight girls taken in one fell swoop?" she asked. "Who are they? Where do they come from?"

Lothar scowled. He had had enough of this choosy, retired whore.

"Since when do you care about pedigrees?" he shot back. "You're not running a charm school! Sometimes I believe you're going soft! I don't know who they are, and I don't care! Stop wasting my time! Do you want to see them, or do I contact your competitors?"

Knowing she had no cards left to play, Mary nodded.

"Good," Lothar said. "Let's go."

Swinging his feet off the desk, he stood. Mary retrieved her heavy purse from the floor. The kisa inside it jangled together enticingly. Mary winced. The fat jailor smiled.

Lothar escorted her to the doorway. Mary squared her shoulders and started following him down the dark hallway. She had taken this walk before, and always for the same reason.

Taking a deep breath, she tried to prepare herself for the kinds of things she would encounter along the way.

FROM HER PLACE NEAR THE CELL'S FAR WALL, MALLORY LOOKED down at the empty dishes. Although the food and water had been evenly divided, there had been very little for any of them individually. The bowls had all been licked clean; not a drop of water remained. If their sustenance didn't improve, what magical powers they had remaining would soon be gone.

She suddenly winced as the pain came again—sharp, stabbing, humiliating. She still hurt in secret places where the guard had probed her. Even so, her exhaustion was so great that it easily rivaled her discomfort. Closing her eyes, she leaned against the dank wall.

She suspected that the hour was late, but there was no way to be sure. All the girls other than she and Ariana were huddled together in one of the cell's corners, fast asleep. A brutish guard paced back and forth on the other side of the barred door. Other than his footsteps and the squeaking rats, this part of the prison was quiet.

Mallory trudged across the room to join Ariana. Her friend was again sitting on her knees, staring at the latest symbols and numbers she had scrawled across the wall. The piece of charcoal she held had become much smaller, prompting Mallory to wonder what they would do when it was gone. She gently placed one hand atop Ariana's shoulder. Ariana turned her dirty face up to her.

"How goes it?" Mallory whispered.

Sighing, Ariana ran one forearm across her brow. "Don't get too excited," she warned, "but I may have it."

Mallory eagerly went to her knees to look at Ariana's calculations. Then she groaned inside when she saw that the tightly spaced numbers and symbols stretched for more than three feet.

"Can it be shortened?" she asked.

Unsure of her answer, Ariana pushed her tongue against one cheek. "Perhaps," she answered. "But I'm not the one to do it. Only a fully realized wizard or sorceress could shortcut this mess. For our use, I'm afraid it must stand as is."

Mallory understood Ariana's concern. In order to master a spell, one had to commit the formula to memory until recalling it was second nature, and then activate it in a split second. Ariana's work would be difficult for Mallory to absorb, and time was running out. The other way to perform a spell was to recite the formula verbatim, in the form of an incantation.

Hearing footsteps, Mallory looked to the door. The guard passed by without looking in. She turned back to Ariana.

"Have you tested it?" she asked.

Ariana shook her head. "No," she answered flatly. "I didn't dare."

"Why not?"

"The other girls' gifts aren't as strong as ours," Ariana said. "You and I are the only two who might succeed. Either of us will only have enough strength for a single try. After that we may never have enough power again.

"Worse yet is the sound it is sure to produce, should it work," Ariana went on. "This place is very old. Everything is covered in rust and grime. If I were to test it just as the guard happened by—well, you get the picture."

Sadly, Mallory had to agree. "What do you suggest?" she asked.

Ariana thought for a moment. "We should reverse roles," she said.

Mallory looked surprised. "Why?" she asked.

"I am the one who wrote the spell, not you. I know it better. If it works for me, then you can perform the part I was to do and entice the guard. I know it's not what we agreed on, but it seems the only way."

For several long moments, Mallory considered Ariana's suggestion. "Do you think you can do it?" she asked.

Ariana sighed. "There's only one way to find out. But I can summon only enough energy to try once, so I'll do it by incantation rather than memory. That way has the greatest chance of success."

Ariana thought about what was at stake, then looked Mallory in the eye. "You're our leader," she whispered. "What do you want me to do?"

A concerned look came over Mallory's face. She stared back at the other girls. All six were fast asleep. Even Magdalene, their resident troublemaker, was out. Mallory looked back at Ariana.

"If there was ever a time to try, it's now," she whispered. "The girls are all asleep, so they won't react and make any noise. If you succeed, we'll wake them. If you fail, they don't have to know."

Standing, Mallory looked to the door. "Wait for my signal," she said. "It will come when the guard is farthest away." Ariana nodded her understanding.

"Good luck," Mallory said.

"And you," Ariana answered back.

Mallory waited until the guard passed by again, then she quickly tiptoed to the door. Placing her face against the dirty bars, she watched him walk away for as long as she could. When she lost the angle on him and he slipped from view, she waved one hand. Concentrating with all her might, Ariana started whispering her calculations. Remembering what Master Duncan had so often told her, when she reached the end of the formula she closed her eyes, then envisioned what she wanted to happen. With her heart in her throat, she cocked her head to listen.

Squeaking as they went, the rusty tumblers in the door's lock started to turn over.

Knowing that the spell was only halfway finished, Ariana held her breath. Eutracian locks always turned over at least twice before they released. She winced as she heard the tumblers scrape again, even louder this time. In the quiet of the prison, they seemed deafening. Terrified, Ariana shot a glance at Mallory.

Mallory heard the guard's footsteps abruptly stop for a moment, then start again. They came faster now, growing louder with every step.

Racking her brain, she hurried to the rear wall, then grabbed up the tin pot in which the gruel had been served. Putting a vacuous look on her face, she started absentmindedly scratching the pot against the wall, as if the relentless boredom had finally overcome her and she needed to do something, anything, to alleviate it. The scratching didn't sound altogether like the rusty tumblers, but it was all she could think of.

As the curious guard stopped before their door, Mallory kept on with her mindless scraping. Out of the corner of one eye she saw him grab the door bars, then peer in as he searched the cell. Ariana kept her face to the wall. Mallory held her breath.

The guard finally sneered at Mallory's foolishness. After what seemed an eternity, he let go of the door. Mallory blessed the rusty hinges that had kept it from shifting at his touch. Saying nothing, the guard turned, then continued his patrol.

Wide-eyed, Ariana looked at her. Mallory let go a sigh of relief.

It was time to wake the others. They hadn't a moment to lose.

MARY'S DREAD GREW AS SHE FOLLOWED LOTHAR DOWN THE TORCH-lit hallways. Today's walk was in an unfamiliar direction. She had never visited this part of the prison before.

The dingy cells along the way held prisoners of both sexes. Some had been imprisoned for so long that their clothes were mere tatters and their bodies had wasted away to slumping sacks of bones. Mary lowered her head as she tried to ignore the pervasive stench of human waste.

Many of these wretched souls had gone mad. Some pointed, laughed, or howled insanely as Lothar and Mary walked by. Others, their eyes wide with terror and hopelessness, lunged at the bars. Still others sat huddled in their cell's corners, babbling incoherently. Signs of physical torture showed plainly on their bodies.

Mary was comforted to know that her two most trusted girls back at the bordello knew where she was, in case Lothar tried something unexpected. That was always the case when she visited here. Even so, as she traveled deeper into this wretched place, she became more frightened.

Her mouth suddenly dry, Mary clutched her purse so tightly that her knuckles went white. She was about to tell Lothar that she wanted to go back when he stopped before a wooden door at the end of the hall. It was made of massive oak planks and was fortified with iron cross braces.

Lothar dropped his cigar and crushed it beneath one shoe. He smiled.

"Just a little farther," he said. "I promise the trip will be worth it."

He produced a brass key from his vest pocket and shoved it into the door's keyhole, then turned it over.

Lothar pulled on the squeaky door. A circular stairway led downward. More torchlight shone from the depths; the sounds of a faintly cracking bullwhip and distant screams wafted up the stairs. The stench rising to meet them was nearly overpowering. Lothar beckoned Mary across the threshold and onto the mildewed landing.

Lothar locked the door behind them. The brass key went back into his pocket. Without further ado, he started down.

Having come this far, Mary knew she could never double back against the jailor's will. Wondering whether she would ever be heard from again, she reluctantly followed him down the stairs.

MALLORY SHOOK SCARLET'S SHOULDERS GENTLY. AT SEVEN SEAsons of New Life, Scarlet was the youngest among them. "Wake up!" Mallory whispered.

Rubbing her eyes, Scarlet scowled sleepily. Ariana busily awakened the other five girls. Once they were all on their feet, Mallory told them to crowd around as she explained the plan. Several of them started to jump up and down and squeal with delight.

That was the last thing Mallory needed. Putting a finger over her lips, she hushed them. For once, even the disagreeable Magdalene obeyed.

"Do you all know what to do?" Mallory asked. Eager nods came from all around.

Mallory looked anxiously toward the door. She had waited until the guard passed by before waking the girls. He was due back soon. Less than an hour ago, there had been a change of shift. To her dismay, the guard patrolling the hall was now the same filthy brute who had abused her earlier. At first that had unnerved her. But now she planned to use it to her advantage. She looked anxiously at Ariana.

"Are you ready?" she asked.

Ariana nodded, but there was a worried look in her eyes. "Be careful," she whispered. "We will have only one chance at this!"

Mallory took Ariana's hands into hers. "I know," she answered. "Be sure they're ready to move at a moment's notice!"

Mallory walked to the door. She was trembling. Taking a deep breath, she tried to calm herself. Ariana had done her part; now it was her turn. She had to be convincing, no matter how much it disgusted her.

Mallory soon heard the guard's footsteps returning. She hiked up one side of her skirt, then grabbed the door with both hands. As the guard neared, he leered at her. Mallory forced herself to smile.

"Why don't you stop for a while?" she asked coyly. Suddenly it was all she could do to keep from becoming ill. Even so, she moved her smiling face nearer to the dirty bars.

The skeptical guard stopped, then glanced toward the cell's far wall. The other girls looked fast asleep in one corner, huddled up against each other as they tried to stay warm. Turning his furtive eyes back to Mallory, he looked her up and down lasciviously.

"What do you want?"

Mallory edged closer. She could smell his stink again, but she held fast.

"I want more of what you did yesterday," she whispered. "I liked it."

She looked back to the girls like she was making sure they were asleep. When she swiveled back around she suggestively rubbed one hip against the door.

"Don't worry," she whispered. "Nobody will see. This time it will be just you and me." She temptingly spread her legs. "Come closer," she said enticingly. "I'll let you do whatever you want."

The guard couldn't believe his good fortune. His predatory eyes shining, he leaned toward the door.

Mallory quickly summoned the craft, then used it to treble her strength. Shoving the door open with everything she had, she slammed its iron bars straight into the guard's forehead.

To her horror he simply stood there for a moment with an amazed look on his face. Blood ran into his eyes. Then his eyeballs rolled up in his head. He fell flat onto his back, unconscious.

The girls ran to her. Mallory looked into Ariana's eyes.

"Does any of your power remain?" she asked urgently.

Ariana shook her head. "Not much," she whispered. "But I'll do what I can!"

Mallory looked at Magdalene. "We three will lead, and the younger girls will follow us. Do you understand? All right, then," Mallory said to everyone. "Let's go!"

The younger girls following along behind them, Mallory, Ariana, and Magdalene stepped out into the hall. Wondering what might await them, they summoned whatever powers they had left.

Mallory looked first to the left, then to the right. Both ways looked the same—dark, looming, endless. She stepped over the guard's body and started leading the girls leftward, down the hall.

May the Afterlife watch over us, she prayed.

WHEN MARY REACHED THE LAST STEP, SHE LOOKED DOWN THE hall to see an intersection looming up ahead. Five separate hallways branched away from its center. It was illuminated by wall torches. The torches' flames cast spectral shadows across the floor and walls.

A guard sat there at a desk. He seemed bored, half asleep. When he saw Lothar approaching he quickly cleared his throat and sat upright.

The cracking bullwhip and the desperate screaming seemed much louder now. Mary found herself fervently hoping that Lothar's route wouldn't take them past the torture session. That was something she wasn't prepared to see.

Just as they neared the desk, a strange-looking streak of blue lightning came out of nowhere to hit the guard squarely in the chest. He was propelled backward with such force that he was lifted into the air and slammed against the rear wall. He hit the floor hard. Blood ran from his ears and nose. Smoke drifted lazily from his burned skin and clothing. Stunned by what had just happened, Mary and Lothar simply stood there, staring. As the smoke cleared, the guard looked dead.

Calling out for help, Lothar started running toward the stricken guard. Suspecting that Lothar had just made a mistake, Mary wisely stayed back.

As Lothar reached the desk he turned to look down the facing hallway. His eyes went wide with surprise. Before he could react another blue bolt came streaking through the air. Like the first one, it hit its target squarely in the chest. The bolt slammed his great bulk into the air.

Lothar landed hard on his back atop the desk with his arms and legs dangling limply toward the floor. His eyes were closed, and his tongue protruded from between his teeth.

Not knowing what to do, Mary stood frozen in the moment. From behind her she heard the sounds of voices and running footsteps. She quickly turned to look.

Far down the dimly lit hall, she could barely see a group of guards charging toward her. They were shouting angrily and carrying torches. When she turned back to look at Lothar, her eyes went wide.

Eight dirty girls stood squarely in the intersection. All of their eyes were locked on her. They looked like starved, desperate animals. What remained of their filthy clothing looked oddly like some type of school uniform. Mary watched as the blond girl in the front narrowed her eyes and pointed one arm at her. Suddenly, Mary understood.

These were the girls Lothar wanted to sell to her. They were of the craft, and trying to break free. *And they believe I'm with Lothar!*

She immediately went to her knees, then put her hands into the air. From behind her the sounds of the guards' boots were getting nearer by the moment.

"Don't hurt me!" she screamed. "I'm not one of them! I want to leave here as badly as you do! But without my help, you'll never find your way out!"

When the blond girl slowly lowered her arm, Mary rose to her feet and ran to Lothar's body.

The girls watched skeptically as Mary gingerly fished about in his vest pockets. His clothing still smoked from the blast. Praying that Lothar's brass key hadn't melted, she finally found it. To her relief it looked intact. Then she felt herself being spun around by the shoulders and stared directly into the blond girl's eyes. The girl's strength had been amazing.

"Who are you?" the girl demanded.

"There's no time!" Mary answered. She held the key before the girl's face.

"More guards are coming!" she protested. "Our only chance is to help one another! You command the craft, and I know the way out! Come on—we must go now!"

The blond girl looked skeptically at a girl with dark hair. After several precious moments the two of them finally nodded. With the eight girls hot on her heels, Mary charged down the hallway leading toward the circular staircase.

The guards entered the intersection, then skidded to a stop. They looked in horror at Lothar's body, then ran after Mary and the girls.

Mary knew that they didn't have much of a lead, and that the girls would be weak from lack of food. With Lothar out of action, she tried not to think about what the guards would do to them if they were caught. Clutching the key like it was her very life, she ran as fast she could.

She reached the stairway, and charged up it. After conquering several steps, she finally dared to look back to check on the girls. The six younger ones soon reached the steps and started up. She was terrified to see the older blonde and brunette standing at the bottom.

"Hurry!" Mary screamed at them. The two girls looked up at her.

"Go on!" the blonde shouted. "We'll be right there!"

Her mind a panicky jumble, Mary shoved the key into the door, then gave it a turn. Pushing for all she was worth, she swung it open. She ushered the six girls through like a distraught mother hen. Then she went back onto the landing and looked down again.

Mallory looked down the hall. Within seconds the guards would be upon them. She looked into Ariana's eyes.

"Are you sure this is going to work?" she shouted.

Ariana shook her head. "No!" she answered. "But it's the best idea I have! Are you ready?"

Mallory nodded. Each girl raised her arms.

"Remember, they must be close enough so that they can't stop in time!" Ariana warned. "Wait . . . wait . . . now!"

The two determined girls summoned their remaining powers. At first nothing happened, nearly causing them to panic. Then the floor between them and the onrushing guards was bathed in an azure glaze. The guards saw it, but they couldn't stop in time and went skidding right into it. They came to unexpected, abrupt halts, the gluelike substance holding them fast. Some stopped so quickly that they came out of their boots and flew through the air, only to have their bodies stick when they hit the floor. Several of their torches and weapons went flying.

Charging up the stairway, the two girls made sure to coat the steps behind them as well. Near the top, they turned to look. Mallory put one hand over her mouth; Ariana's jaw dropped.

Being novices in the craft, the girls hadn't stopped to wonder whether the substance they created might be flammable. The torches the guards dropped had set the azure glaze afire, turning the entire floor into a raging inferno.

Unable to escape, the guards shouted and begged as the roaring flames approached. Screaming madly and flailing their limbs, one by one they started burning alive. As Mallory and Ariana stood there watching, the sickening stench of burning flesh rose to greet them.

Snaking its way toward the circular stairway, the rampaging blaze set fire to the first step, then began madly chasing them up the stairs. Mallory and Ariana turned and ran for their lives up the last two steps, then charged through the huge doorway.

Mary swung the door shut and locked it. Smoke quickly started seeping through the gap at the bottom and along the door frame.

"We have to run away from here!" one of the younger girls screamed.

"No!" Mary shouted back. "You must do as I say! There is no time to explain! *Walk* behind me in single file! Whatever you do, don't talk and don't run!"

Not knowing what else to do, Mallory nodded to the girls. They nodded back.

Just as the massive door started to come ablaze, Mary led her young charges toward the prison foyer.

The foyer was the only marginally attractive room in the prison. As she led the girls across the shiny marble floor, she nodded politely to the guards stationed there. Smiling, the guards nodded back.

Deciding to be of service, a guard walked to the double doors and held them open for the madam and her new charges. As they quietly walked through, he even went so far as to bow. Bowing back, Mary fought hard to contain a grin.

The nine females sauntered out of the prison and into the busy street. Night had fallen, and the oil streetlamps burned brightly.

Praying that the girls would have the good sense to remain quiet, Mary quickly hailed a passing carriage.

Six of the girls were able to sit inside; two had to climb atop the roof. Reaching up, Mary handed the driver more kisa than he had seen in a week. He beamed a toothless smile down at her.

"Where to, m'lady?" he asked. Hearing the question, Mallory stuck her head out of one of the carriage windows.

"To the royal palace!" she ordered.

When Mary gave her a questioning glance, Mallory scowled back. "I'm giving the orders now," she said quietly.

Mary shook her head. Wasting no time, she climbed up to sit with the driver.

"The royal palace it is," she repeated.

With a crack of the driver's whip, they were off.

CHAPTER XI

WHEN TRISTAN REGAINED CONSCIOUSNESS HE FOUND HIMSELF supine on a dewy field. His weapons poked sharply into his back. The night was clear and the stars burned brightly overhead. As he sat up, his head swam sickeningly.

"Do not be alarmed," said a hollow voice. "The sensation will pass. As we travel together it will no long occur."

Tristan looked around. Only a few meters away, the Sippora River lay impossibly still, and the three red moons reflected calmly atop its waters. He saw flat grasslands stretching for leagues in every direction, suggesting that he was somewhere on the fields of Farplain.

A campfire burned nearby. A bit farther on, two unsaddled horses stood tied to a tether line. One was Shadow. A freshly dressed venison hindquarter rotated without support above the crackling fire. Its enticing aroma filled the night air.

Dark and unmoving, a figure sat cross-legged by the fire. A

pewter vial hung from a silver chain lying around his neck. Xanthus' axe and shield lay beside him on the ground.

The prince stood on wobbly legs. He quickly drew his dreggan. After taking two steps toward Xanthus, he suddenly remembered the failed result when Faegan had attacked the Darkling. Tristan looked for a time at Xanthus' unmoving form, then sheathed his sword.

"A wise decision," Xanthus said. "Come sit by the fire."

Tristan looked around warily. Other than the lone campfire, he saw no other lights on the plains. He soon noticed that the night creatures did not sing. The Farplain winds were notorious for their consistency, but tonight the air was uncommonly still. Save for the usual sounds from the campfire and the tethered horses, everything was eerily quiet. Then Tristan noticed the field grass. All around the entire campsite, the vegetation was dead.

Tristan walked tentatively toward the fire. He was desperately hungry. The smell coming from the roasting meat made his stomach growl, but he dared not try any.

"Where are we?" he demanded.

Xanthus turned toward him. His eyes glowed eerily.

"We are the equivalent of one day's ride northwest, along the Sippora's banks," Xanthus answered. "It is still the night of your masquerade ball. Thanks to the craft's wonders, we traveled this far in mere moments."

"Where are you taking me?" the prince asked.

"We travel to the azure pass," Xanthus answered. "How long it takes us to arrive, and what occurs when we do, depend entirely on you."

"How can that be?"

"Your ignorance is understandable," Xanthus said. "I will be happy to enlighten you. But first you must eat. Sit down, *Jin'Sai*. I am not your enemy."

Realizing that escape was probably impossible, Tristan reluctantly took a seat by the fire. He watched a roasted venison piece tear itself away from the slowly rotating hindquarter. It floated through the air to land in his lap. He refused to touch it. Xanthus smiled.

"Bring you all this way only to poison you?" he asked. "I believe not. If I wanted you dead, you would be. Eat. Our journey is long; you will need your strength."

Tristan bit warily into the meat. To his relief it seemed all right. He started eating greedily. As soon as he had finished, another piece was delivered to him, along with a wine flask.

When he finished, he wiped his mouth and looked back at the Darkling. He anxiously eyed the pewter vial hanging from the being's neck. Tristan silently prayed that Xanthus understood the stone's full importance. His mind filled with unanswered questions, Tristan looked back into the glowing eyes.

"You steal the Paragon, attack Faegan, and then abduct me!" he snarled. "Yet you say that you are not my enemy! If that's true, your way of making friends is a strange one! Who are you?" he demanded. "Why am I your prisoner?"

"You bear no chains that I can see," Xanthus answered. "You are not, nor will you ever be, my prisoner. You came willingly."

"I accompanied you only under the threat that more atrocities would occur if I did not!" Tristan shot back. "What sort of sick game are you playing?"

"It's no game," Xanthus answered. "But there are rules, I assure you."

Tristan watched as Xanthus caused a log to float through the air and land atop the fire. The prince turned furtively to regard the axe and shield. As he found himself wondering about them, his curiosity did not go unmissed by the Darkling.

"You still have your weapons," Xanthus said. "Moreover, you are free to ride away anytime you choose. I will do nothing to stop you. But you won't go, and we both know why."

"The Paragon," Tristan said.

"Yes," Xanthus answered. "But there is more to it than that. You haven't grasped the problem's entirety. Observe."

Tristan cringed as he watched the pewter vial float up and away from Xanthus' form. Its top slowly opened. The Paragon and its gold chain lifted free from the vial. Tristan shuddered as he realized that the stone was probably ready to accept a new human host. He also knew that the period between hosts was always the stone's most vulnerable time.

The Paragon dripped cave water as it twinkled beautifully in the firelight. As Tristan expected, the stone quickly started to lose its color. Unless it was given a human host soon, it would die.

Tristan's reaction was immediate. Lunging for the stone, he tried to grab it with both hands.

Just as he neared the Paragon it flew away and its chain landed securely around Xanthus' neck. It twinkled enticingly against the Darkling's black duster.

Seething, Tristan sat down again. Xanthus smiled.

"You could have done that while I was unconscious," Tristan said. "Did you wait simply to taunt me?"

"It was merely an object lesson in our respective gifts," Xanthus answered. "Moreover, you needed to be conscious to see what happens next."

To Tristan's horror, Xanthus caused the pewter vial to turn over, pouring its cave water onto the ground. As Tristan watched the liquid soak into the dead grass his anger finally boiled over.

Hoping to confirm his suspicions, he lunged for Xanthus' axe. To his amazement the Darkling did nothing to stop him. Just as Tristan raised it over his head to strike Xanthus down, the awful realization hit him. Tristan suddenly stopped. With the axe still held above his head, he stared hatefully into the glowing eyes.

Xanthus smiled. "I see you have finally grasped the enormity of your problem," he said calmly.

Feeling impotent, Tristan could only stand there, shaking with rage. He lowered the axe.

"Yes," he admitted.

"Explain it to me," Xanthus said. "Before we travel farther, I must know that we understand one another."

"You already know what the answer is!" Tristan growled.

"I'm sure I do," Xanthus said. His politeness in the face of Tristan's helplessness was driving the prince mad. "Tell me anyway," Xanthus insisted. "Do this small thing for me, and I will then answer some of your many questions."

"Even if I somehow took the stone from you, I couldn't prepare it for a new host," Tristan snarled. "The stone would die. For the time being, I'm forced to accept that it must stay around your neck."

"Well done," Xanthus said. "But there's more to it than that, isn't there?"

"Yes," the prince answered.

Tristan dropped the axe. Even if the Darkling's axe could somehow kill Xanthus, it didn't matter anymore.

"And that is?" the Darkling asked.

"Even if I find a way to kill you, I mustn't," Tristan breathed hatefully, "because there is no fresh cave water with which to prepare the stone for a new host. If you die, the stone dies with you."

"Well done," Xanthus answered. Strangely, he seemed genuinely pleased. "The Heretics said that you are a quick study," he added. He turned his eyes back toward the fire. "Even so, a very important aspect of our relationship eludes you."

"Just what is that?"

"As we travel, you must serve as my protector," Xanthus answered.

The preposterous notion nearly made Tristan laugh. "That's nonsense!" he protested. "I've seen your abilities! Faegan's bolts passed straight through you! No doubt physical weapons would as well. In addition you command the craft. I understand the need for you to live—at least until I have found a way to reclaim the stone. Then I will kill you gladly, if I can. Even so, your warrior abilities far outstrip mine! So why would you need my protection?"

"Calm yourself," Xanthus said. "Sit down, and I will tell you."

Knowing he had little choice, Tristan again sat by the fire.

Xanthus looked into his eyes. Tristan found the experience unnerving. No matter how many times the Darkling gazed at him, he sensed it would always be this way.

"It is in fact true that I may require your protection at certain times," Xanthus said. "If you want to ensure the Paragon's survival, you will give it. Our journey to the pass will be a dangerous one."

"I don't understand."

"I am a binary being," Xanthus said, "created by the Heretics for only one purpose—to tempt you into coming with me. My Darkling half is mere spirit. At certain times, my horse and my clothing are equally ethereal. My specialized gifts allow me to function in your world as though I had physical substance when I choose to do so, and to employ the craft even while the Paragon is immersed in cave water. What you see of me now is only part of what I truly am."

Tristan had never heard of a binary being. Nor could he understand why Xanthus was telling him these secrets.

"If that is true, what makes up your other half?" Tristan asked.

"My other half is human," Xanthus answered. "Although my human half also commands the craft, when I am in that form I am mortal, just like the wizards and sorceresses of your Conclave. You must therefore stay by my side and protect me. If I am attacked while in my human form I might die, and the Paragon would die with me."

Tristan considered Xanthus' words. The irony that the Darkling presented was infuriating. The idea that he might be forced to protect the same dark being that had slaughtered the innocent citizens of Charningham angered him to the core.

"Why would the Heretics grant you human form," he protested, "when it contributes to your vulnerability?"

"Think," Xanthus replied. "The answer you seek is hiding in plain sight."

Tristan suddenly realized that Xanthus was treating him much the same way Wigg and Faegan often did, after he asked a question about the craft. They would sometimes keep the answer from him, forcing him to reason it out on his own. But despite the Darkling's surprisingly quiet nature, this creature was no friend.

At first Tristan couldn't imagine what the answer might be. Then Xanthus turned to him again, showing what little there was of his face. There was no skin, no bone, and no hair. The orbs floated hauntingly in the hood's depths, accompanied only by teeth that were exposed whenever Xanthus opened his mouth. A mere spirit, he had said.

Tristan looked down at the Paragon hanging around the Darkling's neck. Its deep, bloodred color had returned, signaling that it had accepted Xanthus as its new host. Suddenly the prince understood.

"You say your Darkling half is mere spirit," he mused. "If that's true then your spirit side likely contains no flesh, bone, or blood. If it has no blood, then your Darkling half cannot provide the host needed by the Paragon. That is accomplished only by your human side. That is why the Heretics gave it to you. Not because they wanted to, I suspect, but rather because they were forced to do so if you were to successfully take the stone."

"And . . . ?" Xanthus asked.

Tristan tried to make sense of Xanthus' inference. He found sitting beside a campfire and talking craft theory with a mortal enemy maddening. It was like he was somehow being fattened up for the kill, and could do nothing about it.

"Your human half, even though I cannot see it, must coexist at all times with your darkling half," he said. "If it did not, the stone would die."

Tristan understood now. Xanthus' human side sustained the stone, while his Darkling side—the side that he showed—provided the invincibility needed to carry out his mission. In turn, the stone provided the bait Tristan must follow, or risk the Paragon's death. If that happened, magic would disappear forever.

Looking at the ground, he shook his head. The Heretics' plan was elegant, foolproof. Like it or not, he had no choice but to follow this monster.

"But why must I go willingly?" he asked. "A being with your gifts could easily kidnap me, forcing me to come."

The glowing smile appeared for a moment. "Like the way the misguided Coven abducted your sister?" Xanthus asked. "Only to warp her mind until it was nearly unrecognizable? And all so that she would do their bidding as little more than a common slave? No, *Jin'Sai*—the Heretics are not so crude. True, they wished for Failee's success, for it would have furthered their overall cause. But brilliant as the First Mistress was, they easily saw the flaws in her plan—flaws compounded by her madness. Nor were Nicholas or Wulfgar successful against you, despite the Heretics' guidance."

Xanthus paused for a moment as he caused another log to land atop the fire.

"Even I cannot answer why you must go willingly," he added. "But I suspect that it has to do with your *true* nature, and why you are upon the earth. Only the Heretics know such things. When you finally stand before them, they will tell you."

Tristan suddenly felt a rush go through his blood. His next words came only as a whisper.

"Do you mean to say—?"

"Yes," Xanthus interrupted. "If you accompany me through the pass, you will finally come face-to-face with one of the two factions that know all there is about you and your sister's existences. Neither is what you believe, *Jin'Sai*. Your wizards, although brilliant, have been wrong in many respects."

His mind racing, Tristan stared into the fire. If he followed Xanthus through the azure pass, the many secrets he so longed to unravel might be his. But he also realized that if the Heretics wanted him in their midst, their reasons wouldn't be benign. His blood, although still untrained, was supposedly of the highest quality the world had ever seen. As much as he wanted answers, surrendering his person to the same beings who had originated and perfected the Vagaries was unthinkable.

He had to devise some way to take the Paragon from Xanthus and escape. But what if he found no way to take the stone? Would he watch Xanthus disappear into the pass with it forever? Or would he follow him, giving both the stone and himself over to the Heretics?

Something told him that he must do what he had always done when faced with an enemy of the Vigors. He would fight against what they wanted, simply because they wanted it.

"I won't follow you," he said softly.

"The Heretics warned me that this would be your stance," Xanthus said, "at least at first. I understand your need to kill me and to take the stone. That's simply the nature of your blood. But again, you're forgetting something."

"What?" he asked.

"The Paragon's theft was meant to induce you to follow me, at least at first," Xanthus answered. "The Heretics have been watching you since your birth. They might know you better than you know yourself. They suspected that you would struggle against their wishes, simply because they worship the Vagaries. Your stubborn nature precedes you, *Jin'Sai.*" Xanthus looked into the fire again.

"Let us be honest with ourselves," he went on. "You will stay with me until we reach the pass because it is in the craft's best interests for you to do so. But your heart tells you that when we arrive, you should refuse to go in with me. Why? Because you believe that your blood must not fall into the Heretics' hands. The Heretics expected as much. They knew that another, even more potent inducement needed to be found. That is another reason for my Darkling side."

"The atrocities," Tristan whispered.

"Yes," Xanthus answered. "There is a village near here called Everhaven. It will be our first stop. If you continue to resist going through the pass, what I will do there will be but the beginning."

Tristan's anger rose again. Even though he knew it was impossible, he wanted to kill Xanthus with his own two hands. How sweet it would feel to crush the Darkling's throat and watch the blue light abandon his venomous eyes. Remembering that attacking Xanthus would prove pointless, he tried to calm himself.

"Why must the torture start tomorrow," he asked hatefully, "when we have yet to reach the pass?"

"Yet another object lesson," Xanthus answered. "As we go, you will be forced to see what horrors will occur until you consent. You must resign yourself to this, *Jin'Sai.* The wheels are in motion, and neither of us can stop them. There is no other choice."

Tristan stiffened as he watched the Darkling reach into one duster pocket. What Xanthus produced was surprising. It was Tristan's black ball mask, somehow magically ferreted away by Xanthus before they left the palace. The Darkling handed it to him. Not knowing what else to do, he took it.

"Why give me this?" Tristan asked.

"The Heretics have been gracious enough to offer it," Xanthus answered. "I suggest that you respect their wishes. When morning comes, you may find that you want it—perhaps desperately so."

"I still don't understand," Tristan protested.

"But you soon will," Xanthus said ominously. "It will take us several days to reach the pass because we will be traveling on horseback, rather than by the craft. Unless, of course, you decide to honor the Heretics' wishes. If you do, I promise you that the wonders you will behold will dwarf your wildest dreams. Consent and I will take us there in the blink of an eye. Refuse, and the atrocities will continue. As I said when you first awoke—how long it takes us to arrive, and what happens when we do, depend entirely on you."

Tristan looked around. The river was still unmoving, the wind nonexistent, the night creatures silent. He looked back at the Darkling.

"Why does nature still in your presence?" he asked. "I have never seen anything like it."

"The phenomenon has to do with *K'Shari,*" Xanthus answered. "But that is a topic for another time."

Tristan looked down toward the fire. He realized that he was still holding the mask, and shoved it beneath his vest. Soon another question occurred to him.

"If your Darkling half protects you from harm, yet you never show your human half, then how could an enemy possibly kill you?" he asked. "It still seems that you don't need my protection."

"I did not say that my human half is never shown," Xanthus answered, "but there are only two reasons why it appears. Unlike my Darkling half, my human half needs food, water, and sleep to survive. My human half sleeps while unrevealed. But when we take our meals together, I must appear to you that way."

"What is the second reason?" Tristan asked.

"The second reason is more . . . complex," the Darkling answered. "It has to do with proving my devotion to the Heretics. From their places on the Tolenkas' other side, certain of them watch our every move, and hear our every word. They consider your arrival of the utmost importance. Because it was previously impossible to conquer the Tolenkas, never before has anyone—not even a *Jin'Sai* or a *Jin'Saiou*—had this opportunity. For that reason alone, I suggest that you be judicious in your decision. As I said, they see everything. Proving my loyalty to them as they watch is the other reason they granted me a human side."

"How do you prove your devotion?" Tristan asked.

The Darkling turned to look at him. Tristan found the glowing eyes boring into his brain again.

"Through the acceptance of pain," Xanthus answered simply. "But ask no more questions this night, *Jin'Sai*. As we travel there will be ample opportunities for you to learn what I have to teach you, humble as such things might be. Sleep now; you will need your strength. Have no fear. I will watch over you until the cock crows. Then we will start for Everhaven."

Tristan gazed blankly into the fire. Xanthus' unthreatening nature continued to surprise him. It was almost like the Darkling had become his teacher. The calm, talkative being by his side seemed little like the creature that had killed the citizens of Charningham and caused such terror in the Great Hall. Despite his ominous words, the Darkling's recent demeanor had become almost fatherly, caring.

With Xanthus' mention of sleep, Tristan suddenly realized how tired he was. Could he rest safely? With escape and killing Xanthus impossible, what else was there to do? As Xanthus had said, if the Darkling had wanted him dead, he would be.

Unable to hold his eyes open any longer, he lay by the fire with the black masquerade mask pressing against his skin. He fell asleep immediately.

Xanthus ended the spell he had surreptitiously used to put Tristan to sleep. He looked over to see the *Jin'Sai*'s sharp features gently highlighted by the fire, then stared back out across the vacant plains.

There is so much for you to learn, Jin'Sai, *if only you will agree to follow me through the azure pass. But you cannot see that. Considering the many things I must do to convince you, you will remain difficult. Come with me and your wildest dreams will be fulfilled. Refuse and your entire world will suffer peril such as it has never known.*

Amid the ominous quiet, Xanthus started the long wait for dawn.

CHAPTER XII

DEEP IN THE REDOUBT, WIGG LOOKED WITH SADNESS INTO FAEGAN'S face. His old friend was still unconscious. The First Wizard had been sitting by Faegan's bedside for the last three hours. As night marched inexorably toward day, Wigg's concern deepened.

Faegan's face was pale. His breathing was little more than a ragged collection of wheezes and gasps, and he was bathed in sweat. Jessamay stood quietly beside the First Wizard. She hadn't said so, but she doubted that Faegan would last the night. Shailiha and Tyranny were also there, keeping vigil.

Rather than accept rooms in the palace, Faegan had taken up residence in the massive labyrinth belowground. He wanted to be near two of the things he loved most in the world—the Redoubt research facilities, and the fliers of the fields.

Faegan's private rooms were spacious and welcoming. A fire burned warmly in the hearth. A large desk sat to one side, and its top was littered with texts, scrolls, and other craft tools. Patterned rugs and specially chosen artwork tastefully adorned the room, and elaborate floor candelabras held brightly burning candles.

When Faegan wasn't knee-deep in some craft riddle, he could usually be found in the flier aviary. Seated on the spacious balcony, he would watch for hours as his beloved butterflies swooped and darted about the spacious chamber.

It was on that same balcony that Shailiha's only active Forestallment had unexpectedly come alive. It was a day that the princess would never forget. As she now sadly watched the wizard fight for his life, she doubted that they would ever share that balcony again.

After the incident at the ball, Shailiha had quickly ordered the Acolytes of the Redoubt and Duvessa's warrior-healers to tend to the injured ball guests. She had then commanded Traax to immediately take a flying phalanx of warriors to the azure pass, to see whether Xanthus and Tristan might arrive there.

The remaining Conclave members were in agreement that the pass was where Xanthus had probably entered Eutracia. Shailiha had her doubts about whether the warriors could stop the Darkling from taking Tristan back through it, but they had to try. Following Xanthus was impossible, because he had vanished, taking Tristan with him. Stopping him at the pass was their last, best chance.

Faegan groaned, and Wigg reached down to place a gnarled hand on his friend's forehead. After a time Wigg removed his hand. He looked at Jessamay.

"His fever has returned," Wigg said gravely. "When it broke earlier, I had hoped it was for good. But he grows weaker by the moment."

Faegan moaned again and started thrashing about like he was in the midst of some awful nightmare. Wigg and Jessamay had seen this several times during the last three hours. Clearly, there was more going on than Faegan's struggle to survive.

Wigg lifted the covers and looked at Faegan's mangled legs. After being captured by the Coven during the Sorceresses' War, Faegan had been tortured for days. Failee had ordered that his legs be shredded by the craft until their muscles, nerves, and blood vessels lay exposed down their entire lengths. Since then they had been useless to him, causing exquisite, never-ending pain.

One wasn't often reminded of Faegan's legs, because his robe always hid them. Faegan had been able to overcome some of the pain by using the craft to partition it away in his mind. It was a constant struggle, and one that he sometimes lost. He had tried for the last three centuries to formulate a spell that might heal them. But even his great intellect had failed to unravel Failee's particular brand of wickedness.

Faegan cried out again, louder this time. With tears in his eyes, Wigg looked over at Jessamay. They each knew why the crippled wizard was suffering so. Unconscious and on death's door, Faegan's mind had lost its ability to control his leg pain.

After lowering the covers, Wigg again leaned down to put a hand on Faegan's forehead. The injured wizard soon calmed, which told Wigg that his spell was taking hold. Sighing, Wigg stood upright.

"This is the third time I have had to assuage his agony," Wigg said worriedly. "I fully understand that he is weak and fighting for his life. But my spells should be longer lasting. I was not affected during Xanthus' attack. Therefore, any spell that I conjure should sustain itself until I choose to end it. But each of my pain-cessation charms has mysteriously withered away. As they die, I can literally feel them slipping from my grasp. I can already sense the new one starting to erode, and I have never seen its like. It is almost like my spells are somehow being crowded out."

Wigg looked toward the room's far side. Still dressed in their ball gowns, Shailiha and Tyranny were talking worriedly and drinking wine. Tyranny anxiously smoked one cigarillo after the next while she paced around the room like a caged tigress. Wigg was about to admonish her, then thought better of it; everyone worries in his or her own way.

Wigg's immediate concern was to help Faegan regain consciousness. When struck by a craft bolt, the victim often died outright. If one wasn't killed, the main threat became withering bodily functions, because of the massive energy that had surged through the organs and nervous system. The secondary issue was skin burns. In many ways, it was like being struck by lightning. The longer the unconscious state persisted, the less the chance for recovery.

Faegan's torso had been badly burned. Luckily, his face had been spared. Wigg had treated the burns. Provided Faegan lived, they would heal.

But the First Wizard was at a loss about how to strengthen

Faegan's fading life force. Wigg had tried everything he knew to buttress it. Even so, Faegan's heartbeat, breathing, and brain activity had all fallen to critical levels, and they were sinking ever lower. If they became further depressed, death would be inevitable. Hoping that a potion might halt the downward spiral, Wigg had ordered Abbey and Adrian to rush to Faegan's herb cubiculum, to see what they might come up with.

Leaving Jessamay to watch over Faegan, Wigg walked over to Shailiha and Tyranny. The look on his face was discouraging. He poured himself a glassful of wine.

Tyranny finally stopped pacing. Blowing smoke from her nostrils, she tossed her spent cigarillo into the fireplace. She gave the First Wizard a hard look.

"Will he live?" she asked.

Wigg took a long slug of wine, then shook his head. "Only if Abbey and Adrian can come up with something unprecedented," he answered. "His heartbeat is almost nonexistent, and his lungs barely rise and fall. It might be only a matter of time."

Jessamay walked over to join them. There was obviously something on her mind.

"What is it?" Wigg asked anxiously.

"I have an idea," she said.

Wigg put down his wineglass. "What is it?"

Jessamay pointed to the cluttered desk sitting in the corner. "A blood criterion and a signature scope sit over there," she said. "I believe we should examine his blood. It can't hurt."

Wigg scowled. He was willing to do anything to help Faegan, but he failed to see how Jessamay's suggestion would help.

"We can," he answered, "but it won't tell us anything. You know as well as I that blood signatures always look the same, whether the subject is ill or not. So what do you hope to learn?"

"I have no idea," Jessamay answered. "That's why I believe we should do it."

"Very well," Wigg answered. "As you say, it can't make things worse."

He turned to Tyranny and Shailiha. "Fetch me some blank parchment," he said. "Then clear the desk, except for the criterion and the scope."

Eager to contribute, the women hurried to the desk. Shailiha shuffled through the drawers while Tyranny cleared off the desktop. Holding up a clean parchment sheet, Shailiha looked over at Wigg.

"We're ready," she said.

"Place the parchment on the desktop," he said. Shailiha did as he asked.

Wigg walked back over to the bed. Faegan remained calm, but Wigg knew it wouldn't last. Reaching down, he lifted Faegan's hand. The First Wizard summoned the craft.

A short incision formed in Faegan's palm. Liberating one blood drop, Wigg caused it to hover in the air. The wound closed. With a short wave, Wigg sent the blood across the room to land on the thirsty parchment.

Wigg went to the desk and sat down. He drew the scope nearer and positioned the parchment beneath it. When he was satisfied, he stared down through the lens.

He adjusted the scope over the paper until the wire crosshairs embedded in its lens split the signature into four perfect quadrants. As expected, the scope showed Faegan's blood signature leaning far rightward. The curved lines forming half of the signature came from his mother. The other half, containing straight lines and sharp angles, was from his father.

Wigg sighed. "It's just as I expected," he said as he continued to read the signature. "His recent trauma is not evidenced here. Perhaps the criterion will tell us something, but I doubt it. Either way, I—"

Wigg suddenly stopped speaking. His mouth fell open.

"What is it?" Jessamay asked.

Wigg quickly raised one hand, demanding silence. The three curious women crowded nearer. After a time, Wigg lifted his face.

"I beg the Afterlife . . . ," he whispered.

"What is it?" Jessamay asked.

Wigg stood from the chair. "Look for yourself," he said. "Please tell me I'm dreaming."

Taking a seat, Jessamay looked down through the lens. At first she noticed nothing unusual. Then she saw the source of Wigg's amazement. Confused, she looked up at him.

"How is this possible?" she asked. "You told me that neither your signature nor Faegan's carried Forestallments."

Wigg stared into Jessamay's eyes. "That's right!" he answered. "At least not until now!"

Wigg caused a small incision to open in his hand. A blood drop lifted from it to land on the parchment. Sitting down, he quickly repositioned the scope, then looked through the lens. Anxious moments passed. Finding himself at a loss to explain things, he slumped back in the chair.

"As expected, my blood carries no Forestallments," he whispered.

"I don't understand," Shailiha said. "When did Faegan grant himself a Forestallment?"

"Don't you see?" Wigg answered. "He didn't!"

"How can you be so sure?" the princess asked. "He's forever tinkering around down here. Maybe one day he—"

"No, no!" Wigg interrupted. "Don't you see? He couldn't possibly have done this!"

"Why not?" Tyranny asked.

Jessamay looked at the two women with knowing eyes. "The answer is simple," she said. "We don't know how."

"She's right," Wigg said. "We have the Scroll of the Vigors, but we do not know how to imbue its Forestallment formulas into one's blood."

"Then how did Wulfgar come by them?" Tyranny asked.

"There can be only one answer," Wigg said. "Someone at the Citadel possesses the needed skill. How he or she learned is another matter."

Wigg turned to look at Faegan. He was grateful to see that the crippled wizard was still calm. He looked back at the three women.

"You haven't grasped the larger question, have you?" he asked.

"I have," Jessamay said quietly. Worry showed on her face. "Who granted the Forestallment to Faegan's blood?" she asked.

"Who indeed?" Wigg said. "There can be only one answer."

Shailiha suddenly understood. A look of astonishment overcame her face.

"Xanthus," she breathed, scarcely believing it herself. "But how—when?"

"I believe the Forestallment was granted to Faegan's blood when Xanthus attacked him," Wigg answered. "The Darkling's bolt carried the calculations. When the bolt's energy shocked Faegan's system, the Forestallment calculations entered his blood. Faegan gave Xanthus the perfect justification to do this when he attacked him. Remember, Xanthus said that his powers came directly from the Heretics. Is it so difficult to imagine that the Darkling could do such a thing? Before he went with Xanthus, Tristan wisely deduced that it had not been Xanthus' intention to kill Faegan, because the bolt struck his chair, rather than Faegan's person. Xanthus' attainment of *K'Shari* supposedly means that he never misses his intended mark. Xanthus left Faegan alive on purpose, so that he might carry the Forestallment."

"By imparting the spell into Faegan's blood that way, the Darkling intended us to discover it later," Shailiha mused. "He wanted us to find it during our efforts to heal him. But something doesn't figure. Why would Xanthus bother to grant Faegan a Forestallment, when he must have also known that the bolt carrying it might kill him?"

"There might have been no choice," Wigg said thoughtfully. "It could have had something to do with the high power requirements needed to perform both acts simultaneously. In doing so, Xanthus took the chance that Faegan would survive."

Wigg looked back over at his injured friend. "If Faegan dies, his blood signature will also die. We might never know what this Forestallment does."

When Wigg looked back at the three women, there were tears in his eyes again.

"What I am about to tell you will be shocking," he added softly, "but it needs to be said. I will do everything in my power to save him—you know that. But if he dies, it might be for the best."

Shailiha was immediately outraged. "What are you talking about?" she shouted. "Have you suddenly gone mad? The man lying in that bed is your greatest friend!"

"Of course he is," Wigg answered calmly. "But you're forgetting something. Xanthus is a Vagaries servant, sent here by the Heretics. He said so himself. After hearing that, do you really believe that Faegan's new Forestallment is something benevolent? Why else would Xanthus do such a thing, if not to advance the Heretics' cause? I humbly submit that you're wrong, Princess. I agree that Xanthus wants Faegan to live. But he wasn't hoping that we'd find the Forestallment. Instead, he was hoping that we *wouldn't.*"

"Why?" Tyranny asked.

Jessamay turned to look at the three others. Her face had gone white.

"So that he might create an enemy in our midst," she whispered. "The new Forestallment carries several branches. Even now one might be slowly altering Faegan's signature to the left. Just imagine—a wizard with Faegan's power, secretly controlled by the Vagaries and possessing Forestallments we know nothing about. He could destroy everyone before we knew what hit us."

Stunned, Shailiha looked back over at the injured wizard. She couldn't imagine Faegan as an adversary. But she had to respect the possibility. Until Tristan came home, the hard decisions would be hers. She suddenly felt the world lying heavily on her shoulders, but she adamantly resolved to take up where Tristan had left off. She looked sternly into Wigg's eyes.

"Despite his blood, Faegan is still one of us," she said. "We will make every effort to heal him. If he dies, he dies. There may be nothing we can do about that. If he lives, we will watch him closely. I want his blood signature examined every few hours. If any changes are detected, we will deal with them then."

Wigg found himself smiling at her. Shailiha had made the wise and moral choice. In the world of the craft, that was not often a simple thing.

"Well done," he said.

Just then the doors opened. Everyone turned to see Sister Adrian and the herbmistress Abbey standing there. They were both out of breath from hurrying. Abbey held a dark-colored vial in her hands.

The women scurried across the room. Abbey gently passed the vial to Wigg.

"We did the best we could under the circumstances," she said, trying to catch her breath. "Adrian and I put every type of stimulant into it that we could find. In fact, I worry that it might be *too* potent. If Faegan's heart has been damaged, he might not survive it. Then again, if the potion isn't strong enough, it won't work. Time is running out. If this doesn't succeed, we won't have the luxury of another chance."

Wigg walked the vial to the other side of the room. Jessamay followed him. As he held it to the firelight, they examined it closely. Like they had a life of their own, the potion's violet undertones moved about of their own accord. Wigg removed the vial's top, then cautiously sniffed its contents. Recoiling smartly, he scowled. He quickly shoved the stopper back into place. Looking back at Abbey, he was almost afraid to ask.

"What on earth did you put in here?" he demanded. "It smells awful!"

"The best of the best," Adrian answered. "We used crushed nether root, oil of ground black adder, and dried patchouli leaf, to name a few. They're all very strong stimulants. A single taste in these combined dosages might keep you awake for a week. Patchouli is especially noted for strengthening the heartbeat. But the resulting mixture tended to thicken. So we added some Slippery John blossom, to make sure that the mixture wouldn't morph from its liquid state into a colloidal suspension. That's what makes it move on its own. The liquid form will be far easier to digest, resulting in greater effectiveness."

Adrian suddenly blushed. "The Slippery John blossom was my idea," she added softly.

"And a good one," Abbey said.

"You must hurry, my love," Abbey warned Wigg. "Given its volatile nature, this bastard concoction of ours may have a brief shelf life."

Wigg looked tentatively at Jessamay. She thought for a moment, then nodded her concurrence.

"I agree," she said. "It seems we have no other choice."

Just then they heard Faegan moan and start thrashing about again. It was clear that Wigg's charms were wearing off.

Wigg looked at Jessamay. "I will need your help," he said.

"Of course," she answered.

They hurried to the bedside. Faegan's convulsions were wilder now, causing the covers to fall off. That shocked the others. None of them had seen Faegan's gruesome legs. Abbey, Adrian, and Tyranny looked to the floor. Determined to watch, Shailiha forced herself to hold fast. The princess finally saw with her eyes what her heart knew Faegan had to continually endure. She had never believed it possible that her respect for the old wizard could strengthen, but it did.

Wigg looked at Jessamay. "Follow my instructions exactly," he ordered. "I will conjure another spell to ease his pain. As I do, summon the craft to open his mouth. Remember, Faegan is immensely powerful. Despite his weakened state, it might take everything you have. I will conjure another spell to keep his throat open. Then I will administer the potion. Are you ready?"

"Yes," Jessamay answered.

"Good," Wigg said. "Let's start."

Suddenly Wigg had another thought. He turned to look at Abbey. "Assuming this potion works, how long will it be before it takes effect?" he asked.

"Several minutes," she answered. "After that, things will happen fast. Because it is a stimulant, the potion might temporarily raise his power. You might have to control him as it goes about its work."

Shaking his head, Wigg rolled his eyes. "*Now* she tells us!" he grumbled.

Wigg summoned the craft, then placed one hand on Faegan's forehead. Almost at once the crippled wizard started to still. After Faegan had calmed, Wigg looked over at Jessamay.

"You may start," he said.

Calling the craft, Jessamay summoned the needed spell. Faegan's mouth parted a bit, then stopped. His unconscious mind was fighting Jessamay. Concentrating harder, she managed to open his mouth a bit more, but not much.

"Is that the best you can do?" Wigg asked.

Jessamay nodded. "Even in his weakened state, his gifts are exceptionally strong."

Wigg caused the vial to leave his hands. It floated to a place just above Faegan's blanched face. Then the stopper lifted free and the vial moved toward Faegan's lips. Changing his commands slightly, Wigg used the craft to start pouring the mixture into Faegan's mouth, a little at a time.

Wigg was forced to stop twice because Faegan started choking. Finally the violet mixture was gone. Wigg caused the empty vial and its stopper to fly across the room and land on the desk. Precious minutes ticked by. The silence in the room was palpable.

Faegan suddenly stirred. He groaned again, then screamed.

It's starting, Wigg realized. *May the Afterlife grant that we have done the right thing!*

Faegan's thrashing came again, this time more violent than ever. Wigg quickly surmised that the potion was working, rather than his pain spell wearing off so soon.

But Wigg hadn't shared his greatest fears with the others. He saw the danger as being two-sided. In Faegan's unconscious state, his mind might lash out to use the craft any way it could, with no regard to the consequences. If Abbey was right about the potion raising his powers, matters could become worse.

Wigg was even more concerned as to whether Faegan's new Forestallment had been activated by Xanthus when the Darkling had used his azure bolt. To Wigg's mind, the idea that Xanthus had activated it before leaving with Tristan seemed likely. If Faegan could already employ his new Forestallment, even in his unconscious state, it might prove disastrous. If he awakened and used it, he could be unstoppable.

We might be waking a horrific monster of the craft, Wigg worried. *But what's done is done.*

Without warning, Faegan sat straight up in bed with his eyes open—even though Wigg sensed that his friend was still unconscious. Wigg stood aghast as he watched Faegan ominously raise his arms and, laughing insanely, start using the craft.

Almost at once the room started to shake. Ancient dust and mortar came loose from among the shifting stones to fall like so many gray snowflakes. Then the shaking started. It soon seemed like the entire Redoubt was coming apart.

The walls buckled, the ceiling drooped, and the floor heaved. Then rumbling sounds came, quickly becoming so loud that the First Wizard could barely hear himself think. Two ceiling stones let loose, to hit the floor with a thunderous crash, narrowly missing the four women standing near the door.

Artwork tumbled haphazardly from the walls. All the standing candelabras fell over, and two wildly swinging crystal chandeliers let loose to come crashing down. Wigg saw several worried Minion guards come charging to the doorway, but there were no orders he could give them that would help. The structure's trembling had become so great that it was nearly impossible to remain standing. As various furnishings caught fire, dense smoke started filling the room.

Wigg looked frantically to the women near the doorway. "Get out!" he screamed. "Climb the stairs to the palace!"

The women ran from the room, and the Minion guards followed behind them. Only Jessamay and Faegan remained with Wigg.

Faegan laughed again, then turned his wild eyes toward the door. As he saw the women escaping, he pointed one hand in their direction. Almost immediately several more stones loosened from the hallway ceiling to come crashing down. Wigg heard a scream, but he couldn't tell from whom it had come. Dust and debris filled the hall.

As yet more wall and ceiling stones continued to fall, a terrible thought seized Wigg. Could Faegan's relentless destruction of the Redoubt be what Xanthus had wanted all along? Was Faegan conscious and doing this awful thing intentionally?

Wigg's mind reeled before the terrible possibilities. The Tome, the Scroll of the Vigors, and the Well of the Redoubt were all here, to say nothing of the Archives, the Flier Aviary, the Hall of Blood Records, and the Redoubt Nursery. The destruction of the Redoubt and its many treasures would be a disaster that the Vigors could never survive, and would produce an unprecedented victory for the Vagaries. If Faegan was doing this purposefully, he was committing suicide, and taking Wigg and Jessamay with him.

Wigg looked frantically over at Jessamay. He could tell that she was using the craft to her utmost, in a try to keep Faegan from destroying everything. But she couldn't start to match his power. Wigg tried adding his gifts to hers, but even then it was no use.

As the Redoubt continued to come apart, Wigg suddenly found himself faced with an unspeakable dilemma. He knew he either had to wait and see whether Faegan stopped, or kill him and save the Redoubt. Amid the noise and smoke, Wigg's mind was torn by the awful choices.

Wigg decided that the destruction had to be stopped, no matter the price. With tears in his eyes he raised one hand and pointed it at Faegan. Realizing what was about to happen, Jessamay looked at Wigg in astonishment. For the craft's sake, Wigg hardened his heart.

Just then Faegan's eyes rolled back in his head and he collapsed, falling heavily back onto the bed. The Redoubt's rumbling quieted, and the shaking stopped. Mortar dust continued to drift down gently. Everything in the room seemed covered with the lung-choking stuff.

Coughing deeply, Wigg again placed one hand atop Faegan's head. The crippled wizard's heartbeat was strengthening, and his breathing was more regular. Color was returning to his face.

Coughing, Jessamay tried to wave away the falling dust. "Did it . . . work?" she asked hoarsely.

"Perhaps," Wigg answered. "It might be too soon to tell."

Calling the craft, Wigg and Jessamay extinguished the fires and caused the smoke to vanish. Faegan's quarters were a shambles. Brushing off his robe and hair, Wigg walked to the door and ventured into the demolished hallway.

Wigg's most immediate concern was finding a safe way out. His heart fell when he saw the debris-laden hallway. Each direction was sealed off by tumbled stones. A few enchanted wall torches still blazed in between the two obstructions.

Walking down the hall, he was relieved to find a light shaft coming from an opening between two massive blocks. At least there was fresh air to breathe. Satisfied, he returned to Faegan's chambers.

Jessamay gave him a worried look. "Can we get out?" she asked.

"Eventually," Wigg answered. "We could use the craft to move some of the stones. But frankly, I'm too tired. I say we wait and let the Minions dig us out! If I know Ox, they've already started!"

Wigg looked over at Faegan. "How is our patient?" he asked.

"His bodily functions continue to strengthen, but he remains unconscious," Jessamay answered.

Sighing tiredly, Wigg nodded. "Come have some wine," he suggested. "We've earned it."

As Jessamay walked over, Wigg rummaged around in Faegan's cabinets. He finally found a bottle that hadn't been smashed. Jessamay took two intact glasses down from the same shelf. Calling the craft, she freed them from their dust.

Wigg opened the bottle, then poured two glassfuls. He held his up in a toast.

"To Faegan," he said.

"To Faegan," Jessamay answered. "And here's hoping that the Redoubt hasn't been too badly damaged."

They sat in silence for a time, drinking their wine and simply feeling glad to be alive. A curious look crossed Jessamay's face. It did not escape the First Wizard. He smiled tiredly.

"I'd know that look anywhere," Wigg said. "It hasn't changed in three centuries. Go ahead—ask me."

Like she didn't know where to start, Jessamay took a deep breath. "Would you have killed him?" she asked simply.

Taking another sip of wine, Wigg looked over to Faegan, then back at her again. "I don't know," he answered earnestly. "Nor do I know whether he would have killed me, had our situations been reversed. I suppose we never will. Just the same I—"

"What in the name of the Afterlife have you done to my quarters!" a deep voice suddenly bellowed from across the room.

Wigg and Jessamay looked up to see Faegan. Wide-eyed and alert, he was sitting up in bed. Mortar dust rained from his beard and hair. They hurried over to him.

"I demand an explanation!" Faegan thundered. "What's going on here?"

Wigg gave Jessamay a wry look. "I believe it's safe to say that he's back," he said.

"How do you feel?" Jessamay asked Faegan.

Gathering himself up, Faegan looked like he couldn't possibly imagine why they would be asking such a foolish question. He quickly took stock of himself.

"I feel fine!" he said. "As a matter of fact, I've never felt better! I could eat nails!"

"That's the potion talking," Jessamay said with a smile.

"What potion?" Faegan demanded. "What in blazes are you saying?"

"What's the last thing you remember?" Wigg asked.

Faegan searched his mind. "Xanthus," he breathed. "The Great Hall . . . The Darkling killed a flier. . . ." A worried look suddenly commanded his face. "Tristan?" he asked.

Wigg shook his head. "He's with Xanthus. We don't know where they've gone. But I'm willing to hazard a guess."

"So am I!" Faegan said. "We have to stop them! Wigg, no matter what happens to us, we simply must—"

Faegan suddenly froze in midsentence. His abrupt silence worried Wigg. Concerned that his friend might be relapsing, he edged closer. There was a strange, searching look in Faegan's eyes. Reaching out, he grasped Wigg's arm.

"What is it?" the First Wizard asked.

"Such a wonder . . . ," Faegan breathed. A smile overcame his face. "It's absolutely miraculous! The calculations are exquisite. . . ."

"Tell us," Wigg said.

His eyes full of wonder, Faegan looked into Wigg's eyes. "It seems I have somehow acquired a new gift," he whispered. He gripped Wigg's arm tighter. "This will change so much! But how . . . why . . ."

Wigg shot a knowing glance at Jessamay, then looked back at Faegan. "It seems we have much to tell one another," Wigg said. "Why don't you go first?"

Faegan nodded. As he started explaining, the distant sounds of Minion hammers drifted to their ears.

CHAPTER XIII

"YOU SIMPLY *MUST* TAKE US TO THE WIZARDS!" MALLORY PROtested. "We have come so far! If you tell them who we are, they'll let us in, I just know it! We're the girls from Fledgling House!"

Standing before the imposing drawbridge gates, Mallory looked longingly through the wrought-iron bars and toward the palace's inner ward. It was a strange feeling, she decided.

For the last three days she and her friends had been trying to free themselves from locked doors and stone walls. Now they desperately wanted those things to become part of their new life. With Mary and the other girls standing around her, she returned her gaze to the Minion guard standing on the gates' opposite sides. His grim expression fostered no optimism among them.

An unusually cold night beset them. To Mallory's relief, their carriage ride had been uneventful. But that didn't mean that Lothar's guards weren't chasing after them. If they trailed them to the palace, they could surely weave a convincing story about how Mary had abducted the girls for her own purposes. Worse, the winged guards might decide to return them to debtors' prison. A story told by a brothel madam and eight wayward girls would never stand up against whatever lies Lothar's prison guards might concoct.

As the girls shivered in the cold, Mallory again looked cravingly beyond the wrought-iron gates. Standing thirty feet high, the twin gates were adorned with huge golden lions, superimposed with equally golden broadswords. The palace lying beyond looked warm and inviting. Bright torchlight highlighted the walls, turrets, and manicured foliage.

Warriors of each sex roamed the shadowy grounds and the barbicans. The warriors seemed to be in some type of panic. Some were running about and shouting out orders, while others carrying various hand tools were being quickly ushered inside the palace. The frantic scene would prove unnerving to anyone—to say nothing of eight young girls who had never visited this place, nor seen creatures like these.

Suddenly Mallory slipped a little. Reaching out, Ariana helped her stand upright again. What strength Mallory once possessed had been largely depleted by the prison escape. She was so hungry and tired she could barely remain conscious. If only she could display some use of the craft, then the winged creatures might believe her. But calling the craft had become impossible for them all.

From the gates' other side, the Minion guard, Jannicus, glowered disparagingly at the ragtag group.

"I have my orders!" he said. "No one is to be allowed entrance. There has been a disturbance in the palace. I suggest that you return in a few days. By then it might be possible to grant your request."

Defiant, Mallory glared at the gigantic creature. Aside from the beasts that had carried the girls and Martha away from Fledgling House, she had never seen anything remotely like him. But if they served and protected the castle, they had to be the wizards' friends.

Suddenly Mallory had taken all she could bear. They had come too far and suffered too much to be stopped now, a mere hundred or so paces from their goal. Grabbing the gate with both hands, she started to shout.

"Let us in!" she screamed with what meager strength remained. "Let us in! Let us in! Let us in!" Soon the other seven desperate girls took up the chant.

"Let us in! Let us in! Let us in!" they chimed, all of them jumping up and down at once.

It quickly became apparent that the girls weren't about to stop shouting anytime soon. Scowling, Jannicus backed away warily and unsheathed his dreggan. *Human children can be so unpre-*

dictable, he thought. *Minion young know better than to behave so rudely.*

He didn't want to harm them, but he had his orders. Even his shiny sword did nothing to discourage them. Finally realizing how ridiculous he looked, standing there with his sword drawn against eight young girls, he angrily sheathed his weapon. As he wondered what to do, Jannicus cast a helpless look toward the Minion guard stationed nearby. His equally perplexed companion only shrugged his shoulders.

"Let us in! Let us in! Let us in!" the girls screamed.

Just then he sensed someone running up behind him. Turning, he found himself standing face-to-face with Ox.

"What go on here?" Ox shouted angrily, trying to make his voice heard above the din. By this time the insistent girls had climbed onto the gates and begun collectively rattling them with everything they had as they kept up their relentless chant. They soon caught the attention of more warriors behind the walls. The embarrassing ruckus was gaining momentum.

Blushing noticeably, Jannicus clicked his heels. "I, uh . . . well, you see, sir . . ."

Growling, Ox shoved Jannicus out of the way and unsheathed his dreggan. Being careful not to harm the girls, he banged the dreggan's blade loudly against the iron gate.

"Quiet!" he screamed.

The girls finally stilled. Shaking his head, Ox walked closer.

"Why you want enter palace grounds?" he asked angrily. "This not be good time!"

"We are the trainees from Fledgling House!" Mallory said weakly. "We *must* see the wizards!"

A strange look came over Ox's face. "You be from Fledgling House?" he asked incredulously. Ox's expression turned skeptical, and he rubbed his chin. He inched closer.

"What be your name?" he asked.

"Mallory," she answered hopefully. "What's yours?"

Mallory's forthrightness surprised him. He scowled again.

"I be Ox," he answered simply. "If you be from Fledgling House, then who there be your master?" he asked.

Mallory beamed. "His name was Duncan!" she said.

Ox pursed his lips. "He be alive or dead?" he asked, testing Mallory further.

A sad look crowded its way onto her face. "He's dead," she answered softly. "We all loved him."

Starting to believe, Ox narrowed his eyes. "And matron?" he asked. "What be her name?"

"Martha!" several girls cried out in unison.

Ox's jaw fell, and he turned quickly to glare at Jannicus. "Let girls in!" he bellowed.

"But sir . . . !" Jannicus protested. "We have strict orders not to allow—"

"Unless you want go on permanent report, you let girls in!" Ox protested. "I take all responsibility!"

After clicking his heels, Jannicus unlocked the heavy gates, then swung them wide. The eager girls didn't need to be asked twice. They poured through quickly with Mary following along behind.

When Ox saw Mary, he scowled. Placing one hand on her shoulder, he stopped her.

"Who you be?" he asked.

Mallory reached to touch Ox's arm. Again surprised by her boldness, Ox turned to look at her.

"That's Mary," Mallory said. "It's all right—she's a friend."

Finally deciding, Ox grunted. "Very well," he said. "She come, too." His stern demeanor resurfaced. Scanning their faces, he glowered into every pair of eyes.

"Girls be *quiet*!" he warned. "You scream no more!"

"We'll be quiet, I promise," Mallory answered. *We're finally here,* she thought. Hardly able to contain her happiness, she smiled at Ariana.

Ariana beamed back. "You did it, Mallory!" she whispered. "We made it, after all!"

Ox grunted again, sternly reinforcing his demand for quiet. Knowing better than to argue, Mallory and Ariana eagerly nodded. As the gate doors squeaked closed behind them, the huge warrior started leading the wide-eyed group toward the palace lights.

MARY AND THE GIRLS HAD BEEN ORDERED TO SIT IN A ROW OF NINE elaborate chairs set alongside a hallway wall. Armed with curved swords and shiny golden pikes, three winged warriors stood guard over them, watching their every move. Closing her eyes, Mallory laid her head back against the chair's plush upholstery.

She luxuriated in the warmth. She could scarcely remember the last time she had been comfortable. It must have been a different place, a different life. She looked down at her tattered school dress. Once it had been new, and had stood for something. She had been proud to wear it. But sitting here in the imposing majesty of this place, the dress's poor condition embarrassed her.

Gazing down the row, she saw that the other girls looked as bad as she. She spat onto her palms and rubbed some of the dirt from her face. Then she used her fingers to comb the knots from her hair. There could be no telling who might come to them, and she wanted to look as presentable as she could.

Mallory took another look around. The palace was very busy, an unnatural sense of urgency prevailed. Cooks, liveried servants, and musicians scurried up and down the halls, each carrying the tools of his or her trade. More curiously concerned warriors hurried here and there.

Formally dressed men and women wandered about aimlessly, like some recent tragedy had befallen them. Some were strangely tearful and carrying what looked like elaborate ball masks. Aside from its grandeur, the scene wasn't at all what the Fledgling had expected.

Mallory saw two figures approaching. At first she took them for wayward children, searching for their parents. But as the pair neared, Mallory's eyes widened and her jaw fell. She elbowed Ariana and tilted her head in the strangers' direction. Ariana became equally astonished.

The little man was about three feet tall. The woman by his side was a bit shorter. He wore a pair of blue bibbed overalls atop a red work shirt. His hair was red, and an equally scarlet beard adorned his wizened face. A black watch cap sat jauntily on his head. His upturned shoes had seen considerable use. A corncob pipe jutted from between his teeth; one of his hands possessively grasped an ale jug. As smoke curled lazily from the rough-hewn pipe bowl, his penetrating eyes carefully regarded Mary and the eight young girls.

If these two little people were palace servants, the woman by his side seemed more appropriately dressed. Her intelligent face was as wrinkled and worn as the man's bibs. Her wiry gray hair was collected in a severe bun in the back. The sharp, calculating eyes were bright blue. Over her simple gray dress she wore a white apron.

Her shoes were sturdy, no-nonsense things, their laces tied in double knots so that she needn't be bothered with retying them during the course of her busy day. Thick calluses marked her palms. Everything about her proclaimed the simple values of practicality and common sense. Whoever she might be, she was a hard worker.

Oddly enough, the woman was pushing an elaborate stroller. But Mallory knew that she was far too old to be the child's mother. Then she saw that a golden lion and broadsword adorned the stroller, which prompted her to wonder even more. The gurgling child inside was female and seemed to be nearing two Seasons of New Life. Mallory could easily see how protective the little old lady was of her young charge.

Mallory shook her head. The man, woman, and child formed an unexpected and incongruous trio. This was certainly proving to be an interesting night.

Mallory was about to speak when Ox approached. He pointed a muscular arm at the girls.

"These be the ones," he said.

The little old lady barely reached the warrior's knees. "And Princess Shailiha?" she asked worriedly. Her voice sounded nearly as stern as the warrior's did.

"Princess, Sister Adrian, and Tyranny all notified," Ox answered. "They were supervising digging, but be coming now."

Mallory watched the little man take a practiced, one-handed gulp from his jug. He then smoothly transferred his pipe from one corner of his mouth to the other without touching it. Both actions came as naturally to him as drawing his next breath.

"What about the wizards and the sorceress?" he asked.

"Ox not sure," Ox answered worriedly. "Maybe Shailiha know."

"As a matter of fact, I do," they all heard a voice say.

Mallory looked up to see a woman exiting another hallway. Long blond hair graced her shoulders. Her blue gown was strangely covered with some form of gray dust. Her eyes were hazel and resolute, her jaw firm. A gold medallion carrying the imprint of the lion and the broadsword hung around her neck on a golden chain. Having lived at Fledgling House since the age of five, the girls had seen few grown women. They stared at her in awe.

A huge violet-and-yellow butterfly sat perched atop one of the woman's shoulders. Mallory had never seen anything like it. Gently folding and unfolding its diaphanous wings, it seemed to be quite at home with its mistress.

Two more women arrived. One was wearing a dusty red gown, and her hair was short and dark. Where the first woman seemed regal, the second appeared more dangerous, predatory. Then Mallory regarded the third woman. As she immediately recognized the stranger's clothing, her heart skipped a beat.

The third woman was wearing a dark red robe. The robe was collected in the middle by a black knotted cord. There could be no mistaking it, for Mallory had been aspiring to that same costume for the last thirteen years. The third woman was a graduate of Fledgling House.

The woman in the blue gown turned to look at the butterfly perched atop her shoulder. "Hover, Caprice," she said simply.

The miraculous butterfly immediately soared toward the ceiling to start making lazy circles in the air. Something told Mallory that wherever the woman in the blue dress ventured, so did her obedient creature.

The butterfly mistress regarded the girls narrowly. "Which of you is Mallory?" she asked.

Mallory sprang to her feet. "I am Mallory of the House of Esterbrook," she said. "And if it might please the court, whom am I addressing?"

The beautiful woman clasped her hands before her. "I am Princess Shailiha," she answered simply.

A collective gasp came from the girls, and the blood rushed from Mallory's face. She had never dreamed that she might one day stand toe-to-toe with someone from the royal house. Immediately remembering her etiquette, she curtsied, then bent to kiss the back of Shailiha's gloved hand.

"An honor, Your Highness," she said as she stood back up. "Please forgive our appearances. We have come far and suffered much."

Hoping that she wasn't overstepping her bounds, Mallory added, "In case you are unaware, I regret to report that Master Duncan is dead. Martha was spirited away by strange flying creatures. We do not know what became of her." Turning, she looked down the row of disheveled girls. "We eight are all who remain of Fledgling House," she added sadly.

Shailiha gazed sternly into Mallory's eyes. "How old are you?" she asked.

"At nineteen Seasons of New Life, I am the oldest," Mallory answered.

"Are you really who you claim to be?" Shailiha pressed. "I have no time for frivolous escapades. Lying will do you no good—we have ways of determining whether you tell the truth."

"We are indeed," Mallory answered respectfully but firmly. "A simple check of our blood signatures against the parchments in the Hall of Blood Records will prove it." A concerned look suddenly came over her.

"We are desperately worried about our fathers," she added. "Long before Fledgling House was attacked, they stopped visiting us. No reason was given. Not one of us has seen her father for nearly two years. Can you tell us if they are all right?"

Mallory's words pulled hard on Shailiha's heartstrings. If these forlorn girls were who they claimed to be, how could she tell them that their fathers had become traitors? Or that she, Tristan, and the mystics had been actively hunting them down and killing them, if need be? She looked thoughtfully into Mallory's worried face.

"If you are who you claim, your answers will come soon enough," she said.

Mallory was disappointed, but she understood. "Very well," she answered.

Shailiha continued to regard the plucky girls. If they were indeed refugees from Fledgling House, Martha had trained them well in the social graces. But Shailiha knew that it wouldn't do to reveal too much before she knew more. Until Wigg, Faegan, and Jessamay were freed from the Redoubt, she would have to wait.

Then an idea came to her. There was another way to determine their identities. It would not be as conclusive as blood records, but in the wizards' absence it would take them one step closer to the truth.

Shailiha looked at Mallory. "Please be seated," she said.

As Mallory reclaimed her chair, Shailiha walked to stand before Mary. "Who might you be?" she asked.

Following Mallory's example, the brothel madam stood and bowed. "I am Mary of the House of Broderick," she answered respectfully. "I am but a loyal servant who saw fit to help these girls in their time of need. I'm afraid my story is a long one."

Shailiha nodded. "Not so long as theirs, I'd wager," she answered. "Until all of this is sorted out, you will also remain our guest."

Leaving the group seated along the wall, Shailiha ushered the others out of earshot. She looked at Sister Adrian.

"Do you recognize these girls?" she asked quietly.

Adrian shook her head. "No," she answered. "Then again, there's no reason why I should. I have been gone from Fledgling House for more than twelve years. If Mallory is indeed nineteen, we would have missed one another."

"Pardon me, Princess," Shawna said, "but what of Wigg, Faegan, and Jessamay? Will they be all right?"

Shailiha nodded. "They are unharmed. The Minions are digging them free as we speak. Overall, we were lucky. It seems that Faegan's unconscious attempts to destroy the Redoubt were limited to his quarters and their immediate surroundings. There is much work ahead of us to restore the damage, but the Redoubt's many treasures are safe."

"There seems little more that can be done tonight," Tyranny said.

Shailiha looked over at the disheveled girls. "That's not altogether true," she said. She looked at Adrian.

"For the time being, I want you to oversee the girls' welfare," she ordered. "If they really are from Fledgling House, you will have the most in common with them. Until we are sure, under no circumstances are they to interact with the boys in the Redoubt Nursery, nor are you to answer any questions they might have regarding their fathers. See to it that they are bathed, clothed, and fed. Then assign them quarters. Let them rest. Tomorrow you may show them the palace. But under no circumstances are they to enter the Redoubt. I want them under the constant supervision of both you and those three warrior guards. The same goes for that woman calling herself Mary. We know even less about her."

Adrian nodded. "In the meantime, shall I question the girls about Fledgling House?" she asked. "It might go a long way toward proving or disproving their stories."

Shailiha shook her head. "I have a better way." She looked at Ox.

"I want you to fetch Martha," she said. "Wake her, if you

must, but bring her here as soon as you can. Tell her it's urgent. After Celeste's death she took up residence in the city. Sister Adrian will give you her address. She returns to the palace from time to time, to visit the boys in the Redoubt Nursery. If these girls are who they claim to be, Martha will know. In the meantime I want everyone to go back about his duties. I believe this night is far from over."

Shailiha looked wearily down at her daughter Morganna. The child had fallen asleep in the stroller. The princess looked back at Shawna.

"Care for Morganna while I cannot," she said. "In the space of a single night, my responsibilities have become legion."

Tears started welling up in Shawna's eyes. She quickly brushed them away.

"On my life," she answered softly. As she looked at Shannon the Small, her no-nonsense demeanor returned.

"Come on, old man!" she growled. "You heard the princess! There's plenty more work to do! And if you don't keep that pipe smoke away from the child, I'll kick your arse from here to Shadowood!"

As the group separated, Tyranny stayed with the princess. Producing a cigarillo, the privateer struck a match and lit it. After luxuriously inhaling the smoke, she glanced disparagingly at her ball gown.

"Do I have your permission to get out of this ridiculous getup, Your Highness?" she asked with a grin. "My seagoing attire suits me far better."

Shailiha nodded but did not smile.

Tyranny pursed her lips. "It's Tristan, isn't it?" she asked. "I know. I'm worried about him, too."

Shailiha grasped the gold medallion hanging around her neck, then looked into Tyranny's eyes. "Yes," she answered softly. "I fear we may never see him again."

Saying nothing more, Shailiha looked to Caprice and gave her a silent command. As the princess and the privateer left the hallway, the yellow-and-violet flier followed dutifully overhead.

Chapter XIV

"Awaken, *Jin'Sai,*" said a hollow voice. "It is time to greet the dawn."

Tristan stirred, then sat up. At first he didn't recognize his surroundings. Then he saw the familiar campfire burning in the cold morning air, and he knew. He instinctively checked his weapons to find that they remained in place over his right shoulder.

Looking farther, he saw the sun breaking over the eastern horizon. The Sippora still refused to flow, the birds did not sing, and the wind remained still. Shadow and another mount stood a short distance away, still tied to the night line.

His back to the prince, Xanthus sat in the early-morning light. His weapons lay beside him. As Xanthus turned, Tristan braced himself to confront the Darkling's hideous face.

Although he wore Xanthus' clothes, the being before Tristan was human. The unremarkable face regarded him calmly. Waving one hand, the stranger called the craft, and breakfast materialized. It landed softly atop a blanket that had been stretched out beside the fire.

Tristan looked down to see plates of quail's eggs, ham, and sliced brown bread. A churn of yellow butter sat nearby, as did a pot of hot tea and two teacups. Tristan looked back into the unfamiliar face.

"Xanthus?" he asked softly. The man nodded.

"In human form," Tristan mused.

"Yes."

Xanthus lowered the hood of his robe to fully show his face. He then took an egg and struck it against a plate. After peeling it, he started eating. Tristan watched the silver pot rise into the air to pour two cups of steaming tea. As Xanthus sipped his tea, Tristan regarded him narrowly.

Save for his hands and face, the Darkling looked as he did before. He wore the same black robe, duster, trousers, and boots. The Paragon still hung around his neck. Tristan was relieved to see that the stone's color remained vibrant, showing it had accepted Xanthus' human side as its new host.

The prince looked closer at the Darkling's face. Had Tristan met this fellow anywhere else, he would have scarcely noticed him. The visage implied strength, but was also sensual-looking. Brown, almost black eyes rested above a straight nose. The mouth was wide and the lips full. The chin showed a deep cleft, and his rather wavy hair was brown. Had he not been some abomination of the craft, he might be anyone.

Tristan looked skeptically at the food, then back at Xanthus. The Darkling smiled.

"We might be together for some time, *Jin'Sai,*" he said. "You must learn to trust me."

Deciding he had no choice, Tristan took a sip of the excellent tea, then filled a plate with food. After dipping a bread slice into the butter, he ate hungrily. He soon felt the forgotten ball mask rubbing against his skin. Reaching beneath his vest, he removed it. Xanthus eyed it knowingly.

"Before this day passes, you will come to hate me even more," he said. "But less, I suspect, than you will hate me tomorrow."

Putting down his plate, Tristan regarded the mask, then turned his eyes back toward the Darkling. He had never visited Everhaven, but he already mourned its citizens' fates.

"Must it be this way?" he asked angrily. "Is there nothing I can do—short of going through the azure pass—that will dissuade you from this madness?"

"No," Xanthus answered. "I have given you all the needed explanations. It is time to decide."

Tristan looked at the mask. "I know why you gave this to me," he said. "You wish me to remain anonymous as I watch the atrocities. What I do not know is why."

"The answer is simple," Xanthus said. "If and when you return from the other side, the Heretics want no animosity existing between the populace and their prince. Only recently have your fellow Eutracians come to again accept you as their legitimate regent. Should they recognize you while I go about my work, your family house would carry the stain for all time. Such an unfortunate occurrence would prove problematic."

"Why do the Heretics care about such things?"

"All in good time, *Jin'Sai,*" Xanthus answered.

"You just said, 'if and when *you* return from the other side,' " Tristan mused. "Assuming that I follow you into the pass, won't you be returning with me?"

"No," Xanthus answered. "Once I take you to the other side, my work is done."

"What will happen to you?" Tristan asked.

"My existence's sole purpose is to bring you to the Heretics," Xanthus said. "After that, I do not know what will happen to me. I will be rewarded in some way, I suppose."

Tristan looked thoughtfully into Xanthus' human face. He couldn't help but notice that in this form, the Darkling seemed less evil, less remote. If there was any chance that Xanthus might be dissuaded from his mission, it would be now.

But which side controls the other?

Waving an arm, Xanthus caused the breakfast things to vanish. Then the fire went out. The tack lying nearby rose skyward and secured itself onto the horses. Xanthus' axe and shield rose to meet his saddle.

"It is time to go," Xanthus said. "What is it to be, *Jin'Sai*? Shall I take us to the azure pass in a single heartbeat? Or do we go to Everhaven?"

Heartsick with worry, Tristan looked around. As far as he could see, the Farplains fields lay barren. He couldn't kill Xanthus, nor could he escape him. His only two choices were to give himself over to the Heretics here and now, or to helplessly stand by while the Darkling tormented the Everhavians. He looked beseechingly into the strangely human face.

"Don't do this!" he said softly. "I beg you!"

"The time for begging is over," Xanthus answered. "Choose."

His heart breaking, Tristan closed his eyes. "No," he answered. "Not now, not ever."

Xanthus sighed. "Very well," he said. "But one day you *will* follow me through the pass. Your love for humanity will demand it."

Reaching back, Xanthus pulled his robe hood up over his head. Tristan watched the craft's aura form around the Darkling. Soon Xanthus' face and hands melted away, to be replaced by his hideous spirit form. The awful eyes in the hood's recesses stared menacingly at the prince. The combination of the glowing orbs and what was about to happen in Everhaven made Tristan's skin crawl. The evil had returned.

"Mount your horse," the Darkling said. "Take care not to lose your mask."

The two riders climbed aboard their mounts. As the reins untied themselves from the tether line, the line disappeared. Saying nothing more, Xanthus started riding north. His heart heavy, the prince had no choice but to follow.

As the riders left the forlorn campsite, the Sippora started running again, the birds sang, and the wind was reborn.

AS THE VICTIM SCREAMED, TRISTAN TRIED TO TURN HIS FACE AWAY, but could not. Aside from blinking, he could not otherwise close his eyes. From behind the black mask, tears ran freely down his cheeks. *What madness . . . and I am partly to blame!*

From the start of the horrific spectacle, Xanthus had used the craft to take away Tristan's ability to speak, and to move his body. The prince could move his head, but only to suggest yes or no. Before incapacitating him, Xanthus had ordered Tristan to sit in a simple wooden chair, from which he could clearly view the Darkling's grotesque handiwork.

The grisly scene had been going on for hours, and the eager Darkling showed no signs of stopping. The naked man being tortured to death was today's fourth such victim. No one needed to tell Tristan that the poor fellow would soon join the first three already in the Afterlife. But that mattered little to Xanthus. The room was filled with people from whom to choose.

On reaching Everhaven, Xanthus had acted quickly. Calling the craft, he invoked a spell summoning every man, woman, and child to the town square. Tristan had been amazed by the enchantment's powerful grasp.

Spellbound, the unseeing citizens had all trudged to the same spot. Xanthus had then ordered as many as possible to enter the community hall. Those remaining outside simply stood waiting in the sun with vacuous looks on their faces. Tristan and Xanthus entered last.

The hall was a simple structure and was built of fieldstone, mortar, and wood. It was there that the town fathers called the people together to decide important issues, and to share the kingdom's news. Large candelabras hung from the rough-hewn rafters. Wooden pews sat in neat rows, and their lengths were filled with entranced spectators. Stained-glass windows lined the walls, and a dais sat at the room's far end. Standing on the dais and alongside Tristan's chair, Xanthus went about his grisly work.

Waving a skeletal hand, Xanthus inflicted another round of torture. A terrible banging sound came, followed by a scream that filled the air, then faded into nothingness. Sobbing followed. Tristan watched as yet more blood dripped lazily to the floor. Seemingly unfazed, the spellbound citizens sat quietly in their pews as they watched.

Conjured by Xanthus, a massive wooden altar lay on the dais. It was rectangular in shape and measured about one meter high. The dried blood of past victims lay splattered across its sides and top. Sturdy ropes bound the victim's head, torso, and legs to the altar top.

Wooden planks lay along the man's sides, stretching from his hips to his feet. Ropes bound the boards tight against the man's legs, pushing them together. A wooden wedge had been driven between the victim's knees. A bloody wooden mallet, its business end wound with harsh rope, hovered in the air. Nearby lay a wide-mouthed bucket filled with common salt.

Tristan could only watch as Xanthus caused the bloody mallet head to again grind itself into the salt, then hauntingly rise to a place high above the victim. Saying nothing, Xanthus paused in his work to look at the prince. His mind nearly mad with guilt, Tristan thought for a moment, then sadly shook his head.

With another wave, Xanthus caused the mallet to come down with amazing force.

The mallet drove the wedge deeper into the shrinking space between the man's knees, squeezing his limbs against the planks and crushing the flesh and bone. The mallet's salt sank into the fresh wounds.

The man screamed insanely. His eyes bulged from their sockets, and his neck cords strained so tightly that they looked like they might snap apart. After the screaming stopped, the sobbing began again.

Xanthus caused the bloody mallet to again dip into the salt bucket, then resume its place high above the altar. He looked at Tristan. So that the crowd could not hear what he had to say, he silently revealed his thoughts to Tristan's mind.

"*What is it to be,* Jin'Sai?" Tristan heard the Darkling's voice say. *"How many more must die because of your childish stubbornness? Follow me into the azure pass, and this will stop. Follow me, and the many answers you seek will be yours."*

Tristan again looked at the suffering man atop the altar. *Who is he?* he wondered. *And who am I, to have the power of life and death over others?*

"*You are the* Jin'Sai," Xanthus answered. *"Like every* Jin'Sai *before you, you have been born into the dark worlds of magic, manifest destiny, and pain. You are still unable to control your magic or your destiny. But you can control this man's pain. Say yes,* Jin'Sai, *and save him."*

Tristan sobbed openly. He was close to believing that the fault was his, and that had he found a way to murder this abomination of the craft, this would not be happening.

"Yes," Xanthus whispered silently. *"This is indeed your fault. But there is time to rectify your sins. Come with me and I will heal this man, making him as he was before. Resist me, and he will die a horrible death."*

Tristan gazed at the desperate victim's face. The man would never know who Tristan was, or that it had been he who had signed his death warrant. Finally deciding, Tristan looked directly into Xanthus' glowing eyes and shook his head.

Tristan watched in horror as the mallet again came down to squarely strike the wedge. More bone cracked, more blood spurted forth, and more screaming filled the air. This time the damage was so severe that yellow bone marrow oozed from between the boards and the altar top and went slipping down the altar's sides. The last blow rendered the man's knee joints little more than useless sacks of crushed meat, marrow, and bone. This time the trauma proved too much. As his head slumped to one side the man gasped his last and died.

Xanthus looked at the prince. "Four is enough for one day," he said. "I will grant you a different entertainment tomorrow. Perhaps it will make you more agreeable."

Ignoring the corpse, Xanthus came to stand in the dais's center. Soon the craft's azure glow surrounded him. Tristan watched the Darkling reach into one duster pocket and produce something. After removing his duster and his robe, Xanthus dropped them to the floor. In his human form, the Darkling slowly turned to face Tristan.

For the briefest moment, Xanthus seemed to regard the prince with sadness. Then his expression hardened. He turned away.

Naked from the waist up, the Darkling's human muscles glistened in the candlelight. In one hand he held a black knotted cord. After taking several steps across the dais, he faced northwest and sat on his knees. For several long moments the Darkling bowed his head.

His self-inflicted penitence started slowly. Lashing his naked back, Xanthus opened up wound after gaping wound. As the blows quickened, his blood started flowing down his back and onto the floor, mingling with that of his victims.

As the lashings continued, Tristan suddenly found that he could close his eyes. That must have been Xanthus' doing, but he was at a complete loss about why.

If I can shut this out, I will, he thought, as more tears streaked down beneath his hated mask. *Since the Coven's return, I have witnessed the horrors of a thousand lifetimes. I needn't watch this.*

As the knotted line continued to split Xanthus' skin, the enchanted townspeople watched blankly. Tristan of the House of Galland shut his bleary eyes.

CHAPTER XV

AS HE WINGED THROUGH THE AIR, TRAAX SEARCHED THE COUNTRYside for landmarks. He had pushed his airborne phalanx hard and without pause in his attempt to reach the pass as fast as possible. He knew that Shailiha was right. The *Jin'Sai*'s life could hang in the balance.

It was midday in Eutracia, and the sky was clear. The sun hung directly overhead, warming the warriors' wings. If their endurance held, they would reach the pass within the hour. Traax smiled. It would be good to see Gaius again.

Traax was proud of the warriors flying with him. After receiving his orders from Shailiha, he had asked for volunteers. There had no been no shortage from whom to pick. The fifty accompanying him were the best of the best.

He hoped that his chosen warriors could fly to the pass nonstop, yet arrive fresh enough to fight. So far, they had proven him right. Time was of the essence. Traveling light, they bore no supply litters. When they reached the pass they would live in true warrior style, taking what they needed from the land.

Realizing that he was thirsty again, Traax reached back to grasp his canteen. Minion warriors could go for days without food, but water was a constant need. Knowing that they were nearing their destination, he gulped down all that remained.

Seeing their commander drink, the fifty obedient warriors followed suit. A revered Minion tenet stated that a commander must be willing to personally suffer whatever he demanded from his charges. Conversely, while on a mission no subordinate could take rest or sustenance until his leader did so first. There were many warrior ranks, but they all shared this common bond. It was more than good discipline. It was a matter of honor.

Traax could easily have navigated his way to the pass by following the gouge left by the once-rampaging Orb of the Vigors. But taking that meandering path would have wasted valuable time. He had therefore chosen to fly by dead reckoning. Prominent landmarks, the position of the sun, and wind variables had determined the way.

Traax was one of the best navigators in the entire Minion force. More important, he had faith in his abilities. Unless he missed his guess, they would soon fly directly over Fledgling House. Covering the distance from there to the pass would be brief. Confident that he was on the right course, he allowed his mind to drift back to the pleasant time just before he had assembled his troops.

Hearing of his imminent departure, Duvessa had rushed to join him in his quarters. Dried blood from the masquerade ball victims still showed on her hands, forearms, and armor. A white feather lay stitched across a red one on her chest armor, indicating her premier rank as a warrior-healer. Reaching out, Traax pulled her to him.

"Was it bad?" he asked.

Duvessa nodded. She was a handsome Minion female, and

she considered Traax her equal. Besides leading all the Minion healers, she also commanded the female warriors. She bore the mantles well.

Duvessa briefly closed her eyes. "We and the acolytes did all we could for them," she answered, "but Faegan's bolts were powerful. Who could have guessed that it would pass through the Darkling like that? Five died straightaway. Three were human and two were Minion. Twelve more were seriously wounded. The survivors' destinies lie with the fates. How is Faegan?"

Traax's expression darkened. "He will live," he answered. "But when he realizes how many he accidentally killed and wounded, I fear he might never be the same."

Holding up her hands, Duvessa regarded the dried blood. "Such strange beings, these humans," she said. "Some are gifted with the craft and some are not. They are not as physically powerful as we. But their loyalty and honor can be equally strong. Sometimes I believe we share more with them than we know. As our blood mingles with theirs, I cannot tell them apart."

Traax looked thoughtfully into her eyes. He had known many Minion females. But not one had possessed the strength, the heart, or the ability to love that this one did. Since her first husband's death and her subsequent mourning period, she and Traax had been together. During that time she had never asked for more than he had been able to give.

Duvessa placed her palms on Traax's chest. Concern showed on her face.

"Come home safe," she said. "I know you have defeated many enemies. But this Darkling possesses gifts that baffle even the wizards. I am forced to agree with Shailiha. The pass is the likely place where he entered Eutracia. If that is true, it will also be his way back. You might come face-to-face with him again."

"Then let it be so," Traax answered quietly.

The realization that he must leave her crowded in on him again. How would it affect him, he wondered, should he lose this woman? She had become his reason for being, second only to his allegiance to his *Jin'Sai*. Searching her eyes, he decided.

"Stand back, my love," he said gently.

A confused look crossed Duvessa's face. She did as he asked.

Stretching his back, Traax snapped open his dark wings, then gently closed them around her. Among their kind, such a revealing gesture occurred rarely. Her heart in her throat, she returned his gaze.

Opening his wings again, Traax repeated the gesture. *Can this be happening?* Duvessa asked herself. *I hadn't dared to* hope. . . .

Traax parted his wings once more. As Duvessa felt them closing about her for the third time, a tear left one eye.

There could be no mistaking his meaning. According to Minion custom, the first time his wings surrounded her, he was saying how much he honored her. The second time confirmed his love for her. The third time told her that he wanted them to marry.

"Are you sure?" she asked.

"Yes—with all my heart."

"Then my answer is yes," she said softly. She had never meant anything more deeply.

Their personal bond was sealed. But according to Minion custom, two more things needed be done to announce their betrothal.

With his wings still surrounding her, Traax extended a hand to unclasp a gold pin attached to the chest area of his leather body armor. Soon after the Minions were released from the Coven's domination over them and they came under Tristan's aegis, the *Jin'Sai* had allowed them to marry according to their wishes and without permission from a higher authority. Traax had seized on the idea of showing intended betrothal among the Minions by ordering the warrior goldsmiths among them to fashion two distinct types of pins. Each pin was round in shape and it held a jewel in its center. The pin worn by unattached males held a bright, round turquoise, while the pin for the single females secured a round, red ruby in its center.

After unclasping his turquoise pin, Traax attached it to Duvessa's armor. Then Duvessa returned the gesture, attaching her ruby pin to Traax's armor. From this moment until their wedding day, every Minion would know that she was his, and he hers.

How he had wished he could have lain with her then, but he knew he had to leave. Taking a deep breath, he held her closer. He would soon become a husband. If the fates allowed, he might become a father, as well. After giving his intended a farewell kiss, he hurried to assemble his troops.

His mind returning to the present, Traax looked down at his body armor. He smiled. Duvessa's ruby pin remained stubbornly in place, despite the forces buffeting against it, trying to shake it loose. *Just as our union will be,* he thought.

Just then he saw his second-in-command fly up alongside. Traax looked over to see the warrior point toward the ground.

Nestled peacefully among the emerald fields, Fledgling House lay directly below. The Tolenka Mountains could be seen just beyond. Traax nodded his understanding and he watched the warrior slip back into formation.

They soon spied the gorge left by the orb. Traax knew they were close enough to the pass so that the still-smoldering canyon could effectively guide them. Changing course again, he gave up some altitude. Before long, they found the remains of the magnificent pine forest that had once lined the mountain base.

It was a chilling sight. For as far as the eye could see, the forest's charred remnants climbed the craggy mountainside. Wispy smoke could still be seen escaping the ruins. Angling his flight path to accommodate the sloping terrain, Traax climbed to follow the earth's ominous scar.

A few moments later, he saw the dead bodies. The ravaged Minion camp had been stationed on a grassy field, just east of where the charred forest started.

Raising one arm, Traax ordered his warriors to hover. His phalanx quickly gathered around him. After displaying a series of hand signals, he watched the warriors draw their swords. With their fifty-one blades shining in the sun, the warriors retracted their wings and started down.

Splitting into two groups, they landed and ringed the campsite. Looking around warily, they snapped their tired wings back into place. Traax led his two most senior officers into the camp.

Aside from the dead bodies, there was little to see. The warriors stationed here had lived simply, just as Traax's would do until they were relieved. Six tents stood nearby, their unsecured canvas doorways flapping about in the wind. The remains of a wild boar—its half-eaten body now crawling with hungry flies and wriggling maggots—lay skewered over a long-dead campfire. Various tools, weapons, and akulee jugs lay wherever they had been dropped. As Traax and his officers walked toward the stinking bodies, they were forced to cover their noses.

Traax squatted down and looked at a dead warrior. He did not know him. The victim was still holding his dreggan, but the blade was not bloodied. The warrior's lower abdomen and the surrounding grass were covered with blood. His internal organs lay alongside him, with some of their entrails still attached to the torso beneath his armor. Showing no distinction between animal or warrior, flying carrion feasted here as well.

Bending closer, Traax could see no puncture marks in the warrior's body armor. He scowled. Unbuckling the chest armor's brass fasteners, he lifted it from the body. The grotesque sight took him aback.

As best Traax could tell, the warrior's abdomen had literally exploded from the inside out. The image was grisly, unexpected. After dropping the armor back into place, he stood.

Traax turned to look up the mountainside. As always, the Tolenkas' mysterious peaks disappeared into misty fog. From their deep crevasses, silvery glaciers beckoned.

The pass is up there, he thought. *When we reach it, I suspect that what we find will be equally discouraging.*

"Shall we examine the other five bodies, my lord?" one of the officers asked. Torn from his thoughts, Traax turned.

"Yes," he ordered, "but I believe you will learn that they all died the same way." He pointed to the dead warrior. "Notice how his armor bears no marks. The craft was at work here."

"Xanthus?" the officer asked.

"Yes," Traax answered. "Princess Shailiha was right. The Darkling entered Eutracia through the azure pass. He butchered this force on his way to the palace. Assuming he and the *Jin'Sai* have not already come this way, they soon will. If we do not want to suffer the same fate as our dead brothers, we must be ready."

Traax looked hard at the two officers. "Come to attention!" he ordered.

Stiffening, they quickly clicked their boot heels.

"Hear me well!" Traax said. "Make camp here. We will use the abandoned tents. Find a clean water supply. I suspect that glacial runoff from the mountains will be the safest. Take these dead bodies a good distance from the camp and cover them. Build the proper funeral pyres. I will take half our force to secure the pass. When I return, we will give our dead the funeral they deserve."

The warriors again clicked their heels. "We live to serve!" they shouted in unison.

Walking back to the phalanx, Traax selected half of his warriors. Leading the twenty-five troops skyward, he turned to fly alongside the orb's charred path.

Staying on track was more difficult this time, because the dark gouge blended well with the charred earth. Even from their height, the warriors could smell the scorched trees and brush. *It smells like death,* Traax thought. As he climbed higher he strained his eyes, trying to find the azure pass.

Suddenly he saw it. Twinkling icy blue, its shimmering face stretched high into the fog. The Tolenkas' dark granite walls lay tight against its sides. Like they were begging to be released to the outside world, white light shards shot to and fro within its luminous depths. Again drawing their swords, the warriors warily landed about twenty paces downhill.

Motioning with his sword, Traax led his warriors closer. The heat was greater here, and warm cinders crunched beneath their boots. When they reached the five bodies, Traax let go an angry sigh. All the warriors lay dead.

Bending over, Traax unfastened the armor of one corpse and he looked at the warrior's wounds. They were much like those the base camp victims had suffered. Standing, Traax sadly shook his head. After looking around he gathered his warriors.

"There is not enough material here to build suitable litters," he said. "I want ten warriors to fly back to camp. Construct the litters there then return with them. After we have taken these fallen heroes back, we will cremate all our dead at once. Then we will take a well-deserved rest. Go now and hurry back."

Ten warriors quickly took to the sky. Sheathing his dreggan, Traax watched them go.

Looking around, he spied another dreggan, its blade deeply embedded into a partly burned tree trunk. Walking over, he grabbed the sword's hilt. With a mighty heave he yanked it free.

Traax held the blade to the sun. Like the other one he had examined, this blade was unstained. More than ever, he was convinced that these deaths had been Xanthus' doing.

Beckoning his warriors to follow him, he walked to the pass. As they neared they were forced to narrow their eyes against the light. Standing before its majesty was nearly blinding, yet it gave off no heat.

His curiosity piqued, Traax gently inserted the dreggan blade into the shimmering azure wall. Like the pass was made of gossamer, the sword entered it effortlessly. From the wall's opposite side, light shards danced to the metal blade like gathering Parthalonian fireflies. Retrieving the weapon, he again inspected it.

The shiny blade showed no sign of having violated the pass. He reached out to find the razor-sharp blade still cool to the touch. Perplexed, he shook his head. He looked over at his warriors.

"No one is to come closer than ten paces to this wall," he ordered. "Is that understood?"

At once the warriors clicked their heels.

"You may rest," he said.

Sheathing their swords, the grateful warriors started making themselves at home in their predecessors' makeshift camp. They knew the litters would not be long in coming. His expression darkening, Traax looked back at the wall.

You were here, you bastard, he thought. *My gut tells me so. You killed a dozen of my warriors then blithely went on to murder innocent Eutracians. Now you are on your way back and bringing the* Jin'Sai *with you. I do not know how to stop you from taking Tristan into that azure void, but I must find a way. I believe all of our lives depend on it.*

Turning back, he looked down the charred hillside and then to the ruby pin that Duvessa had secured to his armor. He couldn't help but wonder if he would ever see her again. Gritting his teeth, he closed his eyes.

This was far from over.

CHAPTER XVI

AS HE WATCHED ENVELOPERS BY THE HUNDREDS UNDULATE THEIR velvety sides, Reznik smiled. At first, traveling this way had seemed frightening.

He would have preferred sailing in comfort, aboard one of

Serena's war frigates. But the Citadel queen had ordered what remained of her fleet, manned by some of the consuls who had remained behind with her, to sail west and search for the *Jin'-Sai*'s Black Ships.

At first she considered ordering the envelopers to perform the search, for they could range faster than her frigates. But Serena decided on her ships for the job, because her envelopers could not detect endowed blood. Most of her envelopers had stayed behind, guarding her island fortress from above.

As always, Reznik had been given no choice but to agree with his queen's dictates. But as his confidence in the envelopers' abilities grew, he soon enjoyed being carried through the sky.

Looking down, he watched the Sea of Whispers pass beneath him as its restless waves crashed against the Parthalonian coast. He hungrily breathed in the bracing sea air. Looking west, he saw that night would soon fall.

His group had been traveling north for eight hours, continually hugging the shoreline to avoid Necrophagian territory. This course also lessened the chances that they might meet the *Jin'-Sai*'s fleet. Reznik's impending experiments were paramount to the Heretics' plans and had to be protected at all costs.

Reznik again regarded the hundreds of envelopers surrounding him. Despite their closeness, he could barely see them for their clever camouflage. Their backs were the color of the ever-shifting sea; their undersides perfectly mimicked the cloudy sky. Shaking his head, he marveled at them.

Many more enveloper pairs flew nearby. Between each pair stretched an azure net filled with supplies. Each net's opposite sides were held fast to the envelopers' backs by an especially clever spell. The elaborate spell calculations had been Einar's handiwork, with Reznik consulting. Sitting on a net between another enveloper pair, Einar flew along beside him.

Reznik turned to look rearward. Dozens more camouflaged envelopers followed, each pair also connected by a net. More blue-robed consuls and Valrenkians sat in the nets, as did the various craft tools and treatises needed to conduct their experiments. Between another enveloper pair lay the consummately precious Scroll of the Vagaries. Reznik had cringed when he learned how it was to be transported. But as his fears for his personal safety subsided, so too did his concern for the scroll.

Waving an arm, Einar ordered a course change. Avoiding the

port town of Everstill, the thousands of envelopers turned east. Soon they crossed the shoreline to go soaring over Parthalon proper. As green fields stretched beneath them, the envelopers' backs quickly changed to mimic the new terrain.

Soon we will reach the great lake, Reznik thought. *If things go as expected, Parthalon will be ours.* The greedy partial adept could hardly wait. Grinning, he eagerly rubbed his hands together.

An hour later, Reznik could distinguish a huge lake lying in the distance. To his relief, he had seen no Parthalonians. That was welcome, because they wanted no alarms to go out. For the time being their mission was secret, but that would soon change.

Before the group departed, Serena and Einar had told him about the lake, and why it was so important. Even so, he was surprised by its massiveness. Its cold depths were said to be bottomless. As the envelopers descended, it came into better focus.

The lake's waters were dark, and its shoreline highly irregular. A light breeze rippled its surface. Approaching from the west, Serena's forces had also purposely avoided Trinity Downes, the town situated on the lake's southern shore.

Waving a hand again, Einar ordered his envelopers to land at a spot on the western shore. No Parthalonians were about. As darkness fell in earnest, Einar, Reznik, and the handpicked consuls and Valrenkians jumped from their nets to the ground.

Einar pointed one hand toward the envelopers and relieved them of their nets and cargoes. In a flash they soared skyward. Their soft undersides quickly blended into the night, replete with perfectly simulated clouds and stars. Reznik looked back at Einar.

"It is time to bring them," the consul said.

"How can you be sure that they have all gathered here, in one place?" Reznik asked.

"Queen Serena has made it so," Einar answered. "Failee, First Mistress of the Coven of Sorceresses, was the one who first conjured these creatures. In her madness, she did so purely as an act of vengeance, in the event that her try to convert Princess Shailiha to be her fifth sorceress failed and caused her death. With her demise, these creatures would be unleashed in retribution upon the Parthalonians. The prince and Wigg defeated the Coven, killing the four sorceresses, and Failee's spell was soon activated." Pausing to gaze at the lake, Einar slipped his hands into opposite robe sleeves.

"With the beasts' arrivals, pristine lakes suddenly sprang up all over Parthalon, to provide them refuge as they went about their grisly business," he added. "The violent legacy Failee so painstakingly bequeathed to the world has been ravaging Parthalon ever since and fulfilling her warped sense of vengeance. The beasts' numbers soon became so great that even the Minions occupying the newly rebuilt Recluse have been largely ineffective at controlling them. They breed so quickly that there are more than ever before. They survive by feeding off terrified citizens."

"Why hasn't the *Jin'Sai* exterminated them?" Reznik asked. "To us, the people living here are little more than unendowed cattle. But Tristan's misguided love of the Vigors forces him to care for them, does it not? Should he summon all of his forces here, even beasts in these numbers could not prevail."

Einar smiled evilly. "That is true," he answered. "But the prince and his wizards have been exceptionally busy of late—first with Nicholas, then Wulfgar, and now the Darkling. They have had little time for such lesser matters." Smiling, Einar turned his attention to the crowd as a whole.

Happily, and in a louder tone, he announced, "As you will soon see, Failee's hateful legacy is about to become our gain. Her creations are perfect for our plans."

Scowling, Reznik bristled at not being told these things sooner. Serena had told him that, in the interests of security, Einar would inform him as events unfolded.

As the specially selected consuls and Valrenkians stood by, Einar lowered the hood of his robe. His expression was calm, bordering on smugness. Clearly, Einar was the only mystic Serena trusted with all the puzzle's pieces, and he reveled in it. But the clever Valrenkian was starting to put those same pieces together for himself.

"It must be a powerful spell that can both collect the beasts and bind them to our wishes," Reznik mused. "How did our queen come by it?"

Einar smiled in the darkness. The wind stirred, rippling the lake surface. *A small portent of things to come?* Reznik wondered.

"Can't you guess?" Einar asked back.

Suddenly Reznik understood. He smiled. "I know that Failee possessed the Vagaries scroll during her exile here in Parthalon—at least for a while," he answered. "The spells allowing the beasts' creation and control over them must have come from it."

"Precisely," Einar answered. "Now the scroll is ours. Thanks to her ability to commune with the Heretics, Serena also possesses the scroll's index, allowing her to choose the Vagaries Forestallments at will. As the Heretics revealed their plan to her, she realized that these creatures would be of great use to us. After indexing the scroll she invoked the needed formula. Her gifts have become so strong that she can activate spells over vast distances. At her command, all of Failee's beasts have converged here. This lake is the only landlocked water body large enough to hide them all. Our queen's timing is perfect. Because the *Jin'Sai* travels with the Darkling, the Conclave is confused, and fearful for his existence. As a result, they will be slow to act."

Einar smiled. "They have every right to fear for their precious *Jin'Sai,*" Einar added. "The Darkling takes him to a place from where he might never return."

"There are many things that you and the Citadel queen understand, but have yet to divulge," Reznik pressed. "Why does the Darkling lead Tristan to the azure pass?"

Einar smiled again. "All in good time," he said. "All you need know for now is that you and certain of your fellow Valrenkians are here because you possess skills and knowledge that we consuls do not—skills like those involving certain knowledge of the human form, and specialized herb and oil usage. Our early experiments together at the Citadel are proof of that. We are about to forge a new future, you and I. But first I must summon the beasts."

Einar walked to the shoreline. The other adepts followed. Reaching the shore, Einar raised his arms and closed his eyes.

The lake waters started to churn. As Failee's creations rose to the surface, the breath rushed from Reznik's lungs. He had never seen such monsters. Had they not been firmly under Einar's control, he would have been terrified.

The beasts obediently lumbered from the lake to stand in the magenta moonlight. Each was covered with black, velvety hair, much like that of Eutracian sea otters. Their backs were at least as high as the humans were tall. Their bodies were easily five meters long, and large around. Each of their four feet was scaly and reptilian, ending in sharp, webbed claws that looked especially suited for tearing.

They seemed to be some grotesque amalgam of creatures. Each head ended in a pointed nose, much like a rat's. The large eyes scanned everything with an intense, seemingly intelligent hatred. An unusually wide, thin mouth lay just below the nose; ratlike ears sat on either side of the heads. The tails were barbed all along their lengths and ended in points, much like arrowheads. Despite the presence of gills they breathed the night air normally, leading Reznik to guess that they also possessed lungs, and could survive either on land or underwater for as long as they liked.

Soon thousands of them had lumbered ashore. As they stood in the cold night air, steam rolled off their coats. Angry at having been disturbed, many hissed and snarled. Reznik saw row after row of razor-sharp teeth glint in the moonlight.

Satisfied, Einar turned to look at the other mystics. "I give you Failee's swamp shrews," he said simply. "Every one of them ready and willing to do our bidding."

As the beasts snarled and glared, Reznik smiled. "They seem hungry," he said.

Einar nodded. "No doubt," he answered. "They need to be fed. I know just the place."

Closing his eyes, Serena's lead consul sent a mental order to the circling envelopers. In moments they all landed. Reznik reconnected the nets to their backs; the cargo was quickly reloaded, and the adepts again took their places. Einar looked at the shrews.

"Follow us," he ordered. "We must reach our next destination before dawn. There you may feed to your hearts' content."

The enveloper pairs lifted into the sky. Using hand signals, Einar ordered them to fly low, so that the shrews could better follow the glowing nets. With the envelopers flying in circles so as not to lose them, the shrew legions lumbered along behind.

Serena's ominous forces turned northward.

CHAPTER XVII

"IT'S TRUE," WIGG SAID. SHAKING HIS HEAD WITH WONDER, HE looked around the table. "The eight girls who practically barged their way into the palace last night are indeed Fledgling House survivors," he added. "I had given them up for dead."

Wigg sat back in his chair and looked thoughtfully at Sister Adrian. "It seems your burdens just increased," he said. "Not only will you continue to teach your selected acolytes to empower the Black Ships, you must also oversee the continued training of both the girls and the boys. You are about to become an even busier woman."

Pausing for a moment, Wigg rummaged through a pile of parchments lying before him. He found the one he wanted, and skimmed the page.

"Ah, yes," he said. "Here she is—Mallory of the House of Esterbrook. She is the oldest among them. She also seems to be the group's leader. I suspect that her training will finish soon. The others' passages into sisterhood will take longer. In any event, they are your responsibility, Adrian. With all the consuls turned to the Vagaries, these young girls and their male counterparts represent the Vigors' future. Train them all well."

Adrian positively beamed. Having these Fledglings safely ensconced in the Redoubt with the boys meant that the acolyte and consular orders would survive long after she and her contemporaries had perished. She considered it a dream come true.

"Thank you, First Wizard," she said respectfully. "Tell me—do the girls know that they have been positively identified?"

Wigg shook his head. "No," he said. "I thought we might bring them here to tell them. Besides, it's time they saw the Redoubt and met the boys. Since you are First Sister, perhaps you would like to break the news yourself. It seems only fitting, don't you agree?"

Adrian was so pleased that she didn't know what to say. As

usual, Abbey sat beside Wigg. Touching his hand, she placed her lips close to his ear.

"That was wonderful of you," she whispered. "Sometimes you can be quite a pushover. A very *old* pushover, but a pushover, nonetheless."

Leaning toward her, Wigg smiled. "Don't tell these women that!" he kidded back. "I have not lived among such powerful females for more than three centuries! I need to keep all the authority I can!"

Wigg, Shailiha, Abbey, Adrian, Jessamay, and Martha sat around a large meeting table. Caprice perched quietly atop Shailiha's chair back. After confirming the girls' identities, Wigg had summoned the women to the Hall of Blood Records. It was late afternoon of the day following the disastrous masquerade ball. But in the windowless Redoubt, time seemed meaningless.

Shailiha looked around at the chamber's grandeur. This room was the Redoubt's largest. To her mind, it was also the most impressive.

The floor and ceiling were of black marble, especially imported from the province of Ephyra. Encompassing all four walls were row after row of mahogany pull drawers, each with its own solid-gold handle. Each drawer was labeled with a gold plaque. The sliding compartments held copies of endowed persons' blood signatures, sometimes referred to as blood-birth records, arranged alphabetically. Many of the fragile documents were more than three centuries old.

The table at which the five of them sat was huge, and constructed of highly polished mahogany. It was but one of many such tables here. Soft lighting was supplied by solid-gold oil lamps. As is often the case in places of learning, an indefinable mustiness hung in the air.

During the preceding night, the Minions had managed to clear the rubble and start the necessary rebuilding. After being freed from Faegan's damaged rooms, Wigg and Jessamay had taken samples of the girls' blood. They had then come here, to check the girls' signatures against their blood-birth records. Sure enough, their identities were verified. Wigg and Jessamay had then used a signature scope to ensure that the signatures leaned rightward and held no Forestallments. Each was as it should be.

Wigg looked across the table at Martha. The compassionate

matron smiled back joyously. She could hardly wait to be reunited with her girls. Martha's hair had been gray for more days than she could remember, and her once-girlish figure was long gone. But her pride in her Fledglings remained steadfast.

Wigg knew that of everyone here, Martha would be the happiest to see the girls. She had practically raised Adrian—and all the rest, for that matter. Her husband, Duncan, had patiently taught the craft's secrets to every girl crossing Fledgling House's threshold. But Duncan had been brutally killed by Nicholas' agents as Tristan's son tirelessly constructed the Gates of Dawn. On Martha's return to the palace, Wigg had asked her to tutor Celeste. Celeste's unexpected death had devastated the kindly matron nearly as much as it had the First Wizard.

"Where is Faegan?" Shailiha asked. "Is he too weak to attend this meeting?"

"Oh, he's well enough," Wigg answered. "His burns are healing nicely. I granted him another strong anti-pain enchantment, so that he could go straight to work. At this moment he is ensconced in a Redoubt laboratory, trying to unravel the secrets of his new Forestallment. I promised him that we would join him after this meeting."

Wigg turned to Adrian. "What are the girls' conditions?"

Adrian smiled. "Considering all that they have suffered, they seem well," she answered. "They are terribly thin, but that will change. The gnome wives spent all last night making new uniforms for them. Like the boys being taught here, they have been assigned personal quarters. Shawna has to keep bringing them so much food that she's exhausted! At the princess's suggestion, this morning I gave them a palace tour. They're overwhelmed."

Then Adrian's expression darkened. "I have heard their story," she added sadly. "It seems that there is an evil in Tammerland with which we must deal."

Her interest piqued, Shailiha leaned forward. She was clearly tired. Sleeplessness and worry had left dark circles below her eyes.

"What do you mean?" she asked.

"With all due respect, I must defer to Mallory, Your Highness," Adrian answered. "After she told me, she asked if she could inform you herself. It seems that you have made quite an impression on her."

"Then it's time we summoned them," Shailiha said. She looked toward the doors. "Guard!" she called out.

At once the twin doors opened. Two sturdy Minion warriors strode briskly into the room, walked to Shailiha's side, and came to attention.

"Bring the Fledgling House girls," she ordered. "Tell them they have nothing to fear."

The guards snapped their boot heels together. Leaving the room, they shut the doors.

Wigg looked concernedly at Shailiha. As acting regent, she would have to make another difficult decision, and quickly.

"Before the girls arrive we must discuss their fathers," Wigg said gently.

Shailiha nodded. "We will try to break the news in the kindest possible way. Even so, it will be difficult for them to accept. Many of their fathers were killed by people at this very table. Of those remaining alive, we cannot say how many are serving Serena and the Vagaries. Neither explanation will be a welcome one."

Wigg looked down at the tabletop for several moments, then back into the princess's eyes.

"There's more than that," he said dryly.

"What do you mean?" Abbey asked.

"I'm talking about the consuls imprisoned here in the Redoubt," Wigg said. "After each one was captured, Faegan and I examined his blood. As expected, because of Nicholas' influence each of their signatures leans significantly leftward. Jessamay looked into their eyes, further confirming our findings. Luckily, not one holds Forestallments. We also used the craft to enter their minds, but our efforts produced little. With Wulfgar's death, they appear leaderless. In any event, they know nothing of Serena's plans, or of Xanthus' appearance. I wish they could have told us more, but there it is." Pausing for a moment, Wigg looked around the table.

"The moment we took each consul, a forgetfulness spell was enacted over him, negating his magic use," he added. "For security reasons, each was locked away in his own windowless quarters. Two armed warriors guard every consul's door. The consuls clearly know who they are, and they still owe their allegiance to the Vagaries. We compared their signatures to the blood-birth records stored here. In several cases, our findings yielded interesting results."

"How so?" Shailiha asked.

Sighing, Wigg sat back in his chair. "Some of the girls' fathers are imprisoned here, including Mallory's."

"Did you know Mallory's father before he was captured?" Adrian asked.

"Yes," Wigg answered. "I knew them all. The selection process was intimate. Each Directorate of Wizards member had a hand in it, as did Queen Morganna. After all, it was at Morganna's insistence that Fledgling House came into existence."

"What is the consul's name?" Shailiha asked.

"Nathan of the House of Esterbrook," Wigg answered. "At forty-three Seasons of New Life, his blood is strong and his intellect keen. Just as I suspect Mallory's are."

"Can the consuls' blood signatures be changed to lean rightward once more?" Abbey asked. "Jessamay's was."

"Perhaps," Wigg answered. "But I believe that should wait until the threat from Serena has been dealt with."

For several moments, silence again filled the room. Wigg looked into Shailiha's eyes.

"What are your orders, Princess?" he asked.

Shailiha didn't hesitate. "Only Mallory will be told. I believe that she is the only one mature enough to fully bear up under the news. We will let her see her father, if she chooses. But we will tell her about him in private. If she wishes to inform the other girls later, that will be her decision."

As her thoughts turned to her brother, Shailiha's face saddened. "I take it there has been no word from Traax?" she asked.

"No," Wigg answered. "But we must not give up hope. It is possible that Traax's group has yet to reach the pass, or that they were distracted by something important along the way. Traax is an able warrior. When he has something newsworthy to relate, he will send a messenger."

Shailiha couldn't help addressing the darker question. "Do you believe we'll see Tristan again?" she asked softly.

Wigg laced his fingers together. "I do not want to offer false hope, Princess. But your brother is a resourceful man, and it seems that the Heretics have some plan for him. At the very least they want him alive and unharmed."

"I suppose you're right," Jessamay added. "All we can do is wait and see."

"No," Shailiha said adamantly. "We can do more than that. We will attack the Citadel, just as he asked us to do. As we speak, Tyranny is readying the Black Ships. We sail as soon as possible."

A knock came on the door. Calling out, Shailiha granted permission to enter.

The doors opened to show the eight Fledglings, accompanied by the warriors Shailiha had sent to fetch them. Each girl wore a uniform like the one she had donned at Fledgling House—a white blouse, a blue-and-gray plaid pleated skirt, and shiny black shoes. Each crisp blouse carried a bright red image of the Paragon embroidered over its wearer's heart.

Like they had just encountered another world, the Fledglings gazed wide-eyed into the magnificent Hall of Blood Records. When they spied Martha, their decorum vanished.

"Martha!" they screamed. "Martha! Martha!" Charging around both sides of the table, they joyously deluged her.

Hugging her girls incessantly, Martha soon had tears running down her face. Shailiha wisely decided to let the affectionate reunion run its course.

When things had quieted, Shailiha politely commanded the girls' attention. Suddenly remembering themselves, Mallory and Ariana blushed. Shailiha looked at the two guards.

"Please seat our guests," she ordered. When more chairs had been situated at the table, the girls took their places. Leaving the room, the guards shut the doors behind them.

One by one, Shailiha smiled into each new face. She then nodded at Adrian.

"We have learned that you are indeed who you claim to be," the First Sister said. Lifting her hands, she graciously gestured about the room. "Welcome to the Redoubt."

The girls beamed. "Thank you, First Sister," Mallory said. "On behalf of all the Fledglings, it is an honor to be here."

Shailiha smiled. *She is indeed their leader,* she realized. The princess gave Mallory a thoughtful look.

"Sister Adrian tells us that you have told her your story," she said. "I would like you to tell the rest of us. But before you do, would each girl please give her name?"

One by one the girls identified themselves. They were Mallory, Ariana, Magdalene, Deirdre, Carol, Daisy, Constance, and Scarlet. Suddenly remembering Duncan, Mallory gave Martha an apologetic look.

"I'm sorry," she said. "We loved Duncan very much."

Martha nodded wistfully. "Don't be sorry," she answered. "What happened was not your doing. Duncan would be happy to know that we are all back together again."

Shailiha looked at Mallory again. "Now then, please tell us your story," she said.

Mallory nodded. She spoke for a full hour, beginning the tale with their departure from Fledgling House. Even though the part about being in debtors' prison personally embarrassed her, she left nothing out. After finishing she sat back in her chair.

Mallory's story clearly enraged Shailiha. Leaning closer, the princess looked into the Fledgling's eyes.

"Do you believe Lothar is dead?" she asked.

Mallory shook her head. "I don't know. Ariana and I combined our bolts, so it's possible. He was unconscious and his clothes were smoldering. I believe several guards died, though. They had to—the flames overtaking the floor were too intense."

Shailiha looked over at Wigg. "Did you know that such things were going on?" she asked.

Wigg scowled. "Not to such a degree. But for as long as I can remember, our justice system has been seriously flawed. The debtors' prison will be a good place to start forcing some changes." Looking wryly at the door, Wigg thought about the Minion warriors standing on its other side.

"And I know just how to go about it," he added. "By the way—who is the woman who brought the girls here?"

Adrian started to speak, then looked down at her hands. She blushed noticeably.

Smiling, Wigg leaned forward in his chair. "Out with it," he said.

"It seems that Mary is Tammerland's foremost brothel madam," she answered. "She has apparently acquired girls from Lothar in the past."

"Are you telling us that she is also a slave trader?" Shailiha asked. "If so, then she is no better than Lothar."

"Not exactly," Adrian answered. "True, she has paid Lothar for girls. But she always offers them their freedom. It seems that she is some kind of angel of mercy—despite her occupation."

"How curious," Abbey said. "Does she expect a reward?"

"No," Adrian answered. "I believe that she was simply glad to have been of service. To hear her tell it, she hates Lothar as much as anyone."

"The proverbial whore with a heart of gold?" Shailiha asked rhetorically. "How interesting. . . . When next you see her, thank her. Reward her for her kindness, then send her on her way."

"As you wish, Your Highness," Adrian answered.

Knowing that her next task would be difficult, Shailiha looked at the Fledglings. "It is time to tell about your fathers," she said. "I'm sorry, but this will be painful to hear."

Shailiha gently told them the full story—first about how their fathers had been turned to the Vagaries by Nicholas, then the tale of Wulfgar, then how the Conclave had used Satine's list to hunt down the consuls hiding in safe houses. She told them that some of their fathers might still live, serving Serena at the Citadel. Last she related how Xanthus had taken the prince, and that the Citadel was about to be attacked.

By the time she finished, all the girls had teary eyes. But they also bore the news bravely. The princess looked at Martha.

"These girls have been through enough for one day," she said. "Please return them to their quarters."

As the girls rose to leave, Shailiha touched Mallory's arm. "Please stay," she said softly.

Mallory immediately obeyed her princess and reclaimed her seat. Once Martha had ushered the girls out, Shailiha looked Mallory in the eyes.

"We have information particular to you," she said gently. "We wanted to inform you in private. You will find it bittersweet."

Mallory didn't know what to say. After searching every face at the table, she looked back at Shailiha.

"Is it about my father?" she asked, her voice breaking.

"Yes," Shailiha answered. "But take heart. Nathan lives."

Mallory tried to hold back her tears. "Where is he?" she asked.

"He is imprisoned here in the Redoubt," Wigg answered. "Like the other consuls, he now practices the Vagaries."

Thunderstruck, Mallory sat back in her chair. Like a true acolyte, she did her best to regain her composure.

"Do you wish to see him?" Wigg asked. "Before you answer, please be aware that he is probably little like you remember. Nor do we know how he will react to your presence. Seeing him again might be disturbing."

"I don't know . . ." Mallory answered. "I've wished for this moment for so long. But now . . ."

"Take all the time you need," Wigg said. "Perhaps waiting is for the best, anyway. Besides, there's someone else you must meet. I promised we would join him after we concluded our meeting."

Mallory wiped her eyes. "Who is it?"

"Another wizard," Wigg answered. "He is amazingly eccentric, not to mention brilliant. I believe you'll like him. He's working on something special." He gave Mallory a wink. "Perhaps by now he's ready to explain his findings to us lesser mortals."

Wigg stood and walked to her chair. He graciously held out his arm. "Shall I escort you?" he asked.

Mallory cleared her throat and smiled again, then stood and wrapped one arm through his. "It would be my honor," she answered.

Without further ado, Wigg led the group from the room. Shailiha was the last to go.

Fluttering from her perch atop Shailiha's chair, Caprice took to the air. As she followed her mistress through the open doors, the warriors closed them behind her.

Chapter XVIII

Tristan untied the canteen from his saddle and opened it to take a drink. No matter how much he consumed, the same amount of water always remained—telling him that Xanthus was using the craft to ensure that the canteen stayed full. After retying it to his saddleback, he looked up at the cloudless sky.

It was late afternoon, and the sun would soon disappear behind the western horizon. Riding side by side, they had traveled northwest all day, along the Sippora's western bank. Tristan was surprised to notice that today the foliage lying before them did not wither. The river did not still, and the birds and insects still chirped their customary sounds—all despite Xanthus' presence.

Since yesterday, they had met no one. Tristan was grateful, for Xanthus would surely have tortured them. They had stopped only once, to rest their horses and take a midday meal. The Darkling had said next to nothing all day, leaving Tristan alone with his thoughts.

The more Tristan considered his plight, the less convinced he became that he was making the right choice by fighting the Darkling's wishes. If Xanthus had been granted time enchantments, the passing days would mean nothing to him. How many more would die? Could the alternative be worse?

Turning in his saddle, he tried to look at Xanthus' profile. There was little to see of the grotesque face, hidden as it was by the Darkling's hood. Despite how much he hated Xanthus, Tristan found the silence maddening. Seeking answers, he guided Shadow closer.

"Why don't the grass and flowers die today?" Tristan asked. "Does the answer have something to do with your human half?"

Xanthus did not look over. "In a way," he answered. "But no more than it concerns my Darkling side."

"I don't understand."

"We are far from Tammerland," Xanthus said. "I sense no imminent danger, so my *K'Shari* is not being employed. The phenomena to which you refer are simply its by-products."

"So your *K'Shari* is not ever-present," Tristan mused. "Rather, you call on it during times of danger—like during the masquerade ball, or when you are torturing a victim. Then your *K'Shari* becomes active and the foliage dies. But why would a simple martial discipline cause such strange happenings? Does it have to do with the craft?"

"There is nothing simple about it," Xanthus countered, "but I see no harm in explaining its basics." Turning toward Tristan, the Darkling's glowing eyes bored themselves into his.

"*K'Shari* is a state of martial enlightenment that can be gained in two different ways," Xanthus explained. "One method is to devote one's life to mastering the combative arts. Once the physical side has been perfected, the needed mental training may start. In your world's entire history, *K'Shari* has been gained by only a handful of practitioners. There were so few that the art nearly died out. These days, only one such Eutracian possesses the skill. So far, not one of this master's students has succeeded in reaching their teacher's degree of enlightenment. If one does not succeed soon and the master dies, *K'Shari* might vanish from your world forever."

"Who is this great teacher?" Tristan asked.

Ignoring the question, Xanthus looked forward again.

"Very well," Tristan said. "At least tell me about the other method of gaining *K'Shari.*"

"The other way is available only to those owning endowed blood," Xanthus answered. "That is how I attained the gift. Simply put, it can be granted by Forestallment. The needed calculations are found in both scrolls of the ancients."

Thinking to himself, Tristan sat back in his saddle. "That does not answer my question," he pressed. "When your *K'Shari* is employed, why do the plants die, and the creatures still? It's almost like they know, somehow."

"In a way, they do," Xanthus answered. "When *K'Shari* is summoned by a craft practitioner, the effect is far stronger. The calmness is so pervasive that it affects nearby life-forms and forces of nature. Wind and water stop flowing. Nonsentient life-forms like plants and trees slow so much that some wither and die. Moderately sentient beings—like animals, insects, and birds—are also slowed or simply flee. Humans don't sense the effects, but they do observe these highly unnatural occurrences. As I travel away, the pervasive calm moves with me. The rivers and wind flow again after I leave, and the creatures return."

After riding for a time in silence, the Darkling asked, "Have you decided to join me on the other side, *Jin'Sai*? How many more must die before you come to your senses?"

Tristan remained silent.

"Very well," Xanthus said. "It seems I must add an incentive."

Tristan stiffened. "What do you mean?"

"The next time an opportunity avails itself, you will aid me in my tasks," Xanthus answered. "That should make you more agreeable."

Suddenly enraged, Tristan brought Shadow up short. He glared hatefully at the Darkling. "I won't do it!" he shouted.

Xanthus also stopped his horse. Like he was tutoring some insolent schoolboy, the Darkling shook his head. "Tell me, *Jin'*-

Sai—during the brief but eventful time you have known me, have I ever made a false threat?"

Tristan's jaw hardened. "No," he answered softly.

"Just so," Xanthus said. Saying nothing more, they got their horses moving again.

An hour later, they came to some structures sitting along the Sippora's western bank. Tristan saw a thatched cottage, a barn, and a water-powered gristmill. The gristmill's paddlewheel was being turned by the swiftly moving Sippora. Xanthus stopped his horse.

The Darkling smiled. "There can't be many people there," he said, "but it will do for today. It's such a pretty picture. I wonder if there are any children about."

Tristan couldn't believe his ears. *"Children?"* he wailed. "You cannot mean that!"

Xanthus glared back at him. "You're in no position to give orders!" he growled. "That is, unless you accompany me to the pass this instant!"

Tristan hung his head. "I *can't*!" he whispered. "You know that!"

"Then hide your face, *Jin'Sai,*" the Darkling ordered. "Because of your stubbornness, more innocents are about to die."

His hands shaking with rage, Tristan reached beneath his vest to produce the hated black mask. After securing it over his face, he followed Xanthus toward the unassuming buildings.

The house was a simple one. It was built of fieldstone and mortar, and its roof was neatly thatched. By the look if it, it held only a few rooms. A colorful bantam rooster arrogantly squired his hens about the yard. The house was surrounded by a split-rail fence, and a stone walkway lined with wildflowers wound its way toward the front door. No lights shone through the cottage windows, nor did smoke curl from the chimney top, though Tristan guessed they would when darkness fell and the night air cooled.

As expected, the barn was larger. Its wooden doors hung open. Numerous grain sacks lay stacked against the inner walls, and its upper story was filled with hay and straw. A small corral was attached to one side, and three strong plow horses roamed its confines. Tristan knew that the horses would be used to turn the great millstones during the Season of Crystal, should the Sippora freeze over.

The mill was large, even by provincial standards. The square, two-story building was painted red. The gristmill's paddles continually dipped into the quickly moving Sippora only to rise and fall again, and their connecting wheel lay attached to the mill sidewall facing the river.

The owner had cleverly multiplied the current's power by placing dams in the river, thereby concentrating the water flow. This created a narrower, more rapid current to more speedily rotate the wheel. Pull levers led from the shore to a series of sliding dam doors, to adjust the current's course and speed. With each revolution the paddlewheel squeaked pleasantly.

Xanthus dismounted and beckoned the prince to do the same. They tied their horses to a corral rail. Xanthus immediately started walking toward the mill. Tristan warily followed.

To the prince's relief, there was no one inside. The floor was deeply littered with crushed grain husks. Turned by the paddlewheel, a flat, circular under-stone supported a smaller one, grinding against its topside. Another lever system provided the means to lift the upper-stone from its mate.

Had people been working here, they would have been crushing grain between the two stones. The grist would then be sacked and sent downstream on barges to such cities as Tammerland and Far Point. Business seemed good for the mill owner, for dozens more grain sacks lay stacked against the walls, waiting to be emptied. As the squeaky paddlewheel revolved, the comforting smells of crushed wheat, corn, and barley filled the air.

For the first time since meeting Xanthus, Tristan smiled. "How disappointing for you," he said nastily. "There is no one here to kill."

Smiling back, Xanthus turned his glowing eyes toward the prince. "Is that so?" he asked. "Then why do the horses remain in the corral, and their saddles still hang on the barn wall?"

Just then they heard a door squeak open on the mill's western side. With the setting sun at his back, a man stood squarely in the doorway. He held a pitchfork in his hands. Ignoring the Darkling for the moment, he glared straight at Tristan.

"No one wears a mask unless he plans to rob you!" he growled.

His voice was elderly, but strong. Standing his ground, he raised the pitchfork a bit more. He defiantly spat a dark wad of chewing tobacco toward the husk-covered floor.

"State your intentions," he ordered, "or I'll kill you where you stand!"

Xanthus didn't hesitate. Raising one hand, the Darkling called the craft. The pitchfork was torn from the man's hands to fly across the room; its tines embedded themselves into the opposite wall.

Xanthus moved his fingers. At once the man was lifted into the air. As Xanthus brought him closer, the helpless miller stared back in disbelief.

"Who . . . what . . . are you?" he whispered.

"I am from another world," Xanthus answered. Using his free hand, he pointed to the prince. "This man in the mask is my assistant," he added. "As an incentive to help me change his stubborn ways, he is going to help kill you."

"Are you . . . a wizard?" the man asked.

Xanthus smiled. "No," he answered. "I am more powerful than any wizard ever born."

Xanthus closed his eyes. He was summoning *K'Shari,* Tristan guessed.

Walking outside, the Darkling caused the terrified man to follow him through the air. His heart in his throat, Tristan went with them. As Tristan neared the river, his suspicions were confirmed.

The Sippora had stopped flowing, as had the wind. No creatures stirred. Like they had been frozen in time, the chickens and the horses stood stock-still. With no current to power it, the paddlewheel squeaked to a slow stop. The total stillness felt deadly.

Waving one arm again, Xanthus caused the man to go flying. The miller landed hard, facedown atop the paddlewheel's zenith. His head was facing downstream, and his arms and legs hung over the wheel's opposite sides. Xanthus quickly generated a wizard's warp, holding the man fast.

With tears gathering in his eyes, Tristan looked at the elderly miller trapped atop the wheel. He appeared to be about sixty Seasons of New Life. He was dressed in simple farm clothes, and his body was still lean from years of hard work. His face was tan, his jaw strong. His thick hair was silvery-gray. In some ways, he was reminiscent of the First Wizard.

Xanthus looked at Tristan. "Shall we start?" he asked. "This time you're going to participate."

Other than going to the azure pass, Tristan knew there was nothing he could do or say that would change the Darkling's mind. Clearly, Xanthus would continue with these gruesome killings until Tristan relented. Even so, all the prince could do was to shake his head.

"Very well," Xanthus said.

The Darkling closed his eyes. Tristan soon realized that Xanthus was no longer summoning *K'Shari.*

As the Sippora quickly regained its strength, the paddlewheel started to turn. Screaming, the miller headed down toward the rushing water.

As he went under, the struggling miller tried to hold his breath. Coming out on the other side, he gasped desperately for air while trying to regain his senses. As the wheel turned and the man started to go under again, the Darkling looked at the prince.

"It seems the wheel is moving too fast," he said. "You are going to slow it for me, keeping him under longer."

Tristan looked at the Darkling like he was insane. "If you must kill him, it will be without my help!" he shouted. Looking back at the wheel, he saw the man submerge for the second time.

"Is that right?" Xanthus asked. "Let's see if I can persuade you."

As the mill owner came out of the water for the second time, it was clear that he was weakening. Gagging and coughing, he looked at the Darkling with glassy eyes.

Raising one hand, Xanthus called upon the craft to adjust the levers controlling the dams. As the current was directed away from the wheel, it stopped turning. This time the wheel stopped with the miller in an upright position along one side.

Xanthus stepped closer. He looked up at his victim. "Tell me," he asked, "how many hide inside the farmhouse?"

Shivering uncontrollably and trying to catch his breath, the miller shook his head. "There is . . . no one!" he shouted. "I live alone!"

Xanthus nodded. "I see," he answered. "Since that is the case, you won't mind if I look for myself."

Suddenly an even greater sense of panic overtook the helpless captive. "What are . . . you going to do?" he begged.

Saying nothing, Xanthus turned toward the house. He raised one arm.

The farmhouse immediately erupted into flames. Soon the front door burst open. Screaming wildly, an elderly woman and young girl ran through the door. Just as they passed the split-rail fence, the entire structure went up in a raging fireball. In mere moments there was nothing left of it.

Seeing the man atop the wheel, the woman fell to her knees and started wailing. The terrified girl clutching the older woman's arm looked to be about eight or nine Seasons of New Life.

Xanthus looked at the mill owner. "Your wife and daughter?" he asked.

"My . . . wife and granddaughter," he answered weakly. "Do what you will with me, but please don't harm them! They're all I have left of my family! My son and daughter-in law were killed during the failed try to invade Eutracia!"

Xanthus pointed to Tristan. "All your fates depend on this man," he said. "You should be pleading to him, not me."

The miller turned his head to look at Tristan. His desperate eyes stabbed their way into the prince's heart.

"Please!" he cried out. "I beg you! Whatever he wants from you, you must give it!"

Xanthus walked closer to the prince. "Indeed," he said quietly. "Who are you, to let these innocents die? Come through the pass, *Jin'Sai,* and I'll let them live."

Completely overcome, for a moment Tristan believed that his helplessness would drive him mad. Unlike the other victims, this was the first time that one had begged him personally. His heart breaking, he looked hatefully into Xanthus' glowing eyes.

"No," he whispered.

Xanthus shook his head. "Because you continue to be obstinate, it is time for your direct participation." Xanthus pointed to the lever system on the riverbank.

"Throw the levers to open the dams," he ordered. "When your victim is fully submerged, close them again, leaving him under."

Balling his hands into fists, Tristan shook them at the sky. "No!" he screamed. "I refuse to help you in this madness!"

Taking another step closer, Xanthus glared at him. "Do as I say, *Jin'Sai,*" he whispered. "If you continue to refuse, I'll start on the child."

Tristan frantically turned to look at the girl and her grandmother, then back at the miller. His mind was awash with guilt about what might happen next, and his body shook uncontrollably. Finally deciding, he shamefully looked at the ground.

"I will go with you," he whispered, his voice breaking.

What have I just done? he asked himself. He looked at the Paragon, still hanging around Xanthus' neck and shining brightly in the setting sun. *By saving these people, have I also destroyed the craft?*

Xanthus smiled. "Well done," he said.

Releasing his wizard's warp, Xanthus sent the miller crashing into the river. His wife and granddaughter ran to him and helped him ashore. Although he seemed near death, Tristan guessed that he would live.

As Tristan sadly looked west, the smell of charred wood teased his nostrils. Looking past the ruined house, he saw the snowcapped Tolenkas sparkle in the setting sun. *What will it be like on the other side?* he wondered.

He looked hatefully back at the Darkling. The glowing eyes regarded him calmly.

The glow of the craft again surrounded Xanthus. His persona soon melted away to be replaced by his human side. As the prince took in the sensual face, for the briefest moment he thought he saw tears in Xanthus' eyes, but then they were gone.

Xanthus took the black knotted cord from his duster. He removed his duster and robe, then dropped them to the ground. Turning west to face the Tolenkas, he sat on his knees in the dirt.

The one hundred self-imposed lashes came across his back accurately, deliberately. Soon his azure blood ran down to be absorbed by the thirsty dirt. When it was over, Xanthus stood. He put on the robe and duster. The glow came again, restoring his Darkling side. The stunned miller and his family could only look on in unbelieving horror.

Xanthus walked to the prince. The glowing eyes seemed even more self-assured.

"It's time," he said simply. "Mount your horse. You are about to witness such wonders as you've never dreamed possible."

Tristan did as he was told. Wheeling Shadow around, he took a last look at the family he had saved.

But at what cost to the world? he wondered.

The miller's sobbing wife held her husband and granddaughter close, like she couldn't believe they had survived. As she looked at the prince, he saw that her teary eyes were a soft, limpid blue. Bowing her head, she tacitly gave him her heartfelt thanks.

Mounting his horse, Xanthus prodded the stallion to a place

alongside Shadow. The two riders started toward the Tolenkas and disappeared.

CHAPTER XIX

SOMETIMES THE PAIN SEEMS TOO GREAT FOR EVEN MY HIGHLY ENdowed blood to withstand, she thought. *She closed her teary eyes. But with the Heretics' help, our plan has been set in motion. Soon my grief will be avenged.*

Serena opened her eyes and looked around the room. Like every morning, the lush, red rose petals covering the crypt floor were fresh, and their familiar scent filled the air. The dawn's first rays streamed in through the open skylights, and songbirds could be heard greeting the morn. As always, two specially chosen handmaidens stood quietly in the room's far corners.

Lifting her gown, Serena strode through the petals to stand by the altar. Out of respect for her daughter and the man who had fathered her, she completed this sacred pilgrimage twice each day. The Vagaries queen looked down at the dead body and lovingly touched the child's cold face, just as she did each time she visited here.

Just then she sensed the Heretics touch her mind. She smiled, for she knew why they called to her. During their previous communion, they had promised to let her watch the slaughter. Eager to be informed, she went to her knees and closed her eyes.

"I am here," she said silently.

"Your servants have reached their next destination," the many voices said at once. *"As we reveal the scene to your mind, joyously behold the Vagaries' power."*

Unmoving and her eyes still closed, Serena gasped aloud as the vision revealed itself. It soon became so clear that she found it difficult to believe she wasn't part of it all.

It was morning in Parthalon, and the sun's rays were coming

up over the eastern horizon. Einar and Reznik lay on their stomachs in the dewy grass atop a hill. They were looking down on the Ghetto of the Shunned—the same city that for more than three hundred years had imprisoned all those deemed undesirable by the late Coven of Sorceresses.

The Ghetto's walls stood tall and dark. Its drawbridge was raised. A dank moat encircled the city. By the *Jin'Sai*'s order, the Coven's flags had all been removed. From their places atop the hill, Serena's mystics could see movement on the guard paths lining the barbican.

With the Ghetto firmly in Conclave hands, Tristan had ordered all the long-suffering prisoners freed save for those infected with leprosy. The disease had been conjured by the sorceresses three centuries ago, in their bid to subjugate the nation. Once the sorceresses' goal had been met, the diseased and anyone else deemed a threat to the Coven's rule had been relegated there, to linger until death. The *Jin'Sai*'s Minions were the perfect Ghetto overseers, for in her manic attention to detail Failee had granted them immunity to the disease. Ten thousand battle-hardened warriors lived there, helping to administer the city and protect its dying inhabitants.

Reznik looked behind him. A short way down the hill's opposite slope, swamp shrews and envelopers by the thousands waited silently. Their backs mimicking the ground, the envelopers were hardly visible. The Valrenkians and consuls also waited nearby. Their tools, books, and the consummately precious Scroll of the Vagaries lay farther down the hill.

Although the air was cool, Reznik sweated nervously. He had never been associated with so vast an undertaking. He looked anxiously at Einar.

"I tell you again that the Minions will see us!" he whispered. "They might not detect us from the catwalks, but a flying patrol is bound to go overhead sooner or later! We must act!"

Einar smiled confidently. "Take heart," he whispered back. "We will not be seen, I promise you."

Turning, the consul looked down the hill. Raising one hand, he gathered the envelopers' attention.

"Protect!" he whispered simply.

Einar watched in awe as some envelopers quickly obeyed. Their moving shapes little more than slightly noticeable shimmers, they grouped together to form a tight, circular wall around the shrews, consuls, and Valrenkians. As the wall grew, more envelopers took to the air, forming a dome over their allies. Soon the wondrous construct was completed, causing partial darkness inside.

Looking down its length, Reznik could barely see the others waiting here with him. The incredible hiding place stretched for nearly half a league and looked to be about ten meters high. Suddenly understanding, he smiled at Einar.

"The envelopers' backs will mimic the terrain surrounding us," he said. "To anyone happening by, our entire force will be unnoticeable! How marvelous!"

"Exactly so," Einar answered. Standing, he brushed the grass from his robe. "It is time to give the order."

Einar walked to the cone's leading edge. At his command, two of the envelopers forming the cone separated slightly. Einar looked out between them to see another hovering nearby, awaiting its orders. Camouflaged as it was, Einar could barely see it.

"Go!" he whispered. "When we see your signal, others will follow! Remember—not one leper is to be harmed! You will know them by their yellow robes!"

Smoothly undulating its velvety body, the enveloper took to the air. Thousands more followed. As they headed for the Ghetto, Einar and Reznik watched as best they could from their perfectly camouflaged blind.

Still on her knees and her eyes closed, Serena smiled. *Perfect,* she thought.

"I BEG THE AFTERLIFE, THAT'S NO WAY TO THROW AN AXE!" YAKOV shouted angrily. It always perplexed him whenever his junior officers didn't perform to his high standards.

"It's a good thing for you that our *Jin'Sai* wasn't here to see such a pathetic effort!" he added.

Stomping to the target, with a great heave he yanked the axe free from the tree trunk. The other officer's throw had gone high, missing by a good foot the red circle Yakov had painted on the trunk. Mumbling to himself, he walked back to where the others were standing.

There were six more Minion officers in attendance. These seven formed the usual nighttime drawbridge detail. Another complement of warriors had just relieved them. Whenever the bridge was raised, drawbridge duty became notoriously boring.

Even those manning the catwalks above had stopped to gleefully watch the throwing and drinking contest.

Yakov's group was glad to be off duty. During the previous night's boredom, good-natured challenges had been raised, and from those challenges bets quickly arose. Added to this had come Yakov's boast that he could not only outthrow every man in his squad, but that he could easily outdrink him, as well—and do both at the same time. During the night, his boasting had attracted many takers.

Walking back with the axe, Yakov reached down to grab an akulee jug. He hoisted it on his forearm and took a long swig. A wet belch erupted, followed by raucous laughter. He placed the jug at his feet and sloppily wiped his mouth and beard with the back of one hand. Turning to look at his younger charges, he smiled greedily. He could already imagine the kisa that he would win today.

Wavering back and forth from drinking so much akulee, Yakov looked at the target. He narrowed his eyes. Swinging the axe over his head, with a deep grunt he let it go.

Its blade a blur, the axe twinkled briefly in the morning sun, then cleaved the center of the target. Cheers erupted. Proudly holding out his hand, Yakov collected several kisa from each of the other officers. As he went to collect the axe, the others started grumbling about their losses.

Suddenly they heard Yakov scream. Turning to look, they saw that he had somehow vanished. They quickly unsheathed their dreggans, but could find no threat. Then they saw Yakov's boots hauntingly standing alone near the base of the tree.

Another muffled, bloodcurdling scream arose. Somehow appearing out of thin air, the coins Yakov had just won went clinking to the ground around his boots. Then his body armor and weapons also fell from thin air. Finally his polished bones collapsed noisily onto the pile. Then total pandemonium rained down on the unsuspecting city.

Thousands more envelopers, their bodies camouflaged from both above and below, sailed over the walls and through the streets. Ignoring the yellow-robed lepers, they attacked every Minion warrior they could find. Smashing their way through windows and doors, they mercilessly ransacked every building.

The bewildered warriors never stood a chance. From all over the city, they cursed and struck out against an enemy they couldn't see. Muffled screams filled the air as one by one the enveloped warriors disappeared.

As they started to understand their plight, some Minions started blindly swinging their blades through the air in hope of randomly cutting down their invisible foes. In a few cases they succeeded, and the envelopers lost their camouflage to go crashing hard to the earth. But the warriors were succumbing in droves, and literally dissolving as they died.

Yellow-robed lepers tore hysterically through the streets while others took shelter in the buildings. Minion blood became so prevalent that it started painting the dirt and running down the gutters. Fires broke out as the envelopers tipped over oil lamps in their relentless search for prey.

Two specially selected envelopers soared toward the inner wall securing the drawbridge, found the chains holding the drawbridge in place, and wrapped their camouflaged bodies around them. In moments, several chain links dissolved on each side.

With a heaving groan the heavy wooden drawbridge came crashing down, spanning the dank moat. Wooden shards and metal pieces went flying into the air. With its main entryway breached, the city's fate was sealed.

From his hiding place atop the hill, Einar smiled. The falling drawbridge was the signal he had been waiting for.

"Go!" he called out to his remaining envelopers.

At once the protective cone dismantled, and its freed envelopers started soaring toward the beleaguered city. Turning to look down the hill's backside, Einar smiled at his eagerly waiting swamp shrews.

"Attack!" he shouted joyously. "But remember—the lepers are not to be touched!"

Not to be outdone, the snarling shrew herds rumbled down the hill. Thundering across the damaged drawbridge, they greedily tore into whatever warriors remained standing.

Cautiously biding his time, Einar smiled as he listened to the screams. After another hour or so, the city quieted. Smoke drifted ominously over the city walls. Then a few dozen envelopers obediently soared back to their master. Rippling their sides, they landed gently on the dewy grass.

Wasting no time, Einar quickly reconjured the glowing nets. The Valrenkians and consuls loaded their cargoes and took their places. Einar and Reznik joined them. Soon they were all flying toward the smoking city. Using hand signals, Einar ordered the envelopers to soar over the barbican. Reznik was no stranger to the suffering of others. But the scene below him made his skin crawl.

Minion bones, armor, boots, and weapons lay everywhere. Many building entrances and windows were smashed in because of the envelopers' relentless pursuits. Drying blood lay pooled in the streets, alleys, and gutters. Fires raged, and thick smoke blackened the sky.

In many places, warriors' internal organs and limbs lay strewn about, starkly exemplifying the shrews' brutal hunger. Unable to believe that their protectors had been vanquished, traumatized lepers wandered about aimlessly. Leper parents separated from their children called out frantically, trying to find their missing offspring.

Hearing a sharp scream, Einar turned to see a ravenous shrew shaking a Minion back and forth like a rag doll. With a sharp cracking sound, the shrew's jaws savagely closed, breaking its victim's back. It dropped the dead warrior to the dirt, ripped open the warrior's body, and started devouring the Minion's organs.

Looking skyward, Einar called the craft to augment his sight. Even so, he could barely see his envelopers. On the ground, ravenous shrew herds thundered through the streets. Both species were scouring the city for stragglers. Einar knew that whenever one was found, the warrior would be dealt with quickly. Signaling again with his hands, Einar ordered his envelopers down.

Landing in the inner ward, Einar jumped from his net, then looked around. He couldn't have been more pleased. He turned to look at his Valrenkians and consuls.

"Call on the craft to get those fires under control!" he ordered. "We still need the buildings to temporarily house the lepers. Once you are sure that no warriors remain alive, start taking a detailed census. Before I leave here, I must have an exact count! And repair that drawbridge! Soon all of Parthalon will know we've arrived!"

As the screaming quieted, Einar's servants quickly went about their duties.

Just then Einar and Reznik heard a woman crying. Soft and

low, the sound came from somewhere nearby. Curious, they walked across the street to an abandoned storefront.

Shoving aside the smashed door, they walked in. A leper woman sat huddled in one corner. A young girl was there with her. Their yellow robes had been charred and torn during the frenzy.

Beckoning Reznik to follow him, Einar walked closer. As the two mystics neared, the mother and child cowered farther into a dirty corner.

"Do not be frightened, my child," Einar said. "Please stand. Let me look at you."

The woman stood on trembling legs. Her terrified eyes looked into his.

Einar guessed her to be about twenty-five Seasons of New Life. But given her advanced condition, he knew he could easily be wrong. She was little more than skin, bones, and raging sores. Her daughter seemed equally ill. Placing his hands into opposite robe sleeves, he looked over at Reznik.

"How long, do you guess?" he asked. "Your talents in these matters supersede mine."

Reznik looked deeply into the mother's eyes, then examined the poor quality of her hair and nails. He thought to himself for several moments.

"She has two moons, at best," he answered. "The child will last a bit longer."

Reaching out, Einar touched the woman's ravaged face. He smiled. "Do not despair, my child," he said. "Although you will soon perish, your deaths will serve a greater good. You see, your kind is exactly what we need."

Leaving the mother and child behind, the two mystics walked outside. The fires were coming under control, and the shrews and envelopers were returning to the square. Knowing that the Ghetto could never accommodate all his servants, Einar ordered them to leave and guard the perimeter. The envelopers obediently soared over the walls, and the bloodied shrews lumbered back across the partly destroyed drawbridge.

Einar had meant what he said—soon all of Parthalon would know of the attack on the Ghetto. Those warriors still alive on this side of the Sea of Whispers would be sure to respond. They too would have to be dealt with, long before the Conclave heard about what was happening.

The first part of the plan had succeeded brilliantly. But to ensure success, the next phase would have to go equally well. As soon as he had his leper count, Einar would take the next step.

Smiling at Reznik, he beckoned him over to where the frightened lepers were being gathered. As morning drifted into midday, the two mystics started helping with the census.

SMILING, SERENA OPENED HER EYES AND RAISED HER HEAD. SHE stood and looked down at her daughter's endowed corpse.

After touching Clarice's face once more, she turned and left the crypt.

CHAPTER XX

AS HE HEADED TOWARD FAEGAN'S LABORATORY, THE FIRST WIZARD was highly preoccupied. Mallory's revelations about the debtors' prison had infuriated him. The more he thought about it, the angrier he became. As he stomped down the Redoubt halls his robe went flying, and the others had to hurry to keep up. Only the Afterlife knew how many other Eutracians the corrupt jailor had abused. Wigg was eager to set things right.

Shailiha, Abbey, Adrian, Mallory, and Jessamay followed him. As they went, they briefly pointed out various Redoubt areas to the young Fledgling. Still stunned by her surroundings, Mallory looked at everything with wide eyes.

Wigg finally stopped before a large oaken door. Whooping laughter came from the other side. Scowling, he shook his head, then turned to look at the women.

"There's no telling what he's up to in there," he said. "Prepare yourselves."

Opening the heavy door, Wigg ushered the women into the room.

Faegan sat in the new wheeled chair the Minions had made for him. Cackling joyously, he sailed about the laboratory. He seemed so pleased with himself that he hardly noticed his visitors. Laughing gleefully, he finally stopped to hover before the First Wizard.

The group regarded Faegan narrowly. For her part, Mallory had never seen anyone remotely like him. A delighted look overcame her face. Scowling, Wigg crossed his arms over his chest.

"Is this some gift your newfound Forestallment has granted you?" he asked. "Soaring around rooms faster than ever?"

Normally the crippled wizard would have shot back a sly retort. But this time he just laughed again, then gleefully started spinning his chair in circles.

"No, you old fool!" he shouted as he went round and round. "My miraculous Forestallment is far more than that! From this day forward, our world is forever changed!"

"What are you babbling about?" Jessamay demanded. "Stop that spinning and explain yourself this instant!"

Shaking her head, the sorceress looked over at Abbey and Adrian. "Are you sure that your concoction hasn't finally put him around the bend?" she asked under her breath. Wondering the same thing, all the partial adept and First Sister could do was look back sheepishly.

Faegan finally stopped spinning. He grinned at Jessamay. "Do not worry, good woman!" he said. "Aside from a few burns, I'm right as rain!" As Faegan lowered his chair to the floor, Mallory looked around.

The Fledgling House facilities had been meager compared to Faegan's. The laboratory was spacious. Many tables stood about, each littered with beakers, bottles, texts, and scrolls. More bottles holding dried herbs and precious oils could be seen locked behind glass in specially constructed cabinets. In one corner, a brass blood signature scope and criterion sat atop a wooden stand. A hearth lay along one wall, its fire burning merrily.

Looking farther, Mallory saw huge parchments filled with detailed scribbling hanging on the walls. A framed reference chart displaying the craft's many esoteric symbols lay on a nearby easel. The room's entire rear wall was taken up by a strange black panel. It was literally covered with Old Eutracian, the glowing, azure script shining brightly against its background. Oil chandeliers provided welcoming light.

Then Mallory's eyes fell on what she guessed was the Scroll of the Vigors. Its beauty took her breath away.

The massive, unrolled document hovered in the air. One end was secured to a solid-gold rod. Snaking its way around the room, the fragile vellum appeared to be one meter high by about twenty meters long. Sadly, parts seemed burned away. Both sides were covered with Old Eutracian craft formulas. They were the most detailed ones Mallory had ever seen.

Looking closer, she saw dark vertical lines dividing the entire scroll into sections. The various parts were by no means equal in length. Numbers in Old Eutracian stood at each section's top, identifying one section from another. Smaller numbers ran vertically down each section's left-hand margin, referencing the scroll's many lines.

Curious, the First Wizard looked at Faegan. "Why have you unwound the scroll?" he asked.

"First things first," Faegan answered. He wheeled toward Mallory and looked at her new uniform. "I take it you are a Fledgling House girl?" he asked.

Mallory curtsied. "Yes, sir," she answered respectfully. "I am Mallory of the House of Esterbrook."

He bowed at the waist. "I'm sure they have already told you about me!" he said. Then he shot her a conspiratorial wink. "Don't believe everything you've heard! Welcome, Mallory! We meet on an auspicious day!"

"It's time you told us what's going on," Shailiha demanded.

"Right you are!" Faegan exclaimed. Beckoning them to follow him, he wheeled his chair toward the far wall.

Mallory stared at the black panel. Its depths looked endless, seductive. Sensing her curiosity, Faegan wheeled closer.

"It's called a visage board," he said. "It's usually employed for teaching purposes. I keep one here because it helps me think. Observe."

Faegan waved one hand. In the twinkle of an eye, the board's writing disappeared. He turned to look at the inquisitive group, then gestured toward the hovering Vigors scroll.

"Very well," he started. "We believe that at one time this scroll held every Vigors Forestallment calculation known to mankind. Some parts have been burned away. We also know that a Forestallment is a calculation of the craft, especially designed to be placed into an endowed person's blood. Such Forestallments might be time-activated—that is, brought to life at a specific time. Or they might be event-activated—destined to activate concurrently with its owner's performance of some predetermined deed. When imbued into the blood signature they form branches, leading away from the signature proper. Their purpose is to grant their owners immediate powers. This negates the tedious classical training usually needed to reach the same results." Turning to stare at the unwound scroll, Faegan paused.

"Yes, yes!" Wigg interjected. "We all understand that! Tell us something we *don't* know!"

Returning to the moment, Faegan smiled. "I have just outlined the scroll's positive aspects. Answer me this—what has always been the scroll's greatest *drawback*?"

"Its calculations number in the thousands," Abbey answered. "But they are not labeled. Nor is there any other known way to find their physical location on the scroll. Even if one knew that a certain calculation was written there, it might take years to find—if not longer."

Faegan triumphantly pointed a bony index finger into the air. "Precisely!" he exclaimed. "Those days are at an end!"

"What do you mean?" Wigg asked.

"The Forestallment Xanthus granted to my blood has provided me with the index to the Scroll of the Vigors," Faegan answered.

Stunned, the others looked at him in silence. Wigg seemed especially skeptical.

"Prove it," the First Wizard said.

Faegan smiled. "Very well," he said. "Wigg, please describe a power that you have long coveted, but do not possess. He gave the First Wizard a wink. "Go ahead," he goaded him. "Tell us your oldest, deepest wish. If its formula exists on the scroll, I'll find it. I'm reasonably sure about what it is."

Wigg's answer was immediate. "You know full well what it is," he said. "Ever since we blew up my father's laboratory those three centuries ago, I have always wanted to be able to perform alchemy. It has long been my wish to give the results to Eutracia's various charities."

Faegan smiled. "That's right," he answered. "Before we find out whether such a formula exists, I must call forth the index. I will display it for everyone to see."

Faegan turned and pointed at the visage board. Calling the

craft, he concentrated mightily. To Mallory's astonishment, azure words in Old Eutracian started forming in its depths. Soon the entire board was full, its last line literally running off the board's lower-right corner.

Having been trained in Old Eutracian, she read the words easily. A title lay above the index proper. It read:

To all ye who seek the scroll's secrets know this: Behold the index; its titles, subtitles, and formulas lay before you. Use the knowledge well, our children. These twenty-five facets of learning have been left behind as an instrument to guide you in the perfect, wondrous knowledge that is the craft.

Pointing to the board, Faegan again summoned magic. The board's text started rolling upward, showing ever more words. Augmenting his power, Faegan forced the lines to rise faster. To Mallory's lesser gifts, the lines were soon little more than a continuous azure blur. Soon the text started to slow, then stopped altogether.

Faegan walked closer to the board and used the craft to highlight a specific passage. As Mallory deciphered it she was astounded. It read:

Various formulas for the science of alchemy. Scroll Section 19; Subsection 58; lines 347 through 954.

Faegan immediately wheeled his chair over to the scroll. Rolling his way down the hovering scroll's length, he found section number nineteen. After finding the proper subsection, he quickly started scanning the aforementioned lines. Suddenly Faegan whooped for joy.

"It's here!" he shouted. "I beg the Afterlife, it actually exists!"

Then he backed away from the scroll. Looking toward the visage board, he waved his hands. The index promptly vanished. In its place, an azure craft formula materialized.

The formula took up nearly the entire board. Mallory was stunned by its vast complexity. Before today, she had had no idea that such wonders existed.

His face radiating pure joy, Faegan turned his chair around to address the astonished group. He gestured to the visage board.

"I give you the formula for converting lead into gold," he said simply.

They all walked toward the board. For a long time no one spoke as they read the formula. Clearly, its solution had been formulated by an amazing mind.

His mouth hanging open, Wigg shook his head in wonder. "Can it be true?" he whispered. He looked at Faegan with unbelieving eyes. "Have you really unlocked the scroll's vast teachings?"

Faegan looked up at the First Wizard. "Yes, my friend," he answered softly. "As I told you when you first entered the room—from this day onward, our world is forever changed."

"Forgive me, Faegan," Mallory said. "May I ask a question?"

Turning his chair toward her, the crippled wizard smiled into her eyes. "By all means, my dear," he said.

Mallory again looked at the seemingly endless formula. A skeptical look crossed her face.

"How is it that you could read that vast formula only once, then perfectly transfer it to the visage board? To my mind that was miracle enough."

Smiling, Faegan gave her another wink. "That has to do with a little gift I possess called Consummate Recollection," he answered. "I'll be happy to explain it to you sometime."

Stepping closer to the visage board, Sister Adrian looked at the glowing formula. "Faegan," she asked, "could you please revisit the scroll's index? When it showed earlier, something caught my eye."

"Of course," he answered.

Waving one hand, he caused the long formula to scroll downward. Soon the index reappeared. Adrian walked closer. Scanning the index title, she concentrated on the last sentence. She read a portion aloud.

" 'These twenty-five facets of the craft have been left behind . . . '," she quoted. When she turned around there was a knowing smile on her face.

"The scroll being divided into twenty-five 'facets' is no coincidence, is it?" she asked.

"Indeed not," Faegan answered. Delighted that she had figured it out, he let go another cackle.

"Of course!" Shailiha said. "Each of the twenty-five scroll

sections relate to a corresponding facet in the Paragon! They include the Causal, the Sympathetic, the Kinetic, and so on!"

"Correct!" Faegan said. "The formula for alchemy comes from Section Nineteen—the Transformations Section. Now you understand that the index's purpose is to first identify the Forestallment's facet as it relates to the Paragon. Then it tells us where the formula one seeks can be found on the scroll. It is complex in design. But for those understanding its workings, it is relatively simple to use. It also leads me to another conclusion."

As Faegan sat back in his chair, it became clear that he had more to tell. Pulling on his beard, he looked up at them thoughtfully.

"I know that look," Jessamay said. Walking over, she gazed down at him. "What haven't you told us?" she asked softly.

"There is more to my new gift," he answered. "Not only does my Forestallment grant me the index to the Scroll of the Vigors, but also the index to the Scroll of the Vagaries."

The room fell dead silent. For several moments the Conclave members looked at him in awe.

"I beg the Afterlife," Wigg breathed. Grabbing Faegan's chair, he turned it around. "Are you sure?" he asked.

"Yes," Faegan answered. "Just as the Ones wrote an index cataloging their Forestallments, so did the Heretics. I now command each."

"At last!" Shailiha said eagerly. "We are finally on an even footing with those who would use the Vagaries Forestallments against us! We can choose our gifts, just as our enemies do, then use the Vigors calculations against them!"

Faegan wheeled over to the princess. "Your Highness, as tempting as your conclusion might seem, it is not valid," he said sadly.

Shailiha was crestfallen. "I don't understand," she protested. "We have the Scroll, and we have the index! Why can't we fight fire with fire?"

"Because despite this wealth of new information, we still do not know how to place Forestallments into blood signatures," Jessamay answered. "But I find it difficult to believe that the Ones would create this vast index, only to mistakenly omit the very information that makes the formulas usable."

Then she suddenly grasped the answer. She looked at Faegan.

"You know, don't you?" she asked. "When they created the scroll, the Ones did not forget."

"No," Faegan answered, "they didn't. Do you really believe that such inordinately intelligent beings would make such an obvious mistake? I don't."

"What are you two talking about?" Wigg demanded.

"Don't you see?" Jessamay answered. "The instructions for imbuing a Forestallment into one's blood were at one time indeed written on the Vigors scroll—in the area that was destroyed! Until we can somehow acquire that secret, our scroll—despite Faegan being granted its index—still has little use for us."

Their hopes dashed, the Conclave members regarded one another sadly. *It seems that for every two steps forward regarding the craft, we must always take a step backward,* Shailiha thought. Still, she believed that there had to be a way.

"How do we go about finding this information?" Shailiha asked. "Surely beings as wise as the Ones would have created a duplicate scroll."

"Not necessarily," Faegan answered. "They did not do so with the Tome or the Paragon. Worse, our world is an exceedingly large place. Much has yet to be explored. If they did produce a duplicate scroll then hid it, the odds are that it will never be found. Remember—we found the Caves, the Tome, and the Paragon quite by accident."

An astonished look came over Abbey. "It all makes perfect sense," she breathed.

Walking over to the herbmistress, Wigg took her by the shoulders. There was a faraway look in her eyes. "What is it?" he asked.

"Don't you see?" Abbey asked back. "Think back to that night on the palace roof when Wulfgar was defeated the first time. The scroll was partly destroyed. The Ones knew that—they were watching. Once they were finally able to commune with Tristan, they told him that he must recover the other scroll!"

"I don't understand," Wigg said. "Surely the Ones know that we would never use the Vagaries Forestallments!"

Impressed by Abbey's reasoning, Faegan wheeled his chair closer. He looked up into Wigg's face.

"She's right," he said. "But you misunderstand her meaning. It isn't the Vagaries Forestallment formulas that the Ones wish us to possess—it's the information that goes along with them! Just as we assumed that the information was once written on our scroll, it must be written on the other one, as well!"

Suddenly Wigg understood. "The spell allowing Forestallments' embodiment into endowed blood," he breathed. "It must be the same for both craft sides!"

"Precisely!" Faegan exclaimed. "If we can take the other scroll, so much will become possible! Just imagine—every Vigors Forestallment finally ours to command! Our power will increase exponentially!"

"Even so, one question remains," Wigg said seriously. "Why would a Vagaries servant like Xanthus imbue your blood signature with both scroll indexes? It makes no sense! Surely he must know what a help they will be to us!"

"Equally intriguing is his reason for choosing Faegan," Jessamay added. "Why him, and not another endowed Conclave member? We were all present at the masquerade ball."

"The answer to your second question is simple," Faegan said. "He chose me because I alone possess Consummate Recollection. After having read the entire Vigors scroll, I will be able to call from memory first the index, then any formula I choose—all without needing the scroll in my presence. The advantages would be astounding."

But as quickly as Faegan's face came alight with joy, his expression darkened. He looked with concern at the other Conclave members.

"There is of course another possibility," he added, his gravelly voice trailing away again.

"What is that?" Shailiha asked.

"Xanthus' unexpected gift to me could be nothing more than a cleverly designed trap," Faegan mused.

"How so?" Adrian asked.

"By granting me the indexes, Xanthus has dangled a tantalizing prize before us—one that he knows we cannot afford to ignore," Faegan answered. "Our seduction is even more enticing, given that the Ones ordered Tristan to take the other scroll. Suppose Serena has tainted the information in the Vagaries scroll, for example. Or perhaps the entire scroll we secure from the Citadel is some ingenious, spell-ridden forgery, designed to somehow harm us the moment we unlock its secrets! Remember, Krassus tried to do that very thing when he supplied us with but one small vellum corner taken from the Vagaries scroll. Just imagine what the entire document could do!"

Thinking, Faegan looked down at his hands. "For some unknown reason, it seems that both the Ones and Xanthus share the same desire of us," he said quietly.

"What desire is that?" Adrian asked.

"The answer is simple," Faegan said. "They both want us to take the Citadel. But I cannot imagine that their reasons for wanting this could be the same. How curious . . ."

Wigg looked over at Shailiha. He knew that the decision would be a difficult one, but it was hers to make. "What are your orders, Princess?" he asked.

Shailiha turned to Adrian. "How much longer before your acolytes can fully empower the Black Ships?" she asked.

The First Sister smiled. "Grant us three more days," she answered. "In return, we'll give you the fastest vessels the world has ever seen."

Shailiha nodded. "Very well," she said. She looked at Wigg. "In the meantime, we are going to visit a certain Eutracian jailor."

Wigg smiled. "I was hoping you would say that."

Mallory stepped toward the princess. The look on her face was polite but firm. "With all due respect, I have a request, Your Highness," she said.

No one needed to tell Shailiha what Mallory wanted. If the roles were reversed, Shailiha knew that she would be asking for the same thing.

"You want to accompany the raiding party to the prison," Shailiha said. Reaching out, she took Mallory's chin into one palm. "Are you sure that you want to return to that hideous place?"

Mallory set her jaw; her blue eyes grew flinty. "With all my heart," she answered.

For a moment her mind returned to the day the lecherous guard had abused her. In her heart she believed that until she dealt with him personally, the terrible experience would forever color her life. She also believed that he was still alive.

"I have a personal score to settle," she answered softly. "Besides, from what I gather, not one of you has ever been inside the prison. I can show you the way to the dungeons. I'm stronger now, and I won't let you down. Grant me this wish and I will forever be in your debt."

For several moments Shailiha looked at Mallory, trying to decide. *What if Mallory kills him?* the princess wondered. Shailiha wasn't convinced that the guard deserved to die. Worse, if she allowed Mallory to kill, both she and the young acolyte would carry the scar forever.

Then she remembered something Tristan had once told her, after saving her from the Coven. True courage, he'd said, was continuing to follow your heart, even when others disagreed. It seemed that the young acolyte already understood that. Deciding to trust her, Shailiha looked down into Mallory's eyes.

"Permission granted," she said. "And may the Afterlife look after us."

Chapter XXI

Sitting by the campfire, Traax gazed into the sky. Night had fallen, and the three red moons shone brightly across the heavens. What remained of the mountainside's trees cast macabre shadows that reached like malformed fingers across the sloping terrain. Stirred by the wind, the smell of Minion blood lingered.

Lifting an akulee jug, Traax took another drink. They all needed the rest, for the flight to this place had been exhausting. He was immensely proud of his troops. No other fighting force on earth could have traveled so far so quickly.

After his troops had returned with newly constructed litters, they'd loaded the dead, then flown back to the base camp. Laying the fallen alongside their murdered brothers, the funeral detail lit the traditional pyres. The flames roared for hours.

Satisfied that his base camp troops had hunted down enough food and found a potable water supply, Traax had ordered twenty-five warriors to return with him to the pass. Supplies were loaded onto the empty litters and brought along. Traax had sternly ordered the base camp commander to inform him immediately if intruders were seen.

Traax stretched out on the ground beside the fire. Several warriors were sleeping. Three scouts stood guard downhill, and four more watched the shimmering pass. Traax had given stern orders that no one stray from his post.

Just then he saw his three scouts rush into camp. Sensing trouble, he came to his feet.

Before Traax could speak the lead scout covered his mouth, telling everyone to remain quiet. Then the scout pointed to one ear and one closed eye, indicating that he had heard something, but seen nothing.

One by one the warriors silently woke their brothers. Soon everyone was on his feet. The campfire was extinguished, and magenta moonlight reclaimed the scene.

Drawing his dreggan, Traax listened intently. No night birds sang and no creatures stirred. But that meant nothing, because quietness had blanketed the mountainside from the moment his group had arrived. Then the night wind stilled eerily.

Again looking to his commander, the first scout formed a V with two fingers, then pointed his hands toward the ground and wiggled them, signaling that the sound had come from two horses' hooves. The warrior standing beside him nodded his agreement, then pointed down the sloping mountainside.

Satisfied that the threat was real, Traax pointed at some fighters and gestured upward. Their beating wings nearly silent, five warriors stealthily took to the sky. Smiling grimly, Traax was suddenly glad that he had picked these troops personally.

Traax pointed his dreggan toward the ground. Recognizing the order, every warrior quickly took up a handful of charred earth, rubbing it onto his blade so that it wouldn't shine in the moonlight. After a final signal from their commander they fanned out. Expertly becoming one with the charred forest, the warriors waited.

As the anxious moments passed, Traax started to wonder whether his scouts had been wrong. Then the sound of horse hooves rose up the mountainside. Gripping his dreggan tighter, Traax strained his eyes in the moonlight. Still he saw nothing.

Soon an azure cloud formed. As it neared, the horse steps

grew louder. The cloud faded to show two glowing eyes hanging menacingly in space. Soon Xanthus and his mount took form.

Sitting astride his stallion, the Darkling held his axe in one hand and his shield in the other. He stopped his horse about twenty paces downhill. His impatient stallion snorted and pawed the charred ground.

Traax could not see the prince. But even with Xanthus' mount standing still, the Minions soon heard another horse approaching. A second azure cloud formed.

Traax watched spellbound as Tristan appeared from its depths. Riding up alongside Xanthus' horse, the *Jin'Sai* pulled Shadow to a stop. The misty cloud from which he had emerged quickly vanished. Still crouching in the darkness, the Minions waited tensely.

Xanthus turned his awful gaze toward the prince. "It seems that your Conclave hasn't given up on you," he said quietly. "The craft tells me that twenty Minions hide there in the darkness. Another five circle the sky. If you want them to live, call them off. I can kill twenty-five as easily as one."

Tristan glared at the Darkling. "If I order them to stand down, do you promise not to hurt them?" he asked.

Xanthus returned his gaze back toward the camp. "Yes—provided none try to kill me, or to rescue you. I expect you to honor our bargain. If you refuse, your Minions will die. Either way, I grant you some time alone with them before I approach."

Tristan spurred Shadow forward. He soon saw the abandoned campsite. Stopping his horse, he looked around.

"Sheathe your weapons and show yourselves!" he shouted into the night. "This is an order from your *Jin'Sai*!"

Knowing that Tristan's words superseded all else, the warriors obeyed. Tristan soon heard the familiar sound of dreggans sliding into their scabbards.

Traax showed himself first. Then the five flying warriors landed and the rest came out from hiding. Traax hurried to his lord's side. Casting a wary glance downhill, he saw that Xanthus had not moved.

Traax looked worriedly at Tristan. His face drawn and pale, the *Jin'Sai* seemed exhausted. "Are you well, my lord?" Traax whispered.

"Well enough," he answered. "It is good to see you, my friend.

There is no use in whispering. Because he commands the craft, Xanthus probably hears everything we say."

Looking around, Tristan acknowledged the other warriors. Their faces grim, it was clear they were spoiling for a fight. "Xanthus says that there are twenty-five warriors here with you," Tristan said. "Is that true?"

"Yes," Traax answered. "Another twenty-five wait at the base camp, making fifty in total."

Tristan looked around at the anxious warriors. He knew that his next order would be nearly impossible for them to accept, even from him.

"Drop your dreggans!" he shouted. "You have no chance against the Darkling."

Even though the order had come directly from their *Jin'Sai,* at first the warriors hesitated. Then the razor-sharp swords started falling to the ground. Looking down at Traax, Tristan saw that his second-in-command had not complied.

"You too," he added sadly.

Traax looked aghast at Tristan. To a Minion, the mere idea of surrendering one's sword was blasphemy. "But *why,* my lord?" Traax asked. His incredulity was such that his voice had become little more than a whisper.

"We are fifty-one warriors!" he protested. "If we all attack at once, I know that we can kill that bastard! You have but to give the word!"

Tristan shot Traax a determined look. "We cannot defeat him!" he answered. "I have seen the things he can do! I have no choice but to go with him through the pass!"

Stupefied, Traax took a step backward. "But Xanthus serves the Vagaries!" he argued. "Only he knows what will happen to you on the other side! You mustn't do this!"

Tristan gazed deeply into Traax's eyes. For everyone's good, the order had to be followed. "Commander!" he said sternly. "Drop your sword!"

Knowing he must obey, Traax took a deep breath. His dreggan fell to the ground.

"Does Faegan live?" Tristan asked anxiously.

Traax nodded. "Yes," he said. "He was badly burned, but he will recover."

"Good," Tristan said. "What about the ball guests he accidentally injured?"

"Several Minions and humans were killed outright, and some survivors still lie near death. The Minion healers and the acolytes are doing all they can for them. Shailiha ordered us to come here, to intercept you."

Turning in his saddle, Tristan looked down the moonlit hillside. Xanthus was still keeping his word. The prince turned back to Traax.

"I expected as much," he said. Then Tristan saw the ruby pin attached to Traax's body armor. He fully understood the custom. He managed a slight smile.

"That betrothal pin comes from Duvessa, I'd wager," he said.

Traax nodded. "She does me a great honor."

"In truth, you honor each other," Tristan answered.

Reaching beneath his vest, Tristan produced the hated black mask. He held it to the moonlight for a moment before handing it to Traax. A confused look overcame the warrior's face.

"Xanthus insisted that I wear it," Tristan explained. "He didn't want me recognized while he committed more atrocities. I'm glad to be rid of it. When you see Shailiha, give it to her." Tristan leaned down on his saddle pommel. "I assume that because you are here, the Conclave has yet to set sail for the Citadel," he said.

"They had not done so when I left. I cannot vouch for after that."

"After I am gone, I want you to fly back to the palace," Tristan ordered. "Tell the Conclave what happened here. Shailiha must attack soon! Every second we wait, our position weakens. I am more convinced than ever that our answers lie across the sea."

Worry crowded its way onto Traax's face again. "Is there truly no other way?"

"Not that I can find," Tristan answered. "If I refuse, he will keep on killing. Worse, we might lose the Paragon forever."

Wondering what fate awaited him, Tristan looked past Traax toward the shimmering azure wall. His jaw hardened.

"I will do everything in my power to return," he added softly. "Tell Shailiha that I love her. In my absence—be it a day or forever—you are to follow her orders like they were my own. In the event of her death, the wizards command you."

"Your time is up, *Jin'Sai*!" they suddenly heard Xanthus call out. "I am about to approach! If your warriors resist me, they will die!"

Spurring his stallion onward, Xanthus neared the campsite.

As the Darkling neared, the prince could sense every warrior tensing, each desperately wanting to pick up his sword. To Tristan's relief, not one did.

Xanthus glanced around at the discarded dreggans. Looking at Traax, he smiled.

"Very sensible," he said. He looked over at Tristan. "The Heretics await you. It is time to go."

Tristan gave Traax a final look of farewell. "Remember my orders," he said. "Do not try to follow us."

It was rare to see Minion weakness. Even so, Traax's eyes were damp. Collecting himself, he clicked his boot heels together. "I live to serve!" he said.

Tristan looked at Xanthus. "I am ready," he said.

Shimmering brightly, the pass stood about twenty meters up the hillside. As the helpless warriors watched, Xanthus spurred his stallion toward its splendor. Tristan followed.

The azure glow was nearly blinding. Even so, it gave off no heat. Just like the first time Tristan had come here, white light shards danced to and fro within its limitless depths.

Raising his arms, Xanthus called the craft. A white vertical line formed on the center of the wall. Xanthus spread his arms, and the pass divided into two halves. Gazing in, Tristan saw only blackness. Xanthus looked over at the prince.

"It is our time, now," he said softly. "No other *Jin'Sai* or *Jin'-Saiou* has ever been so privileged. Take care not to leave my side. Alone, your death is inevitable. I will place a spell over our mounts so they remain calm, and do our bidding. Come, *Jin'Sai*. Together we will make history." Spurring their horses forward, Tristan and Xanthus entered the darkness and disappeared.

The azure wall closed behind them, leaving the Minions alone again in the night.

Chapter XXII

Leaning back in his chair, Lothar winced. His burned chest and abdomen hurt like blazes. The escaping girls either hadn't had the power or the will to kill him, but they had come perilously close. He still had no idea who they were, or how they had become proficient in the craft. Had he known they were gifted, he would have kept them drugged until concluding their sale.

Glowering down at his raw chest, Lothar lamented his bad luck. He could only imagine the wondrous services those endowed creatures might have plied on their clients, had they somehow been convinced to follow Mary's chosen profession! And with extraordinary selling prices, to match! But he would never know. Not only had the girls slipped through his fingers, but several guards had burned to death during the escape. The guards would have to be replaced, and that was always expensive. It wasn't just anyone who was willing to work here.

Lothar unbuttoned his shirt and reached across the desktop to pick up a bottle of balm the neighborhood healer had given him. He poured some into one palm, and reached beneath his bandages to rub more onto his badly scalded torso.

The girls' bolts had nearly killed him. After lying unconscious for several hours, he had finally awakened, screaming in agony. The guards had called for a healer. Lothar would live, but would be scarred for life.

But ever true to his nature, his grief had quickly turned to greed. This was a new day; there was work to be done and fresh profits to be stolen. Despite his painful condition he intended to make the most of it.

Returning his attention to the matter at hand, he placed the lotion bottle back atop the desk, then gave the torturer another nod. The man in the black mask was the same fellow who had performed the public dunking and provided him with the debtors' next-of-kin list several days before. As the torturer resumed his work, another scream filled the air, then wafted its way down the prison halls.

Lothar sat in a dank stone room. Four leering guards stood nearby. Near one wall a man sat behind another crude desk. His left arm lay tightly stretched across the desktop and his body was tied to his chair.

The hooded torturer sat across from him. Bolted down to the desktop, a manacle encircled the prisoner's left wrist. A hinged iron device encased his left thumb. A broad, rusty turnkey protruded from the device.

Several of the debtor's relatives sat in chairs on the other side of the room. Selected from the prized next-of-kin list, they had been "asked" to attend this session by Lothar's guards, and told to bring all their money. They knew that Lothar could be vengeful. Not one dared refuse, lest something even more dire happen.

The point of this gathering was simple. Unless they paid off not only their relative's debts but also their own, they would soon find themselves sitting in the torture chair. It was the morning following the girls' escape, and Lothar could afford to take his time.

Realizing their plight, some of Lothar's "guests" had tried to pay up even before the session had gotten started. For them, the mere sight of the muscular fellow in the black hood had been incentive enough. But because of his foul mood, Lothar had decided to give them a demonstration anyway. Because he had to suffer, so did everyone else. Smiling, he nodded at the torturer again.

Grasping the thumbscrew key, the hooded man gave it another quick turn. This time bones snapped. Blood ran from the device to drip lazily onto the table. Screaming madly, the prisoner jangled in his chair. But the jailor was not in a forgiving mood. He glared at the cowering relatives.

"Shall we continue?" he asked. "We have lots of time. After all, he has nine digits left. Nineteen, if one counts his toes." Sitting back, Lothar lit a cigar, then sent the smoke toward the ceiling.

"Then again, we could stop," he added, casually regarding the cigar's glowing end. He looked over at the cowering relatives.

"If you agree to pay a bonus—say, an extra twenty percent above and beyond your current debts—you may all walk out of here right now," he offered. "For those of you who do not have enough kisa on hand I will accept a signed promissory note, certifying that the adjusted sum is now the legally recognized amount. Interest adds up, after all! So do we have an arrangement? Or do we keep going?"

Tired and beaten, the weary relatives started shuffling toward Lothar's desk. One by one, they paid all they had. Those who could not meet the ludicrous extortion demands signed detailed documents obligating them to make regular payments to Lothar or be immediately incarcerated. As the travesty continued, a smiling guard witnessed each signature.

Just then Lothar heard shouting from down the hall. It sounded like guards' voices, mixed with others that he didn't recognize. An explosion followed, shaking the prison. Dark smoke started filtering into the torture room, making it difficult to see.

Coughing, Lothar rose gingerly to his feet. He glared at the guards. "Don't just stand there, you idiots!" he shouted. "See what's going on!"

The guards drew their swords, and rushed into the hallway. Lothar followed them as far as the door, where his guards disappeared into the smoke.

Soon Lothar heard more shouting, followed by clashing sword blades. Silence reclaimed the prison. Holding his breath, Lothar waited. As fear gripped him, his cigar fell to the floor and his knees trembled noticeably.

Suddenly a dozen Minion warriors rushed into the room. Holding their dreggans high, they quickly ringed the walls. Some of their blades were bloodied. There was no sign of Lothar's guards. The startled jailor glared at the warriors.

"How dare you!" he shouted. "You have no business here! Wait until the Conclave hears of this intrusion!"

Just then more people stepped from the smoky hallway. Lothar saw an old man in a gray robe, several more Minions, and a tall blond woman. Suddenly recognizing the First Wizard and the princess, he nearly choked.

Wigg calmly walked to stand before the fat jailor. Waving one hand, he caused the smoke to disappear. The First Wizard's eyes bored directly into Lothar's. Swallowing hard, the jailor tried to smile.

"Do you know who I am?" Wigg asked quietly.

"Uh, er . . . of course!" Lothar stammered. "The First Wizard himself! This is indeed an honor!"

"I cannot say that the feeling is mutual," Wigg answered dryly.

He looked around the room. When he saw the torture victim his face went scarlet with rage. Pointing to the thumbscrew, Wigg called the craft. The device unhinged itself. Then the bolts holding the wrist manacle to the tabletop ripped loose, freeing the debtor. Wigg moved his fingers, causing the thumbscrew to fly across the room and into his palm. He held it before Lothar's face. It was still dripping blood.

"And this?" he asked. "A tool of your trade, I presume?"

"Certainly not!" Lothar protested. "Time after time I have told my guards to never use such things, but they won't listen! In fact, I had just entered the room! Now that we're both here, together we can put a stop to it!"

Tossing the thumbscrew aside, Wigg pursed his lips. "I see," he said. "And what about slave trafficking, eh? I suppose you have never pursued that dubious practice, either?"

Lothar held up his palms. "On my life, no!" he shouted. "I am a sworn officer of the court! I would never do such a thing!"

Glowering, Wigg stepped closer. Knowing that it would hurt, he poked an index finger into Lothar's chest. The jailor winced. "You're no longer an officer of *our* court," Wigg breathed.

Another warrior entered the room, walked up to Shailiha, and clicked his heels.

"Your report," the princess said.

"This place is a madhouse!" the warrior answered. "The prisoners are being held in deplorable conditions. Many are close to death. The surviving guards have been locked away. Torture rooms abound. But there is some good news." The warrior grinned straight at Lothar, then back at his *Jin'Saiou.*

"We found that fat bastard's ledgers," he announced proudly. "We also have the safe in which he keeps his fortune. After some Minion inducement, it opened easily. It holds more high-denomination kisa than we could count in a fortnight."

Wigg glared at Lothar. "Those funds are supposed to be repaid to whomever they are rightfully owed!" he growled. "You have been stealing from the citizenry, haven't you? Then you hoard it here, where you can best protect it!"

"No!" Lothar insisted. "I was going to distribute those monies on the new moon, just as I always do!"

Wigg poked Lothar's chest again. "Don't insult me, you fool," he said. "It's doing nothing for my mood."

Shailiha turned to the warrior. "Bring her in," she said simply. The Minion promptly disappeared down the hall.

Soon another person entered. As she walked into the room, Lothar's eyes widened with fear. It was one of the girls who had nearly killed him!

Mallory pointed at the jailor. "That's him, all right," she said. "He was going to sell us into slavery." Looking at his bandages, she smiled. "You got off easy," she said. "Had we been stronger, you'd be dead."

Shailiha turned to the Minion officer. "Take that torturer away and lock him up with the guards," she ordered. "See to it that all the prisoners are released and escorted to the palace. Feed them, then have their injuries looked at by the acolytes and Minion healers. We will hear their stories later."

The officer clicked his heels, then ordered the other warriors to escort the wounded man, his stunned relatives, and the torturer from the room. With terrified eyes, Lothar looked beseechingly at the First Wizard.

"What about me?" he pleaded.

"We'll get to you in a moment," Wigg answered. "But first, Mallory has some unfinished business." Looking over at Mallory, he nodded.

Mallory stepped closer to Lothar. It was clear that she enjoyed seeing him tremble. "The guard who watched over us," she said. "The one with the scar down one cheek . . . What is his name?"

"Why do you want to know?" Lothar asked.

Mallory stepped nearer. *"The name,"* she demanded.

"Ivan," Lothar answered.

Mallory turned to look at Shailiha. A cool, demanding presence had overtaken the young acolyte.

The princess hesitated for a moment. She barely knew this girl. Should she trust in Martha's and Duncan's teachings? If she gave Mallory permission to act, what would the young woman do? Shailiha knew that there was nothing deadlier than an adept who controlled the craft, but could not control his or her emotions. The princess finally nodded.

"Thank you," Mallory said softly. She looked at the Minion officer. "If he still lives, find Ivan and bring him here," she ordered.

Unsure whether he should accept orders from a Fledgling, the warrior looked to his *Jin'Saiou.* Shailiha nodded. The warrior quickly marched down the hall.

Anxious moments passed. Lothar was about to protest his innocence again but apparently thought the better of it. Then Ivan and the Minion officer entered the room. Pressing his sword tip against Ivan's back, the officer prodded him toward the center of the floor. When Ivan saw Mallory, he smiled.

"Hello, my pretty," he said arrogantly. "Come for some more, have ya?"

Mallory walked closer. "No," she answered quietly. "Fall to your knees."

"I don't think so."

Taking a step closer, Mallory raised one arm. Suddenly the guard felt a crushing weight atop his shoulders, forcing him to the floor. Even so, he looked up at Mallory with defiant eyes. She took a step back.

Still unsure about what Mallory might do, Wigg looked worriedly at Shailiha. The princess held her breath.

Mallory raised her arms again. Calling the craft, she closed her eyes.

But as everyone watched in silence, nothing seemed to happen. *Perhaps Mallory is still too weak for whatever she had planned,* Shailiha guessed. She gave Wigg a questioning look, but all the First Wizard could do was offer one in return.

Opening her eyes, Mallory looked Ivan in the face. "Stand up," she said quietly.

The guard stood. "What's the matter, sweetie?" he asked. "Couldn't use the craft, after all?"

"Unlace your trousers," Mallory said.

A confused look crossed Ivan's face. "What for?" he demanded.

Mallory raised her arm again. "Just do it," she growled, "or I'll kill you where you stand!"

The guard untied his britches.

"Pull them down," Mallory said.

Looking around the room, Ivan hesitated.

"Do it!" Mallory shouted.

Finally he complied. Everyone in the room started howling. Ivan screamed hysterically and nearly fainted away. His testicles had vanished.

Trying to control her laughter, the princess again looked at Wigg. Smiling, the First Wizard shook his head and rubbed his brow.

"You bitch!" Ivan shouted hysterically. "What have you done?"

"That should be obvious," Mallory answered. "Be thankful that I left your other part intact for . . . convenience's sake. Although from what I see, it wouldn't be much of a loss."

Finally Ivan had withstood all he could. His dark eyes rolling back into his head, he fainted onto the floor. Lothar immediately fell to his knees.

"Mercy, First Wizard!" he screamed. "From this day forward you can trust me to do anything you ask!"

His grim gaze returning, Wigg stepped closer. "I wouldn't trust you to take your next breath," he answered.

Lothar started sobbing. "What will happen to me?" he asked.

"With the princess's indulgence, I'm going to imprison you here," Wigg answered. "We will study your ledgers. I'm sure their tally will match what we find in your safe. The funds will be redistributed among the debtors' payees. Aside from a rotating group of Minion warriors who will feed you, this shop of horrors is officially closed."

Wailing uncontrollably, Lothar fell to the floor.

Wigg watched Mallory walk over to Shailiha. The Fledgling bowed respectfully.

"Thank you for your trust," Mallory said. "At first I wanted to kill him. Then I came on a better idea. But if Your Highness believes Ivan's punishment too cruel, it can be reversed."

The princess smiled. "That won't be needed," she answered.

"By the way," Wigg asked, "how did you manage that? Master Duncan never taught you such a spell, I'd wager!"

A sheepish look overtook Mallory's face. "Master Faegan taught me," she admitted. "When the idea came to me, I revisited him late last night in his laboratory. Something told me I might still find him there. After meeting him the first time, I realized that he seemed like the type who might agree with my idea. When I explained it to him, he positively cackled!" Then Mallory bit her lower lip. "Was it wrong of me?" she asked.

Snorting a laugh down her nose, Shailiha placed one hand atop Mallory's shoulder. "Well, it wouldn't do to make a habit of it," she said.

"It's time to go," Wigg said. "Our work here is done."

As they turned toward the door, Lothar staggered to his knees. "When will I be released?" he demanded.

Stopping in midstride, Wigg turned around. "Never," he answered quietly.

As they walked down the hallway, the fat jailor's screaming followed them for a time, then faded away.

III

THE ENVOYS

Chapter XXIII

It is not only for ourselves that we fight the Vagaries, but also for those who left behind so many treasures—such as the Tome, the Paragon, and the Scroll of the Vigors. We fight to preserve the legacy of the Ones Who Came Before.

—WIGG, FIRST WIZARD OF THE CONCLAVE OF THE VIGORS

Smiling to himself, Einar watched his servants go about their work. From where he and the others waited they could see only glimpses of the fighting, but they knew it would be intense. Serena's lead consul had no doubt about the outcome.

Peering out from another camouflaged cone formed by his envelopers, Einar looked to the sky. It was midday in Parthalon. Dark clouds were forming, and it would rain soon. He hoped to take his latest victory before the storm broke.

Some of his consuls and Valrenkians had been left behind to oversee the Ghetto while a contingent of envelopers and swamp shrews protected them there. By the time this new prize had been secured, those left behind would be well along in their part of the plan.

Although the distance between the Ghetto of the Shunned and this new place was short, Einar had taken great care that his forces not be seen. The Parthalon population was most concentrated in the north. Though Einar knew that the populace could give him no real trouble, it was in his best interests to remain unnoticed—at least until this second goal had been secured. He knew it would not fall as easily as the Ghetto. But taking this place was paramount to the Heretics' plan, so it had to be done. Smiling again, he returned his gaze to their newest prize. They would capture the Recluse.

Built with slave labor more than three centuries past, the Recluse sat on a high island in the middle of a lake. The large water body surrounding it rippled slightly in the freshening wind. The castle was reached by a long bridge, which was the only way in or out.

The wooden drawbridge meeting the lake bridge was lowered, and flanked on either side by high barbicans. Just beyond, the outer courtyard areas would be filled with desperately fighting Minion warriors. Beyond the first two gate towers were another two towers. Another portcullis stood between them, banning entrance to the inner ward. These two gate towers seemed to be the only opening in the walls surrounding the castle. They also protected the fore-buildings and keep, the Recluse's innermost sanctuary. Unlike the dark and foreboding towers and outer ward areas, the architecture at the Recluse's heart looked more refined.

Even Einar stared in awe. The Recluse had to be at least half again the size of the royal palace in Tammerland. And that didn't include the huge secret areas belowground—the reason this place was so valuable to him. Einar couldn't imagine how many different rooms and hallways there might be. From each corner turret, a flag carrying the *Jin'Sai*'s heraldry waved proudly.

The majestic structure had been partly destroyed when the *Jin'Sai* defeated the Coven. Einar was forced to admit that the Minions had done a superb job of restoring the structure to its original glory. It was also said that this was where the *Jin'Sai* had married Celeste, the First Wizard's only child.

Thank you for rebuilding the Recluse, Einar thought. *We will put it to good use.*

Just then he saw an enveloper approaching. Fluttering its sides, it landed gently before the cone. Pushing two envelopers aside, Einar walked from the cone's darkness and into the midday light.

The consul thought for a moment. "Is it safe to enter the Recluse?" he asked. The enveloper answered with a dip of its head.

"Good," Einar said. "It is time to inspect our newest prize."

Einar ordered the enveloper cone dismantled and watched as the litters were again loaded. Soon he, Reznik, and the others were winging their way toward the smoking Recluse. Soaring over the castle walls, even Einar was surprised by the immense carnage. As the litters settled in the outer ward, their passengers jumped to the ground.

Although the envelopers and shrews had devoured most of

their victims, Minion bodies still littered the castle. Blood ran deep across the stone floors. The occasional dead shrew and enveloper could also be seen, but not in enough numbers to affect Einar's plans. Some interior areas were afire.

Still rooting out survivors, angry shrews roamed the Recluse freely. Despite using the craft, Einar could barely see his envelopers. But he knew they would also be looking for stragglers.

Whenever a surviving warrior was found he was devoured on the spot. Minion screams occasionally filtered down the Recluse hallways to fade away in the spacious outer ward. Here and there a dead, white-winged Gallipolai could be seen among the other victims. Einar knew that more than three thousand warriors had guarded the Recluse. Most were dead. Any survivors would soon join them in the Afterlife.

Einar and Reznik suddenly heard some unusual grunting sounds then smelled an overpowering stench. Before they departed the Citadel, Serena had warned them about the shrews' strange habits. But until seeing it for themselves, they hadn't fully appreciated their grotesqueness.

Many satiated shrews had already started coughing up their victims' bones and clothing. Given the shrews' huge numbers, the regurgitated piles—not to mention those left by the envelopers—were forming all too quickly. Soon the Recluse would be littered with them. Unless they were cleared away, disease would follow. Einar didn't hesitate. Summoning his remaining Valrenkians and consuls, he pointed to the growing piles.

"Use the craft to vanish those leavings!" he ordered. "Unload the craft tools and extinguish the fires! We need this place intact!"

As they set about their work, a consul approached. He bowed. His name was Actinius. A heavyset man in his mid-forties, he was Einar's consular second-in-command.

"My lord," he said. "By your order, a group of shrews are holding some Minion survivors at bay."

"Good," Einar answered. "The warriors will prove useful. Do you know where they are?"

The consul smiled. "One need only to follow the blood trail."

"Show us," Einar ordered.

Actinius immediately started leading them across the bloody outer ward, then toward the fore-buildings and keep. Walking up the majestic steps, they entered the grand foyer. Despite having been wrecked by the fighting, the room's original beauty was apparent.

The foyer was three stories high. Overhead, skylights showed dark, passing clouds. More than one dozen variegated columns stretched their way to the ceiling, and the floor was a black-and-white checkerboard affair. Tables, sofas, and chairs—now damaged and smeared with blood—lay scattered about. Wrecked paintings and ripped tapestries hung drunkenly on the walls.

A curved staircase stood against the room's far side. Its upper landing split off into two opposite directions, each leading to the various second-floor rooms. Minion dead also lay here, as did the odd shrew and enveloper. Walking across the floor, the three mystics did their best to avoid the blood.

As Actinius led them upstairs and down a hallway, Reznik suddenly understood why Einar had ordered that some Minions be spared. The Recluse was vast; finding the chambers they needed would certainly prove problematic. Once they were located, his collaborations with Einar could start in earnest. If they could finish their research in time, the world would be theirs to command.

As they approached the hallway's end they heard snarling shrews. The consul stopped before an open doorway. Leading the others into the room, Einar looked around.

The once-elegant bedroom was a wreck. Like the Recluse's foyer, this chamber was spacious and pleasant. A large four-poster bed stood against one wall, its sheets and bedcover ripped to shreds. Most of the furniture was overturned. Einar noticed that the windows' stained glass had been destroyed, allowing the midday breeze to harass the patterned curtains. He turned to look at the captured warriors.

Two snarling shrews held four Minions at bay. Severely wounded, three were too weak to fight. Unable to rise, they sat on the floor, trying to stanch their wounds.

The exhausted fourth warrior gallantly protected his brothers. Waving his dreggan, he was doing his best to keep the shrews at bay. Einar noticed that the shrews had wisely trapped the Minions in one corner, preventing them from taking flight through the smashed windows.

Einar stepped closer. Looking at the warriors' armor insignia, he was delighted to learn that each fighter held considerable rank. He was pleased, because they would probably have the information that he needed.

Einar boldly walked to stand between the warriors and the shrews. Without taking his gaze from the warriors, Einar ordered the shrews to back off. The snarling beasts retreated toward the door. The warrior protecting the others glared hatefully at Reznik, then Einar.

"What is your name?" Einar asked. His voice was controlled, almost courteous.

"I am Derrick," the warrior answered. He raised his sword a bit higher. "Who are *you*?" he demanded. He was so exhausted he could barely speak. "Why have you attacked us?"

"My identity is of no consequence to you," Einar answered. "But your rank as a Minion officer matters greatly. The Recluse is vast—therefore I require a guide. Although it's beautiful, most of this place means nothing to us. Our only reason for being here is to gain access to Failee's research chambers."

Smiling, Einar placed his hands into opposite sleeves of his robe. "You are going to show me those secret doorways," he added quietly.

Laughing, Derrick lifted his sword point higher. "Never!" he shouted. "Because you command the shrews, it is clear that you serve the Vagaries. Serena is no doubt your queen. We would gladly die before helping you!"

Einar shook his head. "You don't understand," he said. "I was once one of the First Wizard's most powerful consuls. My gifts have only grown since then. Allow me to show how vulnerable you are."

Stretching forth one hand, Einar called the craft. To his great surprise, Derrick suddenly felt his dreggan handle become warm, then hot. Soon it was too scalding to hold, forcing him to drop it to the floor. He watched in awe as the dreggan melted at his feet, forming a pool of liquid steel and gold. Enraged, Derrick glared at the consul.

"Now then," Einar said calmly. "You will escort us to the lower regions."

The warrior remained defiant. "No," he answered quietly.

"Then perhaps another object lesson will help," Einar replied.

Pointing one hand toward the bleeding warriors, Einar again called the craft. An azure bolt loosed from his fingertips to go tearing across the room. Striking a wounded warrior in the forehead, the bolt blew his cranium apart. Blood, bone, and brain matter flew into the air and splattered against the rear wall. Einar lowered his hand.

"Do as I ask or your two remaining friends will suffer the same fate," he warned.

Gritting his teeth, Derrick shook his head. "Do what you will," he said. "Our answer remains the same."

Frustrated by the warrior's stubbornness, Einar again raised his hand. Then a thought came to him. There was a simpler way to get what he wanted. He had never entered a Minion mind. It would prove interesting.

Summoning his powers, Einar invoked the spell allowing him to control the warrior's consciousness. Reznik and Actinius watched with rapt curiosity.

Suddenly the warrior's head snapped back, and his eyeballs rolled up in his head—sure signs that his mind had been overtaken. Reznik and Actinius marveled at their master's talent. Being able to penetrate another's mind was a rare skill.

Satisfied, Einar lowered his hand. Weak from blood loss, the other warriors could only watch.

"Now then," Einar said, "do you know where the secret entrances to the lower regions are found?"

"Yes," Derrick answered thickly.

"How many are there?" Einar asked.

"Seven."

"Good," Einar answered. "You will show us each one."

"Yes," the warrior answered.

Einar smiled. "There's a good fellow," he said. He turned to look at Actinius. "After we have gone, kill the other two any way you like."

Actinius nodded. "With pleasure," he answered.

"Now then," Einar said to Derrick. "You may lead the way."

With Einar and Reznik in tow, Derrick walked numbly from the room. Leading them back to the grand stairway, he started down. As they took their first few steps, Minion death screams rang out from the bedroom above.

Two hours later, six secret entrances had been discovered and marked. As Derrick led them toward the seventh, Einar smiled. This had been a productive day.

Derrick stopped partway down another hallway. Reaching up, he grabbed an oil lamp sconce attached to the wall and gave it a sharp tug. As the sconce angled downward, an oaken wall panel slid open. Using the craft, Einar burned a mark into the wall just below the sconce, identifying it for later use.

Like the other disguised passageways, this one's steps led down into darkness. Suspecting that the First Mistress would have lined the stairway with radiance stones, Einar waved a hand. At once a pale green light illuminated the way. He looked past the helpless Derrick and into Reznik's eyes.

"I'm going down," he said. "I want you to return to the outer ward, then issue the needed orders. Have the craft tools and the Scroll of the Vagaries sent down immediately. Above all, ensure that the Recluse is protected." Then he looked over at the helpless warrior.

"Feed him to the shrews," he ordered. "In his current state he will give them no trouble. Be sure that no Minions remain alive, then join me in the lower regions. We are about to make history." Without further ado, Einar disappeared into the depths.

"Come with me," Reznik ordered Derrick. Having no choice, the officer followed along.

On reaching the outer ward, Reznik called the shrews, envelopers, Valrenkians, and consuls together. After ordering the craft tools and the Scroll of the Vagaries taken to Einar, he selected several consuls to come forward.

"You are to fly back to the Ghetto," he said. "Tell our comrades that they may start the shipments." Pausing for a moment, he looked at the remaining consuls and Valrenkians.

"Continue to clean the Recluse and set things right," he said. "Once that task is done, join Einar and me in the lower regions. The important work is about to start."

To Reznik's delight the Valrenkians and consuls started cheering and shaking their fists in the air. He happily joined in. After today nothing could stop them.

Reznik looked at the shrews. Their numbers were so great that they filled the outer ward, spilled across the drawbridge and lake bridge, and out onto Parthalonian soil.

"As many of you as possible will hide yourselves in the lake!" he ordered. "The rest are to patrol the surrounding area. Devour any strangers who come near!"

Snarling and hissing, the shrews lumbered from the castle grounds. Walking to the drawbridge, Reznik watched as shrews by the hundreds submerged into the lake. As the surface stilled, he smiled.

Returning to the outer ward, Reznik raised his hands to the sky. He couldn't see the envelopers, but he knew they were there.

"Cease your camouflage so that I might see you!" he shouted. At once the sky filled with envelopers, their gray, sleek skin fluttering in the wind.

"Half your numbers are to patrol the sky above the Recluse!" Reznik ordered. "The rest are to become one with the castle! Go!"

Some envelopers dutifully sailed upward, again disappearing as they took on the sky's and clouds' exact likenesses. The others soared toward various places on the castle's structure. Landing flat against the walls, turrets, guard paths, and keep, they soon blended in perfectly with their surroundings and disappeared.

After ordering Derrick to remain where he was, Reznik walked across the drawbridge, then traversed the lake bridge to stand on Parthalonian soil. Looking back at the Recluse, he smiled.

It was amazing. The castle appeared just as it did before the attack. Any force trying to approach would be drawn in by its normalcy, then cut to ribbons before they realized what was happening. Even the *Jin'Sai*'s entire Minion army could never take this place.

As he walked back across the bridge, he saw a litter carrying consuls soar over the castle walls, then turn southward. From his perspective it looked strange in its loneliness, because the envelopers carrying it could not be seen against the sky.

On walking halfway across the drawbridge Reznik stopped and looked at Derrick. With a glassy, absent look in his eyes, the warrior stood exactly where Reznik had left him. The Valrenkian beckoned him forward. Removing a knife from his belt, he grinned wickedly into the warrior's eyes.

"Good-bye, you winged freak," he whispered.

With one sure stroke he cut the warrior's throat, then pushed him into the lake. Hungry shrews rushed to the surface. Teeth flashed briefly, then the warrior disappeared beneath the waves.

Wiping the blood from his knife, Reznik headed for the inner ward. Just as he started up the foyer steps the impending storm broke, sending a cleansing shower down onto everything. Soon the castle's interior would look as normal as its outer walls.

Whistling a happy tune, he started the walk toward the secret passageway.

Chapter XXIV

As Tristan rode alongside Xanthus, panic gripped him. He could sense the Darkling, but all he could see was a muddled form, matching his forward momentum. He also sensed his horse and saddle moving under him and the reins in his hands, but there was no sound. Even their horses' hooves were silent. The azure air was thick and heavy, like the densest cloud.

Tristan tried to speak to Xanthus. Smothered by the dense atmosphere, his words arrived only as whispers and went nowhere. Then he remembered Xanthus' warning.

"Take care not to leave my side," the Darkling had said. *"Alone, death is inevitable."*

Trying to regain his composure, Tristan did his best to keep Shadow near the Darkling and his mount. But because the azure depths were limitless, he couldn't gauge how far they had traveled, or how long they had been here. After a time an unseen force snatched up his reins. Shadow came to a stop. Tristan tried to call out again, but the result was the same. He peered forward into the gloom.

A golden pinprick appeared up ahead. Growing in size, it formed a pinwheel that started revolving. The sensation was dizzying. Soon it encompassed the entire area before them. With a roaring sound it suddenly imploded, taking the azure fog with it. As Tristan gazed into the distance, his jaw fell.

The forbidding landscape was something straight from a nightmare. The lifeless ground was rust-red, as was the angry sky. Lightning continually streaked across the heavens, its accompanying thunder so loud that he thought his eardrums might burst.

Grotesque mountains loomed all around. Steaming geysers sprayed boiling water high into the sky. The ground rumbled and shook, hurling rocks down the craggy mountainsides. There were no trees, no foliage, and no creatures—just barren desert wasteland that stretched into infinity. Red dirt maelstroms whirled angrily, burning Tristan's skin like red-hot needles.

Tristan heard another strange sound, then gasped as a gigantic sinkhole developed, its closest edge not ten meters away. The gaping hole quickly widened, pulling nearby rocks and soil into oblivion. Then the roaring heat hit him fully.

This bizarre world was a living blast furnace, its fiery atmosphere so intense that sweat started pouring from Tristan's skin. Soon his clothing was soaked, and his dark hair lay matted against his head. Even though Shadow was at rest, the horse's chest and neck were already lathering. Xanthus turned to look at Tristan. For some reason, the Darkling had taken on his human form.

Tristan was about to speak when a lightning bolt struck a nearby peak, exploding it into rubble. Shadow suddenly reared, nearly throwing Tristan to the ground. Then the stallion started dancing wildly, disobeying Tristan's every command. Soon Xanthus' mount became equally frenzied.

The Darkling jumped from his horse. Removing two blankets from his saddlebags, he tied one over Shadow's eyes, then did the same for his mount. The horses started to calm. Xanthus urgently beckoned Tristan to dismount. When the prince's boot soles hit the ground, the heat seeping through them nearly caused him to faint.

Tristan glared hatefully at the Darkling. He was now certain that this entire journey had been a ruse, designed to draw him into a horrible death. But when he saw Xanthus' worried expression, he realized that something had gone horribly wrong.

"Where are we?" Tristan shouted. He could barely hear his own voice above the raging elements. "This place can't be what you promised!"

Struggling against the wind, Xanthus placed his lips against Tristan's ear. "It's not!" he shouted back. "The Heretics have activated the Borderlands! Their struggle against the Ones must have escalated! Magic has no use here!"

Just then the wind howled and another dust storm arose, sending more whirling soil toward them. Raising their arms, they tried to shield their eyes. After what seemed like an eternity the maelstrom passed. Xanthus pointed to a mountain range lying against the horizon.

"There is where we need to go!" he shouted.

Narrowing his eyes, Tristan looked into the distance. His heart fell. Leagues of deadly wasteland loomed in between. They would never get across it alive. Then he turned to look behind him. To his horror, all he saw was more endless, heat-baked desolation.

"Can we go back?" he shouted.

"No!" Xanthus answered. "To survive, we have to go forward! You must trust me!"

"I don't understand!" Tristan shouted back. "What are the Borderlands?"

Ignoring the question, Xanthus grabbed the horses' reins then beckoned Tristan to follow him. Bent against the raging wind, they started for the horizon.

Never had the prince traveled across such deadly terrain. As they plodded desperately along, more sinkholes surfaced here and there, nearly sucking them into oblivion. With every step, sweat ran from their bodies, threatening death from dehydration. Wind and sand tore at Tristan's skin like hot knife blades. The ground shook so violently that he went down twice, the scalding earth burning his palms as he fell. Each time he stood he had no choice but to somehow go on. Wherever Xanthus was taking him, he knew he would never live to see it.

After about an hour, Xanthus stopped. Nearly unconscious, Tristan staggered to his side. Xanthus pointed to a nearby slope.

"There!" he shouted. "Do you see it? That dark spot in the mountainside—I think it's a cave!"

Tristan strained his eyes. After a few moments, he saw what Xanthus meant. But given all the swirling dust, Tristan couldn't be sure. Only going there would tell the tale.

Without waiting for Tristan's response, Xanthus started trudging toward their new destination. Summoning his remaining strength, the prince followed.

After another grueling walk they finally arrived. Looking up, Tristan nearly fell to his knees with relief. A huge cave entrance loomed before them, its edges smoothed by the constantly blowing sand. Wasting no time, they led their horses inside.

The cave's interior was immense. Dark red stone lined the walls. As they walked deeper, Tristan and Xanthus turned a corner to see the tunnel's end. The cave's entrance was far too high to seal with rocks to block out the terrible sandstorm, but being around the bend gave them some relief from the elements. The wind moaned as it swirled its way into the cave's depths, then back out again.

His throat parched and his skin burning, Tristan looked around. To his dismay there was nothing to be found. No food, no water—just bare stone and the constantly moaning wind. Reaching to his saddle he untied his canteen to take a welcome drink.

Almost as soon as he started drinking, the Darkling ripped the canteen from his hands. Surprised, he glared at Xanthus.

"What are you doing?" he growled. "I am near death with thirst!"

Xanthus looked back at him calmly. "I know," he answered. "So is my human side. But there is a long way to go before we reach the mountains. Some food remains in my saddlebags, and we have a certain amount of water. Crossing the Borderlands is our only hope. To succeed, we must ration what we have left." Xanthus thought for a moment. "Unless things change," he added softly.

"What are you talking about?" Tristan demanded. "What in this awful place might possibly change?"

Ignoring the question, Xanthus closed Tristan's canteen.

"I agree about the food!" Tristan shouted. "But you charmed the canteens to constantly replenish themselves! Why can't we drink all we want?"

"I have already told you why," Xanthus answered calmly. "Magic has no meaning here. My spell over the canteens no longer works."

So tired he couldn't stand, Tristan sat on the ground. He looked up at the Darkling with angry eyes. "What do you mean?" he demanded. "What in the name of the Afterlife are the Borderlands?"

Xanthus sat down across from the prince. As the wind moaned, the Darkling looked into Tristan's eyes.

"There is so much that you do not know—that *no one* on your side of the world knows," he said. "You are right about one thing: This place is not our destination. Once we entered the azure wall, we should have arrived among the Heretics. When I saw that we were crossing through azure fog, I knew it had all gone wrong. Even so, there could be no turning back. I have done all I can to keep us alive, *Jin'Sai,* and I will continue to do so. Even though you believe I'm your enemy, you must trust me. I'm all you have."

Suddenly an alarming thought struck Tristan. His eyes darted to the Paragon hanging around the Darkling's neck. To his great relief, it looked as vibrant as ever.

"If magic has no meaning here, why is the Paragon still alive?" he asked.

Xanthus looked down at the stone. Cupping it lovingly in his hands for a moment, he looked back at the prince.

"All the craft's spells are made useless here," Xanthus answered. "The Borderlands purpose is to create a deadly environment, protecting the Heretics from the Ones during an intense attack. The environment is meant to be severely hostile—so hostile that if we survive it, we will be the first. It is also said that dangerous creatures—designed by the Heretics to withstand these elements continually wander the Borderlands, hunting for the Ones. But that is not to say that magic does not *exist* here, just because those who enter cannot call forth spells. The fact the Paragon still lives proves that."

Tristan looked unbelievingly at Xanthus. "Do you mean to say that the Heretics are powerful enough to have *created* this place?"

"Yes," Xanthus answered. "Their ability to conjure and dispel the Borderlands is aeons old. But in all that time, the Heretics have needed to summon its protection only twice before. We seem to be witnessing the third time. Summoning the Borderlands is a drastic measure. The Ones must be making a particularly savage attack. Had I known that the Borderlands had been summoned, we would have waited longer in your world. Unless the Borderlands are dispelled soon, our chances of surviving are not good."

"If the Borderlands protect the Heretics from the Ones, then why don't the Heretics summon it constantly?" Tristan asked.

"Although their gifts dwarf anything seen on your side of the world, even they are not all-powerful," Xanthus replied. "The energy needed to sustain the Borderlands is beyond our imagination. Even the Heretics cannot summon it indefinitely. But the last two times they called it forth, it served its purpose admirably."

Tristan scowled. "What do you mean?"

"The Heretics survived," Xanthus said. "When the Ones' armies tried to advance, they were annihilated by the elements."

"Are you telling me that right now—out there, somewhere—

an army of the Ones is advancing on the Heretics?" Tristan asked.

Xanthus nodded. "There can be no other reason, save for one."

"What might that be?" Tristan asked.

Again refusing to answer, Xanthus shook his head. Even so, Tristan was starting to understand—if only a little.

"When the Ones draw near, the Heretics summon the Borderlands," Tristan mused. "Suddenly engulfed, the Ones are without their magic, and they perish from the elements." He looked curiously at the Darkling. "If that is always the case, why do they continue to try?"

Xanthus shook his head. "You speak about such things like they were an everyday occurrence," he said. "Remember, over tens of thousands of years, until now the Borderlands have been conjured only twice. Perhaps the Ones have discovered what they believe is a way to overcome the Borderlands. In any event, the timing bodes badly for us. It seems that we have arrived during another great campaign."

"A place where magic exists, but its use is impossible," Tristan said to himself. Suddenly understanding something else, he looked into Xanthus' human face.

"That is why your human half shows, isn't it?" he asked. "Here in the Borderlands, you can't sustain your Darkling persona." Tristan gave the Darkling a deadly looking smile. "If I chose to, I could kill you right now."

"Yes, you could," Xanthus answered calmly. "But you won't, and we know why."

Just then the wind picked up. Howling loudly, it sent more red dust into the cave, reminding them of what waited outside.

"Do the dust storms ever abate?" Tristan asked. "If so we would stand a far better chance."

"I do not know," Xanthus answered. "Like you, this is my first experience here."

Thinking for a moment, Tristan became curious about something. "If no army of the Ones has ever successfully crossed the Borderlands, then how can we?" he asked. "Surely they would come far better prepared."

"True," Xanthus answered. "But we have an unexpected advantage that they never enjoyed."

"What is that?"

"Remember what I said about our being propelled vast distances in the space of a single heartbeat?" Xanthus asked. "We moved through the azure fog for some time—too long, in fact. The Heretics granted me a unique Forestallment. It is designed to take me through the pass to the Eutracian side and also bring us back to them again—each action occurring in the twinkle of an eye. Instead, the azure fog imploded and we ended up here. I believe that was attributable to the Borderlands being summoned simultaneously to our journey. In effect, it blocked our way. We traveled an amazing distance—but not far enough. Through a quirk of fate, I believe that when we exited the fog we were already far across the Borderlands. If that is true, we may have already come much farther than the Ones' armies ever have."

"What caused us to exit the fog when we did?" Tristan asked.

"As the Borderlands formed, magic became increasingly ineffective. When the craft ceased to matter, my powers became inert. The result was that we had no more momentum. The azure fog imploded, leaving us somewhere in the Borderlands and short of our true destination."

Disheartened, Tristan looked at the ground. Even during his darkest days fighting the Coven he had never felt so defeated. He was stranded in a nightmarish wasteland with a Heretical servant who possessed the Paragon. Worse, things would be building to a climax in Eutracia. He hoped that Shailiha had set sail for the Citadel by now. Whatever *now* meant in this place, for it was clear that nothing could be taken for granted here in this monstrous construct. He looked back at the Darkling.

"Is time the same here?" he asked. "Is a day still a day, a year still a year?"

"I do not know," Xanthus answered. "It is said that there is no day or night in the Borderlands. The Heretics designed it that way, to confuse and tire the enemy. If that is true then time cannot be measured, and has no meaning."

Xanthus handed the canteen to the prince. "Take a small sip," he said. "I will do the same." Despite their grave circumstances, the Darkling managed a slight smile. "In this place where I cannot call on magic, we are finally on equal terms."

Opening the canteen, Tristan drank. The life-giving water momentarily soothed his parched throat. He handed the canteen back to the Darkling so that Xanthus could do the same.

"We should sleep before journeying onward," Xanthus said. "Then we will see."

Tristan was forced to agree. Removing his weapons, he lay them on the ground within easy reach. He stretched out on the cave floor. Closing his eyes, he did his best to relax. Even so, because of the howling wind and the many questions worrying his mind, sleep was a long time in coming.

Once Tristan slumbered, Xanthus walked around the bend and stared out the cave entrance. To his dismay everything about the raging Borderlands was the same. Sighing, he looked to the ground.

My masters did not foresee this, he thought. *Why would they, when the last Borderlands appearance was more than two thousand centuries ago? But now, all might be lost because of one unforeseen coincidence in time. I must get the* Jin'Sai *to safety! The craft's future depends on it! But if the Ones are on the march, it could change everything.*

Xanthus turned away from the Borderlands and walked back into the cave.

CHAPTER XXV

"I NEED THOSE SHIPS READY TO SAIL!" SHAILIHA SAID. SCOWLING, she stared across the table.

"Every day we wait, Serena grows stronger!" the princess added. "If the spell granting Forestallments to endowed blood can be found in the Scroll of the Vagaries, our mission to the Citadel is even more urgent than before!"

Calming herself, Shailiha took another sip of tea. It was strong and hot—just the way she liked it. She was sitting in her private quarters. Before retiring the night before, she had asked Wigg, Faegan, Abbey, and Adrian to join her for breakfast. There were things she wanted to discuss without conducting a full-blown Conclave meeting.

Hearing Morganna call her, she looked down. Her daughter had started walking, her pudgy legs taking her across the floor faster than the princess ever thought possible. Shailiha watched as the child turned to waddle back toward her. Like her mother, Morganna was bright and inquisitive, her eyes always drinking in the world's wonders. With a nod from the princess, Shawna the Short scooped up the toddler, then took her from the room.

It was early morning. The dawn had broken clear and bright, its golden rays streaming in through the open balcony doors. Despite the lovely day, a sense of gloom seemed to dishearten everyone, and the magnificent breakfast Shawna had brought remained largely untouched.

Shailiha looked across the table at Adrian. Because of the princess's outburst, an apologetic look commanded the First Sister's face. Shailiha reached out to touch the acolyte's hand.

"I'm sorry," she said. "I shouldn't have snapped at you that way. I suppose it's because I'm so worried about Tristan. I feel powerless as we wait to sail, and it's driving me mad. I believe the *Jin'Sai* was right—Serena has much to do with his disappearance. The Citadel must be taken soon."

"I understand, Your Highness," Adrian answered. "Rest assured that the acolytes I have chosen are nearly trained. The delay is my fault. I know we should be ready, but I realized that we would need more than six sisters. Just give me two more days, and the others will be trained."

Wigg put down his fork and wiped his mouth, then looked across the table at Adrian. The First Wizard respected her immensely, but this was the first time he had heard about needing extra acolytes to empower the Black Ships.

"There are only six vessels," he said. "Why have you decided that we will need more than six acolytes?"

"There are two reasons," Adrian answered. "First, we must cross the sea without using Faegan's portal. The ships are too large. The last time he tried, Faegan could barely transport Tyranny's lesser frigates. When I explained my concerns to him, he agreed. We concluded that the Black Ships must sail part of the way to the Citadel atop the waves because the sisters will tire. It will mean a slower trip, but there it is."

"What is the other reason?" Shailiha asked.

Picking up her teacup, Adrian thoughtfully cupped it in one palm. "Attrition," she answered grimly. "I understand that Wigg and Jessamay will be accompanying us. Even so, if we lose more than two acolytes in battle, I will need other craft practitioners to take up the slack. The last thing we want is to leave Black Ships behind for Serena to capture and turn against us."

Shailiha was impressed. Looking at the others, she saw that they were equally glad to have the young acolyte in their midst. Smiling, Abbey leaned over to place her lips near Wigg's ear.

"That little scenario escaped you, didn't it, old man?" she asked chidingly. "It's a good thing there are some intelligent women around to advise you two wizards! Only the Afterlife knows how an all-male Directorate managed to operate for so long!"

Abbey's words had not escaped Faegan. He cackled a bit, then winced from his burns. Pushing his tongue against an inner cheek, Wigg sighed.

"Except for training the extra acolytes, are the ships ready to sail?" Shailiha asked.

"Yes," Adrian answered. "As you already know, Tyranny's crewmembers have returned to their civilian lives."

Shailiha understood. Several days before the Darkling's appearance, at Tyranny's suggestion Tristan had issued an order. Tyranny's crewmembers had been released from service, then replaced with Minion troops.

Because so many warriors had been lost in past campaigns, Tristan had at first rejected the privateer's suggestion. But then she'd reminded him that her crewmembers were volunteers, who could quit at any time. Their ranks were already thinning. Besides, Tyranny added, the Minions handled the Black Ships equally well if not better than her men—not to mention that they had vastly superior fighting skills. Tristan had finally agreed.

During the last few days, Tyranny had not only been overseeing the ships' provisioning, but had also been selecting the warriors who would crew the vessels. Scars, her loyal first mate, would remain by his captain's side. Before bidding her crew good-bye, Tyranny had given each one a handsome bonus. The ceremony had been tearful.

It had also been decided that while at sea Tyranny would command the vessels—provided Shailiha concurred with her orders. The attack on the Citadel would fall under Shailiha's direction.

Every Conclave member save for Tristan, Abbey, and Faegan would be sailing with them.

"What about the Necrophagians?" Shailiha asked the table at large. "We will surely pass through their territory. When we meet them they will demand the usual forty dead bodies before we can cross. I simply refuse to ask the Minions to train to the death to provide payment, as we have done before."

"I am hoping that we acolytes will be able to fly the Back Ships high enough so that the Necrophagians will not be able to reach us," Adrian answered. "But that theory remains untested. We will know once we arrive."

Two more days, the princess thought. *Then we go to the Citadel. It is such a secret, foreboding place. I pray that this time we will find the answers we seek.* After taking another sip of tea, she looked at Faegan.

"Have you learned anything more about your new Forestallment?" she asked.

His expression thoughtful, the crippled wizard placed his palms flat on the tabletop. "Yes and no," he answered. "Although I can use the index easily, as you know, the scroll does not mention the formula needed to install the spells into endowed blood. I employed my Consummate Recollection to discover whether the Tome mentions it. It does not. With each passing day I become more convinced that the formula was written on the scroll section that was burned away. Having all these Forestallment formulas at my fingertips but being unable to use them is maddening! If we are right about the other scroll and you can bring it home, our abilities will be enhanced beyond description."

A thought came to the princess. Her expression suddenly keen, she leaned across the table.

"Xanthus commands the craft," she mused. "He said that if Tristan agreed to accompany him through the pass, they would travel great distances in the space of a single heartbeat. It's entirely possible that his Heretic masters granted him the ability to safely cross over and back by Forestallment, is it not?" Suddenly realizing her logic's full ramifications, she gazed hard at the wizard.

"Does the Vigors scroll index refer to such a spell?" she asked.

Smiling broadly, Faegan laced his fingers. "I thought you'd never ask," he answered softly. "It does indeed."

For several moments no one spoke. Wigg found his voice first. "Do you mean to say that—"

"That's *exactly* what I mean," Faegan interjected. "If you can bring me the spell making Forestallments usable, we might be able to safely enter the pass, then follow Xanthus, should he lead Tristan into its depths. Moreover, we might finally conquer the Tolenka Mountains—provided the Vigors orb cut its way through to the other side before returning to Eutracia. But the truly intriguing question is why a Heretic servant would provide us with the Vigors scroll index. It simply makes no sense."

Insistent pounding suddenly came on the door. Shailiha turned. "Enter!" she called out.

The doors parted to show two Minions. Between them they supported a stricken warrior. It was Traax. He appeared to be unconscious. Shailiha quickly beckoned the warriors to bring him into the room.

Traax seemed near death. His body was soaked with sweat and his wings drooped so weakly that they dragged across the floor. Traax's eyes were closed and his head lolled uselessly on his chest.

"Put him on the bed!" Wigg shouted.

The warriors quickly obeyed. Hurrying over, Shailiha looked down at the unconscious warrior. For the first time she saw the ruby pin attached to his body armor. Like her brother, she understood its meaning.

"How did this happen?" she demanded of the two warriors.

"We watched him tumble from the sky to the palace courtyard," one warrior answered. "He struck the ground with such force that I find it hard to believe he still lives. Even so, we could find no broken bones. We immediately sought out your guidance."

"Bring Duvessa here at once!" Shailiha ordered the warriors. After clicking their heels, the Minions ran from the room.

Everyone crowded around the bed. Wigg placed a palm on Traax's forehead. He closed his eyes. When he opened them again, the First Wizard seemed encouraged.

"He will live," Wigg said. "But he suffers from extreme exhaustion and dehydration. We need to bring him back to consciousness quickly. If he remains this way much longer he might never return."

Wigg turned to Abbey. "Do you have anything that might help?" he asked. "I would prefer to use the craft only as a last resort."

Hurrying back to the table, Abbey took up her herbmistress's satchel. After rummaging through the bag she produced a vial, then hurried back. Reaching out, Faegan took it from her, then held it to the light. There were several bright green leaves imprisoned inside. He looked up at Abbey.

"Fresh nosegay?" he asked. Abbey nodded. "A good choice," Faegan said.

He handed the vial to Wigg. "This should work," he said. "If not, you will need to summon the craft."

Holding the vial at arm's length, Wigg unscrewed its top. The First Wizard coughed. Even at that distance the leaves' odor was potent. He gently held it under Traax's nose.

With a great start, the warrior coughed loudly then gasped for air. After thrashing about a bit he finally calmed. "I live to serve . . . ," he said absently then collapsed again.

"Once more," Faegan said.

Wigg returned the bottle to Traax's nostrils. Groaning, the warrior sat up and angrily waved the bottle away. His eyes opened. Wigg smiled.

"Welcome back," he said. "For several moments you had us worried."

"Water . . . ," Traax said weakly.

Abbey went to the table, then returned with a glass. Snatching it from her hands, Traax started drinking greedily. After finishing he lay down on the bed.

"The *Jin'Sai,*" he said softly. "I saw him."

"Where?" Shailiha asked urgently. "Was it at the pass?"

Traax nodded. "Xanthus was still with him. They materialized out of nowhere. Tristan ordered us to surrender. He said that he had no choice but to go with Xanthus through the pass or more citizens would die. I watched them disappear into the azure wall."

Her heart breaking, Shailiha looked away. After a time she looked back at Traax. "What else can you tell us?" she asked.

"The first warrior group sent to guard the pass was killed by Xanthus," Traax answered. "We found their bodies scattered everywhere. I'm sure they died like the heroes they were."

"Is there anything else?" Wigg asked.

Traax nodded. "Tristan said he would do everything in his power to return to us, but that we must attack the Citadel soon—with or without him. He said to tell the princess that he loves her.

Should Shailiha die, command over the Minions and the Conclave goes to the wizards. I returned alone. The remaining warriors continue to watch the pass."

The room went quiet again. As Wigg thought about Tristan being taken to the Heretics, he momentarily closed his eyes.

"There's something else," Traax added. Reaching beneath his body armor, he produced Tristan's black ball mask. Shailiha recognized it immediately. The warrior handed it to her.

"Tristan wanted you to have that," Traax said. "He said that Xanthus forced him to wear it while the Darkling committed his atrocities."

Tears started running down Shailiha's cheeks. Turning away, she held the mask to her breast and walked onto the balcony. Abbey started to go to her, but Wigg stopped her with a shake of his head.

"I know that one better than you ever will," he said softly. "Give her a moment alone." Abbey nodded.

Suddenly Duvessa ran into the room. Seeing Traax, she hurried to the bed. Her dark eyes searched his face. "Hello, my love," he said.

Reaching up, Traax touched the ruby pin attached to his body armor. Despite his exhaustion he managed a smile.

"Your token stayed with me all the way there and back," he said. "It's a good omen for our upcoming marriage. But I hadn't planned to announce our betrothal this way. I'm sorry to disappoint you."

Smiling, she stroked his long hair. "It's of no matter, my lord," she answered. "Welcome home."

Standing alone in the morning sun, Shailiha steadied herself as she wiped her eyes. Holding the mask in one hand, she grasped the gold medallion hanging around her neck with the other. For some reason she had never been able to understand, whenever she and her twin brother were separated, holding the medallion gave her a small measure of relief.

She looked out over the manicured grounds that her late mother had so loved. She could almost see the Eutracian queen, tending her gardens as Shailiha's father, the king, watched. They were all dead, killed by the Coven. If she also lost her brother, Shailiha knew her heart could never stand it.

Tristan, her mind whispered. *Where have you gone?*

Chapter XXVI

Turning over in his sleep, Tristan groaned. His body was stiff and sore. His skin stung hotly from being blasted by windblown sand. As he slowly awoke, he thought he sensed something odd. *Impossible,* his tired mind said. He tried to go back to sleep but couldn't.

Slowly opening his eyes, he sat up. His weapons were still beside him. Curled up on the floor a short distance away, Xanthus lay asleep.

Still tired and groggy, Tristan stood. That was when he first saw the strange substance lying on the cave floor. Picking some up, he rubbed it between two fingers.

It was snow.

As he stood, he suddenly realized how cold it had become. As always, the wind moaned through the desolate cave. But this time it brought a mind-numbing frostiness—a chill so deep that it froze his lungs and rattled his bones. His breath exhaled as ghostlike vapors. Looking to the horses he saw that they had sidled up against one another, trying to keep from freezing to death. The red cave walls had become shiny with frost. As the cold sank into his core, he started to shake.

After quickly strapping his weapons into place he ran toward the cave entrance. Rounding the bend and skidding to a halt, he looked out with unbelieving eyes.

As far as Tristan could see, the Borderlands were buried in deep, white snow. The wind was as fierce as before. Rather than red dust, it carried giant snowflakes the size of his hand. The swirling crystals were so large that their patterns could be seen before they hit the ground.

The mountain ranges were no longer red. Dark and ominous, their snow-covered peaks reminded him of the Tolenkas. The sky had changed as well. No longer red and angry, every color of the rainbow swirled faintly through its vastness, like mother-of-pearl.

"Do not be deceived," he heard a voice say from behind him. "Although it is more beautiful, this sudden shift in the Borderlands is equally deadly."

Tristan turned to see Xanthus. The Darkling did not seem surprised by what he saw. He held two saddle blankets in his arms. He handed one to the prince.

Understanding, Tristan took one, then removed a throwing knife from its quiver. After cutting through the blanket's center he put his head through the hole, letting the blanket drape over his upper body. Taking Tristan's knife, Xanthus did the same with his blanket. They returned their eyes to the amazingly changed valley.

"This is what you were talking about, isn't it?" Tristan asked.

"What do you mean, *Jin'Sai*?"

"When we first entered the cave," Tristan answered. "You said that we would have to ration the water, 'unless things change.' "

"Yes," Xanthus answered. "We now have all the water we want—unless the Borderlands morph again."

Using one hand to shield his eyes from the pearly sky, Tristan looked toward the distant mountain range lying against the horizon. The gap Xanthus had referred to earlier still seemed a thousand leagues away.

"We'll never survive it," Tristan said softly.

"Probably not," Xanthus answered. "But we must try. It's our only hope."

Tristan turned to look at the Darkling. "How is this possible?" he asked. "Only hours ago this place was a scorching wasteland."

"As with all things in the Borderlands, the transformation was caused by the Heretics," Xanthus answered. "Magic may not be employed by those who tread here, but from far away the Heretics can control the elements."

"Why foster such a change?" Tristan asked. "The red wasteland was deadly enough."

"Perhaps, but consider my next words carefully," Xanthus answered. "If an army of the Ones tried to cross the desert they would surely come prepared. That would mean vast amounts of water, food, and proper clothing. If the Borderlands suddenly change into what you see now, the Ones' water and food will freeze, and their clothing will become woefully inadequate. Their chances of survival would lessen drastically. Without magic to change the nature of their supplies, they would only perish faster. It's a clever trap, don't you think?"

Although the Borderlands had been created by the Heretics to slaughter the Ones, Tristan had to marvel at this impersonal way to kill. The Borderlands was an ingenious weapon, devised by a race that was vastly superior to his. He could only imagine what their other powers might be like.

"You come from the Heretics' midst," he said. "Do they look like us?"

"If you live, you will see them. If not, it won't matter. That's enough discussion for now. Pack your canteen tightly with snow and saddle your horse. We must head for the mountains."

On returning to the cave's end they saddled their mounts. After packing their canteens, they led the horses to the entrance.

Nothing had changed. The falling snow swirled, and the mother-of-pearl sky gleamed with every imaginable color. As they led their mounts from the cave, the Borderlands' new form of cruelty hit them full blast.

The wind slicing through Tristan was so cold that he thought his lungs would literally freeze. He found that if he took measured breaths, it was easier. Xanthus climbed onto his horse; Tristan did the same. The Darkling started leading Tristan down the slope and toward the seemingly unreachable gap.

The snow was deep, making the going even harder this time. Shadow stumbled often as he waded his way along, and anything except a trudging pace was impossible. Frost formed on the riders' brows and lashes, making it difficult to see. When his unprotected hands went numb Tristan flexed them incessantly, trying to delay frostbite.

The wildly blowing wind simultaneously created and destroyed huge snowdrifts, their white dunes sometimes appearing, then vanishing in seconds. Sometimes Xanthus chose to climb them to stay on track. Other times they were so high that he and the prince had no choice but go around, losing valuable time. Tristan looked back to see whether Shadow was leaving marks in the snow. Immediately after the heavyset horse abandoned his tracks, they filled in again.

As the time passed Tristan nearly fell asleep. He finally resorted to slapping himself to stay awake. He knew from his

Royal Guard training that falling asleep in the cold was a fatal mistake. But even the tough Royal Guard lessons had never prepared him for anything as brutal as this.

After climbing another high snowbank, Xanthus stopped his horse. Coming up alongside, Tristan gave him a questioning look. The Darkling pointed into the distance.

Tristan gasped. At first he was sure he was hallucinating, due to the terrible cold and lack of food. Closing his eyes, he opened them again. To his amazement, the scene remained the same.

Xanthus indicated that they should retreat a bit, so that their horses couldn't be seen. Tristan obeyed. Leaving their mounts behind, they crawled back to the snowdrift's summit and peered over the edge.

Far in the distance, a massive army tried to forge its way across the Borderlands. But because of the swirling snow and the vast distance, the force appeared to be little more than a dark line against a white canvas.

His eyes wide, Tristan looked over at Xanthus. "Is that the Ones' army?" he shouted, trying to be heard above the wind. His heart was beating so wildly at the prospect of finally seeing the Ones that for a moment he thought it might burst through his chest.

"It's probably only a small patrol," Xanthus answered. "They might have become separated from the main body when the Borderlands changed, and lost their way."

"That's a *patrol*?" Tristan shouted against the wind. "But their numbers are huge!"

"Yes," Xanthus answered. "You will find that the scale of conflict on this side of the Tolenkas dwarfs anything you have ever experienced. Your Sorceresses' War lasting three centuries was a mere skirmish compared to what goes on here. If you are lucky enough to survive the Borderlands and then go home again, your perspective on war will be forever changed."

Tristan looked back down at the slowly moving columns. For a moment his curiosity was so great that he hardly felt the searing cold. Watching the army as best he could, he tried to estimate its size.

It was impossible to be sure, but the slowly moving force seemed to be at least a league wide by several leagues long. Tiny pinpricks of color could be seen here and there—war banners, he guessed. Taken as a whole, from this distance the army looked like a great dark snake, gradually winding its way through the snow.

"Why do you say that they are lost?" Tristan shouted. "It seems that they travel toward the mountain gap, just as we do."

Xanthus looked over at him. "I say that because our destination is a well-kept secret," he shouted back. "That army travels in the same direction by sheer coincidence. Given the Borderlands' huge scale, it's astounding that we would cross paths at all."

Then Xanthus' expression hardened. "I know what you're thinking, *Jin'Sai,*" he shouted. "That you could render me unconscious while I'm in my human state, then somehow hurry to join the Ones as they trudge across the snow. Don't try it! Your plan won't work!"

Tristan scowled. It was almost like the Darkling had read his mind.

Xanthus pointed at the slowly moving columns. "They are as good as dead!" he shouted. "They just don't know it yet! They are heading off into nothingness! The only refuge for thousands of leagues in any direction is where I am leading us. It would be a complete impossibility for that struggling army to find it. Your only chance to remain alive is to stay by my side. I know that you hate me, but I have never lied to you. Assuming you could reach them you would only die, just as they will!"

As the freezing wind tore at him, Tristan's anger and frustration boiled up to such a point that he started pounding the freezing snowdrift with his bare fists. He glared hatefully at the Darkling.

"Someday I will kill you," he growled. "And I'll enjoy it!"

His voice had been nearly drowned out by the raging wind. But Xanthus understood.

Before the Darkling could respond, Tristan felt the ground start to shake, followed by an earsplitting cracking sound. Tristan and Xanthus immediately turned to look back down into the valley.

To his horror, the prince saw gigantic cracks forming in the snow. Starting at the mountain bases on either side, they came from several directions at once as they stretched fingerlike across the valley. Like the army columns, they had to be at least a league wide. As they tore across the landscape, snow by the ton tumbled into their quickly forming abysses. Even from where the prince and Xanthus lay watching, the fissures' depths seemed endless. There were at least eight, with more forming by the moment. Amid the shaking ground and the terrible noise, Tristan held his breath. The fissures were heading straight for the Ones' struggling army.

The columns tried to scatter to avoid the coming threat, but the snow was far too deep for them to move quickly enough. His eyes wild with disbelief, Tristan watched helplessly.

Soon the fissures converged toward one point—the army's center. With a mighty crash the ground beneath the columns started collapsing.

Watching the awful spectacle from such a great distance was strange. As if in slow motion, the Ones tumbled into the fissures' vast abysses. And then there was nothing, save for a gigantic, dark crater lying in the valley's center.

Tears started streaming down Tristan's face. As his rage took over he raised his fists toward the heavens. "No!" he screamed.

But the only answer was his lonely voice, ricocheting off the mountain walls. He fell to his knees and hung his head. After a time he glared at the Darkling.

"Was that your doing?" he demanded.

Xanthus shook his head. "No," he answered. "You know that here in the Borderlands, I am as powerless to cause such things as you are."

"Tell me the truth!" Tristan shouted back. "I refuse to believe that was a coincidence!"

"No, *Jin'Sai,* it was no coincidence. But it wasn't my doing, either. What you just saw was an act of war, performed by the Heretics."

Tristan got to his feet and walked closer toward the drift's edge. He stared down into the valley. Only the huge, dark circle remained in the snow. It was easily the size of Tammerland, if not larger.

He was about to speak when he heard another rumbling sound. The circle was disappearing. With a massive crash the crater closed in on itself, then it was gone. Snow soon washed over the scene, and rapidly forming drifts left no trace of what had happened.

Tristan still couldn't believe that hundreds of thousands of Ones had been destroyed in seconds, simply because of an order given by the Heretics. Xanthus was right. If he survived to see his homeland again, his perspective about war would be forever changed. But this did not seem like war. This was mass annihilation, on a scale so vast that it could scarcely be fathomed.

"It is time to go, *Jin'Sai,*" Xanthus said. "There is nothing for us here." The pair mounted their horses and again headed toward the distant mountains.

Three hours later, Tristan was near death. Struggling to stay in his saddle, he could no longer feel his feet, hands, or face. His exposed skin had turned blue. Xanthus was little better. If they didn't find shelter soon, they would perish. Too weak to stay in his saddle, the prince finally fell from his horse.

Tristan crashed to the snow and lay like the dead. Shadow immediately stopped to walk stiffly back to his master. Nudging Tristan with his nose, the stallion let go a loud whinny.

Xanthus stopped. Seeing the prince lying in the snow, he went back. He jumped down from his horse to examine him. The *Jin'-Sai* was dying.

Xanthus looked around. There was no shelter for as far as he could see. Looking across the valley, the gap in the mountains seemed no closer.

There was only one thing left to do. The measure was drastic. It would keep them alive a little longer, but would also lessen their overall chances.

Finally deciding, Xanthus reached down and drew Tristan's dreggan from its scabbard. His hands were so useless that he could barely hold the heavy sword.

He lowered his head for a moment. Then he raised the shiny blade high over his head. With all his remaining strength, he lashed out.

The dreggan's razor-sharp blade came around in a perfect arc, catching Xanthus' horse unaware. The blade sliced the stallion's throat easily, nearly severing his head from his body. Blood erupted from the open wound to fall red onto the snow. Letting go a tortured scream, the horse fell dead to the ground.

Rushing to the horse's carcass, Xanthus used the dreggan to slice open its belly. Steam filled the air as the horse's innards slid out onto the snowy ground. Working quickly, he found the major artery leading from the horse's heart, then slit it open with one of Tristan's knives. Carefully squeezing the artery, he emptied as much warm blood into his canteen as he could.

Then he cut out the heart. Slicing its base, he pumped it between his hands, also squeezing its blood into the canteen. Xanthus then cut the heart into pieces.

Rushing back to Tristan, he dragged the prince's body near the dead horse. Xanthus sat in the snow beside Tristan. Propping Tristan's head in his lap, he poured the warm blood into the prince's mouth.

His eyes still closed, Tristan instinctively sensed the warmth. Soon he was drinking eagerly. Xanthus saved some for himself, then also drank.

Taking up Tristan's knife, Xanthus finished gutting the horse, then shoved the steaming innards to one side. He had no worry about wasting the organs or meat, for they would soon freeze. Grabbing Tristan's useless hands, he thrust them into the horse's still-warm body cavity. Placing the heart pieces into his duster, he saved them for later. Then he slid his hands into the horse's abdomen alongside Tristan's.

Soon Xanthus' hands came alive again. The life-giving heat was like a welcome drug surging through his system. He removed his hands, then positioned Tristan's body lengthwise along the horse's wound and shoved the prince as far back into it as he could. Knowing that there was nothing else he could do, Xanthus leaned back against the dead horse to wait.

The Jin'Sai *will either live or die,* he thought. *But he must live—live to meet my masters. But even as he hovers near death, there remains so much I cannot tell him. Things he deserves to know but might never learn.*

Looking toward the distant mountain range, Xanthus' heart fell. The *Jin'Sai* was right. They could never travel that far—especially with one horse gone. If Tristan regained consciousness they would take some horse meat with them. But Xanthus feared that death was just around the corner.

Xanthus looked down into Tristan's face. *No* Jin'Sai *has ever come this far,* he thought. *Is this where our journey will end?*

Just then another blast of whirling snow sliced its razor-sharp coldness through the Darkling. Pulling his duster closer, Xanthus waited.

Chapter XXVII

"I know that this was my idea," Shailiha said to Wigg as they walked down the Redoubt hallway. "But looking back on it, it's impossible to know how Nathan will react. Mallory has already been through so much!"

"We gave her the option," Wigg answered. "She has chosen, and we must honor her decision. Martha told me about it, just after Traax's return to the palace. But when Mallory meets with her father, there is one condition on which I must insist. I want this done in strictest privacy. There is no reason for the other endowed girls or boys to see what the consuls have become. I believe Mallory is the only one mature enough to cope with the experience."

Shailiha agreed with the First Wizard's requirement. She also agreed with his assessment of Mallory. The Fledgling's behavior at the prison had impressed everyone. She could have killed the abusive guard, but she hadn't. Instead she'd found her own solution, and it had been a clever one. Looking up, Shailiha saw that Caprice was still flying along overhead.

After walking another quarter hour they stopped before large twin doors. Just above the doors, Old Eutracian words were elegantly carved into the wall. Shailiha couldn't read Old Eutracian, but she knew about the room's importance. Opening the doors, they walked into the Consuls' Nursery. Caprice fluttered in behind them.

The word "nursery" was a misnomer, and everyone familiar with the Redoubt knew it. "School for the Gifted" would have been a more proper phrase. The princess enjoyed coming here, for this place always buoyed her spirits. The craft's future practitioners were being taught in these rooms. In some ways she always felt a bit jealous when visiting, because like Tristan, she was eager to start her training. As Wigg accompanied her toward the floor's center, she looked around.

Twenty-one boys and eight Fledgling House girls were being schooled here. Each child was the handpicked son or daughter of a consul. The princess fervently hoped that the students' numbers would grow. But with the remaining consuls under the Vagaries' influence and Fledgling House abandoned, the nursery's fate was anyone's guess. *At least we have this many we can guide,* she thought.

Shailiha saw several red-robed acolytes among the youth. First Sister Adrian was not here, having returned to the coast to finish the sisters' training to empower the Black Ships. But Martha was happily scurrying about, tending to the children's needs. Shailiha smiled. The nursery was a secret, self-contained world all its own.

Shailiha watched a group of boys and girls practice some lesser craft arts. An acolyte stood before them, monitoring their progress. The boys wore dark trousers and shoes. Like the girls' blouses, the boys' white doublets carried a red embroidered image of the Paragon directly over their hearts. Then Shailiha thought about Mallory. The acolyte would surely be eager to finish her early training and take her sisterhood vows. Here among so many children, she probably felt ancient.

The nursery's main room was spacious. Adjoining rooms for instruction and play led off from it. Unlike the other Redoubt chambers, the nursery walls were paneled in wood and painted with bright, playful colors. A visage board took up one wall, its surface covered with azure writing and complex formulas. Scrolls, texts, and instructional charts were in abundance. All in all, the atmosphere was lively and inventive. Shailiha loved the sounds coming from happy children, and there was no shortage of them here.

Looking around, Shailiha searched for Shawna the Short. At Shailiha's order, Shawna had started bringing Morganna to the nursery each afternoon so that the toddler could interact with other endowed children. Shawna had enthusiastically agreed.

"Shawna," the princess called out. "We're over here!"

On seeing the princess, Shawna waved. She looked back down at Morganna, who was sitting on the floor and batting at some toys. The gnome picked her up and walked over to the princess. When Morganna saw her mother, the toddler's eyes lit up. Shailiha took her in her arms.

Wigg smiled. "She seems to like this place," he said.

"That she does!" Shawna answered. "The princess's idea was a good one. But I must keep Shannon and his awful corncob pipe and ale jug out of here! He loves Morganna so much that he follows us everywhere we go! But he also knows that if he walks through that door, I'll brain him good!"

Shailiha laughed. She knew how protective Shawna was of Morganna. Whenever the child was in Shawna's care, the princess never worried. She also knew how Shawna ruled the roost over her henpecked husband. One afternoon in the palace kitchens, the princess had seen Shawna try to take a frying pan to Shannon's skull, simply because his boots had been dirty. Had Shawna been able to catch up with him, Shailiha was sure that Shannon would have ended up with a massive goose egg.

Knowing how much Morganna enjoyed the fliers, Shailiha ordered Caprice to flutter about the toddler's head. Stretching forth her arms, the child beamed. Taking care not to be injured, the yellow-and-violet flier hovered teasingly just beyond reach.

Shailiha and Wigg saw Mallory approach. The Fledgling bowed.

"Good afternoon, Your Highness and First Wizard," she said. "Thank you for honoring my decision."

Smiling at the Fledgling, Shailiha shifted Morganna's weight in her arms. "You're welcome," she answered. "But we have some things we want to discuss first." She reluctantly handed Morganna over to Shawna, then looked back at Mallory.

"Shall we go?" she asked. Mallory nodded eagerly. Shailiha looked at Shawna. "I will order Caprice to stay here with the children," she said.

Shawna nodded. Grasping one of Morganna's pudgy arms, she used it to wave good-bye.

The trio left the nursery and walked down the hall. Because Wigg knew far more about the captured consuls than she, Shailiha decided to let him do the talking. She gave the First Wizard a nod. Trying to decide where to start, Wigg cleared his throat.

In a compassionate voice, Wigg asked, "Tell me, Mallory, how long has it been since you've seen Nathan?"

"About a year and a half," Mallory answered. "He used to pay me regular visits at Fledgling House, then he simply stopped coming. I was terribly worried. Soon we girls realized that none of our fathers were visiting. When we asked Master Duncan why, he said he had no idea. He was clearly worried by it. But

I've learned here that the consuls were taken away by Nicholas and turned to the Vagaries."

"That's right," Wigg said. Continuing on, the First Wizard clasped his hands behind his back. "Please refresh an old wizard's memory," he said. "Do you have brothers or sisters?"

"I am an only child."

"Ah, yes," Wigg replied. "And where is your mother?"

"She died during my birth," Mallory answered.

Shailiha reached over to touch Mallory's hand. "I'm sorry," she said. "I know what it means to lose one's mother."

"It's all right," Mallory said. "Since I was five, Martha has been my mother. The royal palace is much like Fledgling House, only bigger. We Fledglings already feel at home here—especially with Martha nearby."

"I want to caution you," Wigg said. "When you see your father, he will not be like you remember. I want you to stand in the hall while the princess and I go in. If I think it's all right, I'll let you join us. But under no circumstances are you to enter without my permission, or let him embrace you. If I order you to leave the room, I want you to do so immediately. Is that clear?"

"Yes, First Wizard. What if he tries to use the craft against us? Should I be prepared for that?"

"No," Wigg answered. "His gifts have been neutralized. With me in the room he cannot harm us, and he knows it."

"How is that possible?" Mallory asked.

"He has been granted an enchantment of selective forgetfulness," Wigg said. "All his memories regarding craft use have been wiped clean. It's a painless process, I assure you. He remembers everything, save for spells and formulas."

On rounding the next corner they came to two Minion warriors guarding a door. The warriors snapped to attention.

"Has everything been quiet?" Wigg asked.

"Yes, First Wizard," a Minion answered. He smiled. "Save for some loud cursing from the door's other side, that is."

"I'm not surprised," Wigg said. "He's highly willful."

Looking at the lock, Wigg called the craft. The centuries-old tumblers turned over once, then twice more. Pointing to Mallory, Wigg looked at the Minions.

"Guard this Fledgling," he ordered. "I will call for her when the time is right." Each warrior clicked his heels. Wigg pushed open the door and walked in. Shailiha followed.

Nathan's quarters were modest. There was a bedroom, a sitting room with a fireplace, a washroom, but no windows. Nathan sat before the fire. Putting down the book he had been reading, he rose and walked nearer. Shailiha heard the door close behind them and the tumblers turn over again.

Nathan was tall, handsome, and well built. At forty-three Seasons of New Life, his hair was already a flattering salt-and-pepper affair. He wore a neatly trimmed mustache, and an inverted, whiskered triangle adorned his lower lip's underside. His dark blue robe hung loosely on his frame. The consul's eyes were light blue, his jaw firm. Vertical smile lines lay deeply embedded in his cheeks.

Although he could not employ the craft, Nathan was clearly not intimidated by his august visitors. Shailiha guessed that he had been a powerful consul, and she easily recognized some of Nathan's qualities in his daughter. Shailiha had to admit that had Nathan not been a Vagaries servant, she might have found herself attracted to him. Nathan calmly looked Wigg up and down, then did the same to Shailiha. As his eyes met hers, the princess couldn't help but be impressed.

"Good afternoon, *First Wizard,*" Nathan said. "Or whatever it is you're calling yourself these days." His voice was smoky, controlled. He looked at Shailiha again.

"And the princess herself has also deigned to visit," he added sarcastically. "Normally I would offer you some wine. But as you can see, I'm fresh out."

"Sit down," Wigg ordered.

Walking into the sitting room, Nathan took a seat before the fire. Wigg and Shailiha chose two upholstered reading chairs and sat down across from him. Looking into Wigg's eyes, Nathan came right to the point.

"You have no idea about what to do with me, do you?" he asked bluntly, "or my brothers whom you have also imprisoned in this monstrous Redoubt? Stripped of our abilities to use the craft, we were once among your closest allies. Then we were brought to the light by the *Jin'Sai*'s firstborn son—the most perfect being the world has ever seen. How ironic! Admit it, First Wizard—you and your Conclave are stymied. Your ludicrous morals forbid killing us, and you don't know how to turn us back to your insipid Vigors."

Leaning across the table, Nathan glared into Wigg's eyes.

"Tell me," he whispered ominously. "How many consuls do you keep prisoner here? Enough so that if we found our way to freedom, we might cause you trouble again? What a delicious thought!"

"You're right in a way," Wigg answered. "We have come to discuss your future. But there are things that you do not know."

"Such as . . . ?" Nathan asked.

"We have recently attained several advancements in the craft. We might soon be able to return you and your brothers to the Vigors after all. You were once a powerful, compassionate consul—one of the best I ever saw. You were a good father, too." Pausing, Wigg purposely let the reference to Mallory build tension.

For a moment, a distinct sadness came over the consul. Then his smug demeanor returned. He sat back in his chair.

"Ah, but I'm not alone in that interminable sorrow, am I, Wigg?" he countered. "I always loved Mallory! Nicholas might have taken my daughter, but at least her death served a purpose. Rumor has it that the *Jin'Sai* killed your whore daughter, simply by sleeping with her. I hear that Celeste's death was slow and painful. How sad that must have been for you! Had Failee been alive she would have been intelligent enough to keep that from happening! Better alive with Failee than dead in your uncaring arms, eh, *First Wizard*?"

Even Wigg hadn't been prepared for such a highly personal insult. Shailiha watched the rage build in his face, then subside as he fought it down.

"I haven't come here to discuss my personal life," Wigg replied. "Rather, I wish to discuss yours."

Nathan narrowed his eyes. "What are you talking about?"

Wigg walked to the door. Calling the craft, he unlocked it, then walked out. Muffled voices could be heard coming from the hallway. Wigg soon walked back to sit at the table. Saying nothing, he stared hard at Nathan.

Nathan glanced skeptically at Shailiha, then back at Wigg again. "What's going on?" he demanded.

Leaning forward, Wigg laced his fingers together. "Even though you have become a traitor, what happened to you was not your fault," he said. "I doubt that anyone—including Faegan and me—could have resisted Nicholas' power. That's one reason why we tried to take as many consuls alive as we could. One day you might return to the Vigors. I hope with all my heart that can happen. Just as important, I want you to understand that you have an incentive to do so—one that you didn't expect."

Nathan shook his head. "You fool!" he answered. "Had you ever been exposed to the Vagaries, you would know that nothing in this world could ever persuade me to rejoin your cause!"

Wigg nodded slightly. "We'll see," he said. He turned to look over one shoulder. "It's all right!" he called out.

Nathan gasped as Mallory entered the room. She instinctively wanted to run to him. But remembering Wigg's warnings, she stopped when she reached the sitting room door. Tears started flooding her eyes.

"Come, Mallory," Wigg said. He reached out one arm. "Sit beside me."

The Fledgling took a seat between Wigg and Shailiha. Drying her eyes, she looked at her father. He had changed. The mustache was new, and his hair was grayer. Her heart ached for him as she thought about what he had become.

"Father . . . ," she said, her voice cracking. For the moment that was the best she could do.

"Mallory," Nathan breathed. "Is that you?"

Smiling, she nodded. "In the flesh," she answered.

Nathan immediately started to leave his chair. Acting on caution's side, Wigg summoned the craft to force the consul back down. Nathan glared at Wigg, then returned his gaze to his daughter.

"I thought you were dead," he breathed, "killed at Fledgling House along with all the other girls!"

"That's what Nicholas told you, isn't it?" Wigg asked. "He wanted all the consuls to believe that their children were dead."

"Why would he do that?" Shailiha asked.

"My guess is that he had another use for the children, after taking their blood to help build the Gates of Dawn," Wigg answered. "It would have been something he didn't want his consuls to know about. Because he died during the Gates' collapse, we might never know what he had in mind. Things are probably better left that way."

Wigg's expression hardened. "Unless you would care to shed some light on the subject," he added.

Still overcome by his daughter's appearance, Nathan shook his head. "No," he breathed. "Nicholas never told us."

"Don't lie to me," Wigg said. "You know better than most that I can force the truth from you."

Nathan finally took his eyes from Mallory to look at the wizard. "He told us nothing about this—I swear it. Had I known Mallory was alive, I would have moved heaven and earth to find her!"

Just then Nathan saw the red Paragon embroidered on Mallory's shirt. He glared angrily at Wigg. "Why does my daughter still wear her Fledgling House uniform?" he demanded. "It was my understanding that the academy was abandoned!"

"Don't you remember?" Wigg asked. "Thirteen years ago you came to me on bended knee, asking that your daughter be admitted to Fledgling House. You even went so far as to petition Queen Morganna. It is only right that you know that Mallory's Vigors training continues, here in the Consuls' Nursery. You might also be interested to know that twenty-eight other consuls' children attend school there. The next time you see your daughter, she might be wearing a red acolyte's robe. That's what you wanted, is it not—for her to wander Eutracia as you once did, doing good deeds for the populace?"

Nathan looked like he might explode with rage. "You bastard!" he snarled. "How dare you oversee my child's rearing? I demand that you stop polluting her mind this instant! She's not your charge, and you know it! Her care and training are to be immediately turned over to me!"

Fighting Wigg's warp, Nathan did his best to stretch forth his arms. Shailiha got the distinct impression that if he could, the consul would gladly choke the First Wizard to death. Wigg calmly returned his gaze.

"If you don't do as I demand, one day I will kill you," Nathan breathed.

Mallory was stunned to hear her father speak that way. The First Wizard had been right. This was not the man she once knew.

Wigg sat back in his chair. "You're in no position to give orders," he replied. "Besides, whether Mallory's training continues or not, you've sworn to kill me anyway. Your late master demanded it. But you and I know that you'll never get the chance."

His jaw set, Wigg leaned closer. "You need to understand the seriousness of your situation, Nathan," he said. "Only two things can happen to you and your consular brothers. Either the Conclave finds a way to reverse the damage done to your blood signatures and brings you all back into the fold, or you remain imprisoned here in these rooms until the day you die. I'm sorry, Nathan, I truly am. But that's how things are."

Nathan looked beseechingly into Mallory's face. "You mustn't listen to them!" he shouted. "I'm your father! You have to believe me!" Tears started filling his eyes. He tried to reach an open hand across the table toward her, but it was no use.

Knowing better than to reciprocate without Wigg's permission, Mallory looked at the First Wizard. Wigg thought for a moment, then nodded.

Reaching out, Mallory took her father's hand. It felt strong and warm, just like she remembered. But he was different now, and she knew she must always remember that.

"Are you well?" Nathan asked. "You look so thin."

"The trip to Tammerland was difficult," Mallory answered. "But I'm all right. You must learn to accept that this is what I want—what I've always wanted, ever since my first day at Fledgling House."

Nathan pulled his hand away. "Then so be it!" he said angrily. "But understand something, you foolish neophyte! So long as you wear that Paragon on your shirt and continue to love the Vigors, you're no daughter of mine! Unless you are willing to devote your blood to the Vagaries, you're dead to me! Until that day comes, don't darken my door again!"

Nathan's words went through Mallory's heart like a knife. Even so, she refused to be persuaded. She shook her head.

"The Vigors are my chosen path," she answered. "I can only hope that one day you will return to us. You might yet be the father I once knew."

Nathan shook his head. "Get out!" he shouted. "All of you!" The consul turned away.

Looking at Mallory and Shailiha, Wigg nodded. While Nathan stayed behind, Wigg escorted the two women to the door, then released Nathan from his warp. Mallory stopped to look back.

"Good-bye, Father," she said gently. Nathan didn't answer.

As the door shut and the tumblers turned over, Nathan gazed into the fire. After a time, tears came. Burying his face in his hands, he slowly hung his head.

Chapter XXVIII

Tristan's head still lay in Xanthus' lap as the warm horse blood surged through his system. The prince slowly opened his eyes. Amid the howling wind and snow, the Darkling smiled.

"So you decided to come back after all!" he shouted.

Looking around, Tristan was shocked to see that his body had somehow been shoved into a horse's gaping abdomen. Revolted by his situation, he started frantically squirming his way out. As Xanthus pushed him back, Tristan realized that he was too weak to fight the Darkling's wishes.

"You still need what little warmth the carcass can provide!" Xanthus shouted. "When no more remains, we will try to go on again!"

"What happened?" Tristan asked thickly. His mind was groggy, but he could see that the Borderlands remained in their wintry state.

"You fell unconscious from your horse," Xanthus shouted back. "You were near death. To keep you alive, there was no choice but to kill my stallion and use his blood and body heat to keep you alive."

Suddenly concerned for Shadow, Tristan saw his stallion standing a few feet away. The horse was failing. Motionless in a knee-deep drift, his eyes were closed and his head drooped toward the ground. His back was blanketed with snow.

Shoving his hands into the dead horse's body cavity again, Xanthus discovered that it had finally gone cold. He looked back at the prince.

"Can you walk?" Xanthus shouted at Tristan. "We need to get moving while we still can!"

Tristan nodded. Crawling away from the dead horse, the prince rose shakily to his feet. As he pulled his blanket closer around him, Tristan tried to look through the swirling snow and toward the mountain gap. When at last he saw it, his heart fell. It looked as far away as when he and Xanthus had first exited the azure pass and stepped into the blistering desert.

Xanthus walked over to retrieve Shadow's reins from the deepening snowdrift. The horse came along weakly. After helping Tristan into the saddle, Xanthus started leading them toward the mountain gap.

We won't last long, the Darkling realized. *But* we *must try.*

An hour later, Xanthus stopped. He looked up at Tristan. The prince's hair and shoulders were covered with snow, and he had fallen asleep again. At least this time he was somehow staying in the saddle. Reaching into a duster pocket, Xanthus removed one of the raw heart pieces he had been saving. He would eat half, then give the rest to the prince. Just as he bit into it, he sensed an eerie calm.

The wind had suddenly died. With nothing to blow them about, the giant snowflakes fell straight to the ground. Then they stopped forming altogether, their sudden disappearances granting a clear view of the pearly sky.

The Borderlands were starting to change again, but Xanthus had no clue about what form they might take next. Pulling on Shadow's reins, he brought the horse to a stop. Still asleep, Tristan did not open his eyes.

Like he was frozen in place, Xanthus stood warily in the snow, waiting and watching. He needed to be sure before using up Shadow's last measure of strength. Then he saw the water forming around his boots.

Knowing he hadn't a second to lose, Xanthus mounted the horse behind the prince. Spurring Shadow for all he was worth he turned the stallion hard to the right, away from the distant mountain gap and toward the nearest mountain slope.

Shadow struggled across the valley as fast as he could. But trudging through the heavy snow while also carrying two riders was nearly impossible. Suddenly the valiant stallion stumbled.

Neighing wildly, he went down on one side, throwing Tristan and Xanthus to the snowy ground. As he got up, the Darkling didn't waste time looking back, for he knew what was coming. If Shadow couldn't outrun it, they were dead. The stallion finally fought his way back to his feet.

Lifting the prince, Xanthus somehow got him into the saddle; then he climbed up. Whipping the reins against Shadow's flanks,

Xanthus again charged the horse toward the bordering mountains.

As they reached the slopes, the Darkling heard a rushing sound chasing after them. Knowing that he couldn't waste precious seconds to stop and look, he spurred Shadow up the rocky mountainside. The going was even slower here, because one false step from Shadow would send the horse and riders plunging to their deaths. But the higher they climbed, the less snow there was with which to contend. Soon Xanthus could hear Shadow's iron shoes banging against solid rock.

Only then did he finally stop the horse atop a wide, rocky ledge. He wheeled Shadow around, then looked behind himself to see that Tristan was still unconscious. He slapped the prince hard across the face. Xanthus was desperate for Tristan to see what was happening, because he believed the spectacle would strengthen the *Jin'Sai*'s will to live.

At first Tristan didn't come around. After harshly slapping him again, Xanthus grabbed the prince's shoulders and shook him. The intense rumbling sound also helping to rouse him, Tristan slowly opened his eyes. Xanthus pointed down into the valley. The Borderlands' snow was melting.

But more than just the snow was morphing. The sky was slowly turning from ghostly white to heavenly blue. Speechless, Tristan watched as fluffy clouds arrived. Within seconds a bright, yellow sun formed, bathing the valley in its warmth. Then Tristan's numbed mind fully appreciated the immense noise, and he saw its cause.

As the temperature soared, the mountain snow melted, sending a gigantic wall of water rushing toward the valley. Majestically crashing and tumbling, it slammed its way along the valley floor in a torrent more powerful than any storm that had ever bedeviled the Sea of Whispers. Snow lying on the mountainside high above Tristan and Xanthus turned to warm water and came cascading down, showering them.

As the water brought Tristan fully to his senses, he joyously stood in the stirrups and raised his arms to the sky, bathing in its life-giving warmth. Opening his mouth, he drank greedily. He was about to let go a delighted shriek when he saw Xanthus dismount. The Darkling motioned that Tristan should do the same.

Soaked to the skin, Tristan walked to stand alongside the equally drenched Darkling. Tristan took a moment to rub

Shadow's face. Neighing softly, the horse seemed all right. Xanthus touched Tristan's shoulder, then pointed toward the valley. As the water shower falling over them slowly abated, Tristan looked down.

The valley waters were receding to show dark, rich soil. Soon the water was gone, to be replaced by another miracle.

Tristan watched in amazement as the Borderlands burst forth with new life. Emerald grass shoots sprung fingerlike from the valley floor, growing to their full height in mere moments. Deep blue rivers materialized to meander their way across the land. Waterfalls burst from the craggy mountainsides, their crystalline waters cascading down into idyllic pools lying at the bases of the mountains ranges.

Hearing more rumbling, Tristan saw trees sprout quickly from the ground, their unfamiliar species so many he couldn't start to count them. Some grew to astounding size before blossoming with leaves and fruit, while the ground surrounding them literally burst open to accommodate their hugely expanding root systems. Just when he thought the process might be finishing, sentient life-forms appeared.

Exotic birds appeared in the sky. Strange-looking insects buzzed and hummed, their swarms busily congregating on the colorful flower blossoms that now ranged so freely across the valley floor. Herds of strangely exotic beasts suddenly materialized to mill peacefully about. Stunned, Tristan simply tried to take it all in. It was like walking into a dream. He turned to look at Xanthus. The Darkling had returned to his spirit form.

"This is the Heretics' doing, isn't it?" Tristan asked.

Xanthus said, "The Borderlands have been dismantled. As I am sure you have gathered, magic has returned."

"Why would they do this now?" Tristan asked.

"The answer is simple," Xanthus said. "With the Ones' army destroyed, the Borderlands are no longer needed. What you see before you is but a small part of this world. But beautiful and welcoming as it might be, it is time for us to go."

After they climbed atop Shadow, Xanthus guided the horse down the mountainside. Luxuriating in the sun's warmth, Tristan nearly forgot his troubles as he simply relished being alive. On reaching the lush valley floor, Xanthus guided Shadow to a nearby tree.

Tristan was amazed by it. The trunk and branches were bright scarlet, the leaves light blue. Pendulous fruit hung heavily from its branches, bending them nearly to the ground.

Xanthus raised one hand. Two fruit pieces separated from the tree to come sailing through the air. They each caught one. The fruit's skin was black, with pink spots. Tristan had never seen its like. They jumped down from the stallion to stand in the lush grass.

Xanthus smiled. "Eat," he said simply.

Taking a throwing knife from its quiver, Tristan sliced open the fruit to find sumptuous, dark red meat and mustard-yellow seeds. Its aroma was intoxicating. Wasting no time, he started gorging himself. Even Shawna's pies had never tasted so sweet.

When he had finished, Tristan started to throw away the collected seeds. Grabbing his arm, Xanthus took them from him.

"Watch," the Darkling said.

Placing the seeds onto his palm, he blew them into the air. Tristan watched as the craft carried them far away to fall in the deep grass. Almost at once they started sprouting. Within moments a new grove appeared, its trees identical to that from which they had picked the fruit.

"Amazing," Tristan breathed. "What is this place called?"

"That is for the Heretics to answer," Xanthus replied. "You will meet them soon enough."

Tristan turned to look at the faraway mountain range. Even though he and Xanthus had survived the Borderlands, they seemed no closer to their goal.

"How can that be?" Tristan asked. "We still have so far to go!"

"As I said, *Jin'Sai,* with the Borderlands' passing, magic has returned," the Darkling answered. Xanthus raised an arm. "Behold."

Tristan turned to see the azure pass forming. This time it stood on its own, without granite walls bordering its sides. Just like before, it seemed to shimmer with life. Tristan looked up to see that its upper limits stretched into infinity.

"So your Forestallment can summon the pass and also allow us safe entry?" he asked.

"No," Xanthus answered. "The pass was nearby all the time. We couldn't see it in the Borderlands because magic was useless. In truth, our destination lies far beyond that mountain range. Mount your horse, *Jin'Sai.* The Heretics await us."

Xanthus climbed into the saddle, and Tristan jumped up to sit behind him. The Darkling turned Shadow toward the azure wall. They entered, and then they were gone.

As they traveled through the pass, the same sensations as before flooded over the prince. Azure fog beckoned limitlessly. He could sense Xanthus sitting before him and Shadow moving beneath him, but little else registered. When he tried to speak his words were as useless as before. Also like before, time seemed to have no meaning. As the immeasurable journey continued, Tristan tired again. The last thing he would remember was trying to stay conscious and not fall from his saddle.

"AWAKEN, *JIN'SAI*," A VOICE SAID. "YOU HAVE TRAVELED FAR AND suffered much to reach us. No other *Jin'Sai* or *Jin'Saiou* has succeeded as you have. Awaken, and behold."

Slowly opening his eyes, Tristan lifted his head. He looked around to become amazed beyond description. Then he saw the unfamiliar faces.

"Welcome, *Jin'Sai*," one said. "Welcome to Crysenium."

CHAPTER XXIX

AS A HANDMAIDEN PULLED A TORTOISESHELL HAIRBRUSH THROUGH Serena's dark ringlets, the queen of the Vagaries looked down at her dressing table. Her withered red rose lay before her. Raising her head to stare out her sitting room window, she saw that the dark sea was calm as its waves gently lapped against the rocky shore. The sky was clear, its endless stars twinkling brightly.

But she knew that this peacefulness would soon change. A war was coming—one that would finally end the Vigors for all time. Its stentorian call would come the day the Conclave sailed for the scroll. They had no choice but to try.

She smiled. The prize the Conclave sought was no longer on the Citadel's shores. They would waste their efforts, their forces, and their Black Ships, giving Einar and Reznik more time to succeed in their orders. For now she would obey the Heretics' orders and remain on the island to guard the Citadel and her lifeless child. Looking into the mirror, she reached up to touch the handmaiden's wrist.

"That will be all," she said. "You may retire."

The servant placed the hairbrush atop the dressing table and bowed. "As you wish, mistress," she said. Leaving the queen's chambers, she closed the door behind her. Serena again looked out over the sea.

As she thought about Wulfgar, tears came. She had loved him more than life. Even though she was the Citadel's undisputed ruler and she commanded many souls, she felt desperately alone. These chambers had provided her and her husband with many happy moments. Clarice had been conceived in these rooms. But now these chambers represented only loneliness. Instead of a family's laughter, only silence reigned.

The fact that all those living on the island with her were mere servants only added to her isolation. They were needed to achieve her goals, but they meant nothing more to her than that—especially the crude Valrenkians. She looked forward to the day when the Heretics' triumph would be complete, and she could kill the inferior partial adepts. There would be no room for half-breeds in the new order. But until then she needed them, so she would wait. Victory would also bring the Heretics' total dominion over the known world, and they had promised that she would rule all the lands east of the Tolenkas. Eager for her prize, she relished the possibilities such an august position offered.

Even so, with Einar, Reznik, and all her envelopers gone, she had growing concerns about how her island was to be defended. The Heretics had told her that when the time was right, she would be informed. But it had been days since they last revealed themselves to her mind. Their continued silence increased her restlessness.

Thinking, she lovingly took up the dead rose. The Citadel's defense would be explained to her soon, she knew. Until then she had to be patient, and trust in the Heretics' infinite wisdom.

She detested this benign calmness before the storm, for it did nothing except accentuate her solitude. On Wulfgar's death, at first her heart believed that what little they had shared would last a lifetime. Their love had been that strong, that deep, that rooted in common goals. At first, she had been right.

But as her life became taken up with honoring the Heretics' wishes, other needs resurfaced. She soon missed more than Wulfgar's leadership. She yearned for the commanding way that he had always taken her. Her psyche needed it, longed for it, and demanded it. But there was no one here worthy of granting such intimacies to a widowed queen.

Then she remembered the spell that Einar had told her about, just before leaving the Citadel. Because of its highly intimate nature, at first he hadn't known whether to speak of it. After careful thought he'd decided that Wulfgar would want her to have it, to do with as she pleased. And so it was with no small measure of trepidation that he had visited the queen's private chambers to discuss it.

At first Serena was shocked by Einar's forthrightness. He went on to say that he had happened on the unique calculations among the thousands of other spells, during his perusal of the Vagaries scroll. As she heard him out, her objections gradually softened. In the end she finally accepted the small parchment bearing the elegant symbols and numbers.

Honoring Wulfgar's memory, she had never read the parchment. Doing so would somehow be adulterous, disrespectful, she reasoned. But as another night passed with no one to comfort her, she found herself tempted. Perhaps she would only read the formula. Surely that could do no harm. She lay down the rose and opened her inlaid jewelry box. She called the craft, then levitated the wrinkled document within into the air. With a turn of her wrist she caused the paper to unfold itself.

Bathed in the candlelight, the Old Eutracian formula appeared to have been written by a female hand. As she sat reading the calculations, she marveled at the synchronicity of events that had delivered this wonder to her.

Who was she, Serena wondered—*this woman from aeons ago who had decided to add such a unique formula to the scroll? Although they speak to me, there is still so much I do not know about the Heretics. But this brilliant lady from another place and time has somehow reached out across the ages to offer up this teasing nostrum in my hour of need. Did she ever use it? Had she tragically lost her lover, as I did? Does she somehow watch me from the Afterlife even now, as I consider this temptation?*

Increasingly seduced by the intriguing calculations, the queen of the Vagaries took a deep breath. Standing, she grasped the parchment from the air, then looked to the sea again. Finally she decided. *Forgive me, my love,* she thought.

After memorizing the formula she placed the parchment back into the box, then walked to her bed to lie down. As its lace crinkled against the bedcovers, she was reminded that she still wore her black mourning gown. Taking a deep breath, she summoned the spell.

She watched as the room's light started to change. Unafraid, she willingly embraced the violet hue washing over her. Music came to her ears, its melodious strains permeating her psyche. Her mind started drifting pleasantly, her need quickly strengthening while her guilt at having enacted the spell strangely faded away. Soon she was possessed by a hunger even more irresistible than before.

The unexpected stirring in her loins started slowly, warmly. She wanted to reach down, but then stopped herself as she realized that there was no need, for the magic washing over her grew more enticing by the moment. As the sensation swelled she could almost feel Wulfgar holding her, taking her, whispering in her ear.

Soon her urgency reached a crescendo. Aching to be taken by it, she let the spell enslave her. The result seemed never-ending as she fell into its rapturous embrace. Crying out, she lost all track of time. It seemed the overpowering contractions might never end.

Then the spell slowly left her. The music stopped, the violet light vanished, and her heartbeat slowed. *Wondrous,* she thought.

The queen turned her head to one side and fell into a deep sleep.

"SERENA," SHE HEARD THE VOICES CALL AS SHE LAY SLEEPING. *"Awake to do our bidding. There is much for you to learn."*

Stirring from her sleep, she looked around. Several hours had passed, and the room's candles had nearly burned to their bases. Calling the craft, she brought flame to three fresh ones in various places about her chambers. She left the bed and went to her knees, then bowed her head and closed her eyes.

"I am here," she responded silently.

"The Conclave is nearly ready to sail," the Heretics' voices said. *"Circumstances demand that you be shown how to defend the Citadel. Rise, and do as we say."*

She came to her feet.

"Go to the lowest Citadel region," the voices commanded. *"You know the place. Go alone."*

"As you wish," she answered. She left her chambers and entered the hallway.

There were few consuls or Valrenkians about at this late hour, save for those standing guard. Her appearance surprised them. *Our queen is restless this night,* some thought as she walked through the shadows.

Serena entered the moonlit courtyard and trod down one of the many covered porticoes before coming to an old door. Made from solid oak, its iron cross braces were deeply layered with crimson rust. Calling the craft, she caused it to open. Its hinges protested loudly. Once she was on its opposite side she closed it again.

Remembering what the Heretics had said about coming alone, she locked the door from the inside with an especially convoluted spell. She brought light to the oil lamps lining the steps. Lifting her skirt, she started down.

Although the curved stairway seemed interminable, Serena was not afraid. She and Wulfgar had come here once before. They had been out exploring the Citadel one day soon after their marriage. On reaching the bottom they had found only an abandoned stone room. In the end their search had given them nothing but a good laugh. Unable to imagine why the Heretics would want her to go there, she dutifully continued on.

Reaching the last step, she looked around. The nondescript room was just as she remembered. Square and spacious, it was carved from the surrounding rock. There was no other way in or out besides the stairway she had exited. The room was barren save for several oil lamp sconces hanging on the four walls. A shiny metal light reflector lay attached to the wall behind each one. Waving an arm, Serena brought the lamps to life, flooding the room with a golden glow. She waited.

"Well done," the voices said. *"Walk to the wall facing you."*

She walked across the room to stand before the far wall. Like the other three, its surface was unremarkable.

"Touch the wall," the voices said. *"As you do, enact the same spell you would employ when using a visage board."*

Having spent much time in the Citadel Scriptorium, she was familiar with visage boards. Reaching out, she touched the granite wall and called the proper spell.

At once the wall's right side started to change. The stone morphed into a smooth black visage board. As she watched in wonder, four separate formulas written in Old Eutracian rose from its depths. The azure symbols twinkled brightly against their dark background.

"Good," the voices said. *"Summon the first spell, then the second one. But never bring the third or fourth ones unless told to do so."*

Marshaling her concentration, Serena employed the first spell. Without waiting to see the results, she then called forth the second one.

"Back away from the wall," the voices ordered her. She immediately obeyed.

The wall's entire left side started changing. The rough granite vanished to show another dark panel, its right edge bordering the visage board. Larger than the first, this one stretched from the floor to the ceiling. Then the second spell took hold. As the black panel became transparent, a bright light appeared, illuminating the area on the panel's opposite side.

Stunned, Serena took several steps backward. Her hands flew to cover her gaping mouth. What she saw was impossible. She was looking directly into the Sea of Whispers.

The vision before her was wondrous, overwhelming. She suddenly realized that the lengthy stairs she had descended had brought her to a place far below the ocean surface. The seafloor partly pressed against the panel's opposite side. As the second spell brightly illuminated the depths, she stared in wonder at the sea's untold mysteries.

The water was a brilliant blue. Fish and other exotic sea creatures swam, crawled, and scurried across the ocean floor. Their strangeness both fascinating and beautiful, most were alien to her.

Like they were being caressed by some unseen hand, undersea waves gently undulated the colorful foliage. Multicolored coral grew in abundance. Starfish and shellfish trudged slowly across the sandy bottom, while shadows created by fish swimming overhead crawled over the scene, adding to its mysterious elegance. The occasional fish, eel, or other sea creature would sometimes approach the panel and seem to stare blankly at her, only to turn and swim away again. Entranced, Serena could have stood there watching for hours.

"Four years, Serena," the Heretics said to her.

"I don't understand," Serena answered.

"It took us four years to create the wonder you see before you. That is what you were wondering, is it not?"

Surprised, Serena nodded. *"Yes,"* she answered.

"Summon the third spell."

Serena did so. At once the seascape started changing. The ground outside the panel rushed toward her, like she had somehow gone into the water and was sailing over the seafloor. As the journey quickened she became dizzy, even though she herself did not move. Finally the onrushing landscape slowed, then stopped to show a different underwater scene.

The seafloor had become dark and highly irregular. A high underwater cliff lay before her, its leading edge facing west. It seemed as tall as the Citadel itself before sharply dropping off into a dark infinity. Confused by what she saw, she could only look and wonder.

"The ledge you see is many leagues west of the Citadel," the Heretics said to her. *"Listen closely as we explain what happens with the fourth spell's onset."*

As Serena listened she became astounded. *Could such a thing be possible?* she wondered. *How could I, a far weaker craft practitioner than the Heretics, ever summon such power?*

"When the time comes, all you must do is summon the last spell," the Heretics answered. *"It will then perform all that is called for to defend the Citadel. The fourth spell has never been enacted. Even so, it is as strong as the day it was first conceived. Now you may rest easier, knowing how your island home will be protected. If the time comes that the spell is needed, we will tell you."*

"I understand," she said.

"Command the first three spells in reverse," the voices ordered. *"Return everything in this room to what it once was."*

Serena walked back to the visage board and cast the first three spells in the opposite order from which they had been summoned. The seascape rushed back to its original place on the ocean floor. Then the bright light illuminating the ocean went out and the viewing panel disappeared. Finally the visage board vanished. In their places the granite wall reappeared.

"Do you fully understand your duties?" the voices asked. *"The Vagaries' future and the Citadel's defense might soon depend on you performing these deeds properly."*

"I understand," she answered. *"If needed, all will happen as you have ordered."*

Walking back to the stone stairway, Serena turned to take one last look. Everything about the room was just as it had been when she first arrived. *Astounding,* she thought.

Waving one hand she extinguished the wall sconces and started up the stairway.

CHAPTER XXX

AS TRISTAN TOOK IN HIS NEW SURROUNDINGS, THE MORE HE SAW, the more astounded he became. He was lying atop a silken bed. Xanthus stood beside him, the Darkling's human face staring down at him worriedly. The Paragon still shone brightly as it hung around Xanthus' neck.

Turning his head, the *Jin'Sai* saw a group of beings crowded around his bed's foot. Men and women were in attendance. Each was elderly and wore a glistening white robe.

It took Tristan several moments to find his voice. "Are you the Heretics of the Guild?" he asked.

An elderly woman approached to stand by his bedside. She was tall and graceful, with long, gray hair. Her face was attractive, her expression calm. Her brown eyes seemed to bore their way into his.

"I am Hoskiko, one of Those Who Came Before," she answered. “Five brothers and sisters of my order are here with me. The other six males and females you see are Heretics of the Guild. We welcome you in peace. You are the first *Jin’Sai* to reach us. Our world has long awaited your arrival.”

Tristan shook his head. “This can’t be!” he protested. “The Guild and the Ones are at war! I saw an entire army of the Ones destroyed by the Heretics! Why would bitter enemies like yourselves gather together?”

A man stepped forward. Like Hoskiko, he was elderly. His presence was commanding. His hair was gray, his chin strong. There was a resolute look in his eyes.

“It is precisely *because* we are enemies that we gather together,” he said. “My name is Faxon, and I am a Heretic. Like Hoskiko, I lead five specially selected brothers and sisters of my order. But we six Heretics did not kill the Ones’ army—others of our sect did that. We detest violence. Taken as a whole, we are the twelve Envoys of Crysenium.”

Tristan didn’t understand a word of what Faxon said. But he knew one thing—Xanthus had deceived him. He looked up at the Darkling with hate-filled eyes. Grabbing Xanthus’ duster, he roughly pulled him closer.

“You liar!” he said. “You told me you were taking me to the Heretics! Had I known that the Ones would be present, I might have come sooner! Innocent lives could have been spared!”

An immensely sad look overcame Xanthus’ face. To Tristan’s great surprise the Darkling went down on one knee before him and bowed his head. He started to speak, but Hoskiko waved a hand, cutting him off. Surprised by Xanthus’ reaction, Tristan released him.

“Did Xanthus lie to you?” Hoskiko asked Tristan. “Perhaps—but if he did, it was only by omission. If you must be angry with someone, be angry with us Envoys. He was only following our orders.” Hoskiko smiled at the Darkling.

“He did his job exceedingly well,” she added. “You see, Xanthus serves all twelve of us.”

Tristan felt a shudder go through him. Had Wigg, Faegan, and the late Directorate somehow been horribly wrong about the Ones? Xanthus was a servant of the Vagaries—he had said so himself. If the Ones were partly responsible for sending the Darkling through the pass, did the Ones also worship the Vagaries? His mind filled with unanswered questions, the *Jin'Sai* stared worriedly at the twelve figures in the white robes.

Sensing his confusion, Hoskiko took him by the hand. Her touch was warm, reassuring. "Do not fear," she said. "No harm will befall you here. It's true that we purposely deceived you. But you must understand that not only were our motives just, but highly needed. After we tell you why you have been summoned, you will go home to Eutracia. We are about to burden you with a sacred mission. Whether it takes a day, a year, or your entire lifetime to finish, it must be done. If you are successful, you will forever change not only every living being's future, but that of the craft, as well."

Trying to understand, Tristan took a deep breath. "Are you speaking about Shailiha's and my destinies?" he asked. "The destinies that are so often mentioned in the Tome?"

Hoskiko nodded. "The same," she answered.

"I already know that my fate is to combine the craft's two sides," Tristan said. "If I should fail or die in my attempt, the burden falls to Shailiha. What I do not understand is why or how this is to be carried out."

"The Tome has always been unclear on that point, has it not?" Faxon said. He gave Tristan a compassionate but also critical look that reminded him of Wigg. "Even your wizards are the first to admit that things are not always what they seem—especially about the craft."

"First things first," Hoskiko said. She held out one hand. "Come with us. There is much to discuss."

Tristan stood from the bed. At first his legs were wobbly. Looking around again, he found his surroundings awe-inspiring. "Crysenium," he said softly. "That must be an Old Eutracian word. Where are we?"

"Let us sit," Hoskiko answered. "Then we will explain."

Hoskiko took him by the hand. As they walked across the floor, Xanthus and the other Envoys followed. Walking farther, Tristan still couldn't believe the place's overpowering majesty. It was like being inside a palace made of azure glass.

They were crossing a huge circular room. It seemed to have been built of some sort of crystalline material, almost giving one the impression that it was made of ice. But that was not so, he realized, because the room's atmosphere was warm and welcoming.

The spherical chamber was stunning. Azure columns by the dozens reached high into the air, their scrolled tops seeming to support nothing. There was no ceiling, and the sky overhead was blue, with white, fluffy clouds floating through it. The smooth floor and concave walls were made of the same shimmering material as the columns. A lovely melodious sound—much like that produced by wind chimes on a breezy day—wafted gently through the air.

Although the room was open to the sky, no wind blew though the chamber, nor could Tristan detect any of the normal outdoor sounds one might expect to hear. Then he caught sight of some curved, reflected sunlight high above, and he understood. There was in fact a roof. Made of a clear material, its surface stretched from sidewall to sidewall, covering the entire room. It was breathtaking.

As they walked farther they entered a long hallway. Soon they came to another circular room constructed of the same material as the first one. Tristan saw several closed doors situated in the curved walls. They led to living quarters, he suspected.

At the room's center sat a round, pure white table encircled by fourteen equally beautiful chairs. Half of the circular wall was devoted to the same transparent material that formed the ceiling in the other room. A beautiful pastoral view, much like the one he and Xanthus had just left behind, beckoned from the other side. Tristan again saw many exotic and unfamiliar plants, birds, and creatures. The scene was mesmerizing.

Hoskiko beckoned everyone to sit. As Tristan took a chair, Hoskiko and Faxon sat on either side of him. Xanthus and the remaining ten Envoys also took seats. Tristan eagerly started to ask a question when Hoskiko touched his hand, requesting that he remain silent. Understanding, he nodded.

Clearly, Hoskiko and Faxon would control these proceedings. The two mystics seemed to possess a quiet, innate power. Wigg, Jessamay, and Faegan each commanded the same type of dignified respect. But in Hoskiko's and Faxon's cases, Tristan sensed it far more strongly. Despite his overpowering need for answers, he resolved to be patient.

"First we will introduce ourselves," Hoskiko said. "You have already become familiar with me, Faxon, and Xanthus." She looked across the table to the other ten Envoys. "For the *Jin'Sai*'s edification, will each of you please state your name, and which order you represent?" she asked. "So that the *Jin'Sai* will understand us, we will speak only in his eastern dialect, rather than our own. Is everyone agreed?" Each Envoy nodded his or her consent.

One by one the Envoys told Tristan who they were, and to which order he or she belonged. The three female Ones were Hoskiko, Mitsu, and Sakura. The men were Ichiro, Rinji, and Suzu. Of the Heretics, the men were named Faxon, Arvid, and Balsius. The Heretical women were Alma, Emilia, and Kristin. The Heretics sat as a group on Tristan's right; the Ones sat on his left. Directly across the table from Tristan and separating the two groups sat Xanthus.

"You are wondering where you are," Faxon started. "The explanation is not an altogether simple one." Placing his hands flat atop the table, Faxon chose his next words carefully.

"Simply put, in Old Eutracian, Crysenium means 'Place of Peace,' " he explained. "Crysenium is not a country, a province, or even a city. It is a stand-alone construct of the craft, lovingly built and maintained by the gifted people you see at this table. Crysenium serves but one purpose—to secretly welcome you into our midst. Until Crysenium existed, we could not guarantee your safety. We painstakingly built Crysenium just after the Orb of the Vigors sliced through the Tolenka Mountains, joining the world's two sides."

"Where are we?" Tristan asked.

"We are even deeper inside the territory where Borderlands sometimes rage," Hoskiko said. "Even so, the Borderlands occupy but a small portion of our world's total landmass. Xanthus has already explained your journey, and what you endured to reach us. We therefore know that you already understand the Borderlands' changing nature. Had we known that an army of the Ones was advancing, we would have waited, then sent Xanthus to fetch you later, when it was safer. As a group, we humbly apologize for the hardships you endured."

"You say that you created Crysenium deep inside the Borderlands," Tristan said. "It seems that you must have used magic to do so. But Xanthus told me that magic was of no use in the Borderlands."

"True enough," a female voice said from the table's other side. "But there is more than one way to skin a cat, as you on the world's other side are so fond of saying."

It had been Alma who had spoken. Alma was easily as old as Hoskiko, with short gray hair. Even from across the table her eyes bored into Tristan's.

"I don't understand," Tristan said.

"Even though magic is useless when the Borderlands are activated, the vast majority of time the area is the way you see it now, through this room's window," Alma said. "Crysenium was constructed quickly during those conditions, under cover of a spell allowing us to cloak our work. With the construct finished, another spell ensured that Crysenium remains cloaked. It's true that the Heretics watch for intruders like the army you and Xanthus saw annihilated. But because of the vast distances involved, smaller groups of people are far more difficult for the Heretics to notice. The Heretics use the Borderlands to search for and destroy great enemy hordes—not groups of ten or twelve. Even so, we took a huge risk in building this place. Luckily, our spells held and we were successful. As long as our cloak remains in place, Crysenium is invisible to the Heretics. The Heretics rarely venture here, so this region is perfect for our needs. Rest assured that we have deceived them. If not we would be dead, and Crysenium destroyed. The more fanatical Heretics are not ones to leave stones unturned." She smiled again.

"Besides," she added, "the deadly Borderlands are the last place they would search for a secret craft construct."

Tristan was stunned. "Do you mean to say that you risked your lives to build this place just for me? Why would you do that?"

"So that we could finally meet with a *Jin'Sai* in secrecy," Faxon said. "Even though the Ones and the Heretics remain embroiled in a deadly war, what happens on your side of the world is equally important. Three momentous developments have recently intersected in time. That is why you have been brought here. We must act quickly, for such a wondrous set of occurrences might never merge again."

"What are they?" Tristan asked.

"The first is the creation of the azure pass," Suzu said. A member of the Ones, he sat on Tristan's left side. A gray, bushy beard adorned his face.

"The cutting of the pass through the Tolenka Mountains by the Vigors orb was an event much heralded by the Heretics," Suzu added. "Despite appearances it was a random, unexpected occurrence. We know of no other force in the world powerful enough to have done that. In any event, the unexpected result of Wulfgar's failed plan was the Tolenkan pass. When they learned of it, the Heretics were overjoyed."

"Why?" Tristan asked.

"Because for aeons the Tolenkas had been insurmountable, even to the Ones and the Heretics," Hoskiko answered. "Unfortunately, the pass exited this side of the Tolenkas in Heretic-controlled territory. At long last they had found a way to enter your side of the world, while the Ones could not. Now they can much more easily influence Eutracian and Parthalonian history. As an additional assurance that only they might use it, they immediately flooded the pass with convoluted magic. A special Forestallment is needed to safely navigate its length. Should anyone enter the pass without the Forestallment's protection, death is immediate."

Tristan looked across the table at the Darkling. "And Xanthus' blood carries that Forestallment," he mused.

"That's right," Hoskiko answered. "It also protected you."

"You mentioned three important events," Tristan said. "What are the other two?"

"One is your world's discovery of how to alter the lean of a blood signature," Faxon answered. "That is a major leap forward in your primitive understanding of the craft."

"And what is the third development?" Tristan asked.

Leaning forward, Faxon stared intently into Tristan's eyes. "With the coming of the pass, the Heretics saw it as a way to capture you, and keep you from fulfilling your destiny," he said. "Among all the *Jin'Sai*s ever born, you have come closest to honoring the Tome's prophecies. The Heretics knew that your wizards would never allow you and your sister to enter the pass at the same time. But if they could first tempt you, they would then try to seduce Shailiha. And so they hatched a plan—one that involved Xanthus, and that they believed you couldn't resist. In the end, it nearly worked. Had it not been for us twelve Envoys, you would be in the Heretics' grasp this moment."

Tristan looked across the table at the Darkling. "So the Heretics sent you to Eutracia to steal the Paragon and commit atrocities until I agreed to accompany you through the pass," he said. He looked at Hoskiko. "But you said that Xanthus serves you all," he protested. "What did you mean by that?"

"You have been told only part of Xanthus' story," she answered. "Rather than take you to the Heretics, he followed our orders and brought you here. No matter what you think of him, he is the only reason you're still alive."

"That might be," Tristan said. "But not one of you has answered my first question. Why do the Ones and the Heretics sit peacefully together at the same table? Don't tell me that all this has been done simply to save my life. You want something, and for some reason you need my help to get it."

Hoskiko reached out to touch Tristan's hand. "You must hear us out," she said gently. "The three concurrent events we mentioned have granted us an unparalleled opportunity to finally secure peace between the two orders. That is why we built Crysenium. That is also why we brought you here."

"That still does not explain why Ones and Heretics sit together at this table," Tristan pressed.

Leaning closer, Faxon searched the prince's face. "The simple truth is that not all the Heretics think alike anymore," he answered. "We six represent a larger splinter group, hungry for peace. Unknown to our other Heretic brothers and sisters, our secret group is growing. But the fanatics who so vastly outnumber us wish to see the Vigors wiped out forever. That is why they have been meddling in your world's affairs, *Jin'Sai.* They want to stamp out the Vigors wherever they find it. You and your sister have done amazingly well in your efforts to stop the Heretics' destructive plans. But your struggles against them have been mere skirmishes in the overall battle between light and dark. For hundreds of generations, untold numbers of Ones and Heretics have been fighting and killing one another. And for what reason? we Envoys ask ourselves. The Ones know why they fight—the Heretics are so unrelenting in their attacks that the Ones must battle back simply to survive. The War of Attrition has been going on for so long that either side can scarcely remember why it started." Pausing for a moment, Faxon sat back in his chair.

"Despite my wish for peace, I am still a high-ranking member of the Imperial Order," he added. "That is our military wing. During my career I have ordered the deaths of countless Ones. Perhaps that is why I want a resolution so badly. Once I started discreetly making my feelings known, I was amazed to learn how many other Heretics shared my concerns. Soon a secret splinter group was born. The other Heretics here with me can all be trusted, *Jin'Sai.* They each want peace as badly as I do. That is why we call ourselves Envoys. We need help—help that only you or Shailiha can grant us."

"But how can I, a person of untrained blood, ever hope to help *you*?" Tristan asked. "Your powers and skills dwarf even those of my wizards!" Turning to look at the table as a whole, Tristan's eyes searched every Envoy's face. "It's time you told me why you have brought me to this place," he said. "It's a story I've been destined my entire life to hear."

Hoskiko nodded. "We know," she said, "just as we have been waiting for aeons to welcome a *Jin'Sai* into our midst, and to tell the tale. We are responsible for your and your sister's existences. In turn, you and she are responsible for helping our world, here so far away. It has been this way since the War of Attrition started. With your coming, we hope to change things. We need each other—perhaps more than at any moment in our history. Please listen carefully as we explain your destiny's true meaning." Reaching out, she lovingly placed one hand against his cheek.

Gently, she said, "In many ways, it's not what you have been led to believe."

CHAPTER XXXI

"YOU STILL HAVEN'T SAID WHY YOU'RE TAKING US FOR A CARRIAGE ride at this hour, old man," Abbey chided Wigg. She playfully poked one elbow into his ribs. The First Wizard winced. "What are you up to?" she asked.

Even though she was as confused as the herbmistress, Shailiha smiled. "I agree," she said. "The least you could do is to tell us what's going on. You were so secretive back at the palace!"

Tyranny would be next in line to complain. Sitting beside the princess, she crossed her arms and scowled at the First Wizard.

"Scars and I should be with the fleet—not out on some midnight joyride!" she protested. "Much remains to be done! We sail for the Citadel tomorrow, you know! Or have you lived for so many centuries that your memory is finally starting to go?"

Shailiha snorted a short laugh down her nose, but Tyranny found no part of this mysterious trip amusing. She lit a cigarillo and angrily blew the smoke toward the carriage roof.

Scowling, Wigg took his gaze from the passing street to regard the three strong-willed women traveling with him. They could certainly be a handful. Worse, once they learned why he had asked them to come, there would be no end to their questions.

It was a cool, pleasant evening. Streetlamps cast their welcoming glow across the nondescript coach-and-four as it rattled its way down a busy Tammerland thoroughfare. Scars sat up top driving the team.

Letting go a sigh, Wigg gathered his gray robe closer against the chilly night air. He had chosen this garden-variety coach from the palace stables because he wanted no heraldic adornments giving away its passengers' identities. The First Wizard cleared his throat.

"I'm killing two birds with one stone," he replied. "First, I wanted to talk to you about Tristan. I needed a private place in which to do it, so I chose this coach ride. Moreover, we head to a place where I hope to unravel a riddle. You will find it interesting.

"Besides," he went on to say, "had I not brought you along, then told you all about it later, there would have been no end to your caterwauling! Faegan agreed that this trip was needed, but he chose to stay behind to remain immersed in his work."

At the mention of her brother, Shailiha leaned closer. "What are you talking about?" she demanded.

"The fact is, Faegan, Jessamay, and I believe Tristan might return soon," Wigg answered.

"What!" Tyranny exclaimed. "How could you know that?"

Pursing his lips, Wigg looked thoughtfully down at his hands. "We can't know for sure," he answered. "But we have reasoned it through, and we believe we're right."

Abbey gave him a wry look. "Out with it," she said, "or we'll have to gang up on you."

Wigg took a moment to gather his thoughts. "We all know that

Xanthus could have killed Tristan that night during the masquerade ball, but he didn't," he answered. "That means that the Heretics need him for something. Then there is this equally strange business about the Darkling granting the index forestallments to Faegan's blood. Perhaps even more important, the Darkling spoke about Tristan's possible return. If that comes true, Faegan and I believe that Xanthus might be needed to guide Tristan home again. The azure magic that fills the pass still has us baffled—it's like nothing we have seen before. But we are reasonably sure that a unique spell is needed to safely navigate its depths. Moreover, we have reason to believe that the Heretics alone control the pass, because no Vigors servant has exited it. If that is all true and Tristan returns, we might have to take some unusual steps on his behalf."

"What do you mean?" Shailiha asked.

"When next we see the *Jin'Sai* he could be a changed man," Wigg answered soberly, "and perhaps not for the better. Why would the Heretics want him? He is untrained in magic, so he cannot add to their craft knowledge. They might want his blood to somehow help win their long-standing war against the Ones—but Faegan, Jessamay, and I can't imagine how. In the end, we can come up with but one logical reason why they would summon him into their midst, only to return him to us."

Although she was immensely interested in Tristan's welfare, Shailiha was hesitant to hear what Wigg had to say. Finally her curiosity overcame her worry.

"What is it?" she asked.

Thinking, Wigg looked out the window for a time. When he returned his gaze to them, his expression was grim.

"Simply put, they want to interfere with his destiny," he said. "And yours as well, Princess. Somehow they want to keep you and your brother from combining the craft's opposite sides. If they return him to us a changed man, they might well succeed in doing just that."

"But if that is the case then why return him to us at all?" Tyranny asked. "Simply keeping him on their side of the world would do that."

"Yes," Wigg answered, "but perhaps at a far greater risk to them, and with less effectiveness."

"But how so?" Abbey asked. "What Tyranny said seems sensible enough."

"At first glance, it is," Wigg answered. "But you are forgetting something. The Ones also exist on the world's other side—or so we believe. If that is the case, then—"

"The Ones might somehow rescue Tristan from the Heretics," Shailiha mused. "He would then become *their* ally. It might make more sense for the Heretics to change his thinking in some way, then send him back. If his blood was gifted with their Forestallments, he could do incredible damage to the Vigors."

"Precisely," Wigg said to the princess. "The azure pass might be just the thing the Heretics have been wanting for aeons. They once sent *K'tons* through the pass to serve Wulfgar. One can only guess what might come next. Tristan, perhaps, with a Vagaries army all his own and bent on destroying the Vigors? Only time will tell."

The travelers went quiet for a time as they considered Wigg's ominous warning. Finally Abbey broke the silence. "You said that should Tristan return, we might have to take some unusual steps," she said. "What did you mean?"

"If the prince comes home, we must watch him closely and perform regular examinations of his blood signature before we can rest assured that he is unaffected," Wigg said. "We might even be forced to affect his memory, then lock him away, as we have done with the traitorous consuls. Such things are painful to imagine, I know. I don't like it any more than you, but there it is."

Her heart heavy, Shailiha looked out the carriage window. Tristan becoming their enemy was frightening in the extreme. Moreover, since his disappearance she felt immensely guilty about doing so little to try to find him.

But she also knew that Jessamay and the wizards were right. Trying to send someone through the azure pass without first knowing its secrets might be a death sentence. Worse, should the Heretics detect any tampering with the pass's magic, they might somehow close it. That could make Tristan's return impossible, imprisoning him on the other side forever. Then she remembered his last words to her, just before he disappeared with the Darkling.

"Promise me that you will attack the Citadel!" he had ordered. In truth that was all she could do. But with the Black Ships sailing tomorrow, she felt like she was abandoning him. She turned back to Wigg.

"Where are you taking us?" she asked.

Sitting back in the seat, Wigg folded his arms across his chest. "I want to learn about *K'Shari,*" he said simply. "I think it has more to do with our problems than we might suspect. Faegan believes that besides a lifetime of martial training, the gift might also be granted by Forestallment. In fact, using his newly acquired index Forestallment, he has discovered scroll calculations to that effect. Perhaps that's how the Heretics granted the skill to Xanthus. I know someone who might be able to shed some light on the subject. But it's been a long time—I'm not sure I'll be granted an audience."

"Is learning about *K'Shari* worth our time and trouble tonight?" Tyranny asked. "We sail tomorrow!"

"I understand your concern," Wigg answered. "But we need to learn all we can about Xanthus, and any weaknesses he might have. I believe we haven't seen the last of him. And I have another reason for making this visit." The wizard's face grew wistful.

"The truth is that I need to offer my belated condolences to someone," he said. "Since Wulfgar's defeat, I have been negligent in that responsibility. And by coming with me, you will learn about another facet of Eutracian history. By previous agreement, the late Directorate swore never to speak of it. I am without question violating that promise. But the Directorate is no more, and I have resolved to do this thing." His mind made up, the First Wizard stubbornly gazed out the window again.

The three women looked at one another with confusion. Shailiha was about to ask Wigg another question when Abbey shook her head. For the next quarter hour they rode in silence. As Scars finally brought the coach to a stop, Shailiha looked out the window.

The peasant-class neighborhood was shabby and forlorn. Street light was in short supply. The ramshackle houses lining either street side seemed to drunkenly lean up against one another for support, giving the princess the distinct impression that if one collapsed, the others would fall like dominoes. Whores seductively prowled the corners, while dark male figures lingered in the shadows. She couldn't imagine an acquaintance of Wigg's living here. The First Wizard quickly exited the coach and shut the door, purposely leaving the women behind.

Shailiha scowled. "I thought you said you were taking us with you!" she protested.

Pulling his robe closer, Wigg looked up and down the street. "If I am allowed entrance, I'll request that you three be admitted with me," he said. "Scars will stay with the coach. If you see me signal, you may come. Should anyone approach you, order Scars to charge the carriage up the—"

Suddenly Wigg stopped. After looking at the three perturbed women then up at the glowering Scars, he shook his head.

"On second thought, I'm more afraid for anyone trying to give you trouble than I am for you four!" he said. "Just wait here!" Turning away, he strode toward the house.

Shailiha peered at the ramshackle structure. It seemed much like the others, save for a wooden sign hanging perpendicular to the street. Craning her neck, she was surprised to see that the sign carried no words. One side bore the carved likeness of a snake; its other side carried a sword.

Wigg walked up the steps. Still hoping that he was doing the right thing, he knocked on the door. The door soon creaked opened to show a young man dressed in a dark robe. Golden light streamed from the house's interior to cast Wigg's elongated shadow onto the street.

"May I help you?" the fellow asked.

"I humbly request to see your master," Wigg said. Knowing better than to say more, he remained still.

"Why?" the man asked.

"I am an old friend," Wigg said. "I admit that my visit is unexpected. But if you tell him that Wigg is here, I believe he will see me. I have brought three friends who also seek admittance. Our visit carries some importance."

"It's late," the man said. "He sees no one at this hour."

From their places inside the carriage, the women could see that Wigg was having difficulty getting inside. It wasn't like the First Wizard to take "no" for an answer, Shailiha realized. If this was that important to him then why didn't he use the craft?

Then she watched Wigg do something odd with his robe—something she didn't understand. As he did, the craft's azure glow appeared. The young man's eyes quickly became as large as hen's eggs. Wigg smiled politely.

"Now then," he asked, "may we come in?"

"Uh, er—yes, yes of course," the fellow answered. In his hurry to open the door wider, he nearly tripped over his robe.

Turning toward the carriage, Wigg waved the women forward.

Once they were atop the steps, Wigg snatched the cigarillo from Tyranny's mouth and threw it into the street. The privateer scowled.

The man beckoned them inside. The house's interior wasn't what the ladies had expected. The foyer was small, but well lit and immaculately clean. The walls were constructed of wooden panes. Covered with paper, the uniform panes made it difficult to identify the doorways.

The man bowed to Wigg. "Please wait here," he said.

After Wigg returned the bow, the man slid open one of the well-disguised doors, then disappeared, smoothly closing it after him.

Tyranny looked around. "What is this place?" she asked. "I've never seen anything like it."

"Nor are you likely to again," Wigg answered softly. "It's important that no one speak unless first addressed. I'm not sure about what kind of reception we might get, so do as I say. And above all, take no provocative action. Despite the fact that I command the craft, doing so will likely get you killed."

Shailiha shot a questioning glance at Tyranny and Abbey. The privateer scowled again; Abbey simply shrugged her shoulders.

The paper-paned door silently slid open and the same young man stepped into the foyer. "The master will see you," he said simply. "Follow me."

Everyone stepped through the door to see a long hallway stretching before them. Like the foyer, its walls were made of paper panes. On reaching the hallway's end, the man stopped. He bowed to Wigg.

"He awaits you," he said.

Wigg bowed in return. "Thank you," he answered. His job done, the man walked away.

Wigg looked closely at the curious women. "Remember what I told you!" he whispered. "And if you are asked to speak, keep your voices quiet, and your tones respectful."

Sliding open the door, Wigg led them inside. The room was large. The floor was covered with a straw mat, and the four walls were constructed like those in the hallway. Exotic-looking weapons hung neatly on the walls. Oil lamp sconces provided soft, even light.

In the floor's center, an elderly man sat on his knees. His eyes were closed, and his shaved head reflected the light. He wore a heavy white upper garment that crisscrossed his chest. A black, skirted affair, tied at the top with a narrow cloth belt, covered his hips and legs. His strong-looking hands lay folded in his lap. A dark wooden tray holding a porcelain tea set sat on the floor before him.

Wigg immediately sat on his knees before the stone-still man. Looking up at the women, the First Wizard indicated that they should also sit. They quickly complied to form a line on Wigg's left. While the four visitors regarded their host, the room fell quiet.

As time passed, the accompanying silence became deafening. Wondering how long this might go on, Shailiha cast a curious glance at Tyranny. The privateer questioningly raised her eyebrows.

Finally the man opened his eyes. His gaze was sharp and penetrating. He looked straight at Wigg, then he bowed. Wigg returned the compliment. After looking at each woman, the man bowed to them in turn, then returned his riveting gaze to the First Wizard.

"Wigg," he said softly. "It has been a long time. Because of the Directorate's agreement, I believed we would never see one another again. Yet for some reason you have chosen to violate that accord. In truth, I cannot say that I am sorry. Why have you come, my old friend?"

"Please forgive the intrusion, Aeolus," Wigg said. "I come bearing news—news that only I could bring. For as I'm sure you know, the Directorate is no more."

Choosing not to respond, the man named Aeolus sat stock-still before them.

"Satine is dead," Wigg said gently. "I learned from her tattoos that she was one of your students."

For the briefest moment a hint of sorrow crossed Aeolus' eyes. "Did she die a warrior's death?" he asked.

"Yes."

"I see," Aeolus said. "Who did the deed? Few walk the earth who could have bested her."

"Prince Tristan," Wigg answered. "She had him dead to rights, but she hesitated just before delivering the fatal blow. Sensing the opportunity, Tristan struck. Her death was quick. Were you two close?"

Aeolus nodded. "Satine was like a daughter to me, and perhaps the most gifted student I ever taught. She was a force of nature, that one. But she abandoned my teachings to become a professional assassin. I tried to dissuade her from that path, but I couldn't."

Aeolus knew that his next words would strike directly at Wigg's heart, but the issue had to be raised. The guilt had been weighing on his soul for far too long, and he wanted to be rid of it. He took a deep breath.

"How many Conclave members did she assassinate before the prince killed her?" he asked.

Wigg's jaw dropped, and his cheeks turned scarlet with rage. It took several moments for him to calm before speaking again. Even then, anger flashed in his aquamarine eyes.

"You knew?" he asked, his voice trembling angrily. "Why didn't you warn us?"

"The choice forced upon me by Satine was unfathomable," Aeolus answered. "What's done is done, and I can only ask your forgiveness. When I learned of her plans I begged her to reconsider, but she wouldn't. In the end I had two choices—to not warn you and let fate take its course, or to tell you and ensure that the one I loved most in this world would meet a violent death at my dearest friend's hands." Pausing for a moment, Aeolus looked down at the floor.

"Forgive me, but it is widely rumored that your only daughter recently died," he said. "I am truly sorry for your loss. But tell me—if she had insisted on fulfilling some deadly mission, would you have warned her enemies that she was coming? And if not, can you justifiably condemn me for making the same choice?"

Thinking of Celeste, tears clouded Wigg's eyes. He then blinked them away.

"I understand," Wigg said, "but we lost two dear allies to Satine's skills. One was Geldon, a hunchbacked dwarf with the heart of a lion. He had been invaluable in the Coven's final defeat. The other was named Lionel the Little. He was a Shadowood gnome, and Faegan's most trusted herbmaster. Satine poisoned them, using a clever potion she purchased from a group of partial adepts called the Valrenkians. It caused her victims to go mad, leading them to suicide while she escaped. Faegan discovered it in their blood. Did you teach her that technique?"

Aeolus shook his head. “No,” he answered. “I tried warning her against dealing with Valrenkian slime, but she wouldn’t listen.”

Stunned by what she was hearing, Shailiha cast a quick glance at Abbey. The herbmistress was staring straight at Aeolus. She looked for the world like she had just seen a ghost. Remembering what Wigg had said, the normally inquisitive princess did her best to remain silent.

“How did you find me?” Aeolus asked.

“As I’m sure you know, Minion patrols wander the city, maintaining order,” Wigg answered. “I told them to search out a sign with a serpent on one side and a sword on the other. Only yesterday they told me that they had found it.”

“I see,” Aeolus said. “And who are these lovely ladies?” he asked, turning to look at the women.

Wigg gestured toward Shailiha. “I would first like to present Shailiha of the House of Galland, Princess of Eutracia,” he said.

Aeolus bowed deeply at the waist. “Welcome, Your Highness,” he said. “This is indeed an honor.”

She bowed in return. “Thank you,” she said simply.

“And this lady is Teresa of the House of Welborne,” Wigg said. “You already know Abbey of the House of Lindstrom. All three are Conclave members.”

Aeolus bowed again. Tyranny and Abbey respectfully returned the compliment.

“It is good to see you, Abbey,” Aeolus said. “I am glad that you and Wigg have found each other again. The Directorate was wrong to have banned the partial adepts from Tammerland, but those were difficult times.”

Their mouths agape, Shailiha and Tyranny stared at Abbey with disbelief.

Aeolus reached out to fill five teacups. Everyone took one. After sipping the excellent brew, Aeolus looked at the women, then back to Wigg.

“I can tell by Shailiha’s and Teresa’s expressions that they do not know about me,” he said. He looked back at the princess and the privateer. “If you have questions, I will be happy to answer them.”

Shailiha didn’t hesitate. “Who are you?” she asked. “And how do you know so many old secrets?”

Taking another sip of tea, Aeolus smiled. “The answer is simple," he said. "I was once a member of the Directorate of Wizards."

The princess nearly dropped her teacup. Tyranny's face screwed up with disbelief.

But Abbey only smiled. "It is good to see you, too, Aeolus," the herbmistress said. "You're right—it has been a long time."

"More than three centuries," Aeolus replied. "Wigg was right to grant you the time enchantments. He took a great risk, should the Directorate have found out. But with all of our old friends gone, that no longer matters."

Shailiha finally found her voice. "You were a Directorate wizard?" she asked. "That's impossible! I would have known about you!"

"It was long before your time," he answered. "I decided to leave the Directorate soon after it was formed. I had had enough of war, politics, and magic. I wanted a simpler life. My Directorate brothers graciously agreed to accept my resignation and to continue granting me the time enchantments. You have never heard about me because as part of that agreement, the Directorate resolved that they would never mention me, or our pact. I doubt that even your father, the late King Nicholas, knew about me."

"I have never seen a place like this," Shailiha said. "What purpose does it serve?"

"It is called the Serpent and the Sword," Aeolus answered. "It is a school of martial discipline. I am the owner and head instructor. It is also my home."

"So that is what Wigg meant when he said that Satine was your student," Tyranny offered. "Is that also why she bore a snake tattoo on one arm and a sword tattoo on the other? We saw your interesting sign hanging over the outer door."

"Yes," Aeolus answered. "The sword tattoo indicates weapons mastery, and the snake indicates mastery of unarmed combat. Satine had conquered each discipline. Such experts are few. Before the Directorate was formed, I was a Royal Guard officer. During that time I studied these disciplines. When I left the Directorate I decided to devote my life to carrying on my master's teachings. I still command the craft. But as part of my lifestyle, I choose not to do so."

"There are some things that you need to know," Wigg said to

him. "They will surprise you." Taking his gaze from Shailiha, Aeolus turned his dark eyes toward the First Wizard.

"Faegan and Jessamay are still alive," Wigg said. "They have also become Conclave members. They are well, although Faegan is crippled from being tortured by the Coven, soon after he disappeared. His legs are useless and cause him great anguish, but he controls the pain by partitioning his mind. He searches endlessly for a way to unravel the spell Failee used on him. Unfortunately, he has not been successful."

"I see," Aeolus answered. "I am glad they are with you. Please give them my regards, and my hope that Faegan finds a cure."

"There is something else you should know," Wigg said. "It is vastly important to all we hold dear."

Saying nothing, Aeolus took another sip of tea.

"Thirty-one years ago, *Jin'Sai* and *Jin'Saiou* were born. The Chosen Ones have finally entered the world."

For several moments Aeolus said nothing. Wonderment filled his face. "They have finally come?" he whispered. "Can it be true?"

"Yes," Wigg answered.

"And the azure glow surrounded their twin births, just as the Tome said it would?"

"Yes," Wigg confirmed. "As you know, that was how we could be certain."

"Who are they?" Aeolus asked.

"The *Jin'Sai* is Prince Tristan. The *Jin'Saiou* is Princess Shailiha."

Awestruck, Aeolus looked at Shailiha with even greater respect. "Welcome, *Jin'Saiou,*" he said. "We have awaited your arrival for centuries." Aeolus bowed again. Shailiha bowed in return.

"I have come here for another reason as well," Wigg said. "I need your help."

"You have but to ask," Aeolus said.

"What do you know about *K'Shari*?"

Thinking for a moment, Aeolus poured himself some more tea. After taking a sip he put down his cup then looked at Wigg.

"I am not surprised that you have heard about it," he answered. "However, despite the many legends, to my knowledge I am the only living person in the world who commands the gift.

But I never discussed it with you, or other Directorate members. After all these years, why do you ask about it?"

"The *Jin'Sai* has been lured away by a Vagaries being named Xanthus," Wigg answered, "who is also known as a Darkling, and serves the Heretics of the Guild. Until several days ago, I never knew about such a creature. It was evident that he commanded *K'Shari*. Should he return, I will need to know more about this special talent."

Aeolus shook his head. "I doubt that this Xanthus truly commands the gift," he said. "As I stated, I believe I am the only one to possess it."

"Before arriving at the palace, Xanthus sent Tristan a blank scroll and a freshly cut tree branch," Wigg said. "Witnesses saw Xanthus cut the branch in half in midair."

It was clear that Aeolus was intrigued. "Go on," he said softly.

"Later at the palace he used his gift," Wigg said. "Tossing his axe into the air, he cut a flier of the fields in half while the butterfly was in flight. He never bothered looking at his target. I have never seen anything like it."

His gaze intense, Aeolus leaned forward. "Tell me," he said. "Just before he threw his axe did he say anything odd—an oath, perhaps?"

"Yes," Wigg nodded. "He said: 'My ears hear no begging. My eyes see no pain. My heart feels no remorse.' It is also said that a long time ago, a sword master first showed *K'Shari* to an impudent young Royal Guard officer as a way to spare killing him in a duel. Have you ever heard the phrase or the story?"

Like he was being taken back in time, Aeolus closed his eyes. When he opened them, his expression softened.

"Yes," he answered gently. "You see, I was that Royal Guard officer, and those words were my master's. It was before I met you, and before I learned about my endowed blood. The martial master who saved my life by refusing my stupid challenge was the same man from whom I took over this school. As you know, in my early youth I was a penniless orphan. Joining the Royal Guard seemed the best way to raise myself up from the streets where I lived and begged. But for a long time after that I foolishly felt that I had much to prove—thus the unnecessary challenge to the master. By showing me *K'Shari* he not only saved my life, but forever changed my path, as well. Little did I know that I would one day rise to become a wizard of the Directorate.

Even so, I never forgot him. I never told my fellow Directorate members about the story because I found it embarrassing."

Aeolus gently cupped his tea in one hand. His eyes held a faraway look.

"Despite my earlier misgivings, it seems that you are right," he added. "Someone—or some*thing,* as you describe this Darkling—has also mastered the gift. It takes a lifetime to do so. If what you say about him serving the Heretics is true, then they must have excellent teachers among them."

"Not necessarily," Wigg said. "Faegan has reason to believe that Xanthus was gifted *K'Shari* by Forestallment."

Surprised again, Aeolus put down his teacup. "Do you mean to say that Forestallments exist?" he whispered. "The Directorate's best minds always considered them myth! Even Faegan was unconvinced!"

"Oh, Forestallments exist," Wigg answered. "We continue to unravel their secrets little by little. What can you tell us that might help? I fear we haven't seen the last of Xanthus. Not only does he command *K'Shari,* but the craft, as well."

"I don't understand," Aeolus said. "If he was such a threat, then why didn't you, Faegan, and Jessamay combine your gifts to kill him there and then?"

"Because by then he had already stolen the Paragon," Wigg answered sadly. "We were attending a masquerade ball and didn't have a ready cave water supply, so killing him meant also killing the stone. Normally I would have had some in a vial, hanging around my neck. But as I said, it was a masquerade—the vial was in my chambers. I'm not sure I will ever forgive myself for that blunder. It will never happen again."

"I see," Aeolus answered.

"Why do the plants die whenever Xanthus appears?" Abbey asked. "According to witnesses, the wind also calms, birds and insects stop singing, and rivers refuse to flow."

"Because when he calls his gift he projects a stillness so overpowering that it literally affects the forces of nature," Aeolus answered. "It is the same with me."

"Did Satine command *K'Shari*?" Wigg asked.

Aeolus shook his head. "She knew about the legend, but even she did not know that I commanded the gift. Had she stayed with me, I have little doubt that Satine would have been the first to whom I would have gladly imparted the needed training. She was that good."

"Is there anything else you can tell us?" Wigg asked.

"Only that *K'Shari* is an amazingly potent discipline," Aeolus answered, "one that can be used to either save life or to destroy it. Clearly, Xanthus is a destroyer. If you face him again, my friend, use only the craft. Even you will not be able to defeat him physically."

Abbey scowled. "What do mean by that?"

Aeolus looked at Wigg. "They do not know?" he asked.

"No," Wigg answered. "I had planned on telling them before we left here—provided that you agreed to see me."

"I understand," Aeolus answered.

Standing, Aeolus walked to one wall. With unimaginable speed he grasped a short sword hanging there. His arm a blur, he threw it end over end, straight at Wigg's head.

Shailiha gasped. Even Tristan couldn't summon such quickness. If Wigg couldn't bring the craft soon enough, he would die where he sat.

Raising his arms, Wigg held them wide. Then they all heard a sharp slap. Shailiha's mouth fell open.

Wigg had caught the sword blade between his hands. As though nothing had happened, he calmly laid it beside him on the floor. Relieved but incensed, Shailiha immediately sprang to her feet and pointed an accusatory finger at Aeolus.

"How dare you!" she shouted. "That's the First Wizard sitting there! Had he not been able to summon the craft in time he would have been killed! I could have you strung up from a lamp pole for less!"

Wigg winced at the princess's rude behavior. "Please sit down," he said.

Confused by Wigg's calm acceptance of all this, Shailiha reluctantly did as he asked.

Aeolus smiled. "Excitable, isn't she?" he asked Wigg.

The First Wizard sighed. "As is her brother," he answered. "You have no idea."

"I also demand that one of you tell us why that just happened!" Tyranny exclaimed. "We didn't come here to be attacked!"

"Wigg was never in danger," Aeolus said. "Nor did he use the craft to save himself. You see, it wasn't needed."

"It wasn't needed?" Shailiha protested. "Of course it was! No one is that fast!"

Wigg looked over at her. "Aeolus is right," he said quietly. Standing, Wigg pulled back each robe sleeve. As the craft's familiar glow surrounded him, then faded away, the three women couldn't believe their eyes.

A serpent lay tattooed on Wigg's right upper arm; a sword tattoo had materialized on his other. As the azure glow faded, the tattoos vanished. After rolling down his sleeves, Wigg sat down.

Shaking her head in disbelief, Shailiha simply stared at him. "Satine's arms carried those same symbols!" she breathed. "They can mean only one thing—you're also a graduate of the Serpent and the Sword!" Turning leftward, Shailiha glared at Abbey. "Did you know about this?" she demanded.

Pursing her lips, Abbey crossed her arms. "No," she answered, "I did not. It seems a certain First Wizard has some explaining to do when we return to the palace."

Shailiha looked back at Wigg. Sometimes it seemed that the longer she knew him, the less she understood him. Wizards and their infernal secrets!

"I don't know which question to ask first," she said to him. "Where, when, or why?"

"The 'when' took place several hundred years ago," Wigg answered. "The Sorceresses' War had recently been won. I had just returned from banishing the Coven upon the Sea of Whispers. I'm not ashamed to admit that those were emotional times for me—for all us wizards, in fact. During the Directorate's early days we members made more than our share of mistakes. The newly formed Directorate had just ordered me to cast the traitorous Coven adrift forever. Failee, Succiu, Zabarra, and Vona—I can still see their defiant faces as they stood there on the *Resolve*'s pitching deck, just before I ordered them into that fragile skiff."

Pausing for a moment, Wigg scrubbed his face with his hands. Shailiha touched him on one arm.

"It's all right," she said. "You needn't tell us if you would rather not."

Wigg shook his head. "I knew this would be wrenching, but it was one of the reasons I brought you three here." Collecting himself, he sat up a bit straighter.

"As I said, it was a difficult time for me," he said. "Then I found Abbey and my happiness briefly returned. But when the Directorate foolishly voted to banish all the partial adepts to the countryside, I had another choice to ponder. I could either go with Abbey and start my life over, or stay on as a Directorate wizard and continue to serve the Vigors. I chose the second path. But before watching Abbey go I secretly granted her the time enchantments."

Looking at the herbmistress, he finally produced a brief smile. "It was a decision that I never regretted," he added softly. Smiling back at him, Abbey nodded her thanks.

"Anyway, by then Aeolus was not only a respected Directorate member but also a martial master in his own right," Wigg added. "During that time I needed a newfound serenity that I couldn't find in politics or in the craft. Aeolus agreed to teach me. For the next decade he trained me in the Redoubt, during whatever spare time we could muster."

Wigg looked respectfully into Aeolus' eyes. "I thank you for that," he said. "It was you and your training that helped me to find my spirit again. When I saw Satine's tattoos I realized that she was one of us. I was shocked, but I also knew that I needed to come and see you—not only for the Vigors, but for personal reasons as well."

After taking a deep breath, Wigg continued. "I know how you came to feel about the craft, Aeolus, but times have changed. We must change with them. I don't suppose that you could be enticed into joining the Conclave, could you? Our meeting table still has an empty chair—the one my daughter once held. Full-fledged Vigors wizards are few and far between these days. We could surely use your help. Like Faegan and Jessamay, it would be good to have you at my side again." Pausing for a moment, Wigg turned to look at Shailiha, then back to Aeolus.

"I do not presume to speak on the princess's behalf," he added, "but in the *Jin'Sai*'s continued absence I believe she would heartily accept your membership. The Vigors desperately need our services again. Since the Coven's destructive return and subsequent defeat, our obstacles have been legion. All we hold dear is again in great peril."

For several moments Aeolus looked at the floor. When he returned his eyes to Wigg's, the four visitors could see how much he still respected the First Wizard.

"Thank you, Wigg," Aeolus said. "But my life is here. If I accepted, what would happen to my school? I have over fifty male and female students. Some have devoted their entire adult lives to my teachings, and live in residence here with me. I simply can't pack up and leave."

For several moments the room went still. Wigg looked over at Shailiha. Understanding his intent, she smiled back, then returned her gaze to Aeolus.

"You could relocate the school to the palace," she offered. "The Redoubt already hosts academies for the consuls' gifted children and for the Redoubt acolytes. The Serpent and the Sword would make a welcome addition!"

Shailiha smiled broadly at her next thought. "From what I've seen, perhaps you and your students could even teach the Minions a thing or two about the combative arts!" she added. "That would be a scene worth watching!"

Tyranny smiled. "It would indeed," she muttered under her breath.

A quizzical look came over Aeolus' face. "I know about the Consuls' Nursery," he said. "But who are the Redoubt acolytes?"

Sighing, Wigg smiled. "Like I said, many things have changed."

Thinking, Aeolus rubbed his chin. "I will consider your kind offer," he said. "In the meantime, there is one way I might be able to help."

"What do you have in mind?" Wigg asked.

"You said that Faegan has found the formula for granting *K'Shari* directly to one's blood signature?" he asked.

Wigg nodded.

"Amazing," Aeolus said. "I know nothing about Forestallments. But it occurs to me that simply placing the spell into one's blood might not be enough. *K'Shari* mastery is immensely complex; some purely physical training might also be needed to properly hone the gift. Should you grant it to someone's blood, be sure to send him or her to me before sending them into battle. I would be honored to polish their technique."

Wigg smiled. "Thank you," he said. "We'll keep that in mind." He turned to the three women sitting by his side. "It's time to go," he said. "We have imposed on Aeolus' hospitality long enough."

Wigg came to his feet; Shailiha, Tyranny, and Abbey did the same. Wigg opened the sliding door and escorted the ladies into the hallway, then back to the school's street entrance. Aeolus followed them. As Aeolus opened the front door he turned to face Wigg. The look on his face was thoughtful.

"If you can someday forgive me for your friends' deaths at Satine's hands, I might just accept that Conclave seat," he said. "You're right—times have changed, and we must change with them. Until then, journey safely, and give my regards to Faegan, Jessamay, and the *Jin'Sai.*"

For several long moments Wigg embraced Aeolus. Holding him by the shoulders, the First Wizard looked him in the eyes.

"You're already forgiven," he said, "just as I hope you can forgive me for breaking our accord. And the offer stands."

Leaving the school, the four visitors walked to the carriage. After watching them board the coach and ride away, Aeolus shut the door, then walked back down the long hallway, entered the same room as before, and sat down on the straw mat. The school was quiet, the hour late.

Picking up his teacup, the martial master thought about his old friends, and what it might be like to serve on the Conclave.

CHAPTER XXXII

"BEFORE WE TELL YOU WHY WE BROUGHT YOU HERE, WE MUST FIRST explain Xanthus' part in all this," Hoskiko said to Tristan. Sitting back in her chair, she looked across the table at the Darkling. Tristan saw admiration in her eyes.

"Despite what you were led to believe, he is not evil," she said, "at least not in his present form. When he returns to the Imperial Order they will probably kill him for failing to deliver you. He will tell them that you were lost to him in the raging Borderlands, but that story may not save him. Even so, he accepted this fate when he agreed to help us. As I said before, you owe him your life."

Tristan again looked around the glistening chamber. He was quickly learning that the Crysenium was a maze of well-kept secrets, and his presence was the key that might finally unravel its many mysteries.

After looking into the Envoys' faces, he cast his gaze back to Hoskiko. The prince had no reason to believe that she was lying to him. But Xanthus' terrible atrocities made it impossible for Tristan to believe that the Darkling could somehow be his ally. He regarded Hoskiko skeptically.

"Please go on," he said simply.

"Xanthus is a binary being. He was once completely human, and an officer of some rank in the Imperial Order. That is how he and Faxon came to know each other. His makeup was especially altered by the Heretics so that he might successfully bring you to them," Hoskiko said. "As I told you, it was their intention to take you prisoner, thereby keeping you from your destiny. To help protect his human side and the Paragon's life during his mission, the Heretics also granted him *K'Shari.*"

Despite his august company, Tristan was becoming impatient. "With all due respect, some of this I already know," he said.

Recognizing Tristan's eagerness to learn, Hoskiko smiled. "What you *don't* know is that when the rebel Heretics at this table first approached us, they secretly brought Xanthus with them, and a plan was born," she said. "Before sending him on his mission we drastically changed his blood signature rightward. This way we might convince him to do *our* bidding, rather than follow his original orders. Moreover, the atrocities he committed would be less extreme, yet also satisfy the Heretics' expectations. Our idea worked." Pausing for a moment, Hoskiko again looked at the Darkling.

"The Heretics would be closely watching his progress after he entered Eutracia, so he had to do exactly as they expected to maintain our charade," she added. "Although the Heretics still believe that Xanthus is following their orders, he serves us. But as he went about his atrocities, the guilt consuming his human half became overpowering. Therefore he started flagellating his back. This was his doing, not ours. His reasons were twofold—he wished to pay a deeply felt penitence for the terrible things he was doing, and to trick the Heretics into believing that his self-torture was an act of ritual devotion to the Vagaries. Such rites of self-mutilation are not unheard of in the Heretic culture. It all had to be real, because the Heretics were watching his every move."

Tristan looked across the table into Xanthus' eyes. "You agreed to bring me here," he whispered, "even when you knew that your original masters would likely put you to death?"

Bending forward a bit, Xanthus placed his hands flat atop the table. "Yes," he answered. "The Vigors' cause is too dear to allow one life to endanger it. I have done my part; now I have but to return to the Heretics and meet my fate. You will soon learn your role in this great undertaking. It will be far more difficult and dangerous than mine ever was. I humbly ask that you accept it and fulfill your destiny. Please do not let my death—and the deaths of those innocent Eutracians I was forced to kill—be in vain."

As he realized how wrong he had been about Xanthus, Tristan turned to Faxon. "Must he be returned to the Heretics?" he asked. "Isn't there some way that we can save him?"

Faxon shook his head. "Not and maintain our charade," he answered. "As it is he must return soon, or his tardiness will arouse added suspicions. When he arrives without you at his side, the Imperial Order will be suspicious enough."

"But if they enter his mind, won't they learn everything anyway?" Tristan asked. "In the end, what purpose will all this subterfuge have served?"

"You forget that I am a high-ranking officer of the Imperial Order," Faxon answered. "They trust me implicitly. When I was told by my superiors about their wish to bring you to them, Xanthus' conversion became my idea. From the beginning, it was my plan to secretly bring him to Crysenium. When I take him back, I can help with his fate, but not much. Nor by then will I probably wish to do so. He will be their servant again, and a danger to our cause."

"I don't understand," Tristan said. He turned quickly to look at Hoskiko then back to Faxon again. "Don't you feel any guilt about creating him, only to use him then watch him die some horrible death?"

"We do," Faxon answered. "But to ensure that our gambit works we must do even more to seal Xanthus' fate. Before we allow Xanthus to return to the Heretics we will change his blood signature back to what it once was, then wipe his memory clean of everything we do not want the Heretics to learn. In their place we will provide him with an entirely new host of memories—those that support our subterfuge. In this the Borderlands' appearance, although unexpected, will serve us well. Not only will your unfortunate wandering in the Borderlands explain his being overdue, but they will also provide a plausible explanation for your supposed death. Xanthus will tell them that you fell prey to a great sinkhole, and that your body was unrecoverable. At first they will believe that despite his best efforts, Xanthus simply failed. It wasn't he who activated the Borderlands, after all. Wiping his memory clean will also protect Crysenium's existence."

"And when the Heretics see that I have returned to Eutracia?" Tristan asked. "What then? Won't they know that they have been duped?"

"Yes," someone said from across the table.

Tristan looked to see Mitsu staring at him. She was younger than the others, with an attractive face and a pleasant smile.

"But by then you will be home, and about the mission we shall entrust to you," she added. "When they realize that they have been misled, Xanthus' masters will likely kill him. If all goes as we hope, Xanthus will die believing that he was truly a failure to his Heretic masters. He will never remember the other side of the story—our side, to be precise. We know it's unfortunate, but it's how things must be if we are to succeed."

"You can do that to people's minds?" Tristan asked.

"Yes, *Jin'Sai,*" Mitsu answered. "One day you and Shailiha will also command such gifts."

Tristan shook his head with wonderment—not only at what Mitsu had just said about him and Shailiha, but also at the Envoys' intricate plan. It was foolproof and elegant, he realized. And for some reason it centered on him.

"All right," he said. "I understand *how* you brought me here. What I haven't learned is *why.*"

"This is why," Hoskiko answered simply. "Observe."

Waving one arm, she called the craft. Tiny azure particles soon formed in the air. Waving her hand again, she caused them to start whirling. They formed a mini-tornado that hovered and swirled, then moved to the room's other side. Then the glowing cyclone coalesced to form a staggering panorama. A dozen meters across by several meters high, the colorful image was life-sized and terrifying. Soon sound arose from it to fill the room.

What Tristan was seeing and hearing was so all-encompassing that for several moments he had to close his eyes. When he opened them again, to his dismay he found the scene unchanged.

Across a wide field not unlike those of Farplain, two vast armies charged toward one another. Tristan realized that he was witnessing a battle in the ongoing War of Attrition. He could only imagine the numbers of troops involved—hundreds of thousands in each camp, he guessed.

Some rode towering beasts across the land and through the sky, the likes of which he couldn't start to describe. Entire regiments could be seen doing something even the best Eutracian wizards had always found impossible—they were literally flying through the air toward the enemy. Carrying odd weapons and screaming maniacally, other soldiers ran across the ground at amazing speed. Everything was happening with such frantic quickness that Tristan could hardly take it all in. As the thundering ranks neared, he didn't want to watch, but he found it impossible to tear his eyes away. Then the brave warriors started dying.

The first strikes came from each army's rear lines, as the opposing archers loosed their shafts against one another; the converging arrow clouds were so dense that they literally darkened the sky. Amazingly, every arrow seemed to find an enemy body into which to tear. Screaming and writhing, tens of thousands died on the spot. As the mayhem grew louder, blood ran across the emerald-green battleground.

At first he couldn't believe that such unerring accuracy was possible. But then he realized something more. Many of the warriors must command the craft.

This was no ordinary war among mortals. The War of Attrition was a war among adepts from both sides. Tristan knew that this was what Xanthus had meant when he said that after seeing this world, his perspectives on war and death would be forever changed. The Envoys were right. Compared to what went on here, the war between the Directorate and the Coven was a mere skirmish between light and dark.

As the two armies neared, azure bolts flew through the air. Thousands died on either side; thousands more quickly took up their comrades' abandoned ranks. Amid more explosions, smoke, and carnage, the two great armies finally collided, their forces swarming over each other in a terrible display of wanton death-dealing.

Deciding that Tristan had seen enough, Hoskiko caused the battle scene to vanish. Everyone around the meeting table stayed respectfully silent for a time. Tristan finally looked over at Hoskiko. He shook his head.

"So this is what it is like in your world?" he asked. "I have never witnessed such death and destruction."

Hoskiko nodded. "That was but some of the ongoing struggle. Battles continually rage, and sometimes a siege can last for decades. That scene is being carried out more than two thousand leagues away. Other conflicts go on in the sky and on the water. At this moment, over fifty such battles are occurring. Many are far larger than what you just saw."

Tristan simply sat there for a moment, trying to imagine the war's vast scope. "Your losses are staggering," he breathed. "How can your people continually suffer such decimation yet survive as a race? It doesn't seem possible."

Hoskiko was about to speak when a Heretical Envoy answered for her. "It's all relative," Balsius said. He was a short man, with a long, hooked nose and a kind face. Like Wigg, when speaking he used his hands for emphasis.

"From the Tolenka Mountains that border us on the east, our world stretches for tens of thousands of leagues in every other direction," he said. "By comparison, Eutracia and Parthalon are mere garden plots. Like you, we have our cities, ports, and such—although their splendors would be nearly unrecognizable to your mind. And like you we live, love, care for our children, and hope for a better day. Just as our lands are so much greater, so is our population. The land is almost evenly divided. The Heretics control the north, the Ones the south. The azure pass is found just north of the war border, in Heretic-controlled territory. When activated, the Borderlands run east to west along the border's entire length. Had the orb cut through the Tolenkas farther to the north, constructing Crysenium might have proven impossible. As you might expect, most land battles tend to occur along that north-south border. The struggle you just saw was one such conflagration."

"Do the two separate lands have names?" Tristan asked.

"The Heretic lands are called Rustannica," Faxon answered. "In Old Eutracian it means, 'heretical,' or 'splitting away.' The Ones' lands are named Shashida, or 'homeland of the faith-keepers.' "

"I see," Tristan mused. "And the war has raged ever since the Heretics split away."

"Correct," Faxon answered. "Before the Heretics started their exclusive practice of the Vagaries, we all lived in quiet but fragile harmony. Then the Heretics revolted and started the war. What followed was a miscalculation beyond description."

"What do you mean?" Tristan asked.

"During the war's early years, the Heretics used especially dark magic to influence the forces of nature," Hoskiko explained. "Spells were formulated that allowed them to employ natural phenomena as war weapons. Millions died. To survive, the Ones had no choice but to do the same thing, even though it went against their better judgment. You see, before the war, what you call Eutracia and Parthalon were also part of where we lived. The Tolenkas didn't exist, nor did the Sea of Whispers. The lands encompassing Eutracia and Parthalon were contiguous."

Tristan looked at Faxon with amazement. "How could that be?"

"Once loosed, the magic was far more powerful and difficult to control than either side anticipated," Hoskiko answered. "The Tolenkas unexpectedly rose, and the landmass separated, creating the Sea of Whispers. Since then the environmental and seismic arts have been abandoned by both sides as being far too dangerous. But the formulas are still held in reserve by each side, should either try such madness again. It is said that the Heretics first formulated these spells to create the Isle of the Citadel." Pausing for a moment, she sadly closed her eyes.

"Because such potent magic unintentionally created them, the Tolenkas and the Sea of Whispers hold many secrets—secrets that even we have yet to unravel," she added. "One such mystery is why no one from either side can conquer the mountains. Some say that it is because they are high and the air too thin to breathe—even for us. Others believe that there are darker reasons. But no matter the cause, there is finally a way to cross."

"The azure pass," Tristan said.

"Yes," Hoskiko replied. "That will be your way home again. But time grows short, and we cannot afford to indulge your many questions. It is finally time to tell you why we brought you here."

Sitting quietly, Tristan looked first at Hoskiko, then Faxon. Hoskiko reached out to touch him on one arm.

"Your ultimate destiny is to stop this terrible War of Attrition," she said. "It always has been—just as it has been the destiny of each *Jin'Sai* and *Jin'Saiou* before you who tried and failed."

Hoskiko's words stunned Tristan. "That can't be," he protested. "The Tome clearly states that I am to combine the craft's opposing sides for the betterment of mankind. Besides, how could I ever hope to stop a war that you brilliant Envoys cannot?"

"It has to do with interpreting the word 'sides,' " Hoskiko answered. "Old Eutracian can be a difficult language to grasp, even for those who have spoken it for aeons. Is it so impossible to believe that your wizards might be wrong in how they interpret it?"

Suddenly Tristan understood. "The Tome isn't saying that Shailiha and I must combine the two arts," he breathed. "Instead, I am to combine the two opposite 'sides' that practice those arts—the Ones and the Heretics! I am to somehow bring peace among you!"

"Yes," Faxon said. "You are the first *Jin'Sai* to fully understand."

"But how am I to do this?" Tristan asked.

"You must first understand that the craft's two sides need each other to survive," Hoskiko said. "Without good, evil would not exist and vice versa. Like light and dark, and male and female, each side needs the other to carry on. Each side of the craft must be allowed its existence—even the Vagaries. But to flourish peacefully they must coexist in a world of mystical checks and balances, rather than by warring against each other. If either side should be destroyed, the other will wither and die."

"But if that is the case, then why do the Heretics continue trying to destroy the Vigors?" Tristan asked. "The Coven, Nicholas, Wulfgar—with the Heretics' help, in one way or another they all tried to ensure that only the Vagaries ruled. If what you say is true, their actions make no sense. Was it their goal to wipe out all magic?"

"No," Faxon answered. "The answer has to do with left-leaning blood signatures. Those with signatures leaning far leftward are much more devoted in their fanaticism. Their minds become frantic, chaotic, and unyielding to any philosophy other than their own. Any sense of tolerance disappears. The craft's two sides are much the same, save for this distinction.

"For the most powerful of those who practice the Vagaries,

their worship turns into deadly obsession," he added. "Their minds, hearts, and souls are overtaken by it, and they consider the Vigors' followers to be the evil ones. In essence, they no longer know that what they are doing is wrong, or destructive to the craft as a whole. The Coven of the Sorceresses, Nicholas, Wulfgar, and now Serena were all such true believers, as are the many Heretics who counseled them. Each suffered from this madness. In their frantic need to crush the Vigors, they believe their cause justifies any means. Among the more fanatical leaders of Rustannica that misguided sense of fatalism exists to this day."

"Do you remember Wigg telling you about Failee's madness?" Hoskiko asked Tristan. "She was brilliant, even by our standards. To this day her dark work continues to influence your world. She was not the first to be affected that way. Aeons ago, when the Heretics split away, their improper Vagaries use sometimes caused the same madness in them. Sometimes it also became psychosexual, as it did with Succiu, Second Mistress of the Coven."

"Because of their immense gifts, the radical Vagaries worshippers hold sway over all others living in Rustannica," Faxon told the prince. "Their kind is comprised of two distinct parts. The governing order is a group of Heretical clerics called the *Pon Q'tar.* They are the true fanatics. The Imperial Order is the *Pon Q'tar*'s military arm. They oversee the war, taking their orders from the *Pon Q'tar* and the emperor. Beneath both these groups live the more ordinary citizens."

"Why don't those with far right-leaning signatures suffer their own madness?" Tristan asked. "That's something I could never understand. Nor could my wizards answer this question."

Faxon smiled. "Ah," he said. "We have finally come to the heart of the matter." Leaning a bit closer, he searched Tristan's face.

"To better understand the answer, consider these questions," he said. "Tell us—is cold the absence of heat, or is heat the absence of cold? In that same vein, is dark the absence of light, or is light the absence of dark?"

Tristan found Faxon's inquiries strange. "What are you talking about?" he asked.

"Have your wizards ever mentioned that chaos is the natural order of the universe?" Faxon asked.

"Yes," Tristan answered, "many times in fact."

"With that idea in mind, consider Faxon's questions, then answer them to your best ability," Hoskiko said.

Tristan thought for a moment. "I suppose that cold is the absence of heat," he said, "and dark is the absence of light."

"Well done," Hoskiko said. "Tell us why."

"Because unlike cold and dark, heat and light are energy forms that must be generated," Tristan answered. "It is like being in a cave. Because the cave's natural inclination is to be cold and dark, it will remain that way until visited by a flame's heat and light."

"And . . . ?" Faxon asked.

"The cold and darkness are therefore the natural order of the universe," Tristan mused. "Without energy to change them, they always prevail." An astonished look suddenly overcame Tristan's face. "I finally understand," he breathed.

Smiling, Hoskiko looked knowingly at Faxon, then back at Tristan. "Tell us," she said.

"When the Heretics split away to practice only the Vagaries, they forever abandoned the Vigors—the craft's side that provides its energy and light. It is being in this perpetual state of ensured 'darkness' and 'cold' that causes the Vagaries practitioners to go mad. Just as dark and light are the natural order of the world, without the Vigors, chaos is the craft's natural state. That chaos soon affects the Heretics' minds."

"Exactly," Hoskiko answered. "They shun the light, warmth, and balance that the Vigors would ordinarily bring. Madness soon follows. As their minds spiral downward, they stop caring about anything else. It is this concept that lent the craft sides their names. The 'Vigors' speak of energy and light; they are the 'vigorous' side. The Vagaries refers to the darkness, chaos, and confusion that follow, should one abandon the light."

"But how does this knowledge help me broker a peace among you?" Tristan asked.

"Before you can help do that, you must first return to Eutracia," Hoskiko answered, "for two important reasons."

Tristan listened as Faxon explained the plan that Serena was carrying out. It was heinous, barbaric. Armed with this understanding, Tristan could see how Serena's success might easily destroy the Vigors, and all that the Conclave held dear. Worse, if the Conclave hadn't already attacked the Citadel, they soon would. His friends would unknowingly be sailing into a death trap. He had to get home as fast as possible.

As he thought about the danger the Conclave was heading into, Tristan closed his eyes for a moment. When he opened them, Hoskiko's expression was compassionate and concerned.

"If you and the Conclave can defeat this final threat to your side of the world, your wizards must then alter your blood signature," she said. "We ask that you then return to us."

"Change my signature in what way?" he asked.

"It must be forced leftward," Faxon answered, "toward the Vagaries. As you know, your wizards and sorceresses have recently acquired that power. Once your signature shows no appreciable lean in either direction, you must return to us through the azure pass. Because your blood has not been classically trained, there is little worry that you will be attracted to the Vagaries."

"Before you leave here, we will grant your blood the Forestallment allowing you to safely summon and navigate your way through the pass," Hoskiko added. "We will remain here until you return."

"And then?" Tristan asked.

"We will all leave Crysenium," she answered. "We will seek out the rebel Heretic network. Together we will go on to attract ever more souls to our cause, until our numbers are such that the *Pon Q'tar* has no choice but to listen to our peace plan. To save the craft, we must bring the Heretics back to the light. Ordinarily this would have been impossible. But with you leading us, we finally have a chance."

"But why should these people listen to me?" Tristan asked.

Faxon smiled. "You're forgetting something. You are the *Jin'-Sai.* For aeons, millions have anticipated your coming. The *Jin'-Sai* willingly changing his blood signature so that it has no appreciable lean will be seen as a monumental, unheard-of act of good faith. Everyone will understand that your intentions carry no bias, and that you are willing to work for the good of both sides. We believe that millions from each side will rise up to hear your word, then drop their swords to follow you. Even the Imperial Order and the *Pon Q'tar* will eventually be forced to listen. Peace is finally possible, *Jin'Sai,* if only you will lead us. If the fanatical Heretics can be reasoned with and again be persuaded to accept the Vigors, Rustannica and Shashida will finally be reunited into one kingdom."

Pausing for a moment, he looked into Tristan's eyes. "It will be a new kingdom," he said softly. "One ruled in peace and harmony by the *Jin'Sai,* his blood signature permanently altered to the vertical. Should you succeed in your destiny, you will rule the combined lands with no bias toward either side of the craft. So will your children, and your children's children, who shall all inherit your blood."

Tristan was speechless. *Can such a thing be true?* he wondered. All of his life he had scarcely been able to imagine himself as Eutracia's leader, much less somehow presiding over such vast, magical lands as these. He looked at Hoskiko with wonder.

"Can your plan work?" he asked her.

Reaching out, she took his hands into hers. "All we know is that this horrible war produces nothing but endless slaughter," she answered. "We realize that the risks are huge, but so are the possible rewards. If it is ever to end, someone must take the first step. The likelihood of the Heretics doing so is nearly nonexistent. That being the case, can we do less than try?"

"Why can't you change my blood signature here and now?" he asked. "Surely that is in your power."

"Altering the blood signature lean of a *Jin'Sai* or a *Jin'Saiou* is a major event in the fabric of the craft," Faxon answered. "Even so, your wizards should be able to do it. But the energy released will be so great that if it were done here, Crysenium might be revealed to the Heretics. Crysenium's existence already balances on a knife's edge. We simply cannot afford to take that chance.

"There is something else that you must know," Faxon said. "When Xanthus attacked Faegan, his intent was not to kill your wizard. Instead, he used his azure bolt to grant Faegan a Forestallment. Faegan is probably clever enough to have learned this. But if not, tell him that the Forestallment grants him the index to both scrolls. He will understand its importance."

Hoskiko looked deep into Tristan's eyes. "Do you accept your mission, *Jin'Sai*?" she asked. "Understand that once you return to us, you might be forced to remain here forever. Should the *Pon Q'tar* sense your presence then close the pass, even we cannot send you home again."

"What about the Prophecies of the Tome?" Tristan asked. "The great book's third and final volume? On its pages it is written that I am to read the entire treatise before joining the two 'sides' of the craft. And that I am to be the only one who will read them. If I come back before doing so, doesn't that fly in the face of everything my wizards believed to be true?"

"Yes—as far as it goes," Hoskiko answered. "But so long as you are with us, your concerns over the Tome do not matter."

"Why don't they?" Tristan asked.

Hoskiko smiled. "Because there is nothing contained in the Tome that we cannot tell you. After all, some of the Tome's authors are in this very room."

Stunned, Tristan sat back in his chair. He looked around the table, then back to Hoskiko. "I accept the mission," he answered.

"Then when you leave Eutracia to return here, say your goodbyes well," Hoskiko said. "It might be the last time you see your loved ones."

"I will," Tristan said.

"Very well," Hoskiko said. "Please close your eyes."

Tristan did as he was asked. Hoskiko placed one hand on Tristan's arm. He soon felt a tingle in his blood. It was not unpleasant, nor did it last long. Smiling, Hoskiko looked at him. "You may open your eyes," she said.

"What just happened?" he asked.

"The Forestallment allowing you to navigate the pass has been added to your blood signature," she said. "Because of our higher gifts, doing this caused you no pain. Nor need you be trained in its use. Once you call the pass forth you will be in its depths. From that point on, all will be revealed."

Hoskiko waved her fingers and caused a folded parchment to appear. It hovered gently between her and the prince. Tristan looked questioningly at Hoskiko. Smiling, she nodded.

Tristan grasped the parchment from the air and unfolded it. Upon it was written a lengthy series of complex numbers and symbols.

"This is a craft formula, isn't it?" Tristan asked.

"Yes," Hoskiko answered. "It is the formula allowing Forestallments to be imbued into endowed blood. Faegan already has the scrolls' indexes. With this additional formula he can accomplish much. But because of your wizards' lesser gifts, if they choose to grant you other Forestallments you will experience great pain."

Thinking for a moment, Tristan recalled the first time that had happened. "That was the case when Succiu placed Forestallments into my blood," he said. "I thought I would surely die from the pain."

"Yes," Hoskiko answered simply.

Tristan folded the parchment and placed it beneath his vest. "Thank you," he said.

Faxon looked across the table at Xanthus. "Come here," he said. Xanthus immediately came to stand between Faxon and the prince. "Give me the Paragon," Faxon said.

Reaching up, the Darkling took the stone and chain from around his neck. He handed them to Faxon. Calling the craft, Faxon produced a crystal bowl filled with red water, then laid the stone within it. As he did, another question came to Tristan.

"Answer something for me," he said to Faxon. "If Xanthus had delivered me to the *Pon Q'tar,* what would have happened to me?"

As he watched the stone prepare for its new host, Faxon shook his head. "Even I am not privy to that information," he answered. "Only the *Pon Q'tar* clerics know. But I believe that we can assume one thing."

"What is that?" Tristan asked.

Faxon gave Tristan a wry look. "You're better off here," he said.

Lifting the stone from the water, Faxon smiled, then placed its chain around Tristan's neck. As it lay wet against his worn leather vest, the Paragon twinkled beautifully.

"Before you go, there is one last thing to be done," Hoskiko said. Reaching out, she grasped the gold medallion hanging around Tristan's neck. For the briefest moment an azure glow surrounded it, then faded away. Hoskiko smiled.

"What just happened?" Tristan asked.

"I have enchanted the medallions you and Shailiha wear," she said. "From this day forward, either of you only needs to envision the medallions and the magic will surface. It would have taken your wizards many years to formulate the needed spell, if ever. Try it, *Jin'Sai.* Close your eyes and imagine the two medallions floating side by side. Then reach down and turn yours over."

Tristan closed his eyes. Soon he was envisioning the two gold discs. In his mind's eye they joined into one.

"Look," Hoskiko said.

Tristan reached down to the medallion on his chest and lifted it to his eyes. He saw Tyranny sitting next to Wigg. It was night-time, and they seemed to be riding in a carriage. Between cigarillo puffs, Tyranny was talking up a storm. After dropping the medallion to his chest, Tristan smiled at Hoskiko.

"What Shai's medallion sees, mine also sees," he said. "Is the same true for hers?"

"Yes," Hoskiko answered. "From this day forward she has but to do the same to reverse the process. But you mustn't lose either medallion. The needed spell lives in the medallions—not in their owners' blood. Because of that, if the spells are employed for long periods at one time or summoned too often, they will die. Worse, should the medallions fall into the wrong hands, anyone of endowed blood might learn to use them. You and the *Jin'Saiou* must guard them well."

"We will," Tristan said.

As Hoskiko stood, the other eleven Envoys did the same. "You must go," she said. "Even now there might not be enough time for you to warn your fleet of Serena's plans."

"I understand," he said. "But I have so many more questions."

"We know," Hoskiko replied. "Had the Borderlands not delayed you, we could have told you more. But the hour is late. Your mission on the world's other side must take precedence. All your questions will be answered when you return to Crysenium. Go, *Jin'Sai.* Your world needs you. And remember—as was the case when you first came here, your return journey could prove dangerous."

"I'll remember," Tristan said.

Turning to Xanthus, Tristan embraced him. Each saw tears in the other's eyes. "Good-bye, my friend," Tristan said. "I will never forget your sacrifice."

"Fulfill your destiny, *Jin'Sai,*" the Darkling answered. "That will be thanks enough."

Tristan turned. One by one he looked at each Crysenium Envoy. He gave them all a brief smile.

"Thank you for the look ahead," he said softly. Closing his eyes, he called forth his new Forestallment.

Suddenly he felt Shadow beneath him. As the azure swirled about him, he smiled.

Amazing, he thought. *And so simple! A child could do it!*

In the space of one heartbeat, Shadow and Tristan stepped through the azure pass's other side and into Eutracia.

As the stunned Minions guarding the pass jumped to their feet, their *Jin'Sai* smiled.

IV

THE HIGHLANDERS

CHAPTER XXXIII

Beware the guiles of highlander lasses, all you well-meaning men who would try to keep your hearts pure and your possessions safe. For such wenches have dark eyes that mystify, ways to make a good man abandon home and hearth, and enchantments galore to make a bad man fall prey to their seductive ways even quicker.

—EUTRACIAN PROVERB

"OVER HERE!" EINAR SHOUTED. "I SEE SOMETHING! GIVE ME THE torch!"

Reznik eagerly caught up to Serena's lead consul. He handed Einar the torch. Raising the flame high, Einar looked around.

For the last two days Serena's mystics had been exploring Failee's labyrinthine research chambers, deep below the Recluse. Unknown to them, they had traveled much farther than Tristan and Wigg had done when they rescued Jessamay from Failee's sorceress's cone. Sometimes radiance stones were in evidence as they went along. In other places they were not, and torchlight was needed.

The underground chambers were far vaster than Einar had anticipated. The farther he went, the more he understood why the Coven had chosen this area over which to build the Recluse. Formed partly by nature and partly by the Coven's handiwork, the lower regions were fascinating.

When Einar realized that exploring this place would take days rather than hours, he had ordered some consuls to accompany him and Reznik. Walking in single file, seven consuls carrying food, water, and torches followed behind.

When they had started this journey there had been eight of them. One consul had already plunged to his death while trying to traverse a rocky stone ledge. The others never heard him hit bottom as he tumbled end over end into the murky depths. His torch still in one hand, his screams had simply faded away into the darkness. Knowing that there was nothing more to be done, Einar had carried on. Not one of the survivors had seen sunlight for the last two days.

Stopping for a moment, Einar stared into the gloom. Like many chambers, this one was a revelation. The cavern was huge. The mystics were standing atop a natural stone bridge. Arching its way over a deep cavern and stretching from one stone sidewall to another, it was a good thirty meters long but less than two meters wide. Formed of crystalline rose quartz, it twinkled beautifully in the flickering torchlight. The chamber's curved sidewalls gracefully arched upward to form a domed ceiling. Multicolored stalactites hung from the ceiling like probing fingers, reaching for the cavern floor. The cool air smelled moist and mildewed. Behind the explorers lay the dark tunnel through which they had just come.

Hearing rushing water, Einar looked down. Given the impenetrable darkness, it was impossible to tell how far the cavern walls descended. Curious, he summoned the craft. After pointing to the torch, he separated part of its flame to form a bright fireball. The torch flickered weakly for a moment, then regained its previous strength. Einar caused the fireball to grow in size and brightness until it was about one meter in diameter. Looking down, he cast it into the depths.

On and on the fireball plunged until Einar saw a subterranean river rushing across the cavern floor. Wide and strong, the river flowed along a smooth trough it had long ago carved into the rock floor. He soon realized that it was probably part of the water table feeding the lake surrounding the Recluse. He also guessed how the amazing quartz bridge had been formed. Its curved underside had been carved out by centuries'-worth of rushing water. Interestingly, a crude wooden boat with two oars lay on the stone floor bordering the river.

Suddenly understanding, Einar smiled. *How clever you were, First Mistress,* he thought. After extinguishing the fireball he again started leading his group across the stone bridge.

Einar knew what he was looking for, but the others did not, for Serena had entrusted only him with the secret. He was searching for one of Failee's untried spells, written just before she had been killed by the *Jin'Sai.* Serena had been told about the spell by the

Heretics during one of their sacred communions. The spell was nearly perfect for their needs, provided it could be found. Serena had also given Einar the description of the chamber in which the spell was hidden, and the incantation needed to reveal its secrets. All of this information had come to Serena by way of the Heretics.

Although the spell represented one of Failee's crowning achievements, it had never been tested. Because of this, Einar and Serena doubted that the spell would work the first time it was tried. That was rare among new spell formulations, even when its author was as brilliant as the First Mistress. Testing and refining the calculations would take time, Einar knew. The spell's unproven nature was also why his forces had been ordered to conquer the Ghetto of the Shunned.

Coming to the bridge's end, Einar saw a door in the facing rock wall. Unlike most in these lower regions, it was constructed of iron. Just above it, an Old Eutracian inscription lay carved into the rock. Deep wall crevices lined either side of the intriguing portal. A circular staircase carved into the rock wall led down into the darkness from the bridge's end.

After brushing aside the mildew and cobwebs, Einar read the inscription. Smiling, he turned to face the others.

"We've found it!" he exclaimed.

Everyone let go a cheer, but Einar knew that his work had just begun. A chamber this important would be protected by the craft. Unless he could avoid Failee's traps, everyone would be killed.

Einar looked at the door again. It seemed simple enough. An iron slide bolt across its middle lay waiting to be shoved to one side. But Einar remained wary.

Looking back, he saw Reznik and the consuls standing in single file, awaiting his orders. He beckoned Reznik closer. Holding his torch higher, the Valrenkian examined the mysterious entryway.

"What do you make of it?" Einar asked. "Our prize lies on the other side."

Reznik rubbed his chin. "That's difficult to say," he answered. "If I wanted to safeguard something behind that door, I would set my trap here. But that isn't the question, is it? The real riddle is the trap's nature, and how it can be overcome."

"Precisely," Einar answered. "Look back and tell me what you see."

Puzzled by Einar's demand, Reznik did as he was asked. "I see what I expected," he answered. "There are seven consuls, some holding food, water, and torches."

"And what else?" Einar asked.

"The stone bridge, of course," he said.

Einar nodded. "Yes—the stone bridge—the only way to approach the door."

"Do you believe that the bridge is enchanted?" Reznik asked. "That seems so obvious."

"Obvious perhaps, but highly effective," Einar said. "I would wager that this seemingly innocent slide bolt is the key that starts the process working. After that, there's no telling what might happen."

Standing back from the door, Einar considered his options. Finally he looked back at Reznik and his consuls.

"I want you to hover in the air!" he ordered. Guessing that this might be beyond the partial adept's gifts, Einar cast Reznik a questioning glance. The Valrenkian shook his head.

"Climb onto my back," Einar said. He didn't have to ask Reznik twice.

One by one the consuls hovered above the bridge. Einar did the same, taking Reznik with him. Pointing to the slide bolt, he called the craft. Grinding loudly against the door, the bolt started moving. Then it unexpectedly stopped before finishing its length of travel.

Surprised by the bolt's stubbornness, Einar raised his power. With a loud bang the bolt finally shot the remaining way across the door face, the sound reverberating through the cavern.

At first nothing happened. Then there came a strange scratching sound. As it became louder, Einar and his consuls hovered in space, awaiting their fates.

Screeching madly, hundreds of vicious bats suddenly swarmed from the wall's crevices. Glowing eyes and furious wings careened in the darkness; yellow teeth snapped and tore at the consuls' hands and faces. Two consuls accidentally dropped their supplies as they tried to wave the bats away.

"Stay calm!" Einar shouted. "It will be over soon!"

Almost as quickly as they had come, the bats disappeared.

Then a rumbling noise started. Just as he had feared, Einar looked down to see the bridge cracking apart.

Traveling the bridge's length, a dark crevasse split the stone formation in two. Then the fingerlike cracks clawed at each of the chamber's sidewalls, separating them from the bridge. With a mighty groan the entire structure crumbled away to plummet into the darkness.

Still hovering in place, Reznik and the stunned consuls looked down. After what seemed an eternity they heard the bridge pieces crash against the cavern floor. Wasting no time, Einar pulled on the iron door handle. Its hinges protesting loudly, the door slowly gave way. Beyond the entryway, only darkness loomed.

Einar looked back at his consuls. "Follow me!" he said.

He glided inside. Using his feet to find the floor, he landed gingerly. Reznik left Einar's back to stand beside him. The consuls entered next, feeling their way along in the darkness. Glad for the respite, they placed their remaining provisions on the floor. As they all stood waiting for Einar's next order, an eerie silence flooded over everything.

Knowing that Failee would have provided radiance stones for such an important chamber, Einar waved one hand. As his suspicions came true, he smiled. The radiance stones embedded in the room's ceiling soon cast their sage-colored glow over everything. Looking to his consuls, Einar saw that most were bleeding from having been bitten. They started tending one another's wounds.

As the room came alight, Reznik scowled. *Have we come this far only to be tricked?* he wondered. *Worse yet, how are we going to go back?* He glanced over at Einar. Oddly, the lead consul seemed unperturbed.

The room they had risked their lives to enter was small and unimpressive. About five meters square, it held no books, scrolls, or furnishings of any kind. The walls were constructed of rough fieldstones, held in place with common builder's mortar. Each stone had writing on it. There was no apparent exit except the door they had just used.

Reznik turned to Einar. "Whatever you are searching for isn't here," he said. "We've been tricked! Worse, how are we supposed to return to the Recluse?"

Einar smiled. "Do not worry about that," he answered. "If I'm right, there is at least one way back. The First Mistress's traps were clever, weren't they? As I suspected, the slide bolt was what activated them. The bats' purpose was to force intruders to fall to their deaths. If the bats failed, the collapsing bridge would finish the job.

"Anyway," Einar added, "not only is there a way back, but what we seek is indeed here. We search for a craft formula, written by the First Mistress. The formula was never recorded in the Vagaries scroll because it remains unproven. The burden falls to us to refine it. Because of its importance, Failee chose to record the spell on a far more permanent medium than fragile parchment."

Reznik looked around. "Do you mean to say that—"

"Yes," Einar interjected. "The formula we seek is hiding in plain sight, recorded on these wall stones."

"But there are so many!" Reznik protested.

Einar smiled. "Not really," he answered cryptically.

Einar recited the needed incantation. As he finished, some wall stones started moving. Grinding against one another, randomly selected stones started sliding forward from the walls. When the process was finished, more than two hundred had come forward. Calling the craft again, Einar concentrated harder. As he did, each selected stone's engravings glowed with azure. Fascinated, Reznik walked closer to examine one.

There was a number written in Old Eutracian at the stone's top edge. It showed the stone's particular order in the formula, he guessed. Below that was a glowing symbol that would be one part of the overall calculation. Backing away, he saw that each stone had been marked with a different number at its top, and either another number or craft symbol below it.

Einar walked to join him. "It is well conceived, is it not?" the consul asked. "Even if an intruder should survive the traps, all he would find is this empty room. Even then, should he read one stone it would be useless without the others. And for that, one needs the incantation. The incantation brings forth only those needed for the spell. All of the other engraved stones are meaningless. It truly is the essence of the phrase 'hiding in plain sight.' "

Einar turned to look at his consuls. It was clear that they were as intrigued as Reznik.

"Start recording the formula," he ordered. "Produce nine

copies. When we leave, I want each of us to carry one. Should we lose more people on the way back, the formula will survive. The symbols' placements in the formula can be found at each stone's top. When you have finished, check your work, then check it again. I have no wish to return."

Producing parchment and quills, the consuls started working. As one pointed at the stones' proper order, others dutifully recorded the numbers and symbols. While the consuls worked, Einar and Reznik walked to the door.

"I'm still at a loss to see how we're supposed to get back," Reznik said.

"Did you not see the circular staircase carved into the wall on this side?" Einar asked. "It leads all the way to the cavern floor."

"And then?" Reznik asked.

"We walk to the river," the consul answered. "A boat lies there. We will let it take us downstream. If Failee was as clever as I believe, the first thing she did after hiding the spell was to produce that staircase and boat. I have no doubt that the river will take us to a safe place."

Looking at the cavern sidewalls, Einar saw something interesting. Smiling, he shook his head. "Wigg's wife was indeed a clever woman," he said.

"What have you found?" Reznik asked.

Without answering, Einar turned back to the consuls. "Someone please give me some water," he ordered. Coming quickly, an eager consul offered up his canteen. Einar opened it. "Watch," he said.

Calling the craft, Einar caused the water to leave the canteen and float in the air. Waving one hand, he poured the water across the expanse left by the destroyed stone bridge. The results were unexpected.

As the water fell it seemed to land in midair, forming a link between the iron door and the tunnel entrance in the far wall. Soon they could see that the bridge had somehow returned. But this time it was largely invisible, its outline revealed only here and there by the water pooled on its surface. At first Reznik didn't understand. Then the partial adept smiled.

"The bridge never collapsed, did it?" he asked. "What we saw and heard was an enchantment designed to fool us into thinking that it had been destroyed."

"Not exactly," Einar answered. "The first bridge did collapse.

Then it reconstituted itself in an invisible form. That was the next part of the enchantment that started when I slid aside the iron bolt."

"But why not make the bridge invisible in the first place?" Reznik asked. "That way, only Failee would dare cross the cavern."

"Because if that were the case, a would-be intruder would come no farther than the tunnel exit and then go back," Einar answered. "The First Mistress wanted trespassers killed, not saved."

"How did you know?" Reznik asked.

Einar pointed to the cavern sidewalls. "When the bridge collapsed, both sidewalls cracked. Look again."

Reznik examined the cavern sidewalls. To his surprise, the cracks were gone. "I don't understand," he said.

"No?" Einar asked. "What other reason could there be for the cracks to mysteriously heal, except for the bridge returning and securing itself to the walls, eh?"

Rubbing his chin, Einar thought for a moment. He smiled. "Failee's traps were even cleverer than I believed," he mused.

"How so?" Reznik asked.

"That staircase is a lure, and that boat down below is another trap," Einar answered. "Seeing that the bridge has supposedly been destroyed, an intruder's only remaining option would be to climb down the staircase, put the boat into the river, and happily be on his way—all the time thinking that he or she had cleverly escaped. We nearly did the same thing! But I doubt that the boat ride would be a pleasant one. I now believe that the boat is enchanted to deliver would-be thieves to their deaths. They might successfully steal the formula hidden in this room, but they would never live to use it. There is no telling how they would die, but I doubt that it would be pleasant."

"So we will return by way of the invisible bridge, rather than by the boat," Reznik offered. Einar nodded.

"How can we be sure that the bridge is truly the safe way out, and that the boat is not?" Reznik asked.

As he placed one hand atop Reznik's shoulder, Einar gave the partial adept a wink. "The answer is simple," he said. "Failee wanted us to see the staircase. She never suspected anyone would discover the invisible bridge. The bridge is what she would have used."

Just then a consul walked up. "Forgive the intrusion, master," he said. "The formula has been successfully recorded."

"Give me a copy," Einar said. The consul handed him a scroll. As Einar unrolled it, he and Reznik read the formula. Reznik's eyes went wide.

"But this looks like . . . Can it be true?" he breathed.

"It is," Einar answered. "Now you better understand why we were ordered to take the Ghetto from the Minions." Eagerly rubbing his hands together, Reznik could hardly contain his glee. At long last this great venture would truly need his services.

Einar handed the scroll to the consul. "How many copies do we have?" he asked.

"Nine, master," the consul answered.

"Good," Einar said. "We're leaving. Pack everything up. Each consul is to carry a parchment."

"As you wish," the consul said.

A quarter hour later, they were ready to go. Einar decided he should be first to test the invisible bridge.

As everyone watched, he took a deep breath, then boldly stepped out into thin air. The bridge held. Waving the others forward, Einar started leading them across. On reaching the other side, everyone let go a sigh of relief. Wasting no time, Einar led them back through the dark tunnel.

The return journey to the Recluse would be long and dangerous. But in just two days' time, Serena's servants would eagerly start their experiments.

Chapter XXXIV

The first Minion warrior to see the prince exit the pass immediately came running to his *Jin'Sai.* He took Shadow's reins into one hand.

"My lord!" he exclaimed. "You have returned!" Suddenly

wondering whether Xanthus was also about to follow, the warrior warily drew his dreggan.

Jumping down from his stallion, Tristan smiled. "Sheathe your weapon," he said. "I'm alone."

Before he knew it, twenty-five warriors were happily engulfing him. At first he thought he might never escape their joyous onslaught. Looking up at the sun, he reckoned that it was midmorning.

"Who is in charge here?" Tristan shouted above the din.

A warrior stepped forward. He promptly went to one knee.

"I am Hector," he said. "I live to serve."

"Stand, Hector," Tristan ordered. "Tell me—how long was I away?"

Coming to his feet, Hector looked into his lord's eyes. Tall and tiger-muscled, he was younger than Tristan had expected the patrol's leader might be. "You entered the pass two nights ago," he answered.

"I see," Tristan answered. "Are there still another twenty-five warriors stationed at the base camp?" he asked.

"Yes, my lord," the warrior answered.

"Where is Traax?" Tristan asked.

"He flew to Tammerland to inform the Conclave of your disappearance," Hector answered.

"Has there been word from Tammerland?"

"No, my lord."

"Follow me to the base camp," Tristan said. "From the warriors waiting there I want you to select your ten swiftest fliers. I leave by litter for Tammerland immediately." Another thought came to the prince. "Tell me," he said, "have your warriors ever built a litter that can safely carry a horse?"

Hector smiled broadly. Understanding what his *Jin'Sai* had in mind, he affectionately rubbed Shadow's face.

"To my knowledge that has never been done," he answered. "But we Minions are excellent craftsmen. I'm sure something can be arranged."

Tristan smiled back. "Good," he said. He looked around at the others. "The rest of you are to remain here," he ordered. "Should anyone or anything come through that pass, send a messenger to Tammerland immediately."

Tristan jumped up into his saddle. Wheeling Shadow around,

he started galloping down the charred mountainside. Taking to the air, Hector followed.

THAT HAD BEEN THREE HOURS AGO. AS TRISTAN RODE THROUGH the air in his hastily constructed litter, the sun was approaching its zenith. Taking another sip of akulee, he watched the emerald fields of Farplain slide by below him. He couldn't remember ever having been so tired, or so overwhelmed by his thoughts. For the first time since leaving Crysenium, he could take the time to contemplate his amazing journey.

Although he had lived it, he could hardly believe what had happened. The revelations told to him by the Crysenium Envoys had been wondrous and at the same time terrifying. He could still see the Borderlands swallowing up an entire army, and the terrible battle scene Hoskiko had shown him. Each had been but a part of the ongoing War of Attrition—a war that he was somehow destined to stop, or die in the attempt.

Despite having accepted this great burden, in a way he had also gained a new measure of peace. After a lifetime of asking questions, he had finally learned some answers. He had many more questions—questions he knew that even Wigg and Faegan couldn't answer. Until he could return to Crysenium, those mysteries would have to wait.

His mind soon turned to the threat at hand. Serena's plan was monstrous. If the Conclave couldn't stop her, he would have neither the will nor the ability to return to Crysenium. Worse, the Conclave would be sailing into terrible danger, and until he reached Tammerland there was no way to warn them. Wigg and Jessamay were powerful mystics, and there was no better sea captain than Tyranny. Thousands of Minion warriors would be sailing with them. Even so, Serena's snare would be nearly impossible to avoid.

Tristan looked at the warriors carrying his litter. They were flying as fast as they could, but a southerly headwind was making the going difficult. Close by but still frightened by his strange surroundings, Shadow danced nervously in his specially constructed litter. Ten more stout warriors bore it aloft. Seeing the stallion being carried through the air was a strange sight, but Tristan was glad he had thought to bring the horse along. If he couldn't reach the coast in time to sail with the Conclave, something told him that he would need Shadow in the days ahead.

Then he suddenly remembered his medallion. Looking down, he saw its gold surface twinkle in the midday sun as it lay beneath the Paragon. He had been so intent on getting home that he had forgotten about his new power. Cursing himself for his forgetfulness, he closed his eyes.

Just as Hoskiko had instructed him, he imagined his and Shailiha's medallions hanging side by side in space. Concentrating harder, he watched them combine into one. He lifted the medallion from his chest and turned it over. Just as Hoskiko had promised, its other side showed a scene. Closing his eyes for a moment, he shook his head. The Black Ships had already sailed.

He looked at the medallion again. It showed Wigg leaning against a Black Ship's gunwale. He was talking to someone, but there no was telling to whom. In the distance Tristan could see the other five Black Ships, flying alongside Wigg's over the Sea of Whispers. Closing his eyes again, he caused the scene to vanish and dropped the medallion to his chest.

Shailiha had followed his orders after all, and Wigg, Faegan, and Jessamay must have successfully trained the acolytes to empower the fleet. He wondered how many Conclave members had accompanied Shailiha. Perhaps all, he realized. The Black Ships were not using the crippled wizard's portal to help them across the sea—Tristan had long known that they were far too large and cumbersome for that. Even so, the ships flew so fast that no Minion warriors could likely catch them, even if they were sent right now and directly from their watch stations along the coast. *May the Afterlife bring the fleet home safely,* he thought.

Clearly, there was no longer a need to force the Minions to fly through the night, as he had first planned. Leaning out of the litter, he shouted new orders that they should land at twilight and make camp. After taking another draft from the akulee jug, he shoved the cork back into its spout. He stretched out on the litter floor. Despite his worry for the Conclave, he was asleep in moments.

"*JIN'SAI,*" HECTOR SAID. REACHING OUT, HE GAVE TRISTAN A GENtle shove. "*Jin'Sai*—wake up! We have landed."

Stretching and blinking, Tristan sat up in the litter. He felt refreshed. Standing, he looked around.

Hector had chosen to land in a grassy depression. A low ridge surrounded it on three sides. Night was falling, and the twenty warriors were starting to make camp. Shadow had been released from his litter and was tethered to a night line. Not far away, the Sippora River burbled noisily.

"How far have we come?" Tristan asked.

"We are a little more than halfway, lord," Hector answered, "just south of where the Sippora branches into two smaller rivers. If we get an early start, we will be home by midday tomorrow. The warriors will soon have the camp set up. Are you hungry?"

Tristan smiled. "Famished!" he answered. "What do we have to eat?"

"We brought an elk quarter from the base camp. It's packed in glacier ice. We also have some fresh vegetables. We'll get started on roasting the elk right away. In the meantime, I'll get some scouts into the air."

Tristan looked at the exhausted warriors who had carried the two litters for so far and so long. The litter holding Shadow would have been particularly heavy, and would be no less so tomorrow. As the warriors tiredly made camp, Tristan saw that their wings literally dragged along the ground.

Tristan shook his head. "They have all flown hard," he said. "Let them rest and eat first, then send them aloft." Rubbing his face, he realized that he hadn't bathed or shaven for two days. He looked longingly at the Sippora.

"In the meantime, I'm going to clean up," he said. "Can a warrior lend me some soap?"

Hector immediately barked out some orders. A warrior soon came running to hand Tristan a bar of the harsh, black soap that the Minions made themselves.

"Thank you," he said.

Smiling, he started walking toward the river. It would be numbingly cold, but that was just what he wanted. Then he would laugh, drink, and eat elk with the warriors until he could do so no more. And tomorrow he would be home.

Sitting on his knees by the river, he dipped the soap and lathered his face. He reached behind his right shoulder and produced a throwing knife. Having no mirror, he shaved his face by feel. When he was satisfied he removed his weapons and clothing. Leaving the Paragon and medallion around his neck, he dove headlong into the rushing Sippora.

The river's coldness took his breath away. After swimming

underwater for several meters he surfaced. His eyes still closed, he stood in the waist-deep water and pushed his hair from his face. He could already smell the enticing aroma of roasting elk as it drifted toward the river.

Tristan opened his eyes. To his amazement he saw a figure before him on the riverbank. It wasn't Minion. The intruder held a sword unlike any the prince had ever seen—and it was pointed right between Tristan's eyes.

"It seems I have you at a disadvantage," the unfamiliar voice said. A smile came.

CHAPTER XXXV

AS ACTINIUS STRODE ACROSS THE RECLUSE'S OUTER WARD, HE pulled his robe closer against the cold night air. Two consuls named Jacob and Aaron followed him.

Actinius scowled. He would have preferred to remain inside where it was warm, but he had an important task to perform. The first of many, he guessed, because Einar and Reznik were finally ready to start their work. As the three men crossed the outer ward, lumbering shrews and partly camouflaged envelopers could be seen prowling and soaring about, their numbers nothing compared to those waiting in hiding as they protected the Recluse.

It was nearly midnight in Parthalon, and the three magenta moons cast eerie shadows across the ward's colorful terrazzo floor. By this time most of the Minion blood had been cleaned away from the multicolored tiles. Walking on, Actinius approached the newly constructed cages.

Hundreds of wooden crates stood in the moonlight. Each crate had been constructed at the Ghetto of the Shunned. Then the crates had been crammed full of lepers and flown to the Recluse by Serena's envelopers. Should more subjects be needed, they too would be brought from the Ghetto. Actinius came to stand before one of the cages. He turned to his consuls.

"Any one of them will do," he said matter-of-factly.

Jacob walked to the cage and unlocked the door. Aaron quickly selected a female prisoner of middle age. She would have been attractive, had leprosy not assaulted her face and body. As Aaron grabbed her and hauled her out, she screamed and kicked at him. Actinius quickly held up one hand.

"Remember our instructions!" he reminded the consuls. "There is to be no craft use. It might compromise our research."

The woman screamed again, then lunged forward to viciously bite Aaron on the hand. Laughing, Actinius stepped closer and rendered her unconscious with a single swipe across the face. She fell to the tile floor. After Aaron slung her across his back, the cage door was locked again and the three mystics returned to the Recluse.

As they climbed the castle's broad steps, the men saw that the Recluse remained busy, despite the late hour. Every oil lamp was lit, and enchanted to stay that way. Consuls and Valrenkians hurried here and there, each following Einar's various orders. More shrews and envelopers prowled the majestic hallways and salons. On reaching the grand foyer, the men turned down one hall, then walked toward the nearest secret doorway leading to the lower regions.

Half an hour later they arrived at their destination. As they walked in, Einar and Reznik looked up from a scroll they were huddling over. Seeing his first test subject casually slung over Aaron's shoulder, Einar frowned.

"Is she dead?" he demanded.

"Only unconscious," Actinius answered. "It was needed."

Einar nodded. "Very well," he said. "But don't do it again."

He pointed to a stone table on the room's other side. "Over there," he ordered. As Aaron placed the body on the table, Actinius looked around.

They were standing in another of Failee's research chambers. Einar realized that it would have been easier to conduct his experiments in a room aboveground, but for security's sake he had decided to work here. Like many of the underground chambers, this room had been cut from the surrounding rock. It was spacious and well lit. Bookcases lined the walls. Its center encircled by a golden band, the precious Vagaries scroll lay atop a table standing in one corner.

A parchment holding Failee's recently discovered formula lay unrolled and suspended by enchantment against another wall. The parchment took up the wall's entire length. Other tables laden with various instruments, books, and bottles also stood nearby. Actinius knew that those were Reznik's things. On the wall over the table, another chart had been hung. It showed a strange, oblong form that was mapped into various sections. Each section was labeled in Old Eutracian.

Einar looked at Actinius. He nodded. The consul walked to the table supporting the unconscious woman. Reaching into the folds of his robe, he produced a waterproofed leather bag. After placing it over the woman's head he pulled its drawstring tight around her neck.

"Be careful!" Einar said. "Do not damage her throat!" Nodding, Actinius loosened the drawstring a bit.

Awakened by her sudden inability to breathe, for several agonizing moments the woman struggled against her murderer. Soon her jangling slowed, then stopped altogether. Actinius removed the leather bag from around her head.

Walking to the table, Einar and Reznik looked down at her. Starving her lungs had been the best way to kill her without using the craft or otherwise damaging her body.

"What is your opinion?" Einar asked Reznik. "Is this subject suitable?"

"Yes," the Valrenkian answered. "This manner of death most closely matches the original victim's." Satisfied with Reznik's answer, Einar went to stand before Failee's elegant formula.

Walking to the other table, Reznik selected an hourglass and a razor-sharp boning knife. Walking back, he bent over the fresh corpse. With one stroke he cut away the woman's rags, then dropped them to the floor. Bending over farther, he placed an ear against her bare chest.

"You may start," Reznik said.

As Actinius turned the hourglass over, Einar started reading Failee's formula aloud. When he finished he walked over to stand beside Reznik. Standing up, the Valrenkian shook his head.

"Her liver will tell us more," he said simply. Taking up his boning knife, he sliced open the dead woman's abdomen.

Fascinated, Einar, Aaron, and Jacob neared to watch the Valrenkian work. Being a partial adept, Reznik possessed skills that they did not—skills that would prove vital to their mission. Among his other talents, Reznik was a haruspex, or "reader of entrails." And because the blood that was so vital to the craft was filtered through one's liver, that organ would best tell them what they needed to know.

For the first time since meeting Reznik, Einar was genuinely glad that the Valrenkian partial adept was a part of their group. Haruspication was an immensely detailed art that called for years of specialized training. It could truly be mastered only by partial adepts, because only they had full access to the Paragon's organic facet. True haruspices were few and far between, and Reznik was perhaps the world's finest. Among his other talents was tasseomancy, otherwise known as tea leaf reading. He was also a shell, smoke, and pendulum scryer, and could use those items for divination.

Reznik lifted the red liver from the gaping abdominal cavity. It dripped blood as he walked it to another table and placed it onto a pewter tray. He then looked up at the diagram on the wall that Actinius had wondered about earlier.

Actinius suddenly understood that the oblong shape depicted there was that of a human liver. The organ in the diagram was sectioned off into various oddly shaped areas. Each section was labeled in Old Eutracian. Silently translating the labels into the present day's dialect, he saw such phrases as "Life Forces," "Aging," "Illnesses," and "Intelligence." Walking nearer, Actinius watched Reznik sit on a stool standing before the table.

First the Valrenkian turned the liver so that its position exactly matched the one in the diagram. He then took up a pair of magnifying spectacles and arranged them on his face. After wiping his hands down the length of his bloody smock, he picked up another knife and methodically started sectioning the liver into pieces matching those shown in the diagram. As the time passed, Einar, Aaron, and Jacob remained watchful. They couldn't help but find their appreciation for Reznik's talents growing with every moment.

Referring to the chart, Reznik segregated the liver section known as "Life Forces." It was an oblong piece about the size of a hen's egg, and looked just like the one in the diagram. Putting it into a separate pan, Reznik placed the first pan aside. Taking up a finer knife, Reznik shaved off a slice. It took several tries before he had the thinness he wanted.

Using a pair of silver tongs, he held the slice to the light. It had been shaven so thin that it was translucent. After placing the slice into another pan, Reznik leaned back and took a deep breath.

"What have you learned?" Einar asked eagerly.

Removing the spectacles from his face, Reznik stretched his back. "Patience, my friends," he said. "I know nothing yet, other than that Failee's spell failed. We need to learn why, and only my herbs and oils can tell us that."

Reznik picked up a leather-bound text. The title on the book's spine read *Haruspication Oils, Herbs, and Elixirs: Their Uses in Deciphering Entrails*. The book was massive, and its page edges were worn and dog-eared. After placing the dusty book on the table, Reznik repositioned his spectacles on his face, then unfastened the book's leather binding straps. He opened it and started leafing through its fragile pages.

After a time he walked to the room's far side. Many shelves lined the wall, each one holding dozens of different colored bottles. These too had accompanied him from the Citadel. He found the one he wanted and placed it into a smock pocket. Locating the other two bottles took longer, but they finally came to hand.

After walking back to the table, he placed the three bottles alongside the tray holding the liver slice. He opened one bottle, then took up an eye dropper. Placing the dropper's end into the bottleneck, he siphoned off a few drops of the precious oil. He then judiciously emptied the dropper's contents onto the liver slice.

A quizzical look came over Einar's face. "What are you using?" he asked.

"Oil of encumbrance," Reznik answered, without looking up. "It's rare. This small bottle alone would bring at least two thousand kisa."

"What does it do?" Einar asked.

"As one might gather from its name, oil of encumbrance slows down certain organic processes," Reznik answered. "Combined with other herbs and oils, it becomes more effective."

Reznik opened another bottle, took a pinch of dried herbs between his fingers, then sprinkled them onto the slice. Sitting back, he waited for the combination to take effect.

"That herb you just added," Jacob said. "What is it?"

"It's a ground root called maiden's breath," he answered. "It grows wild in Eutracia. When dried and pulverized, its orange blossoms are good for many things—especially when added to oil of encumbrance."

His curiosity growing, Einar came closer. After gazing at the slice he looked at Reznik. "How does this particular combination of oil and herbs serve our purpose?" he asked.

"When added together, oil of encumbrance and maiden's breath work to slow the decay process," Reznik answered. "Now we can examine the liver sample at our leisure, without fear of losing its freshness, and whatever message it might tell us."

Reznik picked up the third bottle and held it to the light. The amber container was tightly sealed with a specially hinged lid. He removed the cork and took a wary sniff to test the herb's freshness. The pungent aroma made him recoil.

"This is ground blossom of tansy ragwort," he said, running one finger under his nose. "It is a common ragwort with a yellow flower. It is an aggressive form of weed that is toxic to some cattle." As he removed two pinches from the bottle, the herbmaster smiled. "Eutracian farmers are forever trying to stamp it out," he added. "Little do they know how valuable it can be."

As he had with the other ingredients, Reznik sprinkled this latest addition onto the specimen. Standing, he took a high-powered magnifying glass into one hand. In his other he again took up the silver tongs. Grasping the parchment-thin slice ever so gently, he held it to the light.

"Now then," he said. "We will see what we will see."

Holding up the glass, he carefully examined the specimen. A discouraged look conquered his face.

"It's just as I feared," he said. Looking at Einar, he beckoned the consul closer. "Look through the glass," he said, "and tell me what you see."

Einar did as he was asked. To his surprise, against the backdrop of the oil lamps the translucent slice looked rather beautiful. The red tissue had turned pink, and its depths were shot through with dark, weblike striations. He looked at Reznik.

"It's intriguing," he said. "But what do these marks mean? I suspect that they don't occur naturally, or were there before she died."

"That's correct," Reznik answered. "Look again."

As the consul again looked at the specimen, Reznik leaned closer. "I believe that those striations indicate that Failee's spell is flawed—too weak, probably," the Valrenkian said. "Even so, my guess is that her calculations are taking us along the right path. During our next attempt I will try to raise the spell's power by adding other precious herbs and oils. It might take many tries before I find a mixture that works, but I remain optimistic."

"Will you examine the woman's other organs as well?" Einar asked.

Reznik shook his head. "They would tell us little. And taking another sample from this woman's liver would do no good either, because the result would be the same. I will start formulating the first of what I'm sure will be many recipes. We will force the next subject to ingest it before he or she is killed. Then we will try again."

Reznik walked back over to his table, donned his spectacles, and again consulted the great book that he had used before. As he looked though the pages he took up a quill and started making notes.

For his part, Einar was discouraged but far from defeated. He knew the secret would be found—he could feel it in his bones. But it would take much time and patience, he realized. He looked at Jacob and Aaron.

"Bring us another subject," he said.

As the two consuls left the room, Einar went to look over Reznik's shoulder.

CHAPTER XXXVI

"COME OUT OF THERE!" THE MAN SHOUTED. HIS VOICE WAS DEEP and lively. Although he clearly meant business, he gave Tristan a humorous smirk.

"You look ridiculous!" he added. "It's a pity you have nothing to steal but those meager trinkets lying around your neck!" The bizarre-looking man furtively cast his eyes toward Tristan's weapons, lying just out of reach on the riverbank. "Although that sword with the gold hilt looks tempting," he added dryly.

Standing waist deep in the rushing Sippora, Tristan shivered. Whoever the intruder was, he had him dead to rights. The prince knew there was no point trying to reach his weapons, for he could be easily killed before he left the water.

Tristan watched in dread as the man bent down to grasp the discarded dreggan and knife quiver. After tossing the quiver over one shoulder, the man stood and sheathed his sword. Then he drew Tristan's dreggan, letting the baldric drop to the ground. For some time he admired the magnificent Minion blade in the moonlight.

Tristan quickly looked around. To his dismay, hundreds more equally mysterious figures lined the surrounding ridge. Shivering more violently, he wrapped his arms about himself. He couldn't imagine how so many men had slipped by his Minions. He tried looking past his captor and toward the warrior campsite, but the riverbank blocked his view.

"Who are you?" Tristan demanded. "What do you want?"

"The answer is simple," the man replied. "I want your horse, your gold jewelry, and anything else of value you own. And I mean to get them."

Tristan tensed as he thought about losing the Paragon and his gold medallion. Where in the name of the Afterlife were Hector and his twenty warriors?

"Do you plan on standing in that freezing water all night?" the man demanded. Emphasizing his point, he pointed the dreggan at Tristan. "If so, I hope you have already fathered all the children you want."

Tristan scowled. Naked and dripping water, he walked up the slippery riverbank to stand beside his discarded garments.

"May I dress?" he asked sarcastically. "Or are you going to steal my clothes, too?"

"The rags you may keep," the stranger answered. "I wouldn't wear them on my worst day."

Tristan dressed quickly. Running his hands through his wet hair, he pushed it back from his forehead. He stood there for a few moments, glaring at the man who had so surprisingly appeared.

The figure was imposing, almost theatrical. About Tristan's age, he was tall and muscular. He wore a white, blousy shirt, its full sleeves collected loosely at the wrists. Baggy black trousers were tucked into his soft, laced top-boots. A gray fur vest lay over the shirt, and a brimless hat of the same material sat at a jaunty angle atop his head.

His longish brown hair escaped the hat's bottom here and there, and he wore a neatly trimmed, matching goatee. His sharp jawline and dark eyes glinted in the moonlight. Several gold chains adorned his chest, and many of his fingers bore glittering rings. His free hand rested loosely on a curved hip dagger, its leather scabbard accented with silver filigree. A matching sword dangled from his left hip. The weapons seemed to be a natural part of the man's persona, showing that he knew how to use them.

Tristan suddenly realized that despite not knowing the fellow's name, he understood his heritage. The intruder was a Eutracian highlander. As their eyes met in a contest of wills, Tristan tried to remember what Wigg had once said about them.

The highlanders were as much myth as reality. Living in colorful wagons, they were reputed to be marvelous horsemen. The men did whatever fighting was called for, while their women stealthily performed the thieving and duping of unsuspecting innocents as their caravans traveled from town to town. It was often said that a highlander maid could easily steal a man's purse, horse, and heart all in the same night. The legend went on to warn that the man's purse would be taken surreptitiously, his horse taken quietly, and his heart taken willingly.

It was also rumored that besides speaking Eutracian, these nomads conversed in another language all their own. Their women were said to be remarkably beautiful and intensely sexual beings, possessing notoriously free spirits. The highlanders were rumored to live in tightly knit clans that often warred among each other, usually over territory and ill-gotten spoils that none of them could rightfully claim. Still standing on the riverbank, Tristan glared into the highlander's dark eyes.

"Turn around," the man said. "Put your hands behind your back."

Knowing he had no choice, Tristan did as he was told. He

soon felt his wrists being bound. He turned back to glare at his captor.

"What happens now?" he demanded.

"We return to your poorly guarded campsite," the man said. He again pointed Tristan's dreggan at him. "A surprise awaits you. Move, *dango*!"

Tristan scowled. "What did you just call me?" he demanded.

"Dango," the highlander answered with another smile. "In our world it means 'city dweller.' And if you're thinking it's an insult, you're right."

Cursing himself for letting the Minions rest rather than sending scout patrols aloft, Tristan reluctantly walked the remaining way up the riverbank. After retrieving the dreggan baldric from the ground, Tristan's flamboyant captor prodded the prince forward. Clambering down from the ridge, the other highlanders followed. Tristan saw no women among them.

As they reached the top of the ridge, Tristan couldn't believe his eyes. Although not one looked injured, all twenty Minion warriors had somehow been overcome. Their hands, feet, and wings bound tightly with harsh rope, they sat glumly on the ground around the campfire.

More highlander men surrounded the captured warriors. Laughing at the Minions' expense, they eagerly tested the warriors' unusual akulee and hungrily ate purloined elk meat. All of the warriors' weapons lay nearby in a ramshackle pile. A strange-looking heap of what looked like coarse netting lay beside the captured Minion weapons, along with a loose collection of colorful arrows.

The highlander leader walked up alongside Tristan. "Those flying creatures are yours, I presume?" he asked.

Tristan nodded angrily. "How did you capture them?"

The highlander raised an arm. "Do you see that pile of netting?" he asked. "After sneaking up the ridge, my men attached arrows to the nets, then shot them over your fighters. The arrows carried the nets to the ridge's other side, then buried themselves deep into the ground. We use the same technique to capture herds of deer. Your warriors started to cut their way free, but as they did they were told that we already had you. We described you, then warned them that if they didn't surrender, you would be killed." As the highlander leader turned toward Tristan, a look of respect flashed across his eyes.

"Whatever those winged things are, they're certainly loyal to you," he said. "They collectively offered up their lives so that you might go free." He let go a sudden, short laugh. "I'm not so sure I could say the same for my clansmen!" he added.

"You're highlanders, aren't you?" Tristan asked. "What is your name?"

Smiling, the man bowed sarcastically. As he did, many of his followers laughed uproariously at the prince's expense.

"I am Rafe of Clan Kilbourne," he answered. "Chieftain of the clan. All told, we number just under three thousand. We are camped not more than two leagues away. Had you traveled just a bit farther, you would have flown right over us." Rafe's eyes narrowed. "And just who are you, may I ask?"

Tristan suddenly regretted having asked Rafe's identity. He was about to lie when another of the highlanders rushed forward.

"I know who this *dango* is!" the man growled.

The highlander was huge—almost as big as Scars. But where Scars was muscled, this man was grotesquely fat. He was as colorfully dressed as Rafe, and at least twenty years older. A gray, downward-dropping mustache covered his top lip, and unruly gray hair graced either shoulder. His calloused hands looked the size of small hams. Smiling, he arrogantly placed them on his hips.

"Tell us, Balthazar," Rafe said.

Walking closer, the highlander named Balthazar searched Tristan's face.

"He's Prince Tristan, that's who!" Balthazar shouted. "I'm sure of it! I saw him once in Tammerland. He was younger then, but there is no doubt." Scratching his chin, he looked back at Rafe.

"We should keep this one," he added slyly. "Rumor has it that he commands several wizards. They would surely pay to get him back."

Rafe laughed. "Is that so?" he asked. "My, but this *has* been a fortuitous day!"

Looking down at the captured warriors, the highlander leader thought for a moment then looked back at the prince. "I was going to rob you, then set you and your fighters free," he said. "But I see that you're too valuable to release so easily. It seems you're coming with us."

Rafe came closer and reached out to lift the still-wet Paragon and gold medallion from Tristan's chest. The prince tensed. For several anxious moments the rapacious highlander eyed them hungrily as they lay twinkling in his palm.

Tristan's mind raced. Should he tell him about them? Or would that only pique the bastard's curiosity and make him want them more? Hoping against hope that he was doing the right thing, Tristan remained silent. To the prince's relief, Rafe finally let the jewel and the disc fall back to Tristan's chest. Rafe nodded.

"You must be royalty," he said. "Who else would wear a medallion that carries the heraldry of the House of Galland, eh? I stand convinced. You may keep your baubles, Your Highness. I sense that they will pale in comparison with what your ransom will bring." The highlander chieftain looked at his clansmen.

"We ride back to camp!" he shouted. "There is much to celebrate tonight! We will bring the winged ones along, as well! Ugly as they are, they should be worth something in trade!"

Rafe placed his face only inches from Tristan's. "Nothing is to happen to this one," he added quietly. "It seems he's worth his royal weight in gold."

Amid his men's shouting and cheering, Rafe prodded Tristan toward the ridge's other side. About fifty meters away, hundreds of horses saddled with colorful tack grazed quietly on the emerald fields. When Tristan and the highlanders reached them, the prince was relieved to see Balthazar single out Shadow. To Tristan's surprise, Rafe drew his curved dagger and cut the prince's bonds. Rubbing his wrists, Tristan looked at Rafe curiously.

"I'm not worried about you escaping, Your Highness," he said. "As we ride, we will be all around you. Where can you possibly go?"

Tristan scowled. "I see your point," he answered angrily.

Turning to Balthazar, Rafe heartily slapped a hand down atop his friend's shoulder. "See to it that the winged ones are brought along," he ordered. "Have them walk back, and be sure to bring their weapons—we can always use more. Keep the warriors bound, my friend, and do not underestimate them. We tricked them once. But by the looks of them, I would not wish to try again."

"On my life," Balthazar answered.

After grinning at the prince, Rafe said something to Balthazar in a strange language Tristan didn't understand. Throwing his head back, Balthazar laughed hugely, his fat belly nearly popping the buttons of his riotous silk shirt.

"Everyone mount up!" Rafe shouted. "We ride for home!"

Under Rafe's watchful gaze, Tristan swung up into his saddle. Shadow danced nervously for a moment before settling down. Rafe cast a greedy glance at the black stallion before mounting his dull bay mare.

"That's a beautiful mount!" he shouted at Tristan, his voice barely rising above the hundreds of anxiously milling horses. "I will enjoy owning him!"

Wheeling his mare around, Rafe trotted her southeast. With hundreds of watchful highlanders surrounding him, Tristan had no choice but to also wheel Shadow around and go with them.

HALF AN HOUR LATER, RAFE INCREASED THE PACE. UNFETTERED by fences, woods, or hills, the hundreds of galloping riders struck out across an approaching field with abandon.

Surrounded on all sides by colorful highlanders, Tristan quickly realized that Shadow was easily the equal of their horses. But even though the prince had often been called one of the best horsemen in the kingdom, he was about to be further humbled by his talented captors.

Knowing that they were showing off largely for his benefit, Tristan watched as the highlanders started performing amazing feats of horsemanship. Some leapt from their saddles to stamp their boots against the passing ground, even as their horses kept on charging. They would then launch back into the air, easily finding their saddles again. Others took their reins in their teeth, then stood upright in their saddles to wave their swords. As Tristan watched, he noticed that aside from their other weapons, each highlander also carried a short bow and a quiver full of colorful arrows slung across his back.

Looking ahead, Tristan saw Rafe leering back at him. Well aware that even the best Royal Guard cavalry officers had never been able to perform such feats as Rafe's clansmen, Tristan scowled. Laughing loudly, Rafe faced forward in his saddle again then started leading the hundreds of riders in a gentle turn toward the west. Not to be outdone, Tristan dug his heels into Shadow's flanks.

After a few more minutes of hard charging, Tristan saw a

small rise looming up ahead. Rafe headed straight for it. As they reached the top of the rise, the highlander chieftain held up one hand. Tristan and the clansmen came to an abrupt stop, allowing their horses some rest. Saying nothing, Rafe pointed toward the shallow valley lying below. As Shadow stamped and snorted beneath him, the prince looked down.

Hundreds of highlander wagons stood quietly on the fields below, their colorful wooden wheels and canvas tops stretching far across the moonlit plains. Campfires seemed to burn everywhere, the light from their orange-red flames lighting up the night sky. The smell of pungent food came to Tristan's nostrils, causing his stomach to growl. Seeing the camp's huge size, he could easily believe Rafe's claim about being the chieftain over three thousand men, women, and children.

Turning in his saddle, Rafe waved one of his clansmen forward. Strong and fit, the fellow looked younger than most of the others. As he rode past the prince he gave Tristan a hard stare.

"Lead them down," Rafe ordered. "As usual, no one gains entry to the camp unless his arrow finds its mark." Looking over at Tristan, the highlander chieftain smiled. "The prince and I will stay here and watch," he added cryptically.

With a nod, the young highlander wheeled his horse around to start leading the others down the slope at a full gallop. Hearing the hundreds of pounding hooves, highlander men, women, and children eagerly poured from the campsite to walk out on the plains to watch their comrades approach.

Curious, Tristan spurred Shadow up alongside Rafe's mare. "What's going on?" he asked.

Rafe leaned one arm down on his saddle pommel. His eyes continually locked on the galloping clansmen, he smiled.

"Watch and learn," he said. "You are about to witness an old highlander custom—one designed to keep our skills honed. Any of my men who miss the target will not be allowed to eat tonight, or to sleep with his woman. It is a test of both the horses and the men. There is an old highlander saying, *dango.* 'A clansman can only be as good as the horse he rides.' "

Fascinated, Tristan watched the riders charge down the opposite side of the rise. Then he noticed something odd, lying in the distance. Narrowing his eyes, he saw what looked like several dozen straw scarecrows standing in a long line before the camp. Each one was attached to a pole that had been plunged into the ground. Between the incongruous scarecrows and the approaching riders lay a deep ravine, its depths dark in the twinkling moonlight. Such deadly ravines were not uncommon on the Farplain fields, Tristan knew. Even so, he found it odd that Rafe would choose to make camp near one.

He watched the thundering highlanders suddenly fan out into long, disciplined lines like charging cavalry regiments, one line following behind the next. As the lines formed, the riders reached over their backs to retrieve their deeply curved bows. Then each one removed an arrow from his quiver.

The scene bathed in the magenta moonlight was captivating. As the lines of hard-charging highlanders approached the deep ravine, each put his reins between his teeth then notched his arrow onto his bowstring. With no regard for their safety, they kept galloping onward. Should anyone's horse fall short in his jump, death would come quickly to both horse and rider. Mesmerized by the scene, the prince couldn't help wondering how many brave riders would die, simply because Rafe had ordered them to do this bizarre thing.

The idea was simple enough, but would also be very difficult to accomplish. As each rider jumped the ravine, he would loose an arrow at one of the scarecrows. If his horse successfully finished the jump and the arrow found its mark, both horse and rider had proven themselves. Holding his breath, Tristan watched as the first wave of riders thundered onward.

Dozens of arrows flew through the air as the horses leapt over the gorge. Amazingly, not one missed its mark. Flying through the air, the horses crashed down on the other side. The first wave had been successful, but there were many more to follow. Surely they could not all be so skillful, or their horses so sure, Tristan guessed.

As wave after wave of highlanders followed, few of their arrows missed their marks. Mesmerized, Tristan could only sit atop Shadow and marvel at the plainsmen's skill. Finally the last line charged headlong toward the ravine. Not to be outdone by the others, the highlanders shouted wildly through their clenched teeth as they chased toward the abyss. Their arrows notched and their bowstrings pulled, they started leaping their horses over the dark gorge. Just then one of the horses went down, taking another mount with him.

Stepping into a hole dug by some burrowing plains creature,

the stallion's front leg snapped in half like a dry tree branch. Screaming wildly, the horse tumbled to the grass headfirst. Another horse stumbled over him and also went crashing to the ground. They hit hard, horses and riders skidding across the dewy grass and toward the gaping ravine. His heart in his throat, Tristan watched helplessly as the drama played out before his eyes.

As he fell, one rider managed to dig his boot heels into the turf, slowing his momentum. He skidded to a stop at the ravine's edge. But the other rider and the two horses weren't so lucky. Tristan watched in horror as he realized that the second rider's boot was caught in his saddle stirrup. His horse's momentum carrying them unerringly toward the ravine, they tumbled over the side. Unable to regain his footing, the other horse followed.

Tristan and Rafe heard the highlander's distant screams for a time, then all went silent. As their horses pawed the ground and the spectators from the camp anxiously rushed toward the ravine, the once-cheering highlander riders respectfully went quiet.

Tristan's admiration quickly turned to anger. If there was one thing he couldn't abide, it was unnecessary loss of life. He glared at Rafe.

"Tell me," he growled. "Was it worth that?"

Sighing, Rafe did not turn to look at him. "It is our way, *dango,*" he said quietly. "If there is a need to explain it to you, then it is something you would never understand."

Finally Rafe turned, his dark eyes pouring into Tristan's. "Follow me," he ordered simply.

Without hesitation Rafe started galloping down the hill toward the highlander who had been spared. Tristan followed. With one fluid movement Rafe grasped the man's outstretched hand, then hoisted him up onto his horse's back, just behind his saddle. With his last clansman secured, Rafe led Tristan safely around the ravine's far end.

Slowing their horses, they trotted quietly into the highlander camp. Before every wagon, a campfire burned cheerfully. Black pots hung over many of the campfires, their steaming contents sending delicious aromas into the air. As Tristan looked around he saw Rafe's horsemen return to their wagons to be eagerly greeted by their loved ones. Pleasant but odd-sounding music filled the air, sometimes interrupted by the squeals of playful children. Although he was Rafe's captive, Tristan found the carnival-like atmosphere fascinating.

Aside from their exotic clothes and jewelry, most of the women he saw looked quite ordinary. But some were positively ravishing, with dark, seductive eyes, hourglass figures, and long, dark hair hanging to their waists. As he rode by, several of them gave him glances that clearly spoke of sexual curiosity, mixed with an animal-like wariness.

As Tristan accompanied Rafe deeper into the camp, the happy children stopped playing. The highlander men and women looked warily at him from their seats around their fires and from the shadows formed by the canvas wagon tops while the camp elders talked among themselves urgently, using the hushed, guarded tones of their secret language. Greed showing in their eyes, some pointed brazenly at the shiny silver bits adorning Tristan's black saddle and bridle.

Who is this person Rafe has brought into our midst? Tristan could almost hear them asking. *Aside from his saddle, he does not look rich. No outsider ventures willingly into a highlander camp, unless he wants to be robbed. How can he be so stupid?*

Turning his mare left, Rafe led Tristan toward the camp's center. The cleared area was large and encircled by wagons. The wagons' stern ends faced the clearing's center, and their doors had been lowered, their insides showing bedsheets, blankets, and pillows. More tasseled pillows lay on the ground before the wagons, with highlanders reclining on them. A large bonfire burned merrily in the area's center. The highlanders eyed Tristan warily as they watched him ride into their midst.

Rafe pulled his mare to a stop near one of the largest wagons. After the hard ride, the prince was thankful to have his feet back on the ground. A young boy came running to take their reins, then led the sweating horses away. Scowling, Tristan couldn't help but wonder whether he would ever see Shadow again, but there was little he could do about it.

Rafe walked over to his wagon and casually tossed Tristan's dreggan, baldric, and throwing knives inside. He then lowered himself down atop several colorful pillows. Lying casually on one side, he beckoned the prince to do the same. Tristan obliged, sitting cross-legged atop one of the larger ones. Rafe clapped his hands.

Four highlander women appeared. They were all fiercely

beautiful in the same sort of way, giving Tristan the impression that they might be sisters. Each wore a low-cut, high-hemmed frock that left little to the imagination. Each had strings of gold coins around her neck and multiple gold bracelets on her wrists. One carried a large amphora, and another girl carried a tray of glasses. Rafe and Tristan each took one.

Rafe's glass was filled first with a dark, smoky-smelling liquid. Then one of the women filled Tristan's glass. As she did, her long, dark hair brushed Tristan's cheek, giving him the impression that it had happened on purpose. As he watched her seductively walk away, she turned to smile back at him, her teeth flashing in the moonlight. Then she touched one fingertip to her blouse, directly atop her heart. Slapping one hand down on his thigh, Rafe laughed uproariously.

"That one is Yasmin," he said with a wink. "She's famous for her predatory ways. You are unfamiliar with our customs, so I will decipher her meaning for you. Yasmin just suggested that she would like you to share her bed tonight."

Rafe took a discerning sip of the dark brew, then looked mischievously at Tristan. "Are you interested, Your Highness?" he asked. "A woman of such quality deserves an answer."

Before responding, Tristan took a swig of the mysterious drink. At first he recoiled, finding it even more bitter than Minion akulee. But unlike akulee, the taste quickly settled down to provide a pleasant, warming sensation. Guessing that it was particularly strong, he sipped, rather than guzzled the stuff. This was clearly no night to lose his head. He looked over at Rafe.

"I am your prisoner," he answered. "Why would you give one of your most beautiful women to me?"

After taking another sip, Rafe laughed. "You misunderstand, my friend," he answered. "I do not give her away. No one owns a highlander woman. In our world, a woman wishing to serve a man and being subservient to him are two very different things. If she wishes to serve you, she will do so with all her heart. But should she be mistreated, humiliated, or betrayed, you would likely find a particularly treasured part of your anatomy suddenly taken away with a swift slice of her dagger." Pausing for a moment, Rafe took another drink.

"Because Yasmin's offer was made freely, who am I to argue with it?" he added. "Being chosen in this way is truly a great honor. Few *dangos* can make such a claim." Leaning closer,

Rafe gave Tristan a conspiratorial look. "I suggest that you agree with her wishes," he told Tristan. "It will be an experience you will long remember."

Tristan took another drink. He realized he was starting to like the heady concoction. "What do you call this?" he asked, hoping to avoid an answer about Yasmin.

Rafe smiled. "In our language it is called *tachinga,*" he replied.

Tristan gave Rafe a meaningful look. "You treat your enemies well," he said. "Why do you do it?"

"You are not my enemy," he answered. "You ride well, and you drink well. And by the look of those weapons you carried, you also fight well. Your sword blade shows the telltale signs of many hard-fought battles." Throwing his head back, Rafe laughed at his next thought. "And now Yasmin wishes to learn whether you do something else as well!"

Laughing again, then slapping Tristan on the shoulder, Rafe almost knocked the prince over. "Just because I plan on ransoming you doesn't mean we cannot be friends! Tell me, are you hungry? We will dine together!"

Tristan nodded. "I'm starving," he answered. "But before we eat, I must make a request."

Rafe regarded him narrowly. "What is it?" he asked.

"When my warriors arrive, I want them treated humanely," Tristan answered. "They are to be fed and cared for. I value them just as much as you value your clansmen. Surely we can agree on that score."

Rafe nodded. "Unlike you, I do not command an entire nation. But I know what it means to lead, and to earn the respect of my people."

Rafe clapped his hands. Soon the four women reappeared. Yasmin came to stand directly before Tristan. Looking up at her face, he was quickly reminded of her exotic beauty.

She was tall and leonine, with dark, heavily lidded eyes that seemed to look straight into his soul. Her jaw was rather square and her lips full, almost pouting. She stood barefooted before him in a blatantly sexual stance that reaffirmed her earlier intentions. Her long, dark hair was unruly, and hung to her waist. She was an amazingly strong yet also feminine creature, one that he couldn't imagine any man ever truly taming. It would be a shame to break her spirit, he realized. *This one's wild side should be preserved.*

"Bring food," Rafe said simply.

As quietly as they had come, the four women walked away. As Yasmin left, Tristan found himself watching her body seductively sway to and fro. Reaching for the amphora, Rafe refilled their glasses. He smiled again.

"The truly beautiful ones have a way of getting under a man's skin, don't they?" he asked. "Not to mention his heart."

Taking another sip, Tristan thought of Celeste. "That they do," he said softly.

Soon the women reappeared with two trays of food and a large silver bowl. Tristan had no idea what sort of food it was, but it smelled wonderful. The women placed the trays and the bowl on the ground before Tristan and Rafe. One tray held warm bread and freshly churned butter. The other held two bowls of hot stew. Lean cuts of freshly roasted lamb swam in rich brown gravy alongside carrots, potatoes, and onions. Tristan noticed that no utensils had been provided.

Three of the women then walked away, leaving Yasmin standing alone. To Tristan's surprise she sat down beside him on her knees. Wondering why, he shot a questioning glance at Rafe. The highlander chieftain smiled.

"It seems you have made quite an impression," he said. "She wishes to feed you."

Tristan turned to look into Yasmin's dark eyes. Her gaze was intoxicating.

"Thank you, but that won't be needed," he said politely. "I can fend for myself."

Yasmin bored her seductive eyes into his. "I don't do this only for you," she answered. Her voice held a husky quality that he found attractive. "You are unaccustomed to dipping into our hot stew," she said. "You would burn yourself."

Tristan scowled. "Why do you care?" he asked.

Leaning closer, she placed one hand on his thigh. He had to admit that it felt warm, inviting.

"Because should you accept the offer of my bed, I want everything working as it should—including your fingertips," she said brazenly.

Reaching into the hot stew, she grasped a lamb piece between her index finger and thumb then offered it to him. Smiling again, Tristan accepted it.

The food was wonderful, and rather unlike anything Tristan had tasted before. Yasmin served him skillfully. As they feasted and drank, Tristan decided to offer Rafe a proposition.

Given the chieftain's surprisingly friendly nature, the prince was becoming more sure that he and his warriors would eventually be released. But he desperately needed to return to Tammerland sooner rather than later. Moreover, the highlanders impressed him—even though they were scandalous thieves. Such men could be useful, provided they could be controlled. And controlling them meant giving them something. As Yasmin fed him another piece of lamb, he looked over at Rafe.

"What would it take for you to let me and my warriors go this very night?" he asked. "As you said, I am royalty—I need no one's permission to make a deal. If we can come to terms and you release us now, I swear to you that you will be fairly rewarded."

Rafe took another swig of the potent *tachinga* and laughed. "What type of fool do you take me for?" he asked. "Do you really believe that I would release my greatest prize on a mere promise? The clan elders would brand me a fool, or worse!"

Tristan thought for a moment. "How did someone so young become chieftain?" he asked. "I would have expected a clan leader to be much older."

A sad look overcame Rafe's face. After refilling his glass he took another long swig of *tachinga.* Removing his fur hat, he tossed it to the grass, then tousled his hair.

"The same way that it is said you did," he answered sadly. "I inherited the post from my slain father. That is our custom, provided the firstborn son has reached a certain age."

Yasmin held another stew piece before Tristan's face. Smiling, he thanked her then said that he had eaten his fill but that the food was wonderful. Then he turned back to Rafe.

"I'm sorry about your father," he said. "It seems we have more in common than I thought. Even so, I must get home quickly. Eutracia's fate and the fate of the craft of magic depend on it."

Reaching out, Yasmin placed the silver bowl between Rafe and Tristan. The bowl was filled with water and floating rose petals. Following Rafe's lead, Tristan washed his hands and face, then dried them with a cloth supplied by Yasmin.

Rafe scowled. "You need to understand something," he said. "I don't give a tinker's damn about Eutracia, or about the craft. Our way of life has been going on for centuries. My people have seen dozens of monarchs come and go, each one haunted by his supposed worry over the craft. And for what, we ask? As far as we are concerned, the more things change, the more they stay the same. I like you, *dango.* But I seriously doubt that you and your wizards are any different from the fools who have come before you. Unlike some other clans, we are not murderers or rapists. Here, you and your warriors needn't fear for your lives. Even so, you will stay with us until I say otherwise."

Still determined to get home, Tristan thought for a moment. "Of all the things in the world, what is it that you and your clansmen want most?" he asked, still hoping to appeal to Rafe's greed.

Rafe looked thoughtfully across the clearing. "Despite our way of life, my answer might surprise you," he said softly.

"What is it?" Tristan asked.

"Some of us—especially those who have children—wish to finally put down roots," he answered. "They are tired of wandering, being looked down on, and living from hand to mouth. They want a better, more secure life. Not all feel that way, but many do. What I'm trying to say is that we want a homeland of our own."

Tristan gave Rafe a look of surprise. "Do you feel this way?" he asked.

"I have purposely delayed taking a wife and having children, so that I might better lead my people," Rafe answered. "Putting one's personal needs aside is but one of leadership's many burdens. Just now we are in the midst of a fragile truce with a rival clan—one that I am not sure will survive. Until I know my people are safe, my life must remain as it is."

"Suppose I helped you with your troubles?" Tristan asked.

Rafe's eyes narrowed. "How?" he asked.

"Order your entire clan to come with me to Tammerland," Tristan answered. "I can guarantee your safety. You needn't live behind the city walls, if you choose not to. In return for taking me and my warriors home, and granting me one other favor, I will give you your homeland. I will deed your clan any number of acres of land they want, and anywhere they want—all within reason, of course. I will grant the land in perpetuity, along with full hunting, fishing, grazing, mineral, and timber rights. You could even form your own province, should you wish to do so. Choose the right piece of Eutracia, and you could become rich beyond your wildest dreams. Best of all, it would happen legally, including the crown's ongoing protection against rival clans. You could still practice your customs, provided you abandoned all illicit activities. Refuse, and you will remain thieves and nomads, your heirs and theirs perhaps wandering Eutracia forever."

Tristan could see that he had impressed the highlander. "You would do that for us?" Rafe asked incredulously.

Tristan leaned closer. "Eagerly," he answered. "The stakes for our country are that high."

Rafe slugged back the last of his *tachinga.* Staring into the bonfire, he thoughtfully rolled the empty glass between his palms. "And this other favor you mentioned," he said, his wary skepticism returning. "What is that?"

"For a brief time I wish to command your marvelous horsemen in the struggle that is brewing," Tristan answered. "When the fight is over I will release them from my service. I will need every able-bodied rider you can muster. For too long, Eutracia has been without a cavalry regiment. I fear that she will soon need one. Highlanders who might wish to stay and form a permanent regiment would be welcome." Tristan looked hopefully into Rafe's eyes. "What say you?" he asked.

Rafe looked over at Yasmin. It was clear that she was as stunned as her chieftain.

"Even as clan leader I do not have the authority to dismiss your offer out of hand," Rafe answered. "Its ramifications are too huge. I will take it up with the council of elders in the morning. By highlander law, whatever the council says is always done. Soon after daybreak you will have our answer, Tristan," he said, using the prince's given name for the first time.

Tristan nodded. "Fair enough," he said.

Just then they watched the massive Balthazar and several other highlanders push their way past the circled wagons and into the clearing. Walking up, Balthazar reached down to grab the *tachinga* amphora. Hoisting it up alongside his forearm, he took a long sideways drink. After wiping his mouth, he smiled.

"The winged ones will be here in a few hours," he said. "They can be a handful, even when bound! What is to be done with them?"

"See to it that they are fed, and treated with respect," Rafe ordered. "I have promised their master that it would be this way."

"As you wish," Balthazar answered. Turning to the highlanders standing behind him, he barked out some sharp orders in their secret language. They quickly went about their duties.

"Thank you," Tristan said.

Rafe shrugged his shoulders. "A promise is a promise, even among thieves. Now then, it is time for us men to enjoy ourselves!" He looked over at Yasmin. "Would you and your sisters do us the honor of a dance?" he asked.

Coming smoothly to her feet, Yasmin gave Tristan a sly look. "By all means," she answered. She disappeared quickly.

As Balthazar sat down with them, Rafe leaned closer to Tristan. "She has fed you, agreed to dance for you, and offered to share her bed. I can never remember a *dango* being so honored. This is truly a night to remember!"

Rafe again slapped Tristan hard on the back, this time forcing him to cough. For the first time since meeting the highlander, Tristan smiled. The chieftain's manner was so infectious that he simply couldn't help it.

Moments later, Yasmin and her sisters reappeared. They were dressed even more provocatively than before. Aside from the flimsiest of dark material draped over their shoulders and breasts, only diaphanous, blousy leggings covered the lower parts of their bodies. Their feet and midriffs were bare, and they bore bits of gold jewelry that pierced their navels. Each girl wore a sheer veil, draped seductively below her eyes. Looking closer, Tristan saw that they also wore a pair of thumb and finger cymbals on each hand.

The women walked to a place before Tristan and Rafe, bowed, then sat on their knees. They closed their eyes. Rafe clapped his hands.

From somewhere on the other side of the bonfire, lively music started. As it wafted its way across the clearing, the women stood and started their dance. Two of the girls quickly made their way toward other men, while Yasmin and her sister approached Tristan and Rafe.

Tristan had eyes only for Yasmin, just as she did for him. In the firelight, her undulating body was amazingly beautiful. Moving seductively to the music, time and time again she approached him, only to expertly tease his senses then slink away.

Closing her eyes, she raised her slender arms overhead to start tapping her cymbals together. As the music grew louder, her movements became ever more provocative, the clashing cymbals and the alluring sway of her hips marking every beat.

She moved closer again, this time so near that Tristan could smell the enticing perfume sprinkled between her breasts. Slowly sitting on her knees with her naked back to him, she leaned back until her head and chest were in his lap. Like he and Yasmin were the only two people in the world, the entranced prince could hear only the music, smell only her perfume, and see only her beauty. She lifted her body, bringing her mouth nearer his. As if possessed by a spell, Tristan closed his eyes and parted his lips . . .

The scream that tore through the night was chilling. It was a male voice, coming from the opposite side of the clearing. The music stopped abruptly and the dancing girls went stock-still. Yasmin immediately came to her feet.

Standing quickly, Tristan looked at Rafe. Balthazar and the highlander chieftain were already upright. Looking across the campsite, Rafe's eyes held a peculiar mixture of worry and hate. Snapping his head around, Tristan saw the object of Rafe's concern.

A highlander was running toward them. Standing, Tristan coiled up at first, then relaxed as he recognized the fellow who had led the charge toward the ravine. As he neared, Tristan saw that he was carrying something. Yasmin came to stand beside Tristan.

Running pell-mell, the highlander skidded to a stop before Rafe. Looking down, Tristan saw that he was carrying a canvas cinch bag. Tristan froze as he saw the bag's bottom. It was dripping blood.

"Master . . . ," the breathless highlander said. He handed the bag to Rafe at arm's length, like it was full of deadly snakes. "This was just found at the camp's edge!" he exclaimed. "I have not opened it, but I fear the worst."

Rafe untied the bag and looked inside. At once his face blanched and twisted into a terrible grimace. Closing his eyes, he dropped the bag to the ground, then turned his face away.

"What is it?" Tristan asked. Forgetting himself for a moment, he started to reach for the fallen bag. Before he could grasp it, Balthazar roughly shoved him aside. Saying nothing, Balthazar picked up the bag and looked in. A hateful look overcame his face as well. He too dropped the bag like it was cursed.

"Zorian traitors!" he growled. "You will pay for this!" Shaking his fists in the air, Balthazar raged against the night. "Do you hear me, you bastard sons of a thousand fathers? This insult will cost you your lives!"

As other highlanders crowded around, Tristan reached down to retrieve the bloody bag. He did not wish to offend anyone, but he had to know. He pulled the bag open and looked inside.

It contained a severed male head. It was bloody, and cut many times by what had probably been a razor-sharp dagger. The eyes had been sewn shut with bits of coarse leather, and its teeth pulled out by some crude instrument. Clearly, the man had been tortured before being killed. Closing the bag, Tristan respectfully placed it back onto the ground, then looked at Yasmin.

"What does this mean?" he asked.

"Our truce with the Zorian clan has ended," she said sadly. "The head in the bag is that of Casimir, Rafe's brother."

"The Zorians are a rival clan?" Tristan asked.

Yasmin nodded. "They are butchers, rapists, and cutthroats—including their women."

"Casimir was captured by them?" Tristan asked, trying to understand.

"No," she answered. "During a truce it is often customary for each side to exchange hostages. The hostages are almost always persons of importance. As long as the hostages live, so does the truce. By killing Casimir and sending his head, the Zorian elders have ended the truce. A challenge has been made. Rafe has but one choice left to him now."

Looking over, Tristan watched Rafe turn back around. The highlander chieftain's face was resolute. Yasmin placed her lips near Tristan's ear.

"Whatever happens, you must not interfere. This is highlander business. Rafe likes you, but he will tolerate no *dango* intrusions."

Rafe nodded harshly at Balthazar. Understanding, the giant quickly walked away.

"We should sit," Yasmin whispered into Tristan's ear. "We have no part in this."

The prince sat down on the dewy grass. Yasmin sat beside

him. Despite the tense circumstances, he was struck by how comfortable her presence felt.

Balthazar soon returned with a bound prisoner in tow. The man was about Tristan's age. His face was dark and cruel-looking, and his long hair fell about his shoulders. His hands were tied behind him.

Several more Kilbourne clansmen came forward. Two of them carried a thick, rough-hewn pole. They quickly pounded it into the ground before the bonfire. Pushing his prisoner toward the pole, Balthazar viciously shoved the man's back up against it.

The two other highlanders quickly untied the prisoner's hands, then bound them tightly again behind the pole. They then did the same to his feet. Placing a leather strap around the man's forehead, Balthazar pulled the strap tight and tied it, pinning the man's head to the pole.

Rafe picked up the *tachinga* amphora and took a long drink. He carelessly let the amphora drop to the ground. Unsheathing his silver dagger, Rafe walked toward the prisoner.

His dagger hanging loosely from his right hand, Rafe glared at the prisoner's dark face. The bonfire highlighted the man's sharp, unrepentant glare. Aside from the snapping flames, the tense campsite had gone totally silent.

Tristan turned to Yasmin. "Is the man tied to the pole your Zorian hostage?" he whispered.

"Yes," Yasmin whispered back. "He is the Zorian chieftain's second son."

Reaching out, Rafe impassively drew his dagger across the prisoner's offered throat. The man coughed blood for a moment, some of it running down his chest. Soon his head slumped forward. Sheathing his dagger, Rafe took out his sword. With a single stroke, he beheaded the corpse. The head tumbled to the grass.

"It is done," Yasmin whispered.

Picking up the head by its hair, Balthazar held it high for everyone to see. He then walked back to where the canvas bag lay. Removing Casimir's head, he reverently wrapped it in cloth, then handed it to one of the female elders. He put the other head into the bag and knotted the string. Balthazar casually tossed the bloody bag to the young highlander who had first brought it into the camp. As he wiped the blood from his sword, Rafe turned to look at him.

"Dump that trash at the edge of the Zorian camp where they

will be sure to find it," he ordered softly. Bowing, the young highlander picked up the bloody bag and hurried for his horse.

Yasmin leaned closer to Tristan. "Rafe will want to be alone," she whispered. Despite all that had happened, her eyes still held the predatory yearning that had filled them before. As the firelight highlighted her sensual face, Tristan again felt himself drawn to her.

"He will retire to his wagon and so will I," she said. "Things have changed. Much will happen tomorrow." She placed a warm palm against Tristan's cheek. As her lips neared his again, he sensed the heat building inside him. "What is your decision?" she asked. "Will you come with me?"

Reaching out, Tristan clenched some of her tresses in one hand. Closing his eyes, he luxuriated in its wonderful scent. Looking her squarely in the face again, he commandingly pulled her hair, ordering her closer. She smiled. A quick series of master-slave signals shot back and forth between their eyes. *But which of us is the master, and which the slave?* he wondered.

"I . . . ," Tristan said. Then he froze.

A screaming man had suddenly charged into the camp, his sword held high. Dressed all in black and with a black scarf tied across his lower face, he was heading straight for Rafe's back.

"Rafe!" Tristan screamed.

Rafe turned just in time to see the killer coming and he too raised his sword. As the intruder lashed out with his blade, Rafe deftly sidestepped the bow then took the man's head off at the shoulders.

Seconds later, the entire camp erupted into pandemonium. Women screamed, men hollered out urgent orders, and the sounds of clashing sword blades filled the night. Tristan stood and spun around to look.

Figures dressed all in black had invaded the camp. Some on foot and some on horseback, they were cutting down men, women, and children with abandon. No one needed to tell the prince who they were.

As fast as his feet could take him, Tristan ran for Rafe's wagon. Reaching inside, he frantically searched for his dreggan and knife quiver. But just as he found them, he felt Rafe's strong grip on his wrist. As he turned to look at the chieftain, Tristan's face turned into a vicious snarl.

"Don't be a fool!" he shouted. "You need my sword! And if you know what's good for you, you'll order that my warriors be freed and their weapons returned to them! I swear on my life that we will not take up arms against you!"

Cursing, Rafe shook his head back and forth for a moment, then finally relented. He shouted at Balthazar. The huge highlander came running. "Do as the *dango* says!" Rafe ordered him. Running across the clearing, Rafe drew his sword and joined the fray.

Tristan grabbed the giant by the shoulders. "Go to my warriors and free them!" he shouted. "Give them their weapons, then tell them to find me! Tell them it is an order from their *Jin'-Sai*! I know that phrase means nothing to you, but when they hear it they will instantly obey, and not harm you! Go!" Balthazar gave Tristan a confused look, then ran off to do as he had been told.

Wheeling around, Tristan quickly situated the knife quiver over his right shoulder. He drew his dreggan and tossed its baldric aside. Then he heard Yasmin scream.

At first he couldn't find her amid all the confusion, mayhem, and sudden death. By now many wagons were ablaze, fighters were dying all around him, and insane wailing filled the night. Suddenly he heard her scream again, and he whirled around.

About ten meters away, a figure in black had pinned her to the ground. Holding a dagger to her throat, he was viciously trying to tear off what remained of her clothes. Yasmin was fighting back furiously, but Tristan knew that her attacker would soon take what he wanted. Tossing his dreggan from his right hand over into his left, Tristan immediately reached back over his shoulder.

Let my aim be true, he prayed. His right arm a blur, he sent the knife whirling end over end across the clearing.

CHAPTER XXXVII

STANDING AT ONE OF THE BLACK SHIPS' STARBOARD GUNWALES, Shailiha, Adrian, and Tyranny felt the bracing ocean wind against their faces. Although all three women were tired, being at sea again was welcome.

It was just after midnight on the Sea of Whispers. The winds were steady, helping the Conclave make good time as their fleet plowed its way east, toward the Citadel. The sky was clear, allowing the stars to twinkle brightly. Their pitching forms dark as night, the remaining five Black Ships dutifully followed Tyranny's flagship.

Because the vessels had been returned to the Conclave's service, Jessamay had suggested that they be reanointed with their original names. The Conclave had wholeheartedly approved. The Black Ships were once again the *Ephyra,* the *Illendium,* the *Malvina,* the *Florian,* the *Cavalon,* and the *Tammerland.* Tyranny had chosen the *Tammerland* as her personal flagship.

The fleet's departure had come earlier than planned. After returning from their meeting with Aeolus, the three women and Wigg had discovered that the vessels were ready to depart, several hours ahead of schedule. Because time was essential, Shailiha decided to sail immediately.

As usual, Faegan intended to remain behind and concentrate on his research. But the more he thought about the mission, the more the Citadel's untold mysteries beckoned. Moreover, his unique gifts might be needed, because not one Conclave member truly knew what dangers they might be facing. At the last moment he had agreed to come along. As a precaution he had hurriedly packed the specialized craft tools needed to conjure his azure portal, among other wizardly items.

Abbey remained behind. Should the prince return home, Wigg wanted someone in authority to inform Tristan about recent events, including the surprise visit to Aeolus. Although she was disappointed, Abbey had accepted her passive assignment graciously, and had promised Shailiha that she would take good care of Morganna.

Cupping her hands against the wind, Tyranny lit a cigarillo, then tossed the dead match over the side. As she cast an expert gaze over her huge flagship, she smiled.

The Black Ships were plowing through the waves, rather than flying over them. After weighing anchor, Adrian and her acolytes had powered the vessels through the air for several hours. They had made amazingly good time. But the women had eventually tired, forcing the fleet to sail for a time in the traditional way. It would be back and forth like this all the way to the Citadel, Tyranny knew. When the fleet was aloft, little work was needed from the Minion crewmen. But now that the ships were afloat, the warriors were busy.

As she watched them go about their duties, Tyranny had to admit that the Minions were superior to human crewmembers in every way. Male and female warriors swarmed expertly over the ships' decks. Others worked the sails and rigging, adjusting them quickly to the shifting weather conditions. Winging their way aloft, they rose confidently to the great heights commanded by the vessels' towering masts, then hovered as they worked. Unlike human crewmembers, warrior patrols could scout the sea for leagues in every direction, and did so constantly. And perhaps most important, Tyranny knew the warriors' fighting abilities firsthand.

The Black Ships had been loaded nearly to the sinking point with warriors, food, and weapons. If the attack on the Citadel became protracted, these precious cargoes would have to sustain the siege until victory was won. Given how fast the ships were traveling while so heavily burdened, Tyranny could only guess at their speed after some provisions had been consumed, and the vessels became lighter. Compared to the ships and crews she was used to commanding, the Conclave privateer had never felt so powerful or so confident.

A wry look overtook her face as she took a final drag on the cigarillo, then tossed it overboard. She tousled her short hair. *Believing in your own infallibility is a terrible mistake out here,* she reminded herself. *That will get you killed as fast as anything.*

She turned to look at Shailiha. The princess was wearing a gray jerkin with dark trunk hose and black knee boots. A sword hung from her left hip, and a sheathed dagger lay tied down to her right thigh. Her long blond hair was pulled behind her head and collected by a gold barrette. Tyranny secretly enjoyed seeing the princess dressed this way, for it seemed to put the two of them on a more equal footing. The privateer looked at Adrian.

"Why don't you go and get some rest, Sister?" she asked. "You look exhausted."

Adrian gave the other women a tired smile. "I was thinking that exact thing," she answered. "With your permission, Your Highness?"

Shailiha nodded. "Certainly," she answered simply. "Sleep

well. I have a feeling we will need your skills soon enough." With a bow, Adrian walked away. Shailiha gave Tyranny a knowing look.

"So what is it that you do not wish Adrian to hear?" Shailiha asked. As she looked back out to sea, her hair swayed gracefully behind her in the wind. "Given that there are no problems with the fleet, I can only guess that the subject is personal. And if it is," she added quietly, "then it probably has to do with Tristan."

Tyranny nodded. "I'm worried for him," she said.

Turning around, Shailiha leaned her back against the gunwale. Smiling slightly, she crossed one foot over the other. "Oh, I think it's more than that," she said. "You love him, don't you?"

Knowing she had been found out, the privateer nodded. "You're right," she said. "Is it that obvious?"

"Yes," the princess answered. "Especially after hearing what you said to him, just before he disappeared with Xanthus. Tristan's heart still suffers from Celeste's passing, but less so than before. In truth, he might be ready to start another relationship. But there is something else about my brother that you need to understand." Turning back to the sea, Shailiha thoughtfully laced her fingers atop the polished deck rail.

"Until the return of the Coven, Tristan's entire life—and mine as well—had seen nothing but wealth, ease, and privilege." She smiled knowingly. "Many thought him arrogant and spoiled. And in some ways, I suppose that they were right. The strange thing is that he never wanted such pampering. He begged our parents night and day to let him pursue a rough-and-tumble career in the Royal Guard. But of course they could not allow it, for they knew that his path lay in a different direction. That always rankled him, and forced him to feel like his destiny was someone else's to govern. To really know Tristan is to understand how much he hates being told what to do." Shailiha paused for a few moments, thinking.

"Then, in the space of only a few hours, everything changed," she went on. "The Coven resurfaced to capture me and the Paragon. Tristan had to grow up literally overnight, so that he could serve the craft, and what remained of his family and his nation. Now he is the ruler of Eutracia, and I am his successor. But it goes far deeper than that. You and the others probably believe that being royalty somehow makes fulfilling our destinies easier. If you do, you're wrong. Given all the added burdens our offices demand, being the prince and the princess sometimes makes our lives more difficult. Many things weigh heavily on each of us."

Tyranny gave Shailiha a wry look. "So what are you saying?" she asked. "That I should somehow pity you two? I'm sorry, Your Highness. If you expect that sentiment from me, you've chosen the wrong woman."

Shaking her head, Shailiha laughed quickly down her nose. "No, of course not," she answered. "What I'm saying is that if you intend to enter Tristan's heart, go slow. He has many burdens with which to cope. You see, in his earlier, carefree days, he never needed to approach women—they almost always approached him, and he grew tired of it. I have often thought that one of the reasons he was so drawn to Celeste was that she was at first so unavailable to him, and on so many levels. The fact that he was the prince meant nothing to her, and he found that intriguing. It's true what they say, you know."

"What's that?" Tyranny asked.

Shailiha smiled. "That we always want most what we cannot have," she answered.

Tyranny stared at the deck for a moment. "Thank you for that insight," she said. "I never considered Tristan that way."

"You're welcome," Shailiha answered. "But don't come crying to me if he remains aloof! Many women have tried to get truly close, but only Celeste succeeded. Even so, my brother can get under a girl's skin."

"I know," Tyranny said quietly. "I have become one of them." Looking out to sea, the privateer sighed.

"I will be eager to see him again," she said, "if and when he returns to us." Almost immediately, Tyranny regretted her remark. "I'm sorry," she said quickly. "It's just that—"

Giving her a little smile, Shailiha put one hand over hers. "It's all right," she said. "We all miss him. We must remain optimistic. When he finally comes home, we can take turns shouting at him for being away so long!" Both women laughed at that idea.

Just then they saw Traax running their way. Stopping abruptly, he clicked his heels.

"Begging your pardon, Your Majesty," he said, trying to catch his breath. "The wizards are calling an emergency Conclave meeting."

Tyranny's wariness resurfaced. "What is it?" she demanded. "Have our patrols sighted something?"

Traax shook his head. "No, Captain," he answered. "Nor do I know why the wizards deem this impromptu gathering to be of such importance. All I know is that we must go quickly."

"Very well," Shailiha said. "Lead the way." Traax turned and hurried off with the women in tow.

Finally reaching the stern, Traax led Tyranny and Shailiha down a series of hatchway steps. Three decks down he left the stairway to continue along a lamplit hallway, then continued on toward the ship's stern. Finally he stopped before mahogany double doors. Even before Traax knocked, the women could hear shouting coming from the other side. Without waiting for a response, the Minion commander opened the doors and the three of them walked into the room.

The chamber stretching before them was large and sumptuously decorated. Each Conclave member knew this place. Long ago, this suite of rooms had served as the captain's quarters, when the ship had sailed against the Coven in the service of the Directorate. The arrangements were the same aboard each Black Ship. But here on the *Tammerland,* Tyranny had graciously given these chambers over as the Conclave's meeting place.

The room's large rear wall was also the ship's stern. It was laden with opened, wood-slatted windows and intricately carved artwork. A rectangular meeting table sat in the room's center, around which all of the other Conclave members were already seated. Patterned rugs lay atop the hardwood floor, and upholstered furniture had been strategically placed around the room. A doorway in the right-hand wall led off to a bedroom, sitting room, and washroom. Soft light was provided by oil lamp chandeliers, each swinging gently in opposite rhythm to the rocking ship.

As she walked to take her seat at the table, Shailiha was surprised to see Faegan scowl and angrily bang his fists down atop his chair arms. The princess gave Tyranny a questioning glance, but all the equally confused privateer could do was to sit down and shrug her shoulders.

"And I'm telling you that this is my fault and mine alone!" Faegan shouted at Wigg. "I can't believe I was so stupid! We simply aren't prepared! If they were to attack now, our entire fleet might be done for!"

"Don't be so hard on yourself," Jessamay countered. "Not one of us realized it, either."

"What's all this ruckus about?" Shailiha shouted, quickly taking control of the meeting. "Has something happened?"

Wigg laced his long fingers on the table top. "Not yet," he answered. "But we just realized how perilous our situation might already be. Before we explain, you must order that each ship's sails be furled, and that the fleet come to a standstill. If we drift, we drift. It can't be helped. We must not travel any farther east until we have devised a proper plan."

"What are you talking about?" Tyranny demanded. "After making such good progress, why on earth would you want us to *drift*? That is when a warship is at her most vulnerable!"

"Not in our case," Wigg answered cryptically.

"Please explain," Shailiha said.

"It's about the Necrophagians," Faegan answered for the First Wizard. "We believe it possible that they might attack at any time. We must not move farther east until we have devised a plan to deal with them. How foolish we were not to see it before now!"

"We all understand the threat," Shailiha said. "But surely we do not have to worry about it just yet. Everyone knows that Necrophagian territory is in the middle of the sea, a good fifteen days' sail from either coast. With the acolytes empowering the fleet, we have made good time so far. But even I am sea dog enough to know that we couldn't possibly have reached the ocean's midpoint this quickly."

"Normally we would agree," Jessamay said. "But during Wulfgar's second invasion attempt, things changed. In truth, we might already be in Necrophagian territory."

Tyranny leaned forward and gave Jessamay a hard look. "How is that possible?" she asked.

"You're forgetting something," Wigg answered. "Something that the rest of us also neglected before we sailed. During Wulfgar's second invasion of Eutracia, we defeated the *Enseterat,* but not all his servants. When last we saw the Necrophagians, they were still alive. They had followed Wulfgar to a point near the Eutracian coast, where the climactic sea battle between the Minion fleet and the Black Ships took place. If they did not return to their old territory, we might already again be in Necrophagian waters. Either way, we must quickly form a battle plan to deal with them."

"But how did Wulfgar manage to bring the Necrophagians that far west in the first place?" Tyranny asked Wigg. "To call them into his service, he must have had some power over them. Where did that come from? Even Failee didn't seem to control them to such an extent. I don't remember you, Faegan, or Jessamay telling us the answer."

"That's because we don't have one," Faegan said. "At least not one that we believe we can rely on. Because of the relatively short time Wulfgar lived at the Citadel, we can only assume that all of his gifts were granted to him by way of the Vagaries Forestallments. If that is true, then the Scroll of the Vagaries must contain the needed spell to command the Necrophagians. Or perhaps Wulfgar simply bartered with them to do his bidding, as Failee did. He would have been in a position to offer them far more than she could have at the time. In any event, once the Vagaries scroll is in our grasp, we'll know more." Faegan paused for a moment, thinking.

"As you also know, we believe that the Necrophagians are transformed members of the Ones Who Came Before, captured by the Heretics during the War of Attrition," he added. "Instead of killing them outright, our guess is that the Heretics condemned the Ones to the depths, forcing them to do their bidding. We have further theorized that the Heretics did this to add yet another layer of protection to the Citadel. What better way to defend an island than with endowed underwater beings, perpetually lying in wait to devour anyone who came near? But all this remains pure conjecture. Only on reaching and taking the Citadel can we be sure. And you can bet that Serena will have more than one nasty surprise waiting for us when we arrive."

"*If* we arrive," Adrian added. "As you said, first we must deal with the Necrophagians."

Tyranny stood up from the table. "I've heard enough," she said. "I will immediately give the order to furl our sails. I will also order the other ships' crews to do the same. It will put us off schedule, but for the time being it seems that there is no other choice." Shaking her head, Tyranny scowled.

"But allowing warships to aimlessly drift in such a time of danger goes directly against every fiber of my being," she added.

She looked at Shailiha. "With your permission, Princess, I will take my leave."

Shailiha nodded. "Be quick," she said, "and return. We still have need of your counsel."

After giving the members a short bow, Tyranny hurried out the double doors. Almost immediately the Conclave heard her loudly calling out for Scars.

"She's a good woman," Wigg said. "Now then, let's discuss how to deal with the Necrophagian threat. As we have done before, we can ask for Minion volunteers to fight to the death, to supply the Necrophagians their usual bounty of forty dead bodies as payment to sail across their territory. But I think that—"

His face suddenly blanching with surprise, Wigg's eyes went wide. At first Shailiha and the others wondered why. But when Wigg spoke again, they quickly got their answer.

"I beg the Afterlife," Wigg said.

The wizard's breath was coming out in white, vaporous clouds. Then everyone suddenly realized that the temperature had plummeted, causing their breath to also become ghostlike vapors in the unexpected coldness.

Suddenly the *Tammerland* lurched to an abrupt stop. Tilting hard on her bow, the ship's stern literally lifted from the sea. She came to a standstill so quickly that all the furniture slid across the room, the oil chandeliers swung violently, and Adrian and Wigg were launched from their chairs to go tumbling to the floor.

With a tortured groan the *Tammerland*'s black timbers stressed agonizingly against one another as she crashed back to the sea. Then the huge ship rocked back and forth violently, finally finding her equilibrium again. No sooner had Wigg and Adrian scrambled to their feet than a dense fog started rolling in through the stern windows.

Thick and gray, the fog slithered in like predatory snakes. It quickly covered the floor and stuck fast to everyone's clothes and skin. It soon was knee-deep, and everyone became awash in its velvety embrace. Then the unthinkable happened. Out over the sea, more fog formed, then started morphing into a gigantic hand.

Shailiha watched speechlessly as the hand's fingers reached their way in through the stern windows. Glass broke, solid iron window casings snapped apart, and ornate wall carvings went tumbling to the floor. Then the hand closed around the *Tammerland*'s stern to start crushing it like an eggshell.

Splitting into hundreds of shards, the stern's upper section came crashing apart, partly exposing the room to the sea. Salt water immediately started pouring in, threatening to engulf the entire room. Screaming and waving his arms, Wigg ordered everyone to run for their lives. The Conclave members finally reached the door.

Wigg ushered Jessamay, Shailiha, and Adrian through first, followed by Traax. Then the First Wizard and Faegan went through. As the rushing seawater poured into the hallway, Wigg spun around to face everyone.

"Go!" he screamed. "Try to climb the stairway to the top deck! Jessamay, you stay here! Faegan and I need your gifts!" As the sorceress stayed behind, Traax and Adrian started working their way down the flooded hallway.

"What are you going to do?" Shailiha shouted.

"We will try to seal the meeting room from the sea!" Wigg shouted. "But this is no place for you! Go with the others!"

Realizing that she could not help them, Shailiha gave each mystic a supportive look. "Be careful!" she shouted. The rising water in the hallway was nearly at her knees.

"Get out of here while you still can!" Wigg shouted. "Do it now!" Turning away, Shailiha started wading down the hall as fast as she could go.

The seawater rapidly approaching his waist, Wigg turned to look first at Jessamay, then Faegan. As the crippled wizard hovered in his wooden chair just above the rushing water, there was desperation in his eyes.

"We have to try to seal this doorway!" Wigg shouted. "Are you with me?" They both nodded.

"There is no time to discuss this; just follow my lead!" the First Wizard shouted. "If we can contain the water in the meeting room, we might have a chance!" Wigg raised his arms and pointed them at the open door.

At once twin azure bolts streamed from the wizard's hands, pouring their power over that part of the door's surface that was still above the rising seawater. Faegan and Jessamay followed suit, their bolts adding strength to Wigg's.

"Now!" Wigg shouted. "And with everything you have!"

Just as the three mystics started straining to push the door closed, a strange sound came to their ears. Soon it became earsplitting, rising even above the noise of the rushing water.

From somewhere on the mysterious Sea of Whispers, the Necrophagians could be heard making their demands to Tyranny. But unlike every other time the Conclave had encountered the Eaters of the Dead, this time the beings were not demanding the usual forty dead bodies as payment to cross their territory.

They were demanding the lives of everyone aboard.

CHAPTER XXXVIII

TRISTAN HELD HIS BREATH AS HE WATCHED HIS DIRK BURY ITSELF into the shoulder of Yasmin's attacker. His eyes wide with surprise, the Zorian highlander started to pull the knife free, but Yasmin was quicker.

Reaching up, she grasped the dirk's handle, then pulled the knife free and plunged it into her attacker's throat. When she felt the blade tip strike her attacker's neck bones, she pushed it again, then gave it a savage twist. The highlander fell atop her. With a sneer, Yasmin shoved the body off her and onto the ground.

Tossing his dreggan back into his right hand, Tristan ran to her. As he lifted Yasmin to her feet, he saw deep appreciation in her eyes. But this was no time for talk. Standing protectively before her, he quickly cast his eyes around the camp.

The scene was even more desperate than before. Many of the wagons were on fire, and the screams of the dying and wounded filled the night. Dark smoke drifted through the clearing, making things difficult to see. Fighters from both sides struggled everywhere, darting in and out of the smoke like spectral ghosts.

Although they fought valiantly, Rafe's ambushed clansmen were losing the battle. To his dismay, Tristan saw no sign of the Minions. Bending down, he quickly pulled the bloody dirk from the dead highlander's throat, then shoved it into Yasmin's hands. He had no doubt that she knew how to use it.

"Take this!" he shouted. "And stay near me!"

Yasmin shook her head. "I fight my own battles!" she shouted back.

Before he could stop her, Yasmin ran to attack a Zorian highlander who was about to bring his sword down on an old woman. He died quickly, his sliced throat spilling blood into the thirsty dirt.

Tristan was about to shout at Yasmin again, but he wasn't given the chance. Raising his dreggan, he narrowly parried a highlander sword flashing toward him in the moonlight. The two blades struck each other with such force that sparks went flying. Backing up, Tristan tried to gain some maneuvering room. But his attacker was very good, constantly keeping Tristan on the defensive. Time after time their swords clashed, with neither fighter able to find an opening. Finally Tristan feinted with an overhead strike, then quickly changed his sword's direction, swinging its tip across the highlander's legs.

His thigh muscles severed, the highlander screamed and fell to his knees. As his sword slipped from his hands, he dazedly looked up into the face of the man he knew would kill him. Without hesitation Tristan swung his dreggan again, taking the highlander's head off at the shoulders. The dead man's eyes still open, his head toppled to the dirt.

But there would be no time for the prince to consider his victory, or to try to find Yasmin again. As soon as he looked up, another screaming highlander was on him.

HIS DREGGAN IN ONE HAND AND HIS *JIN'SAI*'S MESSAGE STILL RINGing in his ears, Hector took to the sky. Eager to join the fray, the nineteen other warriors followed.

Nothing would ever assuage their shame at having been captured. And Balthazar's strange warning that they attack only those fighters dressed in all-black garb was surprising. But if he and his warriors could kill enough of the enemy, perhaps they might partly redeem themselves in their *Jin'Sai*'s eyes.

Seeing the fighting in the highlander camp's center, Hector led his warriors down.

HIS EYES FLASHING, TRISTAN'S SECOND OPPONENT RUSHED TOWARD him. The prince soon found that this man was an even greater threat than the one he had just killed. Nearly the size of Balthazar, he was far stronger than Tristan. His technique was simple but brutally effective: He rained nonstop blows down on the prince, knowing that Tristan would soon tire, and be forced into a mistake. Then, like a big cat that had finished toying with its prey, the huge highlander would rush in for the kill.

Backing up desperately, it was all Tristan could do to parry the bigger man's blows, say nothing of going on the offensive. Using his quickness, Tristan tried to side-slip the highlander and seize on an opening. But despite his huge size the man moved nimbly, matching the prince's every step. Finally the highlander sensed the growing tiredness in Tristan's arms. Screaming wildly, he raised his sword high, then brought it down with everything he had.

The strategy worked. The sharp blow resonated through Tristan's sword blade and into its hilt so sharply that it stunned his hands, painfully forcing the dreggan from his grip. Tristan frantically dived to the dirt, scrambling to pick the sword up again. But that was just what the highlander wanted. Taking his sword into both hands the Zorian raised it vertically, readying its blade to plunge straight down into Tristan's back.

With the dreggan in his hands again, Tristan quickly rolled over. But when he looked up he knew that he was too late. As the highlander blade came streaking down, a final thought flashed through his mind. *So this is how it ends,* he thought.

Just then Tristan saw something flash through the air, and the highlander's eyes went wide. What was left of his face had become bloody, deformed. A Minion returning wheel had embedded itself into the highlander's face. Starting at the top of the man's forehead, its teeth lay deeply buried diagonally between his eyes and down the length of his face, ending in his chin.

Like time suddenly had no meaning, the highlander dropped his sword to stand there stupidly as blood cascaded down his destroyed face. For a moment his mouth tried to work. But the deadly wheel held his jaws fast, causing his lips to tear even more as he tried to speak. Then he fell over onto his back, dead where he lay.

Tristan scrambled to his feet and looked around. He soon saw Hector, hovering in the air about ten meters away. Tristan gave him a nod. Hector nodded back, then eagerly went about killing more Zorian highlanders in the service of his lord.

The Minion presence finally turned the tide. Hector's warriors were doing just what Tristan would have ordered, had he been given the chance. Hovering above the fray, they used their tactical advantage to hack down every fighter dressed all in black that they could find. As the Minion's bloody dreggans and returning wheels sliced through the air, one by one the enemy highlanders fell. Before it was over, two more died by Tristan's hand.

Finally the battle ended. Physically exhausted and his hands smeared with blood, Tristan wearily drove his dreggan into the ground and leaned down on its hilt. Looking around, he saw that the carnage and destruction were even worse than he had imagined.

Every wagon in sight was afire. Running about the camp, Rafe's men shouted out urgent orders. The healers among them were working furiously, trying to save as many of their stricken clansmen as they could. Other Kilbourne clansmen were systematically searching the campsite, driving their swords into Zorian bodies to ensure that they were finished. Sometimes terrible screams rang through the night from those who had been faking death.

Corpses and body parts from both sides seemed to lie everywhere. Turning, Tristan saw a black-garbed Zorian wandering about blindly. Dazed and in shock, he was cradling his own severed arm like he was looking for someone who could magically reattach it. Turning his gaze toward the stars, he collapsed, his massive blood loss finally securing his eternal peace. As the great bonfire in the clearing's center continued to crackle and burn, horses ran wildly, children cried, and the clan's elderly bemoaned their losses in their strange, secret language.

Just then the Minions landed warily in the clearing. Tristan watched curiously as they immediately formed strict ranks, with Hector front and center. Taking a quick count, the prince realized that all twenty had survived.

Hector suddenly went to his knees and bowed his head. The other warriors followed suit. Hector drew his sword and held the bloody weapon vertically across his palms, humbly offering it up to his *Jin'Sai*. The other nineteen did the same.

Tristan understood the Minion gesture. Having been captured, the warriors believed that they had failed him. By giving up their swords they freely admitted their mistakes, and would gladly accept whatever punishment Tristan chose to mete out—

including their deaths. Pulling his dreggan from the dirt, he sheathed it and walked over.

"Arise, all of you," he ordered. At once the twenty warriors came to their feet.

"I refuse to accept your swords," Tristan said. "The fault for your capture was mine, for not sending patrols aloft." Turning, he looked across the bloody clearing, then back at them.

"Your fighting was exemplary," he added. "It made the difference between victory and defeat. You should feel proud, rather than dishonored. Go now, and do what you can to help the highlanders tend to the wounded."

Like they were of one mind, the warriors sheathed their swords with simultaneous precision. After giving Tristan a look of gratitude, Hector barked out some orders and sent the warriors about their new duties.

"Those flying creatures of yours fight well," a voice said from behind him. "And so do you."

Tristan turned to see Yasmin standing there. She was bloodied and dirty, but seemed unharmed. Reaching out, she handed him the dirk he had given her. He had no doubt that she had made good use of it. After wiping its blood onto his trousers, he slid it back into its quiver. Walking closer, he smiled.

"Are you all right?" he asked.

She nodded. "Yes," she said, "but you aren't."

She took him by his left hand. Tristan looked down to see that he had been wounded. A jagged, bleeding cut ran diagonally across his inner forearm.

"This is deep," Yasmin said. "It must be tended to before infection sets in. Come with me." Taking him by the hand, she started leading him across the ravaged clearing.

They walked for a while until Yasmin came to one of the few wagons that hadn't been destroyed. Lowering its rear door, she bade Tristan to sit on it. Glad to be off his feet, he did as she asked. The beautiful highlander woman quickly went to work.

Reaching into the wagon, she removed an aged wooden box. She opened it to show various healer's tools, some of which Tristan was familiar with. After cleaning the wound she produced a small amber bottle. Uncorking it, she spread the open wound wide, then poured some of the bottle's contents directly onto it.

Shouting with pain, Tristan yanked his arm away. Not to be

outdone, Yasmin scowled, then grasped his wrist again and commandingly pulled it back. She gave him a little smile.

"What in the name of the Afterlife is that awful stuff?" he shouted.

"Aged goat urine," she answered, "tinged with certain herbs. There's nothing better for a wound. Now stop being such a child! I know what I'm doing—I've sewn up plenty of men. Be still and let me do my work!"

Wondering what Abbey and Faegan would say about Yasmin's potion, he finally gave in and let her do her worst. It hurt like blazes as she sewed the wound shut, but he knew it had to be done. Flexing his fingers, he left the wagon door to stand on the ground. He looked at his wound to see that Yasmin's stitches were clean and precise.

"They will leave a scar," Yasmin said. "But from what I've seen of you so far, it already has plenty of company."

Tristan laughed, then pointed to the wooden box of healer's tools. "How did you know those things would be here?" he asked.

"This wagon is mine," Yasmin answered.

Without further ado, she closed the box and put it away. Coming closer, she looked into his eyes and placed her hands onto his chest. As she stared at him, her normally predatory gaze softened into something more curious than commanding.

"Tell me, *Jin'Sai,*" she said. "Do you keep a woman of your own at the palace?"

Startled by her frankness, Tristan took a quick breath. He started to answer her, then he stopped. Instead, he reached up to wipe a dirt smudge from one of her cheeks.

"Where did you hear the phrase, *'Jin'Sai'*?" he asked.

"From your flying warriors," she answered. "But you're avoiding the question."

Remembering Celeste, Tristan looked at the ground. "It's a rather long story, you see, and I—"

"There you are, *dango*!" they suddenly heard Rafe's voice call out. "Leave it to you to be tended to by the camp's most beautiful woman!"

Tristan and Yasmin watched Rafe and Balthazar walk up. They were each holding a *tachinga* jug. Balthazar looked rather drunk. Rafe offered his jug to Tristan.

Smiling, the prince took it, then swallowed a long gulp, followed by another. After wiping his mouth, he gave Rafe a compassionate look.

"I am sorry about Casimir," he said. "I'm sure he was a good man."

Rafe's face darkened. "He was," he answered. "I am also sorry to see him gone. But in the end, his death served a noble purpose. We have taken a Zorian body count. By the looks of it, they came at us with every fighter they had. All but a few are dead. The Zorian threat is no more."

"There are Zorian survivors?" Tristan asked.

Just then a terrible scream rang out across the clearing. It slowly faded away, to be replaced by outright begging. Tristan immediately understood that the Zorian survivors were being tortured to death. He was about to protest when Yasmin's eyes caught his. She gave him a nearly imperceptible shake of her head. Understanding, he took a deep breath and resolved not to speak of it. Highlander business, he realized. He looked back at Rafe.

"What are your losses?" he asked.

Rafe shook his head. "They are very bad," he answered. "Perhaps the worst ever suffered by our clan in one fight. More than half of our wagons are gone. And with them went many supplies, provisions, horses, and other livestock. More than one quarter of my men are dead, and several dozen more are wounded. The Zorian cowards struck down many of our women, elderly, and children. Two of the twelve council members are also dead. But we will somehow go on. We always do."

Taking Rafe by one arm, Tristan pulled him nearer. "Then it is even more important that you and your council consider my offer," he said. "After what happened tonight, we need each other more than ever. At the very least, come with me to Tammerland and let me resupply you with some of the things that you lost. I know nothing can make up for the death of your people. But you owe it to your survivors to take me up on at least that much."

Rafe put one hand on Tristan's shoulder. "I know," he said softly. "To a great extent, we owe you and your warriors our lives. That's why I have called for an emergency elders' meeting to discuss your proposal."

"When?" Tristan asked.

"Now," Rafe answered.

"So soon after tonight's calamity?" Tristan asked.

Rafe took back his jug and swallowed more of the potent *tachinga.* "Can you think of a better time?" he asked back.

Smiling, Tristan shook his head. "No," he answered. "I suppose not."

Balthazar walked up to face the prince. After taking another enormous gulp, he belched loudly. Tristan smiled. The massive highlander would make a good drinking partner for Ox, he realized. Balthazar gave Tristan a crooked smile, showing the absence of several teeth. Leaning in, he poked an index finger into Tristan's chest.

"You fight well for a *dango*!" he said. Closing his eyes, he belched again, this time nearly dropping his jug. "Maybe we won't ransom your scrawny arse after all!"

"Come, all of you," Rafe said. "The meeting will start soon. Then we will see what we will see." He gave Tristan a wary glance. "But I warn you—the elders can be a very uncompromising lot," he added.

Wondering what the rest of the night would bring, Tristan started accompanying Rafe, Balthazar, and Yasmin across the moonlit clearing.

CHAPTER XXXIX

BY THE TIME TRISTAN, YASMIN, RAFE, AND BALTHAZAR REACHED the camp's meeting place, many highlander onlookers had already arrived. Tristan quickly realized that these meetings must be public affairs.

Like in the camp clearing, a large bonfire burned. An iron tripod stood over the bonfire's flames, and a black pot hung from the tripod's apex. A strange white fog billowed from the pot's lip, its clouds disappearing as they drifted gently down.

Some of the surviving wagons had been wheeled to this place. Thirteen chairs, each upholstered in red velvet, stood in a nearby circle. Ten elders sat waiting while three of the chairs remained vacant. It was obvious that news of Tristan's proposal was filtering through the camp, because more curious highlanders were arriving by the moment. Although many were tired and bloodied, they seemed highly interested in this stranger who had killed their enemies as if they had been his own.

Walking toward the circle of chairs, Rafe bade Tristan to follow him. Before Tristan went, Yasmin touched him on the arm.

"Good luck," she whispered. "The elders are stern, but wise. State your case strongly, then be quiet unless spoken to. You are still a *dango,* after all."

After nodding back, Tristan walked to join Rafe. The chieftain indicated that Tristan should sit. Before doing so, the prince thought for a moment. As a gesture of goodwill he unbuckled his baldric and quiver, then laid his weapons in the dewy grass. Only then did he take his seat.

As she watched, Yasmin sensed a familiar presence arrive by her side. She looked over to see Sonya, one of her sisters who had danced with her. Sonya gave Yasmin a coy look, then turned her attention back to the prince as he sat waiting for the meeting to start.

"You have eyes for him," Sonya whispered conspiratorially. "I can tell! Tell me—is he as clever as he is handsome?" She ran her gaze over Tristan, then looked back at her sister. "Does he have brothers in Tammerland?" she whispered eagerly.

Scowling, Yasmin turned to glare at Sonya. "Be still, you harpy!" she admonished her. "I wish to listen!" Smiling, Sonya returned her gaze to the meeting.

Tristan looked politely at the council elders. "Elder" was an apt word, he realized. Each of the surviving five men and five women had to be at least seventy Seasons of New Life, perhaps older. Several of the men had long white beards. The women's hair was equally white, and their faces were deeply creased by decades of hard nomadic life. But regardless of their gender, each clan elder looked commanding. These were people who would not be easily swayed, Tristan realized.

Without ceremony, one of the male elders started speaking in the clan's secret language. He spoke for some time, then finally went quiet. After looking over at Tristan, Rafe came to his feet. He bowed to the man who had spoken.

"I understand, Gunther," he said. He then turned to look at the crowd. "To all those present this night, I suggest that we speak only Eutracian. This *dango* has risked his life for us. It seems only right that he understands what we say."

After conferring with the other elders, Gunther nodded. "Very well," he said. "You may tell us what the *dango* has in mind."

For the next quarter hour Rafe outlined Tristan's proposal. He looked over at the prince several times to ensure that he was delivering Tristan's offer correctly. The prince nodded his agreement but did not speak. Rafe was forceful and concise, just as Yasmin had counseled Tristan to be when his turn came. Rafe was doing a good job, making the prince wonder whether he would need to speak at all. When he had finished, Rafe sat down. Gunther looked commandingly at Tristan.

"Tell us, *dango,*" he said. "In return for commanding our horsemen, will you really give us all the things you promise? Are you in fact the crowned prince of all Eutracia? Or are you merely some poseur commanding a pack of flying beasts?" Even from across the wide circle, Tristan felt Gunther's eyes boring their way into his.

"If you are lying to us," Gunther added menacingly, "we will kill you here and now, regardless of how many Zorians you and your warriors slaughtered. We do not tolerate deceivers in our midst."

Tristan looked over at Rafe. The chieftain nodded. Tristan stood and looked at each elder in turn.

"I am indeed who I claim to be," he said respectfully. "And if your clan follows me to Tammerland and allows me to command your horsemen for a time, I will grant you all that I have promised. You have my word on it."

Not knowing what more to say, Tristan reclaimed his seat. He could only hope that his words had somehow been enough. He was asking much from these people, he knew. But if they would only believe him, they would gain much, as well.

Gunther huddled again with his council members. He looked back at the prince.

"Before making such a huge decision, we will need proof," he said simply.

Tristan's mind raced. He looked over at Rafe for guidance, but the chieftain seemed equally stymied. Tristan looked back at Gunther.

"Proof of what?" he asked.

"That you are indeed the prince," Gunther answered, "and that you are telling the truth about your many promises. Once we have it, we will vote on the matter."

Tristan thought for a moment. Other than his word and the items hanging around his neck, he had little to offer. Standing again, he grasped the Paragon and gold medallion with one hand and lifted them from his chest for everyone to see. They twinkled brightly in the bonfire's orange-red light.

"I bear a medallion carrying the heraldry of the House of Galland," Tristan answered. "There are only two such discs in the entire world. My twin sister, the princess, wears the other. The red jewel around my neck is the Paragon, which allows all magic to flow into those of endowed blood. Surely you have heard of it! Moreover, I alone command the Minions of Day and Night—the flying warriors who helped bring you victory this night. Are these things not enough to prove my identity?"

Shaking his head, Gunther folded his gnarled hands in his lap. "Tell me," he said. "If I suddenly appeared to you wearing two unremarkable baubles and commanding but twenty fighters, would those things be enough for your citizens to suddenly give up the lives they had known for centuries, and follow me into the unknown? I think not! As I said, we need proof. There is one among us who can either verify or dispel your claims. If we summon her, do you agree to honor her pronouncements about you, whatever they might be?"

Tristan looked quizzically at Rafe. Standing, the highlander chief placed his mouth near the prince's ear.

"If you have been lying, you must tell me this instant!" Rafe whispered urgently. "If this goes no further, I might be able to convince the elders to spare your life. But if you have been truthful then I suggest you agree with their demands. The one they will call forth will unquestioningly uncover the truth. She is never wrong."

"Who is she?" Tristan asked.

"Agree, and you will see," Rafe answered. "Until she is summoned, by highlander law that is all I am allowed to tell an outsider about her."

Tristan remained adamant. He looked over at the seated elders. "Then bring her, whoever she is," he said aloud. "I welcome the opportunity to prove myself."

Gunther nodded. "So be it," he answered. He looked at Balthazar. "Go and fetch Arwydd," he ordered. Balthazar obediently disappeared into the crowd.

Tense moments passed. As the bonfire crackled and burned, the pot hanging over its flames continued to spew its mysterious fog. Then Balthazar returned to stand at the crowd's inner edge. The crowd gradually parted, allowing a narrow pathway to form.

At first Tristan could see no one. Then he heard a strange mixture of sounds. As the crowd parted wider, a woman shuffled into the meeting area. Tristan hadn't known what to expect. Even so, her appearance surprised him.

The woman named Arwydd was old and haggard. Her feet and hands were bound by rusty chains. Gray hair fell to her shoulders. Unlike the other highlanders' colorful dress, she wore only a tattered robe. Simple leather sandals adorned her dirty feet. Despite her weathered condition, her brown eyes were bright and missed nothing as they darted around the camp. Her hooked nose rested over a wide mouth. Because she was chained, Tristan guessed that she might be dangerous. Then Tristan discovered another striking feature about the mysterious woman, and his heart went out to her.

A heavy oxen yoke lay slung across her shoulders. Deep and long, the smooth wooden yoke forced her upper body down. Her arms raised to cradle the yoke at either end, the woman shuffled into the circle's center. More chains led from iron rings in the yoke's ends to wrap around her body. The chains collected before her abdomen and were secured one to another by a rusty padlock.

As she trod toward the circle's center, Tristan heard the sounds of tinkling glass. Looking closer, he was again surprised. Many small bottles sat atop the yoke, secured into holes that had been carved into the yoke's upper surface. Suspended from eyehooks, strange-looking iron tools dangled from the yoke's ends. They too knocked lightly together as she walked. Tristan noticed that the tools and bottles were positioned in such a way that they were unreachable to her unless she was freed from her chains. The combination of the clinking chains, tinkling bottles, and dangling tools conspired to form an odd chorus that would surely announce her presence wherever she went.

Tristan was enraged. Thinking that he might have misjudged Rafe, he glared harshly at the highlander chieftain.

"This is barbaric!" he hissed. "How can you allow such a thing?"

Like the other highlanders, Rafe seemed unperturbed by the woman's plight. "Do not be so judgmental before knowing the facts," he answered. "Her situation is not yours to decide."

"Who is she?" Tristan demanded.

"She is a Zorian soothsayer," Rafe answered. "She was captured during one of our raids, when my father led the clan. Because he recognized her talents, he let her live among us. At first we believed that she had accepted us. But then my mother and father suddenly died one night, poisoned. When she was questioned, the old crone gleefully admitted her crime. She laughed about it, dancing in happy celebration before our eyes. It was all I could do to keep the angry crowd from tearing her apart." Rafe's expression hardened as he looked into Tristan's face.

"I became the clan leader the next day," he added softly. "Perhaps more than anyone, I also wanted her dead. But like my father, I recognized her usefulness. Even so, I couldn't allow her to go unpunished. Forever carrying the tools of her trade across her back like a beast of burden was my idea. It somehow seemed right. As you might have already gathered, she cannot reach her possessions unless she is freed."

As he was reminded of his own parents' murders, Tristan's attitude toward Rafe softened a bit. He found himself unable to condemn the chieftain, for he had done far worse in seeking justice for the vicious way the Coven had murdered his mother, and forced him to kill his father.

A sudden worry struck Tristan. "If Arwydd hates you all so much, how can you rely on her to tell the truth?" he asked anxiously. "My life seems to depend on what this crone has to say!"

Rafe gave Tristan a flinty look. "Because she knows that if what she says is learned to be false, she will be killed," he said simply. "We have never known Arwydd to be wrong."

Looking back at the bent-over soothsayer, Tristan groaned. He could only hope that Rafe was right. He would tell the truth, for his life hung in the balance. But his mind was filled with worry.

"Arwydd!" Gunther called out. "Come here!"

The old woman shuffled over to the head elder. Rising up a bit from beneath the crushing yoke, she looked him in the eyes. Gunther pointed to Tristan.

"We need to know whether this *dango* tells the truth," he said. "In return for commanding our horsemen, he has promised us wondrous things. We find his tales difficult to believe. You are to work your skills on him."

Swinging the yoke around, Arwydd looked at Tristan. Her gaze was penetrating. She regarded him for some time before turning back to Gunther.

"I will do what I can," she answered in a gravelly voice. "He is an interesting specimen, that one. To do this properly, I will need two things."

Gunther's eyes narrowed. "And what are they?" he asked.

"I must be unchained," she answered, "for I must have access to my tools and bottles. And I will need three goats. I must perform a sacrifice."

Gunther nodded, then gave Balthazar a commanding look. The huge highlander left the clearing again. As everyone waited for Balthazar's return, Gunther left his chair and walked to the soothsayer. He reached beneath his shirt and produced a rusty key that hung around his neck from a leather string. He unlocked the padlock securing Arwydd's chains. Removing them from her body and the yoke, he dropped the chains to the ground. Arwydd carefully placed the yoke at her feet with her precious bottles facing skyward.

As the mysterious woman was freed, Tristan saw many in the crowd recoil, and frightened children scurried to hide behind their parents. Gunther held a wizened finger before the woman's eyes.

"One false move and you're dead," he growled.

Rubbing her chafed wrists, Arwydd smiled crookedly. For the next quarter hour, Gunther explained Tristan's offer to her.

Turning, Arwydd walked to stand before the prince. Tristan grimaced as she neared. He didn't fear her, but there was something about her that was disconcerting. Tilting her head this way and that, she looked deeply into his eyes. She grasped some of his hair, then made a great show of feeling it and smelling it. After letting go a soft grunt, she walked back to her ox yoke.

Freed from her chains, she had easy access to her tools. From the yoke's underside she selected a pair of scissors, then walked back to the prince. Smiling, she snapped the scissor blades open and shut several times. Unsure of what was about to happen, Tristan gave her a deadly look.

"If you harm me, you won't have to worry about Gunther," he whispered. "I'll kill you before he can stand from his chair."

Saying nothing, Arwydd gleefully snipped away a lock of the prince's hair. She put the hair in a pocket of her robe, then backed away.

Just then Balthazar reappeared. He was shepherding three common goats. The goats bleated as he led them into the clearing. Another highlander followed him. The second fellow carried three tent pegs and a small mallet.

Arwydd pointed to a spot near the fire. "There," she said simply.

Balthazar and his companion set about pounding the stakes into the ground and tying the goats to them. They then returned to the crowd.

Arwydd looked at Tristan. "Select one of the goats," she said simply.

Tristan gave her a skeptical look. "Why?" he asked.

"It is not my job to educate you in such matters," she snapped back. "But if you must know, the task I am about to perform might not be valid unless the subject in question picks the sacrificial goat himself. It makes no difference which one you choose, provided it is you who do it. I suspect that your life hangs on my pronouncements, *dango.* Do you wish to keep arguing with me, or shall I simply tell Gunther that you are lying and get things over with quickly?"

Tristan looked over at Rafe, and the chieftain nodded. "Very well," Tristan answered. "I choose the one in the middle."

Arwydd walked back to her yoke and took up four branding irons and a knife. She shoved the irons' business ends into the bonfire coals. She then walked to the tethered goats. Quick as a flash, she grabbed one of the middle goat's horns, lifted its head, and slit its throat. Bleeding profusely, it wobbled shakily for a moment, then fell dead. Wasting no time, Arwydd starting boning out the goat's hindquarters.

She soon produced four wet bones. Two were from the goat's upper rear legs where they met the hip joint. The other two were the smaller shank bones from between the goat's knee joints and ankles. After wiping them clean with a rag, she walked over to the fire and dropped them into the black pot.

After returning to her yoke she selected a bottle. Uncorking it, she walked back to the fire, then poured some of the bottle's contents into the boiling pot. The strange white fog rose higher, vanishing into the sky and releasing a terrible odor that smelled like rotting flesh. She then reached into her pocket, removed the lock of Tristan's hair, and also dropped it into the pot.

Tristan looked over at Rafe. "Does she command the craft?" he asked quietly.

"No one knows," Rafe answered. "Father always suspected her of it. Most highlander clans have a soothsayer in their midst. But none compare to Arwydd. We are simple folk, and have no way to know if she commands magic."

Using a pair of tongs secured from her yoke, Arwydd retrieved the blanched bones from the pot. After again drying them with the rag, she placed the bones in a line on the ground. Then she removed the first of the irons from the fire. Holding it against the first bone, she branded it on either side. She repeated the strange process with subsequent irons until each bone had been branded twice with its own distinctive markings.

After picking up the bones, she looked at Tristan and crooked one finger at him. Standing from his chair, he walked to her. Except for the sounds coming from the crackling fire, the meeting place was deathly silent. Arwydd's haggard features seemed evil and gloating in the bonfire light.

"I am ready to start," she said. "Be careful how you answer my questions, *dango.* You might lie, but the bones never do."

Tristan nodded. "Go ahead," he answered. "I have nothing to hide."

"Very well," she said. "Tell us your name."

Arwydd looked deeply into Tristan's eyes. For a moment, he felt dizzy. As quickly as it had come, the sensation passed.

"I am Tristan of the House of Galland, prince of Eutracia," he answered loudly, so that everyone could hear.

Arwydd squatted and picked up the bones. She put her hands together, then moved them in a wide circle. As she dropped the branded bones to the ground they clattered into a small pile. Arwydd went to all fours to smell the bones and look at them from several different angles. Then she looked up at Gunther.

"He is who he says," she answered simply.

The crowd immediately let go a collective gasp. As the elders busily conferred, Tristan looked over at Rafe. Rafe grinned back broadly.

Coming to her knees, Arwydd picked up the bones the same way she had done before. She again looked Tristan in the eyes.

"Gunther says that if you are allowed to command our horsemen, the Kilbourne clan will be rewarded in specific ways. Are you speaking the truth?"

Again Tristan's dizziness came, then left just as quickly. "Yes," he answered. Then he paused, thinking. "I will also order my sister and my wizards that in the event of my death, it will be their duty to see that the rewards are given to you just the same."

Arwydd again cast the strange bones to the ground, then crawled around as she interpreted them. It took longer this time for her to form her decision. She finally looked up at Gunther again.

"He tells the truth," she answered. "If he is allowed to command our horsemen for a time, he truly intends to reward you, and in the exact way he mentioned."

This time the spectators positively buzzed with excitement. Tristan imagined them asking themselves if the *dango* would really give so much.

Tristan looked at the elders. From their surprised expressions he gathered that they had fully expected Arwydd to tell them that he had been lying. Confused by her findings, they huddled together urgently.

Rafe leaned closer. "It seems you have caused quite an uproar," he said. "For your sake, it is good that so many spectators attended this meeting. There is no way that the elders can say that something else happened here. Before these gatherings were made public, the elders were not above such trickery. This time they will be forced into taking a vote, whether they like it or not."

Rubbing his chin, Rafe glanced around the circle of august men and women. When he looked back at Tristan, there was a skeptical expression on his face.

"What troubles you?" Tristan asked. "The elders have their proof. I should think that considering all that I'm offering, the vote would be a mere formality."

Rafe sighed. "In your world, that might be the case," he answered. "But highlander logic can be strange. You are asking a great deal of the elders. Despite your magnificent offer, I believe the vote will be close."

As Gunther ordered the elders to stand, Tristan guessed that the vote was drawing near. "Is there anything more that I can do to influence the outcome?" he whispered to Rafe.

"If you could find another last-minute way to help the clan, it might sway some of the undecided elders to your cause," Rafe answered. "But given your limited freedom, I don't know what that would be."

Tristan gave Rafe a sly smile. "I do," he answered.

Without consulting the chieftain, Tristan stood and faced the elders. He was about to make a bold move, but he was willing to risk it.

"Before you vote, I wish to be heard!" Tristan shouted brazenly.

A hush came over the crowd. *The* dango *is either very stupid or very brave to speak to the elders without first having been addressed!* he could almost hear them saying. *What could possibly be important enough to make him invite the council's wrath?*

Gunther wheeled around angrily. "How dare you?" he growled. "Even though Arwydd has validated your claims, you're in no position to give orders!"

"It is about Arwydd that I wish to speak!" Tristan answered. "I mean the council no disrespect. Even so, I fear that your soothsayer is more than she claims to be. I believe she practices the craft's dark side!"

The crowd gasped. Tristan turned to look at the old woman. Her gaze toward the prince turned even more hateful. Gunther gave Tristan a skeptical look.

"How dare you?" he demanded. "You have been in our midst for less than a day, yet you claim to know more about her than we do!"

Walking closer, Tristan held out his hands in a display of friendship. "Allow me to prove it to you," he said. "If I am right, I will have removed a terrible danger from your midst. You have long known that she is treacherous. But I fear that you greatly underestimate her talents, and her resolve to hurt your clan further. I am told that she has already killed Rafe's parents. Don't let her kill again! If I am wrong about her, then you have lost nothing. But if I am right, I will have done Clan Kilbourne yet another service."

Glowering at Tristan, Gunther thought it over. He finally let go a deep breath. "Very well," he said. "But we still believe that she is an asset to the clan. Before I let you prove your charges, I must know what it is you will do."

Tristan smiled. "The answer is simple," he said. "I need only take one drop of her blood."

Screaming with rage, Arwydd pointed an accusatory finger at Tristan.

"Blasphemer!" she shouted. "It is not I, but you who are the deceiver!" Going to her knees, she looked into Gunther's face. "Please don't let the *dango* touch me!" she begged. "He will kill me sure!"

Tristan looked at Gunther. "I don't need to touch her, if that worries you," he said. "Select two clansmen whom you trust, and I will tell them what to do."

Gunther rubbed his chin, thinking. "Very well," he answered. "Rafe and Balthazar, come here." The two highlanders hurried to stand before the head elder. "What would you have them do?" Gunther asked Tristan.

Walking over to where his weapons lay, Tristan retrieved one of his dirks. He returned to hand it to Rafe. The look in Rafe's eyes said that he thought Tristan had just gone mad. Tristan gave Rafe his best look of reassurance. He turned back to Gunther.

"We will also need a piece of blank parchment," he said.

Gunther ordered that a parchment be provided. A highlander quickly brought one. Knowing that it would only strengthen his case if he did not touch it, Tristan asked that it be placed into Gunther's hands. He looked over at Balthazar.

"Bring her," he said.

Grabbing Arwydd by the shoulders, the giant started manhandling her over to where the others stood. She kicked and scratched at Balthazar, and spat in his face. Finally hoisting her over one shoulder, he took no notice as she pounded her fists against his back. Balthazar dropped the soothsayer before the others like she was a sack of grain.

"Hold her by the wrists," Tristan said. He gave Arwydd a harsh look. "If I'm right about you, you know full well what is about to be done. I suggest you hold still, lest they mistakenly cut you more than need be."

Arwydd glared hatefully at the prince. "When this is over, I will kill you," she breathed.

Tristan gave her a sly look. "When this is over, your days of killing will be forever done," he answered.

As Balthazar tightened his grip on her, Tristan looked at Rafe. "Cut as small an incision into her arm as possible," he said. "There is no need to be abusive. Then collect a little bit of her blood on my knife blade."

After nodding at Tristan, Rafe did as he had been asked. A rivulet of Arwydd's blood ran onto the knife.

"Now," Tristan said, "allow but one blood drop to fall onto the parchment that Gunther holds. If I am right, you will see something you never dreamed possible."

Positioning the bloody knife over the parchment, Rafe carefully tilted the blade. One drop fell onto the paper. As the elders gathered around to watch, Tristan smiled.

As he had guessed, a partial blood signature started to form. Twisting and turning with a life of its own, it soon showed a series of sharply angled, intersecting lines. Then the blood died, and stopped moving about the page.

Rafe looked at Tristan like he had just seen a ghost. He and the other highlanders had heard strange stories about the blood of those who commanded the craft. But to see a clan member's blood do the same thing was shocking. Amazed into speechlessness, the elders simply stood and stared. Tristan looked over at Arwydd.

"You're a partial adept," he said. "Your father was a man of fully endowed blood, and trained in the craft. You practice the Vagaries, don't you, Arwydd?"

Arwydd kicked and cursed, but she could not break Balthazar's iron grip.

"Bastard!" she breathed. "I cast a pox on your royal house, and all those who practice the Vigors!" Undaunted by her threat, Tristan laughed.

"I don't understand," Gunther breathed. "If this means she is your enemy, why would she validate your tales?"

"That's simple," Tristan answered. "She had no choice. Like Rafe said, if what she told you didn't come true, she would be killed. Had the tools of her trade been available to her when she was unsupervised, my guess is that she would have killed many of you before making her escape. That's what you dream of, isn't it, Arwydd?"

Taking a step closer, Tristan looked into her eyes. "You made your first mistake when you killed Rafe's parents," he said. "Had you not done so, the clan would have come to trust you, and you might not have been bound. In time you could have gathered all the herbs and oils you needed to practice your arts freely. But your craving for vengeance got the better of you, and you killed the previous chieftain and his wife. Then I arrived to unmask you and seal your fate."

Gunther stepped forward. He again stared down at the newly formed blood signature. "This strange-looking pattern," he said. "That means that she practices the craft?"

Tristan nodded.

"How is it that no other Kilbourne clan member's blood exhibits these strange ways?" Gunther asked.

"One must be trained in the ways of the craft first," Tristan answered. "None of you claim that advantage. You yourself told me that Arwydd was born a Zorian. Clearly, there are parts of her history about which you still do not know."

"Even so, how do you know that she practices the dark side?" Gunther asked.

"Because no Vigors practitioner commits unneeded murder," Tristan said. "But my wizards have other ways of telling, should you want further proof. If you bring her to the palace, we will show you how it is done."

"How did you guess who she was?" Rafe asked Tristan.

"Her use of herbs and oils reminded me of another partial adept I know," Tristan answered. "She serves on the Conclave. Even so, that wasn't proof enough. When Arwydd asked me her two questions, I felt dizzy, and I suspected the craft was at work. I believe she used a technique allowing her to enter my mind. My wizards also perform it, although to a much better degree. But until tonight I didn't know that partials could also perform the spell. This parlor show was just window dressing, designed to fool you all—it always has been. She got her real answers when she entered my mind—not by reading goat bones! As long as she could trick you into believing that she was merely some sort of soothsayer who worked without the aid of the craft, she could continue to show that she was worth keeping alive."

Straining as best she could against Balthazar's iron grip, Arwydd leaned closer and spat directly into Tristan's face. He calmly wiped it away.

"Very clever, Chosen One," she said.

Tristan raised an eyebrow. "That's another mistake," he said. "You just called me 'Chosen One,' " he said. "Usually only those acquainted with the craft know that phrase. So you admit who you are?" he asked.

"Yes, I admit it!" she shouted, knowing that her ruse had finally run its course. "I only hope I live to see the day when you and your wizards are crushed by the Vagaries!"

From their places in the crowd, Yasmin and Sonya gave each other astonished looks. "So the prince *is* as clever as he is handsome!" Sonya whispered.

Scowling, Yasmin poked her sister in the ribs, then returned her gaze to Tristan. "Hush!" she whispered back.

Gunther stepped closer. As he stared at Tristan, there was a determined look in his eyes. "I told you that we tolerate no deceivers in our midst," he said. "I meant what I said." Gunther looked at Balthazar. "Take this traitorous bitch into the woods and kill her," he ordered.

Grabbing Arwydd by one wrist, Balthazar started dragging the screaming woman from the clearing. By now, Tristan knew better than to intervene in highlander business. Even so, he couldn't just stand by and watch her be killed. He was about to risk a protest when Arwydd sealed her own fate.

Twisting violently, she went for the dagger at Balthazar's hip. Pulling it from its scabbard, she plunged its blade into the giant's left shoulder. Like the wound meant nothing, Balthazar acted swiftly.

Letting go of her wrist, he took her head into his hands and give it a savage twist. Tristan took a quick breath as he watched the partial adept's head turn all the way around, her neck bones cracking loudly as it went. Letting go of her, Balthazar stepped back. Arwydd stood there stupidly for a moment; then the light went out of her eyes. She collapsed to the ground like a rag doll, dead where she lay.

Rafe stepped closer to Tristan. There was a deep look of appreciation on his face.

"When you asked to see Arwydd's blood, I thought you mad," he said. "Now all I can do is to offer you my thanks. My parents have finally been avenged."

"I understand all too well," Tristan answered.

Then he saw Yasmin and Sonya approach. After giving Tristan a knowing look, Yasmin went to Balthazar. She grasped the dagger by the handle.

"Gather your strength," she said.

Knowing what was coming, Balthazar nodded. Yasmin quickly pulled the knife from his shoulder. Smiling, she looked at Tristan again.

"It seems that I must sew up more than one man's wounds tonight," she said. As she started leading Balthazar away, she turned and gave the prince a final look. "You know where you can find me if you wish," she said quietly.

Grinning widely, Rafe slapped Tristan on the back. "Your work for the night might not be over!" he said laughingly.

Tristan gave Rafe a smirk. "What about the vote?" he asked.

They turned to see the elders huddling in animated conversation. It went on for some time. Finally Gunther walked back to where Tristan and Rafe were standing.

"Will you vote now?" Rafe asked.

"We already have done so," Gunther answered. "There is no need for you to add your vote, for it won't change the outcome."

"And that is?" Rafe asked.

"Seven to three in favor," Gunther answered. "We have accepted the prince's offer." Gunther held out his hand to Tristan. They shook hands, sealing the deal.

"As of this moment, you have nearly one thousand highlander horsemen on your hands, Your Highness," Gunther said. "The rest of the clan will follow them to Tammerland. I hope you know what you're doing."

Tristan smiled. "So do I," he answered. "But no matter what else happens, know that I will keep my part of the bargain."

"You'd best do so," Gunther warned him. "Clan Kilbourne would make for a determined enemy."

Tristan smiled again as he thought about what Wigg and Faegan would say when the Minion scouts told them that a highlander clan was coming, with Tristan leading them. Both the wizards disliked highlanders, Tristan knew. Making the two mystics comfortable with this new arrangement would take some doing.

Gunther looked at the night sky. "It will be dawn in a few hours," he said. "I suggest that we get some sleep. At sunrise we will bury our dead, then break camp and head for Tammerland. I bid you good night."

Rounding up the other council members, Gunther escorted them from the meeting place. When the crowd saw the elders leaving, they too started walking away. As they left, some looked at Tristan with curiosity, others with worry, and still more with outright scorn. Soon Tristan and Rafe were left alone with only the bonfire, the stars, and their concerns about tomorrow. Looking at the ground, Rafe worried a pebble with the toe of one boot.

"It will take much more than what happened here tonight for you to gain the entire clan's respect, you know," he said. "You have won the right to command our horsemen how and when you wish, but nothing else. The elders and I still govern the clan. You need to remember that."

Tristan nodded at his new friend. Something told him that before too long, he and Rafe would be riding into danger together.

"I know that my powers are limited," he answered. "You have my word that I will not overstep them."

"Good," Rafe said. "Will you walk with me?"

Tristan shook his head. "You go on ahead. I have some thinking to do."

"Very well," Rafe said. "Until dawn, *Jin'Sai.*"

Tristan smiled slightly. "Until dawn," he answered.

Tristan stood alone by the bonfire as he watched Rafe's lean figure disappear among the shadows. Only then did he pick his weapons up from the grass and start his way back into the camp's heart.

As he walked among the wagons and surviving clanfolk, stark remnants of the recent battle again came into view. Dead Zorian bodies still lay where they had fallen, but the Kilbourne dead had been taken away. Blood lay on the ground in random patterns, its darkness shiny against the surrounding grass. Some highlanders were still awake beside their campfires, talking excitedly about what their new lives might bring.

Looking at the sky, Tristan smiled as he saw a silhouetted Minion patrol cross darkly before the three magenta moons. *Good for you, Hector,* he thought. *That's one mistake we'll never make again.*

For better or worse, he realized that he was slowly wending his way back toward Yasmin's wagon. He knew that she would be waiting there, lying in the dark and wondering whether he would come to her. Finally nearing her wagon, he sat down on a stool. A campfire still burned, and an abandoned *tachinga* jug lay near his feet. It seemed that no one else was awake. *That's just as well,* he thought.

After taking a deep drink from the jug, Tristan placed it back down on the ground, then put his head in his hands. Bone-tired, he sat that way for some time, thinking. So much had happened in the last few days that he scarcely knew how to interpret it all. Looking around the campsite, he shook his head.

I beg the Afterlife, he thought, *what have I done? I am about to lead an entire group of people on a life-changing exodus. How will I ever live up to their expectations?*

Then he remembered Celeste.

Tears overtook his eyes; he brushed them away. What would she want for him? he wondered. He remembered her last letter to him, the one she had saved until her death. The letter still lay on the fireplace mantel in his palace quarters, the golden vase holding her ashes standing beside it. That's all that remained of her. Mere ashes, and nothing more. *That's all that will eventually remain of any of us,* he realized. *In the end, all that matters is how we lived, and who we loved.*

Turning, he looked back at the wagon. The canvas flap was lowered; no light shone from inside. Finally deciding, he stood and climbed the wagon's steps. Pushing aide the flap, he went inside.

Lying naked atop the wagon bedding, Yasmin's body glistened in the moonlight. Her long, dark hair was splayed out over her pillow, and her perfume returned to arouse his senses. Lying down beside her, Tristan started to speak. But before he could, she placed her fingertips across his lips.

"There is only one thing to consider," she whispered. Lowering her hand, she looked into his eyes. "Do you want this, *Jin'-Sai*?"

"Yes," he whispered back.

Leaning down, he placed his mouth onto hers.

CHAPTER XL

BY THE TIME WIGG, FAEGAN, AND JESSAMAY FINALLY STRUGGLED their way back to the *Tammerland*'s top deck, the scene before them was so terrifying that they all stopped short the second they cleared the hatchway.

The fog had rolled in over the night sea from seemingly nowhere and everywhere, engulfing the entire fleet. Thick and gray, it clung to everyone's clothes and skin. With the fog's arrival the temperature had plummeted, making everyone's breath appear as ghostly vapors. The wind had calmed, resulting in a glass-smooth sea. Their dreggans drawn, thousands of Minion warriors crowded the fleet's top decks.

Some of the fog had coalesced into massive columns, rising from the water. As the Conclave members knew would happen, the columns had morphed into giant hands, each pair grasping a ship by opposite ends. All the fleet's ships were thus caught. As the Necrophagians' wailing assaulted their ears, Wigg, Faegan, and Jessamay hurried to find the others.

The princess and the captain were standing in the bow with Adrian, Traax, and Scars. Although their insane howling was growing ever louder, the Necrophagians had yet to appear. Tyranny spun around to give Wigg a serious look.

"What about the aft hallways?" she shouted. "Were you able to seal them from the sea?"

Leaning closer, Wigg put his mouth near Tyranny's ear. "Yes!" he shouted back. "But the meeting room is completely flooded! The strain of keeping the spell in place is exhausting the three of us!"

Regardless of the Necrophagian threat, Tyranny was sea captain enough to know that the condition of her crippled vessel came first. She immediately ran to the starboard gunwale, then looked over the side. Her worst fears were quickly realized. Because of the flooding, the flagship was riding dangerously low in the stern, and threatening to go down. Tyranny knew that the trapped seawater was immensely heavy, forcing her to wonder whether the mystics would be able to launch the *Tammerland* into the air.

"We're foundering!" she shouted as best she could above the terrible wailing. "The flooded compartments are nearly sinking us! Even if we unfurl the sails, there is no wind to fill them! Our only hope is to fly away!" Grabbing Wigg by his shoulders, she glared desperately into his face. "Please tell me that you and the others can release us from the Necrophagians' grip and get us aloft!"

Wigg shook his head in frustration. He was about to answer when Shailiha called out. She was standing at the opposite gunwale with an astonished look on her face. The others hurried to her and stared over the side.

The sea around the fleet had begun to bubble and roil, like something was trying to come to the top. Then faces started to form on the ocean surface. The Necrophagians—the ages-old Eaters of the Dead—were coming into view.

Everyone stared in awe at the rapidly forming beings. There seemed to be hundreds of them. Their flesh was a mixture of sea green and dark red and streaked with ancient wrinkles and boils. Where eyes and mouths should have been there were only dark, empty holes. Then the wailing unexpectedly stopped. As the faces drifted ominously among the waves, an eerie silence reclaimed the night.

Faegan looked at Wigg and Jessamay. "Follow me!" he ordered.

Praying that his assumptions about the Necrophagians were correct, he levitated his chair and soared over the gunwale to hover directly above the hundreds of menacing faces. Wigg and Jessamay quickly followed him. As the three mystics hovered in the air, they looked down on the terrible threat.

"You are all about to die!" the Necrophagians suddenly shouted as one.

Their words were so explosive that everyone thought their eardrums might burst. Such torrential wind accompanied the Necrophagians' unexpected statement that the three hovering mystics struggled mightily to keep from being blown far out to sea, their robes and hair flying as the awful wind struck them.

As the angry Necrophagians waited for a response, the terrible wind subsided. Composing himself, Wigg looked down into the awful faces lying just meters below his boots.

"Why must we die?" he asked respectfully. "We have done nothing to harm you. We only ask permission to cross, and we will pay if we must. That is the standard arrangement, is it not?"

"You and the Jin'Sai *are responsible for the death of the* Enseterat*!"* the voices answered. *"You also wish to attack the Citadel. That must not be allowed to happen. We are ordered to destroy you."*

"Ordered by whom?" Faegan asked.

"Fools!" the voices screamed. *"Powers far beyond your ken command us!"*

Faegan suddenly realized that his suppositions about these strange beings might be true after all. That would explain so much! But it would also make crossing nearly impossible.

"It was Wulfgar who freed you from your previous territories as he traveled west on his way to Eutracia, was it not?" Faegan asked. "Then he ordered you to follow him to the Eutracian coast, and to help him in his invasion. But the invasion failed and Wulfgar was killed, leaving you free to roam the sea at last."

Silence reigned again. Faegan cast a knowing glance at Wigg and Jessamay. The First Wizard raised an eyebrow. It seemed that Faegan had struck on something important—something the Necrophagians were uncomfortable dealing with.

"Tell me," Faegan pressed. "With Wulfgar dead, has Serena become your new mistress?"

"Our true masters are the same as they have always been, their magnificence long since ensconced on the other side of the Tolenka Mountains," the voices answered. *"Travelers may form bargains with us, just as Failee and Wulfgar did. But they can never truly rule us. That remains the province of only one group of indomitable mystics, the likes of which your minds cannot grasp. We tell you these things only because you are about to die."*

Like the Necrophagians were suddenly humbled by this new topic, their voices had quieted to their usual whisper. The terrible wind that had once accompanied their screeching also stilled, as did the sea. But the mysterious hands of fog still held each vessel tight in their iron grips.

Fascinated, Faegan lowered his chair closer to the waves. "Who are these great mystics?" he asked. "Are they the Heretics of the Guild? Do you commune with them?"

At first the Necrophagians did not answer. When they finally did, their voices were even softer, like they were speaking of the divine.

"We commune with only the most powerful of the Heretics," the voices answered, *"those in whose blood the highest gifts of the Vagaries flow."*

Intrigued by the Necrophagians' answer, Faegan thought for a moment. "Who are these mystics?" he asked again. Like the Necrophagians, his voice had also become a whisper.

"They are the embodiment of the Vagaries," the voices answered back. *"They are the ones to whom all other Vagaries practitioners bow. They are the* Pon Q'tar.*"*

"You were once members of the Ones Who Came Before, were you not?" Faegan pressed. "Captured in the War of Attrition, you were morphed by the Heretics into the Eaters of the Dead. Then you were ordered to remain in this sea forever, protecting the Citadel by devouring any who dared come near. Some of you even commanded these Black Ships in the service of the Vigors. Isn't that true? Will you not spare an answer, and grant the dying wish of an old, foolish wizard?"

Tense moments passed. *"We do not . . . remember,"* the chorus of whispers answered.

"What is the *Pon Q'tar*?" Wigg asked.

"Enough of this!" the voices shouted back, thunderous again. *"You are of the Vigors! You mean to attack the Citadel! It is time for you to die!"*

Everyone aboard the Black Ships knew what would happen next. Using their massive arms of fog, the Eaters of the Dead would relentlessly pull the vessels under. Then they would greedily consume every living person and warrior, sucking them into their gaping maws. There would be no escape, no reprieve. Unless the three frantic mystics could devise a way to stop it, everyone would die here and now on this sea. Worse, the ramifications of the slaughter would resound through the centuries, perhaps sealing the Vigors' fate forever.

The attack on the Citadel would not happen, and the Vagaries scroll would not be captured. Serena would continue to rule in Wulfgar's stead, free to attempt her still-unknown mission with almost no resistance. And Tristan—should he one day return from the Tolenkas' other side—would be nearly bereft of help to carry on his destiny. There would be no one save Abbey to train him, and as a partial adept she could teach him only so much. There would be almost no surviving Minion armies for him to command. The Redoubt consuls—although imprisoned—would remain in the grip of the Vagaries and present yet another disturbing threat. And perhaps worst of all, the *Jin'Saiou* would not remain alive to carry on the fight for him, should he die.

Everything relied on their living through this, Wigg knew. It has all boiled down to this day, this hour, this second, adrift on a strange sea so far away from home. Trying desperately to devise an escape plan, he looked over at Faegan and Jessamay.

Faegan had the tiniest seed of an idea, but he knew that he couldn't risk telling the others for fear the Necrophagians would hear him. What he needed most was time. Without consulting Wigg or Jessamay, he decided to take the risk.

"Before you take us, I ask one favor," he shouted adamantly. Wigg and Jessamay gave him puzzled looks, but knew better than to ask.

"What is your favor, Vigors wizard?" the terrible voices demanded.

"We have deities to whom we pray," Faegan lied. "We revere them, much like you do the *Pon Q'tar.* Thousands of us are about to die. Please allow us a short time to explain our failures to our fellows, and to ready our souls for the Afterlife. Grant us this small courtesy, and in return I promise that our people will go willingly into your cold embrace."

For a time the waves' swells slapped gently, almost reassuringly against the Black Ships' hulls. Finally the Necrophagians broke their silence.

"Out of respect for the craft, we grant you a time in which to ready your souls," the voices answered. *"But the grace period will be short. Prepare to die, mortals."*

Beckoning Wigg and Jessamay to follow him, Faegan quickly soared up and over the *Tammerland*'s gunwale. The First Wizard and the sorceress landed beside him.

As everyone crowded around Faegan's chair, he closed his eyes and placed his fingertips on either side of his head. Normally the Conclave members would have left him alone to sort out his thoughts, but this time they had no such luxury. Squatting down before his chair, Shailiha took his ancient hands into hers.

"Please tell us that you have a plan!" she whispered urgently.

Faegan opened his eyes, then looked up at Wigg and Jessamay. "If the Necrophagians' hands of fog can hold the Black Ships in place then they must have genuine substance, regardless of their appearance," he said, half to himself. "And if that is true, then they might not be beyond harm." Faegan looked at Tyranny. "I assume that we carry barrels of pitch, with which to repair the Black Ships' hulls?" he asked.

"Of course," she answered. "Each ship carries several."

"Good!" Faegan said. "But it is only the *Tammerland*'s that I need." He then looked at Traax. The warrior quickly snapped to attention. "I want ten barrels of pitch taken to the end of the hallway that reaches the flooded meeting rooms," he ordered. "The water is high belowdecks, making this a nearly impossible job. Even so, it must be done quickly. Once there, you've got to keep the barrels close until I arrive! Go!"

Traax immediately ran off to carry out his orders.

"What in the name of the Afterlife are you doing?" Wigg demanded. "Adding more weight to the *Tammerland*'s stern will only make things worse! We're nearly going down as it is!"

"I know!" Faegan answered. "You must trust me!"

Beckoning everyone closer, he quickly outlined his plan. When he was finished he looked at Adrian.

"I know you're exhausted!" he said. "We all are! Even so, your part in this is vital! If you fail, we all do!"

"I'll do my best," Adrian answered.

Wasting no time, Faegan looked at the waiting Minions and barked out a series of orders. Quick as a wink, one warrior scooped Adrian up in his arms like she weighed nothing. Then hundreds more got busy, sheathing their dreggans and running about the *Tammerland*'s deck in search of stout rope. They soon formed strict lines before the wizards and the sorceress, each one carrying a coiled section of rope slung over his or her shoulder. Finally satisfied, Faegan looked first into Wigg's eyes, then Jessamay's.

"Give me as much time as you can, then send Adrian over the side and the warriors into the air," he said. "This will be a close-run thing!"

"Good luck," Wigg said.

"And to you," Faegan answered back. Leaving his chair behind, he soared toward the ship's stern, then disappeared down the deck hatchway.

Clearly stunned by the audacity of Faegan's plan, Shailiha and Tyranny turned to stare blankly at Wigg. "Can this work?" Shailiha breathed.

Wigg shook his head. "We're about to find out," he answered.

"Your time is up, mortals!" the Necrophagians suddenly screamed. *"You must meet your deaths! There are many thousands of you aboard these vessels. For that reason your flagship will succumb first. Then we will take the others, one by one!"*

Wigg snapped his head around to look at the warrior holding

Adrian. "They're about to sink us!" he shouted. "Go! And may the Afterlife protect you!"

Launching himself into the air, the warrior flew over the port gunwale, then down within meters of the sea. With Adrian in his arms he started flying along the length of the ship and toward the *Tammerland*'s stern as fast as his wings could take him.

Just then the *Tammerland* lurched sickeningly. Wigg looked forward then aft to see that the huge hands were starting to pull her down. As the waterline rose up her sides, the *Tammerland* rocked, and her hull groaned. With a great cracking sound, one mast split in two under the unprecedented stresses to come crashing down, killing dozens of warriors instantly. Wigg ran to the port gunwale and looked over the side. Soon the rising water would conquer the top deck. The stricken ship and all her passengers would be done for.

Suddenly everyone heard an explosion come from the stern, followed by another terrible howl from the Necrophagians. But this time the seaborne monsters were not wailing with anger, Wigg realized. They were screaming in agony. Everyone turned to look sternward, where the warrior carrying Adrian had flown.

Another massive explosion tore through the air, then another and another. Not one of them could see Adrian as she went about her work, but in their hearts they knew that the First Sister would be doing her utmost as she sent azure bolts tearing into the hand of fog that gripped the ship's stern.

After being struck by one more blazing bolt, the Necrophagian arm was finally rent in two, releasing the ship's stern from its torturous grip. As the huge hand tumbled into the sea, dark green blood spurted from the arm's ragged stump. Looking over the side, Wigg saw Adrian and the warrior again soaring low over the waves, this time approaching the *Tammerland*'s bow.

Wigg and the others watched as Adrian, still in the warrior's arms, started attacking the hand holding the bow. Three bolts came in rapid succession, each narrowly missing the ship's hull. They tore into the hand of fog just below the wrist, severing it from the arm. As more green blood spurted from the fresh wound to land in the sea, the Necrophagians again screamed in agony. Her task about the *Tammerland* done, Adrian immediately ordered her warrior to fly her to the other Black Ships, to start the same process and to shout out orders to the acolytes aboard them.

Knowing that the *Tammerland* had been freed, Wigg spun around to look at the lines of waiting warriors. "Now!" he shouted.

At once the warriors started moving. Working swiftly, they tied their ropes to the *Tammerland*'s many mooring cleats, then took off, letting out line as they went. After tying the lines about their waists, they hovered and watched.

With another shout from Wigg, he and Jessamay immediately stopped the spell they were using to help Faegan seal the ship's damaged stern from the invading sea. Faegan would know when this happened because he would feel the far greater strain of trying to sustain the spell alone. He would then abandon the spell and allow it to vanish, and the seawater would again start rushing into the ship's hallways.

At that point Faegan would start his part of the plan—provided the combined efforts of Wigg, Jessamay, and the hovering warriors could take the *Tammerland* aloft. If not, the seawater rushing into the damaged stern would surely sink her before the protective spell could again be conjured, and the Necrophagians would devour everyone aboard.

Raising their arms, Wigg and Jessamay concentrated mightily as they summoned the craft. At the same time the warriors started trying to fly higher, straining with everything they had against the ropes tied around their waists.

Amid the Necrophagians' awful wailing, Tyranny and Shailiha watched as the *Tammerland* rocked violently, then started to rise. Her timbers groaning, she nosed upward, then crashed mightily back down atop the sea, taking many warriors and their lines down with her. Tangled in their ropes, some struggling Minions were unable to get aloft again.

Screaming in triumph, the Necrophagians pounced on the stricken warriors before they could rise from the ocean. Sucked into the gaping maws, most were cut in half as they were eaten. A clear portent of what would come should Faegan's plan fail, fresh blood and severed body parts started bobbing atop the waves.

Trying again, Wigg and Jessamay strived with everything they had as the remaining warriors aloft did the same. The *Tammerland* slowly started to rise. As she did, a desperate thought went through Wigg's mind.

We just might survive this, he realized. *If only Faegan and Traax are still alive.*

AS FAEGAN FOUGHT HIS WAY DOWN THE FLOODED HALLWAY, HE realized that Traax and the warriors he had ordered to bring the barrels of pitch must have surely drowned. The water was so high that only inches of breathable air remained between it and the hallway ceiling.

Putting his mouth as close to the ceiling as he could, he used the craft to help him struggle forward against the rushing tide. He could easily sense that the communal spell holding back the seawater had been abandoned by Wigg and Jessamay. But if they couldn't get the *Tammerland* into the air in the next few moments, all would be lost.

Reaching the hallway's end, he saw Traax and five warriors struggling to stay alive. Their faces nearly touching the ceiling, they were gasping the last of the remaining air as they bravely waited for the wizard. The door to the meeting rooms was wide open, allowing seawater to stream into the ship's hull unabated. Submerging for a moment, Faegan saw the ten heavy barrels of pitch rolling to and fro on the hallway floor. Coming back to take a gulp of precious air, he grabbed Traax by the shoulders.

"Get . . . out, all . . . of you!" he shouted, as some of the rising water went down his throat. Coughing and gagging, he spat it out. "Leave here while you still can!"

Wasting no time, Traax and the others started fighting their way back down the hall. As he watched them go, Faegan was sure that they would never reach the stairway alive.

He took another gulp of air, then submerged again to locate the pitch barrels. Praying that their seals were intact, he used the craft to bring them to the surface but found that the air space was gone, and that the hallway was fully flooded. He quickly invoked a spell to make the most of what air remained in his lungs, but even his gifts would not sustain him for long.

Just then he felt the ship lurch upward at the bow, and he tumbled violently underwater. Higher and higher the *Tammerland* rose until he felt the seawater suddenly rushing in the opposite direction, toward the damaged stern. *It's working,* his oxygen-deprived brain told him. *Wigg and Jessamay are doing it! Just a little more and we'll be aloft!*

As the ship climbed and her hull tilted even more sharply, the trapped seawater rushed violently astern, cascading out the damaged hull and taking all of the room's furniture out with it. Soon Faegan's head was above water again, and he took a life-saving gasp. But he hadn't counted on how forceful the rushing water would become, as it threatened to take him and the barrels into the meeting rooms.

His body nearly vertical in the raging water, he grabbed a passing wall sconce and desperately hung on as he summoned a spell to try and hold the pitch barrels in place. If the water took them out the damaged stern, all would be lost, regardless of Wigg's and Jessamay's success in getting the *Tammerland* airborne. Then the horrible, unexpected pain started. As the seawater rushed aft, searing agony coursed across the exposed nerve endings of his ravaged legs.

He hadn't taken that into account, and the pain's sudden ferocity was overcoming the partition in his mind that had for so long helped him deal with his relentless suffering. Trying to keep the barrels near while also attempting to retain his precious sanity, he screamed aloud.

He did his best to hang on, but he knew that his endowed grip was slipping on both the wall sconce and the barrels. A choice had to be made, and the answer was obvious. If the fleet was to be saved, he would have to stop trying to control the pain and concentrate all his power on his grip and keeping the barrels near. Holding on for dear life, he stopped partitioning off the pain.

Except for his torture by Wulfgar during the *Enseterat*'s first invasion attempt, Faegan had never endured such agony. Screaming insanely, his eyes bulged and his damaged body convulsed as the water rushed by.

Then it was over, all of the trapped water having found its freedom out the damaged stern. Letting go of the wall sconce, Faegan crashed to the floor. Because of the immensely steep angle on the ship's bow, he was forced to use the craft just to keep himself and the barrels from skidding down the hallway, into the meeting rooms, and out the ship's gaping stern.

While sustaining the spell holding the barrels, he allowed himself to slide along the angled floor toward the meeting room door. Seizing the doorknob with one hand as he passed by, he held fast against the ship's sharp angle of climb. He then called the craft to right the barrels and rip their circular tops away one by one. As the ship continued to climb he ended the spell holding the barrels in place and shoved the door open wider, making way for them. As they tore through the doorway and across the floor he used the craft to turn them so that their opened ends faced him.

His body nearly vertical again, Faegan watched the barrels slide on their sides toward the gaping rent in the stern. The timing would have to be perfect, if only his exhausted blood could still summon enough power to make it so. As the barrels tumbled out the stern and into the night sky, he launched consecutive azure bolts at their open ends.

The barrels exploded, setting the raining pitch on fire. Just then Faegan felt the *Tammerland* right herself into level flight. As he sensed his consciousness going, he hoped with all his heart that his timing had been right. Giving up the fight, he fell onto the wet floor.

THE MOMENT WIGG AND JESSAMAY HEARD THE STERN EXPLOSIONS they knew Faegan had been successful. With the seawater emptied from her hull, keeping the *Tammerland* airborne was much easier and she climbed faster. After leveling her off, Wigg shouted out orders to several warriors that they should rush to Faegan and bring him topside. As the warriors hurried away, everyone ran to the port gunwale and looked over the side.

Faegan's plan had been simple in concept, but given the ship's distressed condition it had been nearly impossible to achieve. As they all watched, the flaming pitch rained down on the Necrophagians; screaming, wailing, and the stench of burning flesh filled the night air.

In their mad quest to devour the fallen warriors, the beings had never seen the fiery deluge coming. As the pitch burned atop the water, the Necrophagians caught fire, their faces morphing into even more grotesque, hideously burned embodiments of what they once had been. As they died, they slipped into the deep, their destroyed faces vanishing.

Wigg quickly turned to look at the other five ships. With the Necrophagians dead, the hands of fog that had not been severed by Adrian also went under, freeing the other ships. At once the acolytes empowered the fleet. Soaring into the night sky, the majestic vessels joined the *Tammerland*.

Wigg knew that all the acolytes empowering the ships would

be exhausted. So was he! But he wanted to put as much distance as possible between the fleet and the watery Necrophagian grave site as possible. He told Tyranny so. Then there was also the problem of repairing the *Tammerland*'s damaged hull before she again rested atop the waves. But if he and Jessamay took turns flying her and resting, they could keep her aloft for some time. Smiling, he turned to look at Tyranny.

"How long will it take to repair the stern?" he asked.

"Your best estimate?" she asked Scars.

The giant first mate rubbed his chin, thinking. "If the wizard and sorceress can keep us continually aloft and the Minion carpenters are as good as I have heard, I would estimate about eight hours," he answered. "It won't be pretty, but it will hold." He gave Wigg and Jessamay a hopeful look. "Can you two keep us flying that long?" he asked.

Jessamay gave Scars a wink. "After what we've just been through, that will be the easy part," she said. "But the acolytes empowering the other ships don't have our stamina. We will have to fly in circles above them as they sail the waves and rest. But I agree with Wigg. For the time being, let's keep putting distance between us and what just happened!"

"Very well," Tyranny said to Wigg. "Steer your new course south by southwest, if you please." Then she gave him a broad smile. "I could get used to this," she added coyly. "I rather enjoy ordering wizards around!"

Wigg grinned back at the privateer. "South by southeast it is," he answered.

With that, Jessamay stopped augmenting Wigg's powers. Taking up the rest of the burden so that the sorceress could rest, Wigg altered the ship's course. The other Black Ships immediately complied.

Just then several warriors appeared. They carried Faegan in their arms. As they lowered him into his chair, Jessamay hurried over to check on him. Traax and the warriors who had been in the flooded hallway appeared, as did Adrian. The surviving warriors who had helped to pull the *Tammerland* into the air landed back on deck.

Faegan was exhausted, soaked with seawater, and shivering. Jessamay pushed some of his long salt-and-pepper hair away from his face. Tyranny and Shailiha also hurried over. The princess lovingly took the wizard's shaking hands into hers.

"Your plan worked," she said. "We're free of them!"

"So I see!" he answered, his teeth chattering. "We were fortunate! For a moment there, I thought that—"

Suddenly a torrential wind tore through the night sky, howling and shrieking, from high above. It slammed down atop the Black Ships with such force that it plunged them seaward, threatening to crash them all into the waves. Doubling his efforts, Wigg met the threat in time and righted the *Tammerland* only meters from the sea. Wheeling around, he was relieved to see that the acolytes aboard the other vessels had been equally successful. Each ship had survived, but was now flying along at the same low altitude as the *Tammerland.*

"What is it?" Shailiha shouted. "What caused that strange wind?"

Running to the port gunwale, Tyranny looked first toward the sea, then into the sky. Nothing seemed amiss.

"I don't know," she answered. "I have seen severe wind shears out here before, but nothing so powerful as that. It was almost like—"

Then the sudden wind came again, howling and thundering its way down from the heavens. This time Wigg and the acolytes were better prepared. Even so, it was all they could do to keep their ships steady, to say nothing of gaining altitude. But unlike before, this time the wind didn't abate. It just kept coming, forcing Wigg to use all his powers to keep the *Tammerland* under control. That was when the thunder and lightning started.

As he tried desperately to keep the *Tammerland* steady, a terrible realization overtook the First Wizard. He looked frantically at Faegan. Silently confirming Wigg's suspicions, Faegan nodded back darkly, then pounded the arms of his chair in frustration.

"How could I have been so blind?" he raged into the night. "We have just caused our own deaths!"

As lightning tore across the sky in unbelievable patterns and the thunder roared, the sea became illuminated like it was daytime. Thirty-foot swells started overtaking the already-treacherous Sea of Whispers, their tips smashing into the ships' keels.

This was no sudden storm, Wigg knew. This was the craft at work, and there would be no escape from it. Nor was there time to explain it to the others. *At least we were aloft and our sails were furled when it hit us,* he realized. Had the ships been sailing atop the ocean, the entire fleet would be lost.

Centuries ago, the Necrophagians had been brought under the *Pon Q'tar*'s control by Forestallment, Wigg realized. Now that they were dead, their Necrophagians' Forestallments were being released, just as they always were on the death of their hosts' endowed blood. But the dead Necrophagians hadn't been just any practitioners—they had once been members of the Ones Who Came Before—with powers to match.

Suddenly the memory of the dying sorceresses of the Coven went through Wigg's mind. When they had perished, the release of the sorceresses' combined Forestallments had shaken the mighty Recluse to destruction. But because of the Ones' once far greater gifts, the First Wizard knew that what the helpless fleet was about to experience would be far worse.

Suddenly another lightning flash came, lighting up the night. He looked up in horror to see a terrible sight.

Her acolyte apparently unable to keep control, the *Cavalon* had somehow come to a place directly above and at cross angles to the *Tammerland.* Then the heavens let loose again, sending down another terrible blast of wind.

While Wigg watched in horror, the *Cavalon*'s massive hull came plummeting straight down toward the *Tammerland.* As the flagship's masts snapped in two like so many matchsticks against the *Cavalon*'s keel, all Wigg could do was to brace for the impact, and pray.

V

THE PON O'TAR

CHAPTER XLI

The Heretics are to be feared; that much shall be true for as long as the great schism between the Vigors and the Vagaries goes unhealed. But it is the Pon Q'tar—in all its terrible secrecy and wonderment—that shall remain the even greater threat.

—PAGE 688, CHAPTER II OF THE PROPHECIES OF THE TOME

"DISMISS YOUR HANDMAIDENS," THE VOICES CALLED OUT TO SERENA'S mind. *"It is again time to commune with you."*

At first Serena was surprised by the voices' sudden arrival. Then she smiled as she realized that she shouldn't be. She had hoped that she would soon commune with the Heretics of the Guild. Ensconced as she was on this lonely island, only they could rightfully inform her of recent developments, and her hunger for news grew by the moment.

Turning, she looked at the two handmaidens. "Leave me," she ordered. With deep bows, the women walked to the double doors and quietly showed themselves out.

As she stood alone in Clarice's crypt, Serena obediently waited for the Heretics to address her again. It was just after dawn at the Citadel, and golden rays were starting to shine through the crypt's angled skylights. Like every morning, fresh rose petals littered the floor, their fragrant bouquet filling the air.

Walking to the pink marble altar, she looked down into her dead daughter's face. She gently placed one palm against the corpse's cold cheek. *Soon,* she thought.

"Serena," the voices came again. *"Return your thoughts to us."*

Taking a deep breath, the Citadel queen brought her mind back to the task at hand. *"I am here,"* she answered.

She realized that there was something different about the

voices this time. They remained a chorus of immense beauty, comprised of male and female members. But today they sounded even lovelier and more commanding.

Feeling her endowed blood rise, she found herself drawn to the voices as never before. Overcome by an irresistible sense of reverence, she went to her knees and bowed her head.

"We have news of the enemy fleet," the voices said to her mind. *"The Conclave intends to take the Citadel, and to capture you and the Vagaries scroll. We ordered the Necrophagians to destroy them. But the Vigors wizards and their sorceress are clever. Because of their meddling, the Necrophagians are dead. For centuries they were valiant guardians of the Citadel, devouring many in our cause. But fear not, for with their deaths has come the release of the centuries-old Forestallments we employed to make them our servants. Because of this, the Conclave fleet will probably not last the night."*

Still on her knees and her eyes closed, Serena smiled. *"The Conclave's destruction will be welcome indeed,"* she answered.

"Not all of our news is heartening," the voices added. *"For reasons not yet fully understood, the Darkling has failed to deliver the* Jin'Sai *into our hands. Xanthus was able to tempt him to the Tolenkas' other side but apparently unable to imprison him there. This might be because we were forced to temporarily summon the Borderlands. If the Darkling returns to us, we mean to have our answers. But for now the* Jin'Sai *has somehow managed to return to Eutracia. He has enlisted the aid of others, and he wears the Paragon. But he poses little threat. With the imminent destruction of the Conclave fleet, even he will be unable to affect the outcome of our mission."*

"What of Einar's and Reznik's research?" Serena asked eagerly. *"Does it progress well?"*

"Yes," the voices answered. *"They have found Failee's unfinished spell and have started their work. Even so, we order you to stay at the Citadel. Should the Conclave somehow survive, only you can protect the island and its ancient treasures. Your journey to the Recluse will come soon enough."*

Although she was disappointed, Serena understood. *"Very well,"* she answered. *"I will do as you say. But my eagerness to be apprised of our progress knows no bounds."*

"We understand, our child," the voices said. *"To that end, we are about to grant you a formula of the craft. As you see the azure*

numbers and symbols start to swirl in your mind, do not be afraid."

Serena saw a craft formula appear against the darkness of her closed eyes. The calculation was elegant. As she knew, craft formulas always stemmed from one or more of the Paragon's many jeweled facets. Although this new spell's use escaped her, she recognized it as being one from the Temporal facet.

"Recite the spell, Serena," the voices said. *"Do not be afraid; it will not harm you. Bring it forth while thinking of Einar and Reznik and behold its wonders."*

Serena recited the spell while doing her best to envision Einar and Reznik. For several minutes she concentrated that way. Finally she opened her eyes.

At first she didn't see the pale azure light, and she feared that she had failed. But as the light materialized, it slowly overtook the room. Standing, she turned to look toward one of the crypt's four corners.

The light was forming into a glowing star. Without warning it flashed brightly, then spread out to become an azure cube. Entranced, she stepped nearer.

It was unlike anything she had seen. The newly formed cube was about one meter square and hovered at shoulder height. The blurred scene it displayed was tinged with azure. Just then sounds started coming from it, and its imprisoned image came into sharper focus. As Serena took a quick breath her eyes widened with surprise.

She was seeing and hearing Einar and Reznik as they went about their grisly work in the depths of the Recluse. Starting to understand, she stepped nearer. The scene was ghostly. She was looking through the cube rather than at it. Traces of the crypt's marble wall showed through from the opposite side of the cube.

"It's a miracle," she thought, relaying her wonderment to her masters.

"There are no miracles of the craft, our child," the voices answered. *"There are only things that you have not yet learned. Behold, and view but one of the Vagaries' many wonders."*

Einar, Reznik, and Actinius were standing in a stone room. Research materials lay scattered about, as did variously shaped bottles and vials. The magnificent Vagaries scroll hovered in one corner. To one side, a naked man lay atop a stone table. His skin pallor told Serena that he was dead.

Looking further, she saw that a craft formula hovered in the room and its azure numbers and symbols glowed brightly. It was the most elegant and complex series of calculations she had ever seen.

"Is that Failee's lost spell?" she asked her masters. *"The one that you say Einar and Reznik found?"*

"Yes," the voices answered.

After carefully measuring out some of the contents from two bottles into a shallow mortar, Reznik ground them with a pestle. When he was satisfied he poured some of the mixture onto a pair of weighted scales. After removing several pinches of the mixture and casting them aside, the trays balanced to his satisfaction.

"What's different about your potion this time?" Serena heard Einar ask. His voice was so clear that he might have been standing alongside her.

"The last subject's liver sample made me suspect that ground savannah twig might aid Failee's spell," the herbmaster replied. "It's rare, and has long been known as a potent stimulant. It also warms the blood, making it good for frostbite."

Reznik walked to another table. Taking up a piece of cured leather, he grasped a pair of scissors in his other hand then cut a crude circle from it. He quickly threaded a leather thong around the circle's circumference. He knotted the ends of the thong and pulled on them to create a simple leather bag. Taking up his herbal mixture, he poured it into the bag, drew the thong tight, and knotted the bag closed.

"What is that?" Einar asked.

"It is called an herbmaster's sachet," Reznik answered. "They have many uses, most of them medicinal. In some cases they can be used as protective amulets. But no partial adept has ever put one to such an important a purpose as we."

Reznik walked to the corpse and placed the string around the dead man's neck so that the sachet lay atop his breastbone. He looked over at Einar.

"You may start," he said. "I will call a spell allowing everyone to hear the results."

Looking to the hovering formula, Einar started reciting the incantation. As he did, Reznik started reciting one of his own.

Almost immediately the sachet quivered atop the dead man's skin. Wispy smoke started snaking its way free from the bag.

Reznik was converting the herbal mixture to a vaporous form, Serena realized. The image was so clear and bright that she thought she could almost smell Reznik's burning concoction as it climbed into the air.

Fascinated by the process, Serena watched as the wispy smoke collected to a place just above the dead man's heart. The collecting smoke started whirling into a funnel shape. Its bottom point became no larger than a pinhead, and its top stretched about six inches across. Then the maelstrom's point seemed to somehow penetrate the man's skin, and the whirling funnel disappeared into his body without leaving a wound. Within seconds it was gone.

Reznik removed the sachet from around the man's neck and cast it aside, then started reciting another incantation.

Einar finished his reading and turned away from Failee's unfinished formula to look at Reznik. Moments later, Serena and the others heard the welcome telltale sound. Her heart was overjoyed.

In the silence of the stony room, the dead man's heart was beating again. His lungs started to rise and fall in jerking, staggered lurches. One quivering finger rose from his right hand, then fell again. As the methodical thumping of the man's heart filled the room, Reznik looked up from the corpse to smile at Einar. Serena's lead consul smiled back.

Suddenly the man's eyes opened wide, and he breathed a desperate gasp. His heartbeat stopped. Sighing, Reznik removed his spectacles and scrubbed his face in frustration.

Einar shook his head. "Another failure," he said.

Reznik looked up and arranged the glasses on his face. "To you, perhaps," he said. "But I see it as a success. The subject's heartbeat lasted longer this time, and he raised one finger. I believe the addition of the savannah twig brought his motor skills alive—something to remember for next time. We haven't reached our goal, but we're on the right track."

Einar looked over at Actinius. "Bring us another one. The day is young." He then regarded Reznik. "I suggest that you do what you can to strengthen your potion. The queen will be here soon. She has a personal stake in this process, and will expect nothing less than complete success."

With a nod, Reznik walked to consult a leather-bound volume while Actinius heaved the corpse over his back. Actinius carried the corpse from the chamber. Although her mystics' success had not lasted, Serena was encouraged.

"Our servants continue to advance their knowledge," she said to the Heretics. *"I am pleased. But time is of the essence."*

"Yes," the voices answered. *"You may now conjure the panel to view Einar and Reznik's progress whenever you please. They will never know that you are watching."*

"Forgive me, but I have a question," Serena said.

"You have but to ask, our child," the voices answered.

"The timbre of your voices has changed," she said. *"As you speak to me this time, I find my blood is drawn to you more than ever before. Are you the same beings who first entered my mind to tell me that my husband had perished, and that it had been the* Jin'Sai *who killed my child?"*

"The beings who first contacted your mind were indeed Heretics of the Guild," the voices answered, *"but they were not us. They were lesser practitioners. Because the* Jin'Sai *has returned to Eutracia, we have decided to take up in their stead. We are the supreme masters of the Vagaries. We are the ruling body of clerics known as the* Pon Q'tar.*"*

Serena again went to her knees. *"What are your orders?"* she asked.

"Prepare to use the safeguards the lesser Heretics showed you, should it become necessary to protect the Citadel," the voices answered. *"When the Conclave fleet is resting on the bottom of the Sea of Whispers, we will again reveal ourselves to your mind."*

"On my life," Serena answered.

With that, she sensed the *Pon Q'tar*'s mental link drift away to nothingness. She waved a hand and watched the azure cube disappear.

As she strode through the lush petals and back to the altar, she plucked Wulfgar's dead rose from her gown's cleavage, then bent down, and lovingly stroked it across Clarice's cheek.

After a time, she turned and left the crypt. The marble doors closed behind her with finality, sealing inside the many secrets she hoped would soon change the world.

CHAPTER XLII

AS YET ANOTHER LIGHTNING BOLT SHOT DOWN FROM THE RUMbling heavens, Wigg suddenly felt the *Tammerland* lurch forward. The vessel's unexpected rise in speed was unlike anything he had ever experienced aboard a Black Ship.

Looking up, he saw the *Cavalon*'s dark keel plummeting downward. But because of the *Tammerland*'s unexplained impetus, the *Cavalon* was quickly nearing the flagships' stern, rather than coming down amidships. Even so, there was no doubt that the two Black Ships would collide. The only question was how badly.

With only moments to spare, Wigg frantically looked aft. Straining with everything they had, Faegan and Jessamay were calling the craft, speeding the *Tammerland* to help avoid a point-blank collision. Adding his gifts to theirs, Wigg called on all his remaining power. But even the three gifted mystics could not change the inevitable.

With a mighty crash, the *Cavalon*'s bow crashed down onto the *Tammerland*'s already-damaged stern. As the *Cavalon*'s metal-lined keel smashed a glancing blow into the flagship, the *Tammerland*'s aft deck and gunwales crashed apart, and her stern mast snapped in two to come tumbling down. With a tortured groan, the *Cavalon*'s keel slid across and off the *Tammerland*'s stern. Both ships crashed hard onto the roiling sea.

"Angle her back into the air!" Wigg screamed at Faegan and Jessamay. "We must get airborne again, before she floods with seawater!"

Faegan and Jessamay quickly obeyed. Her bow rising, the *Tammerland* slowly took to the air, struggling against the relentless wind. Wigg looked back to see seawater again pouring from her stern. To his great relief he saw the *Cavalon* also rise. Amazingly, she seemed to have suffered little damage. That was probably because of the iron strip each Black Ship bore along her keel, he realized.

Finally the terrible weather accompanying the Necrophagians' dying Forestallments quieted. The wind returned to normal, and the sea below the *Tammerland* calmed. The sun had started peeking over the eastern horizon, bringing with it the advent of a new day. Seeing that no more seawater was pouring from the *Tammerland*'s stern, Wigg gratefully returned the ship to level flight.

Exhausted beyond measure, the First Wizard looked around. Blessedly, all six Black Ships were airborne. At first glance it seemed that only the *Tammerland* had suffered significant damage. As he set an easterly course, the fleet followed. The other Conclave members ran to meet him.

"It seems we've made it!" Shailiha said. "But what do we do now?"

Tyranny looked commandingly at Traax. The expression on her face told everyone that she was in a foul mood. Nothing incensed her as much as damage done to her precious fleet. She gave Traax a hard look.

"While the *Cavalon* is still airborne, I want you and several others to fly up and check her keel!" she ordered. "Under no condition is her acolyte captain to put her back onto the sea until she has permission from you! When the acolyte can no longer sustain flight, she is to send us a warrior telling us so. If needed, Faegan, Jessamay, or Adrian will relieve her."

Traax immediately snapped his heels and ran off to select several warrior shipwrights whom he trusted. Moments later, he and six others took to the air. Tyranny urgently waved Scars forward.

"Get as many warriors as our stern can hold and get to work on this ship!" she ordered. "Just a few moments ago, you told me that eight hours would suffice! I don't care how much new damage has been done! I want this vessel atop the waves in that same time frame, or else!"

Scars knew that when Tyranny was like this, there was nothing to say about it. He immediately ran aft, shouting out threats and orders that would have reddened the cheeks of Tammerland's most hardened brothel madam.

After angrily tousling her hair, Tyranny took a cigarillo from her vest pocket. Striking a match against one knee boot, she cupped her hands to light it. She took a deep lungful of smoke, then glared angrily at Faegan.

"That was fancy work," she said, "killing the Necrophagians that way. I must say that I've never seen anything like it. But then I heard you castigating yourself. So what in the world just happened out here? Did your wizardly solution make things worse?"

Without waiting for an answer, she turned her glaring attention toward Wigg. "I was told that these endowed ships were impervious to damage!" she said.

Wigg raised an eyebrow. "For the most part, they are," he answered quietly. "But not against each other, or the power of the Necrophagians."

Sighing, Faegan looked up at Tyranny. He was still soaked and shaking from the cold. He knew that Tyranny didn't mean to be harsh with everyone; that was just her way of getting rid of frustration. Even so, she deserved an explanation. His teeth still chattering, he coughed before answering.

"I forgot to take something into account," he answered.

"I'm listening," she said.

"The Heretics apparently controlled the Necrophagians with Forestallments, laced into their blood centuries ago," Wigg answered for Faegan. "When we killed them, their Forestallments died with them. The resulting reaction is always the same—amazing lightning, thunder, and wind. The more powerful the practitioner, the more powerful are the atmospheric events when he or she dies. These were the strongest we have ever seen. We were lucky to survive."

After taking another drag on her cigarillo, Tyranny seemed calmer. Sighing, she tousled her hair again.

"I'm sorry," she said. "It's just that as the fleet's captain, it's my job to get these ships to the Citadel in one piece. Once we're there, the rest of you may give me all the orders you like. But until then these ships are mine."

"I understand," Faegan said. "You carry much on your shoulders. We all do. Even so, in a way, I'm sorry to have killed them."

"Why?" Shailiha asked.

"Because if our assumptions about them are correct, the Necrophagians were once members of the Ones Who Came Before," Jessamay answered. "Given enough time we might have been able to find a way to set them free. They would have been invaluable allies. But we'll never know."

As the sun rose in earnest, a respectful silence fell over the Conclave members. Tyranny dropped her cigarillo to the deck and crushed it beneath her boot. Faegan looked wistfully out to sea.

Shailiha walked over to put one arm around Faegan's shoulders. As she did, the old wizard turned to look at the *Tammerland*'s ravaged stern. He shook his head.

"What have I done?" he breathed.

Squatting down, Shailiha took his hands into hers and looked into his eyes. "You did what you do best," she answered. "You cheated death and gave us the chance to fight the Vagaries another day."

Faegan finally smiled. "Thank you," he said. He looked at Wigg. "The Necrophagians mentioned a group of Vagaries mystics called the *Pon Q'tar,*" he mused. "Have you heard the phrase before?"

Wigg shook his head. "No," he answered.

"Nor have I," Jessamay added.

"How much longer can you keep us aloft?" Faegan asked Wigg.

"Two hours at best," Wigg answered. "That's all I have left in me."

Faegan nodded. "When you can do no more, one of us will relieve you. In the meantime I suggest that we all get some rest. I fear that what we just experienced will pale compared with the greeting we will get at the Citadel."

Just then they all heard saws and hammers working, and Minions urgently ordering one another about. Although the noises were chaotic, they also sounded hopeful.

But as the Black Ship fleet flew east into the rising sun, Faegan's warning about the Citadel clawed at every Conclave member's heart.

Chapter XLIII

"When we get there, Ox want go inside with *Jin'Sai,*" the giant warrior said. His barrel chest puffed out with pride against his body armor. "This may be dangerous place. Me protect you."

Tristan shook his head. "From what Abbey tells me, that's not true. I'll be fine. Even so, this isn't the best of neighborhoods. Someone needs to guard the carriage, and I can think of no one better qualified than you."

A disappointed look came over the warrior's face. "Ox obey," he said. "But Ox no like it."

Tristan gave him a reassuring smile. "I know," he said. "But that's an order."

The prince looked out the carriage window. It was midday, and the sky was sunny. Shannon the Small sat up top, driving the team and doing his best to follow the directions Abbey had given him.

Two days had passed since Tristan had arrived in Tammerland, and he was glad to be home. To save time, he and Rafe had come by Minion litter. The entire Clan Kilbourne was following with their wagons. Hector and the other warriors were traveling with them, providing protection and helping them make the journey. Shaking his head, Tristan found himself wondering for the hundredth time whether he was doing the right thing. Then his mind turned to Yasmin.

Their night together had been wonderful, but it hadn't been love. Rather, it was the urgent, needful joining of two people who wished, however briefly, to explore and possess one another. She had again reached for him in the cozy embrace of her shopworn wagon, and he had obeyed. After awaking in each other's arms, she changed the dressing on his wound and fixed him a hearty highlander breakfast. She had then kissed him and bid him good-bye.

She gave me more than just her companionship, he realized as he watched Tammerland's busy streets go by. *Without knowing it, she also set me free. I will always treasure my time with Celeste. But my heart is again my own.*

Soon his mind turned to other matters. Abbey had been overjoyed to see him, as had Ox and the palace gnomes. But when Tristan had introduced Rafe to the herbmistress and explained his agreement with the Kilbourne clan elders, he had thought Abbey might have a heart attack. She had angrily pulled Tristan aside to demand if he had suddenly gone crazy.

Tristan had been polite but firm. In the end, all Abbey could do was roll her eyes and mutter, "Just wait until Wigg and Faegan get home!" Tristan had smiled at that, saying that her matronly admonishment reminded him of the kind of warning his mother had often given him. It had the same lack of effect then too, he had told her with a smile.

Tristan had refused to argue about the highlanders further, and asked Ox to assign Rafe quarters in the palace. But the prince was no fool. Although he wanted Rafe where he could easily confer with him, he had no plans to allow him access to the palace's many treasures. In the end he had granted Rafe the run of the place, provided he was accompanied by a Minion warrior. Rafe had understood. In his customary style, he laughingly told Tristan that if the roles were reversed, he would do the same.

Over dinner that night, Tristan and Abbey had traded tales. Their talk had gone on for hours. As she listened, Abbey's eyes had grown to the size of hen's eggs. Even though the amazing story came directly from the *Jin'Sai,* she'd found much of it simply too unbelievable for words. Tristan had understood her skepticism. Had these things not happened to him personally, he would have been equally incredulous.

He'd been immensely glad to learn that Faegan had recovered from Xanthus' attack, and that the Conclave possessed the index to the two scrolls. But he was desperately worried for the fleet as it neared the Citadel, and he felt powerless because he could not warn them. He'd been astonished to learn that a Forestallment calculation existed for *K'Shari,* and that some Fledgling House survivors had returned. But what had intrigued him most was Aeolus. With little else to occupy him until Clan Kilbourne arrived or the fleet returned, Tristan had resolved that he would try to meet him.

To that end he had sent a warrior to the Serpent and the Sword with a handwritten parchment, asking for a personal audience the following day. Aeolus had sent word back that he accepted.

Tristan suddenly felt the carriage jerk to a stop. He and Ox climbed out to look up and down the street. The neighborhood had clearly seen better days, forcing Tristan to wonder why a man of Aeolus' character would choose to live here.

After tying the reins around the carriage's brake handle, Shannon left his ale jug behind for once and clambered his way down from the seat. As he came to stand by Ox, his head barely reached the warrior's knee. They were an incongruous pair, to say the least. Even so, Tristan would have been hard-pressed to guess which was the most stubborn. He gave them a commanding look.

"Don't go wandering off," he warned. "I want this carriage here when I return."

Ox obediently clicked his heels together. Shannon's only answer was a sudden puff of smoke coiling up from his corncob pipe.

Tristan turned to look at the house's weathered sign. As Abbey had said, it carried a serpent on one side and a sword on the other. Without further ado he climbed the steps and knocked on the door.

The door opened to show an attractive middle-aged woman. She was dressed in a white long-sleeved blouse that crisscrossed her chest. Her black split skirt spilled down over bare feet. Although her garb wasn't bizarre, Tristan couldn't recall seeing anything quite like it.

"May I help you?" she asked.

"Yes," he answered. "I am Prince Tristan. I have an appointment with your master."

As the woman looked him up and down her eyes lingered briefly on the dreggan hilt and dirk handles showing just above his right shoulder. A martial student's curiosity, he assumed. She seemed unimpressed.

"We are aware of your appointment," she answered emotionlessly. "Come in."

As the door shut, Ox clenched his jaw and stared moodily at the forlorn building. Shannon snickered at him.

"What are you so worried about?" the gnome asked. "He was taking care of himself long before he met you! Best swordsman in the kingdom, he is!"

Ox grumpily folded his arms over his chest, then leaned back against the carriage, giving Shannon the impression that he would wait forever, if need be.

Tristan followed the woman down a long, paper-paned hallway. Everything was just as Abbey had described. But the house's exterior had been deceiving, belying the spaciousness inside. When they reached the hallway's end the woman opened another door and beckoned Tristan through.

Surprisingly, the door led outside again. A beautiful courtyard lay just beyond. The woman turned to Tristan.

"Wait here," she said.

She went down another set of steps and into the courtyard proper. As she did, Tristan took in the interesting scene.

The rear courtyard was spacious and surrounded by a high stone wall. Most of the area was taken up by a perfectly manicured lawn. Pebble pathways snaked through it here and there. A large dogwood tree stood in one of the far corners, its leaves casting welcoming shade. Beneath the tree sat a table and four chairs. But what Tristan found most interesting were the people, and what they were doing.

About forty students of varying ages and both sexes were in training. Everyone was dressed the same way as the woman who had led him here. Standing in strict lines, each person held a wooden staff. A man dressed in similar garb stood before the students, his broad back toward the prince and his bald head shining in the sun. That would be Aeolus, Tristan reasoned. As Tristan watched Aeolus move with effortless grace, something told him that the old master already knew he was there.

Raising his staff high, Aeolus took a practiced step forward, then cut the staff through the air in a perfect circle. At once, every student followed suit. Tristan watched respectfully as the sword training went on for several more minutes. Then the woman walked up to Aeolus and whispered something in his ear. Without turning around, Aeolus nodded.

He laid his staff in the grass, then clapped his hands. With military precision, the students quickly sat on their knees, then bowed deeply at the waist. Aeolus clapped his hands again; then the students disbanded to enter the house through a separate doorway.

Without looking at Tristan, Aeolus took up his staff. He

walked to the table beneath the shade tree and sat down. The woman returned to Tristan's side.

"He will see you now," she said.

"Thank you," he answered. A sudden thought crossed his mind. "Shall I give you my weapons?" he asked.

For the first time since meeting him, the woman smiled. "That won't be necessary," she answered. "You couldn't kill him on your best day."

As Tristan raised an eyebrow she gave him another smile, then entered the house, leaving him and Aeolus alone in the courtyard.

Tristan crossed the grass to come and stand by the table. Aeolus came to his feet and bowed. Unsure of the school's etiquette, Tristan decided to bow in return.

Aeolus smiled. "At long last the *Jin'Sai* is among us," he said. "I have met the *Jin'Saiou,* but I'm sure you already know that. It is a pleasure to be in your company."

"And yours," Tristan answered.

Aeolus beckoned Tristan to sit while he did the same. The prince was glad of the shade.

"To what do I owe the honor of this visit?" Aeolus asked.

Tristan was already impressed with the centuries-old wizard and martial expert sitting across from him. Even so, he had questions. He decided to come straight to the point. He settled into the chair and crossed one leg over the other.

"It isn't every day that Wigg offers someone a seat on the Conclave of the Vigors," he said.

Aeolus nodded. "I'm sure," he answered. "So you came to see me for yourself."

"Yes," Tristan answered. "And I wish to ask you some questions."

"By all means," Aeolus answered.

"Please understand that I welcome your membership, provided my concerns are answered," the prince said. "Your wisdom would be of great help. Our current foes are the deadliest we have ever faced."

"I have yet to decide," Aeolus said, "but I thank you for the offer. What troubles you?"

"Satine," Tristan answered simply. "I was the one who killed her."

A touch of sadness crossed Aeolus' face. "I know," he answered. "I couldn't persuade her from straying from my teachings."

"So I have been told," Tristan said. "I want you to know that I had no choice but to kill her. She was the best I ever saw. I was lucky to keep my life."

Leaning forward, Tristan looked deep into Aeolus' eyes. "I must know that no bitterness lingers in your heart about her death," he said. "If it does, I must oppose your membership. It would be disruptive to the Conclave, and we need all the cohesiveness we can muster right now."

As he sat back in his chair, Tristan remembered what the Envoys had told him about the Heretics' mad plan. Even he could scarcely believe it. Serena had to be stopped at any cost. Should Aeolus choose to join them, he wanted to be absolutely sure about the old wizard's feelings.

"I hold no bitterness toward you," Aeolus answered. "You have told me that you did what you had to do, and I believe you."

Relieved for the time being, Tristan took up his next question. "Tell me," he asked, "are you really as good as they say?"

"Yes," Aeolus answered. "I do not mean to brag. But to state otherwise would be a lie."

"I mean no disrespect, but I find that hard to believe," Tristan said. "Especially considering the amazing tales Abbey told me about your skills."

After giving Tristan a smile, Aeolus stood. Finding himself a bit confused, Tristan stood with him.

"Come with me," Aeolus said.

They walked across the grass for a time. On reaching the courtyard's center, Aeolus stopped and turned to look at Tristan.

"Draw your sword and do your best to kill me," he said simply.

Tristan shook his head. "I understand what you're trying to do," he answered. "It isn't necessary. I ask for no proof other than your word."

Aeolus smiled. "Wigg tells me that you and your sister are very stubborn," he said. "That having been said, I want no doubt to linger about this. Do it, *Jin'Sai*. Unsheathe your sword."

Perhaps it was Tristan's intense curiosity about all things martial that persuaded him. Or it might have been the commanding nature of the old wizard's gaze. But for whatever reason, Tristan found himself reaching behind his back.

The dreggan's handle came surely into his right hand. As he

pulled the sword free, its blade rang in the air and glinted brightly in the sunlight.

"Whenever you're ready," Aeolus said.

Taking a deep stance, Tristan raised the dreggan overhead with both hands, holding its blade parallel to the ground and its tip pointing directly at Aeolus. Surprisingly, Aeolus assumed no defensive posture. He simply stood in place, his dark eyes locked on Tristan's. Swiveling both arms, Tristan brought the blade around with everything he had.

At first the prince was sure that Aeolus was about to die. Standing stock-still, the master waited patiently for the blade to reach him. Then he simply wasn't there.

The heavy blade hummed through the air with such speed that it nearly took Tristan around with it. Looking leftward, he saw Aeolus calmly standing about two meters away. His hands were placidly crossed before him.

"Again," Aeolus said.

Feinting high, Tristan quickly reversed his blade's direction, then brought it around and down. Designed to deprive an enemy of his legs, it was a technique that had served him well in battle.

Again the blade went whistling around, striking nothing. Aeolus had moved to the right this time.

Catching his breath, Tristan glared at him. "Are you using the craft to summon that amazing speed?" he demanded.

Aeolus shook his head. "No," he answered simply. "Now then, one more time, if you please."

Tristan did not wish to hurt Aeolus, but he had become determined to succeed at this in some fashion—even if it only meant his blade touching the master's clothing. Taking the sword into both hands again, he reclaimed his stance.

As quickly as he could he drove the sword's point straight ahead, directly toward Aeolus' abdomen. But like the other times, the sword struck nothing.

Suddenly Tristan felt a sharp pain in his sword hand. He felt himself being launched into the air; then he landed hard on his back. He was dazed, but conscious enough to realize that his sword was gone. The force that had taken him off his feet had been unexpected, irresistible.

As his vision cleared, he raised up onto his elbows. Aeolus was standing over him with his dreggan in his hands. The old master was calmly examining the blade in the sunlight. He looked down at Tristan and smiled again.

"My apologies," he said. "It seems that you have never been taught how to fall properly." Holding one hand out, he helped Tristan to his feet. "That is the first thing we teach here."

Scowling, the prince rubbed the back of his neck. "How did you do that?"

Aeolus handed the sword to him. "It is merely a technique, much like many others," Aeolus answered. "But like all neophytes, you're missing the point of the lesson."

"Which is?" Tristan asked as he sheathed his sword.

"If you cannot kill me while I am unarmed, then how could you ever hope to best me if I had sword in my hand?" Aeolus answered.

Shaking his head again, Tristan smiled. "I stand convinced," he said. "Even so, I have another question."

"By all means," Aeolus answered.

"Do you really command *K'Shari*?" he asked.

"Yes," Aeolus answered. "For me, *K'Shari* was attained only by a lifetime of intense training. But Wigg told me that a Forestallment calculation exists for imbuing the talent directly into one's endowed blood. What an amazing concept! A lifetime of work, condensed and gifted in only a few moments. But as I'm sure you know, little is impossible when the craft is involved."

"With your indulgence, I wish to see proof that you command the gift," Tristan said.

Aeolus nodded. "I understand. But tell me—will you truly recognize it when you see it?"

As Tristan thought back to the times that Xanthus had been forced into torturing and killing innocent Eutracians, his face darkened. "I am all too familiar with its effects," he answered.

Aeolus nodded. "If that is true, then you are one of the world's few," he said. "Wigg told me about Xanthus, by the way."

Aeolus turned to look toward the courtyard's rear wall. Taking a deep breath, he calmed himself.

"My ears hear no begging," he said quietly. "My eyes see no pain. My heart feels no remorse."

At once the courtyard quieted. The singing birds and buzzing insects hushed and the wind stopped, stilling the tree branches. A deathly, almost familiar silence overtook everything, like nature's life forces had somehow ceased to exist.

Tristan took a few steps closer to the martial master and looked into his face. The old wizard's visage showed no strain whatsoever. For Aeolus, it seemed that calling forth *K'Shari* was as natural as drawing his next breath. Even so, Tristan couldn't imagine the degree of hardship, sacrifice, and training that must have been required to reach this level of enlightenment—especially without help from the craft.

"Again, I stand convinced," he said quietly.

Aeolus opened his eyes. Almost at once everything returned to normal. His gaze toward the prince was calm, knowing.

"You burn with curiosity for all things martial, do you not?" he asked.

Tristan nodded. "How did you know?" he asked.

"I can see it in your eyes. Satine had much the same look. It never left her."

Aeolus led them back to the table, and they both sat. As he leaned closer, a concerned look came over his face.

"When the Conclave returns, you have every intention of asking Wigg to imbue your blood with its calculations, don't you?" he asked.

Tristan was taken aback. That was indeed his desire, and had been ever since learning of the Forestallment. He knew that if Serena could be stopped and he returned to Crysenium as the Envoys wanted, commanding *K'Shari* might be immensely useful.

"Yes," he answered. "How did you know?"

Aeolus smiled. "It was by no wizardly use of the craft that I guessed your intentions," he answered. "It was simple logic. Who among us interested in the martial ways would not want such a thing? And to gain it so quickly and easily! What a feat that would be!"

Tristan looked down at his hands for a moment. "Quickly, yes," he answered. "But perhaps not easily. Sometimes imbuing Forestallments into endowed blood causes terrible pain. I know firsthand. Under Failee's orders, the sorceress Succiu placed many Forestallments into my blood against my will, and all at once. They are gone now. But the pain is not something I wish to reexperience. Even so, I believe that *K'Shari* would be worth it."

A faraway look came into Aeolus' eyes. "Succiu," he said softly. "What a beautiful but evil woman. Her devotion to the Vagaries was unquestionable."

"You knew her?" Tristan asked.

"I knew all the sorceresses of the Coven," Aeolus answered, "and Failee best of all. Those were such dark days for Wigg. I am truly glad that he and Abbey have found a measure of happiness."

"I have a request of you," Tristan said.

"And that is?"

"Come take up residence in the palace and train me—if only for a little while," Tristan asked. "Abbey told me what you said about *K'Shari*—about how someone so quickly imbued with its Forestallment might need specialized physical training as well, so as to hone the gift. I'm not asking you to give up your life here and join the Conclave—that is up to you to decide. Nor do I think it wise that I explain all of what we are up against, unless you join us. But I am asking you to do something to help the Vigors in its hour of need."

Aeolus thought for a moment. "Do you have any idea when the Conclave might return?" he asked.

"Not really," Tristan answered. "I ordered them to attack the Citadel, a Vagaries stronghold. None of us knows what awaits them there. I can only hope that they will be successful, and that they will all return safely."

Aeolus sighed, then nodded. "In the interests of the Vigors I will do this thing for you," he said. "But I have conditions."

"Name them," Tristan answered.

"During our training sessions you will abide by my orders," Aeolus said. "We train where I say and when I say. Time might be short before the Conclave returns. You will be a mere beginning student and I the master. During our sessions neither your royal heritage nor the fact that you are the *Jin'Sai* will have any meaning for me. You must be prepared to train like you have never trained before. Nor will you question my orders, no matter how bizarre they might seem. In these things I will brook no disagreement."

"Done," Tristan answered. "Is there anything else?"

"I reserve the right to leave whenever I wish, and again take up my teaching here," Aeolus said, "whether I have done all for you that I can or not."

Tristan thought about that for a moment. After having spent this time with him, Tristan would have preferred that Aeolus stay on and join the Conclave. Wigg was right, he realized. Aeolus would make an invaluable addition to the group. But Aeolus' demands seemed firm.

"Very well," Tristan said. "I accept your conditions. But if duty calls I will feel free to walk away from a training session without your permission."

"Of course," Aeolus answered.

"When can we expect you?" Tristan asked. "I will tell the palace gnomes to make your quarters ready."

"Sometime tomorrow," Aeolus answered. "I need to settle some things here and select a student to carry on in my stead while I am away."

"A Minion warrior awaits me on the street to take me home," Tristan said. "I would be happy to tell him to stay and escort you to the palace tomorrow."

Smiling, Aeolus shook his head. "As you have seen, I have no need of your warrior's protection. I might be old, but I'm not senile. I remember the way to the palace well enough."

Tristan smiled. "Of course," he answered. He stood from the table and reached out his right hand.

"Until tomorrow," he said.

The two shook hands. Tristan found Aeolus' grip firm and dry.

"Until tomorrow," the master answered. "Sleep well, Prince. Shortly after my arrival we will start."

Tristan nodded, then started the long walk back to the house. As Aeolus watched him go, his thoughts turned to the future.

He will be good, that one, he thought. *But he will also be headstrong and impatient. He will want to run when I command him to walk. There is a natural quickness and an inherent ability in him that few possess. Satine was one of them.*

Sighing, Aeolus shook his head. He would never have thought that he would become the willing teacher of the one who had killed Satine. It seemed that his life was about to come full circle.

As the insects buzzed and the birds sang, the old teacher sat there for some time before returning to the house to inform his students.

Chapter XLIV

From the depths of his imprisonment, Xanthus wept. Time had no meaning here, and trying to guess how long he had been in this place was impossible.

Crouching naked on the filthy floor, he had no idea why his revered masters were treating him this way. During his unexpected march through the Borderlands with the *Jin'Sai,* he had seen Tristan suddenly fall prey to one of the red desert's great sinkholes. He had told them that simple truth over and over again, but to no avail.

Deprived of his gifts and condemned to human form only, Xanthus tried to peer into the dark. Even after days of confinement, he could see nothing in the impenetrable darkness. Food was lowered to him by way of an azure column, its brightness stabbing his eyes. During all other times only darkness reigned. Biting rats and his own decaying excrement took up what space the filthy floor had to offer.

Standing weakly, he reached out to touch the unforgiving prison surrounding him. The deep hole into which he had been lowered was cylindrical, and its sidewalls were constructed of rough-hewn stone blocks. He had tried several times to climb the blocks in the darkness, only to fall back again. Realizing that escape was impossible, he had finally given up trying.

Weeping again, he held his head in his hands. *Why have my masters forsaken me?* his soul cried out. *I did my best to fulfill my mission. Yet I find myself here, in this terrible place. The* Jin'-Sai'*s death was not my fault. Stripped of my gifts and my Darkling side, I am totally helpless. Even my command over* K'Shari *has been taken from me.*

Imperial Order Guards had come for him once already. He had been interrogated with such viciousness that he had been sure he would die. All he could tell his captors was the same truth over and over again, for that was all he remembered. After repeatedly bringing him to the cusp of death, they had finally stopped. His interrogators were experts. They could keep him on death's knife edge for years if they chose to.

"Bring that traitorous filth back up into the light," he suddenly heard a voice say from above. "He is to be questioned again."

From high above, an azure light shaft streaked down into the hole, illuminating Xanthus and his dank cell. As the azure gleam struck his light-unaccustomed eyes he cried out in pain.

The descending light shaft stopped about one meter above where he crouched. Tentacles formed at its base, then snaked downward to wrap themselves under his arms. Gripping him by his shoulders, the beam of light started silently lifting him upward. He could do nothing but let it happen.

On finally reaching the top, he fell to his knees. As the light beam started dragging him across the floor, the onetime Darkling fell unconscious.

"WAKE UP, XANTHUS," SOMEONE SAID. THE VOICE WAS MALE. ITS timbre was almost fatherly, caring. "Your last session was not as productive as we had hoped. It is time for another talk."

Still unconscious, Xanthus did not hear him.

"His mind has gone deep," another said. "I suggest you wake him."

At once a jagged bolt tore through the air to strike Xanthus in the face. As his head snapped back he screamed aloud and his body jerked uncontrollably. He slowly came around.

"That's better," one of them said.

Xanthus gingerly opened his eyes. Blessedly, the room was dark, and its contents were bathed in shadows. Looking around drunkenly, he tried to take stock of his situation.

Like the time before, he was seated in a simple wooden chair. An azure glow shone down from above, encircling him. More bands of azure light secured his hands and feet to the chair. Prior experience told him that the craft's harsh embrace would grant no slack. Straining his eyes, he tried to discern what lay before him in the shadows.

Thirteen figures faced him. About three meters away, they sat next to one another behind a rectangular table. Cloak hoods surrounded their shadowed heads, making their facial features indistinguishable. He neared unconsciousness again, and his head slumped forward to his chest.

Despite his grogginess, Xanthus suddenly realized that this time he was not in the presence of Imperial Order troops. A shock went through him as he understood his new interrogators' identities. He was sitting across from *Pon Q'tar* clerics. What little mercy he had experienced before would not be granted again.

"You told us that the *Jin'Sai* perished in the Borderlands," one of them said. "Yet we know that he has returned to Eutracia. Worse, he has sent the Conclave to do battle against the Citadel queen, and to capture the Scroll of the Vagaries. We can see no end to the trouble this might cause. Tell us, Xanthus—how can the *Jin'Sai* be dead in the Borderlands, yet also fighting the Vagaries in Eutracia? Do you mean to say that he has somehow risen from the grave?"

Xanthus closed his eyes. His throat was parched. "Water . . . ," he begged.

"No," another of their voices answered simply. "Not before we have the truth."

Sobbing quietly, Xanthus hung his head.

"Are you secretly in league with the Shashidans?" another voice demanded. This time its owner was female. Its tone was sharp and impatient.

"No . . ."

"How did the *Jin'Sai* manage to take the Paragon from you?" another asked. "He wears it for the first time. Yet another of your failures, it would seem."

"I don't know," Xanthus answered.

"You do!" the voice answered. "You're simply being stubborn to better protect your new friends, isn't that right?"

Desperate to understand why his masters would not believe him, Xanthus shook his head back and forth like a wounded animal. "No . . . ," he rasped. "I'm telling you the truth! The *Jin'Sai* died in the red desert! I tried to save him, but I couldn't!"

Suddenly one of the *Pon Q'tar* clerics banged his fist down on the tabletop.

"Enough of this!" he shouted. "Either you tell us what we want to know, or we will enter your mind again. And this time we will rummage through your brain so savagely that you will beg for death."

"Then kill me if you must!" Xanthus shouted. "It would be a blessing!" Again losing consciousness, he slumped forward in the chair.

"We must examine his memories again," one of the clerics said. "Because the *Jin'Sai* lives, there is clearly more to learn about this mystery."

"No," another male cleric argued. "That has already been tried, and it revealed nothing. If he truly is in league with the Shashidans, his real memories might have been altered, forcing him to believe he is telling the truth. Besides, doing so again might kill him. If he dies, we will never have our answers. We must do all in our power to help Serena succeed."

"What do you suggest?" a different female voice asked.

"Cleric researchers have nearly perfected the spell we need," he answered. "You all know the one I mean."

"The fabled nautilus effect?" another female voice asked. "That spell's existence has been rumored for centuries. Do you mean to say that we are finally nearing its unraveling?"

"Yes," the other answered. "It is supposedly linked to the rare gift of Consummate Recollection. If we are successful it will open entire new vistas about blood signature science. We should have it soon. I suggest we keep him alive and that Xanthus be its first recipient."

One by one the *Pon Q'tar* clerics announced their agreement. Without ceremony they left the room.

The azure bands binding Xanthus disappeared and he fell to the floor. Later he would awaken in the darkness of his cruel prison, only to again wonder why his masters would not believe him.

In three more days he would have his answer.

CHAPTER XLV

"BEWARE, OUR CHILD," THE *PON Q'TAR* CLERICS HAD WARNED. Their words had been haunting, urgent. *"The Conclave fleet has survived the Necrophagians' dying Forestallments. They approach the Citadel as we speak."*

Stunned by the unexpected warning, Serena had immediately gone to her knees.

"You must leave the Citadel at once to join Einar and Reznik at the Recluse," the voices had gone on to say. *"You will be safe there. Take the dead child's body with you, and the Vagaries documents that you have prepared for travel. Just before leaving you must enact the four spells hidden in the bowels of the Citadel. Go quickly. Time grows short."*

Then the voices had vanished, leaving her no opportunity to answer.

Desperate with concern, Serena had immediately summoned the island's most senior consul and issued urgent orders. The other consuls and Valrenkians had also been apprised of the imminent danger. As she ran across the inner ward, panic swept the island.

Docked at the Citadel's underground pier, what few ships Serena still possessed were being frantically loaded with people, goods, and craft tools. Every Vagaries book, scroll, and parchment had been packed into crates days ago, awaiting the order to be moved. Today that frightening directive had come.

Serena reached one of the fortress porticoes and charged along its length until she found the old door. She called the craft and tore it open with such force that it nearly separated from its hinges. Hoping that she would be in time, she ran down the stairs.

When she reached the subterranean room, she quickly brought life to the wall sconces. As the room came alight, she stole precious seconds to reacquaint herself with what needed to be done. She rushed across the room to the far wall, touched it, then called the proper spell.

Soon the wall morphed into the black visage board she had seen before. Four separate formulas written in Old Eutracian hauntingly rose from its depths. Marshaling her concentration, she called on the first two spells simultaneously.

As she hoped, the wall's left side started changing to show another panel. Then the familiar light appeared, illuminating the panel's opposite side.

She was again looking deep into the Sea of Whispers. Its underwater beauty beckoned serenely, belying the frantic exodus taking place aboveground. Looking back at the visage board, she read and summoned the third spell.

Just like before, the shimmering seascape rushed toward her.

Faster and faster it came, until it slowed to show the underwater cliff lying tens of leagues away. Dark and ominous, the centuries-old formation lay waiting to be called on.

Closing her eyes, Serena did her best to calm herself. When she felt sure, she opened her eyes, then summoned the fourth and final spell.

The final calculations, she thought. The ones the Heretics had said never to invoke without their blessing. Even she did not know what they would bring. She knew that she should not linger and watch. Even so, her curiosity demanded that she stay long enough to see what the unknown fourth spell would do.

Almost at once the giant underwater ledge started to shift. Rumbling mightily, it broke free from its resting place to go sliding forward, tumbling into the dark abyss lying before it. Then it was gone, leaving in its place nothing more than a gaping undersea cavern. The whirling debris slowly settled, and the view cleared again.

When it was over, she was sure that she had failed, and panic gripped her. Then she saw something miraculous start to happen. Entranced, she stepped closer to the panel.

A massive wave was being generated by the underwater landslide. Even though the seawater was transparent, the craft brought the wave's form into such stark relief that she could discern it easily. Suddenly its length and depth seemed without limits as it extended west and started rising violently toward the surface. Only then did the Citadel queen fully understand what she had loosed on the world.

As the wave climbed from the seabed she started to turn away. But then she saw something from the corner of her eye, and she looked back toward the panel. In their infinite wisdom the Heretics had woven another facet into the spell.

Dark creatures rose from the cavern created by the cliff's departure. Swirling higher and higher, they accompanied the terrible wave toward the ocean surface. As she watched them go, the Citadel queen smiled.

After causing the viewing panel to vanish, Serena ran back up the stairway to take her place aboard one of the departing ships.

AS TRAAX PULLED HIS DARK WINGS THROUGH THE SKY, HIS thoughts turned to Duvessa. He was glad that she had come on the mission to take the Citadel.

But she had not been amused when he had insisted that she serve on a different vessel than the *Tammerland.* Traax had his reasons for this decision—not the least of which was that he was always distracted when his betrothed was nearby. Duvessa was traveling aboard the *Cavalon,* as were all the female warriors serving under her command. Her healers were divided equally between the ships, so that they could tend to the casualties that might be incurred during the quest.

Looking down at the ruby pin stubbornly attached to his body armor, he allowed himself a smile. *She will be a wonderful wife,* he thought. *We will raise our children to be honorable and strong.*

Traax was leading a scouting party east, high over the waves. Nine more warriors followed behind him in an arrowhead formation. It was their job to scout for enemy ships, and to try and sight the Citadel. Before sending them aloft, Tyranny had said that the fleet had traveled far enough to the east so that a scout patrol might sight the fortress.

But they had not found it, and they were nearing the point of no return for this patrol. Traax's keen dead-reckoning skills told him that after no more than another half hour of flying, they would be forced to return to the ships. Trying to scan as much of the sea as possible, Tyranny had sent other scout patrols along northeasterly and southeasterly routes as well. Traax hoped that the others were having better luck. As he sensed a sudden change in wind direction, he veered a bit south to stay on course. The warriors behind him followed suit.

They had been lucky to survive the Necrophagians. That had been two days ago, and during that time the *Tammerland* had been adequately repaired. With the acolytes rested, the fleet had again taken to the air and made good time. Traax guessed that without interference, what was once a thirty-day sail between continents in conventional frigates had been cut to a mere week in the Black Ships—even less if enough accompanying mystics could keep them in constant flight.

Just then he noticed something strange. For as far as he could see to the north and south, the sea's horizon was rising violently into the air. A huge wave was forming, dwarfing even those that had been created by the Necrophagians' dying Forestallments.

But this wave was different in more ways than its great size. Rising to at least one hundred meters, its tumbling leading edge was heading due west, directly for the fleet. There was no doubt that this wave was a ship-killer of the highest order.

Stopping to hover, Traax held up one arm. The other warriors came to gather nearby. Saying nothing, Traax pointed east.

The wave was rushing toward them at an amazing speed. Traax knew that the swiftest Minion fliers could reach twenty-five leagues an hour and sometimes more. To his dismay, it seemed that the monstrous wave was moving at least that fast. Warning the Conclave meant that messengers would have to return immediately if they were to take advantage of their closer proximity to the ships. But if they couldn't at least match the wave's speed, it would roar beneath them and reach the unsuspecting fleet first. Traax understood that the craft was at work here. Serena had sent this thing at them, and somehow the Black Ships had to survive it.

His mind racing, Traax looked at his warriors. He would send only two, he decided. Should the awful wave change speed or course, he would need reserve warriors to inform the fleet.

"Axel and Valgard!" he shouted. "Return to the ships as fast as you can! Tell the Conclave about this new threat! Warn Tyranny that there is no use changing course to the north or the south to avoid it, because it stretches as far as the eye can see!" Knowing his next order would be difficult for them to obey, he gave them a commanding look.

"Should either of you collapse from fatigue and fall to the sea, the other is forbidden to save him!" Traax shouted. "I know that Minion custom dictates that no warrior be left behind! But as your commander I am countermanding that tradition! Go! The fleet's survival depends on you!"

"We live to serve!" the two handpicked warriors shouted. Then they were gone, winging their way west.

Looking back, Traax and his remaining warriors saw strange beings exploding from the wave's top to take to the air. The warriors were too far away to see what the things looked like. Traax decided that because the creatures were born of the terrible wave, they too must be products of the craft, and therefore a deadly threat.

As the beings collected in the air they circled busily into a dark swarm. Then they started soaring directly toward the hovering warriors.

Traax watched for a few moments, then drew his dreggan; the other warriors followed suit.

CHAPTER XLVI

PAUSING FOR A MOMENT, TRISTAN WIPED THE SWEAT FROM HIS brow. The midday sun was hot, and Aeolus had refused to let him drink. Nor had he eaten since breakfast. His chest heaving, he tried to reclaim his breath. This was only the first day of his training, yet he already found Aeolus' brand of discipline agonizing.

They had been at it all morning. Although Aeolus had been duplicating Tristan's every move, the old man had hardly broken a sweat. Nor was his breathing labored. Seeing Tristan stop without permission, he scowled.

"Again," he ordered.

Lowering his wooden staff, Tristan shook his head. "We have been at this for four hours without a break or anything to drink! Are you trying to kill me?" Leaning over, he put his hands on his knees to take a rest.

Aeolus walked closer and took the prince by the shoulders. He raised him up and looked him in the eyes.

"No, but others have tried, and it seems a safe bet that more will," Aeolus answered. "Just what will you tell your enemy on a hot day, eh? That His Highness needs to stop for a cool drink?" Sighing, Aeolus calmly clasped his hands before him.

"It might interest you to know that there are students twice your age at the Serpent and the Sword who can do this sort of thing all day," he added. "Before clay becomes brick, it must withstand the kiln."

Tristan took another deep breath. "You're starting to sound like Wigg," he said.

"I'll take that as a compliment," Aeolus answered emotionlessly. "Now then—back to work."

"All we've done is trace patterns in the grass like foolish schoolchildren!" Tristan protested. "I thought I was going to learn to fight!"

"Learning to move properly is the key to all that will follow," Aeolus said. "First you must hone such skills as the one you practice now. Only then will we work with live blades. Have you forgotten your failure to strike me down yesterday? Or that *you* came to *me,* asking to be trained?"

"No," Tristan answered grudgingly.

"Very well," Aeolus answered. "Start again." After backing away he clapped his hands, signaling that the exercises should resume.

Save for the Paragon and his gold medallion, Tristan stood naked from the waist up in the blazing sun. Sweat poured from him as he marshaled what energy he had left. Taking a deep breath, he collected his thoughts and recommenced the exercise.

Earlier this morning Aeolus had shown him how to become lighter on his feet as he moved. He had also demonstrated how to travel, swivel, and turn smoothly without bobbing his head and shoulders. The raising or lowering of an enemy's upper torso was a telltale sign of attack, he had said. Learn to recognize its advent and you will gain your first defensive advantage. Learn to move your body without it, and you will have gained your first offensive one.

But Tristan quickly realized that seeing Aeolus do it, and doing it himself, were two very different things. Because he was forced to stay slightly bent at the knees, the exercise was excruciating to his thighs and calves.

Raising his staff for what seemed the thousandth time, Tristan again started a zigzagging path across the grass. The goal was to complete the circuit and end up in the exact spot from which he had started without once looking down. Aeolus had pulled some grass from the ground to mark the exercise's starting and stopping point.

On coming to the circuit's end, Tristan checked his location. He had done better this time, his boots landing less than a foot from the starting place.

Smoothly lowering his staff the way Aeolus had taught him, Tristan looked into his teacher's eyes. Surely the old wizard would have something complimentary to say this time.

"When you can return to the exact starting point while blindfolded and performing perfect sword cuts along the way, you will have finally accomplished something," was Aeolus' only comment. "Even so, it will be but a baby step. Now do it again."

Sighing, Tristan wiped his face and began the exercise anew.

Aeolus had surprisingly arrived at the palace gates before dawn. Tristan had ordered Ox to greet him, but neither of them had guessed that the old man would arrive so early. Ox had shown Aeolus to his quarters, and the master had insisted on waking the prince himself.

Not knowing what else to do, Ox allowed Aeolus entry to Tristan's private rooms. As Aeolus noisily rousted Tristan from his bed, all Ox could do was to offer Tristan an apologetic look. From this day until the Conclave's return, Aeolus had said, he expected the prince to be in the courtyard just before daybreak, ready and eager to train.

As Tristan finished the circuit he saw Abbey and Ox approaching. Hoping that he had just been saved, he let go a deep breath.

"We need to speak with you," Abbey told Tristan. She turned to Aeolus and smiled. "Welcome back to the palace, by the way," she said.

"Thank you," Aeolus answered. "But my stay is temporary."

"What is it?" Tristan asked Abbey. "Has the fleet returned?"

"No," she said. Her expression soured. "It's about Clan Kilbourne. They are nearing the city. Hector wisely flew on ahead of them, so as to inform us. He wishes to know whether you have any orders for him or for the highlanders."

It wasn't often that one saw surprise overtake Aeolus' face. He gave the prince a questioning glance.

"Highlanders?" he asked.

Tristan nodded. "We have an arrangement. In return for a homeland of their own, their horsemen are going to temporarily join the Minion forces as cavalry."

Pursing his lips, Aeolus shook his head. "Highlander cavalry . . ." he mused. He gave Abbey a wry look.

"If that's the case, you'd best hide all the horses and tack, not to mention the palace silverware," Aeolus added. "And a highlander homeland, no less? Wigg's and Faegan's reactions to this development should prove most interesting."

Abbey shook her head. "They're not all that way," she

protested. "I've often bought herbs from highlanders over the years and I've never been cheated or robbed."

After giving Abbey an approving smile, Tristan looked at Ox. "How far is the clan from the city?" he asked.

"They be three leagues away to the northeast," Ox answered.

Tristan thought for a moment. He knew that his agreement with the highlanders would be controversial among the Tammerland citizens. Three leagues was close enough, he decided.

"Tell Hector to fly back," he ordered Ox. "He is to ask the clan elders to make camp where they are. Rafe and I will visit them after I bathe and get something to eat." He thought for a moment. "Have a litter made ready," he added.

Ox's face screwed up. "It be only three leagues," he said. "*Jin'Sai* no take Shadow?"

His legs still burning with fatigue, Tristan shook his head. "No," he answered simply. Out of the corner of her eye, Abbey saw Aeolus stifle a smile.

"We're done for today," Tristan told Aeolus. He handed the master his wooden staff.

Aeolus bowed. "Until tomorrow morning, *Jin'Sai,*" he said.

Abbey walked to Aeolus and threaded one arm through his. "In the meantime, let's you and I have some lunch, then I'll reacquaint you with the palace and the Redoubt," she offered. "Much has changed since you were last here. Even so, our tour should bring back many pleasant memories."

Aeolus smiled. "Thank you," he said. "Is your nerveweed tea still as good as I remember?"

Abbey gave Aeolus a wink. "Even better," she answered. "After all, I've had three more centuries during which to practice."

Ox gave Tristan a hopeful look. "I go with *Jin'Sai* to see highlanders," he said. "Ox never see highlanders before! Everyone say they be thieves!" His face took on a glowering seriousness. "I no let them steal anything!"

Tristan smiled. Knowing how he had disappointed the warrior yesterday, he decided to agree this time. "All right," he answered. "You can come."

After walking to collect his vest and his weapons, Tristan accompanied everyone back to the palace.

Chapter XLVII

As Traax watched the awful things soar toward his patrol party, his hands clenched tighter around his dreggan handle. Without needing to be told, his seven remaining fighters immediately formed a battle line on his right.

His face grim, Traax watched the oncoming swarm climb to a place well above the Minion position. Darkening the sky with their numbers, they caused a massive shadow to crawl across the ocean surface. The swarm would be directly overhead in moments.

There must be thousands of them, Traax realized. He could run, but his warriors were already fatigued and the enemies' speed was great. He decided that it would be better to die here, trying to buy time for Axel and Valgard. There would be little hope of that, but he had no choice other than to try. Axel and Valgard simply had to warn the fleet before the monsters and the giant wave that birthed them could reach the Black Ships. Given the wave's incredible speed, it was the only chance the fleet had. As Serena's monsters neared, the warriors could finally see them for what they were.

Each was about the size of a man, but that was where any similarity to mankind ended. They were dark gray reptilian things. Their bodies were broad and muscular, ending in long, forked tails that bore rows of sharp barbs along either side. Each beast had two muscular arms and their clawlike hands ended in sharp talons. Two leathery wings protruded from each of their backs, propelling them through the air with amazing speed. The heads were goatlike, with dark, beady eyes and two sharp horns protruding from either side of their skulls. As Traax looked closer he was surprised to see that the creatures bore no weapons.

Just then he saw one advance to a place about ten meters ahead of the others. That would be the leader, Traax knew. His jaw clenched as he watched it near. *Come to me, you bastard,* he thought. *It is only right that you and I clash first.*

Knowing it would flash brightly in the setting sun, Traax raised his dreggan blade high. Certain that this would be their last act in defiance of the Vagaries, the other warriors did the same.

Seeing Traax's challenge, the monsters' leader let go a menacing cry. A strange cross between a human scream and a bearlike growl, it resonated loudly through the sky. As the leader cried out, its sharp teeth flashed briefly in the setting sun.

The leader and about twenty others quickly peeled off to dive on the Minions, while the remaining swarm continued, accompanying the huge wave. For what he knew would be the last time, Traax looked down at Duvessa's ruby pin.

Refusing to wait for death, he shouted an order to his fighters to follow him higher. Struggling skyward, the eight warriors rose to meet their fates head-on as the twenty monstrosities plummeted to attack them. With a great clash, the two opposing forces tore into one another.

Three of the enemy and one brave warrior died on the spot, one monster perishing at the point of Traax's blade. Then Traax saw his trusted friend Brutus tumble end over end from the sky. Brutus' right arm was gone, and blood poured wildly from his mouth. But he did not scream as he plunged to his watery grave.

Suddenly Traax heard another of the awful things cry out, and he turned just in time to see one lunging at him. But even he could not raise his sword in time. As he glared into the beast's awful face, his warrior's instinct told him that he was about to die.

Then he saw a sudden flash of silver cross his vision, and the monster's face split vertically into two grotesque halves. Green brain matter tumbled from the thing's split skull as the expertly thrown returning wheel kept on going, exiting the back of the creature's head. Gurgling black blood from its ravaged mouth, the beast tumbled from the sky.

As the fighting raged all around him, Traax stole precious seconds to turn and see who had saved his life. His left arm covered with blood, Yuri gave him a quick nod. Traax nodded back. But their respite would be short-lived.

Traax heard a strange cracking sound, and Yuri screamed in agony. From about four meters away and behind Yuri, one of the monsters had snapped its tail like a bullwhip, wrapping it tightly around one of Yuri's legs and burying its sharp barbs into his flesh.

With a vicious scream it flew a bit closer, then snapped its tail again. To Traax's horror, the thing tore Yuri's leg away at the hip joint. Screaming insanely, Yuri tried to stay aloft. But massive blood loss quickly overcame him, sending him into unconsciousness. He too plunged toward the sea.

Hovering with its tail still entwined around its bloody prize, the thing stared greedily at Traax for a moment. As it sneered at him it raised its talons and let go an insane victory scream. Enraged, Traax went after it.

But just as he started toward Yuri's killer, Traax heard another of the awful cracking sounds rip through the air. A searing pain suddenly shot through his left arm. Another beast's barbed tail had found him from behind. The snarling thing that had killed Yuri dropped the severed leg and rushed toward him, its talons flashing orange-red in the disappearing sun.

Raising his dreggan high with his other hand, Traax turned in the air, purposely tightening the tail's length. The added pain nearly caused him to faint, but it had to be done. Raising his dreggan, he brought it down with everything he had.

The dreggan cut deeply into the barbed tail but did not sever it. More black blood spurted onto his sword hand, threatening to loosen his grip. Raising the sword again, he was finally able to cut the thing's tail completely through.

The beast that had entwined him screamed in pain, then tumbled downward. Turning wildly, Traax sensed that the one that had killed Yuri was still coming for him. His vision a blur as he whirled, he knew that the approaching creature would be so close that it would present a point-blank target. As he finished his turn he automatically shoved his blade forward, even before he saw his enemy.

Traax's guess had been right. The dreggan impaled the creature squarely in the chest, then stopped short as it struck against the thing's backbone. Screaming in agony, the monster gripped the blade with its talons and frantically scratched at it in an attempt to free itself.

Without hesitation, Traax pressed the hidden button on the dreggan's hilt. The clanging blade shot forward. Arching wildly, the impaled monster lifted its head, then screamed again. Holding the sword deep in the thing's gaping wound, Traax viciously rocked the blade up and down, then gave it a savage twist. He felt the thing's backbone crack apart and saw the light die in its eyes. Sneering, he lifted one boot to push the corpse off his sword.

He quickly looked around. Save for one other warrior, the sky was empty. His friend Aldaeous hovered weakly nearby, wounded badly. Deep cuts from one of the thing's barbed tails completely encircled his right thigh.

Flying to him, Traax sheathed his dreggan, then produced a tourniquet band from beneath his body armor. He quickly wound it high around Aldaeous' leg, high near the warrior's groin. As he cinched it tight, Aldaeous grimaced. Seeing his friend's blanched pallor, Traax quickly realized that Aldaeous had lost much blood. He then cinched a tourniquet around his own upper left arm.

Traax took another quick look around. Blessedly, the sky remained empty. They had done it! Eight brave warriors had killed twenty of those awful things, and two warriors had lived to tell the tale. When he and Aldaeous were graybeards, what a story they would have to tell their grandchildren! Then his face darkened as he remembered that they were wounded, and a long way from the fleet.

Without speaking, the warriors instinctively turned westward. The sun was setting in earnest, soon to be replaced by the three red moons and thousands of twinkling stars. Traax knew that he could navigate his way back as well by the stars as by the sun. Then he looked far into the distance, and his heart fell.

He could just see the huge wave and its accompanying black swarm as they continued heading west. During the airborne battle, the wave had roared beneath them and traveled far. Traax could only pray that Axel and Valgard were still ahead of it.

Just then he saw Aldaeous faint and start tumbling through the air. Swooping down, Traax caught the wounded warrior. Aldaeous' eyes fluttered open again.

"Let me perish," he whispered. "You'll never get back if you carry me."

"Be still," Traax said. "We'll make it back, I promise you."

Drooping weakly in Traax's arms, Aldaeous gave him a knowing smile. "What about your order, m'lord?" he asked. He coughed, spitting up some blood that ran down his body armor and dripped toward the sea. Worried for him, Traax clenched his jaw.

"Should one of you collapse, the other is forbidden to save him!" Aldaeous repeated sternly. Closing his eyes, he smiled again. "That's what you said, isn't it?"

"Consider that order countermanded," Traax answered. He gave Aldaeous a quick smile. "And your insubordination is noted," he added.

"Privileges of rank, sir?" Aldaeous asked weakly.

"Something like that," Traax answered. He watched Aldaeous faint away.

Traax could easily have let Aldaeous fall, which would vastly improve Traax's chances for survival. But he didn't.

Unsure of their futures, he carried the stricken warrior back toward the unsuspecting fleet.

CHAPTER XLVIII

CALLING THE CRAFT, WIGG LEVITATED ONE OF HIS WHITE ROOKS, then caused it to hang inverted from the game board's underside. "Check," he said.

Faegan smiled. "Too obvious, First Wizard," he answered. After some thought he judiciously moved his threatened king one space rightward. Now it was Wigg's turn to worry.

The two mystics were sitting in Faegan's quarters aboard the *Tammerland,* playing wizard's chess. The game was much like ordinary chess, but with two important differences. First, the black-and-white game board was suspended in the air. Each of the board's sides held the same number of black and white squares.

Second, each player commanded two armies rather than one. Thus two opposing armies lay atop the board, and another two clung to its underside. Pieces could be moved from one of the board's sides to the other and back again, with the proviso that the player's next move must take place from that board's side.

Smiling, Faegan used the craft to turn over the three-minute sand globe resting near his elbow. As the trapped sand poured down, he looked at Wigg and sipped some more tea.

"I believe that you might be done for this time," he said. "If you aren't careful, I will take one of your kings in four moves."

"Be still!" Wigg demanded. "I'm trying to concentrate! And don't be so cocky! You might win more often than I, but that doesn't mean you will today!"

Suddenly suspicious, Wigg pursed his lips. "Why would you warn me about my king?" he asked.

Faegan cackled softly. "Because it doesn't matter," he answered. "You won't figure it out until it's too late."

Narrowing his eyes, Wigg looked at the board's two sides and considered his options. Faegan smiled as he watched the telltale vein in Wigg's forehead start throbbing—a sure sign that the First Wizard was feeling stressed.

As the two wizards concentrated on their game, all seemed normal with the Conclave fleet. The night sea was calm, and clouds slipped gently across the sky, occasionally blocking the moonlight. Each of the six Black Ships was sailing atop the waves in the traditional way while their empowering mystics rested. For the last two days the fleet had forged ahead without incident.

Tyranny's plan was to wait until all three of her roving scout patrols returned before again ordering the ships into the air. If one of the patrols sighted the Citadel, a course correction might be needed. With the fleet's slower speed atop the waves, an adjustment would be smaller, thus saving time. Two of the patrols had returned but had seen nothing. Traax's group was overdue, but was not so late as to cause concern.

Wigg again called the craft, this time moving a knight from the board's underside to its topside. He reached out and inverted the timing globe.

Faegan scowled. "What in blazes are you doing?" he asked. "That was perhaps the most foolish move I have ever seen!"

Smiling, Wigg sat back in his chair and folded his arms. "Time will tell," he answered.

As Faegan concentrated on the game, Wigg stared thoughtfully at his old friend. Despite his normally jocular nature, Faegan always seemed obsessed about something. Everyone who knew him understood that. More often than not, the crippled wizard's fixations involved some craft mystery that he was trying to unravel. As soon as he succeeded at deciphering one, he always managed to find another to brood over.

But Wigg sensed that there was something else on the crippled wizard's mind—something that bothered him deeply. Moreover, he thought he knew what it was. Faegan had unfinished business to complete, and Wigg guessed that he would not rest until it was done.

Deciding to broach the subject, Wigg first took another sip of red wine. After placing the glass back atop the table he laced his long fingers together.

"You want him, don't you?" he asked. "That's the real reason you decided to come on this mission, rather than wait at the palace for Tristan to return home. You want to find him and kill him with your own hands, and you won't rest until you do."

Faegan reached out to gently tip the three-minute glass on its side, meaning that he wanted a break from the game. After taking another sip of tea, he looked into Wigg's face.

"I thought I was the only one who knew," he said.

"I don't believe that the others realize it," Wigg answered. "They haven't known you for three centuries like I have. But I gather that Jessamay suspects. Little escapes her sorceress's acumen, you know."

"How true," Faegan answered.

"You believe Reznik escaped to the Citadel," Wigg said, "along with the other surviving Valrenkians. I think you're right."

Faegan nodded. "It's the only answer that fits. If so, Serena might have taken them into her employ. It would be to her advantage, after all. Only the Afterlife knows what evil she might be ordering the Valrenkian community to concoct. Of all people, I needn't tell you that Vagaries practitioners have little regard for human life other than their own. The farther we sail, the more apprehensive I become. I fear that the Necrophagians were only the beginning of our troubles."

Wigg was acutely aware of Faegan's hatred for Reznik, even though the two enemy mystics had never met. Being outfoxed by another wizard was hard enough on Faegan's infamous ego. But the humiliation of being duped and nearly killed by a partial adept carried a nasty sting.

His jaw hardening, Faegan looked into Wigg's eyes. "Yes, I want to kill him," he said quietly. "He deserves to die for more reasons than I can count. If we are lucky enough to find him, I want it understood that he is mine."

Wigg nodded. "Very well," he answered. "I will take the liberty of telling the other members. There will be no disagreement."

As he turned to look out one of the ship's portholes, Wigg found his mind returning to Eutracia. He took another sip of the excellent wine.

"What is it?" Faegan asked.

Wigg judiciously rolled the wineglass back and forth between his palms for a moment. "It's Tristan," he replied. "I worry about him constantly. Only the Afterlife knows what that creature Xanthus did with him, or why."

"You are not responsible for Tristan's fate," Faegan answered. "From what you told me, he had no choice. Nor did you have any choice but to let him go."

"I know," Wigg answered. "It's just that—"

Suddenly the *Tammerland* heaved mightily into the air, the angle on her bow easily as sharp as when the ship had violently risen to escape the Necrophagians. Wigg's concentration slipped, allowing the chessboard and its pieces to go clattering to the floor. Just as quickly all the room's furniture slid aft, taking the wizards with it.

His eyes wide, Wigg looked at Faegan. They immediately understood that something must have gone terribly wrong abovedecks. Besides themselves, Jessamay was the only mystic aboard with the power to raise the ship so dramatically. Worse, Tyranny would have never allowed such a violent maneuver unless the situation was dire.

As they tried to hurry for the door, the wizards heard Minion drummers suddenly start hammering out the maritime drum roll called "beating to quarters." It was the clarion call for all Minion warriors while at sea, ordering them to their action posts. Even from several decks below, Wigg and Faegan could hear the sounds of Minion boot heels urgently pounding across the ship's topsides.

Knowing that there was no time for discussion, the two wizards struggled for the door. Finally traversing the sharply angled floor, they clawed their way up the inclined hall and toward the aft stairway.

FROM HER PLACE AT THE *TAMMERLAND'S* STERN RAIL, TYRANNY lowered her spyglass, then looked blankly out across the ocean again. In all her years at sea she had never met such a threat.

"Is it true?" Shailiha asked urgently. "Are Axel and Valgard right about what they told us?"

Adrian and Scars were also standing beside her. Everyone was holding on to the rigging, so as not to fall backward while the *Tammerland* continued her steep climb. Jessamay clung to the ship's wheel and was straining her powers to the utmost to keep the *Tammerland* rising. As the flagship flew higher, her timbers and masts groaned torturously, like they were about to come apart. Tyranny handed the spyglass to the princess.

"Look for yourself," Tyranny answered. "It is beyond your imagination. I doubt we can escape it."

Shailiha quickly brought the spyglass to one eye, then twisted its cylinders to bring the threat into better focus. When she saw the danger her jaw dropped.

About one league away, a deadly wall of water had risen to more than two hundred meters and was heading directly toward the fleet. Just as the two warriors from Traax's patrol had said, the wave stretched to the north and south for as far as the eye could see—even with the aid of the spyglass. The swarming beings that the returning warriors had also warned of were accompanying it.

The warrior manning the *Tammerland*'s forwardmost crow's nest had seen the threats and had quickly rung the warning bell. But because cloud cover sometimes blocked the moonlight, he had not seen them soon enough to do the fleet much good. Then Axel and Valgard had unexpectedly crashed to the ship's deck. They had been nearly dead from exhaustion.

Although the warriors had returned ahead of the wave, they had lost much of their lead to its amazing speed. After hearing their incredible tale, Tyranny knew that there was only one way to survive. The mystic aboard each vessel must force her ship to climb to her utmost while reversing course. Tyranny had immediately issued the orders, then commanded the Minions to their action stations.

Still gasping for breath, Axel had finished his bizarre report with more bad news. Traax and his remaining warriors were surely dead, he said. There could have been no other outcome.

Shailiha absently handed the glass to Scars. After looking for a moment, he used one meaty hand to angrily collapse the spyglass's cylinders. Shaking his head, he gave his captain a grim look.

"We won't escape it!" he shouted. "We weren't given enough warning! Even at our current rate of climb the wave will strike us! You were also right to reverse course, but I fear that our actions won't be enough!"

Scars turned to look at the other Black Ships as they struggled to match the *Tammerland*'s steep climb. He quickly pointed at them.

"Our sister ships are faring even worse!" he shouted. "The acolytes aboard them don't have Jessamay's strength!"

Everyone turned to look at the five struggling warships. Flying behind and below the *Tammerland,* their bows were raised at distinctively lesser angles, hampering their climbs.

As she looked, Shailiha's heart sank. She knew that the acolytes were doing all they could. But if Scars believed that the *Tammerland* would be engulfed by the oncoming wave, the others didn't stand a chance.

"Where are Wigg and Faegan?" Tyranny shouted. "We need them!"

No sooner had the privateer asked the question than the two wizards exited the stern stairway. Holding on to the railing, they struggled their way toward the others.

"What is going on?" Wigg shouted.

Tyranny pointed astern. By this time the huge wave and its accompanying creatures could be seen with the naked eye. Just then a patch of magenta moonlight caught the wave, illuminating its terrifying splendor. It would be on them in moments. As everyone watched, Serena's flying creatures started diving down to start their attack.

"I beg the Afterlife," Wigg breathed.

"What do we do?" Tyranny demanded. "Can you stop it, or turn it away somehow?"

Wigg shook his head. "Its power is beyond our gifts!" he answered. "Our only chance is to outrun it!"

"What purpose do the flying creatures serve?" Shailiha shouted. "Surely the wave is enough to destroy us all!"

Faegan looked up at Shailiha from his wooden chair. It was plain to see that he was as thunderstruck as Wigg.

"Those monsters have but one purpose!" he shouted. "They will attack in force to overwhelm the Minions! If they kill the mystic aboard each ship then the vessels will crash back to the sea, their fates a certainty when the wave rushes over them! That is why they are diving well ahead of it! Order every warrior into the air at once! They have to meet that swarm head-on and somehow keep those beasts from breaking though!"

Shailiha immediately barked out some orders. At once warriors by the thousands left the *Tammerland*'s decks to fly toward the advancing swarm. More soared downward to relay the princess's orders to the other ships. Soon the night sky filled with their beating wings, and thousands of dreggan blades flashed menacingly in the moonlight. Wigg quickly called three more warriors forward.

"Take me, Faegan, and Adrian to three of the other ships!" he ordered them.

"What are you doing?" Tyranny demanded. "We need you here!"

"Not as badly as they do!" Wigg countered. "Jessamay must continue to climb the *Tammerland*! But the weaker acolytes need us! It is the only way! The two remaining sisters that we cannot help will just have to do the best they can!"

Scars, Tyranny, and Shailiha watched the warriors take the three mystics in their arms. The Minions launched into the air and disappeared into the darkness over the stern rail.

Shailiha turned to look at Jessamay. The sorceress was near exhaustion, her legs shaking as she tried to keep the *Tammerland* climbing ever higher. Just then Shailiha heard a terrible noise and turned to look.

As the wave chasing them drew ever nearer, the Minion hordes and the swarming Vagaries creatures clashed head-on.

LOOKING WEST, TRAAX COULD BARELY SEE THE GIANT WAVE AS IT approached the fleet. Straining with everything he had, he tried to fly faster. But blood loss from his wounded arm and carrying Aldaeous had taken their toll. He struggled higher, hoping to find a tailwind, but there wasn't one.

He watched proudly as his warriors soared from the Black Ships' decks to counter Serena's deadly swarm. Like his friend Yuri and the other warriors who had died during the last battle, they would not understand about the creature's deadly tails until it was too late. Desperate with frustration and anger, he screamed out a warning. But from so far away it of course did no good. Exhausted, he looked down at his unconscious friend.

Wondering if Aldaeous was dead, Traax hovered for a moment. Supporting Aldaeous as best he could with one arm, he felt for a pulse. There was none.

He remained like that for some time, wondering what to do. Finally he bid Aldaeous farewell and let go of the body. Tumbling end over end, it splashed into the dark sea.

Just then he heard a mighty crashing sound. Looking west, he saw Minion warriors by the thousands flying headlong into Serena's deadly swarm. Stretching his wings farther, he did his best to again head for the fleet. Then he noticed something else, and his heart fell.

The Black Ships were climbing fast, thereby becoming even more difficult for him to catch. Worse, Tyranny had wisely ordered that the fleet turn west, trying to buy time in their escape from the monstrous wave.

Good, he thought. *Perhaps they'll survive. But by doing so, they have sealed my fate.*

Straining with his last bit of energy, Traax tried to make up the growing distance between him and the fleet. But with each beat of his wings, the ships were pulling away even faster.

He suddenly felt something warm and wet against his skin. Looking over, he saw that his tourniquet had loosened and that fresh blood was streaming down his wounded arm. Exhausted as he was, there was no telling how long he had been bleeding. Reaching over with his right arm, he cinched the tourniquet tighter.

Looking west again, by this time he could barely see the fleet. Before starting out once more he looked down at Duvessa's betrothal pin to find it splattered with blood. He flew on.

Soon his eyes grew heavy, and he knew it was the end. He struggled as best he could to stay in the air, but each wing beat had become tortured, useless.

My wings are so heavy, he thought. *If only I could rest.*

Then the blood loss finally overcame him.

His mind and body finally at the breaking point, Traax tumbled into the sea.

RAISING HER DREGGAN, DUVESSA STRUCK ANOTHER OF THE AWFUL things from the air. After summoning her female warriors to the top deck of the *Cavalon,* she had proudly led them against the swarming mass of creatures. From all around her came the sound of warriors screaming, and the beasts' manic victory cries. The killing was happening at such a frantic pace that blood flew through the air almost in torrents.

Suddenly she saw one of the things snap its tail and wrap it around the waist of one of her warrior-healers. The warrior screamed wildly in pain. Flying to her, Duvessa raised her dreggan, and brought it down viciously.

Even so, the beast's sinewy tail refused to sever. Again and again she cut into it until its victim was freed. She then plunged the dreggan's tip into the beast's right eye. Black blood spurted from the eyeball to splatter against her body armor. Looking down, she saw that it had covered Traax's betrothal pin.

Suddenly a different emotion stabbed her heart, and she knew. It was often said that something in the Minion soul told each one when his or her mate was dying. Some claimed that it was a secret mechanism of the craft, purposely added to the spell Failee had used to create them. Others insisted that it was the Minions' amazing sense of duty, binding each warrior to the other.

No matter the reason, Duvessa knew that Traax was failing, and she could do nothing about it. As tears ran freely from her eyes she harshly collected herself. Screaming, she viciously struck another of the terrible things down, hoping that it had been the one that had attacked her betrothed.

Her chest heaving, she swiveled in the air. Terrible carnage reigned for leagues in every direction. The dark night sky made it impossible to see whether the Minions were keeping the swarm from reaching the Black Ships.

Peering through the dark, she tried to see the fleet but couldn't. Deciding that she must know the ships' fates, she avoided two sidelong skirmishes and flew quickly upward, straight through the melee. Another beast lunged at her; she deftly avoided it. As she flew higher, another tried wrapping its tail around her leg but missed. Ignoring it, she kept going higher.

Finally she broke free of the fight. Here the sky was almost windless. Soaring westward over the raging battle, she finally reached its leading edge. She stopped to hover and looked down.

To the west, the six Black Ships were still struggling skyward. For some reason the *Tammerland,* the *Florian,* the *Cavalon,* and the *Ephyra* were well ahead of the others in their rush to avoid the giant wave. Aghast, Duvessa could only watch as the wave approached the sterns of the two slower ships.

It took the *Malvina* first, its relentless crest crashing down atop her. The ship's bow wildly surfaced; then she exploded from the water to completely turn over in midair. Masts snapped like toothpicks, and all the ship's superstructures were instantly wiped clean from her decks like leaves in a stiff breeze. Then the once-majestic ship broke cleanly in half and the wave engulfed her for the second and final time. Like nothing had happened, the terrible surge kept rushing forward, threatening another Black Ship.

The *Illendium* was next. The wave's incredible power slammed into the ship's aft deck, tilting her vertical. Then the wave slammed flat against her entire topside and tore her apart. With a tortured groan the *Illendium*'s remains were tossed about like pieces of some child's broken toy. Then the wave's crest cascaded over them, taking them and everyone aboard under. From her vantage point high in the sky, all Duvessa could do was watch.

As the wave crashed ever onward, Duvessa screamed with despair. Within moments it would reach the *Tammerland.*

Chapter XLIX

As their minion litter soared high over Tammerland, Tristan grinned at Rafe's expense. *Serves him right,* he thought, *after the way he kept me standing in the Sippora River that night.*

Tristan believed Rafe to be an immensely brave man. But it

was becoming clear that the highlander's idea of travel was sitting atop a horse or a wagon—not flying through the sky in some contraption carried by Tristan's bizarre Minions. As he fidgeted nervously in his seat, Rafe grasped the litter's sides so firmly that his knuckles had gone white.

Ox and Abbey had also come along. Tristan smirked as he heard Ox occasionally bark out seemingly unnecessary orders to the litter bearers. At first Tristan couldn't decide who the gigantic warrior was trying to impress—him or Rafe. Finally deciding that it was probably a little bit of both, he leaned back and watched the scenery go by.

The prince had several reasons for visiting the highlander camp. He wanted to be sure that everyone had arrived safely, and that the Clan Kilbourne elders were content with where Tristan had asked them to stop. He also wanted to order the clan horsemen to the palace, so that they and the Minions could become acquainted with each other's customs and tactics.

Then there was the need to be sure that the clan was properly supplied with food and other goods. Tristan knew the highlanders' ways, and he wanted to stem as much thieving as possible. To that end, his reply to the elders through Hector had suggested that they make camp on the northern bank of the Sippora River. The river would grant them all the freshwater they might need, yet also separate them from the many temptations the capital city would present. Should added food and supplies be needed, he had every intention of ordering the Minions to deliver it.

Tristan looked over at Ox. From the first moment he had met Rafe, Ox had been highly skeptical and perhaps more than a bit gruff. *He has been listening to Abbey,* Tristan surmised. The same sense of distrust had possessed Ox when he had first met Scars, but later the two had become fast friends. Tristan hoped that Ox would also accept Rafe, but he wasn't betting that their friendship would bloom overnight.

Abbey was no happier to be on this journey than Ox. Tristan also had his motives regarding the herbmistress. If there was a key to Wigg's heart, it was she. If he could convince Abbey that his bargain with the clan was a good idea, she might help temper Wigg's protests. Either way, Tristan reasoned, he had nothing to lose by bringing her along. Leaning forward, he decided to have some fun by testing the chilly waters between Ox and Rafe.

"You know," he said to Ox as he thoughtfully rubbed his chin, "if the clan runs low on food I might have to order you and some other warriors to keep them supplied."

Ox gave Tristan a respectful look, then glared angrily at Rafe. "If *Jin'Sai* want Ox to do, Ox will do," he answered. "But if highlanders go hungry, Ox no care. Why they not just steal food? Wigg say they steal everything anyway."

Looking away, Abbey snorted out a laugh. Despite his uneasiness, Rafe laughed too. He gave Ox a wry look.

"I wouldn't worry if I were you," Rafe said. "You Minions are so fearsome that I wouldn't *dare* try stealing anything from you."

Unsure of whether Rafe was being sarcastic, Ox screwed up his face. "Good," Ox finally said. "It best you remember that."

Suddenly the litter banked sharply right. Gripping the litter's side even harder, Rafe started to appear a little green.

"I no worry if I be you," Ox said, doing his best to mimic Rafe's earlier comment. "While Abbey and *Jin'Sai* aboard, warriors no *dare* drop you!"

Beaming at his own cleverness, he smiled, then folded his arms across his barrel chest. Tristan and Abbey couldn't help but to laugh. Trying to quell his uneasy stomach, Rafe scowled back grumpily. *So much for diplomacy,* Tristan thought.

After a time Tristan saw the camp come into view, its colorful wagons dotting the lush fields on the Sippora's northern bank. He was relieved to see that the clan elders had taken his advice.

"Put us down in the camp's center," he ordered Ox. After nodding back, Ox barked out some orders and the litter started downward.

As the passengers disembarked, hundreds of highlanders walked toward them. Looking around warily, Ox stayed close to Tristan. The prince thought about telling him that it wasn't needed, then decided to let the giant warrior persist in his overly protective ways. Tristan cast his eyes around the growing crowd.

He did not see Yasmin, but something told him that she was somewhere near, and that her seductive eyes were on him. He pursed his lips as he partly came to regret bringing Abbey along. Perhaps it was just as well that Yasmin hadn't greeted him, for he didn't need her included in Abbey's report to Wigg. Not to mention what kind of bawdy outbursts Rafe might utter, should he see them together again!

He saw Balthazar and Gunther approach. Gunther was not smiling, leading Tristan to wonder if he ever did. But the look on the elder's face seemed to carry more respect for Tristan than before. Apparently Tristan's unmasking of Arwydd had done much to raise his esteem. The prince reached out and shook Gunther's hand.

"Is everyone safe and well?" he asked.

"Yes, *Jin'Sai,*" Gunther answered. "And you?"

Tristan nodded, then introduced Abbey and Ox. When Gunther extended his hand to the herbmistress, Abbey acted like she was being forced to touch a snake. Tristan cleared his throat and gave her a harsh look. Finally she shook the clan elder's hand.

"It is a pleasure to meet you," Abbey said tentatively.

"And you," Gunther answered. He skeptically raised an eyebrow, reminding Tristan of Wigg.

"I sense that you have your doubts about my clan's arrangement with your prince," he added. "Perhaps we can change your mind during your visit. Anyway, rest easy. Our agreement is not permanent."

Trying to be a bit more cordial, Abbey forced a smile. "I meant no disrespect," she said apologetically.

Tristan looked over at Balthazar. His fists on either hip, the huge highlander was smiling at Abbey's expense. His shoulder was still wrapped in Yasmin's expertly wound bandages.

"And you, Balthazar?" Tristan asked. "How is your wound?"

"Better," Balthazar answered. "Yasmin has a healing touch. But you'd know all about that, wouldn't you?" Laughing, he slapped Tristan on the back.

"What does he mean?" Abbey asked. "Who's Yasmin?"

"A highlander healer," Tristan answered simply. "She dressed my wound." He looked at Gunther again.

"Does the clan have enough food and supplies?" he asked.

Gunther nodded. "We have enough for now. Our horsemen are wondering about your plans for them."

"That's another reason why I have come," Tristan answered. "I want them to travel to the palace. They can live among the Minions, in tents set up on the surrounding palace grounds. But I believe it best that they leave their families here. We do not know when the Conclave fleet will come home. During the intervening days I want the warriors and horsemen to learn each other's tactics. I want them working as a cohesive unit, and the sooner the better."

Balthazar stepped forward. "That brings us to another question," he said to Tristan. "If you are killed, who do we take our orders from, eh?" He pointed at Ox and gave the warrior a disparaging look. "If you believe that we will take our direction from those like him, you think wrong," he added nastily.

Glowering, Ox grabbed the dreggan handle at his side. Freeing the sword a few inches from its scabbard, he took a quick step forward. Tristan quickly shook his head at him. Several tense moments followed as Tristan sized up the situation. This was Balthazar's first test of Tristan's leadership, and the prince knew it.

"The Minions have no more right to order you about than you do them," he answered sternly. "I command you both. In the event of my absence or death, all forces will take their orders from my sister Shailiha. Should she fall, you come under the command of my wizards. In any event, your orders will likely come to you through Rafe, just as my orders to the Minions go through one called Traax. Our foes will be of the craft, and unlike any you have ever fought. If you want to keep your head I suggest that you follow orders, and fully honor your elders' commitment to me."

Commanding stares passed between Tristan and Balthazar. After glancing at Gunther and Rafe, Balthazar finally relented. Snorting out a short grunt of approval, Ox shoved his dreggan blade home.

"Very well, *dango,*" Balthazar said. "We already know that you are a good fighter. Soon we will see what kind of leader you are." Then he turned on his heel and walked away.

Rafe leaned closer to Tristan and gave him a sly smile. "Well done," he whispered. "Balthazar can be difficult to manage. He isn't known for giving his respect and friendship easily. But once he does he will gladly die for you. I believe you know the type."

As he watched Balthazar stomp away, Tristan thought of Ox and Scars. "I do indeed," he answered softly.

Tristan looked at Gunther. "I would like the horsemen assembled," he said. "For the time being they should say their goodbyes to their families. They will be allowed periodic visits back to the camp."

"There is no need to assemble them," Gunther answered. "They are practicing their maneuvers as we speak."

Realizing that this would be a perfect opportunity to show Ox and Abbey what the horsemen could do, Tristan smiled.

"We will go and watch," he said. "Then Abbey and I will return home. Ox and Rafe will wait here until the horsemen are ready to leave. Then they will escort them to the palace."

Rafe grinned; Abbey sighed. Ox gave Tristan an obedient but disappointed look.

"Ox do as *Jin'Sai* say," he answered.

Seizing on the opportunity to badger the warrior yet again, Rafe walked over and put one arm around Ox. He winked at Tristan, then good-naturedly jostled the massive Ox as best he could.

"We'll do fine, won't we, Ox?" he chided.

Ox looked at the ground and growled something unintelligible. Sighing, Tristan looked at Gunther.

"Please lead on," he said.

After nodding back, Gunther started wending a path through the crowd. As Tristan made his way among the highlanders, he saw fewer disparaging looks this time. He took that as a hopeful sign. The highlanders didn't have to like him, but he needed their respect. That was especially true of the horsemen.

Finally Gunther and his group found their way to the crowd's farthest edge. A long green field stretched before them. The highlander horsemen were going through their paces.

Gunther called for chairs, and soon some were brought. Tristan recognized them as the same red upholstered ones the elders had used the night he had exposed Arwydd. When the chairs were arranged in a line before the crowd, Tristan and his group took seats. Abbey sat on his left; the one to his right lay empty.

The late Royal Guard cavalry members had been wonderful riders, but even their talents paled before those of the highlanders. While the Royal Guardsmen had learned their disciplined horsemanship on parade grounds, the highlander riders had developed their skills on rough-and-tumble fields and plains, relying on them not only for their defense, but also to produce much of their food. *That's what makes them better in some ways,* he realized. *They do it because they must, to stay alive on a day-to-day basis.*

Some highlander horsemen held swords; others carried bows.

Recognizing the prince, they stopped their maneuvers and gathered their horses together. After talking for a moment, the colorful riders started lining up across the field.

Rafe sat on Abbey's left. Leaning toward her, he smiled.

"It seems that we are in for a show," he said. Still unconvinced, Abbey said nothing.

A series of targets had been set up midfield. They included straw men and various types of fruit impaled onto poles set into the ground. One by one, the riders carrying bows started galloping toward the straw men.

Yelping wildly, the first one expertly swung out of his saddle, sliding down alongside his horse's right flank. Gripping his reins between his teeth he hung sideways, nearly touching the ground as his horse thundered forward. Tristan was horseman enough to know that this trick was difficult without simultaneously trying to shoot an arrow. He had seen the highlander riders perform before, but he couldn't believe that one could hit his target from that position.

Charging hard, the highlander guided his horse toward one of the straw men. With only his left leg over his saddle to hold him in place, he notched an arrow onto the bowstring. Then he pulled the string back and held it there for a moment before releasing it.

Tristan held his breath as he watched the colorful arrow arc through the air. The rider quickly reclaimed his saddle like he had been born in it, then charged his horse to one side. As Tristan watched, the arrow buried itself squarely in the red heart that had been painted onto the straw man.

The crowd cheered and applauded loudly. Tristan found himself on his feet, raising his fists and shouting in admiration. As the cheering died down he reclaimed his chair and cast Abbey a knowing look.

"Well done for a ragtag group of thieves, wouldn't you say?" he asked.

Scowling, Abbey crossed her arms. "It will take more than that to convince me," she answered.

Tristan smiled. "Then prepare to be convinced," he said.

One after another the highlander bowmen each performed the same feat. Not one missed the mark. Then it came the swordsmen's turns. Shouting vigorously, they started charging toward the impaled fruit pieces.

Like the first riders, they took their reins in their teeth. Tristan watched in rapt fascination as most of them produced not just one sword, but two. Waving their swords in circles, one by one they charged toward the targets.

Rather than approaching one of the targets on either end, the first rider drove for the line's center. Raising each sword high, he cleanly severed two fruit pieces at once, one on each side. As the others followed suit, the same amazing feat was accomplished over and over again.

Their practice done for the day, the riders turned their horses toward the spectators. In a show of respect, they formed battle lines before Tristan's chair. As their lathered mounts whinnied and pawed the ground, the horsemen stared calmly at him, waiting for some type of acknowledgment.

Tristan knew that a respectful gesture was called for. Turning to his left, he beckoned everyone to stand. When he bowed, they did as well. The crowd cheered again.

As the riders walked their horses away, Tristan and his group reclaimed their seats. Gunther clapped his hands. Soon some serving girls brought wine, and trays laden with sweetmeats. Not standing on ceremony this time, Tristan helped himself. When Abbey and Ox did not, he gave them stern looks. Finally they relented and joined in.

"Now do you see why I want them with us?" Tristan whispered to Abbey.

Abbey scowled. "All right!" she whispered back. "I'll admit that they're excellent riders. But are they more than just a carnival act? Can they fight?"

"Yes," Tristan answered. "They are among the fiercest I have ever seen."

Despite viewing the recent demonstration, Abbey shook her head again. "But they're *highlanders,* Tristan!" she protested. Turning to her left, she saw that Gunther was trying to have some semblance of a conversation with Ox. She was sure that the warrior's conversational skills were not taxing Gunther's acumen. She turned back to look at the prince.

"If we don't watch them like hawks, they'll steal us blind!" she added. "When Wigg and Faegan hear about this, they'll be positively livid!"

Tristan took another sip of wine. "I know," he answered. "That's why you're going to help me convince them."

"Why should I?" she asked. "Wigg will believe I've gone crazy."

"Because this arrangement is good for everyone," Tristan answered. "We get these fighters to help us. In return, the highlanders get a homeland and they promise to give up their thieving ways. I'm not naive enough to believe that all will be converted. But if some are, so much the better."

Abbey snorted, laughing. "All right, all right," she finally agreed. "I'll talk to Wigg for you. But don't you dare blame me if it doesn't work!"

Smiling, Tristan lightly clanged his silver wine goblet against hers. "You've got a deal," he said.

Just then Tristan sensed a presence on his other side. He turned to see that Yasmin had slipped into the empty chair on his right. She was dressed beautifully, and her exotic perfume reminded him of recent events that he would rather Abbey didn't know about. He smiled at her.

"Good afternoon, *Jin'Sai,*" she said. She turned her eyes to his bandaged forearm. "How is your wound?"

"It's healing nicely," he answered, "thanks to you."

Leaning forward, Yasmin looked at Abbey. "And who is this lovely lady?" she asked.

For the first time since arriving in the camp, Abbey smiled knowingly. Tristan let go a little sigh of defeat. *With a single glance from Yasmin, Abbey understands,* he realized. *How is it that women always know? Sometimes their unendowed powers of perception rival Wigg's and Faegan's magic.*

Tristan gestured toward the herbmistress. "Abbey of the House of Lindstrom, I'd like to present Yasmin," he said simply. "Yasmin is the highlander healer I mentioned."

"It is a pleasure to meet you," Abbey said.

"And you," Yasmin answered.

The three of them chatted for a time; then Abbey placed her lips near Tristan's ear.

"So that's the highlander healer who helped you, eh?" she asked. She gave him a coy smile. "From the looks of her, I'd say that their men might gladly be wounded! I'm sure Balthazar was right about her healing touch. . . ."

Saying nothing, Tristan sighed and pushed his tongue hard against the inside of one cheek. He decided that it was time to go—for more than one reason. Standing, he gathered everyone's attention.

"Rafe and Ox, you stay here and collect the horsemen," he ordered. "Escort them to the palace as soon as you can. Have them take tents among the Minions and see to any other needs they might have."

Rafe smiled and slapped Ox on the back. "We'll join him soon, won't we, Ox?" he said. Shaking his head, Ox scowled darkly.

After saying his good-byes to Gunther, Tristan looked at Abbey. "It's time to go," he said. Turning to look at Yasmin, he smiled at her, then kissed the back of her hand.

"Until next time," he said. As he let go her hand, her perfume lingered.

"Until next time," she answered back. "I look forward to seeing the palace."

"Uh, er—yes," he answered. Abbey grinned widely again.

After wending their way back through the camp, Tristan and Abbey boarded the litter. Soon six stout Minion bearers had taken them skyward. As Tristan watched the camp grow smaller, his mind turned to the Conclave fleet.

They would be nearing the Citadel by now, he realized. Then he thought about what the Crysenium Envoys had told him. Knowing that he had been unable to warn the fleet, a grim silence overtook him. Seeing the change in him, Abbey leaned closer.

"What is it?" she asked.

"I have something to show you," he answered. "It is time to see what it can tell us."

Reaching down, Tristan lifted the gold medallion from his chest; then he closed his eyes. Unsure of what was happening, Abbey looked at him curiously.

In his mind's eye Tristan envisioned the twin medallions. Just as the Envoys had described, the gold discs started glowing in his mind, then merged to form one.

When Tristan looked again, he saw that Abbey's face had come alive with surprise. He had expected as much. But then Abbey saw the scene depicted on the medallion, and a look of terror seized her.

Quickly turning the medallion up, Tristan looked at it. As he did, his heart skipped a beat.

Chapter L

Amid the howling wind and stinging sea spray, Shailiha and Tyranny held on to the *Tammerland*'s rigging for dear life as Jessamay strained to keep the great ship rising.

Her hands firmly grasping the ship's wheel, the sorceress screamed as she struggled to augment her power. The angle on the ship's bow was so severe that from their places in the stern, all the women could see before them was the looming, nearly vertical deck. As the ship's timbers and masts groaned torturously, Shailiha doubted that the *Tammerland* could hold together for much longer, even if they could avoid the pursuing wave. In the darkness and chaos she had lost sight of the other surviving vessels.

The princess turned to look at the terrible wave chasing after them. Tyranny had done the right thing by changing course and keeping the fleet from hitting the wave head-on. But two of the Black Ships had already been consumed by the wave's awful power, never to be seen again. The *Tammerland* had to be at least one hundred meters in the air and climbing quickly, but the wave was looming larger with every passing second. In moments it would engulf the ship's stern and she would be done for.

Racked with fatigue, Jessamay summoned every scrap of power she could. The stricken ship lurched noticeably higher. Scars helped Tyranny claw her way up the slippery deck to stand beside the sorceress. Once there, the only thing keeping the privateer from sliding aft and tumbling into the sea was her first mate's massive arms—one holding fast to a wheelhouse cleat, the other wrapped around her waist.

Desperate to give Jessamay an order, Tyranny inched closer. By now the thunderous noise and salty spray accompanying the wave had struck the *Tammerland* full blast, drenching everyone and making it nearly impossible to communicate.

"If you can escape the wave, immediately reverse course and

let the ship fall!" Tyranny screamed. "It's the only way she'll survive the stresses! But even then I can't be sure she won't break apart!"

Although she heard Tyranny, Jessamay didn't acknowledge it. Screaming, she somehow granted the stricken ship a final burst of energy.

Just as the wave was about to engulf the stern deck, the *Tammerland* lurched violently higher. Even so, the deadly wave's crest slammed into the ship's stern keel, levering it upward and suddenly returning her level flight. The wave crest surged onward, thunderously smashing its way forward along the length of the keel.

Jessamay immediately did as Tyranny had ordered. As she turned the great ship one hundred and eighty degrees to starboard, the *Tammerland* literally pivoted atop the foaming wave crest. Then Jessamay recalled her spell, allowing the ship to plummet unaided down the wave's back-side.

Pushing Jessamay to one side, Tyranny and Scars quickly took command of the ship's wheel. As the *Tammerland* lurched and skidded down the opposite side of the wave, suddenly everything was reversed. Her bow facing down at a sickening angle, the great flagship nearly heeled over and floundered. Then she righted again to continue tearing down the wave's rearward slope at incredible speed.

Almost as suddenly as it had begun, it was over. With a mighty splash the *Tammerland* plowed into the bottom of the wave's following trough, throwing Shailiha to the deck. For several frightening moments the ship rocked violently as she tried to find her equilibrium. Finally she settled. In the calm after the storm the wind was still, the sea smooth as glass. The clouds had vanished, leaving behind a moonlit sky.

Shailiha stood shakily to see Jessamay collapse to the deck. They all ran to her. Sitting down, Scars lifted the sorceress's head into his lap. Still trembling, Jessamay slowly opened her eyes.

"You've done it!" Tyranny said. "We escaped the wave. You saved us."

Jessamay raised her head a bit. "What about Wigg and Faegan?" she asked weakly.

Running to the port gunwale, Shailiha looked westward. About one-third of a league away, the terrible wave was continuing onward. Just like the *Tammerland,* one after another the *Ephyra,* the *Cavalon,* and the *Florian* had struggled to the pinnacle of the wave's crest.

Following the *Tammerland*'s example, they too reversed course and plummeted down the wave's backside. Each ship threatened to flounder but later righted. Soon they hit sea level, plowing mightily into the wave's trough. After rocking back and forth they too settled down.

Shailiha worriedly looked to the sky again. The battling swarms were smaller now, but still killing each other with abandon. The combatants' forms were merely dark specks, and it was impossible to say which side might be winning. The valiant Minions had apparently kept Serena's creatures from breaking through their lines. *But how many warriors had that cost?* she wondered. Was it enough to tempt those monsters to dive on the ships?

Shailiha took a moment to look overboard. Bodies and body parts from the Minion forces and Serena's monsters littered the waves, as did lakes of blood, pooling on the ocean's surface. As she watched, more carnage from the battle above fell to splash into the dark sea.

Just then she heard the sound of boots landing solidly on the deck. She turned to see that the same three warriors who had spirited Wigg, Faegan, and Jessamay away had brought them back. Wigg and Jessamay quickly stood while the warrior carrying Faegan looked around for the crippled wizard's chair. To no one's surprise, it had apparently been washed overboard. Faegan ordered the warrior to carry him to where the others were standing.

"Is everyone all right?" Wigg asked urgently.

Tyranny nodded. "And you three?" she asked.

"Yes," Wigg answered. "But we lost two ships, and the acolytes who so bravely captained them."

"We know," Tyranny answered sadly. "The acolytes died heroes."

Like they were reading each other's minds, everyone turned their eyes to the sky. The moonlight showed fewer warring specks than before. They soon joined up for a few moments, then started plummeting earthward toward the ships. Wigg gave Faegan, Jessamay, and Adrian a wary look. All their senses on alert, the four mystics immediately raised their arms in defense of what might be coming.

As the thousands of figures neared, Shailiha let go a deep sigh of relief. Blessedly, they were Minion warriors. Not knowing what else to do, those who had been stationed aboard the lost *Malvina* and *Illendium* seemed to be heading for the *Tammerland.* Exhausted beyond all endurance, they crashed haphazardly to the deck. Shailiha gasped as she saw how many were seriously wounded.

Soon the *Tammerland* was awash in warriors. Many were bleeding profusely, and others had lost limbs. Taking up every inch of deck space, they tried their best to be stoic. But even those who were not wounded were so spent that they could barely move. The *Tammerland*'s top deck became slippery with their blood, and soon the air filled with calls for help.

Aghast, Tyranny looked at Shailiha. The privateer was captain of the fleet, but in Tristan's absence, Shailiha was the Minions' mistress.

"What are your orders?" Tyranny asked urgently.

Shailiha thought for a moment. "We will use the *Tammerland* as a hospital ship," she announced. "Have all the wounded who landed on other ships brought here. Use each ship's skiffs if you must. Only then will we truly know how many wounded we are dealing with."

Hearing Shailiha's orders, some warriors who could still fly started heading toward the three other ships as best they could. After looking around the crowded deck again, Shailiha suddenly remembered Duvessa.

"Does anyone know what has become of Duvessa's group?" she shouted.

No sooner had the princess asked the question than more warriors started crashing to the deck. Shailiha immediately recognized the red and white crossed feathers on their chests, telling her that they were Duvessa's warrior-healers.

Then Duvessa fell to the deck. Although exhausted, she looked unharmed. But it was obvious that her group had suffered its share of casualties. She did her best to come to all fours.

Wigg and Tyranny ran to her and helped her to her feet. After surveying the deck, Duvessa's face became grim.

"Can you give us a report?" Wigg asked.

As Duvessa tried to speak she started to faint away. Laying her on the deck, Wigg put one hand to her forehead then called the craft. As he did, it saddened him to see Traax's pin feather still attached to her armor. He gave Shailiha a quick shake of his head. Soon Duvessa's eyes fluttered open.

"What can you tell us?" Wigg answered.

"The battle was . . . indescribable," she answered. "But we managed to beat them back. Some of the beasts survived and retreated east. From what I saw, our losses were heavy. The *Malvina* and the *Florian* went down."

"We know," Shailiha said.

A look of worry suddenly overtook Duvessa's face. She tried to rise up on her elbows, but Wigg forced her back down.

"Where is Traax?" she demanded. "Is he safe?"

Wigg couldn't help but give her a concerned look. Duvessa started to bolt upright but Wigg stopped her again. Panic gripped her.

"Where is he?" she shouted. "Is he dead? I have a right to know!"

"Traax and his patrol are missing," Shailiha answered. "They should have returned some time ago. But that doesn't mean that they are dead."

"How late are they?" Duvessa demanded.

"About two hours," Wigg answered.

"We must send out search parties!" Duvessa insisted. "They have to leave at once!"

Wigg shook his head. "We are as worried about him as you are," he said. "But what you ask is impossible. We sent every warrior into the air to fight off Serena's creatures. Each one returned as exhausted as you—not to mention the many who are wounded and dying as we speak. Although I'm sure that there would be no shortage of volunteers, if we sent a search party out now they would all crash into the sea before they flew ten leagues. We need to concentrate all our efforts on the wounded and dying, and since you are the Minions' premier warrior-healer, we need your help to do that."

Pausing for a moment, Wigg looked commandingly into her eyes. "I promise you that we will send out a search party as soon as we are able. But for now, you must follow orders. It's what Traax would want."

Duvessa finally calmed. "All right," she said. "But when the search starts, I want to be the one to lead it! As his betrothed, I have earned that right!"

Wigg gave her an encouraging smile. "Very well," he answered.

Wigg and Shailiha lifted her to her feet. Without further argument, Duvessa doggedly started organizing the care of the wounded. It would be a massive undertaking.

Just then Shailiha saw two warriors wending their way across the crowded deck. They were carrying a wooden chair on wheels. It looked like it had been quickly hammered together from scrap pieces of rough-hewn wood. The warrior carrying Faegan gently lowered the wizard into it. It wobbled and squeaked a bit as it moved, but it would do.

Wasting no time, Faegan quickly wheeled himself over to where the others were standing. He urgently gathered the other Conclave members closer.

"There are far too many wounded for us to handle on our own," he said, "to say nothing of how many will be coming from the other ships. I have seen several die already during the short time we have been talking. We need help!"

"What do you suggest?" Adrian asked.

"I brought the craft tools needed to conjure the azure portal," he answered. "I am reasonably sure that I can place the portal's exit on or near the palace grounds. We should send the worst of the wounded through and let them be dealt with on the other side. Those who can't walk can be carried through on litters. A sizable Minion force was left behind. Their healers and the Redoubt acolytes will do a far better job caring for them than we. Working together, we will save more of them. Besides, the severely wounded will not be battleworthy for a long time, if ever."

"I agree," Wigg said. "What say you, Princess?"

"He's right," she answered. She turned to Faegan. "Get started as fast as you can. In the meantime, I want Duvessa to start singling out those whom she thinks should go."

Wasting no time, Faegan started wheeling his way toward Duvessa. After conferring with her for a moment he headed for the stern stairway. Shailiha guessed that he would be locked away in his quarters for hours while calculating the needed spell.

Looking around, Tyranny found Scars on the deck's port side, helping to bandage a wounded warrior. She quickly called him over.

"I want a damage report on each of the four surviving vessels," she said, "and I want it fast. Take one of the skiffs. I need to know where we stand." Scars hurried away.

Tyranny turned to look forward. If the other ships had suffered no more damage than the *Tammerland,* the situation was salvageable, but it would take time. Two of her flagship's masts were cracked but still standing, and from where she stood she could see at least four broken spars and much torn rigging. The sails had been furled, so they should have been unharmed. Tousling her hair, she bristled at the notion of again being delayed to effect repairs. She produced one of her dark cigarillos, lit it, then luxuriously exhaled some bluish smoke into the air.

From the throng of wounded warriors, an exhausted Minion officer approached Shailiha. His dark wings drooped so badly that they dragged along the bloody deck. Standing before her, he did his best to come to attention.

"Yes?" Shailiha asked.

"Begging your pardon, mistress," he said. "Some of us officers request permission to burn our dead."

Shailiha thought for a moment. She knew full well that Minion funeral rites involved cremation. She also knew that she could never allow funeral pyres to be built and used aboard the ship—especially in the sizes and numbers that would be needed. She gave the officer a questioning look.

"What do you have in mind?" she asked.

"We will place our fallen onto the sea with their brothers," he said. "We ask that the adepts set the bodies alight. In that way the fires will be contained, and be of no danger to the ships."

Shailiha looked at Wigg. "Can you set fire to the dead without endangering the fleet?"

Taking a step closer, Wigg clasped his hands before him. "Yes," he answered. "But with all due respect I believe that we should be tending to the living."

The princess looked over the ship's side. Bloated and mangled bodies—ally and foe alike—littered the waves. As she turned back to look into the officer's eyes, she found herself disagreeing with the First Wizard. To the Minions, the culture of death was easily as important as that dealing with life, and she would honor it.

"Permission granted," she said. "The mystics will see to your needs."

Immensely grateful, the officer went to one knee and bowed

his head. "Thank you, mistress," he said, "from both our living and our dead."

Shailiha walked to the starboard gunwale and tiredly leaned up against it. After a time she heard bodies splashing into the sea. To her great discouragement, the sounds went on for far longer than she might have guessed.

After a time she saw a broad azure beam extend from the *Tammerland* and streak into the night. Its gentle embrace washed over the sea to collect the bodies together then slowly push them east, a safe distance from the ship.

Almost at once the dead burst into flames. Shailiha turned to see that every warrior who could stand had silently come to attention. Those who were conscious but too severely wounded to stand were being held upright by their fellow warriors. At that moment Shailiha realized she had done the right thing.

Tyranny came to join her at the rail. For a time they watched the corpses burn in silence. As the privateer saw the sun slowly start creeping up over the horizon, she tossed her spent cigarillo into the sea.

"We have survived, but our losses have been great," she said softly. "You are faced with a difficult choice."

"I know," Shailiha answered. "To continue on to the Citadel, or to lick our wounds and go home."

Shailiha cast her gaze farther out to sea. The burning bodies were fewer now, and their roaring flames were starting to ebb.

"But first we must search for Traax," she said.

Turning away from the railing, the two women tiredly went to help with the wounded.

CHAPTER LI

CLOSING HIS EYES, TRISTAN RUBBED HIS TEMPLES WITH HIS FINGERtips. He was exhausted. Worse, he was deeply concerned over the news he had recently gotten. After taking another sip of wine he looked worriedly into his friends' faces.

He was in Faegan's chambers in the depths of the Redoubt. It was the day following his visit to the highlander camp, and the hour was late. Abbey, Aeolus, and a Minion warrior of new acquaintance sat at the table with him. As the prince considered his options, the remains of an ashen log crumbled to its death in the fireplace grate, its sound the only break in the gloomy silence.

While viewing Tristan's medallion yesterday, the prince and Abbey had seen some of the mayhem overtaking the Conclave fleet. Mad with worry, they had wanted to watch longer, but Tristan reluctantly followed the Crysenium Envoys' advice and ended the spell. After that he had paced the palace like a caged animal, fearing for his friends and warriors who were so far out to sea.

Three hours later, Faegan's azure portal had unexpectedly appeared on the palace grounds. As its whirling vortex coalesced, a terrible sight formed. Wounded warriors emerged in droves to collapse on the grass. Some died where they fell.

Tristan had been quickly summoned from his bed. Surmising that the Conclave had sent the wounded home because of their overwhelming numbers, he had immediately summoned Aeolus, Abbey, and every acolyte and Minion healer. Even Mallory, Martha, Ariana, and the palace gnomes were working feverishly, doing what they could to help tend the wounded.

A few hours later the entire palace and its surrounding areas were overflowing with Minion wounded and dying. As Tristan frantically directed the emergency efforts, an unknown warrior approached him, bearing a letter. After telling Tristan he had just arrived through the portal, he went to one knee and humbly handed the correspondence to his *Jin'Sai*.

The letter was addressed to Abbey. But the warrior had been given orders that if the *Jin'Sai* had returned, it should be given to him instead. Tristan recognized the red wax seal immediately. Its imprint bore the lion, the broadsword, and the letters "SG."

He tore the envelope open and read its contents quickly, then looked at the warrior who had brought it. "What is your name?" he demanded.

"Kratos," the warrior answered.

"You were part of the recent fighting that took place over the Sea of Whispers?" Tristan asked.

"Yes, my lord. I killed six of the beasts. I had never seen anything like them."

Tristan's response was immediate. "Are you familiar with the herbmistress named Abbey?" he asked.

"Yes."

"Go to her," he said. "She is in the Chamber of Supplication, tending to the wounded. I want her and the man named Aeolus to immediately join me in Faegan's quarters, in the Redoubt. I want you there too."

Kratos clicked his heels together. "I live to serve," he said. Tristan watched him hurry off.

That had been one hour ago. As he again looked down at Shailiha's letter, he sensed the burden of command that would be weighing so heavily across his sister's shoulders. Before allowing Kratos into the room, he had shown the letter to Abbey and Aeolus. Picking it up, he silently read it again:

Dearest Abbey,

As I write this, we are doing all we can to tend to the thousands of warriors wounded in a recent air battle with Serena's forces. It is plain that there will be far too many for us to treat. We have therefore activated Faegan's portal, so that they can be sent home. We pray that you, the acolytes, and the Minion healers will save as many as you can. Know too that for the next several days, Faegan's portal will reappear at midday, and stay open each time for as long as he can sustain it.

Serena's creatures were beaten back, but at a terrible price. Early estimates show that at least a full third of our warriors are dead or wounded. The Malvina, *the* Florian, *and the acolytes who captained them were lost to a giant wave that we believe was conjured by Serena. The other four Black Ships were damaged, but Tyranny says that they can be repaired. Sadly, a scout patrol led by Traax has gone missing. The longer they are gone, the more we fear them dead.*

As the hours pass, I struggle with the decision about whether to carry on to the Citadel. I will confer with the other Conclave members and decide shortly. If in your judgment more warriors can be spared from the palace, please send them to us. Should there be any news about Tristan please tell us. Besides our many troubles, we all worry for him desperately.

Love,
Shailiha

Letting go a deep breath, Tristan folded the letter, then replaced it into its envelope. After sliding it beneath his worn leather vest, he looked at Kratos.

"What else can you tell us?" he asked.

"Little, my lord," Kratos answered. "The *Jin'Saiou* has explained matters well. The wizards cremated our dead. Everyone worries for the fate of Traax's lost patrol."

On hearing about Traax again, Tristan sadly shook his head. He was glad that Ox was still at the highlander camp, and unable to hear the news.

"Thank you," Tristan said to Kratos. "Your service has been admirable. Please wait in the hall."

Kratos bowed. *"Jin'Sai,"* he said simply. He walked across the room and let himself out.

Leaning his forearms on the table, Tristan closed his eyes. "It's my fault," he said. "Had I come home sooner, I would never have allowed the fleet to sail."

"I don't understand," Aeolus said. "You gave them the order to attack, did you not? Surely you suspected that Serena would have traps lying in wait."

"Yes," Tristan answered. "But that was before I knew."

"Knew what?" Aeolus asked.

Abbey touched Tristan on the arm. "I assume that you asked Aeolus here because you wanted the wisdom of an experienced Vigors wizard," she said. "But even he can't help unless he is fully informed. I suggest you tell him everything that you told me."

Leaning back in his chair, Tristan gave Aeolus a hard look. "Twice now, you have been invited to join the Conclave," he said. "But I still have no answer. If I am to tell you all I know, it will only be after you accept membership. Will you join us or not?"

As Aeolus looked at the tabletop, a sea of emotions both old and new flooded through him. He looked back at the prince.

"Aside from the fleet's predicament, how serious is the overall threat?" he asked.

"It is the worst we have ever known," Tristan said. "It is greater than the return of the Coven, Nicholas' Gates of Dawn, and Wulfgar's effort to pollute and destroy the Orb of the Vigors. I daresay it is even more dire than the Sorceresses' War of three centuries ago. Conflicts and forces are in play that you couldn't start to imagine."

Aeolus looked over at Abbey. "We have known one another for a long time," he said. "I don't distrust the *Jin'Sai*'s word, but I want to hear you say it. Is the threat truly as terrible as he says?"

Abbey nodded. "Yes," she answered. "Unless we stop it, everything we hold dear is doomed."

For several long moments silence filled the room. Aeolus looked into Tristan's eyes. "I accept," he finally said.

Tristan was pleased by Aeolus' answer. But before giving his final stamp of approval, he wanted to be crystal clear about some important points.

"I know how you feel about the craft and your school," Tristan said. "You must promise to live here at the palace, to accept my orders at all times, and to willingly use the craft when needed. Do you agree?"

"Yes," the wizard and martial master answered. Then he gave Tristan a smile. "I also promise to train you nearly to death in your pursuit of *K'Shari.*"

Tristan finally smiled back. "Fair enough," he said. He looked over at Abbey. "The Conclave again numbers ten souls," he said.

Abbey nodded. "So it would seem," she answered, "if Traax still lives." Realizing his oversight, Tristan nodded sadly.

For the next hour, Tristan told Aeolus all about his journey with Xanthus. Aeolus became nearly speechless at the tale. For several moments he looked at Tristan like the prince had lost his mind. "Is what you say true?" he breathed.

"Yes," Tristan answered. "Had I not lived it, I would find it equally incredible."

Aeolus shook his head in disbelief. "Amazing," he said. "And yet, it explains so much. But you still haven't discussed the immediate threat."

Tristan's face became grim. "Simply put," he said, "unless we can stop her, Serena will soon have the ability to simultaneously change every right-leaning blood signature in our world leftward. With everyone of endowed blood so strongly influenced to worship the Vagaries, everywhere east of the Tolenkas, the Vigors will cease to exist. The Forestallment allowing this power is being held by the *Pon Q'tar.* They have yet to trust its calculations to Serena's mind. But when the right time comes, they will."

"I beg the Afterlife," Aeolus breathed. "Abbey told me that Wigg, Faegan, and Jessamay had found the formula allowing them to change blood signature lean. But I never suspected that all the signatures of one type or another could be affected at the same time!"

"Nor did we," Tristan said.

"How is such a thing possible?" Aeolus asked.

"On Wulfgar's death, Serena's unborn child miscarried," Tristan answered. "Before leaving for Eutracia, Wulfgar magically bound his life force to Serena's, so that she would know if he died. But he underestimated the spell's strength. When I killed him, the spell caused the miscarriage and nearly killed Serena. The dead baby was a girl. Serena calls her Clarice. She blames me for her child's death."

"Go on," Aeolus said.

"Serena has enchanted the baby's corpse, ensuring that it won't decay," Tristan said. "The corpse figures prominently in the Heretics' plan."

"But why preserve an infant corpse?" Aeolus asked. "It doesn't make any sense."

"Ah, but it does," Tristan answered. "Before Wulfgar was killed, he spirited the Valrenkians away to the Citadel. Reznik, the most adept among them—and Einar, Serena's lead consul—are conducting grotesque experiments. They are trying to refine a lost spell written by Failee, just before she died."

"To what end?" Aeolus asked.

"To bring the dead back to life," Tristan answered quietly.

For several moments no one spoke. Stunned, Aeolus sat back in his chair. "But why?" he breathed.

"They would use this spell to revive Clarice," Tristan answered.

"But why is the life of one child so important?" Aeolus asked.

"Because that child's living blood is the last piece of the puzzle," Tristan answered. "If Clarice can be revived, she will be the only person in the world who carries the late Queen Morganna's blood that has not been affected by a Forestallment, as mine and Shailiha's have. It would be virgin territory, if you will. Because she is Morganna's descendant through Wulfgar, her living blood will be of great power. It would not be as strong as mine or Shailiha's. But it would reign third most powerful in our world—dwarfing even yours, Wigg's, Faegan's, and Jessamay's."

"Why go to all the bother?" Aeolus asked. "Why don't the *Pon Q'tar* clerics grant the Forestallment calculations directly to Serena's mind now? Then she could imbue the Forestallment into her own blood and morph all of the right-leaning blood signatures at will."

Leaning over the table, Abbey looked into Aeolus' eyes. "Because even Serena's blood, potent as it is, is not strong enough to accept such an amazingly strong Forestallment," she explained. "Only Morganna's blood or some derivative will suffice."

"And Clarice's blood is strong enough?" Aeolus asked. "Even though Wulfgar was your half brother, and his daughter is two generations removed from Morganna?"

"Yes," Tristan answered, "provided her blood has never been imbued with any other competing Forestallments. In this, her blood is unique in the world. On bringing Clarice back to life, she will be the only living person of Morganna's blood walking the earth with a left-leaning blood signature, and controlled by those who worship the Vagaries. When Clarice reaches maturity, the *Pon Q'tar* will provide her mother with the Forestallment allowing all right-leaning signatures to be changed leftward at once. Serena will then grant that Forestallment to her daughter's blood. Clarice will call it forth, forever sealing the Vigors' doom everywhere east of the Tolenkas. It would be about twenty years before this could happen. But you and I know that twenty years is only a blink of an eye in the history of the craft."

Aghast, Aeolus slumped back in his chair. He stared blankly down at the tabletop for some time before returning his gaze to the prince.

"It's monstrous," he whispered. "You're right. This threat eclipses even the Sorceresses' War. I assume that we three are the only Conclave members who know about it?"

"Yes," Tristan answered. "But there is more to tell you. Despite your experiences in the Sorceresses' War, you will find the rest of the tale difficult to hear."

"Please continue," Aeolus said.

"Both the Ghetto and the Recluse have been conquered by Serena's forces," Tristan said. "All the Minion warriors who once manned those strongholds are dead. Serena needed the Ghetto because there she could easily secure large numbers of vulnerable people all at once, rather than having to waste time scouring the countryside for them. The lepers are being taken to the Recluse and used as subjects for Reznik's and Einar's bizarre experiments. They are killing them and using Failee's continually refined formula on them, trying to bring them back to life."

"Aren't they worried that the use of lepers might somehow alter or ruin their experiments?" Aeolus asked.

Tristan shook his head. "No," he answered. "Dead is dead."

Aeolus stared blankly at Tristan. "What will you do?" he asked.

"I will do the only thing I can," the prince said. "I will order the fleet home."

"But by now they must be near the Citadel," Aeolus protested. "Why not let them continue on and capture Serena and her dead baby girl? If they succeed, the threat is ended and the Recluse can be dealt with later."

"For one thing, I fear that there has been too much attrition in the Minion forces for the campaign to succeed," Tristan answered. "Serena is being aided by the Heretics. Two ships have already been lost, and one-third of the warriors are casualties. Our forces need to come home so that they can regroup, and be joined by the highlander cavalry."

"Will you go through the portal to give this order?" Abbey asked Tristan.

Tristan shook his head. "I would like to, but I mustn't," he said.

"Why not?" Aeolus asked.

"You're forgetting something," Tristan said. "Crysenium's existence is a secret, and must be kept that way. If I am captured, the information might be tortured from me. Nor may either of you go for the same reason. For the time being, we must allow no one with the fleet to understand my true motives for ordering them home. To do so could alert those at the Recluse. Instead, I will send a letter back to Shailiha, citing her recent losses as the only reason for my decision. I suspect that given the situation, she might soon come to that decision on her own, anyway. When our forces return we will quickly ready another invasion fleet, including the highlander horsemen. Then we will sail for Parthalon and lay siege to the Recluse."

"We will attack the Recluse?" Abbey asked. "Not the Citadel?"

"That's right," Tristan answered. "We can only guess at whether Serena remains at the Citadel, but we *know* that Einar and Reznik have taken sanctuary in the Recluse. Stopping them from completing the formula will be as effective as capturing Serena and Clarice. Both are needed for the Heretics' plan to work."

Aeolus thought for a moment. "If the *Pon Q'tar* are in possession of a powerful Forestallment that alters all blood signature lean at once, then why haven't they used it against their enemies on their side of the world?" he asked.

"They tried to do so, aeons ago," Tristan answered. "And they nearly succeeded. Luckily, the Ones got wind of it and developed a counterspell. Millions were converted before the Ones could turn the tide."

"Why can't the counterspell be used on this side of the Tolenkas to protect us?" Abbey asked.

"I asked the Envoys the same question," Tristan answered. "Simply put, there isn't enough time. You must remember that our knowledge and power in the craft is infantile compared to that possessed by the Ones and the Heretics. I was told that our learning to employ the spell could take far longer than the time required for Clarice to grow old enough for her blood to accept the needed Forestallment."

Tristan stood from the table, walked to Faegan's desk, and looked through its drawers. He soon produced a parchment, an inkwell, and a quill. After giving the issue some thought, he penned a letter to Shailiha. When he had finished he placed the letter in an envelope, sealed it with hot wax, then removed his signet ring and forced an impression into the fresh wax.

He turned toward the door. "Guard!" he called out.

At once the doors opened. A sturdy Minion warrior entered the room and clicked his heels.

"I need to see Kratos," Tristan said. The warrior bowed, then left the room. Kratos soon appeared. Tristan beckoned him closer and handed him the letter. He gave the warrior a stern look.

"This might be the most important mission of your life," he

said. "When Faegan's portal opens tomorrow at midday, you are to enter it and return to the fleet. Give that letter to Princess Shailiha. She will surely pen another letter back to me. Bring it back as fast as you can. Until then, you are to guard this letter with your life."

Kratos bowed. *"Jin'Sai,"* he said solemnly. As he turned and left the room, Tristan returned to the meeting table.

Silence reigned again. Abbey put one hand atop Tristan's. "Will your stated reason be enough for Shailiha to obey your orders?" she asked.

Tristan turned to look into the fire. "It has to be," he said. He turned back to worriedly look at the herbmistress and newest Conclave member.

"If the Conclave doesn't come home soon," he added softly, "all is lost."

CHAPTER LII

"COLLECT A SAMPLE OF HIS BLOOD," ONE OF THEM SAID. "IT IS TIME to test our latest discovery."

The harsh words awakened Xanthus. As he came around, he found himself in the same room where he had been interrogated twice before. Azure bands again bound him to a simple chair. A glowing light shone down on him from overhead, its stark beacon the only reprieve from the darkness. Although he was weak, Xanthus had yet to be harmed. Their faces bathed in shadow, twelve *Pon Q'tar* clerics again sat at a table across from him.

Xanthus watched with fear as a cleric pointed at him. With his powers gone, he could do nothing but wait for the agonizing pain. But this time the suffering never came. Instead he felt a slight tingling in one wrist, nothing more.

Xanthus looked down to see that he had been bound to the chair with his right wrist upturned. He watched a painless incision form to release a single drop of his endowed blood. The incision closed. As the azure blood drop hovered to a place between him and the clerics, it smoothly evolved into his blood signature.

The male cleric who had spoken seemed to be in charge. Peering through the gloom, Xanthus watched him move his index finger slightly. At once the blood signature obeyed and floated closer to the clerics' table.

"Watch as I bring the needed spell," the lead cleric told the others. "The theory behind the nautilus effect is vastly complex," the cleric added. "Behold."

At once a series of Old Eutracian symbols and numbers started materializing in midair. They swirled about the room for several moments before silently arranging themselves into a horizontally aligned formula. Xanthus tried to decipher it, but he soon realized that its complexities went far beyond his knowledge. Then the formula aligned itself vertically, and the symbol at the line's top revolved several times, twisting the formula into a tight spiral.

Looking closer, he saw that the numbers and symbols had an unusual thickness about them. This formula's configuration was different from every other he had seen. Not only did it carry a vertical orientation, but it seemed to also have a physical, three-dimensional substance about it.

"Beautiful, isn't it?" the lead cleric asked his fellows. "What you see is the product of more than a decade of work by our best Heretic researchers. It couldn't have come at a better time."

The lead cleric pointed at Xanthus' blood signature. It obediently came to rest on the formula's top, then started winding down its length, leaving a blood trail as it went. When it reached the end it stopped.

At once the formula lost its spiral shape, then started curling from the bottom upward, securing Xanthus' blood signature tightly at its center. As it finished winding up, its numbers and symbols vanished.

In their places, outward-facing chambers appeared. Spiraling tightly in a clockwise direction, they looked like those shown if a nautilus mollusk had been cut in half lengthwise. But unlike a naturally occurring nautilus, this one had grown to over two meters across, and held hundreds of individual compartments. The spiraling compartments grew in size as they radiated outward from the nautilus's center. Each compartment held brilliantly colored patterns, like those viewed in a kaleidoscope. As it hovered in the air, its outer shell glowed.

"I give you the nautilus effect," the lead cleric said. "From this day forward, no one of endowed blood will be able to hide his or her memories from us—even if those memories have been altered by the craft."

"Breathtaking," one of the female clerics said.

"Indeed," the lead cleric answered. "Like the sea mollusk, this shell is separated into a series of progressively larger compartments. With the nautilus effect, each successive compartment holds not an ever-growing sea creature, but an ever-growing number of memories, taken directly from the subject's blood. The physical similarity between the naturally occurring mollusk and the nautilus effect is strictly coincidental. Still it makes for a good comparison, hence the name.

"The subject's earliest memories are at the nautilus's center," the cleric added. "Because there are fewer retrievable memories available from one's formative years, the chambers near the center are the smallest. Succeeding chambers grow in size as the subject ages and ever more memories are created and retained in the subconscious. Because these memory chambers arise from one's blood rather than one's mind, our researchers doubt that they can be tampered with. Should Xanthus' memories gleaned in this manner prove different from those we found while searching his mind in the traditional way, we will know that trickery is afoot."

"How are these closeted memories shown?" another of the *Pon Q'tar* women asked. Xanthus could tell that she remained skeptical, despite the wonder hovering before her.

"As is the case with the vast variety of Forestallment formulas, an index spell will be needed," the lead cleric answered. "Our researchers say it should be finished soon, and that it will rely on chronology and subject matter. For example, should one wish to see a subject's adolescent memories relating to his father, the index will select the appropriate time frame from the subject's life, then search for images showing the subject's father. Then the index will sift though the scenes until the requested memory is found. Even without an index, I can give you a nonspecific demonstration here and now. I have but to select a memory chamber, then call forth one of its thousands of scenes."

Xanthus had become so entranced that he had almost forgotten his dire situation. If what they said was true, the gleaming chambers held his entire life's story. But which part was it about to show?

Suddenly one of the nautilus's smaller chambers glowed, and its patterned colors started whirling. Then an azure light shone from the chamber. As the light streamed into the room, a scene formed in its depths.

Xanthus did not remember the particular occasion that was being shown, but he could identify the people in it. One of them was him, around the age of nine or ten. He walked hand in hand between his paternal grandfather and grandmother. The old man's face was kindly, weather-beaten. The woman looked slightly younger. They were strolling through a lively forum. The sun was high, the sky clear.

Xanthus was dumbfounded by what he saw. His grandparents were long dead, and had been named Aaron and Esther. He had loved them with all his heart. By that time in his life he had become an orphan, his parents killed in the seemingly never-ending War of Attrition. It had been his parents' tragic deaths that had eventually convinced him to join the Imperial Order. As he watched the strangely familiar people walk along, he started hearing sounds come from the scene. With this last enhancement, the image took on an eerie life of its own.

The bustling forum was colorful and alive with energy. Hundreds of stalls enticed the many passersby. Each stall's proprietor called out loudly to the shoppers, trying to get them to stop and admire his or her wares. Stern-looking Imperial Order officers strolled watchfully, looking for anyone who seemed out of place. Young Xanthus admired their golden uniforms and the short swords hanging at their hips.

Smiling, Aaron looked down at Xanthus. "Would you like a treat?" he asked.

The boy nodded eagerly. After paying for a candy, Aaron handed it to him. Xanthus placed the whole thing into his mouth. Smiling widely, he looked up at his grandmother, then—

The lead cleric waved one hand. The image vanished, and the azure light fled back into the nautilus's compartment. The compartment's riotous colors stopped whirling. Suddenly brought back to reality, Xanthus returned his gaze to the shrouded *Pon*

Q'tar clerics. The amazing respite into his past had been brief but welcome.

"Do you remember that day?" the lead cleric demanded. Unlike Aaron's voice, the cleric's held no compassion.

"No," Xanthus answered. "But that does not mean it didn't happen. The two elderly people were Aaron and Esther, my paternal grandparents. They raised me after my parents died in the war."

"We know," the cleric answered dryly. Lifting a leather-bound notebook from the tabletop, he held it up for Xanthus to see. "It's all here in your file. You were once a respected member of the Imperial Order. You even rose to become Faxon's personal assistant. He trusted you enough to choose you to bring us the *Jin'Sai*. But you turned traitor and let Tristan escape. What we cannot understand is why you brought him so far, only to let him go. We have spoken to Faxon. Like us, he is beside himself with anger at your betrayal."

"And I keep telling you how wrong you are!" Xanthus protested as he angrily strained against his bonds. "I am no traitor! I saw the *Jin'Sai* die in the red desert with my own eyes! It was not I who conjured the Borderlands! If anyone is responsible for the *Jin'Sai*'s death it is you!"

"Mind your tongue!" one of the female clerics shouted. "There was an army of Ones advancing—we did what we had to! How dare you question our wisdom! We are not some gaggle of low-ranking Imperial Order officers for you to berate! We are members of the *Pon Q'tar*! Any one of us could kill you with a single thought!"

Xanthus' mouth turned up into a sneer. "But you won't," he answered sarcastically. "You need to learn whether I'm telling the truth."

The lead cleric had heard enough. "Guard!" he shouted.

Double doors immediately opened in the wall behind Xanthus' chair. Light streamed in, hurting his eyes again. Two high-ranking Imperial Order officers quickly entered the room. The azure bands binding Xanthus disappeared.

"Take this traitor back to his hole!" the lead cleric ordered. "As punishment for his insolence he is to be denied food for the next two days." The two officers promptly manhandled Xanthus from the room. As the doors shut behind them, the darkness returned.

"When will the index spell be ready?" one of the clerics asked.

"Within another moon," the leader answered. "Then we will have our answers. Even so, the *Jin'Sai* has escaped us. But if Serena succeeds, Tristan and his sister will be of little consequence."

"We have just proven that one's blood signature holds the entire account of its owner's life," he added. "Even we clerics at this table would never have believed that possible. It is often said that the eyes are the window to the soul. But after witnessing the nautilus effect, now I say that the true window to the soul is one's blood signature, in all of its amazing splendor."

"Do you still believe that Xanthus is a traitor?" another of them asked.

Several quiet moments passed before the lead cleric answered. "Only time will tell," he said. "If he is, he will be killed. If not, we might find another use for him after all."

After picking up Xanthus' file from the table, he squired the other clerics from the room.

CHAPTER LIII

AS SHE AND HER WARRIOR SCOUTS SAT ATOP PART OF THE SMASHED deck, Duvessa raised her eyes to the sky. Her heart fell as she realized that the coming darkness would drastically impede her search.

It was early evening of the day following the attack on the fleet. Even the famous Minion battle with Nicholas' forces high over Farplain had not caused so many casualties. As she looked down at the floating wreckage, the premier warrior-healer fervently hoped that she might find some fellow warriors still alive.

Wigg had been right. Had she ordered a search party aloft yesterday, they would not have gotten far before tumbling into the sea. It would have been a Minion suicide mission, pure and simple. Even so, Duvessa knew that there would have been no shortage of volunteers.

As her group had traveled farther east, they had all realized that not even Traax could have stayed continually aloft for this long. Any survivors would be in the ocean, and that only lessened their already meager chances for survival. As she and her warriors had focused their attention on the waves, they found Black Ship wreckage. Each piece had to be investigated. Eventually she and her scouts had landed on a section of aft decking to take a rest.

At first Duvessa had been surprised to see wreckage of any kind. To her mind, the wave had been so tall and strong that no part of either lost Black Ship should have reappeared. But after giving the matter some thought, she understood. After engulfing the ships and breaking them apart, the wave had sent debris tumbling east, down its backside. The trough's impetus had then carried the wreckage even farther.

As Duvessa surveyed the flotsam, she realized that she had no idea from which ship it had come. Not knowing somehow added to the forlornness of it all. It was strange to see it like this, as it wandered the sea by itself. The deck boards were broken or missing in many places and most of the ship's wheelhouse was gone. Sections of tangled rigging still lay about. Finding this wooden island had come just in time, for the tired patrol had been nearing the point of no return when they spotted it. Although it held no sign of Traax's group, the respite it granted was welcome.

As Duvessa tried to decide what to do, she looked at her exhausted male and female warriors. Each had eagerly volunteered. As their commander she had every right to force them eastward until they plunged to their deaths from exhaustion. Despite how much she loved Traax, that was not an order she was prepared to give. If they turned around now, with any luck they would make it back to the fleet. But even the current was against her. Their wooden island was quickly drifting east, adding urgency to her decision.

She thoughtfully touched Traax's betrothal pin still attached to her armor. Finally deciding, she stood and gathered her warriors' attention.

"I'm ordering you all back to the fleet," she said.

The warriors had been expecting this, and each understood her real meaning. She was going to continue searching for Traax's group to her death, if need be. But because they were already at the point of no return, she would not ask them to continue on with her. Yesterday this mission would surely have meant their deaths. Today, if there was a chance the others could get back, she would make them take it.

One of Duvessa's most trusted warrior-healers stood. Her name was Kefira. At twenty-five Seasons of New Life, she was one of the best long-distance fliers in the entire Minion force. Although she regarded her commander with humility, she meant to be heard.

"With all due respect," she said, "we have a suggestion."

Duvessa didn't like having her orders questioned. But out of respect for Kefira she decided to listen. "Speak quickly," she said. "What daylight remains is rapidly fading."

"I will go with you," Kefira proposed. "Two pairs of eyes are far better than one. The others will spend the night here, atop this wreckage. Although it is damaged, it seems to be in no imminent danger of sinking. If you and I have not returned by dawn, those remaining behind will fly back to the fleet. It is a sound tactical decision, mistress. We bore enough food and water to last until morning. By then those staying here will be refreshed and will have a better chance of getting back alive."

Duvessa understood the real reason behind Kefira's plan. Those who stayed behind had no intention of resting. They planned on keeping up the search, using the ravaged deck as a base from which to send smaller patrols north and south. She gave Kefira a grateful look.

"Very well," she said. "But are you sure that you want to accompany me? You're probably signing your own death warrant."

Kefira gave her commander a knowing smile. "I live to serve" was all she said.

Duvessa looked at the others. "You are each in agreement?" she asked. "Any who wish to go back now may do so without shame."

The five males and four females nodded. *Minions to the end,* Duvessa thought. She looked back at Kefira.

"Very well," she said. "You and I will leave at once." While the others stood to honor them, their commander looked into every face. "Thank you," she said softly. Without speaking, her warriors came to attention.

After climbing back into the sky, Duvessa and Kefira made a circle over the shabby wooden island before turning east toward the growing darkness.

CHAPTER LIV

"WE KNOW THE PROBLEM IS A DIFFICULT ONE, PRINCESS," WIGG said. "But we have to decide soon. The repairs to the ships are nearly done. Tomorrow we must be either on our way home, or headed toward the Citadel. There is no middle ground."

Gathered in Faegan's quarters, the Conclave members had been meeting for the last two hours. Tyranny had just reported that the four surviving Black Ships would be ready to sail soon. Most of the severely wounded warriors had been sent by portal to Tammerland. Aside from waiting for the return of Duvessa's patrol, by dawn there would be no valid reason to tarry.

No fresh replacements had been sent from Eutracia, and that worried everyone. Had Faegan's portal malfunctioned in some way, Shailiha wondered, causing the wounded warriors to somehow go to their deaths? Despite the princess's worries, Faegan firmly insisted that his portal was working normally. Or perhaps the palace had been attacked by other forces, Shailiha worried. Those considerations and more plagued her as she considered what to do.

"I say we forge ahead," Faegan said from the other side of the table. "I for one haven't come so far and lost so many brave warriors just to turn tail and run!"

Wigg gave him a hard look. "And it is for those exact reasons that I say we must return!" he argued. "Clearly, Serena knew we were coming! Our advantage of surprise is long gone! We must go home and regroup!"

"Every day we wait, Serena grows stronger," Jessamay added, siding with Faegan. "We need to take the Citadel soon."

Suddenly an urgent pounding came on the cabin door. Shailiha scowled. She didn't wish the meeting to be disturbed. But if there was an emergency, she needed to know.

"Enter!" she called out.

An unfamiliar warrior strode briskly into the room. He held something in one hand.

"Approach," Shailiha said.

The warrior hurried to the table and looked at Shailiha. "Please forgive the intrusion, Princess," he said. "My name is Kratos."

"What is it?" Shailiha demanded.

Kratos handed her a letter. "I was told to give you this," he answered.

Shailiha saw that it was addressed to her. More important, she knew the handwriting. When she turned the letter over, she recognized her brother's seal, and her heart jumped for joy.

"It's from Tristan!" she shouted as she tore it open. She unfolded the parchment and cast her hungry eyes down the page. As the other members waited and wondered, the princess was overcome with happiness. Pressing the letter to her chest, she closed her eyes and let go a deep sigh of relief.

"Don't keep us on tenterhooks!" Tyranny blurted out. The privateer blushed at her outburst, then regained her composure. "What does he say?" she asked.

Looking at the letter again, Shailiha read it aloud.

Dearest Sister,

I have returned to the palace, and I am well. Also know that although no replacement warriors were sent to you, we are not in danger here. For reasons of security I cannot explain my reappearance further, nor can I come to you. You simply must trust me.

Because of the fleet's significant losses, I order you to return to Eutracia at once. Wigg and Faegan will surely wonder whether I have truly come home. After seeing me vanish with Xanthus they are right to be suspicious; they might even doubt whether it was I who penned this missive. With all my heart I tell you that it is me. Should you or the wizards doubt that I have returned, I ask that you follow the instructions written at the bottom of this letter.

Come home soon. Much remains to be done, and time is of the essence.

Your loving brother,
Tristan

Wigg raised an eyebrow. "What are these instructions he mentions?" he asked.

Shailiha handed the letter to Wigg. Not to be left out, Faegan quickly wheeled his chair close to Wigg's, then rudely read the letter from over the First Wizard's shoulder. Scowling, Wigg sighed and shook his head.

Each wizard read the addendum twice. As Wigg sat back in his chair he looked at Kratos. "Did the *Jin'Sai* give you this letter personally?" he asked.

"Yes," the warrior answered.

"How did he seem?" Wigg asked. "I mean, was he himself in every respect?"

"Without question," Kratos answered. "I watched him write the letter. I met with him in the Redoubt, along with Abbey and another man."

Wigg scowled. "What other man?" he asked.

"He was about your age," Kratos answered. "His name is Aeolus."

Pursing his lips, Wigg placed his hands flat on the tabletop. "Well, well," he mused.

"It seems that some things have changed while we were away," Jessamay said.

Wigg nodded. "If Aeolus has agreed to join the Conclave, then so much the better." He picked up the letter again. "The handwriting looks like Tristan's," he said, "and the envelope carries his seal. More important, Kratos has *seen* the prince. But I still have my doubts." He handed the letter to Faegan. "In your opinion, did Tristan write this note? If the person Kratos saw is some kind of impostor, he could be ordering us right into a trap."

Faegan held the page to the light. "I can't tell from this alone," he said. Then he seized on an idea and he cackled softly. "But there's a way to find out."

Reaching across the table he took up a piece of blank parchment. Then he closed his eyes. Everyone wondered what he was up to, but knew better than to interrupt. With his eyes still closed, Faegan lifted the parchment higher. The Conclave members were surprised to see words start forming on the page. After several lines had appeared, Faegan opened his eyes.

Faegan grinned. "I just called on my gift of Consummate Recollection," he explained. "As you know, I am able to perfectly recall everything I have ever seen, heard, or read. I used the gift to reproduce one of the many parchments the prince has signed of late. I then used the craft to duplicate it onto this fresh sheet. This document has to do with recent taxes levied against the province of Ephyra. But it's not the text that interests me." Then the wizard smiled again. "It's the prince's signature I'm after."

Faegan lifted the two pages, then held them side by side to the light. After a time he nodded, then placed them on the table. "As best these old wizard's eyes can tell, the signature on Shailiha's letter is genuine."

As Shailiha looked around the table, she saw that everyone seemed convinced except Wigg. "What's wrong?" she asked him.

"You seem to have forgotten our conversation while we were on the way to the Serpent and the Sword," Wigg answered. "I told you that if Tristan came home, we would have to take measures to ensure that he wasn't under the influence of the Vagaries. That possibility still concerns me. But out here at sea, there is no way to tell."

Faegan thoughtfully cast his eyes to the bottom of Tristan's letter, then smiled. Wigg knew that look. This time it worried him. "What are you thinking?" he asked.

"I'm looking at these instructions Tristan left for Shailiha," Faegan said. "I believe she should follow them."

"And I don't!" Wigg shot back. "The last time we saw Tristan he was being taken away by a creature of the Vagaries! There's no telling what sort of disaster these instructions might produce! For all we know the entire fleet could go up in flames!"

Faegan looked over at the princess and gave her a wink. "What say you, Your Highness?" he asked. "Will you give it a go?"

She reached out and took up Tristan's letter. As she reread the instructions, she had to admit that she couldn't guess what might happen. *Do as I ask,* Tristan had written, *and my reason will be-*

come clear. It seemed that he was referring to the craft. She had not been trained in the craft and possessed but one usable Forestallment, allowing her communion with the fliers of the fields. But she desperately wanted to believe that it was Tristan who had penned this note, so she decided that she would try.

She looked at Wigg. "I'm sorry," she said," but I agree with Faegan." After putting the letter on the table she closed her eyes.

Following Tristan's instructions, Shailiha imagined the gold medallion hanging around her neck. Then she imagined Tristan's medallion hanging alongside hers. To her surprise they combined to form one disc. Shailiha heard people around the table gasp. Worried that Wigg had been right, she opened her eyes.

At first she thought nothing had happened. Then she saw everyone looking at her chest. When she looked down her mouth fell open. A soft, nearly undetectable glow was seeping out from beneath her medallion. She picked it up and turned it toward her face.

The medallion's underside had changed amazingly. On its surface she saw Tristan sitting in his palace quarters. Abbey and Aeolus were there with him. All three seemed to be waiting for something. The Paragon lay around Tristan's neck, but his medallion did not.

Suddenly Shailiha saw her brother's face light up. *He just noticed that we're watching,* she realized. *He has placed his medallion across from him, so that we can see him and the others. Our medallions can reach across space and time! How marvelous! But how, why . . . ?*

She saw Tristan stand. Entranced, Shailiha watched as he came closer to his medallion. Then he held something up for her to see. It was small, made of gold, and twinkled brightly. He smiled at her and nodded. Understanding, Shailiha smiled back. Having seen all she needed, she ended the spell the way the letter's instructions suggested.

"Amazing," she breathed. She dropped the gold disc back to her chest.

"Indeed," Wigg said. "The medallions you and your brother wear have been enchanted in some way. But what did you see when you turned yours up to your face? At that point, the rest of us could no longer view the scene."

Shailiha smiled again. "I think he was counting on that," she said. "I also have no doubt that it was truly him."

"Why?" Faegan asked.

"He showed me a gift that I gave him when he graduated from his Royal Guard training," she answered. "Since then it has been our little secret. Even our parents never knew about it."

"What is it?" Wigg asked.

"A small, golden image of Pilgrim, the stallion mother and father gave to him on the same occasion," Shailiha answered. "I would recognize it anywhere." Smiling, the princess looked around the table.

"As soon as Duvessa's scout patrol returns," she said, "we're going home."

CHAPTER LV

AMID THE PLAINTIVE SCREAMS OF THE DYING, SERENA TURNED TO look at Actinius. She smiled.

"I want all the remaining lepers brought here from the Ghetto," she said. "If we're forced to continue feeding all of our servants in one place like this, we will need them. We might even be forced to gather up citizens from the countryside. But that doesn't matter. Parthalon holds enough souls to satisfy our needs."

Night had fallen several hours ago. Serena and Actinius stood on the guard path atop one of the walls surrounding the Recluse. The Eutracian moons shone brightly down on the lake and the land surrounding the huge castle. As more screams filtered up to their ears, the two mystics looked down at the grisly spectacle.

Shrews and envelopers by the thousands were voraciously feeding on lepers brought from the Ghetto. It was vitally important to keep the beasts alive, even if the Conclave fleet had been destroyed. Once Serena's mission was fulfilled, the shrews and envelopers would serve as her taskmasters, just as the Minions had done for the sorceresses of the Coven. She wanted them to know who was in control, and that it was she who satisfied their needs.

Like Failee, she worshipped the Vagaries and ruled the Recluse with an iron fist. But there would be vital differences between her and Wigg's late wife. Serena would directly serve the *Pon Q'tar.* And her power would dominate two nations, rather than just one.

Only minutes ago, several hundred lepers had been herded through the castle's entryway, across the bridge spanning the lake, and onto the surrounding land. Naked and terrified, at first they had huddled together like they could somehow find safety in numbers. Little had they known that this was the worst thing that they could have done, for it only simplified the beasts' feeding frenzy.

Sensing prey, shrew herds had surfaced from their hiding places in the lake surrounding the castle, and from the nearby bodies of water that had sprung into being after the sudden deaths of the Coven sorceresses. Not to be outdone, envelopers by the thousands abandoned their camouflage and left their hiding places in the air and against the castle walls to join in the frenzy.

In moments the gorging had reached an insane crescendo. Serena knew full well that there weren't enough victims for all her creatures to feed on at once. In fact, she had planned things this way.

After launching the vast tidal wave, Serena had every confidence that the Conclave fleet had been destroyed. But if by some miracle it had not, she wanted her servants hungry, and eager to act at a moment's notice. She had also given instructions that the victims be proffered naked, so as to minimize evidence of the atrocity. The shrews and envelopers left clothing, bones, and footwear behind. After each feeding Serena's consuls were ordered to leave the castle and cause the abandoned bones to vanish. Should Conclave forces approach, she wanted everything to look as normal as possible.

She watched with curiosity as two shrews fought over a screaming, naked man. One had its jaws closed around the man's head, while the other had sunk its teeth deep into his feet. Snarling and struggling, they pulled in opposite directions so mightily that the fellow's head was torn from his shoulders, leaving one shrew to claim the bulk of the prize. The snuffling monster quickly dragged the headless carcass off into the darkness to keep the meal for itself.

A quieter, more muffled type of screaming also filled the air. These sounds were coming from the victims taken by envelopers. As the creatures wrapped their velvety bodies around victim after victim, they absorbed them.

When the feeding session ended, not one human remained. The beasts that hadn't secured someone to feed on snarled and hissed at the others as they all reluctantly returned to their hiding places. The massive shrews submerged; the envelopers again blended in perfectly with their various surroundings. Soon all went quiet.

Serena turned to Actinius. "Send out the consuls," she ordered.

Actinius turned around to look down into the palace courtyard. Several dozen consuls stood there, waiting for his command. After seeing Actinius give them a hand sign, they walked across the bridge and onto the killing field. The place was a sickening maze of regurgitated bones. Blood seemed to lie everywhere, its slick freshness shiny with moonlight against the surrounding grass. The stink rose so high as to reach Serena and the consul by her side.

Serena watched as azure beams streaked from the consuls' hands and into the night. Little by little, all evidence of the recent atrocity vanished and the scene returned to normal. Just then Serena and Actinius heard footsteps. They turned to see a consul approaching.

"Begging your pardon, mistress," he said. "Einar and Reznik request your presence. They wish to give you a report."

Serena nodded. "Very well," she answered. "I will meet them in my quarters."

After giving his mistress a bow, the consul hurried away.

Actinius gave Serena an encouraging look. "I think they are near success," he said.

"Good," she answered. "But with the Conclave fleet resting on the bottom of the sea, their sense of urgency might not be what it once was. I must ensure that is not the case. Come with me. I want you in attendance."

Levitating from the guard path, Serena floated down to the courtyard. When Actinius reached her side, they started for her personal quarters. As she walked across the outer ward's tile floor, the Vagaries queen ignored the cries of those still imprisoned in wooden cages. Walking up the majestic steps, she entered the great castle.

Her journey from the Citadel had been quick and uneventful. After overseeing the mooring of her vessels just south of the port city of Eyrie Point, she had hurried on to the Recluse under consular guard. The remaining consuls, Valrenkians, and Vagaries documents that had accompanied her to Parthalon were still trickling into the Recluse.

Walking up the curved staircase, she and Actinius strode down several long hallways before reaching her private quarters. She had purposely taken the refurbished rooms that had once belonged to Failee, and the irony of that choice hadn't escaped her. The door was partly ajar, telling her that Einar and Reznik had arrived. She and Actinius walked in.

The main room was wonderfully sumptuous. A lovely landscape mural covered every wall. Double stained-glass doors on the room's opposite side lay open to show a huge balcony overlooking the lake. Several hallways led off from the main room to the bedroom, personal library, washroom, and more. Elegantly carved furniture and brightly patterned rugs graced her view, and evening birds could be heard warbling just beyond the exquisite wrought-iron balcony railing.

But as she entered the room she was overcome by a sadness that even her sumptuous surroundings could not assuage. Had Wulfgar and Clarice lived, she would have occupied these rooms as a proud wife and mother, rather than as a grieving widow whose only child was dead. But soon she would have her revenge. For her, its scent hung in the evening air as distinctly as did that of the hibiscus blossoms lying just beyond the windows.

Einar and Reznik were seated at a large table on the far side of the room. Ignoring them, she left Actinius to walk toward one corner. The familiar pink altar had been brought from the Citadel, and the floor immediately surrounding it was covered with fresh red rose petals.

Like so many times before, she reached through the azure aura surrounding Clarice and touched the child's cold cheek. After standing that way for several moments she went to sit with her lead consul and Valrenkian. Actinius joined them.

"Your report?" she asked. Knowing that Einar and Reznik were unaware that she had been viewing their experiments from afar, she was eager to learn whether they might try to deceive her, and lie about their progress.

Einar cleared his throat. "As you are aware, Your Grace, we have found Failee's lost spell. We know that it is the one we need, because we have had some measure of success with our test subjects. But not one has been resurrected sufficiently to regain sustained life. Reznik has augmented the spell with herbs and oils, but it still lacks the potency we need."

"Is it a matter of not having the right ingredients?" Serena asked Reznik.

The Corporeal shook his head. "I do not think so, mistress," he answered. "Rather, it is about having enough time. Moreover, I am working in uncharted territory. Usually, an herbmaster has a previous frame of reference to guide him down the right path. With this work there is none. But given enough time, we will find it."

Serena gave each of her mystics a stern look. "Just because we suspect that the Conclave fleet is destroyed does not mean that you can dawdle," she warned them. "Xanthus failed. The *Jin'Sai* has returned to Eutracia. When he learns of the Conclave's destruction his anger will know no bounds. Although it's true that he is not trained in the craft, he remains exceedingly dangerous, and many Minion warriors still serve him. The *Pon Q'tar* clerics are becoming impatient, as am I. We can afford no more delays. You also need to know that I have ordered the total evacuation of the Ghetto. Not only might we need the Ghetto's additional supplies and inhabitants, but it is far easier to defend one fortress than two. As the people and goods arrive, you will be informed."

"We understand, Your Grace," Einar said. "We will redouble our efforts, and go forward as quickly as possible."

Serena nodded. "Just so," she said. "Leave me and return to your work. I wish to be alone."

As the three mystics neared the door, Serena called out Einar's name. He stopped and watched Reznik and Actinius walk down the hall for a moment; then he turned back.

Einar gave his queen a questioning look. "Yes, Your Grace?" he asked.

"After we are sure of success, you may kill Reznik and all other Valrenkian half-breeds like him," she said softly. "There will be no room in the new order for those bearing a partial blood signature."

Einar smiled. "With pleasure," he answered.

He walked through the door and closed it quietly behind him.

Chapter LVI

Duvessa's heavy wings were telling her that she was quickly nearing another point of no return. As her eyes searched the waves, she was thankful for the bright moonlight that shone down. She looked to her right to see Kefira give her a reassuring smile. The other Minion officer's youth was serving her well, and Duvessa knew that Kefira would be able to continue on after she could not. But that was not an order she would give.

This far to the east, Black Ship wreckage was almost nonexistent. They had seen but one piece—a rather sizable part of a smashed skiff. After briefly resting on it and drinking some water, they had continued on. That had been three hours ago. As Duvessa's wings grew heavier, so did her heart.

Just then she heard Kefira call out. She snapped her head around to see her companion point into the distance. Duvessa's heart leapt in her chest as she strained her eyes to find what Kefira was trying to show her. But she became disheartened again as she identified it.

The Citadel, dark and foreboding, lay against the eastern horizon in the twinkling moonlight. From the two warriors' vantage point, the three moons seemed to float in the night sky directly above it. Had it not been for Kefira's sharp eyes, they might easily have missed it. Then Duvessa realized that there was something odd about the fortress. Slowing her pace, she held up one hand. Kefira hovered beside her.

"Why are we stopping?" Kefira asked.

"There is something peculiar about the Citadel," Duvessa answered.

Kefira cast her gaze into the distance. "I don't understand," she said. "What do you see that I do not?"

"It's what I *don't* see," Duvessa answered.

Suddenly Kefira understood. From what she had been told, at night the Citadel was always brightly illuminated. But this night the great fortress's walls, turrets, and catwalks were bathed only in moonlight. She quickly realized that it had been something of a miracle for her to discover it at all. She looked back at Duvessa.

"Why is it dark?" she asked.

"There can be only two possibilities," Duvessa answered. "Either Serena has ordered the Citadel to be abandoned, or she has purposely ordered no lights to shine. My money is on the first reason."

"But why would she order the place abandoned?" Kefira asked. "It makes no sense."

"It might if she believes that the fleet was destroyed," Duvessa said. "Perhaps her supposed victory was only one part of her plan, and another part is to be carried out elsewhere. That would explain much. Whatever the reason, the Conclave must be informed."

With the discovery of the darkened Citadel, Duvessa suddenly found herself torn between two conflicting choices. The Conclave needed to know about this unexpected development as soon as possible. But the only way to ensure that was to reverse course and abandon her quest for Traax. As she searched her heart, she tried to imagine what her betrothed would have done had their roles been reversed. In the end there was but one answer. She and Kefira would abandon the search.

Just as she was about to give the order, some clouds parted, allowing more light to stream down onto the sea. A shiny moonlit path came to life atop the waves, lying directly between the hovering warriors and the Citadel. Lying on the path was a piece of mast, bobbing atop the water. Wasting no time, Duvessa headed for it.

As they neared they saw that the mast section was long and heavily entangled in torn rigging. Several spars were still attached to it. Suddenly Duvessa thought she saw something else. Redoubling her efforts, she winged her way toward it for all she was worth.

Buffeting the air with their wings, Kefira and Duvessa slowed as they approached. As Duvessa looked closer, the breath caught in her lungs. There was a body lashed to the mast.

Duvessa and Kefira landed to stand atop the bobbing mast as best they could. Duvessa quickly bent down to turn the body over. It was Traax. His skin pallor was ghostly white, and he looked dead. Duvessa quickly understood that he had somehow found this mast, then used the rigging to tie himself to it, so that his face would remain above the waves. He lay chest-down, with one cheek pressed against the cold, soaked wood.

With tears filling her eyes, she quickly unsheathed her dreggan and cut the ropes that bound him to the mast. She turned him over and pressed her fingertips against his neck. There was a very slow, nearly undetectable pulse. Then she saw the tourniquet bound around his upper arm, and she knew.

When his patrol was attacked, he and some others had stayed behind, trying to buy time for Axel and Valgard to warn the fleet. He was suffering not only from exposure but also from massive blood loss. Even if he got immediate care, his chances for survival were not good. Her eyes filled with tears again as she saw her wet, bloodied, ruby pin still attached to his body armor.

But as she looked around, her heart fell again. Tired as she and Kefira were, she doubted that one of them could lift him into the air, and trying to carry his body between them would probably reopen his wound. Then an idea came to her. Cradling Traax's head in her lap, she looked into Kefira's worried face.

"Draw your sword!" she ordered. "We have work to do!"

CHAPTER LVII

AS TRISTAN LOOKED DOWN AT TRAAX'S FACE, AN OVERWHELMING sadness washed over him. Traax lay atop a bed, his body covered by a light blanket. The Minion had been in a deep coma for more than ten days. During all that time, Duvessa had scarcely left his side.

Tristan watched Duvessa apply a wet cloth to the warrior's forehead. Traax's condition was being further complicated by a high fever, and an infection had set into his arm wound. Since finding him lashed to the mast, Duvessa had yet to see him open his eyes. The palace mystics had done all for the warrior that they could, but from this point forward only time would tell. Like Tristan, they checked on him often.

On finding Traax, Duvessa and Kefira had cleverly used their dreggans to cut the spars free from the floating mast. They had then built a crude litter by binding the spars with some of the torn rigging. After they had placed Traax onto the litter they had hardly been able to get it airborne and fly back to where they had left the others. But with more warriors to bear the load, they had found their way back to the fleet. Shailiha had quickly ordered the surviving vessels to turn for home.

After a week at sea, the four Black Ships had returned, arriving three days ago. With the Necrophagian threat gone, the return voyage was uneventful. It had taken an entire day and part of that night for everyone to trade tales. Aeolus had joined in his first Conclave meeting, and everyone had been glad to have him there. Tristan had been amazed to hear the details about Serena's attack on the fleet, but not that the Citadel had gone dark.

As he had expected, when he told his story he was first greeted with outright disbelief, followed by a dense silence that he thought might never end. After the shock wore off, everyone had started badgering him at once and had interrogated him for hours. But like the others, he had more questions than answers. Tristan had then presented Faegan with the Envoys' parchment that held the formula for granting Forestallments directly to one's blood signature. When the old wizard saw it, he whooped for joy like a child with a shiny new toy.

While he waited for the return of the fleet, Tristan spent each morning in training with Aeolus. He was gradually improving, even by the old master's standards. The rest of his time had been devoted to helping the Minions and highlanders learn each other's maneuvers. At first the warriors and highlander horsemen had been highly suspicious of each other. Tristan had expected that. But as they came to appreciate each other's unique abilities, a grudging respect formed between them.

As a precaution, the mystics had used a signature scope to check Tristan's blood signature, while Jessamay had looked deeply into his eyes to confirm their findings. Aside from the Forestallment granting Tristan access to the azure pass, they pronounced his signature to be normal in every respect.

Just then Tristan heard the door squeak open. He turned to see Wigg standing there. Crooking a finger, the First Wizard beckoned the prince into the hall. Tristan went to him.

"Has there been a change in Traax's condition?" Wigg asked.

"No," Tristan answered. "But he hasn't worsened, either." He gave Wigg a questioning look. "Are you and Faegan ready to honor my request?"

Wigg scowled and crossed his arms over his chest. "The others await us," he answered. "But they want another word with you first."

Tristan was well aware of the Conclave's misgivings. Yesterday he had argued with his friends about this subject for hours. He shook his head.

"The answer is still no!" he insisted. "I will not give up on this. You and Faegan are to install the *K'Shari* Forestallment into my blood signature today."

Wigg sighed. "Walk with me," he said. As Tristan and the First Wizard started down the hall, Wigg seemed deeply concerned.

"I can't start to tell you how much the rest of us are against this," Wigg said. "You are the reigning *Jin'Sai,* so if you order us to do it, we will. But we worry about the consequences. We have had the formula allowing the placement of Forestallments directly into one's blood for only a matter of days. Even Faegan has yet to fully understand its workings. Please let us research it further!"

Tristan loved and respected Wigg like the old wizard was his father. But he meant to have his way in this. He had been fascinated by *K'Shari* ever since first hearing about it years ago, during his Royal Guard training. Then he had taken his unexpected journey with Xanthus and returned home to meet Aeolus—the same man the fable described. These two unexpected events had only heightened his need to know.

More important, he had seen firsthand the kinds of things that Xanthus and Aeolus could do, and he wanted those skills for himself. But he fully understood Wigg's concerns. He gave the old wizard a reassuring smile.

"I would think that as an accomplished graduate of Aeolus' teachings, you'd understand how badly I want this," he chided Wigg.

Wigg stopped walking and looked into Tristan's eyes. "That's just it," he answered. "I understand the need all too well. But that doesn't mean that gaining *K'Shari* this way is a good idea. We can't be sure about what the spell will do to you. We can't even know whether it's something the Envoys of Crysenium would object to." One of the wizard's eyebrows went up. "They expect you to return, you know."

Tristan put a hand on Wigg's shoulder. "Thank you for your concern," he said. "But this is going to happen, with or without your blessing. Let's join the others, shall we?"

Knowing that Tristan wouldn't change his mind, Wigg finally gave in. Walking on, they took one of the many staircases down into the Redoubt and eventually arrived at Faegan's quarters. Tristan knocked on the door; then he and Wigg walked in.

As Tristan had requested, only Faegan, Shailiha, and Aeolus were waiting there. They were sitting at a table and talking in hushed, worried tones. Two rolled-up parchments lay atop the table. The prince was relieved that the entire Conclave membership was not present. If the *K'Shari* Forestallment proved painful, there was no need for the others to see him suffer.

Shailiha came to him and took his hands in hers. Her expression was worried, nearly desperate.

"Please don't do this!" she breathed. "I know how badly you want it, but what if something goes wrong?" As she searched his face, tears came to her eyes. "I might lose my only brother," she added softly. "I couldn't bear that."

"You won't lose me, I promise," he answered. Then his eyes took on a knowing, faraway look. "Something tells me that it will be all right. . . ."

He looked over at Faegan. "Are you ready?" he asked.

Faegan nodded. But like the others, he seemed worried. "Yes," the wizard said. "But I must protest this hurried use of—"

Raising a hand, Tristan stopped him in midsentence. "We're going to do this. I assume you want me to be seated?"

"Yes," Faegan answered. Reaching across the table, he took

up the two small scrolls and unrolled them. He handed one to Wigg.

Tristan walked across the room. After removing his weapons and placing them on the floor, he sat in an upholstered chair. He looked at the two wizards.

"I suggest that you bind me," he said.

Faegan nodded. At once azure bands secured the prince's limbs to the chair's arms and legs. He tested the constraints to find that they were as unforgiving as iron manacles.

"You may start," he said.

Before Wigg and Faegan could act, Shailiha returned to Tristan's side. Her eyes had become tearful again.

"Is this worth the risk?" she asked.

"Yes," Tristan answered quietly. "No matter how much pain it might cause me, I want this." He nodded at the wizards; then he looked at Aeolus. Aeolus nodded back.

He understands, Tristan realized, *even if the others do not.*

"Good luck," Aeolus said. Then he gave Tristan a wink. "If this works, you and I will share a unique bond."

By earlier agreement, Wigg would first read the calculations summoning the gift of *K'Shari.* Then Faegan would call the spell allowing the Forestallment to be placed into Tristan's blood. Because they had never granted a Forestallment before, the wizards did not know what to expect, or how long the process might take.

As Wigg started his incantation, Shailiha reached out to take Tristan by the hand. He gave her a reassuring smile, then closed his eyes.

At first Tristan felt nothing, prompting him to wonder whether something had gone awry. After finishing his part, Wigg lowered his scroll. It was Faegan's turn. As the crippled wizard called his spell, pain started roiling up in the prince.

Suddenly every nerve in Tristan's being came afire, and he started to scream. Soon his body was dripping sweat and convulsively dancing like a marionette at the end of unseen strings. His spasmodic jerking became so violent that the chair literally jumped up and down against the floor. Foam dribbled from the corners of his mouth, and his eyes drifted shut. As the pain went through him he gripped Shailiha's hand so strongly that she feared he might break her fingers. But she refused to let go.

Then it was over. Tristan had gone unconscious, and his skin had turned a pale, ghostly white. As his grip slackened, he slumped forward in his chair.

Desperately worried, Shailiha looked beseechingly at the wizards. All three mystics ran over to Tristan. As Faegan ended the spell binding the prince to the chair, Aeolus reached out and caught him in his arms.

"Put him on the bed!" Faegan shouted.

As Tristan lay on the bed, his breathing became desperately ragged and his head lolled to one side. Drool ran from his mouth to fall on the pillow. Wigg placed a palm on Tristan's forehead, then closed his eyes. After a time he removed his hand and looked at Shailiha.

"What is it?" she asked.

"There has been a great disturbance in his blood," Wigg answered. "With the supposed addition of the Forestallment, his blood pounds through his veins quickly, and hotly."

"Will he live?" Shailiha whispered.

Wigg shook his head. "I don't know."

Shaking with worry, Shailiha looked down at her brother with tearful eyes. "I told you not to do this," she whispered angrily, barely able to get the words out.

"What do we do now?" she asked.

"The only thing we *can* do," Wigg answered. "We wait."

THREE HOURS LATER, WIGG, SHAILIHA, FAEGAN, AND AEOLUS were still waiting for Tristan to regain consciousness. With every passing moment, Shailiha became more worried. Knowing that not one of them would leave until they knew more about Tristan's condition, Shawna had brought food and drink. But Shailiha and the mystics had eaten little.

Turning to look back at her brother for what seemed like the hundredth time, Shailiha brushed away a tear. Faegan placed a hand over hers.

"Can't you do anything more?" she asked. "He looks so helpless lying there."

Faegan shook his head. "No," he answered. "As we told the prince yesterday, with the granting of our first Forestallment, we have sailed into uncharted waters. His fate rests with the Afterlife. All we can do is pray, and hope that Tristan hasn't forced us to make a horrible mistake."

Plainly worried, Aeolus placed his hands flat on the tabletop.

Since joining the Conclave, his martial uniform had been replaced by a simple, dark green robe.

"We must shoulder some of the blame for allowing it," Aeolus said. "But one thing is certain. Even without the benefit of *K'Shari,* he is the fastest learner I have ever taught. I believe that his natural abilities surpass even those wielded by Satine. If he survives and the gift of *K'Shari* becomes his, he might become the greatest weapons and hand-to-hand combat master the world has ever seen. I daresay his gifts would quickly dwarf mine." After thinking for a moment, Aeolus gave Faegan a questioning glance.

"Something just occurred to me," he said. "Did the *K'Shari* calculations hold only the ability allowing Tristan to call it forth? Or was a predetermined ability to perform martial techniques incorporated into the formula as well?"

Despite the grave circumstances, Faegan managed a brief smile. "I thought you'd never ask," he answered. "The calculation that Wigg recited did indeed hold weapon and hand-to-hand techniques. As I perused the spell, there were so many that I finally stopped counting them. If he survives, Tristan will not only command *K'Shari,* but I expect he will awaken fully trained in your ways, as well—even though he might not immediately realize that part of it. I doubt that he will need any more of your instruction."

Aeolus shook his head. "Can it be true?" he asked. "That what took me a lifetime to learn can be gained in a matter of moments?"

Wigg nodded. "Our knowledge about the craft has been greatly enhanced while you were away. It would be no exaggeration to say that—"

Suddenly the three men heard Shailiha gasp. They turned to see that she was looking at Tristan.

The prince was sitting up on the side of the bed. Trying to clear his mind, he shook his head back and forth. Then he ran his fingers through his hair, pushing it back from his forehead. As the others went to him, he stood.

Shailiha embraced him and looked into his eyes. "Are you all right?" she asked.

Tristan smiled at her. "Yes," he answered. "I'm not sure that I've ever been better." He looked at Aeolus. "You know what I mean, don't you?"

Aeolus smiled at him. "I do," he answered.

As Tristan's head cleared, he realized that something wonderful had happened to him. His senses were keener, and he could tell simply by standing there that his balance and his coordination had markedly improved. His muscles felt stronger and his confidence surer. In many ways, he felt like an entirely new man. The sensation was glorious, empowering. Without hesitation he walked over to where his weapons lay and started strapping them over his right shoulder.

After he had finished he gave Aeolus a wink. At once the wizard knew what Tristan wanted. He smiled.

"Very well," he said. "But not here."

Understanding, Tristan quickly headed for the door. He hadn't gotten two paces before Wigg's voice rang out.

"Where do you think you're going?" the First Wizard demanded. "We have to examine your blood signature, to make sure you're all right!"

Stopping at the doorway, Tristan turned and shook his head. "Not now," he said. "I have been waiting nearly my entire life for this moment."

Without further ado he and Aeolus left the room, leaving Wigg, Faegan, and Shailiha no choice but to follow them.

On reaching the first floor, Tristan and Aeolus hurried down a corridor and headed for a door leading outside. By now they were moving so fast that Wigg and Shailiha had to trot to keep up, and Faegan had to levitate his chair. Soon Shailiha saw Tyranny and Abbey up ahead, standing next to each other and talking. After Tristan and Aeolus hurried by, the privateer and acolyte gave them all puzzled looks.

"What's going on?" Tyranny demanded.

"I don't know!" Shailiha called out over one shoulder. "If you want to find out, you'll just have to come along!"

Not to be outdone, Tyranny and Abbey joined the chase.

Tristan stopped just long enough to confront a surprised Minion warrior standing guard in the hall. Tristan ordered him to give up his dreggan. With a confused look on his face, the warrior offered up his sword. His curiosity piqued, he wanted to follow along, but knew better than to abandon his post.

Tristan barged through the doors and led everyone outside. He hurried around a palace corner to find a section of manicured ground that hadn't been taken up by Minion wounded. As Aeolus neared, Tristan tossed him the extra dreggan.

Aeolus caught the sword firmly by the hilt. As the others caught up and gathered around, Aeolus tested the sword by twirling it several times, watching its blade catch the afternoon sun. This was the first time he had held a dreggan. Although he found the weapon heavy, he keenly appreciated how finely balanced it was.

Tristan came to a stop in the center of the small courtyard and faced Aeolus. As they stood looking at each other, the others watched. Shailiha looked quizzically at Faegan. Saying nothing, Faegan only shook his head and then looked back at Tristan and the weapons master.

Smiling, Tristan bowed, then raised his sword. But Aeolus did not answer the challenge. Instead, he plunged the dreggan's blade into the ground. His words would surprise the prince.

"No," Aeolus said. "Until you have proven something to me, you are still my student. Lower your weapon."

Tristan did as he was asked.

"First tell me—do you feel it?" Aeolus asked.

Holding his dreggan in one hand, Tristan closed his eyes and spread his arms toward the sky. He inhaled deeply and felt like he could conquer the entire world with nothing but the sword in his hand.

"Yes," he answered, his eyes still closed. "I own it. It is a part of me now."

"Then prove it," Aeolus said.

Raising his free hand, the wizard pointed to a nearby tree. Calling the craft, Aeolus tore a branch from the tree and caused it to hover in the air.

When he heard the sound of the branch breaking free, Tristan opened his eyes and lowered his sword. After looking at Aeolus, he closed his eyes again.

"My ears hear no begging," he said softly. "My eyes see no pain. My heart feels no remorse."

Suddenly everything stilled. The birds stopped singing and the insects quieted. Then the wind stopped, and the grass surrounding the *Jin'Sai* withered and died. It was like nature had somehow decided to end her ceaseless travails. His eyes still closed, Tristan remained still.

With a wave of his hand, Aeolus sent the freshly cut branch

soaring toward the prince. As the branch neared Tristan, it was almost like he could see it coming even with his eyes closed. At the last second he opened them and brought his dreggan blade around in a perfect arc.

Those who saw Tristan's first use of *K'Shari* would never forget it. His blade came around so fast that it was nearly invisible. It severed the branch in midair, and the pieces fell at his feet.

After sheathing his sword, Tristan released his *K'Shari.* As he bent down and picked up one of the branch pieces, the forces of nature came alive again. He saw that the angled end of the branch was cut clean, its fresh surface smooth as glass. He handed it to Shailiha for safekeeping.

Aeolus looked at Tristan and smiled. "So it seems the student has surpassed the teacher," he said. "You have my deepest congratulations."

"Thank you," Tristan said humbly. "But I doubt that I could best you, even now. Your years of training would win out."

Smiling, Aeolus shook his head. "Not if what Faegan told me is true," he said. "He believes that the Forestallment he just granted to your blood also contained hundreds of martial techniques, and that they will reveal themselves as needed, without further training. Who knows?" Aeolus added with a wry smile. "*You* might be able to teach *me* a thing or two at this very moment! And you're forgetting something else," he added.

"What is that?" Tristan asked.

"That of the two of you, your blood is far stronger," Wigg interjected. "True, you each carry the ability to summon *K'Shari.* But it is in your blood, Tristan, that it will burn brightest. So you see—the student has surpassed the teacher after all."

Tristan and the others watched Aeolus reach under his robe. He produced a small white scroll. Its center was bound with a bloodred ribbon. The prince immediately recognized it as the second symbol of *K'Shari* mastery. Tristan gladly took it into his hands.

"I have been waiting for three hundred years to give someone that scroll," he said. "For a long time, I thought it would go to Satine. Instead it finds its way to you, and I'm glad."

"Thank you," Tristan said softly. "I will always honor it."

"Now then," Aeolus said. "There remains but one more thing for me to do."

Although curious, Tristan decided not to ask. Over the last

fortnight he had come to trust Aeolus with his life, just as he did each Conclave member.

"Very well," he said. As he waited, he looked into Aeolus' eyes.

Suddenly the azure hue of the craft blanketed each of Tristan's shoulders, and he knew. The azure glow soon faded.

"What you now bear was my first use of the craft in more than three centuries," Aeolus said. "Wear them well, *Jin'Sai.*"

Tristan looked first at one shoulder, then the other. On one lay a tattooed serpent; on the other lay a sword.

"I will," he said softly. "And thank you."

Tristan looked around to find Tyranny. "When can we sail for the Recluse?" he asked her.

Tyranny smiled. "Three more days should do it," she answered. "Four at the outside."

Tristan turned to look east, toward where the Sea of Whispers lay waiting. As he did, he thought about Serena.

"Good," the *Jin'Sai* answered quietly. "I'm ready."

CHAPTER LVIII

"BEFORE WE START, IS THERE ANYTHING MORE THAT YOU WOULD like to tell us?" the lead *Pon Q'tar* cleric asked. "If you repent, we might spare your life. If not—well, let's just say that your demise will not be a pleasant one."

Although Xanthus knew it would do no good, for several moments he strained against his bonds. Finally giving up, he looked across the shadowed room.

"No," he answered. "My allegiance to the Vagaries is unshakable. You know that! That's why you chose me for the mission! All I can tell you is the truth, and I have already done so!"

"Very well," the lead cleric answered. "Then what happens next will be on your head."

Xanthus glared at the twelve hooded faces behind the table. For the last thirteen days he had been confined to his stinking hole. He had nearly gone mad with loneliness, and the sensory deprivation had been so great that the only way to count the passing days had been when his guardians fed him. When they finally pulled him from the hole, he thought that the azure light coming from above would surely blind him.

As he again sat bound to the chair, he took stock of himself. His black robe was torn and reeked of his own waste. The beginnings of a dark beard had surfaced on his face, and his brown hair was matted and knotted. He was filthy, defeated, and completely alone in his plight—just the way the clerics wanted him to be.

Xanthus cringed as he watched the lead cleric point a finger at him. At once an incision opened in one of his wrists and a drop of his endowed blood was freed. The cleric caused it to float to a place midway between him and Xanthus. Soon the drop morphed into Xanthus' blood signature.

Alongside the signature, azure numbers and symbols started materializing into a craft formula. Like before, the formula turned to the vertical, and the blood signature started sliding down its length. No one needed to tell Xanthus what was coming. He watched the beautiful nautilus form, its spiraling, colorful compartments growing in size as they radiated outward from its tightly wound center.

He had wondered about the nautilus often during his confinement. Although he had seen its wonders with his own eyes, he still found them difficult to believe. As the nautilus finished forming, he suddenly understood why he had been brought back after so long. The Heretics had perfected the nautilus index.

In a way, Xanthus was glad. He was not an enemy of the *Pon Q'tar,* nor could he imagine ever becoming one. He had meant what he said about being loyal to the Vagaries. Had he felt otherwise, he never would have accepted the mission to seduce the *Jin'Sai* into the pass. He welcomed the coming of the index. If it helped the *Pon Q'tar* find the precise memories they were searching for, then the truth would come out, and they would realize that what had happened to Tristan was not his fault. Perhaps they might even release him, and allow him to return to his post as Faxon's assistant in the Imperial Order.

Xanthus watched as another glowing craft formula appeared

in the air. It was the longest one he had ever seen. He tried to read it. But like the first formula, its vast complexities were lost on him.

"Behold," the lead cleric said. "I give you the nautilus index. Watch as I demonstrate its use." The cleric raised his arms and pointed his hands at the formula.

"I wish to view the memories in the nautilus," the cleric commanded.

Xanthus soon realized that the cleric was speaking directly to the glowing spell, rather than to the people in the room. He had never heard a mystic verbally address a raw craft formula this way, nor had he known that such a thing could be done. Then he remembered what the cleric had said about this spell having been wrought by the very best Heretical minds.

"Specifically, I wish to view only those images dealing with the subject's recent time in the Borderlands," the cleric added.

The spell immediately obeyed. Like it possessed a mind of its own, it flew across the room and wound its length around the hovering nautilus. At once a bright azure light shot from the nautilus's largest chamber and streamed into the room.

Like the time before, Xanthus watched his memories unfold. As the cleric had ordered, the scene playing out showed him and Tristan exiting the pass to unexpectedly arrive in the terrible red desert. Xanthus anxiously watched the blazing heat start to overcome him and the *Jin'Sai.* The searing wind birthed red dust maelstroms that bothered their eyes and stung their skin. The wind's howling noise was terrible; and great sinkholes opened before them, threatening to take them into oblivion with every step. Then Xanthus watched Tristan turn and shout a question to him. Just as he remembered, he answered.

It will happen soon, Xanthus realized. *At any moment a sinkhole will open in the desert floor and take the* Jin'Sai. *And the* Pon Q'tar *will realize that I have been telling the truth.*

But rather than see Tristan die, he watched incredulously as he and the *Jin'Sai* started trudging toward the distant mountain peaks. He felt his endowed blood turn to ice water.

This cannot be! Xanthus thought. *It didn't happen this way!*

With a wave of one hand, the lead cleric caused the scene to speed up. Soon Xanthus saw himself and Tristan enter a cave. They talked and later fell asleep. Then Xanthus saw himself awaken and go to the cave entrance to find the prince standing there. After donning blankets, they led their horses from the cave to start trudging through the deep snow.

"Stop!" the cleric called out angrily.

The amazing scene froze in place, and the sound quieted. As he sat bound to the chair under the harsh light, Xanthus suddenly felt even more naked and alone.

"So it seems that you were lying after all," one of the female clerics said to him. There was no mercy in her voice. As he wondered about his fate, Xanthus started to shake with fear.

"We all know that we morphed the Borderlands into a polar state to trap the army of Ones that was approaching," she added. "After that, the red desert did not reappear. We again have irrefutable evidence that the *Jin'Sai* survived, rather than perished, as you say he did. You are a liar and a traitor to the Vagaries, Xanthus. And because of your treachery you will meet a horrible death."

Xanthus was beyond any rational understanding of what he had just seen. Weeping, he lowered his head.

"But it didn't happen that way," he sobbed. "I swear it."

"The nautilus seems to disagree," the lead cleric answered. "And we have it on good authority that the nautilus never lies." He calmly looked back at the shining craft construct.

"Recommence," he ordered. "Move swiftly."

The scene started changing again, this time moving faster. Xanthus saw himself and Tristan nearly die from exposure, and he watched incredulously as he killed his horse and used its steaming innards to keep Tristan alive. Then they trudged on again through the nearly waist-deep snow. But Xanthus couldn't believe what he was seeing, and he remembered none of it.

Suddenly the Borderlands disappeared to show Rustannica in its natural state. The ability to use magic had returned. After he and Tristan ate and drank, they disappeared into the azure pass. When he watched himself and the *Jin'Sai* exit the pass, Xanthus' mouth fell open.

As the onetime Darkling and the *Pon Q'tar* clerics watched and listened, all of Crysenium's secrets were gradually revealed.

Xanthus' fate was sealed.

VI

THE MOTHER AND CHILD

CHAPTER LIX

What is it, I wonder, that creates such a deep, unshakable bond between a mother and her child? Is it simply love, a desperate need, or something else? For even if she should somehow forever lose that child, the bond between them—although invisible, intangible, and indescribable—will always remain unbroken. And she will carry it in her heart until her dying day.

—SERENA, REIGNING QUEEN OF THE VAGARIES

"YOU KNOW, SOMETIMES YOU AMAZE EVEN *ME*," RAFE SAID. AS HE stared out to sea, he offered Tristan his *tachinga* bottle. Tristan took a swig, then wiped his mouth and handed the bottle back.

"What do you mean?" Tristan asked.

"I never thought you would get the Clan Kilbourne elders to agree to your scheme, but you did," Rafe answered. "And unmasking Arwydd that way was no small victory, either—at least to us highlanders. But then you accomplished the greatest feat of all." After taking another drink, Rafe laughed and slapped Tristan on the back.

"And what was that?" Tristan asked.

"Why, getting those three miserable wizards to let us highlanders come along!" Rafe answered. "In all my days I have never met such irascible old men! They make the Kilbourne elders seem positively affable! Aeolus isn't so bad, I suppose. And I suspect that Faegan might be amusing, once one gets to know him. He at least carries a twinkle in his eye. But that Wigg is surely a caution!"

Tristan laughed. "I know," he said. "He's been around for more than three hundred years. To say that he's set in his ways would be the greatest understatement of all time. He is a very moral man, and he doesn't take kindly to thieving highlanders.

The best way to get on his good side is to prove to him that you can control your vices—at least until this campaign is over."

"I suppose so," Rafe said. "But my men are getting restless. All I can say is that it's a good thing there's nothing on these giant tubs worth stealing!"

"You're probably right," Tristan answered laughingly. "But even if you did find something, you'd have no place to hide!"

Rafe laughed again and reached beneath his fur vest to produce a dark plug of chewing tobacco. After biting off a piece, he offered the plug to Tristan. Tristan winced and shook his head. Rafe shrugged his shoulders, then spat some dark spittle over the *Tammerland*'s side. Another slug of *tachinga* followed.

Tristan couldn't help but like Rafe, even if the highlander was a crook. Rafe had never lied to him, and his riding and fighting abilities were wonderful—as were those of each of his horsemen. Tristan supposed that if there was such a thing as a gentleman thief, Rafe was it.

As his thoughts turned to the campaign ahead, Tristan looked out over the moonlit sea. The fleet was sailing atop the waves while the mystics rested for the night. The ships' black sails were full, and each foresail carried a bright red image of the Paragon.

Ten days had passed since Tristan had been granted the *K'Shari* Forestallment, and the fleet had been at sea for eight of those days. Because the Necrophagian threat was gone, the Black Ships had made good time. Tyranny estimated that they would reach the coast of Parthalon by dawn. From there the ships would fly overland to the Recluse.

Few aboard the Black Ships could sleep this night, in anticipation of what the next day might bring. Many warriors and highlanders prowled the decks, talking among themselves and sharpening their weapons. Wigg's, Faegan's, Aeolus', and Jessamay's powers had kept the fleet in the air for much of the journey. Wigg empowered the *Tammerland,* Faegan the *Ephyra,* Aeolus the *Florian,* and Jessamay the *Cavalon.*

Blessedly, Traax had regained consciousness. True to his warrior nature, he had insisted on coming. But it remained unclear whether he would be ready to fight, because his arm hadn't fully healed. Duvessa still watched over him and was doing her best to make him rest. But if Tristan knew Traax, the warrior would soon be up and about—if for no other reason than to prove his worth to his *Jin'Sai.*

Tristan took a moment to look up and down the *Tammerland*'s massive hull. The Black Ships were loaded nearly to the sinking point with food, water, Minions, and highlanders and their horses. This time every Conclave member had come, as had every acolyte, save those needed to watch over the nursery.

For the first few days the highlanders—including the stalwart Balthazar—had been deathly seasick. That had pleased Ox to no end, and he had teased Balthazar unmercifully. But as the two giants' mutual training had progressed, a grudging form of respect—and perhaps even a budding friendship—had started to flower between them.

Tristan still hadn't gotten used to seeing the colorful highlanders wander about the decks. *This is the most ragtag group that I have ever assembled,* he thought as he watched the restless waves. *But in some ways it might be the best.*

Of all the highlanders, only Rafe had been told the full nature of the mission. When Tristan had explained it, Rafe was stunned. The chieftain had no real knowledge of magic, and that had complicated Tristan's task. But Rafe had promised that when the time came, he and his horsemen would follow Tristan's orders to the death. Tristan believed him.

Despite the massive forces he commanded, Tristan was desperately concerned about the battle ahead. Serena would not surrender the Recluse easily. Given that the Scroll of the Vagaries was hers, there was no telling what dangers she had conjured to protect herself and the body of her dead child. One thing remained certain. If Clarice could be brought back to life and Serena could spirit her away before the Conclave could attack, the world as they knew it would be forever changed. It wouldn't happen today, tomorrow, or presumably even a decade from now. But one day Clarice would gain enough maturity to understand the Heretics' wishes and to call forth the craft, thereby ensuring that the Vigors would be no more.

Tristan was also disturbed because he had no real battle plan about how to take the Recluse. He and the other Conclave members had spent hours trying to formulate one, but to no avail. They were familiar with the Recluse and its surroundings, and that was an advantage. But because they were so unsure about the threat they faced, they had finally decided to approach the castle cautiously, and then make their plans.

Deciding to shelve his troubles for a while, the *Jin'Sai* took a bracing lungful of sea air. He still felt wonderfully powerful and alive. He assumed that he would keep these sensations for as long as his blood carried the *K'Shari* Forestallment. He also believed that Faegan had been right about the Forestallment granting him immediate training in a variety of weapon and hand-to-hand techniques. He could almost feel them stirring in his blood as they lay waiting to be unleashed.

Looking down at his bare shoulders, he saw the tattoos Aeolus had given him. He wore them with pride. Aeolus had also been right about something. He and Tristan shared a unique bond. It was one that the others—including Wigg—didn't fully understand.

Just then Tristan saw Rafe look in another direction and smile. Tristan turned to see Tyranny coming across the quarterdeck. The magenta moonlight highlighted her tousled hair, and a cigarillo was pressed between her lips, its lit end glowing in the night. As she neared, Rafe looked her up and down, then turned back toward the prince. He spat some more tobacco bits overboard.

"A beautiful woman," he said quietly. "In some ways, she reminds me of Yasmin. Her nature can sometimes be deadly, and she approaches the world on her own terms. Such women can easily steal a man's heart. The predatory ones are the best, don't you agree, *dango*?"

Tristan suddenly thought about Celeste. These days he was glad to find his heart filled with fond memories of her, rather than only the pain of what might have been. But Celeste had been different from Tyranny and Yasmin. Shaking his head, he looked back at Rafe.

"That's not always true," he answered quietly.

As Tyranny approached, she tossed her cigarillo into the sea. She gave Rafe a respectful look.

"Would you please excuse us?" she asked. "I need to speak with the *Jin'Sai.*"

Rafe bowed. "Of course, Captain," he answered. He offered Tristan a final pull on his jug. After Tristan declined, Rafe walked away.

Tyranny turned to look out over the shifting ocean. "There is something I need to tell you," she said quietly. When she turned around her eyes searched his face, like she was trying to guess his feelings.

Tristan suspected what was coming. If he was right, this would be hard for her. She could use a sword and command an oceangoing vessel with the best of them. But when it came to showing her innermost emotions she oftentimes faltered, just as he did. Rather than ask, he decided to let her take her time. Quiet moments passed.

"I love you," she said simply, honestly. As she spoke, he saw a glimmer of hope flash in her eyes.

"Forgive me," she said. "The truth is that I simply can't help it. It started slowly, that day I rescued you from one of Wulfgar's slaver frigates. It has only grown since then. I'm sorry you lost Celeste. I loved her too, and I mean no disrespect to her memory. But I need to know how you feel about me."

Aware that he was about to break her heart, Tristan closed his eyes for a moment.

"I understand, but we can't be together that way," he said, trying to tell her as gently as he could. "I care for you, you know that. But my heart still searches."

He sensed her pain, and he could tell that she was bravely trying not to cry. True to her nature she blinked hard, conquering her impending tears.

"Is it because I serve on the Conclave?" she asked. "That didn't keep you from loving Celeste."

"I know," he answered. "But that is precisely why it cannot happen again. Celeste died while on a Conclave mission that I commanded. In some ways, I will forever carry that guilt. For everyone's benefit, I simply cannot place my heart—or another Conclave member's heart—in that position again."

Reaching out, he placed one palm against her cheek. As he felt her tears run among his fingers, she closed her eyes and reached up to press his hand closer.

He knew that telling her this way—rather than reminding her of what they each knew to be true—would be the kindest. When Tristan had found the Scroll Master, the young man had told him that there would be another woman for him, and that he would know her when he saw her. She would be the true love of his life, and she would bear his children. Since that day he had known that Tyranny was not the one. Nor was Yasmin, who had so unknowingly helped restore his heart.

"I want you to know that had we met in another place or time, things might have been different between us," he said. "There will always be that much. As it is, I can only ask that you respect my feelings."

Tyranny nodded and swallowed hard. "My heart suspected that this was how it would be," she said. "But I had to know."

She took a deep breath and gave him another searching look. Coming closer, she kissed his cheek.

"I hope you find her, *Jin'Sai,*" she said softly. "Whoever she is, she's a lucky woman."

Saying nothing more, she turned and walked away. After watching her go, Tristan turned and looked back at the moonlit Sea of Whispers.

Whoever she is, he thought, echoing Tyranny's parting words. *But will I ever find her?*

The *Jin'Sai* remained alone at the ship's rail for a long time, wondering.

CHAPTER LX

DAWN WAS COMING QUIETLY TO PARTHALON, BUT EVERYONE TAKing refuge in the Recluse knew that the peacefulness would not last. The coming day would be momentous.

Serena stood quietly in her private chambers. Outside her balcony, the sun crept above the eastern horizon, flooding the inky sky with light. Einar and Reznik were there with her.

Serena walked over to the pink marble altar. Clarice still lay atop it, but today no red rose petals adorned the floor, the altar, or her corpse. Their scent could interfere with his formula, Reznik had warned. As an added precaution, the dead child was naked.

As she reached down to touch Clarice's face, Serena shivered with fear and joy alike as she thought about what would soon happen. Her two servants knew better than to intrude on her private thoughts during moments such as this. Their queen had suffered much to see this day. This would be done in her way, and in her time.

Early yesterday Einar had hurried to her bearing the good news. *We have done it!* he said. Failee's spell and Reznik's accompanying potion were finally ready. They had tried it on the last five lepers remaining at the Recluse. After killing them, they had successfully revived each one.

At the queen's insistence, five more subjects had been tested. But these persons had not been lepers. They had been female newborns, hastily abducted by Serena's consuls from nearby towns and villages, and then flown to the Recluse by envelopers. Their terrified parents had fought back as best they could, but they stood little chance against the craft. Most died while trying to save their babies.

Under the queen's merciless gaze, Einar and Reznik had strangled each of the wailing infants to death, then successfully brought them back to life. Only then did Serena agree to try the process on Clarice. The revived baby girls had been carried to the top of the fortress walls and tossed alive into the moat. The hungry shrews had devoured them greedily, leaving no evidence of the queen's crimes.

Serena turned to look at Einar. She knew that time was of the essence, for the Heretics had been keeping her informed of the *Jin'Sai*'s quick progress across the sea. Only three hours ago they had again touched her mind to tell her that the fleet was sailing overland, and that Clarice must be brought back to life quickly. Einar and Reznik's success had not come a moment too soon. The hiding shrews and camouflaged envelopers had also been warned of the *Jin'Sai*'s imminent arrival.

Serena glared into Einar's eyes. "Are you *sure*?" she demanded.

Einar nodded. "As sure as we can be," he answered. "More testing would be prudent, but we have no time. After we finish here we must see to the defense of the Recluse. Only when your child is revived and the *Jin'Sai* has been destroyed can we finally relish our victory."

"Very well," she said. "You may start. But if you harm Clarice rather than give her life, I will kill you both."

As Serena backed away, Einar and Reznik nervously approached the altar. Einar waved a hand, and Failee's spell materialized in the air. It twinkled beautifully as it quietly hovered above the altar. As Reznik removed something from his butcher's smock, Serena recognized it as a herbmaster's sachet. Reznik placed the sachet on Clarice's chest, then quietly backed away.

Einar started to recite Failee's spell. Wispy smoke soon rose from the sachet and started to whirl into a little maelstrom. Then the maelstrom entered the skin of the child's bare chest, leaving no mark. As they watched and waited, quiet reclaimed the room. Serena held her breath.

Suddenly Clarice's chest started to rise and fall, and she coughed. Color quickly returned to her gray skin. Then her arms and legs wriggled about and she started crying. As tears streamed down her cheeks, she stretched her arms higher, and her blue eyes opened in an instinctual search for her mother.

Reznik looked over at Einar. Knowing better than to speak during this momentous event, Einar only smiled. The two servants humbly backed away.

Lunging for the altar, Serna lifted her squirming child and held her close. As she did, Clarice's wispy, dark hair quietly brushed against the dead rose secured in Serena's bosom.

Reunited at last, Serena's heart cried out.

Crying, laughing, and then crying again, Serena turned to her mystics. Tears ran freely down her face.

"Well done," she whispered.

She stood that way for some time, rocking her child and lovingly remembering the man who had fathered her. Clarice's crying soon quieted into a soft gurgle.

Serena turned to the door and sharply called out. One of the trusted handmaidens she had brought from the Citadel obediently entered the room. Her name was Dagmar, and she would serve as Clarice's nanny and wet nurse. She smiled when she saw the revived child. When Dagmar neared, Serena reluctantly handed Clarice to her. The queen gave Dagmar a grave look.

"If she perishes, you perish," she warned ominously.

Cradling the reborn child in her arms, Dagmar bowed. "Yes, Your Grace," she said.

Just then Serena sensed a familiar sensation start to grow in her mind. "Leave us," she said to Dagmar.

After giving her queen another bow, the wet nurse took the

gurgling child from the room. As Einar and Reznik watched, Serena went to her knees.

"I am here," she said.

"You have done well," the *Pon Q'tar* said to her. *"But your greatest trial is about to start. Your child has been reborn, but it is too late for you and her to flee. So now you must do everything in your power to protect her. The Black Ships approach. But the Recluse defenses are strong, so make the Conclave come to you. Defend Clarice and the Recluse with your life, if need be. Destroy the* Jin'Sai *once and for all."*

"On my life," Serena answered.

When she sensed the clerics' presence fading away, she came to her feet. Just as she was about to address Reznik and Einar, Actinius burst into the room.

"Forgive me, Your Grace!" he exclaimed. "An enveloper patrol has sighted the Black Ships! They can be seen from the tops of the castle walls!"

"I know," Serena answered quietly, surprising them all.

The three mystics saw a look of grim determination come over their queen. They had finally given her the one thing she wanted most in the world, and they knew that she would do anything, sacrifice anything, to protect her child. She gave her servants a commanding look.

"Hurry!" she said to them. "You know your orders!" At once all four mystics ran from the room.

The battle for the Recluse was about to start.

CHAPTER LXI

FROM THE BOW OF THE *TAMMERLAND,* TRISTAN USED TYRANNY'S spyglass to look north. What he saw worried him.

Under his orders, the four Black Ships had stopped at a point south of the Recluse and about three hundred meters away. Wigg was still empowering the *Tammerland.* At the *Jin'Sai*'s order the ship hovered twenty meters in the air. Faegan, Aeolus, and Jessamay soon positioned the other three vessels to hover in a battle line on the *Tammerland*'s starboard side. As the rising sun cast its rays over the vessels, the massive Black Ships twinkled ominously in the growing light.

Tristan lowered the spyglass and turned to look at his friends. Save for Jessamay, Faegan, and Aeolus, all of the Conclave members—including Traax—were present. Rafe, Scars, Ox, and Balthazar were also there, waiting for orders. Thousands of Minion warriors and highlander horsemen crowded the ships' decks, every fighter eager for the battle to start. Thousands more waited belowdecks. So far, the fleet had met no resistance.

Tristan handed the spyglass to Wigg. "Give me your opinion," he said.

Wigg took the glass and focused its lenses on the Recluse. After a time, he shook his head.

"It looks deserted," he said. "But every instinct in me says that it's not. It's a trap."

"I think you're right," Tristan agreed.

Shailiha took the glass from Wigg to see for herself. To her surprise, the Recluse looked abandoned. Under normal circumstances, Minion warriors would have prowled the guard paths lining the tops of the walls. The drawbridge would have been lowered, and more warriors would be seen guarding the drawbridge and the arched bridge stretching over the island's lake. Other warriors would have been flying patrol in the sky. But today not one could be seen, and the wooden drawbridge was raised. All the blue-and-gold flags displaying the heraldry of the House of Galland had been lowered. An ominous stillness commanded the entire structure and the surrounding land.

Seeing the Recluse like this was eerie, Shailiha realized. In some ways, its seemingly abandoned state was even more foreboding than if it had been swarming with Wulfgar's once-powerful demonslavers. She lowered the glass and looked at Tristan.

"What are your orders?" she asked him.

Tristan leaned against the gunwale, thinking. He was about to speak when Wigg beat him to it.

"Serena might want us to risk it all on a full frontal assault," the wizard said. "And I must admit that it's a tempting idea. But I would caution against it. We still don't know what kind of strength she has gathered behind those walls. If her forces outnumber us, we could lose this battle soon after it starts."

Tristan agreed with Wigg. But he also trusted Traax's opinions in such matters. He looked toward his battle-hardened commander.

"And you, my friend?" he asked. "What do you say?"

Leaving Duvessa's side, Traax walked closer. Although the warrior was up and about, his left arm was still bandaged. The look on his face was thoughtful, cautious.

"I agree with Wigg," he said. "If there are too many of them and we attack in force, we could lose everything. Better to let a small group of warriors approach the castle and draw them out to test their defenses. It could be a suicide mission, but we might learn much."

Tristan gave Traax a wry look. "And I suppose you want to lead them?" he asked.

Traax smiled. "Who better?" he asked. "My left arm might be weak, but my wings and my sword arm are fine."

Tristan thought for a moment. "We could send a force of one thousand," he mused. "That would be small enough not to weaken us badly should the group be vanquished, but perhaps large enough to draw the enemy out. As you say, we must find out what we're up against." The *Jin'Sai* went quiet again as he looked back at the distant Recluse.

"All right," he said to Traax. "You may lead them. But I want half of the warriors to walk toward the castle while the rest circle above, protecting them from the air. That way we might learn what threats await us on the ground *and* in the sky. If you meet overwhelming odds, sound a retreat. Leave as soon as you have assembled your group."

Tristan turned to Ox. "You're in charge of relaying our plan to the other ships," he ordered. "Be quick about it. Tell Faegan, Jessamay, and Aeolus that they are to take no action without my direct order." In a flash, Ox and Traax were gone.

Taking a deep breath, Tristan looked back at the solitary Recluse. *Soon we will know,* he thought. *But I fear that Serena's response will be swift and deadly.*

Shortly after that, the Conclave members watched the Minion forces soar away from the *Tammerland*. Traax led the ground forces. With their dreggans drawn they landed warily, then started to advance on the Recluse. The other five hundred stayed in the air as their eyes scanned the sky and the warriors beneath them. Like Tristan had ordered, the flying warriors circled slowly so as not to gain distance on the ground troops.

As the probing warriors approached the Recluse, Tristan looked over at Shailiha. She gave him a short smile, telling him that she agreed with his decision. After nodding back he took the spyglass from Wigg.

His face grim, Tristan watched his troops cross the field and near the halfway point to the Recluse. Still there was no resistance. As the troops advanced, Tristan started wondering if the castle was indeed abandoned. He lowered the glass and looked down at the deck, thinking.

Had Serena already managed to revive her dead child? If so, had she fled? He knew that she would probably not return to the Citadel, for the Conclave was well acquainted with its existence. With the help of her rogue consuls, she and Clarice could easily hide in Parthalon until Clarice was the proper age for the other part of the Heretics' mad plan. The Conclave might search for decades and never find her. Suddenly he heard the sounds of battle, and he looked to his troops.

Rising from the castle lake and surrounding ponds, thousands of snarling swamp shrews raced toward the approaching warriors. At first Tristan was startled, but then he remembered that the Minions had battled shrews before. Raising the glass back to one eye, he watched the shrews and the warriors tear into each other.

Hundreds died on either side as shrews eagerly devoured their victims and frantic warriors cut the snarling beasts down with abandon. Twisting the spyglass cylinders, Tristan looked closer to see two shrews attack a struggling warrior. Pouncing on him from behind, they tore the warrior's legs away, then dragged off the upper half of his body to start greedily feeding on him.

But five other warriors had seen his plight and took to the air. They soared over the two shrews to hack them apart with their dreggans. Amazingly, the warrior that had been torn apart was still alive, writhing in agony on the bloody grass. As a fellow Minion came to stand over the stricken warrior, Tristan knew what would come next. Without hesitation the warrior raised his sword high, then brought the blade down hard into his fellow soldier's heart, ending his pain.

Tristan tried to find Traax but could not. As the battle progressed, Tristan tensed. His highly outnumbered ground troops were losing. He soon wondered why a retreat hadn't been called, also forcing him to fear that Traax might have been killed. Blood and body parts from both sides lay everywhere as the killing went on unabated.

Tristan lifted the spyglass toward the five hundred warriors circling the sky. When he saw them fold their wings into place behind their backs, he knew why. Confident that no threat existed in the air, they couldn't continue to watch their fellows being slaughtered. Plunging vertically into free fall, the warriors went to the aid of their stricken brothers.

Feeling more confident, Tristan lowered the glass and nodded. *This will help even the score,* he thought. *If they can kill all the shrews, we will sail for the Recluse.*

Raising the glass again, he turned it on the castle. Suddenly he saw something that he didn't understand. Twisting the lenses, he brought the majestic fortress into sharper focus.

At first he thought he must be dreaming. Parts of the castle walls looked like they were *moving.* Stunned, he watched thousands of small wall areas start to shimmer and shift. Soon they somehow lifted away to blend into the morning sky. Then they were gone. Had he not been looking directly at the castle walls as they departed, he might never have seen them. His heart pounding, Tristan shoved the spyglass into Wigg's hands and pointed to the sky.

"Look there!" he shouted. "Augment your eyesight and tell me what you see!"

Wigg hurriedly put the spyglass to one eye. At first the wizard saw nothing. Then he applied all the power he could spare toward sharpening his vision. Even using his gifts he could barely see the thousands of shimmering shapes flying through the air.

Taking on the exact hue of the sky surrounding them, they started diving down onto the flying warriors plummeting to help those on the ground. As they lost altitude and Wigg's viewing angle on them changed, the shimmering shapes started changing color to perfectly mimic the green grass over which they flew. Wigg shuddered as he realized that the unsuspecting warriors would never see them coming.

Then Wigg saw Minion warriors suddenly start disappearing.

They weren't being cut down by whatever was attacking them. Instead, they simply *vanished*!

Trying to regain control over his emotions, Wigg twisted the spyglass cylinders to follow one warrior's progress and see what might happen. He soon got his answer.

Like so many others, the warrior was nowhere to be seen. Looking closer, Wigg found the lower parts of the warrior's boots, but nothing else of him. Then the boots were hauntingly lifted a meter or two off the ground. They shook violently for a few moments, then fell back to earth and lazily toppled over. To Wigg's utter amazement, the warrior's body armor, weapons, and bones materialized out of nothingness to fall into a ragged pile. He thought he saw a shimmering shape move, then nothing. Somehow, the grotesque pile was all that remained of a once-living, breathing warrior.

When Wigg lowered the glass, there were tears in his eyes. "You must order a retreat," he told Tristan.

Tristan snatched the glass from Wigg to try to see what had so disturbed the wizard. But without the benefit of Wigg's gifts, he couldn't identify the threat. All he could see were scores of Minion warriors suddenly disappearing from view. Looking farther, his blood ran cold when he saw the growing piles of Minion weapons, armor, and bones. He was about to order a Minion bugler to fly to them and blow retreat when from afar he suddenly heard its call. Traax or some other designated warrior must have ordered it, he guessed. He was relieved to hear it.

As the few remaining warriors started retreating, it seemed that they were not being pursued. Letting go victory cries, the shrews lumbered back to submerge into the Recluse's lake and surrounding ponds. Unseen by Tristan and his forces, Serena's envelopers returned to the sky and again flattened against the Recluse walls, perfectly mimicking their color and texture.

Tristan scanned the killing field. The once-proud group of one thousand volunteers had been cut down to several score, and most of them were wounded and bloodied. Realizing that the defeat had been total, the *Jin'Sai* sadly lowered the glass and closed his eyes. As the battered Minions started finding their way back aboard, Duvessa and some of the Conclave members rushed to tend to their wounds.

Tristan turned to look at Wigg. "What just happened?" he breathed.

Wigg shook his head. "I am as much at a loss to explain it as you," he said. "But Faegan, Jessamay, and Aeolus were also watching. I suggest that you order them to the *Tammerland.* Perhaps they can shed some light on this mystery."

"I have your mystery right here," they suddenly heard a familiar voice say.

They turned to see Traax standing there. He was covered from head to foot in some kind of dark gray slime. Four warriors stood by his side. In their arms they held a highly unusual creature.

At a gesture from Traax, the warriors dropped the strange carcass to the deck. With the thing's death, its camouflage had gone. As Tristan hurried closer, Traax sheathed his dreggan, then pointed to the beast. Tristan had never seen anything like it.

"I was lucky," Traax said. "When that thing surrounded me, I was sure that I would die. That is all the warning those bastards give. Two of my officers saw it morph and rushed to my aid. Not knowing what else to do, they started hacking at it with their swords. Being smothered by that monster was not an experience I would care to relive."

Wigg squatted to look at the dead beast. After a time, he stood and walked to Tristan.

"I have never seen one of these," he said. "It deserves further examination."

"First things first," Tyranny interjected. "How much longer can you and the others keep the Black Ships hovering?"

"For a few more hours, at best," Wigg answered calmly.

"What?" Tyranny exclaimed. "The only known body of water large enough to accommodate all the Black Ships is Dark Lagoon, and that's hours away!" Shaking her head, she snorted a laugh down her nose. "I suppose we could put them all down atop the lake surrounding the Recluse," she suggested sarcastically. "But I doubt that Serena would approve! So what do you expect us to do?"

"Don't fret," Wigg said. "I know of an appropriate spell that will help us. It was formulated three centuries ago, as the ships were being designed. I didn't suggest it sooner because I wasn't sure whether Tristan was going to order the ships to attack the Recluse. When Faegan, Jessamay, and Aeolus see what we're doing, they will follow suit."

Tyranny folded her arms across her chest. "Then I suggest that you get on with it!" she ordered. "This I have to see!"

As Wigg walked to the starboard gunwale he brusquely ordered the warriors out of his way. Curious, Shailiha walked to stand beside Tristan and Tyranny.

"What is he going to do?" she asked. Tristan just looked at his sister and shook his head.

Looking over the side of the ship, Wigg raised his arms. At once bolts loosed from his hands to fly toward the ground. All the Conclave members walked closer to watch.

As Wigg's bolts struck the earth, great mounds of soil exploded into the air. On and on the process went, until Tristan guessed what the wizard was doing. He smiled as he watched, knowing that Tyranny and Shailiha still hadn't grasped the concept.

Wigg finally finished his task and lowered his hands. Everyone could see that the stress of keeping the massive ship airborne and performing his strange digging had exhausted him. But if Tristan was right, there was only one more thing for Wigg to do, and then he could rest.

Raising his arms again, Wigg strengthened his spell over the ship. The *Tammerland* started moving. But rather than rise higher into the air, she kept her altitude and drifted to port. Tristan again looked over the side of the ship to see that he had been right. Wigg had used the craft to dig a deep cradle in the earth that perfectly matched the shape of the *Tammerland*'s hull.

Wigg slowly lowered his hands. The *Tammerland* descended, and her hull lowered ponderously into the earthen cradle. Her timbers creaked as she shifted; then she finally settled to a perfect level both forward to aft, and bow to stern.

"We used this technique to great effect during the Sorceresses' War," Wigg said. "Sometimes we would burn away small stretches of forest, then dig these cradles and lower the ships into them. The surrounding foliage served as wonderful hiding places when the Coven's forces were on the march."

"Well I'll be!" Tyranny said. "Well done, First Wizard."

Just then they heard more explosions, and they turned to look. As Wigg had promised, Aeolus, Faegan, and Jessamay were doing the same thing. Soon all four Black Ships had settled into their forgiving earthen cradles.

Tristan looked over at Traax. "I want patrols sent aloft at once," he ordered. "And ring all four ships with ground troops. If the slightest threat is noticed, alert me immediately."

Traax came to attention and clicked his heels. "I live to serve," he answered. He hurried away to give the orders.

As Traax walked off, Tristan returned the spyglass to his eye and gazed at the Recluse. Because he was already familiar with shrews from his previous visits to Parthalon, he was far more worried about the new creatures that Serena had conjured.

The unexpected creatures' abilities to camouflage themselves would greatly impede his attempt to take the Recluse. If their numbers were strong enough, sailing the ships over the Recluse walls might be impossible. And he had already seen the results when he had attacked with a small force. Wigg had cautioned against a full frontal attack, and at first Tristan had agreed. But now he wasn't so sure. They had just proven that sending forces against the Recluse piecemeal was suicide. What he needed was to find another way in, but there wasn't one.

As he scanned the fortress an idea formed in his mind. Lowering the spyglass, he looked down at the deck, thinking. He knew his concept had merit, but he would need advice from his mystics before deciding. He turned to look at Tyranny.

"Order Faegan, Aeolus, and Jessamay aboard," he said. "Bring them and Traax to the meeting room. We need to talk." He pointed to the dead creature on the deck. "And have them bring that disgusting thing along," he added.

Without further ado he led his remaining Conclave members aft, then down the stern stairway to await the others.

CHAPTER LXII

"YOU CAN PROPOSE THE SAME THEORY ONE HUNDRED TIMES MORE, but our answer will still be the same," Wigg said to Tristan. "You idea is sound, I'll grant you that. But we just can't find a way to make it work."

All of the Conclave members sat around a table in the stern

meeting room of the *Tammerland.* They had been discussing the taking of the Recluse for the last two hours. They all agreed that Tristan's idea had promise. But as Wigg said, it seemed impossible to carry out.

Tristan understood that the gravest threat to an attack on the Recluse were the new creatures at Serena's command, and their unusual ability to camouflage themselves. Traax had agreed. But he had also suggested that unless the beings' numbers were overwhelming, they might be conquered if only they could be seen. Sadly, an examination of the dead creature Traax brought back to the ship had revealed little about its endowed workings.

Tristan's idea was simple in concept. If Serena's flying creatures could be covered with some form of substance, then they could be seen, allowing the Minions and highlanders to attack them on equal terms. The prince had hoped that his mystics could somehow provide a way to do that. But after two hours, they were still searching for an answer.

Worse, even if they could overcome Serena's servants and get close to the Recluse, they still had to find a way in. Soaring over the walls was probably the only option. But Serena's consuls would without doubt be stationed atop those walls and would use the craft against them—probably in the form of azure bolts. If any of the mystics empowering the ships were killed, then his or her vessel would crash, and perhaps never rise again.

Faegan placed his hands flat atop the table, thinking. "The first problem with Tristan's idea is securing enough of some substance to cover all of Serena's flying beasts," he said. "And that is further complicated by the fact that we have no real idea how many of them exist. Those that killed the warriors this morning might have been only a smattering of the total number. Worse, getting the stuff close to the Recluse would be impossible without being attacked again. And even then the substance would have to be somehow spread out in a huge, high pattern, because we cannot see the enemy. We could hope that they might fly through it and thereby reveal their forms, but that is highly doubtful. There are simply too many variables that remain unaccounted for."

Tristan watched Shailiha picked up her wineglass and thoughtfully roll it between her palms. He knew that look—he had seen it all of his life.

"What is it?" he asked. "Do you have an idea?"

"Perhaps," she answered. She looked at Faegan. "You say that you would need a great deal of some liquid substance to make Tristan's idea work," she mused. "Are you saying that you four could never conjure that much—even if the acolytes helped?"

"It's highly doubtful," Faegan answered. "And even if we did, Serena would see it as we tried to move it closer to the Recluse. Moving that much so far and so fast would probably be impossible in itself."

Shailiha thought for a moment. "Would water work?" she asked. "By that I mean, could you use the craft to color it, and make it sticky, somehow?"

"I suppose," Jessamay answered. "But why do you ask?"

"Because the lake surrounding the Recluse is full of it," she answered. Realizing that she had seized on something, the princess leaned forward over the table. "If you could add color to it and change its composition, could you four lift it into the air and cause it to spread out?" she asked.

Aeolus' eyes narrowed. "Perhaps," he said, rubbing his chin, "if each of us tried to lift only his or her share. But even then it would be a monumental undertaking."

Shailiha looked at Abbey. "Can you come up with a concoction that would spread quietly if placed into the lake water and would then change its color and consistency only when you ordered it to? And then could you somehow make it explode on command?"

"Perhaps," Abbey said. "But I would need Faegan's help. I have most of my herbs and oils aboard. Provided we can come up with a basic formula, your other requirements could then be incorporated with various spells."

"Good," Shailiha said. "Then this is what I propose. . . ."

As the princess outlined her plan, Tristan smiled. It was truly ingenious. But even if it allowed his forces to overcome Serena's flying creatures and the shrews were also dealt with, that still didn't grant them entry to the Recluse. The fortress walls were several meters thick, and probably impervious to azure bolts. And despite the Recluse's size, its outer ward wasn't large enough to accommodate landing even one of the ships behind the fortress walls. Then there remained the problem of Serena's consuls.

While he glumly thought about the Recluse's seeming invulnerability, a curious thought struck him. As the idea took shape, he turned it over in his mind. After Shailiha finished explaining her idea, Tristan looked at Wigg.

"Tell me," he said, "can you, Aeolus, Faegan, and Jessamay empower the Black Ships if you are *inside* of them?"

Wigg rubbed his chin. "I don't think it has been tried, but I can't see why it wouldn't work," he answered. "Because we needed to see where we were going, we always chose to empower them from abovedecks."

"And could you use the craft to temporarily provide certain parts of the ships with extra fortification?" Tristan asked.

"I suppose so," Wigg answered. "But what are you suggesting?"

Tristan started to explain his plan. The more he described it, the more he realized how well it might follow Shailiha's idea. The strategies would need split-second timing, but they just might work. When he finished speaking he sat back in his chair. To his relief, everyone approved.

One hour later they had a fully formed attack plan, and the Conclave mystics went to work.

CHAPTER LXIII

GARVIN WAS SMALL FOR A MINION WARRIOR. BUT WHAT HE LACKED in stature he more than made up for with courage. He was also resourceful, a good swordsman, and a fast flier. Because of these admirable traits, Traax had suggested him for a vitally important mission. To help him hide in the night sky, his exposed skin and his shiny weapons had been rubbed with charcoal.

The entire Conclave had questioned him for more than an hour before finally agreeing on him as their choice. As he stood on the *Tammerland*'s moonlit deck, the importance of his impending mission began to sink in. In the finest Minion tradition he was ready to do his best, no matter the cost to himself.

It was nearly midnight of the evening following the failed probe of the Recluse defenses. All the Conclave members were on deck to see Garvin off, as were throngs of anxious Minions and highlander horsemen. Tristan would soon order a group of warriors to conduct a diversionary tactic designed to draw Serena's servants away from the Recluse. If the diversion failed, Garvin knew that he would probably be killed.

It had taken Faegan and Abbey all day and part of the night to produce the small amount of fluid that he would soon carry. It was precious, they had told him. The highly concentrated formula had exhausted Abbey's supplies of certain herbs and oils, ensuring that producing another batch would be impossible. The campaign for the Recluse and the future of the Vigors relied on Garvin's success. There would be no second chance.

Garvin looked to the night sky. The *Jin'Sai* was standing beside him as they waited for the right time to send him aloft. If a suitable cloud formation formed, Garvin could perhaps use it to hide in. As he looked west, it seemed that he was about to get his wish. He pointed skyward.

"Look there," he said to the others. "That might do."

Tristan stared at the passing clouds. They were dense and moving east to west.

"What do you think?" he asked Traax.

Traax nodded. "I agree," he said. "If we don't take advantage of this formation, we might not get another one."

"All right," Tristan said to Garvin. "Hide in those clouds and travel with them as they move. Stay close enough to their lower edges so that you can see the ground. When the diversion starts, you know what to do."

Tristan held out the precious glass tube. It was about four inches long by one inch wide. A simple cork secured its top. The dark green formula trapped inside swirled and eddied with a life of its own.

Garvin carefully took the tube from Tristan and secured it in a leather pouch tied around his waist. He clicked his boot heels together.

"I live to serve," he said quietly. "And I won't let you down."

Tristan nodded. "Go," he said softly. "May the Afterlife be with you."

Everyone watched Garvin leave the deck and soar into the sky. Following his orders, he headed east and climbed quickly.

They soon lost track of him as he approached the cloud formation.

Tristan turned to Ox. "Now comes your turn," he said. "Take your force and head slowly for the castle's southern face. Give them plenty of time to see you. When the shrews attack, fight them for a short time, then sound a retreat. We will surely lose some warriors to Serena's shrews and camouflaged creatures, but that can't be helped if we're to give Garvin enough time. Go, and good luck to you."

Puffing out his barrel chest, Ox clicked his heels together and smiled. He turned to gather his warriors. In moments he and three hundred others had landed on the ground to start skulking toward the moonlit castle.

As he watched them go, Tristan clenched his jaw. There was much about this plan that he didn't like, but it was the best that he and his Conclave had been able to devise. For Garvin to succeed, Ox and his group had to entice Serena's creatures far from the Recluse. Even so, Gavin would have to perform his part of it quickly, and without being seen.

Tyranny walked across the deck to stand beside Tristan. Trying to calm her nerves, she produced a cigarillo and lit it. After taking a deep lungful of smoke she reached out to take his arm, then gently tugged him to one side.

"Good luck," she said simply.

"Thank you," he said. He gave her a searching look. "No hard feelings about our earlier conversation?" he whispered.

After taking another drag on her cigarillo, she shook her head and tousled her hair. Finally she smiled.

"No hard feelings," she whispered back. "But I have to be honest with you. I still haven't given up. One of these days, you'll come around to my way of thinking."

Tristan let go a short laugh, then looked back at the Minion warriors moving across the moonlit field. Almost at once the action started.

Shrews by the thousands ominously surfaced the lake surrounding the Recluse. As they snarled wildly, their breath streamed out in ghostly vapors and their teeth and steaming coats glinted in the moonlight. They immediately started thundering across the killing field.

Tristan held his breath as he watched Ox and the warriors staunchly obey their orders. Holding their dreggans high, they stopped advancing and formed a tight phalanx as they braced for the onslaught.

Wait, Tristan thought, as he watched the brave warriors hold their ground. *Wait, wait . . . now!*

Like Tristan had willed it from afar, the warriors launched into the air just as the shrews reached them, then started hacking at the monsters from above.

Tristan anxiously raised Tyranny's spyglass to look closer. *Remember your orders, Ox,* his mind warned. *Don't remain in the fray for too long!*

Just then he saw warriors start disappearing into thin air, and he knew that Serena's other monsters had left the castle walls to join the attack. That was what he had wanted to happen, but it also added much to the danger his warriors faced.

Sound the retreat! Tristan's frantic mind begged as his fingers closed harder around the spyglass. *You must do it now, before you are completely overcome!*

Suddenly he heard the distant bugle call come floating across the field. As the warriors started flying back, Tristan raised the spyglass to the sky.

HIS WINGS FOLDED BEHIND HIS BACK, GARVIN PLUNGED EARTHward in a nearly vertical free fall. As ordered, he had waited for the diversion to start before he left his hiding place in the clouds.

Turning his attention from the battle, he focused on his landing place. It was to be on the Recluse's north side, putting the castle directly between him and the fighting. As he neared the structure he could see that the consuls and Valrenkians had abandoned their posts along guard paths atop three of the four walls. To a man they had gathered on the southern wall top to raucously watch the fighting and to cheer the vicious shrews onward. The *Jin'Sai* had predicted that their attention would be firmly locked on the killing field, and he had been right.

As he neared the north shore of the lake, Garvin unfolded his wings to slow his descent. He landed silently on the grass, then snapped his wings into place behind his back. Looking around, he quietly drew his dreggan. As the Conclave had hoped, the area on this side of the Recluse seemed deserted. Knowing that there was no time to lose, he used his free hand to remove the glass tube from his waist pouch and silently crept toward the lakeshore.

"For the formula to work, you must pour the contents into the water bit by bit, until it is gone," Faegan had told him. *"Then return the tube to your pouch and leave as quickly as you can."* In the quiet of the night, Garvin started to uncork the tube. Then he heard a soft splashing sound.

He froze, trying to listen. He could hear faint cheering still coming from the southern wall top, but nothing else. Then the splashing sound came again, followed by a low, snarling growl. He cautiously turned to look behind him.

About fifteen meters down the lakeshore, a shrew stood glaring at him. Its coat was wet and steaming in the cool night air. The beast's breathing was ragged, and blood dripped from a wound in its right shoulder. Garvin quickly gathered that the wound had probably been incurred during yesterday's failed try to probe the Recluse. Another bloody gash from a Minion dreggan ran vertically between the beast's dark eyes.

Garvin quickly guessed that the shrew had stayed behind to lick its wounds. Worse, it might be just one of many such wounded monsters taking refuge in the lake. Not one member of the Conclave had taken this possibility into account.

As the shrew stood there snarling at him, Garvin wondered why it didn't attack. Perhaps it was wounded too badly, or its eyesight had been adversely affected. He had no idea whether shrews could communicate with their masters, but he couldn't take the chance. The beast had to die. But his mission must come first.

Deciding to risk it, he took a step closer to the shore.

The shrew immediately snarled, louder this time. But it did not move. As he held the shrew's gaze, Garvin took another step.

The unpredictable shrew snarled, then charged a few paces and stopped again. Despite its wounds, its speed was incredible. As the terrible thing glared at him, its teeth glinted in the moonlight and more blood ran from its shoulder to drip lazily onto the ground.

If he could steal one more pace, Garvin knew that he would be close enough. Holding his breath, he took the final step. Reaching slowly across his body with his sword arm, he tried to uncork the tube without laying down his dreggan. After a few moments the cork wiggled free and Garvin dropped it to the grass. He held the tube at arm's length and started gradually pouring the wizards' formula into the lake.

That was when the shrew's instincts took over, and it charged.

Garvin sidestepped and quickly put his thumb over the open end of the tube. Then he brought his dreggan down and around, aiming for the preexisting wound in the monster's shoulder. As the shrew went past him he felt a searing pain in his sword arm. The shrew skidded to a stop about five meters away in the slippery grass.

When the shrew turned to face him, Garvin could tell that his aim had been true—the beast's wound was far deeper and longer than before, and blood was literally spurting from it with each beat of the thing's dark heart. In truth he didn't know what was keeping the monster's front leg attached to its shoulder.

He stole a precious second to glance at the tube. Most of its formula had gone into the lake, but a bit remained in the tube's curved bottom. With one eye locked on the shrew, he starting dribbling the rest of the formula into the water. But before he could finish, the thing attacked again.

Again he tried to sidestep the shrew, but this time he wasn't quick enough. The monster brushed against his body, throwing him to the ground on his stomach. To his horror, the tube slipped from his hand but blessedly landed upright in the grass. He lunged for it, but at the same time the shrew bit viciously into his right thigh.

Desperate to recapture the vial, he tried crawling forward. In retaliation the monster thrashed his leg viciously about, and bit deeper into his flesh. He knew that the beast's strength and size would soon win out, but he had to somehow finish his mission.

Lunging forward with everything he had, he felt his thigh muscles tear away, but the vial finally came into his hand. Turning it upside down, he poured the remaining formula into the lake.

I can die now, he thought, *like the warrior I was trained to be.*

But then the beast did something amazing. It let him go.

Garvin turned as best he could to look at the shrew. The monster wobbled drunkenly as its jaws loosened from around his thigh. For several tense moments it slowly lifted its awful head and glared at him. Then it collapsed onto its wounded side, dead from blood loss.

His chest heaving, Garvin did his best to stand. The searing pain nearly caused him to faint away, and he dropped the vial. Much of his outer right thigh was gone, some of it still lodged between the shrew's pointed teeth. His right arm was bleeding badly. He reached under his chest armor to produce two tourniquets, then wound them tightly around his wounds.

He was terribly weak from blood loss, but his wings had not been injured and the fleet was close. Suddenly remembering what Faegan had said about not leaving any evidence behind, Garvin nearly fainted again as he picked up the empty vial and returned it to his waist pouch.

It was all he could do to get airborne. He knew that a direct flight path back to the Black Ships would probably mean the difference between him living or dying. But he dutifully chose to follow orders and backtrack along the more circuitous route that had brought him here. His mind light-headed and his muscles feeling like they were made of lead, Garvin did his best to head west.

After finally crashing to the deck of the *Tammerland,* he lived just long enough to tell his tale.

CHAPTER LXIV

AS DAWN BROKE THE FOLLOWING DAY, TRISTAN NERVOUSLY PACED the bow of the *Tammerland.* The Conclave's plan was clever, but not without its weaknesses. Everything would have to go exactly as planned, and each player in the scheme would have to do his or her job perfectly. This time Tristan would commit all his forces. If the attack failed, there would be no second chance.

He sadly looked down toward the deck. Black sailcloth had been wound around the corpse lying there. Tristan had known Garvin for only a few hours, but he had liked him. Garvin had finished his mission successfully, but that didn't guarantee that Faegan and Abbey's formula would work. Either way, the sailcloth was a fitting burial shroud. Later on, Garvin's corpse would be cremated, alongside the other warriors who would fall this day.

Carrying two cups of hot tea, Shailiha appeared by Tristan's side. She gave him one and they stood together drinking for a time, watching the fog lift from the blood-soaked killing field. Dark and foreboding, the castle seemed to crouch threateningly atop its mist-shrouded island like a giant spider. Shailiha gave her brother a supportive pat on one arm.

"Soon," she said simply.

"Yes," Tristan answered. "Your idea is brilliant."

"As is yours," she answered. "But for us to take the castle, both plans have to work, don't they?" After taking another sip of tea, she gave him a short smile. "We make a good team," she added softly. Tristan smiled back at her, then looked down the length of the *Tammerland.*

Thousands of warriors stood topside, waiting to attack. Far more filled the *Tammerland*'s lower areas. Gathered on the ship's bottom deck, the highlander horsemen waited nervously astride their mounts. The ship's giant rear hatch had been lowered, allowing them easy access to the ground. The Minions aboard the *Ephyra,* the *Florian,* and the *Cavalon* were also waiting, and ready to strike at a moment's notice.

Tristan cast his gaze toward the rising sun. Although attacking at night was tempting, the Conclave members knew that it had to be done in sunlight. Even if Serena's flying creatures could be marked, they would be difficult to find in the dark. And so the Conclave had nervously waited for the sun's rays to break over the eastern horizon before launching the attack.

Tristan watched as the remaining Conclave members wended their way through the warrior and highlander throngs. As they crowded around, he smiled at them. Each had his or her own special skills, and they would all be needed today. Tristan again looked at the sun and decided that the time was right. He turned back to face the Conclave.

"Each of you knows your orders," he said, "so there is no need for me to repeat them. Faegan, Aeolus, and Jessamay, it is time to take to your ships. Wait for the signal before starting your spells." The three mystics gave the prince a farewell look, then left to command their respective vessels.

Wigg came to stand beside the *Jin'Sai* and *Jin'Saiou.* The look on his face was concerned, thoughtful.

"We of the craft have never tried anything like this before," he said. "Our plan might easily fail. But I can think of no finer practitioners to attempt this than Faegan, Aeolus, and Jessamay." He placed his gnarled hands on Tristan's and Shailiha's shoulders. "We will try our best," he said.

"We know," Tristan answered. "In the end, that's all any of us can do. It's time to get started."

Tristan turned toward Traax and Rafe. "Take your forces afield and form your ranks," he said. "You know your orders. Remember, we are committing everything to this attack. It will be all, or nothing. Once your advance starts, move fast. But don't charge until you see my signal."

Traax came to attention. "I live to serve," he said. After giving Duvessa a look of farewell, he ran off to carry out his orders.

Rafe responded by giving Tristan a final slap on the back. "No matter what happens, it was a pleasure knowing you, *dango*!" he said, then walked off to join his horsemen belowdecks.

Wigg moved a bit closer to Tristan. "I might have been wrong about those highlanders," he admitted softly. Tristan's only answer was a smile.

After a time, Tristan saw his forces gather on the field. Their great numbers would soon be easily visible to the enemy, and he was counting on that.

With their weapons gleaming in the sun, thousands of Minions stood in tightly formed phalanxes. Traax and Ox were at their head. Ahead of the phalanxes were hundreds of mounted highlander horsemen, their colorful clothes in direct contrast to the Minions' dark hair and body armor. Knowing that they were about to go into battle, the highlander warhorses pawed the ground and strained against their bits and reins.

We will soon know, Tristan thought as he looked back at Wigg. *May the Afterlife be with us.*

He gave Wigg a nod. Wigg nodded in return.

The First Wizard raised one hand. An azure bolt shot from his fingertips and went flying into the air, signaling that the attack should start.

At once the highlander horsemen charged toward the Recluse while half the Minions flew low cover. The other half ran across the ground behind them. It was a breathtaking sight. Even from the deck of the *Tammerland* Tristan could feel the ground tremble as his forces gathered speed and tore for the Recluse. To draw

Serena's forces out as quickly as possible, the highlanders and Minions started screaming out insults and epithets of every conceivable kind.

As expected, shrews again surfaced from the lake to face their foes. Snarling and shaking their heads, they thundered toward the approaching Conclave forces. As the two terrible armies charged, Tristan turned his spyglass toward the Recluse walls. Wigg remained by his side, waiting for Tristan's next order.

Come, you bastards, the prince's mind begged.

And then he saw them. Like the time before, thousands of small areas on the Recluse walls started shifting, telling him that Serena's flying creatures were about to join the battle. Now there could be no reprieve, no turning back from the Conclave's plan.

"Do it!" Tristan shouted at Wigg.

At once the First Wizard loosed another azure bolt into the air. This time it was a signal to Faegan, Aeolus, and Jessamay. Then Wigg raised his arms, just as Tristan knew the other three Conclave mystics would be doing. As the prince turned his gaze to the lake surrounding the Recluse, he held his breath.

The entire lake started rising into the air. It was the singlemost stunning display of the craft Tristan had ever seen.

The formula Faegan and Abbey had concocted had three stages, and each one had to work perfectly for the plan to succeed. First, at Faegan's command the formula would spread quickly throughout the lake. Then the formula would be called on to hold the lake in its original shape as the mystics lifted it into the air. Finally, it had to change the color and consistency of the lake water.

As the water rose from the lake bed, Tristan was stunned to see that it was indeed keeping its shape. Its inner border matched the fortress walls, while its outer border conformed to the lakeshore boundaries. Not only were thousands of tons of water being lifted into the air, but also everything it contained. Without warning, the mystics allowed wounded shrews, rocks, fish, and water vegetation to go crashing back to the empty lake bed. As the oddly shaped ring of water rose toward the Recluse's wall tops, Tristan smiled as he watched Serena's stunned consuls and Valrenkians leave their posts and run for their lives.

Soon Tristan saw the suspended lake water surrounding the Recluse turn dark red. The crimson liquid was stunning as it twinkled with the craft and literally hung there in space. Now there was only one more thing to be done.

Tristan looked over at Wigg to see that the First Wizard's face had reddened mightily from the strain, and that his entire body was shaking. Then he saw Wigg partly relax. Tristan knew that without the First Wizard's powers, Faegan, Aeolus, and Jessamay would be working harder to keep the lake aloft, but it couldn't be helped. As Wigg pointed his arms toward the Recluse and brought the final part of the spell to bear, Tristan again looked toward the hovering body of water.

With a thunderous crash, the lake water exploded.

Crystalline beads of sticky, red water burst forth in every direction, flooding the Recluse walls and deluging the sky. The red drops flew high and wide, bathing everything they touched in their crimson embrace.

When Tristan saw thousands of red shapes suddenly leave untouched spots behind on the walls, he knew that his mystics had succeeded. Because the endowed water landed atop the creatures' skin, even if their color changed they would still be seen. Unfazed, the thousands of red flying creatures did their duty to the Vagaries, and started hurtling through the sky toward Tristan's forces.

At last! Tristan rejoiced. *We can finally meet them on equal terms!*

He lowered his spyglass and trained it on the battlefield. Following Tristan's orders, Rafe's riders were well out ahead of the low-flying Minions and the warriors charging on foot. Tristan's plan called for the highlander riders to charge directly through the spaces between the shrews' undisciplined ranks and kill as many as possible on the first pass. Those shrews still alive would be dealt with by the warriors on foot, while those higher up would busy themselves with the red creatures. Tristan held his breath as the two opposing forces on the ground and in the air rushed toward each other.

One hundred meters, he thought. *Seventy . . . forty . . . ten . . .*

With a thunderous clash, the two armies tore into each other.

Hanging sideways from their saddles, Rafe's highlanders courageously threaded their charging mounts among the onrushing shrews and launched arrow after arrow at the snarling beasts. Hundreds of shrews went crashing to the earth. Then more fell, and more after that. By the time they reached the warriors, their ranks had thinned. As the highlanders rode thorough the ragged ends of the shrew lines, they reclaimed their saddles and wheeled their horses around. Waving their sabers this time, they charged to attack the beasts from the rear.

As the remaining shrews met the warriors, the Minions on the ground started hacking into the beasts. Grateful that the first part of his plan was succeeding, Tristan turned his attention to the air campaign.

Because the airborne warriors could finally see their opponents, they could fight them in earnest. Soon dead envelopers and warriors started falling from the sky to oftentimes crash haphazardly atop the Minions and the shrews fighting below them. Sometimes only clothing, weapons, and wet bones fell, marking the death of another warrior. Soon the battlefield was strewn with carnage of every conceivable kind.

As Tristan watched the battle unfold, his right hand tightened around the spyglass. He longed to be with his forces. He could feel the *K'Shari* Forestallment calling out to him, demanding to be used. But he knew that for now his place was on the bow of the *Tammerland,* overseeing the battle. Taking a deep breath, he lowered the spyglass and turned to look at the worried Conclave members. Now there was nothing to do but wait, and see which way the tide of battle turned.

The massive carnage would go on for three more hours. In the end, the Conclave forces would triumph. As Tristan watched his bloodied warriors and highlanders return from the battlefield, he closed his eyes in gratitude.

But he knew that even now it wasn't over. Although Serena's forces had been weakened, he had every confidence that she had kept some in reserve for a last-ditch effort to defend her child. He was sure of it, because it was what he would have done. Worse, Serena's mystics and Valrenkians probably outnumbered his mystics. Even so, there was no time to lose.

As soon as the *Jin'Sai* could regroup his tired army, he would attack the Recluse for the final time. They would either take it, or die trying.

Chapter LXV

"You fools!" Serena shouted angrily. "How dare you suggest that the Recluse is impregnable? Didn't you see what happened out there this morning? We grow weaker while the Conclave grows stronger!"

As she paced the confines of her sumptuous chambers, the Vagaries queen was beside herself with rage. She turned to look at Dagmar. The handmaiden sat in a chair on the room's other side, suckling Clarice. The loving scene softened the queen's expression briefly, but she soon turned back to again glare at her contrite servants.

The Conclave's idea to mark her envelopers had been completely unexpected. Einar and Reznik had not been able to devise a way to remove the red stain from the creatures' skins. From this day forward the envelopers would be prime targets for the *Jin'Sai*'s troops.

Worse, more than half of Serena's envelopers and shrews had been killed in the latest attack. Although the Conclave's losses had also been heavy, she correctly guessed that they were not as serious as hers. But Serena still held several tactical advantages.

Einar and Reznik were partly right—the Recluse would be exceedingly difficult to conquer. As far as she knew, there were no ways in or out through the castle's lower regions. The walls were more than three feet thick, making them nearly impervious to attack. And although the water surrounding the Recluse was gone, the wide, muddy lake bottom that had been left behind would be very difficult to slog across on foot.

She also knew that each of the Black Ships was too large to set down in the castle outer ward. The Black Ships could bring the remaining Minion warriors near so that they could try to fly over the walls. But for the *Jin'Sai*'s mystics to effectively use their gifts against her, they would eventually have to put the ships at rest. From the guard paths she had watched the Conclave mystics dig the ships' earthen cradles. The technique was clever, but would be very time-consuming to perform while under attack. Should the Conclave try to do it near the castle, her consuls would quickly take advantage of their vulnerability and strike down on them from above.

"With all due respect, Your Grace, there are two things regarding Clarice that need our attention," Einar said, interrupting her thoughts.

Serena narrowed her eyes and looked at her lead consul. "What do you mean?" she asked.

"First, we must remove the spell that you conjured about Clarice after your tragic miscarriage. As I recall, it was designed to preserve her body while we furthered our research. Now that she is reborn, keeping it in place might harm her."

Serena nodded. "Very well," she said. "What is your second suggestion?"

"During my perusal of the Scroll of the Vagaries, I found mention of a 'partial' time enchantment," Einar answered. "I read the formula, and it appears valid. I suggest that Clarice be immediately protected by its workings."

Serena scowled. "What are you talking about?" she demanded. "There is no such thing as a *partial* time enchantment."

As Einar walked toward Dagmar and Clarice, he dropped the hood of his robe to show his sharp features and intelligent eyes. Dagmar had finished suckling the child, and she was gently rocking the baby in her arms. For a moment Einar lovingly reached down to stroke Clarice's downy hair.

"Ah, but there is such a spell, Your Grace," he answered. Placing his hands into the opposite sleeves of his robe, he turned to face his queen.

"As we know, a time enchantment carries two distinct parts," he said. "One part stops the aging process. The other protects the subject from disease. We had always thought that the two were inseparable. They aren't."

Serena was intrigued. She highly respected Einar's intelligence. Moreover, she trusted him. But if her daughter was to be involved, she would need proof.

"Can you show me the calculations?" she asked.

"Of course," Einar answered.

The consul produced a parchment from the folds of his robe. He unrolled it and started reading aloud. At the same time he caused the formula's glowing numbers and symbols to hover in the air for his queen's inspection.

Serena walked closer and read the calculations. What she saw surprised her. It was indeed a formula for a partial time enchantment. Unlike the full spell, this one held only those calculations that would protect Clarice from disease, and it had been formulated to work independently of the half that halted the aging process.

She immediately understood how this could greatly benefit her child. Granting Clarice a full-time enchantment would be counterproductive to the Heretics' plans, because it would keep her from maturing to an age that would allow her to consciously employ the craft. But if Serena could forever protect her daughter from disease, the advantage would be enormous.

She looked back at Einar. "You are sure about this?" she asked.

Einar nodded. "Yes," he answered. "The child's health should be protected—especially because the Recluse was recently inhabited by lepers. The choice is yours. But should you proceed, I suggest that you first dismantle the other spell. Despite the strength of Clarice's blood, I would not wish to see the two calculations entwine in a subject who is so young and vulnerable."

"Of course," Serena answered.

She walked to the balcony, thinking. She would remain that way for some time before deciding. Finally she turned back to look at Einar.

"Very well," she finally answered. "I agree that it should be done. But after I dismantle the first spell, I want you to apply the partial time enchantment. You are more familiar with its workings."

"As you wish, Your Grace," Einar answered.

Serena's lead consul could barely contain his delight. Finding the spell had been a stroke of luck. Not only would it protect the child, but it would further cement Serena's bond with him. He had no doubt that after the war was won, he would become a high-ranking official in Serena's new order.

He looked at Dagmar. "Bring the child to me," he said.

Under Serena's watchful eye, Dagmar stood and carried the squirming baby to the consul. Einar looked at his queen.

"With your permission, Your Grace?" he asked.

Serena nodded. From his place on the other side of the room, Reznik watched with rapt fascination. After handing the child over to Einar, Dagmar walked to stand beside the herbmaster.

Einar cradled the child in his arms. She cooed quietly as he looked down at her.

"Whenever you are ready, Your Grace," he said.

Serena closed her eyes and started to dismantle the spell. She did so carefully, taking great pains to be sure that the convoluted formula had been completely eradicated. After she opened her eyes, she hurried over to check on her daughter.

Einar smiled. "Well done, Your Grace," he said. "There seem to be no ill effects."

Glad to see that the child had not been harmed, Serena lovingly took Clarice into her arms. She rocked her gently for a time before looking back at Einar.

"You may proceed," she said. Einar could easily detect the ominous warning her voice carried. "But if any harm befalls her, you will die," Serena added.

"I understand," Einar answered.

Closing his eyes, he folded his hands before him and recalled the needed incantation. Although it was much like the one used for granting a full-time enchantment, it held subtle differences. Einar began the incantation:

"Your health shall remain forever true,
"Your strength and vitality shall always shine through.
"Of neither disease nor sickness shall you fear,
"Nor the world's wasteful processes seem so near.
"From this moment on you shall walk with new life,
"Free of all ills, and with them, their strife."

Serena watched as the familiar azure glow of the craft appeared all around the child. Then it faded away, leaving the room as quickly as it had come. She carefully examined Clarice for signs of distress. There were none. In fact, the child's color seemed to have improved, as had her overall vitality.

Looking into her mother's face, she wriggled about happily and smiled. Like she knew that she shared a sacred bond with the withered rose tucked into the bodice of Serena's black mourning gown, Clarice reached out and touched it with her delicate fingers.

She is truly Wulfgar's child, Serena thought. Delighted by what she saw, Serena fought back tears as she looked at her trusted lead consul.

"Thank you," she whispered. "Please leave me now; I wish to be alone with my daughter. Unless I miss my guess, the *Jin'Sai* won't be long in coming. Should our sentries see the slightest movement from the enemy, I am to be informed at once."

"Of course, Your Grace," Einar answered. He led Reznik and Dagmar from the room and closed the door behind him.

As Serena lovingly rocked Clarice, to anyone who did not know her, she could have been any contented mother, anywhere in the world. But she wasn't. She was the reigning queen of the Vagaries, and she would soon lead her side of the craft in a historic battle that would be remembered though the ages.

Worried for the fate of her only child, Serena closed her eyes.

CHAPTER LXVI

AS TRISTAN READ TRAAX'S BATTLE REPORT, HIS HEART FELL. Nearly a quarter of his warriors were dead, as were a third of the highlander horsemen. Rafe, Ox, Scars, and Duvessa had survived, but even they had been shaken by the recent battle's savagery. Despite his losses, Tristan planned to start the final assault on the Recluse within the hour.

From the bow deck of the *Tammerland,* Tristan looked out over the bloody field. The midday sun was bright. Flies and carrion birds had started gathering on the corpses, to avail themselves of the unexpected feast. Wigg and Shailiha stood quietly beside Tristan, waiting for him to give the order. Aside from the three of them, the *Tammerland*'s topside was deserted. So were the topsides of the other three Black Ships, resting nearby in their earthen cradles. Seeing the vessels' decks without warriors or highlander horsemen atop them suddenly seemed strange, the prince realized.

By his order, every fighter waited in the sweltering areas belowdecks on their respective ships. So too did Adrian's acolytes, whom Tristan had been holding in reserve and whose numbers had been equally divided among the four vessels. As the ships neared the castle he wanted everyone hidden from attack until the last possible moment. Faegan, Aeolus, and Jessamay were aboard their vessels. When they saw the *Tammerland* lift into the air they would immediately empower the ships and follow her.

Tired of battle plans and casualty reports, Tristan angrily tore up the parchments he was reading and cast them to the wind. The pieces flew away as quickly as had the warriors' and horsemen's lives accounted for on their pages. He looked down at the deck, thinking.

The Black Ships had been readied according to his plan, the fighters were itching to go, and the Conclave mystics knew their jobs. There was nothing left to do but to give the order. As he thought about the impending battle, he could feel his *K'Shari* Forestallment churning his blood as never before, begging to be unleashed. But as he stared back at the mighty Recluse, his heart remained unsure.

Taking a step closer, Wigg put one hand on Tristan's shoulder. "There is nothing more to be done," he said quietly.

Shailiha gave her brother a supportive smile. "Wigg is right," she said. "It's time."

Tristan took a deep breath. "All right," he said. "Let's go."

Tristan led Wigg and Shailiha toward the bow hatch and down the stairway. One deck down, he exited the steps and entered a hallway.

After escorting Wigg and Shailiha into a specially prepared room, Tristan shut the door. He knew that Faegan, Aeolus, and Jessamay would be seated in similar chambers aboard their respective vessels as they waited nervously for the *Tammerland* to lift into the air. Adrian and all the acolytes stationed aboard the *Tammerland* were there waiting for them. Tyranny and Abbey were also present.

Tristan glanced around the room. The aft wall was flat and held the door through which they had just come. The sidewalls curved with the ship's hull, and their opposite ends joined to form the point of the ship's bow. Tristan had ordered Minion carpenters to cut rectangular viewing ports into the hull, one on each side of the bow joint. Each window was a meter wide by half a meter high, and was angled to provide an excellent view forward. As he and Shailiha neared the port window, Wigg and Tyranny walked to the starboard one. Tristan gave Wigg a knowing look.

"Are you ready?" he asked. "Remember, we must have as much momentum as possible for this to work."

Wigg nodded. "I understand," he answered. "And may the Afterlife be with us."

Tristan turned and looked at Sister Adrian and the acolytes. He knew that they were nervous; everyone was. But he also knew that when the time came, they would do their duties.

"And you?" he asked them. "Is each of you ready to do her part? If you don't work as a team, thousands will die needlessly. Remember—do not use your gifts until you hear my order. Until then you must save your power."

"We understand," Adrian answered for the group. Then the normally staid First Sister gave Tristan a wry smile. "Let's go and kill some Vagaries servants," she added softly.

The First Wizard turned his attention toward his window. Wigg raised his hands. Almost at once the *Tammerland*'s great bulk lifted from her earthen cradle and into the air. Soon the ship was flying over the bloody battlefield and heading straight for the Recluse.

As the *Tammerland* gained momentum, the aft door opened and Traax appeared. "The other ships are also in the air, my lord," he said. "They are matching our speed and following us in single file."

"Good," Tristan answered. "Alert me at once if anything changes. Otherwise, you know your orders. And good luck."

Traax clicked his heels and hurried from the room. Tristan turned back toward Wigg. The wizard was shaking noticeably as he tried to grant the *Tammerland* all the speed that he could.

Soon the ship started to shake, and her timbers groaned from the strain being placed on her. Tyranny shot Tristan a worried glance. As the Black Ships tore over the body-strewn battlefield, Tristan unsheathed his sword; Shailiha and Tyranny did the same.

Just then they all heard an explosion, and the ship rocked violently. While Wigg struggled to keep the *Tammerland* on course,

Tristan looked to the Recluse. The expected bombardment had started.

From atop the fortress walls, Serena's consuls were hurling azure bolt after azure bolt toward the attacking fleet. The bolts came in such great numbers that their combined glow lit up the sky. Wigg had confirmed that the Black Ships were built to withstand a certain amount of endowed bombardment. But even he couldn't be sure if they would hold together if Serena's consuls attacked in force.

Suddenly another azure bolt slammed into the ship, this one striking the deck directly above Tristan and his friends. The topside planks shattered, then speared threateningly down into the room as pointed shards of black wood rained down. The bolt's power forced the ship to angle down dangerously, and nearly plow headlong into the earth. Straining to his utmost, Wigg righted her again. Suddenly another bolt went whizzing by to narrowly miss the starboard bow. With a great explosion it plunged into the ground and exploded. Tons of dirt and sod went flying into the air. As the bombardment intensified and the explosions grew louder, everyone in the room hung on and hoped for the best.

With the coming of the bombardment, Tristan worried about how the other ships were faring. The single-file formation had been his idea. The narrower their profile facing Serena's consuls, the less damage the ships would incur. But this strategy also made the *Tammerland* the prime target. Faegan commanded the next ship in line. If the *Tammerland* went down, the crippled wizard would lead the charge.

Just then another bolt hit the flagship, this one sending her plummeting out of control. Tristan watched in horror as the *Tammerland* angled downward so steeply this time that all he could see from his window was bloody grass, and the scattered bodies left behind on the battlefield.

Adrian didn't want to go against Tristan's orders, but she knew there was no choice. She immediately raised her arms. As she and Wigg strained mightily, Tristan felt the *Tammerland*'s bow start rising. He held his breath as he wondered whether it would come up in time.

Just as the ship leveled she hit hard and her metal keel plowed a gouge in the earth. As the *Tammerland* skidded dangerously across the bloody grass, Shailiha and some of the acolytes were thrown to the floor. Straining with everything they had, Wigg and Adrian managed to take the violently weaving ship skyward again.

Azure bolts rained down with greater ferocity, and the ship suffered another direct hit, forcing her to rock sickeningly. Tristan heard a mast crash down atop the deck above. Then another mast crashed, this one landing atop the bow area. To his horror, he suddenly smelled smoke. He spun around to see a dark plume drifting down through the damage that had opened up in the deck above, and he knew.

The sizzling azure bolts had set the *Tammerland* afire. But with no warriors stationed topside, little could be done about it. Acrid smoke poured into the room, and everyone started coughing. The acolytes were able to use the craft and rid the room of smoke. But the fires above had already become so intense that there was little the women could do about them.

Coughing violently, Tristan helped Shailiha stand, then looked out the starboard window. So many azure bolts were raining down that they seemed to crowd out the sky, and they thundered into the earth in such numbers that the air was literally filled with smoke, flying dirt, and clumps of sod. Tristan strained his eyes to look at the Recluse. Wigg had them dead on course again, and the blazing *Tammerland* was picking up speed.

Then another bolt hit the flagship, nearly throwing Tristan and Shailiha to the floor. The *Tammerland*'s groaning timbers and the fire raging topside made him wonder what was keeping her together. He helped his sister to her feet.

Tristan looked toward the Recluse again. The time had come. He turned toward the waiting acolytes.

"Now!" he shouted. "You must do it now!"

The acolytes immediately called the craft and joined their powers. Raising their arms, they sent azure beams forward to fortify the bow joint where the port and starboard walls met. As the beams saturated the walls and their connecting joint, the black exterior of the ship's bow started to glow with an icy blue.

Tristan snapped his head around to look out the starboard window again. As the ship closed on the Recluse, he nodded to Tyranny. She quickly gazed over Wigg's shoulder to help him stay on course while the wizard strained to give the vessel every last bit of speed.

"Come five degrees to port!" she screamed. His muscles nearly cracking, Wigg steered a course correction.

"Too far!" Tyranny shouted. "Come back two degrees!"

A sense of helplessness gripped Tristan as he realized that he no longer controlled the situation. Now everything depended on Wigg, Tyranny, and the acolytes. Wrapping one arm around Shailiha, he grabbed a wall cleat and braced himself. He looked out the window again. The great ship was still dead on course and gaining speed.

"Steady!" he heard Tyranny shout. Amid all the noise and explosions, her voice might as well have been a distant whisper. "Steady . . ."

Forty meters to the Recluse, Tristan guessed. *Thirty, twenty, ten . . .*

With a massive crash, Wigg set the *Tammerland* down directly atop the stone bridge spanning the muddy lake bed. Sparks flew from her metal-lined keel as she screeched agonizingly against the rough stones and tore across the bridge toward the Recluse.

In a massive explosion of wood and iron, the *Tammerland*'s bow plowed straight into the Recluse drawbridge.

Everyone was thrown to the floor as the fortified bow smashed through the wooden drawbridge, obliterating it. As the ship jammed her bow through the stone drawbridge arch, her abrupt stop brought her stern into the air. Then her keel crashed back down atop the wide bridge in a cacophony of broken wood, split stone, and mortar dust. Tristan held his breath as he wondered whether the bridge would hold the ship's weight. It did. But with no cradle in which to rest, she would soon heel over to port or starboard on her deeply curved hull. If she rolled too far, all could be lost.

Tristan scrambled to his feet and ran to his window. His plan had worked! The *Tammerland*'s bow had obliterated the raised drawbridge, and it protruded deeply though the stone archway that had once surrounded it.

Suddenly the *Tammerland* started to heel far to port. With her bow still held fast by the archway, it was being literally twisted away from the ship's hull. As her massive black timbers groaned and snapped, the room holding Tristan and his group started to drunkenly roll. In mere seconds the *Tammerland* would break away from her bow altogether, heel all the way over, and tumble off the bridge. Tristan frantically turned to look at Wigg and the acolytes.

"Now!" he screamed. "Bring her about!"

Wigg and the women raised their hands again. While azure bolts continued to rain down and fires still raged topside, they struggled with all their might to free the ship. To his delight, Tristan suddenly felt the *Tammerland* right herself and move astern. With a great wrenching sound, she freed her bow from the stone archway. As the ship retreated, the archway lintel and parts of its surrounding walls fell in, accompanied by shards of black, battered wood.

At once Wigg and the acolytes rotated their arms, and the massive ship pivoted in the air to again land atop the bridge. But this time her stern faced the castle. Tristan felt her settle; then he heard the huge stern door drop open and his fighters start charging off the vessel.

Tristan ran to take Adrian by the shoulders. "You know your orders!" he shouted. "You must stay aboard and keep the *Tammerland* balanced on the bridge until everyone is off! Then get out of here! After that, if you have no choice but to let her tumble onto the lake bed, do it!"

"I will!" Adrian shouted. "And good luck!"

Tristan and the others left the room to go charging down the hallway. They finally reached the stern stairway and ran down to the *Tammerland*'s lowest deck.

By the time they reached the stern launching area, pandemonium reigned. Just outside the lowered hatch, azure bolts were exploding everywhere, and warriors and red envelopers were crisscrossing the air between the ship and the castle. Minions by the hundreds were hurtling themselves off the hatchway deck, trying to get airborne. Struck down by azure bolts or quickly seized by envelopers, many died before they could snap open their wings. Angry shrews prowled the muddy lake bottom, greedily feeding on fallen warriors both living and dead. So many screams cut through the air that they combined to form an uninterrupted cry of anguish.

Tristan stared out the hatchway to see the remains of the drawbridge archway. Behind him, hundreds of mounted highlander horsemen waited for the first waves of warriors to clear a path so that they could charge across the bridge and into the Recluse.

But shrews by the hundreds stood in their way atop the bridge, fighting the Minions and making an advance impossible.

When the warriors realized that their *Jin'Sai* had arrived, they quickly cleared a pathway for Tristan and his group. They soon reached the stern hatchway. Just meters away, shrews, envelopers, and Minions were dying in droves as the terrible battle seesawed back and forth atop the bridge and smoke-filled air. As his hand closed tighter around his dreggan, Tristan searched the sky.

Where are you? his heart begged. *We need you now!*

Just then the sky went black as the keels of the other three Black Ships loomed overhead. With the acolytes aboard them empowering the vessels, Faegan, Jessamay, and Aeolus were finally free to do some death-dealing of their own.

At once azure bolts tore from gunwales of the Black Ships to strike the Recluse. Following Tristan's orders, the acolytes were keeping their ships high. This meant that the only targets Serena's consuls had were the ships' keels, while the wizards and the sorceress rained destruction from above.

Azure bolts tore into the guard paths lining the tops of the castle's red-stained walls. Parts of the barbicans exploded, bringing screaming consuls down with them. Many were on fire as they fell to the mud and the floor of the inner ward. Then more bolts rained down, this time tearing into the herds of shrews barring the castle side of the bridge. Shrews and warriors alike exploded and blew skyward. Tristan mourned the warriors, but he knew that their deaths couldn't be helped. Soon a gap in the fighting opened up, allowing a brief window of opportunity to cross the bridge and storm into the Recluse. Refusing to wait any longer, Tristan turned around to look searchingly at the women he cared so much about. Then he turned to Wigg.

"Watch over them," he said.

"On my life," Wigg answered.

After giving Shailiha a final look of farewell, Tristan turned to face the fighting. Closing his eyes, he raised his arms and called on his *K'Shari* Forestallment. At once he felt it surging through his blood, strengthening his heart and calming his mind for battle.

But this time he sensed something more. The hundreds of martial techniques the Forestallment held suddenly burst through his mind and his nervous system, granting him their immediate use. Opening his eyes, he was about to charge across the bridge when he heard a familiar voice.

"Not so fast, *dango*!" Rafe called out. "Let me give you a ride!"

Tristan turned to see Rafe and his highlanders charging down the path opened by the warriors when their *Jin'Sai* had entered the room. As the highlander chieftain neared, Tristan smiled.

Tristan stretched out his left arm. As Rafe charged by, their two hands locked in a firm grip. With his *K'Shari* Forestallment active, the *Jin'Sai*'s movements had become one with him, like there was no longer any need for conscious thought. Tristan effortlessly threw himself up onto the horse's back, just behind Rafe.

Their swords held high in the afternoon sun, Tristan and Rafe charged across the bridge and into the heart of the Recluse.

CHAPTER LXVII

AS THE BATTLE FOR THE RECLUSE RAGED ON, SERENA STOOD ON her knees in her private chambers. She was exhausted, and her fingertips were badly scorched from throwing azure bolts. Her once-immaculate black mourning gown was smeared with the blood of both her allies and her enemies, but her precious withered rose remained tucked in her bosom.

She had personally directed the defense of the castle until the monstrous Black Ship had rammed the drawbridge. Then she had left her post to take refuge in her rooms, and to check on her baby daughter. Einar and Reznik were still somewhere among the fighting. She prayed that they were alive, and helping to turn the tide. After dismissing Dagmar and checking on Clarice, she had immediately assumed a posture of supplication.

It was not fear for her life that had brought her here. Rather, it had been to beg communion with the *Pon Q'tar.* With the castle walls breached, she needed their guidance. But she also knew that if she remained amid the chaos and noise, she might not hear their wondrous voices should they touch her mind. And so she had retreated to the relative quiet of her rooms to pray for a sign. Suddenly it came.

"Serena," the melodious voices called out. *"Take heart. We are here."*

She was overjoyed to hear them. Their powerful presences immediately strengthened her resolve.

"The walls are breached," she answered. *"What am I to do?"*

"Do not fear," the *Pon Q'tar* voices answered. *"Do as we say, and you and your child will be saved."*

"I await your wisdom," she replied.

"If the Recluse becomes untenable, you must save yourself," the voices said. *"The spell that we are about to grant you is powerful, and is meant only for you and your child. Use it to escape the Recluse."*

"But what of Einar and my consuls?" she asked. *"Are they to flee with us?"*

"No," the voices answered. *"From the beginning, they were only a means to an end. That is part of what true devotion to the Vagaries means. Now that Clarice lives, all of your conjured servants, your consuls, and your Valrenkians account for nothing. All that matters is that you and your child escape, and that Clarice grows to womanhood so that the other part of our plan can come to fruition. Despite your fears, it is not too late. Be still, our child, while we impart the needed calculations into your mind."*

Serena waited. Soon a riot of swirling, azure numbers and symbols appeared in her mind's eye. She tried to read the spell, but found it far beyond her comprehension. Then the calculations unexpectedly vanished. She tried to call them back, but couldn't. Worried that she had somehow lost them forever, panic struck her heart again.

"I do not understand," she said. *"How am I to use the spell if I cannot recall it?"*

"All is as it should be," the voices answered. *"The spell is too powerful and important to fall into Conclave hands. Should you be captured, your enemies will not be able to draw it forth, for we have sent it far too deep into your mind for their meager abil-*

ities to retrieve. Even so, we will be able to return it to your ken. You need not understand its workings—you need only to read the calculations aloud in Old Eutracian. But until the battle's outcome is known, wait where you are, where it is safest. It is still possible that your forces will turn the tide. But if not, we will revisit your mind, and your escape with your child will be ensured."

With that, Serena knew that the *Pon Q'tar* had gone. Her hope and courage renewed, she walked to the balcony and calmly looked down on the fighting.

As the *Pon Q'tar* had told her, it seemed that the battle still might be won by her forces. The shrews and envelopers fought savagely and in huge numbers. Looking farther, she could no longer see the Black Ships. *Perhaps they have been destroyed after all,* she hoped. Many of her consuls still lined the wall tops. Black smoke rose into the air as the sounds of the screaming and the dying drifted to her ears.

She watched the terrible battle with renewed faith, for she now understood that its outcome was of no real importance. Once she and Clarice escaped, the wondrous *Pon Q'tar* would protect them for all eternity.

CHAPTER LXVIII

THE MOMENT TRISTAN AND RAFE CROSSED THE BRIDGE AND ENtered the Recluse's inner ward, Tristan jumped down from Rafe's horse. The *Jin'Sai* had a mission to fulfill, and it didn't include the highlander chieftain. Landing warily on the bloody floor, he spun around and took stock of the situation.

Tristan's assault on the Recluse had deteriorated into complete pandemonium. This wasn't a battle of disciplined warrior phalanxes, or of Minion officers shouting out crisp orders. It was a massive street brawl, and each fighter struggled only for himself. Dark smoke and the stench of spilled blood filled the air with their all-too-familiar scent. Dead shrews, Minions, and envelopers lay everywhere. The desperate fighting had completely overtaken the Recluse and darkened the sky; and Minion and highlander bones, clothing, and weapons lay in grotesque, wet piles scattered across the ward.

Tristan stole a precious moment to look toward the wall tops. Although most of the guard paths had been damaged, some were still intact and manned by consuls. The consuls were using their strategic advantage to cast azure bolts down on the Minions and highlanders both inside the castle walls and those still pouring across the bridge.

Tristan's priority was to find Serena. His heart told him that she would be somewhere atop the walls, commanding her remaining consuls. But because of the smoke and confusion, he would need to get up there to know for sure.

He quickly looked around to find stone steps attached to an inner wall. They led up to the guard paths, but they lay on the other side of the ward. Tightening his grip on his dreggan, he decided to try to reach it.

Just as he started running across the ward, a pair of enraged shrews charged out from around one corner of the Recluse granary. Their bloody teeth flashing, the beasts snarled and thundered straight toward him. Tristan's response was immediate and unthinking.

The *Jin'Sai* dropped his dreggan, then reached his right arm over his shoulder to grasp two throwing knives. Without hesitation he placed one knife into his left hand while keeping the other knife in his right. Raising his arms, he simultaneously threw the two blades at the charging shrews.

The knives flew so quickly that they seemed little more than spinning, silvery flickers. A blade buried itself into one shrew's right eye; the second one tore into the other shrew's left eye. To Tristan's amazement, the knives kept going and burst out the back of the shrews' heads, killing the beasts instantly. Then the bloody knives traveled across the ward and plunged into the facing wall of the granary. They hit the stone wall with such force that they cracked it in two from top to bottom. Tristan suddenly remembered the momentous night in the Great Hall when the Darkling had killed the flier of the fields. Xanthus' axe had gone on to strike one of the hall's marble columns and had nearly cracked the structure in half.

The *Jin'Sai* instinctively pointed his arms toward the throwing knives. They quickly levered loose from the wall and flew back across the inner ward. Like he had been practicing the technique all his life, he calmly used both hands to catch the knives by their handles and returned them to his shoulder quiver. Then he looked down at the dreggan lying at his feet. Without thinking, he lowered his right hand and opened his palm. The shiny sword immediately jumped into his hand, hilt-first.

Despite the danger all around him, for several moments Tristan simply stood there, marveling at the things he had just done, and how easily they had come to him. He hadn't been trained to throw dirks with his left hand, and his technique had never mustered such unbelievable force. Nor had he any idea that he could will his weapons to return to him. But he knew that this was no time to analyze his new gifts. Determined to never be surprised by his *K'Shari* gift again, he charged across the ward and started racing up the sidewall steps.

He reached the southern guard path and climbed up without incident, but the situation atop the castle walls was as deadly as that in the inner ward. As he searched for Serena he saw more shrews prowling the paths, viciously protecting their endowed masters. Hundreds of red-stained envelopers filled the sky, swooping low and wrapping their velvety sides around struggling Minion warriors and highlander horsemen. To his dismay, Serena was nowhere to be seen.

Tristan quickly looked down the wall's outer side. To his relief, Faegan, Jessamay, and Aeolus had succeeded in following his orders. Knowing that they would have no time to dig earthen cradles into which to set the Black Ships, he had ordered them to set the vessels down atop the soft, muddy lake bed. As expected, each ship tilted hard toward starboard or port. But they were largely intact, and Minion troops still poured from their hatches to join the fight.

Tristan suddenly froze as something told him that an enveloper was swooping toward him from behind. Its velvety sides extended, it was about to blanket him in its deadly embrace. He didn't have to turn around to confirm the coming danger, for he *sensed* it with certainty.

Standing his ground, he took his sword into both hands and

waited, purposely drawing the creature in. Suddenly he felt a strange tingling sensation in his arms, but there was no time to question it. Swiveling around, he raised his dreggan high and brought it down with everything he had. As he did, a strange, icy-blue glow flashed across his vision.

The dreggan severed the stunned enveloper from top to bottom like it had been made of parchment. But the sword had done more than cut. It had also *burned* its way through the monster's flesh with a searing heat so intense that it had nearly cauterized the thing's wound at the same time. Tristan watched azure smoke drift from the nearly surgical slash, and he smelled burning flesh. Split and smoking from cranium to tail, the enveloper tumbled to the lake bed. Then Tristan started blankly at his bloody dreggan and blanched with wonderment.

The blade of his sword glowed with the azure hue of the craft. As the tingling sensation in his arms and hands faded away, so did the glow of the blade. Knowing better than to question what had happened, he swiveled around again, looking for his next challenge.

Suddenly an azure bolt came tearing his way. Launched from a wounded consul standing on the same guard path, it flew over the inner ward and straight toward him. Tristan whirled at the last moment, narrowly avoiding the bolt's searing heat.

With a deafening explosion, it slammed into one of the nearby barbicans, blasting it to bits. The concussion threw Tristan to the guard path as mortar dust and broken stone rained down on him. Then he heard a scream, and he groggily turned to look.

Through the clouds of settling dust he saw the enraged consul extend his arms and start running at him. Snarling and baring its teeth, an angry shrew charged along beside its master. Dazed from the blast, Tristan struggled to his feet. As he did the consul loosed another bolt.

Tristan instinctively raised his dreggan and held it before him. The bolt struck the dreggan and was immediately entrapped by its blade. Trusting his *K'Shari,* Tristan whirled the blade twice in a great circle, then stopped it dead and pointed it at the shrew. The bolt shot from the blade and screamed along the guard path, hitting the shrew squarely in the chest. Bursting into a thousand pieces, the shrew simply disappeared. Even so, the consul hadn't stop charging. Raising his arms again, he prepared to throw another bolt. Tristan raised his sword and braced himself.

But this time the consul lacked the needed power. Exhausted from the fighting, when he tried to summon another bolt, only a soft, azure light arced from his hands. Before it could reach Tristan it fell short onto the guard path, then sizzled away into nothingness. Undeterred, the enraged consul kept coming. As he neared he pulled a dagger from the folds of his robe and raised it high.

Quick as lightning, Tristan sheathed his dreggan, then spun around toward his attacker's unarmed side and grabbed the consul's wrist. He spun again and launched the consul off his feet and into the air. The consul hit hard atop the stone pathway. Tristan kicked the dagger from the consul's hand and put his boot to his attacker's throat. The consul tried to use his gifts to escape, but his endowed power was clearly spent.

Tristan drew his dreggan. Because he needed information from this man, he had resisted the urge to kill him. He glared down at the consul's sharp, hawklike features.

"What is your name?" he demanded.

The consul's only response was to turn his head as best he could and spit on Tristan's boot.

As Tristan's determination rose, the tingling sensation returned to his sword arm, and the dreggan blade glowed again. He slowly moved the blade's lustrous point toward the consul's face, and the mystic's eyes widened with amazement.

"Your name!" Tristan demanded.

Still the consul did not answer.

Determined to get his information, Tristan swiveled his boot and forced the consul's cheek flush against the pathway. Then he touched the dreggan's glowing blade to the man's exposed temple. The consul immediately started to scream. As azure smoke and the smell of burning flesh drifted upward, the *Jin'Sai* drew the blade down the consul's cheek, forever branding his face.

"Einar!" the man screamed. "My name is Einar!"

Tristan lifted the blade. "Where is your queen?" he shouted.

Despite his searing pain, the consul did not answer. Einar probably feared Serena's wrath far more than that of the *Jin'Sai,* Tristan realized. He decided to change the consul's opinion.

Tristan moved the glowing sword point away from Einar's face. At first the consul showed a great sense of relief. But as Tristan moved the blade toward Einar's throat, the consul's eyes widened with horror.

Starting at the neckline, Tristan touched the dreggan blade to the consul's blue robe, and the cloth immediately started to burn. As the blade traveled toward Einar's feet, the two halves of his robe fell away, leaving him naked. Tristan calmly placed the glowing blade tip directly above Einar's exposed genitals. The consul nearly fainted with fear as he felt the heat engulf his groin.

"Where is your queen?" Tristan snarled.

"She's in Failee's previous quarters!" Einar screamed. "She went there to try and commune with the *Pon Q'tar*! That's all I know!"

"Take me there," Tristan growled. He started to raise his boot from Einar's throat.

"That won't be needed," Tristan suddenly heard Shailiha say. "I learned the way while I was imprisoned here."

Tristan spun around to see Wigg and Shailiha standing behind him on the guard path. They looked exhausted.

Wigg's robe was singed and torn, and his fingertips were scorched black. Shailiha's doublet and breeches were smeared with blood; a jagged wound lay in her right hand. Her thigh dagger was gone, and her sword blade was heavily bloodied. Her face was filthy with sweat and smoke residue. The blond hair Tristan loved so much, tied behind her back and secured with a gold barrette, was so dirty that she could have been a brunette. She had done her share of killing, he realized. Relieved to see that they were alive, Tristan let go a deep breath.

"And the others?" he asked anxiously.

"They were all alive, last we saw them," Shailiha answered. "But that was some time ago."

Wigg looked down at Tristan's glowing dreggan. As his blood calmed and the tingling sensation left his arm, it no longer surprised Tristan to see his dreggan stop glowing. Wigg looked back into Tristan's face.

"Interesting," he said simply.

Tristan took a moment to look around. It seemed that the fighting on the wall tops had all but ended. As he turned back toward Einar he placed the point of his blade against the consul's bare chest, then removed his boot from his throat. Wigg stepped beside Tristan to look down at the traitor.

"Hello, Einar," he said calmly. "It's been a long time."

"Not long enough, you bastard," Einar answered. Despite his perilous situation, he gave Wigg a nasty smile.

"You might find Serena," he said. "But you'll never capture her. Her powers have become as strong as yours, *First Wizard*—or whatever grandiose title you're giving yourself these days. Serena's daughter has been reborn, and Serena will do anything to protect her."

As the battle quieted, Tristan pulled Einar to his feet. But as he came up, the consul produced another dagger from inside the folds of his severed robe and thrust its blade straight toward Tristan's neck. Shailiha gasped; even Wigg realized that there was no time to summon the craft.

As the silvery blade neared Tristan's jugular, the prince slid leftward. Grasping Einar's dagger hand, Tristan twisted it, then drew it in a large circle. Before he knew what was happening, he had thrown Einar headlong from the guard path.

Screaming wildly, the consul hit his head on the stone steps, breaking his neck. He landed on the inner ward's tile floor with his head lying at an unnatural angle against one shoulder. Einar's death had taken less than three seconds.

Shailiha looked at Tristan's sword, then she searched her brother's face like she was seeing both for the first time. "How . . . ?" she asked.

"This isn't the time to discuss it," Tristan answered. "We need to go." With Shailiha in the lead, they ran across the guard path, down the stone steps, and started across the inner ward.

Although the battle had quieted on the wall tops, the savage fighting in the Recluse proper forced Tristan to realize that his assault could still fail. Minions, envelopers, highlanders, and shrews still waged desperate war against each other, and as yet neither side sensed victory.

As they neared the palace steps, more than once Wigg was forced to kill ravaging shrews, and Tristan's glowing blade cut two swooping envelopers from the air. On the way they came across Ox, Traax, and a group of warriors. The *Jin'Sai* quickly ordered them to follow along. Soon their party reached the marble steps, and they charged up into the Recluse.

The search for Serena had begun.

Chapter LXIX

Under Tristan's orders, Faegan, Aeolus, and Jessamay were also searching for Serena as they cautiously prowled the Recluse's second floor. Like everywhere else, the fighting there was a terrible mixture of smoke, magic, and sudden death.

Shrews and envelopers still controlled the Recluse, but the tide was slowly turning. Faegan had ordered a dozen Minion warriors to follow his group up the stairs. Not to be outdone, Rafe and twenty of his highlander riders had spurred their horses up the foyer staircase to follow along.

Blood smeared the second-floor walls, and the hallway floors were littered with bodies from both sides. Smashed furniture, torn paintings, and ripped draperies lay everywhere. Stained-glass windows were scattered in pieces around their broken window frames. Levitating his chair as he went, Faegan led the charge. The hallways were so wide that Aeolus, Jessamay, and several warriors could run alongside him.

Faegan soon saw an intersection up ahead. The area was huge. Five massively wide hallways joined ends there, creating a pentagonal sitting area. The center of the intersection was open and overlooked the marble floor below. A huge ceiling mirror hung directly above the intersection opening, reflecting a fountain sitting on the first floor. The fountain water shot high into the air, climbing up through the intersection opening before falling back. An intricately carved wooden railing protectively lined the intersection's five angled sides. It was a beautiful part of the Recluse that incongruously belied the brutal ugliness taking place elsewhere.

As Faegan and his party neared the intersection they suddenly heard screeching sounds. Searching for prey, dozens of envelopers soared upward from the first floor to careen through the intersection's open center. At once the sitting room became a riotous madhouse.

The Conclave mystics immediately raised their hands. Azure bolts struck many envelopers, killing them instantly. But soon the flow of envelopers became a constant stream, forcing Faegan to admit that his group could not overcome them. Just then the warriors started charging ahead to engage the envelopers.

"No!" Faegan shouted at the warriors. "There are too many of them for you to kill! You must come back!" As the warriors returned, Faegan looked anxiously at Aeolus and Jessamay.

"Unless I miss my guess, the beasts will gather for a coordinated assault!" he warned them. "Then we will act!"

As they waited and watched, it became clear that Faegan was right. Soon the intersection was full of envelopers, ominously circling the massive room. So many were gathering that Jessamay could imagine no way to survive their impending onslaught. While more soared up from the first floor to join the whirling maelstrom, she frantically looked at Faegan.

"Whatever you have in mind, you must do it soon!" she shouted.

Faegan shouted out a quick series of orders to Jessamay and Aeolus. *It worked once, so it should work again,* he reasoned. *But we must perform our parts to perfection, or we're all dead.*

Envelopers finally stopped rushing up from the first floor. Knowing that they hadn't a second to lose, Faegan gave the order, and the three mystics raised their arms.

Faegan acted first by sending an azure bolt toward the ceiling mirror. On hitting the mirror, the reflected beam streamed straight down into the water swirling in the massive fountain. Calling on the same spell that Wigg had used for the Recluse lake water, Faegan commanded the fountain water to keep its shape and lift into the air. The ring of water quickly levitated to the second floor, engulfing the surprised envelopers.

Twin beams shot from Aeolus' and Jessamay's hands. The beams hit the ring of water, and it started twinkling with an icy blue. Then it instantly froze solid, trapping all the envelopers in midflight.

As Aeolus and Jessamay lowered their hands, Rafe trotted his horse through the warrior ranks to stop beside the mystics. He had seen many amazing things this day, but this feat stunned him most of all.

"I beg the Afterlife . . . ," he breathed.

The huge, frozen ring imprisoning the envelopers revolved

gently in the air. Rafe correctly guessed that it revolved because of the momentum it had gathered when the circling beasts first entered it. He turned his incredulous gaze toward Faegan.

"Are they dead?" he asked.

Faegan rubbed his chin. "I don't know," he answered. "If not, they soon will be. We will sustain the spell and let them freeze to death."

"Reznik!" a male voice called out from the floor below. They heard boot heels running across marble.

"Einar is dead!" the unfamiliar voice shouted. "If you want to live, you must come with us!" As he heard the words, Faegan stiffened.

Reznik.

Without hesitation, Faegan flew his chair into the sitting room. Narrowly missing the hovering ring of ice, he launched over the railing and soared down toward the first floor.

Aeolus and Jessamay realized that they had no choice but to go, too. As they levitated over the railing they heard two thunderous explosions boom out. The Minions dutifully followed the mystics. Unable to go with them, Rafe and his riders charged their horses back down the hallway in search of more prey.

When Aeolus and Jessamay landed on the first floor they saw two dead consuls with their heads blown apart. One lay on the floor. The other hung on a wall, his chest impaled by an iron sconce bracket. Bits of the smashed globe the bracket had once held lay on the floor, beneath the dead consul's dangling feet.

Faegan sat nearby. His arms were raised, and dark smoke drifted from his scorched fingertips. He faced a trembling man trapped in a nearby corner. The fellow was a fat, greasy-looking creature, and he wore a bloody butcher's apron.

Aeolus and Jessamay immediately suspected that the man was Reznik. As they stared at him the Minions descended. Looking around warily, the warriors confirmed that this part of the Recluse was peaceful. Even so, the sounds of fighting going on elsewhere eerily drifted toward them.

Faegan glared at the man in the corner. "You're Reznik," he growled. "You do not wear a blue consul's robe, and I heard your name called out from the room above."

Reznik cowered before the wizard. "I am he," he said. "Please don't kill me!"

"Is Serena's child reborn?" Faegan demanded. Knowing that there was nowhere for the Valrenkian to go, Faegan lowered his arms.

"Yes . . . ," Reznik answered.

"Where are they?" Faegan asked.

"I don't know," Reznik answered.

"Don't lie to me, you piece of filth!" Faegan shouted.

For a moment Reznik beseechingly cast his eyes around the room like he was searching for someone to take pity on him. No one took the bait. He looked back at Faegan.

"If I answer, will you spare my life?" Reznik countered.

"I'll consider it," Faegan answered.

As Reznik tried to decide, he started shaking, and a stream of urine ran down one of his legs to form a puddle on the marble floor. He nervously wiped his damp palms down the front of his bloody smock.

"Serena and Clarice are on the second floor, in Failee's previous quarters," he finally answered.

"I have ways of finding out if you're telling the truth," Faegan warned him. "If I think you're lying to me, my methods of making sure can be most unpleasant."

"It's the truth, I swear it!" Reznik pleaded. Suddenly a more confident look overcame the Valrenkian's face.

"I just remembered something else," he said. "You're a member of the late Directorate of Wizards! You took vows against murder!" Suddenly surer of himself, Reznik laughed at Faegan's expense. "Because I am not attacking you, you must take me alive!" he added brazenly. When he heard no response he decided to press his advantage.

"Since that is the case, let me tell you something else, *wizard,*" he added nastily. "I enjoyed making those potions for Satine, and I reveled in the fact that she killed your precious Geldon and Lionel! I have tortured and killed hundreds during my career, and I loved every minute of it! My only regret is that you didn't die with so many of your Minions in those traps I left behind in Valrenkium! I spit on their graves, you useless cripple!"

Sure that he had found the secret to his survival, Reznik held out his hands. "Go ahead, *wizard,*" he said snidely. "Take me into custody."

Faegan had become so incensed that he trembled with rage. He raised his hands and pointed his scorched fingers at the Valrenkian. Aeolus started to make a move toward stopping him, but Jessamay quickly touched him on one arm. His face grim, Aeolus took Jessamay's advice and decided not to interfere.

If there had been any mercy in Faegan's heart for the Valrenkian, Reznik's boasting had just destroyed it. Taking a deep breath, Faegan decided.

"You're wrong on two counts," he said quietly. "First, I was never a member of the Directorate of Wizards. And second, I never took their vows." He raised his hands a bit more.

Reznik's look of terror quickly returned. "You said that if I told you where Serena and Clarice are, you would let me live!" he pleaded.

"No I didn't," Faegan answered quietly.

Before Reznik could protest, Faegan launched twin beams at him. The beams quickly blanketed Reznik's body and lifted him into the air.

Faegan moved his arms. The twin beams threw Reznik violently across the room and headlong into a wall, breaking the Corporeal's right arm and leg in grisly compound fractures. Then the bolts threw him across the room again like he was nothing more than some broken doll. Screaming wildly, Reznik smashed into the marble fountain. His skull split open, killing him instantly. As Aeolus, Jessamay, and the warriors looked on, the room fell silent.

After folding his scorched hands in his lap, Faegan lowered his head.

Chapter LXX

As Wigg escorted Shailiha down the second-floor hallway, worry crowded into his mind. Tristan, Ox, Traax, and several warriors followed them.

Wigg knew that finding Serena's private rooms wasn't the

problem. What truly concerned him were the unknown dangers awaiting them there. Serena was a powerful sorceress. She would savagely defend herself. Most of all, she would protect her daughter to the bitter end.

But Wigg had an even greater worry. Serena and Clarice might have already escaped. The lower regions of the Recluse were riddled with unexplored areas. There could be secret passages leading from there to the relative safety of the countryside. If Serena and Clarice were already gone, they might never be found.

Shailiha slowed as she neared the next hallway corner. Stopping, she held up one arm, then turned to look at the others. There was no fighting here, and things were quiet. *Too* quiet, she realized.

Wigg quickly looked around the corner, then pulled back. Double doors laden with gilt filigree stood at the far end of the crimson-carpeted hallway. After ordering everyone to be still, Wigg closed his eyes and concentrated. Soon he opened his eyes.

"Besides us, I sense only two owners of endowed blood," he whispered. "They are each immensely powerful, and one dwarfs the other. Logic says that Serena and Clarice are behind those doors. It must be they, for it's highly doubtful that any consul would have blood that strong." Wigg looked meaningfully at Tristan and Shailiha.

"I suspect that the more powerful blood belongs to Clarice, your half niece," he added.

Tristan's response was immediate. "We must try to take them alive," he said, "especially Clarice. Too many in our family have already died. She shares the blood of the House of Galland, and she is an innocent in all of this. I will not abandon that part of her blood which is my own."

"I understand your feelings," Wigg answered. "But you must also remember what the Envoys of Crysenium told you. The child possesses a left-leaning blood signature. Although she is untrained, she poses a great threat to the future. If killing her becomes the only option, we must take it."

"What do you propose?" Shailiha asked.

"Serena will be expecting us to break down the double doors," Wigg answered. "Instead, I'm going to surprise her. Most of the rooms on this floor have balconies. I'll order Ox to come with me, and we'll search until we find one. He will then fly me toward Serena's chambers. Her rooms likely have a balcony, too. If so, I'll burst them open with the craft. That will distract Serena from the doorway. When you hear the noise, come running and knock down the doors. We will try to take her and the child alive."

Tristan thought for a moment; then he looked at Shailiha. The princess nodded her agreement. Tristan looked back at Wigg.

"All right," he said. "But hurry!"

Using the craft, Wigg quietly unlocked a nearby door. He and Ox went in. After a time they came back out to enter another room. This time they did not reappear.

"What are your orders?" Traax asked his *Jin'Sai*.

After taking a quick look at Serena's double doors, Tristan shook his head. "I have little to add," he answered. "For now we will wait and listen for Wigg's signal. Then we will charge for the doors and hope for the best. Remember, I want them alive."

As they waited, a deathly stillness overcame the hallway.

"IT IS TIME," SERENA HEARD THE *PON Q'TAR* CLERICS CALL OUT TO her mind. *"The Recluse is lost. Go to the crib and collect the child."*

Serena dutifully walked across the room and picked up her daughter. As the queen held her baby close, Clarice cooed sweetly. Serena lifted her head.

"We are ready," she replied silently.

"Good," the voices answered. *"We will now retrieve the needed spell from your consciousness."*

Serena closed her eyes. At once the amazingly complex formula appeared in her mind's eye.

"Start reading the formula aloud in Old Eutracian," the clerics demanded. *"Soon you and the child will be free."*

Serena dutifully started reciting the formula.

WITH HIS ARMS TIGHTLY WRAPPED AROUND THE WARRIOR'S STOUT neck, Wigg held on as Ox launched from the balcony and took to the air. Ox followed Wigg's instructions and flew toward Serena's chambers.

As they approached, they saw that her balcony doors were closed. Wigg ordered Ox to back off a bit and hover in the air. Using his right hand, the First Wizard pointed to doors of wrought-iron and glass. At once an azure bolt flew from his scorched fingertips. The bolt exploded the doors into a cacophony of flying glass shards and twisted iron.

Carrying the wizard in his strong arms, Ox immediately headed for the balcony.

THE MOMENT TRISTAN HEARD THE EXPLOSION, HE LED THE CHARGE down the hallway. With the coming danger he could feel his *K'Shari* rising again. Three meters from the doors he instinctively launched into the air. Flying feet first, he crashed the doors down, then landed in the room on all fours, like a cat. Raising his dreggan, he frantically looked around.

Wigg and Ox were rushing in from the balcony. On the other side of the room, Serena calmly held Clarice in her arms. The queen's eyes were closed. Seemingly oblivious to the invasion, she was reciting some kind of incantation in Old Eutracian. Fearing the worst, Tristan frantically looked at Wigg.

"Stop her!" Tristan screamed.

As Serena finished reciting her spell, she turned and gave Tristan a smile that sent a chill down his spine. To his horror, he saw that her image was fading. Somehow she and Clarice were going to escape his grasp after all! As he stood there powerless to stop her, she and her child became increasingly translucent.

The narrow azure bolt that Wigg sent flying was designed to strike the queen's head and spare the child she held. But as it neared Serena, instead of destroying her it passed straight through her—just like Faegan's bolt had done to Xanthus, the night of the masquerade ball. Wigg's bolt flew on to explode deafeningly against the room's far wall.

As Serena's and Clarice's forms became increasingly transparent, Tristan stood in awe of the craft. He knew that the members of the *Pon Q'tar* were somehow spiriting them away, and that there was nothing he could do to stop it.

Without warning, Serena and Clarice burst into flames.

Screaming madly, Serena clutched her child closer to her breast. Astonished beyond words, Tristan and the others could only stand by and watch as the queen staggered toward the balcony. As she struggled they could also hear Clarice's sickening cries as she burned to death in her mother's arms.

Serena turned and looked straight into the *Jin'Sai*'s eyes. An intense hatred rose from their fiery depth to strike at his very core. Then Serena and Clarice collapsed onto the balcony floor to form a pile of black ash. Dark, wispy smoke rose from the remains.

Shailiha came to take Tristan by the hand. Neither of them completely understood what had just happened, but the results were clear. The threat was gone, but they had failed to save Clarice.

Shailiha, Tristan, and Wigg walked onto the balcony to stand beside the dark mound. The wind came up and started to scatter the ashes into oblivion.

"What just happened?" Tristan breathed. "Did she kill herself and take her child with her?"

Wigg shook his head. "I don't know," he answered. "In truth we might never comprehend it fully. What little I could hear of her spell was so convoluted that even I didn't understand it."

Tristan looked over the balcony and down toward the fighting. His troops had finally taken the upper hand. He called Traax to his side.

"Get down there and finish it," he said. "Try to take the remaining consuls alive. But if they continue to resist, kill them. I want every one of Serena's surviving shrews and flying creatures put to the sword. And get me a casualty report as soon as you can, including any deaths or injuries suffered by Conclave members."

Traax clicked their heels. "It shall be done," he said. He and the other warriors left the room.

Tristan sadly looked to the sky. "It will come any time now," he said quietly. He put one arm around his sister and held her close. As he did she laid her tired head on his shoulder.

"Yes," Wigg answered, "just as it always does."

The sky started to darken. Soon the heavens became black as night, and the wind howled incessantly. Then the lightning started, its bright tentacles streaking down in unbelievable patterns. Thunder tore from the sky to shake the very foundations of the Recluse. With Serena's death had come the death of her blood. And with the death of her blood, her Forestallments were leaving.

In his mind's eye Tristan could see the young Scroll Master standing in the miraculous Well of Forestallments, watching as Serena's gifts went to join those of so many endowed others who had perished in the name of the craft. He could imagine her azure death mask forming as the Forestallment calculations that had once graced her blood signature took their place below it, in one of the thousands of gleaming, azure cases. *Might they come to rest beside Celeste's?* he wondered.

Soon the heavens quieted and the trembling earth stilled. Tristan looked down to see that the pile of ash had been taken by the wind, never to return.

There are still so many unanswered questions, he thought. But one thing remained certain. He had to return to Crysenium—perhaps for all time.

Unsure of his future, he held Shailiha closer.

CHAPTER LXXI

"IT IS BY THIS RITUAL THAT THESE TWO SHALL BE JOINED, AND MAY their union never be rent asunder," Tristan announced as he read from the wrinkled parchment. "As a gesture of the love and respect that exists between you, I now ask that the traditional tokens be exchanged."

Tristan looked up from his parchment to gaze around the Great Hall. The room looked as resplendent as it had the night Xanthus had come to take him away. He gladly stood on the dais with several dozen other people. It was a happy day.

Traax and Duvessa had asked that their *Jin'Sai* perform the ceremony, and Tristan had heartily agreed. All of the Conclave members were present, as were the palace gnomes. The room was packed with Minion well-wishers. Rafe, Balthazar, Scars, Martha, and the elders of Clan Kilbourne were also in attendance. The fliers of the fields fluttered colorfully overhead, and a string quartet sat nearby, ready to play.

The Great Hall was lavishly decorated with flowers and potpourri, their combined scents wafting delicately into the air.

Each of the stained-glass windows was open, and a late-afternoon breeze drifted into the room. Tables laden with food, wine, akulee, and *tachinga* sat along one wall. Every dish had been lovingly fussed over by the ever-industrious Shawna the Short like her life had depended on it.

A path of yellow rose petals lay on the floor, leading away from the dais and across the hall. A Minion honor guard in dress uniform lined each side of the path. After a nod from Tristan one of the officers shouted out a crisp order. At once they all reached to their hips and drew their dreggans. Lifting their shiny blades high, they smartly crossed them over the pathway.

Traax and Duvessa stood arm in arm at the opposite end of the pathway. Shailiha and Morganna stood directly before them. Shailiha held her daughter's hand to keep her from falling. In her other hand the princess held the two warriors' betrothal pins. At a gesture from Tristan, the quartet started to play. He then nodded at Shailiha.

The princess looked down at her daughter. "Time to go," she whispered.

Morganna looked delightful in her red velvet dress, white leggings, and shiny black shoes. A wreath made from violet everscent blossoms encircled the crown of her head. As Morganna and Shailiha approached, Tristan realized how much the child was starting to look like her grandmother. Walking up the dais steps, Shailiha and Morganna came to stand beside Tristan. The prince looked at the betrothal couple and smiled.

As Traax and Duvessa approached, one by one the Minion warriors lining the petal-strewn path clicked their heels. It was an impressive display, meant to honor the union that was about to take place. When Traax and Duvessa reached Tristan, they knelt before their *Jin'Sai*. Tristan again looked to the parchment that outlined the traditional Minion service.

"You may exchange tokens," he said to them.

Shailiha placed the two pins into Morganna's hand. They were the same two that Duvessa and Traax had exchanged earlier, when he had first asked that they be joined. Like the warriors who were about to be married, the pins had been through much, but they had survived.

"Come along now," Shailiha whispered to Morganna.

As the princess ushered her daughter toward the happy couple, Morganna seemed a little afraid. She stared wide-eyed at Traax and Duvessa as she tentatively offered up the pins. The warriors gently took them from the little girl's grasp.

Duvessa gave Morganna a wink. "Well done," she whispered.

For the first time since entering the Great Hall, Morganna giggled. As Shailiha escorted her daughter back to their places, Duvessa and Traax looked up at their *Jin'Sai.*

Tristan looked into their eyes. "You may begin," he said.

Traax snapped open his wings and gently surrounded Duvessa with them. They again exchanged betrothal pins like they had done the first time. No longer needing the parchment, Tristan rolled it up and handed it to Wigg.

"You are now mates for life," Tristan said. "May the Afterlife watch over you, and grant you a happy and fruitful union."

With that, all sense of decorum vanished. Everyone deluged the happy couple, and the sounds of laughter and applause filled the air. Bottles were uncorked, and glasses were filled and raised in what would soon become toast upon toast. Tristan joyfully embraced Traax and Duvessa.

As it happened, Rafe and Ox had been standing beside each other during the ceremony. It was rare to see emotion overtake a Minion warrior, but Rafe noticed that Ox's eyes had become shiny. Realizing that this was too delicious an opportunity to pass up, Rafe reached into one pocket to produce a frantically patterned highlander handkerchief. He elbowed Ox in the ribs and handed it to him. As Ox scowled and took it, Rafe could hardly keep from laughing.

"What this be for?" Ox demanded.

"It's meant to dry your eyes with, you dunce!" Rafe said. "It's the least I could do in your time of need! But I thought big Minion warriors like you weren't supposed to cry!"

As he growled some ancient Minion epithet and blinked maddeningly, Ox scowled again and shoved the ridiculous handkerchief back into Rafe's hands.

Two weeks had passed since the taking of the Recluse. Three of the four Black Ships had been too badly damaged to sail. But given enough time and care, they would be repaired and brought home. The *Ephyra* was still seaworthy. She and Faegan's portal had returned everyone to Eutracia except for several Minion phalanxes ordered to stay behind and complete the repairs to the Recluse and the fleet.

The fight for the castle had been successful, but costly. Luckily, every Conclave member had survived. Some had suffered wounds, none of which had been life-threatening. Many of Tristan's warriors had died, and nearly half of Rafe's horsemen. But even the highlanders agreed that the struggle had been worth it.

On Tristan's return, the Clan Kilbourne elders had demanded three thousand uninhabited acres of prime timber and grazing land northwest of Hartwick Wood. Wigg and Faegan had cringed when they heard about it. But a deal was a deal, and Tristan had gladly agreed. The needed papers had been drawn up and signed by Tristan and the camp elders.

Spells of forgetfulness had been placed into the minds of the surviving Valrenkian adults, and Tristan had ordered that they be taken to the Tammerland debtors' prison, to serve life sentences with Lothar and his guards. After much discussion, it was decided that the best place for the Valrenkian children was the Tammerland orphanage, where they could become wards of the state while they awaited adoption. Word had it that many had already found good homes.

The Conclave mystics were still at a loss to understand what had happened to Serena and Clarice. All they knew for certain was that the Vagaries queen and her infant daughter were dead. The Scroll of the Vagaries had been recovered and was now safely ensconced in the Redoubt. Despite a thorough search, no trace of the formula used to bring Clarice back to life had been found, but scores of priceless Vagaries texts and scrolls had been recovered.

Tristan looked around the room. He found the celebration bittersweet, as he knew everyone secretly did. Tonight he would leave by Minion litter for the azure pass. Once there, he would use the Forestallment granted him by the Envoys to take him back to Crysenium.

As requested by the Envoys, his blood signature lean had been painstakingly altered to the vertical by Wigg, Faegan, and Jessamay. The process had been agonizing, but he seemed to suffer no ill aftereffects. He needed to go, for Crysenium was where his destiny lay. But the fact that he might never return still haunted him.

Wigg and Shailiha were especially depressed about his imminent departure. For that reason he had decided to take them as far as the pass. During his final Conclave meeting, he had made it abundantly clear that in his absence Shailiha would rule not just the Conclave, but the Minions and all of Eutracia, as well.

This celebration is as much a farewell for me as it is a wedding ceremony for Duvessa and Traax, he thought. *After tonight, will I see this palace or any of these people ever again?*

Just then Wigg walked up. After taking a sip of wine he looked Tristan in the eyes. The Paragon twinkled brightly as it lay against the wizard's chest. Wigg's expression was sad, searching.

"I know this is somewhat premature," Wigg began. "But I just wanted to say that—"

Tristan quickly held up one hand. "I know," he replied quietly as he looked into the old wizard's aquamarine eyes. "I will never forget you, either."

Wigg was about to speak again when a group of about forty men approached. They were of varying ages, and some had young girls and boys accompanying them. Each one reverently went to his knees and bowed his head before Tristan and Wigg. Tristan looked knowingly at the First Wizard, then back at them.

"Do not kneel before us," Tristan said. "Please rise. All is forgiven."

One of the men walked forward. He looked into Wigg's eyes.

"On behalf of us all, we wish to thank you and the *Jin'Sai* for saving us," he said. "We owe you our lives, and the lives of our children."

"No apology is needed, Nathan," Wigg answered. "It is to the Vigors' benefit that you and your fellow consuls have been returned to the fold."

With tears in her eyes, Mallory approached. She curtsied toward Tristan and then toward Wigg.

"Thank you for bringing my father back to the Vigors," she said. "I thought I had lost him forever."

Things have come full circle, Tristan thought as he looked at the talented Fledgling. *So much has changed, yet so much remains the same.*

With the return of the Conclave to Tammerland, it was decided to try to bring the traitorous consuls back into the fold. Because the lean of their blood signatures had been so drastically altered, the Conclave mystics suspected that moving them rightward would be a long and painful process for the consuls to endure. They had been right.

It had taken two weeks of arduous work, but it had been worth it. Just as Adrian was the First Sister of the Acolyte order, the newly restored Consular order would now need a First Consul. Although he had yet to be told, the Conclave had unanimously voted to grant Nathan the post. Consuls in dark blue robes were finally prowling the Redoubt once more. But now they shared the underground labyrinth with the acolytes.

Feeling the need to be alone, Tristan excused himself. He walked across the floor, then went through one of the doors and onto the stone patio that surrounded the Great Hall. After a time he heard the sounds of boot heels. Without turning around, he knew that Tyranny was approaching.

They stood silently watching the sun set for a time. When she finally turned toward him, there were tears in her eyes. Her left arm was in a sling and she limped a bit, but her wounds would heal. True to form, she commandingly blinked her tears away.

"I'm not very good at good-byes," she said quietly. "So I thought I would do it now."

Tristan gave her a short smile. "I know," he replied. "I'm no better."

Tyranny gave him a soft kiss on one cheek. "Good-bye, *Jin'-Sai,*" she said. "You will be missed."

"And good-bye to you," he answered. "I hope to see you again one day." Then he gave her another little smile. "Take good care of my Black Ships," he added.

Tyranny started to answer, but she was suddenly too overcome. After giving him another kiss, she simply walked away.

While the merriment continued in the Great Hall, Tristan noticed that the sun had nearly disappeared.

Soon, now, he thought.

Chapter LXXII

As Tristan stood looking at the gleaming azure pass, a shudder went through him. He was about to abandon everyone he held dear and ride into an uncertain future. Suddenly the price of fulfilling his destiny seemed high indeed.

Wigg, Shailiha, and the warriors who had been posted here stood with him. The night was clear, and dawn would come soon. The stout litter bearers had flown all night. Another litter had brought Shadow along. Because Tristan and Xanthus had entered the pass on horseback, the prince thought it best to do so again.

His good-byes to everyone back at the palace had been emotional. After the wedding celebration had quieted, a receiving line had been formed in his honor. Tristan had walked down the line, bidding each person farewell and sometimes giving them last-minute orders. When he finally turned to walk away, there hadn't been a dry eye in the room.

Tristan looked up toward the mountain peaks lining either side of the pass. The Envoys had revealed some of the Tolenkas' secrets to him, but he knew that many more remained to be learned. As always, the shining pass rose so high that it disappeared into the fog gathering around the mountaintops.

Knowing that it was time to go, he turned and looked at Wigg and Shailiha. He walked over to Wigg and embraced him.

"Thank you for everything that you have taught me," he said. "When all is said and done, there are no words. . . ."

Wigg brushed away a tear. "I know," he said.

"Watch over my sister as you would me," Tristan said, trying to give the wizard a smile. "That is my last order to you."

"On my life," Wigg promised, his voice cracking a bit. "Stay safe."

Tristan turned to take Shailiha in his arms. Despite her best efforts to be brave, she was shaking, and tears filled her eyes.

Scowling, she composed herself and grabbed either side of his worn leather vest like she was never going to let go.

"Must it be this way?" she asked.

"Yes," he answered. "You know that as well as I. This is what I was born to do."

"But what will I do without you?" she asked. She finally managed to give him a short smile. "After all, I've gotten pretty used to having my brother around."

"You'll do what I would do, if I was still here," he answered. Tristan looked over at Wigg.

"Do you see that old man standing over there?" he asked. "Value his wisdom and guidance, and that of the other Conclave members. That is why I chose them. But also know that sometimes even the mystics can be wrong. When you make decisions, always follow your heart—even if some of your advisors disagree."

"Will I see you again?" Shailiha asked.

Tristan smiled. "You're forgetting something," he answered. He reached down and lifted the gold medallion from her chest. "Any time you want to visit me, call forth the spell," he said.

A look of hope crossed the princess's face. "Our medallions can bridge the western world to ours?" she asked.

"Yes," he answered. "I believe that is why Hoskiko provided us with the spell. She knew how difficult my leaving Eutracia would be."

"I love you," Shailiha said. Her voice was little more than a whisper.

"And I love you," Tristan answered. "But now I must go."

Tristan walked over to where Shadow stood waiting, then threw himself up into the saddle. Like he knew where they were about to go, the spirited black stallion danced about a bit before settling down. Wigg walked over to Shailiha and put one arm around her.

When Tristan looked down at them, his heart was in his throat. "I love you both," he said softly. "Never forget that."

Tristan wheeled Shadow around and headed for the pass. He stopped Shadow and raised his arms, calling on the Forestallment granted to him by the Envoys.

Wigg and Shailiha watched in awe as a white line formed on the face of the pass. Starting at the bottom, it soon climbed the surface of the pass to disappear into the clouds. Then the pass parted into halves, revealing a dark, seemingly limitless emptiness beyond. Without looking back, Tristan spurred Shadow into the abyss.

Then the pass closed, sealing the *Jin'Sai* and its many secrets within.

CHAPTER LXXIII

AS ON HIS OTHER JOURNEYS THROUGH THE PASS, TRISTAN COULD feel Shadow moving beneath him, but he could hear nothing and see only azure. A dense fog surrounded him, its depths so all-encompassing that it appeared limitless.

Just then Shadow stepped from the fog. As the azure mist surrounding him disappeared, Tristan looked around. He was indeed in Crysenium. The room was the same one in which he had awakened during his first visit.

Relieved that he had arrived safely, he dismounted. Shadow danced nervously as the stallion took in his new surroundings. Tristan rubbed Shadow's head and the horse calmed. After tying the reins to a nearby column, the *Jin'Sai* looked around.

The crystalline, spherical chamber looked exactly as before. Dozens of azure columns rose from the shiny floor and reached high into the air. The transparent ceiling showed a beautiful blue sky overhead. Determined to find the Envoys, he started to take the short walk to the meeting room where he had learned so many revelations.

"Welcome back, *Jin'Sai,*" a voice said. "I am glad that you have returned."

Tristan spun around to see Xanthus in his human form. Xanthus still wore the familiar black leather duster with the dark robe beneath it. As he walked toward the prince he held his axe and shield in his hands.

"Xanthus," Tristan breathed. "You're alive. . . ."

"So it would seem," the Darkling answered. When Xanthus spoke, he spun his axe with one hand, its blade turning so quickly that it hummed through the air.

Tristan suddenly felt his *K'Shari* rising without having been beckoned. He tried to stay calm by reminding himself that Xanthus was a friend. But he soon realized that it was no use. Deciding to trust his blood, Tristan eyed Xanthus warily.

"Where are the Envoys?" he asked.

"They await you in the meeting room," Xanthus answered cryptically.

Tristan instinctively stepped backward to gain some breathing room. It did not go unnoticed by Xanthus. Spinning his axe again, he smiled.

"You see," he said, "I am no longer the Envoys' servant. After Faxon and I returned to Rustannica, the *Pon Q'tar* discovered the deception. By the way, Faxon is dead. He died screaming like the traitorous pig that he was."

A chill went down Tristan's spine as he realized that his *K'Shari* had been right to warn him. "You are again a servant of the *Pon Q'tar,* aren't you?" Tristan asked. "But when we said our farewells, you were firmly committed to the Envoys. The Envoys were about to change your memories with such finality that their deception would prove impossible to unravel, even by the *Pon Q'tar.*"

"All that is true," Xanthus answered. "The Envoys did alter my memories. But they underestimated the *Pon Q'tar* clerics. The clerics have devised a new spell called 'the nautilus effect.' They used it to uncover my true past—the past that the Envoys tried to hide."

"What is the nautilus effect?" Tristan asked.

Xanthus shook his head. "I am not at liberty to say, *Jin'Sai.* But I will tell you this much: The *Pon Q'tar* have returned my blood signature to its original, deeply left-leaning state. I again serve them, and they have granted me a final chance to redeem myself. When I told them that you would return, they decided to send me back to kill you, rather than take you in. You have learned too much, you see. They want there to be no chance whatsoever of you contacting the Heretic rebels—even to the point that they are willing to give up the notion of taking you alive."

"What killed Serena and Clarice?" Tristan demanded. "Did the Vagaries queen commit suicide and take her child with her?"

"Of course not, you fool," Xanthus answered. "The *Pon Q'tar* killed her."

"Why would they do that?" Tristan breathed. "The *Pon Q'tar* had so much invested in her. . . . They had such plans for Clarice. . . ."

"True," Xanthus answered. "But as the Recluse became untenable, the *Pon Q'tar* knew that it would be far better for Serena and Clarice to perish, rather than to fall into the hands of the Conclave. Serena trusted the *Pon Q'tar* completely. They exploited that trust to trick her into using a spell to end her life and the life of her child. By the way, marking the envelopers and crashing one of your Black Ships through the Recluse drawbridge were very clever tactics. The *Pon Q'tar* clerics were impressed."

"The Envoys will never let you take me," Tristan protested.

"I think that they will," Xanthus answered cryptically. He smiled again and raised his axe.

"You are about to die, *Jin'Sai,*" he said. "You can either try to defend yourself, or simply let me kill you with one blow and grant you a quick death. Either way, your head goes back with me to Rustannica."

Tristan narrowed his eyes. "Why would you attack me with your axe when you could easily kill me with the craft?"

When the Darkling didn't answer, Tristan realized that he was onto something. He looked into Xanthus' eyes.

"The *Pon Q'tar* clerics still don't trust you completely, do they?" he demanded. "Despite their discovery of the so-called nautilus effect, they aren't entirely sure that the Envoys didn't plant some other spell or device into your being that remains to be found. Because of those misgivings, they stripped you of your gifts before sending you back to Crysenium. They want you to kill me, but they have limited your abilities in case you are still a traitor.

"I'm right, aren't I, you hideous freak?" Tristan pressed. "Your craft powers have been compromised! That's why you must appear to me in human form! The only way that you can kill me is by physical force! Because you plan to kill me with your axe, I suspect that they took everything from you but your gift of *K'Shari*! Because they know that I do not command the same gift, they believe that I will be an easy kill for you! Tell me, Xanthus—how does it feel to be the *Pon Q'tar*'s castrated lapdog?"

To Tristan's surprise, Xanthus smiled again. "Well done," he said quietly. "They told me that you were a quick study. But you left something out. They promised that when I kill you, they will return all my past gifts to me. Moreover, I will be granted an even higher rank in the Imperial Order."

"And you believed them, you fool," Tristan answered. "Didn't the way they betrayed Serena tell you anything?"

Xanthus' smile vanished. "You had best let me kill you quickly," he warned. "You cannot defeat me. I command *K'Shari,* and you do not."

Tristan drew his sword. With his free hand he slowly reached beneath his vest and produced something. He held it up before Xanthus' eyes. It was the blank scroll that Aeolus had given him to confirm his mastery of *K'Shari.*

Tristan had meant the scroll to be a symbolic gift to the Crysenium Envoys, marking his safe return. But now its symbolism would serve a far more deadly purpose. He tossed the scroll at Xanthus' feet. As the *Jin'Sai* started to circle his enemy he raised his weapon.

"My ears hear no begging," Tristan whispered. "My eyes see no pain. My heart feels no remorse." The *Jin'Sai* immediately felt his gift wash over him, empowering him and calming his center for the coming fight.

As the realization sank in, Xanthus stood stock-still for a moment. Knowing that there could be no going back, he too recited the three phrases and started to circle his opponent.

"I understand," he said softly. "Since the first moment I saw you, I somehow knew that it would come to this."

"As did I," Tristan answered.

Xanthus' first strike came so fast that Tristan barely saw it coming. Slipping to one side, the *Jin'Sai* dodged the axe and brought down his dreggan. But Xanthus recovered quickly and lifted his shield. Sparks flew as Tristan's dreggan struck it and slid harmlessly off to one side. Their first clash proving inconclusive, the warriors circled each other again.

Within an instant, they struck at each other simultaneously. With an earsplitting clang, Tristan's blade and the Darkling's axe came to a quick stop as Tristan's blade caught in the joint where Xanthus' axe head joined its handle. Struggling mightily, each stood his ground, trying not to be the first to back away.

Suddenly their weapon blades started to glow with the azure hue of the craft, and there came a thunderous explosion. Azure smoke rose, and the two combatants were thrust away from each other to go skidding across the shiny floor.

Tristan came to a stop on his back. He looked up through the haze just in time to see Xanthus rushing at him. His azure axe twinkling in the light, Xanthus brought it down with everything he had.

Tristan rolled hard to the right. With a great crash, Xanthus' axe barely missed the *Jin'Sai* and split the floor's entire length in half. The massive concussion resonated through the walls and caused the transparent ceiling to shatter. Crystalline shards rained down into the room.

As Xanthus struggled to free his blade, Tristan jumped to his feet and brought his dreggan whistling around. But Xanthus again blocked it with his shield. Finally the Darkling's axe came free and Xanthus attacked again, forcing Tristan to back up.

As the battle seesawed back and forth, the fighters quickly neared where Shadow was tied, causing the horse to rear nervously on his hind legs as far as his reins would allow. Soon Tristan found himself being forced toward the hallway entrance.

As they passed though the crystalline door frame, it split thunderously apart. Several more cracks split the hallway walls, and lengthened violently to match the combatants' forward progress. Tristan could only guess that these phenomena were being caused because two *K'Shari* masters had called on their gifts simultaneously. But he couldn't risk thinking about that now.

The whirling axe came around again, but this time Tristan raised his dreggan a fraction of a second too slowly. Xanthus' blow resonated so harshly through the dreggan blade and into Tristan's hands that the sword fell from his grip to go clattering to the floor. Xanthus immediately kicked the dreggan past Tristan and sent it skidding down the hallway.

Tristan was tempted to turn his back on Xanthus and go chasing after his sword, but every instinct told him not to. Knowing that he finally had Tristan trapped, Xanthus smiled. Tristan watched him raise the glowing axe.

Having no choice but to completely trust in his gift, for the first time Tristan surrendered his entire being to his *K'Shari*. As he did, the downstroke of Xanthus' axe seemed to slow to the point that sidestepping the blow was effortless. The nature of Tristan's next move was revealed to him with crystal clarity. He reached behind his right shoulder.

The two throwing knives came into his right hand so quickly that he had grasped them even before Xanthus finished his strike. He took one dirk into his left hand.

Tristan lashed out. As he backed away, he heard a scream.

One knife handle protruded from each of Xanthus' eyes. Screaming again, the Darkling waved his arms and staggered about blindly. Blood ran from his eye sockets and down onto his black robe. His axe and shield stopped glowing and went clattering to the floor. Then he fell forward, dead where he lay.

His chest heaving, Tristan stood there for a moment, staring at Xanthus' bloody corpse. Facing certain death and having no other alternative had finally forced him to learn how to let go, and to trust his new gift entirely. It was a lesson he wouldn't soon forget.

When he walked to collect his dreggan, he thought he heard someone softly call out. As he picked up his sword he heard the wind moaning through the shattered ceiling in the other room, but nothing else.

"Tristan," someone whispered. This time there could be no mistaking it.

Holding his sword high, he crept down the hallway. He took a deep breath and stepped quickly into the next room.

The meeting chamber was a bloodbath. Eleven of the twelve Envoys lay dead. Azure blood was splattered everywhere. Bodies and body parts were strewn about the room, and the transparent panel that had once graced part of the curved wall had been destroyed. Dark smudges dirtied much of the chamber, telling Tristan that azure bolts had been used in the recent battle.

But if they are all dead, who called my name? Tristan wondered. He was about to check each body for signs of life when he heard the lone voice call out again.

"Jin'Sai," a woman whispered.

Tristan looked across the room to see Hoskiko lying on the bloody floor. She had raised herself up onto her elbows and was trying to crawl toward him. Sheathing his dreggan, he ran to her and cradled her in his arms.

A deep wound lay beneath Hoskiko's once-immaculate white robe. Dried blood lay crusted on the garment and in her long gray hair. Her eyes were losing their luster. As she gently reached up to touch his face, she smiled.

"You're alive . . . ," she said. "I heard the fighting. Did you kill Xanthus?"

"Yes," he answered gently. "What happened here?"

"The Imperial Order came," she answered. "When the *Pon Q'tar* learned about Crysenium, they sent them to destroy us. Xanthus came with them. We tried to fight back, but there were too many of them."

"How did you survive?" Tristan asked.

Hoskiko managed a weak smile. "I fooled them," she answered. Then she coughed, bringing up some blood. As Tristan felt his heart tear in two, he held her closer.

"I used a spell to slow my heartbeat and mimic death," she said. "It might have been cowardly of me, but I had to stay alive long enough to see you return. There is so much that you still do not know. . . ."

"I don't understand," Tristan said. "If the Imperial Order was here, why didn't *they* kill me? Why would they leave, and trust the job to Xanthus?"

"Because Xanthus had been compromised by the Envoys, he had become more expendable," she answered weakly. "You must always remember that the *Pon Q'tar*'s paranoia knows no bounds. But there is another reason why the Imperial Order left so soon after finishing their dirty work. They boasted about it as they watched the others die."

"Why?" Tristan asked.

"With what strength I have remaining, I am cloaking your blood," Hoskiko answered. "At the same time, the *Pon Q'tar* is trying to sense your blood from afar. When I die, they will succeed. If they sense it long enough, they will know that Xanthus failed to kill you. Their only choice will be to summon the Borderlands to destroy you and Crysenium. That is why the Imperial Order didn't wait." Raising herself up a little, she looked sternly into Tristan's eyes.

"You must leave here immediately!" she begged him. "When

I die, the *Pon Q'tar*'s rage will know no limits! The form the Borderlands will take will be savage, and all-encompassing!"

"I will take you with me," Tristan insisted.

"No!" Hoskiko answered. "I am too far gone—we both know that. My time is over!"

"But where am I to go?" Tristan asked. "If Crysenium is destroyed, I will die in the Borderlands!"

"Go home!" Hoskiko said weakly. "Call forth the Forestallment that we granted to your blood and go back to Eutracia! But you must leave quickly! As the Borderlands near, magic will become useless and you will lose your ability to call forth the Forestallment!"

Tristan's mind raced as he turned to look through the empty space where the viewing panel had once been. The deceiving scene on the other side remained idyllic. But if Hoskiko was right, it would soon become a living nightmare.

"All right," he said. "I'll go back. But I'll never forget you."

"What you must remember above all is the true nature of your and Shailiha's destinies," she said. "Because the *Pon Q'tar* knows that you finally understand this, they will do everything they can to keep you from coming back. Despite their great power, they fear the coming of you and your sister more than anything in the world. You must find a way to cross the Tolenka Mountains, or to conquer the polar ice caps that imprison the Sea of Whispers to the north and the south. Return and seek out the Heretical splinter group. Only then can you start to heal the terrible wounds on this side of the world."

Tristan nodded. "Somehow I will find a way," he answered.

As he held her, he saw a tear leave Hoskiko's eye. She weakly reached up to touch his face.

"You are the first *Jin'Sai* to reach us," she said softly. "And now that you have, we failed you. There is so much that we had planned to tell you—so much that you and your sister deserve to know." As Hoskiko coughed again, Tristan could see that she was nearing the end.

"The rebel group you seek is called the League of Whispers," she said. "That is all I can tell you about them, because only Faxon knew their many secrets. But before I die, there is something else that you should know. It's about your parents, Nicholas and Morganna. They weren't . . ." She gasped. "They weren't . . ."

His eyes wide with anticipation, Tristan clutched Hoskiko harder. "They weren't *what*?" he shouted. But then Hoskiko closed her eyes, and her head fell to one side.

He knelt there for too long, mourning the loss of the Envoys and wondering what Hoskiko might have told him about his late parents. Then the rumbling noises started, and they suddenly brought him back to reality. He gently placed Hoskiko's body on the floor and quickly turned to look out the gaping hole in the wall.

The Borderlands were forming.

Tristan stood aghast as he watched the sky darken. Suddenly the ground shook violently, and Crysenium trembled with it. To his horror, the distant earth was starting to heave itself upward into dozens of volcanic cones. As more cones erupted, they started forming a path toward Crysenium.

The dark cones erupted so quickly that they rose to maturity in a matter of seconds. With their coming, Crysenium shook even more violently, and part of the meeting room ceiling came crashing down.

On reaching their complete heights, all the volcanoes erupted into raging infernos, spewing tons of ash and molten lava into the air. As the lava cascaded down their dark sides and poured across the valley, it immediately vaporized everything it touched. In only moments it would engulf the entire structure.

For the last time, Tristan looked at the other dead Envoys, then back down at Hoskiko. She seemed peaceful, and finally at rest. Leaving the room, he tore down the hallway as fast as he could.

By now Shadow had become nearly mad with fear. Tristan ran across the shattered floor and untied the stallion. He threw himself up into the saddle just as the molten lava touched one of Crysenium's outside walls.

With a mighty explosion, the crystalline wall burst into flames and crumbled inward, allowing the lava to invade the room. Several columns crashed down, narrowly missing Tristan and Shadow. As lava washed across the shattered floor, Tristan wheeled Shadow around. Praying that it would still work, Tristan called on his Forestallment.

The azure mist blessedly appeared, but he knew it wouldn't last long. Spurring Shadow for all he was worth, he charged the stallion headlong into it.

The silent, dense fog surrounded him again, and at first he

thought that he was safe. But then he felt the searing heat, and he knew. As Shadow galloped beneath him, Tristan turned to look. The lava flow was chasing after them.

All he could see was a huge, blurry wall of glowing red rushing after him, but he knew that it could be nothing else. He did his best to spur Shadow faster, but in the whirling midst of the Forestallment he couldn't tell if the horse was gaining speed. The heat was becoming more unbearable by the moment, and he suspected that the lava would soon reach them, engulfing them forever.

Suddenly Shadow burst out the other side of the azure pass and into the charred forest. The sudden change in footing surprised the horse and rider and sent them tumbling to the ground.

Tristan launched high over Shadow's head as the stallion hit the ground and skidded through the dark ash covering the forest floor. Then they went crashing straight into the Minion campsite that lay just beyond. Startled warriors ran and took to the air as Tristan and the neighing horse took down two tents, then barreled through the campfire before coming to a stop. Stunned into speechlessness, the warriors ran to help them.

The Minions lifted Tristan to his feet. He seemed dazed but unhurt. Shadow rolled over and stood shakily. Then Tristan came to his senses, and he suddenly remembered the lava flow.

"Everyone into the air!" he screamed. "One of you must take me aloft!"

One of the warriors immediately took Tristan into his arms, and they all quickly went aloft. When they had reached a height of about ten meters, Tristan told them to hover and turn toward the azure pass. Soon the ground started to shake, and everyone heard a great rumbling sound. When Shadow sensed the returning danger he turned and galloped wildly down the mountainside.

Tristan and the warriors watched in amazement as the azure pass started changing color. As the glowing red lava neared it, the pass morphed from bright azure into green, and then from green into glowing red. With a thunderous rumble, the lava finally reached the face of the pass. Suddenly the pass immediately exploded outward, and was no more.

Amazingly, the lava did not rush into the forest. Instead, it halted its forward advance and started rising up, filling the mountain gap left behind by the destroyed pass. Higher and higher it rose, until, like the pass had once done, it too became lost in the clouds. Then Tristan and the warriors watched as it somehow cooled immediately and turned to dark granite. It was like the pass had never existed.

Tristan ordered the warriors back to the ground. After finding an overturned camp stool he righted it and sat down. As the stunned warriors surrounded him, their commanding officer knelt beside his lord.

"Jin'Sai," he breathed. "What just happened?"

Tristan took a deep breath and looked back up at the monolithic mountains that still held so many secrets.

"A dream just died," he answered quietly. "And a new one has been born."

Epilogue

The hour was late as Faegan pushed his chair on wheels down the Redoubt hallways. Alongside him hovered the Scroll of the Vigors, the Scroll of the Vagaries, and the Tome of the Paragon. There were few acolytes or consuls about at this hour. But those who did cross his path bowed to him reverently as they watched the fabled wizard and the three priceless documents continue on down the halls.

With the threat from Serena and Clarice gone, Faegan hoped that he would have some peaceful time to study the newly acquired Vagaries scroll. Having their indexes would be a marvelous advantage. For the sake of convenience he had decided to place all three documents under lock and key in the same place. Wigg and Shailiha had agreed. After seeing Tristan enter the azure pass, the First Wizard and Shailiha had returned by Minion litter only several hours ago. Because of their sadness, Faegan had kept his meeting with them brief.

Finding the room he wanted, Faegan stopped, as did the three documents floating alongside him. Faegan called the craft and listened as the tumblers in the lock turned over once, then twice more. He opened the door and wheeled himself into the Archives of the Redoubt. The huge library was the single greatest repository of craft books and scrolls ever collected in one place.

The Archives occupied a vast room of Ephyran marble, one of the most beautiful in the entire Redoubt. The square room measured at least two hundred meters on each of its four sides, and was seven stories tall. Each story was surrounded by a railing that overlooked the central area. Each level was lined with books from top to bottom, and a magnificent set of stairs with a brass railing ran up and around to each of the floors, granting access to the thousands of books and scrolls. Several hundred finely carved desks, reading tables, and upholstered chairs lined the main floor. Soft, golden light was supplied by a combination of oil sconces and desk lamps, all enchanted to burn continually and without smoke.

As Faegan entered the room he was pleased to see that no one else was about. With a wave of one hand he commanded the doors to close and the tumblers to lock.

Faegan thought for a moment about where to store the three precious works. He knew that no one granted access to the Archives would try to harm them, but he wanted them protected, just the same. Finally he seized on an idea.

Raising his hands, he called the craft. Almost at once the three documents rose higher into the air, then settled in a row against a bare area of the room's far wall. With another wave of his hand, he encased them in a glowing, azure box mounted directly to the wall.

He would of course reveal the spell calculations to the other mystics on the Conclave, but to no one else. Now he could check on the documents anytime he chose, and they would still be easily accessible. Faegan found himself wondering how long it had been since the three amazing artifacts had been so near one another.

Perhaps centuries, he thought. *If in fact they ever were.*

Happy with his invention, he let go a little cackle as he let himself out of the room. The massive double doors closed. Had someone been inside the Archives to listen, he would have heard the tumblers in the door locks turn over once, then twice more.

Unknown to anyone, the three documents suddenly started to glow. As they brightened, selected books and scrolls on all levels of the Archives started to take on the same azure hue.

After this night of nights, the craft would never be the same.

Read on for an exciting excerpt from

RISE OF THE BLOOD ROYAL

the next book in
THE DESTINIES OF BLOOD AND STONE
by Robert Newcomb

AS TRISTAN, SHAILIHA, AND JESSAMAY RUSHED TOWARD THE Archives entryway, the intense white light coming through the open doors nearly blinded them. Groping about with his free arm, Tristan found one of Shailiha's hands and gripped it.

Just then the wondrous light began to dim. His vision clearing, Tristan saw the crippled wizard Faegan sitting in his wooden chair on wheels, his arms upraised. His face showed intense concentration; sweat had broken out on his brow. His arms shook from the great effort he was expending as he summoned the craft.

Aeolus, Wigg, and Abbey stood by Faegan's chair, their arms also raised.

"What's happening?" Tristan whispered to Jessamay. He let go of Shailiha's hand and quietly sheathed his dreggan.

"I don't know," Jessamay whispered back.

After tense moments, the azure glow vanished at last, and Tristan gazed in amazement at the scene before him.

Books, scrolls, and parchments had been ripped from their shelves and covered the first floor in massive piles. Tristan couldn't begin to imagine how long it might take to set things right.

Tristan beckoned Jessamay and Shailiha to follow him.

Trying as best they could not to trample any documents, they slowly walked over to where Wigg, Aeolus, and Abbey stood beside Faegan's chair.

"What happened here?" Tristan asked.

Faegan twisted around and looked sadly into Tristan's face. The ancient wizard wore his familiar black robe. His unruly gray hair lay parted down the middle and reached nearly to his shoulders. Much of his face was covered by a shaggy gray beard, and his lustrous green eyes seemed to bore straight into Tristan's soul. The prince could see that the normally mischievous wizard had been deeply sobered.

"I don't know exactly *what,*" Faegan answered. "But I believe I know *why.*"

Faegan swiveled his chair around and pointed to the wall on the far side of the room. Everyone turned to look.

Tristan knew that Faegan had brought the Tome—the primary treatise outlining the study of the craft—and the Scroll of the Vigors and the Scroll of the Vagaries here to the Archives for safekeeping. The wizard had used the craft to magically secure them within a five-sided transparent wizard's box high against the marble wall. Only the Conclave mystics had been entrusted with the complex formula that could dismantle the dimly glowing box.

Tristan had approved of Faegan's elegant solution. To the best of Faegan's knowledge, the azure box was impervious to everything except the spell that allowed for its dismantling. But *something* had gotten through. More than the box was illuminated. The Tome and both scrolls were glowing with the same bright white light that had only moments earlier engulfed the chamber. As Tristan gazed at the unprecedented glow, trepidation grew in his heart.

Fascinated, Shailiha stepped nearer. "What is that light?" she breathed.

Wigg shook his head. He was dressed in his customary gray robe. His iron-gray hair was pulled back from his widow's peak into a braid that fell down his back. Despite his advanced age, his tall form remained lean and muscular. His strong hands were gnarled and elegantly expressive, and his craggy face and aquamarine eyes showed deep concern. Sighing, he placed his hands into the opposite sleeves of his robe, then turned to the princess.

"As Faegan said, we don't know," he answered. "Logic dictates that the glow coming from the Tome and the Scrolls has something to do with whatever made such a mess of this room. It took a mighty force to do this. But only the Afterlife knows how or why."

Wigg turned his gaze back toward the glowing box that held the three precious documents. "We can only hope that the box protected them," he added. "Luckily, it seems to be intact. And except for the glow, they appear unharmed. But I suppose that there is only one way to know for sure."

He turned back to look at his old friend. "What say you, Faegan?" he asked. "Do you think it prudent that we dismantle your invention and take a look?"

Faegan, lost in concentration, didn't reply. His eyes were closed and his head was bowed slightly as he pressed his fingertips against his temples.

Tristan understood what Faegan was doing. The wizard was one of the rare few who commanded the gift of Consummate Recollection, allowing him to perfectly recall everything he had ever seen, heard, or read from his birth more than three centuries ago right up to the present. Faegan was almost certainly mentally reviewing the Tome, to learn whether it might shed light on this evening's strange turn of events.

After a time, Faegan raised his head and opened his eyes. His face was pinched with worry.

"The Tome mentions this phenomenon," he said quietly. "Truth be told, until this moment I never gave it much importance. That is because the Tome does not specifically name the three documents that when placed side by side will cause this effect. Now the answer has been revealed. It is only by the greatest chance that we possess all three at the same time. This might be the first moment in history when they have been this close to one another."

"Do you mean to say that your conjured box caused all this?" Jessamay asked.

"No," Faegan answered. "The box is only a means of protection. Still, there is no telling what might happen if it is dismantled. Let me recite the proper Tome passage so that you might better understand."

Closing his eyes again, he leaned back in his chair and spoke:

AND SO IT WILL COME TO PASS THAT IF CERTAIN RELICS ARE PLACED IN CLOSE PROXIMITY TO ONE ANOTHER AND LEFT TO REST, THE RESULTS WILL BE OF VAST IMPORTANCE FOR THOSE TRYING TO UNRAVEL THE SECRETS OF MAGIC. THE AREA SURROUNDING THEM WILL SLOWLY TAKE ON AN AURA THAT WILL GRADUALLY ENGULF THE DOCUMENTS, CAUSING THEM TO GLOW. PRECEDING THE GLOW A GREAT WHIRLWIND WILL COME, MARKING THE ADVENT OF THE SPELL. AFTER THE PASSING OF THE WIND, THE THREE RELICS WILL GIVE UP MUCH WHEN THEY ARE OPENED.

Faegan sighed and sat back in his chair. He opened his eyes.

"What does it mean?" Abbey asked.

Abbey was nearly as old as Wigg, Faegan, and Aeolus. She too was protected by time enchantments. Like Jessamay, she did not look her age. The herbmistress and partial adept was wearing a simple plaid dress that covered her shapely figure. Her long dark hair was sparsely streaked with gray and her sensual face showed a strong jaw, deep blue eyes, and dark eyebrows. Three hundred years earlier she had been Wigg's secret lover, before the late Directorate of Wizards banished all partials from Tammerland. During the dangerous hunt for the Scroll of the Vigors, Wigg and Abbey had found each other again, and had been together ever since.

"As you all know, the Tome is often difficult to understand," Faegan answered. "I have long believed that the Ones fashioned it to be purposely obscure, so that it would confound friend and foe alike. It seems that we have yet another riddle to unravel."

"What is the code to which the quote refers?" Tristan asked. "Could it be that there is much more to the Tome and the Scrolls than we know?"

Wigg raised an eyebrow. "Have you ever known that *not* to be the case?" he asked. He looked back at Faegan. "You still haven't answered my question," he said. "Do we dismantle your box, or not?"

Faegan turned toward Aeolus. "What say you, Aeolus?" he asked. "We have yet to hear your opinion."

Before answering, Aeolus walked toward the glowing box. He stopped about two meters away and looked at it carefully.

Aeolus was the most recent addition to the Conclave. Once a powerful Directorate Wizard, he had grown tired of war, politics, and the craft and had resigned his membership to pursue a private life teaching martial arts. But by necessity he had become involved in the search for the Scroll of the Vagaries and the struggle against Serena. In the end he had accepted Tristan's and Wigg's offers of a seat on the Conclave.

Three centuries earlier, Aeolus had been granted a time enchantment at the age of eighty Seasons of New Life. Like Wigg, he remained lean and muscular, despite his physical age. His head was shaved and his dark gray beard closely trimmed, and his dark eyes never missed a thing. Out of respect for his late Directorate brothers, he wore a gray robe.

After regarding the box for a time, Aeolus looked at Faegan. "Does your spell incorporate any dangerous components that might harm the documents if it is reversed?"

Faegan shook his head. "No," he answered. "But owing to the need to protect the documents, the spell I conjured is tremendously strong."

Aeolus turned to look at the box again. "My greatest worry is what will happen when the documents are again exposed to the environment of this room," he mused.

"I concur," Faegan said.

"I don't understand," Tristan interjected. "Why would the room harm them? The white light has done its work and it is gone. Aside from the usual oil lamps, the only light comes from the documents themselves."

Faegan gave Tristan a grave look. "That's not true," he said. "The white light is still with us."

Perplexed, Tristan looked around. "I can't see it," he protested.

Wigg shook his head. "Just because you cannot see it doesn't mean that it isn't here," he replied. "We tried, but even our collective gifts could only dim the light to a point that it cannot be seen by those untrained in the craft."

"It's true, Tristan," Jessamay added. "I can still see it."

"So what does all this mean?" Shailiha asked.

"My wizard's box, transparent though it is, might have blocked some of the light from the documents. By conjuring the box, I might have inadvertently hampered the spell. It seems clear to me that the spell was intended to bathe the documents in the light at its brightest. We have no way of knowing what might happen if the Tome and the

Scrolls were first partially exposed and then are fully exposed to the light."

As Tristan considered the mystics' concerns, he was again reminded of what a tangled web the craft was. Clearly, the decision whether to continue was a huge one.

Should the documents already be damaged beyond use, the Conclave's struggle to ensure the safety of the Vigors and bring peace to the lands west of the Tolenkas would suffer an unimaginable setback. It was true that Faegan had read the first two volumes of the Tome and could probably recite them verbatim to a consul scribe, but that might take years. And because Faegan had not yet fully read the Scrolls, most of the precious forestallment formulas they held would be lost forever. Perhaps worst of all, the Prophecies—the third and final volume of the Tome that only Tristan was destined to read—would also be destroyed.

He looked back at Wigg. "Although I am the nation's sovereign and the leader of the Conclave, I must leave this matter to those who command the craft," he said. "Only you four have the knowledge needed to decide."

Wigg nodded. "I agree," he answered. He looked at the others. "What say you all?" he asked.

Faegan took a deep breath. "We can't leave the Tome and the Scrolls up there indefinitely," he said. "We need them too badly. We could wait for the spell to subside, but that might never happen. I say we liberate the documents and take our chances. I understand that the risk is huge, but what other choice is there?"

"I agree," Jessamay said.

"As do I," Aeolus replied.

"Very well," Wigg said. "Faegan will dismantle the box. And may the Afterlife grant us luck."

Faegan swiveled his chair to face his invention, then

closed his eyes and raised his arms and began his spell of reversal.

For several long moments the box glowed brighter. To Tristan's relief, the three sacred documents inside did not. Slowly, the sides of the box came apart and vanished. Tristan held his breath as Faegan reversed the last fragments of the spell, freeing the three relics from their places high against the wall.

As Faegan opened his eyes and lowered his arms, the Tome and Scrolls suddenly flew toward the center of the room. Tristan looked worriedly at the wizard.

"Was that your doing?" he whispered.

"No," Faegan replied. "What happens now must be the purview of the Ones."

To everyone's amazement, the documents began to spin. Faster and faster they went, until their forms became little more than glowing blurs. Then there was a great explosion, and an intense wind sprang from nowhere.

All the fallen Archives documents went flying into the air. As the precious books and the papers whirled about, three explosions followed in quick succession. Their immense force took the visitors off their feet. Tristan landed hard beside Faegan's overturned chair. He turned his head to see the wizard lying beside him.

Tristan groggily did his best to look through the whirling paper blizzard. He could barely see that the Tome and the Scrolls had stopped spinning. But something else was happening. The three relics were emitting some type of azure dust. The quickly growing cloud grew and grew until it engulfed the room.

As the azure cloud drifted over him, Tristan sensed his consciousness slipping away. He tried to look around; it seemed that everyone except him and Faegan had been overcome.

Tristan managed a last look at Faegan. The old wizard's face showed great delight.

"The legend is true . . ." Tristan heard Faegan faintly whisper, as if the wizard's voice was drifting to him from some faraway place. "Subtle matter exists . . . subtle matter exists . . ."

Unable to stay conscious, the prince finally surrendered.